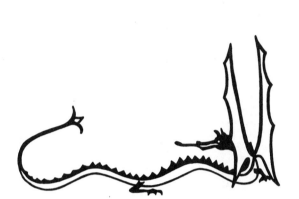

THE ANNOTATED HOBBIT

*A portrait of J.R.R. Tolkien, probably taken
by Elliot & Fry in London, October 27, 1937*

THE ANNOTATED

HOBBIT

REVISED AND EXPANDED EDITION

ANNOTATED BY

Douglas A. Anderson

◈

THE HOBBIT

OR THERE AND BACK AGAIN

J.R.R. TOLKIEN

Illustrated by the Author

HOUGHTON MIFFLIN COMPANY • BOSTON • NEW YORK

2002

I cannot imagine a pleasanter old age than one spent in the not too remote country where I could reread and annotate my favorite books.

—André Maurois

What we read with pleasure we read again with pleasure.

—Horace

Contents

Preface to the Second Edition   xi

INTRODUCTION   1

1. AN UNEXPECTED PARTY   29
2. ROAST MUTTON   60
3. A SHORT REST   87
4. OVER HILL AND UNDER HILL   100
5. RIDDLES IN THE DARK   115
6. OUT OF THE FRYING-PAN INTO THE FIRE   137
7. QUEER LODGINGS   161
8. FLIES AND SPIDERS   191
9. BARRELS OUT OF BOND   222
10. A WARM WELCOME   241
11. ON THE DOORSTEP   255
12. INSIDE INFORMATION   267
13. NOT AT HOME   289
14. FIRE AND WATER   302
15. THE GATHERING OF THE CLOUDS   314
16. A THIEF IN THE NIGHT   326
17. THE CLOUDS BURST   333
18. THE RETURN JOURNEY   346
19. THE LAST STAGE   355

Appendix A. The Quest of Erebor   367
Appendix B. The Runes   378
Bibliography   380
Map of Wilderland   399

Acknowledgments

A book like *The Annotated Hobbit* could not be compiled without the help of many people, and I would like to express my thanks here. Foremost I am grateful to Christopher Tolkien for allowing me to reframe his father's book with criticism and commentary, and additionally I have greatly benefited from his comments and suggestions. I also owe a special debt to my friends Christina Scull and Wayne G. Hammond, who shared with me some of their research for their forthcoming *J.R.R. Tolkien: A Companion and Guide,* and also helped in many other ways.

Of institutions and organizations, I would like to express my thanks for assistance from Matt Blessing, archivist, the Memorial Library, Marquette University, Milwaukee, Wisconsin; Christopher W. Mitchell and Marjorie Lamp Mead of the Marion E. Wade Center, Wheaton College, Wheaton, Illinois; Dr. Judith Priestman of the Bodleian Library, Oxford; and the University of Notre Dame Library, South Bend, Indiana.

At the Houghton Mifflin Company, people (past and present) who have been very helpful (and patient beyond the call of duty) include Clay Harper, Austin Olney, Ruth Hapgood, Becky Saikia-Wilson, and Rhiannon Agosti.

Others who helped on specific points or assisted in various ways include Fred Biggs, Richard E. Blackwelder, Alexandra Bolintineanu, David Bratman, Brad Brickner, Diane Bruns, Humphrey Carpenter, Deborah Benson Covington, John L. DiBello, Michael Drout, Charles B. Elston, Verlyn Flieger, Steven M. Frisby, John Garth, Charles Garvin, Peter Geach, Peter Glassman, Glen H. GoodKnight, Martin Hempstead, Thomas D. Hill, Carl F. Hostetter, Ellen Kline, Chris Lavallie, Dennis K. Lien, Abbe Lyons, Michael Martinez, Richard Mathews, Charles E. Noad, John D. Rateliff, Becky Reiss, Taum Santoski, Dr. William A. S. Sarjeant, Tom Seidner, Tom Shippey, Babbie Smith, Susan A. Smith, Stacy Snyder, Donn P. Stephen, Priscilla Tolkien, Rayner Unwin, Richard C. West, Kelley M. Wickham-Crowley, Gene Wolfe, Reinhold Wotawa, Nina Wyke-Smith, Ted Wyke-Smith, Jessica Yates, Manfred Zimmermann, and Henry Zmuda.

For assistance with various aspects of the translations of *The Hobbit,* and the foreign illustrators, I am grateful to Mikael Ahlström, Felix Claessens, David Doughan, Jim Dunning, Mark T. Hooker, John Kadar, Victor Kadar, Mari Kotani, Gergely Nagy, René van Rossenberg, Arden R. Smith, Anders Stenström (Beregond), Asako Suzuki, Makoto Takahashi, and Takayuki Tatsumi.

Preface to the Second Edition

The Annotated Hobbit was first published by Houghton Mifflin Company in September 1988, in recognition of the fiftieth anniversary of the first American publication of *The Hobbit.* A British edition, published by Unwin Hyman, appeared in 1989.

In the fourteen years since the first edition was compiled, many volumes of previously unpublished writings by Tolkien have appeared. Additionally, the amount of secondary material on Tolkien, including books and articles, has increased at a staggering rate. In revising and updating *The Annotated Hobbit*, I quickly realized that a wholesale revision was in order. This, in my view, called not for a new approach to the process of annotating the book itself, but for a readjustment of my earlier methodology and its application to the many advances in Tolkien scholarship.

In general, I have preferred to keep Tolkien's own views about his writings in a position of central importance. My annotations start from there and move outward to the biographical and historical context. The goal of annotation itself is usually considered to be illuminating a text, but I have also attempted to give more information about Tolkien's life, his friends and associates, his literary interests, and his other writings so that a better cumulative portrait is achieved. The result is that some annotations may seem to stray beyond an immediate relevance to the text, but I do feel such slight wanderings are both justifiable and worthwhile.

Every section of this new edition of *The Annotated Hobbi*t has been revised, updated, and rewritten, but the new edition differs from the earlier one only slightly in content and arrangement. The most immediately apparent change is that all of the notes about Tolkien's revisions to the text of *The Hobbit,* originally placed in an appendix, are now integrated with the other annotations into the main body of the book. (The details on the various editions of *The Hobbit* that Tolkien revised are given in the second section of the bibliography at the end of this book.) One item new to this book is "The Quest of Erebor," Tolkien's retelling of the story of *The Hobbit,* originally intended to be part of an appendix to *The Lord of the Rings* but omitted for reasons of length; it was first published in a variant form in *Unfinished Tales.* To the bibliography I have added the section "Selected Criticism of *The Hobbit*" in order to call attention to other critical approaches. Some of the articles referenced there are highly interesting in their own right, but their arguments are complex and not easily condensed to make an-notations. A good example is Paul Edmund Thomas's "Some of Tolkien's Narrators," an excellent analysis of Tolkien's narrative voice that should be read in its entirety.

In my annotations and throughout this book I have referred to a number of works that are vital to any study of J.R.R. Tolkien, referencing them by a short abbreviation rather than a full title. A list is given below, and the full details of publication can be found in the first section of the bibliography at the end of this book.

ARTIST: *J.R.R. Tolkien: Artist and Illustrator* (1995), by Wayne G. Hammond and Christina Scull.

BIBLIOGRAPHY: *J.R.R. Tolkien: A Descriptive Bibliography* (1993), by Wayne G. Hammond, with the assistance of Douglas A. Anderson.

BIOGRAPHY: *J.R.R. Tolkien: A Biography* (1977), by Humphrey Carpenter.

HISTORY: The twelve-volume series *The History of Middle-earth* (1983–96), edited by Christopher Tolkien.

LETTERS: *The Letters of J.R.R. Tolkien* (1981), edited by Humphrey Carpenter, with the assistance of Christopher Tolkien.

"Nomenclature of *The Lord of the Rings*": In *A Tolkien Compass* (1975), edited by Jared Lobdell. Tolkien's notes for translators, originally written in 1966–67.

PICTURES: *Pictures by J.R.R. Tolkien* (1979); revised (1992), edited by Christopher Tolkien.

"Silmarillion": The word "Silmarillion" in quotation marks refers more generally to the body of Tolkien's writings that concern the earliest legends of Middle-earth. In italics, as in *The Silmarillion,* the word refers specifically to the book published in 1977, edited by Christopher Tolkien.

DOUGLAS A. ANDERSON
March 2002

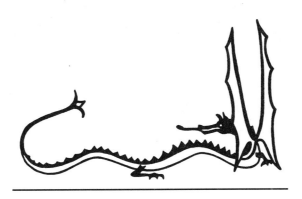

THE ANNOTATED HOBBIT

Introduction

Tolkien once said that his typical response upon reading a medieval work was not to want to embark on a critical or philological study of it, but instead to write a modern work in the same tradition.[1] And similarly, to an interviewer in 1965, Tolkien said that he "hardly got through any fairy-stories without wanting to write one [himself]."[2]

These statements, in a broad sense, serve as a good entry point in studying Tolkien and his works. For with an understanding of Tolkien's background and his literary interests there follows a greater appreciation of what he achieved in his best-known works, *The Hobbit* and *The Lord of the Rings*.

John Ronald Reuel Tolkien was born on January 3, 1892, in Bloemfontein, South Africa, the son of Arthur Reuel Tolkien, a bank manager, and Mabel Suffield. Both of his parents were from the Birmingham area in the Midlands of England.

Arthur had proposed to Mabel while they both still lived in England, but soon afterward he obtained a post with the Bank of Africa, and their wedding took place in Cape Town. J.R.R. Tolkien, known as Ronald, was their first child; a second son, Hilary Arthur Reuel, was born two years after Ronald.

In 1895, Mabel Tolkien returned to England with her two children, ostensibly for a short visit, but also because of concerns over young Ronald's health. Arthur Tolkien, who had remained in South Africa, became ill in late 1895, and died soon afterward.

Mabel stayed in England, raising her children near her own family in the Birmingham area. In 1900, Mabel converted to Roman Catholicism, much to the consternation of her Protestant relatives, who withdrew their support. Mabel struggled on her own, instructing her children in the Catholic religion. Her health faltered, and after she died in 1904, Father Francis Morgan of the Birmingham Oratory became the guardian of the two Tolkien boys.

The boys were educated at King Edward's School in Birmingham, where Ronald won a scholarship in 1903. Around 1910, Ronald met another orphan, a young woman named Edith Bratt who had rooms at the same boarding house where the Tolkien boys lived. A secret relationship developed between Ronald and Edith, but once it was discovered by their guardians, Ronald was forbidden to see or to speak to Edith until he reached the age of twenty-one.

Tolkien went up to Exeter College, Oxford, in

The house at 20 Northmoor Road, Oxford, where the Tolkien family lived from January 1930 through early 1947. Tolkien's study was on the ground floor, occupying the room at the lower right, with windows (seen above) facing to the west and windows facing south (to the right), not visible in this photograph. Tolkien's desk sat before the south-facing windows.[3]

the autumn of 1911. He first read classics but soon found his interests leading him to study Comparative Philology as well as other languages, like Finnish, and to begin creating a personal language that he would later call Quenya or Elvish.

In 1913, on his twenty-first birthday, Tolkien resumed his relationship with Edith Bratt. He took a Second Class in Honour Moderations, and owing to his bent for philology he achieved a First Class in English Language and Literature in June 1915.

Immediately afterward he joined the Lancashire Fusiliers and trained as a soldier. Ronald and Edith were married on March 22, 1916, before Tolkien was sent to the front in France that summer. Tolkien spent some months in the trenches of the Somme, experiencing firsthand the horrors of World War I. Eventually he contracted trench fever, and he was returned to England, where he spent most of the remainder of the war. Ronald and Edith Tolkien's first child, John Francis Reuel, was born in 1917.

Near the end of the war Tolkien accepted a position on the staff of the Oxford English Dictionary, then being compiled in Oxford. In 1920 he was appointed Reader in English Language at the University of Leeds, and the family moved north. A second son, Michael Hilary Reuel, was born in 1920.

Tolkien's first major professional publication, *A Middle English Vocabulary,* appeared in 1922. It was designed for use with Kenneth Sisam's anthology, *Fourteenth Century Verse and Prose* (1921). With this and other such work and his experience on the *Oxford English Dictionary,* Tolkien was becoming one of the most accomplished philologists of his time. In July 1924, he was promoted to professor of English language at Leeds, and a third son, Christopher Reuel, was born later the same year.

A major edition of the Middle English poem *Sir Gawain and the Green Knight,* co-edited by Tolkien and E. V. Gordon, appeared in 1925. Soon

In 1972 Tolkien presented his desk to the organization Help the Aged, so that its sale could benefit this charity. In a letter of July 27, 1972, presented with the desk, Tolkien wrote, "This desk was bought for me by my wife in 1927. It was my first desk,[4] and has remained the one that I chiefly used for literary work until her death in 1971. On it *The Hobbit* was entirely produced: written, typed and illustrated." The desk is now housed in the Marion E. Wade Center at Wheaton College in Wheaton, Illinois.

A report of J.R.R. Tolkien reading a paper on "Norse Sagas" to the Literary Society at King Edward's School, Birmingham, on February 17, 1911, from the *King Edward's School Chronicle,* March 1911 (26, no. 2) pp. 18–19.

afterward, Tolkien was elected the Rawlinson and Bosworth Professor of Anglo-Saxon at Oxford. His fourth child (the only daughter), Priscilla Mary Reuel, was born in 1929. *The Hobbit,* written for his children, appeared in 1937.

Tolkien held the Rawlinson and Bosworth Professorship until 1945, when he was elected the Merton Professor of English Language and Literature at Oxford. The long-awaited sequel to *The Hobbit, The Lord of the Rings,* was published in

three volumes in 1954–55. He remained a fellow of Merton College until his retirement in 1959. His wife Edith died in 1971, and Tolkien himself died, following a brief illness, on September 2, 1973.

Tolkien's attraction to medieval languages and literature began very early. While a student at King Edward's School, Tolkien read *Beowulf,* first in a modern translation and then in the original Anglo-Saxon. He went from there to the Icelandic sagas, some in translations by William Morris, and to the prose *Edda* of Snorri Sturluson, and the *Elder Edda,* a collection of Old Norse mythological and heroic poems. He encountered the Finnish *Kalevala* in 1911. At Exeter College his interest in the works of William Morris deepened. That Morris had also been an undergraduate at Exeter probably fueled Tolkien's interest, and he found Morris's narrative verse and the late prose romances (some of which are interspersed with poetry) especially to his liking.

Tolkien read and studied the entire corpus of early Germanic languages and literatures, specializing in Old English, Old Norse, and Middle English. From the Middle English period Tolkien's interests included the works of the poet Geoffrey Chaucer (1340?–1400), as well as the anonymous fourteenth-century author of *Sir Gawain and the Green Knight, Pearl, Cleanness,* and *Patience.* One of Tolkien's special areas of scholarship was the West Midlands dialect of Middle English, as found in the *Ancrene Wisse,* a book of religious instruction for women who chose to live the religious life in small cells built alongside churches.

Tolkien's interest in sharing such enthusiasms led him to form a Viking Club at Leeds, which met to drink beer and read sagas; and back in Oxford he founded an Icelandic club, the *Kolbítar,* which consisted of a group of dons that met from 1926 through around 1930–31 in order to read aloud to one another Icelandic sagas, translating impromptu. Tolkien's friend C. S. Lewis was a member of the *Kolbítar* (or Coal-biters — the men who sat so near to the fires as to seem to bite the coals), as was Nevill Coghill, both of whom would also become members of the Inklings, the group of Oxford writers who met regularly to read their own compositions to one another. In fact, the Inklings (whose name originally came from an undergraduate group that met from around 1931–33) seems to have developed as a group directly from the earlier *Kolbítar* meetings.

Tolkien's own literary creativity found expression from very early on. His interest in languages is seen in the invented language Animalic, which Tolkien and two cousins devised as adolescents. It was one of the first of the many languages Tolkien invented, which were often constructed with great complexity.

Perhaps as a result of his mother's tutoring, Tolkien was also very interested in painting, drawing, and calligraphy. A full study of his artwork, spanning many decades, can be found in *J.R.R. Tolkien: Artist and Illustrator,* by Wayne G. Hammond and Christina Scull.

In 1910 Tolkien also began to write poetry, and around the time World War I began, Tolkien encountered the following lines in *Crist,* an Anglo-Saxon poem by Cynewulf:

Ēalā Ēarendel,   engla beorhtast,
ofer middangeard   monnum sended
                    (*Crist,* lines 104–5)

Hail Earendel   brightest of angels,
over middle-earth   sent unto men

The word *Ēarendel* is usually glossed as meaning "a shining light, or ray," and some scholars

have thought it refers to a star. Tolkien felt that Earendel might have been the name for Venus, the evening star. Years later, in a letter of December 18, 1965, written to Clyde S. Kilby, Tolkien referred to this couplet from Cynewulf as "rapturous words from which ultimately sprang the whole of my mythology."[5]

Tolkien's mythology was also an outgrowth of his invented languages, for he felt that in order for his invented languages to grow and evolve as real languages do, they must have a people to speak them, and with a people comes a history. Tolkien called his invented world Middle-earth, which is simply a modern alteration of Old English *middangeard,* a word for the world we inhabit. Tolkien peopled his world with elves, men, and other creatures, while his two main Elvish languages, Gnomish (which later became Sindarin) and Qenya (later spelled Quenya), became rooted in an imaginary history.

Tolkien wrote "The Voyage of Earendel the Evening Star," the first poem of what became his invented mythology, in September 1914. And for the next few years his mythology primarily found expression in lexicons, grammars, and poems. In early 1916, he offered a collection of his poetry, entitled *The Trumpets of Faerie,* to the London publishers Sidgwick and Jackson, but the book was turned down. Soon afterward he began writing prose versions of the invented mythology, calling the assembled stories *The Book of Lost Tales.* These prose versions are the originals of what became Tolkien's "Silmarillion," the legendarium that he worked and reworked throughout his entire life. The complex evolution of these tales and legends is evidenced in the twelve volumes of Christopher Tolkien's series, *The History of Middle-earth* (1983–96).

Tolkien began writing for children in 1920 with the first of what became for many years a series of illustrated letters, addressed to his own children, ostensibly written by Father Christmas and telling of events at the North Pole. The earliest letters are fairly simple, but around 1925 they began to grow in length and complexity, as Tolkien inevitably evolved a mythology around Father Christmas and the various elves, gnomes, and polar bears of that region. A selection of these letters appeared in 1976 as *The Father Christmas Letters,* edited by Baillie Tolkien. A much-expanded edition appeared in 1999 under the title *Letters from Father Christmas.*

Around 1924, Tolkien began telling tales to his children, sometimes writing them down. One of these early efforts is "The Orgog," an unfinished tale of a strange creature traveling through a fantastic landscape. Another, a short novella called *Roverandom* that was published posthumously in 1998, was first told extemporaneously to his children in September 1925 but apparently was not written down until around Christmas 1927. *Mr. Bliss,* an illustrated booklet published in a facsimile edition in 1982, was written in 1928, according to a summer diary of Michael Tolkien's, though the only surviving manuscript appears to date from the early 1930s.[6]

Around 1928 Tolkien began a series of poems that he titled "Tales and Songs of Bimble Bay," set around an imaginary seaside town called Bimble Bay. Tolkien wrote six poems in this series, three of which appear in this book.[7] And the earliest version of *Farmer Giles of Ham* probably also dates from the late 1920s, around the time just before *The Hobbit* was written.[8]

In his essay "Whose *Lord of the Rings* Is It, Anyway?," Wayne G. Hammond gives an excellent evaluation of Tolkien's children's stories:

The significance of Tolkien's children's stories has not been fully appreciated. They gave him opportunities (or excuses) to experiment with other modes of storytelling than the formal prose or poetry he used in writing his mythology. In a children's story he could be unashamedly playful, even childlike, with words and situations. Not for the serious *legendarium* was a red-haired boy named Carrots who had strange adventures inside a cuckoo clock, or a villain "Bill Stickers" and his nemesis "Major Road Ahead." Not for posterity, either, since Tolkien seems never to have set these stories on paper, or not to a great extent. . . . *Mr. Bliss* has layers of social satire, and (as far as we know) is Tolkien's only experiment with the picture book, in which art and words have equal weight. In the "Father Christmas Letters" he could indulge his talents for painting and drawing, calligraphy, and languages. *Roverandom* began as an invention to comfort young Michael Tolkien who had lost a toy, and Michael and his brother John who were frightened during a storm. . . . *Farmer Giles of Ham* likewise began simply, as a family game played in the country around Oxford, but it appealed to Tolkien's love of wordplay and of place-names, and he subsequently enlarged it for publication. (*Canadian C. S. Lewis Journal,* Spring 2000, p. 62)

The Hobbit represents the first coming together of these various facets of Tolkien's writings — his poetry (there are sixteen poems in *The Hobbit,* plus eight riddles); his artwork; the peoples and places from his invented mythology (Elrond, Mirkwood, and the Necromancer, Sauron); and the style and accessibility of his writing for children, together with a kind of playfulness drawing on his professional knowledge of medieval languages and literature. All of these come together and blossom in *The Hobbit,* while similarly they would bloom in *The Lord of the Rings.*[9]

Tolkien himself claimed that *The Hobbit* was derived from "previously digested" epic, mythology, and fairy story. We can name some such sources: *Beowulf,* the fairy-tale collections of Andrew Lang and the Brothers Grimm, works by

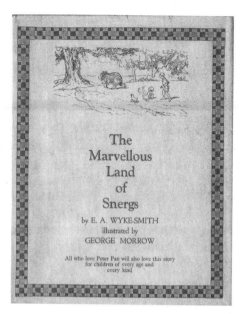

The dust jacket (with maroon printing over a light pink background) of the British first edition of *The Marvellous Land of Snergs,* by E. A. Wyke-Smith, published by Ernest Benn in September 1927. A somewhat breathless blurb on the front flap (probably written by the book's editor, Victor Gollancz, who worked at Benn's before founding his own publishing firm) describes the book as follows:

> The book opens with a description of a Settlement for Superfluous Children. A little to the north of the Settlement Vanderdecken and his crew are in shore quarters; the *Flying Dutchman* anchored close by. To the south are the amicable if unintelligent Snergs, some off-shoot of the pixies. Rather naughtily Joe and Sylvia run away, and in the company of Gorbo—of all Snergs least intelligent—get mixed up with magic and find themselves *the wrong side of the river.* Escapes from Golithos, an ogre imperfectly reformed; from Mother Meldrum, that sinister witch; from the wicked King Kul; and the rescue by Vanderdecken and the Snergs, fill a joyous volume.

The *Times Literary Supplement,* on November 24, 1927, called it "a cheerful and satisfactory book." *The Marvellous Land of Snergs* was reprinted in 1996 by Old Earth Books of Baltimore, with an introduction by Douglas A. Anderson concerning Wyke-Smith and his writings. (Photograph courtesy of Peter Glassman of Books of Wonder, New York.)

Edward Augustine Wyke-Smith (1871–1935). Wyke-Smith was a British mining engineer and an adventurous world traveler. In the 1920s he published eight novels, four of which were for children. Wyke-Smith also published a number of stories for children in the various annuals edited by "Herbert Strang" and published by Oxford University Press. *The Marvellous Land of Snergs* was his final book. This photograph was taken around 1925, when Wyke-Smith had completed *The Marvellous Land of Snergs.*

E. H. Knatchbull-Hugessen, Rudyard Kipling, William Morris, and George Macdonald, especially the latter's *Princess and the Goblin* and its sequel *The Princess and Curdie.* The single influ-

ence that Tolkien called a conscious one was his own "Silmarillion" legends. Another, more obscure influence was *The Marvellous Land of Snergs* (1927), a children's book by E. A. Wyke-Smith. This story concerns the adventures of a Snerg named Gorbo. Snergs are "a race of people only slightly taller than the average table but broad in the shoulders and of great strength."

The land of the Snergs is described as "a place set apart," where a small colony has been established for children who have been taken away from their abusive or neglectful parents. The story centers on two children, Joe and Sylvia, who, along with Gorbo, proceed on a rambling adventure into unknown lands. They encounter various troublesome and curious characters, such as Golithos, a reformed ogre who has become vegetarian and no longer eats children, and Mother Meldrum, a sinister witch who is also a wonderful cook.

Tolkien admitted in a 1955 letter to W. H. Auden that *The Marvellous Land of Snergs* was "probably an unconscious source-book! for the Hobbits, not of anything else" (*Letters*, No. 163). But this statement fails to convey the esteem in which Tolkien once held the book. In the drafts for his famous lecture "On Fairy-Stories" he wrote, "I should like to record my own love and my children's love of E. A. Wyke-Smith's *Marvellous Land of Snergs,* at any rate of the snerg-element of that tale, and of Gorbo the gem of dunderheads, jewel of a companion in an escapade."

The playfulness and humor of *The Marvellous Land of Snergs* are strongly suggestive of *The Hobbit,* as the following excerpt demonstrates:

> [The Snergs] are great on feasts, which they have in the open air at long tables joined end on and following the turns of the street. This is necessary because nearly everybody is invited — that is to say, commanded to come, because the King gives the feasts, though each person has to bring his share of food and drink and put it in the general stock. Of late years the procedure has changed owing to the enormous number of invitations that had to be sent; the commands are now understood and only invitations to stay away are sent to the people who are not wanted on the particular occasion. They are sometimes hard up for a reason for a feast, and then the Master of the Household, whose job it is, has to hunt for a reason, such as its being somebody's birthday. Once they had a feast because it was nobody's birthday that day. (*The Marvellous Land of Snergs*, p. 10)

There are other similarities between the two books, in theme and in a few specific incidents. *The Marvellous Land of Snergs* remains a delight-

This illustration by George Morrow, from *The Marvellous Land of Snergs,* shows Gorbo the Snerg leading Sylvia and Joe (and their dog, Tiger) through the Dark Woods. Morrow (1869–1955) was a well-known illustrator for *Punch*, a magazine to which Wyke-Smith also contributed. Morrow's graphic style, concentrating on people and facial expressions, complements Wyke-Smith's prose very well. Morrow also illustrated Wyke-Smith's three other children's books, *Bill of the Bustingforths* (frontispiece only), *The Last of the Baron,* and *Some Pirates and Marmaduke,* all published in 1921.

ful book, and fans of *The Hobbit* will find much to enjoy in it beyond the Tolkien connection.

The history of the actual writing of *The Hobbit* is best told by first studying the surviving manuscripts, typescripts, and proofs now held in the Memorial Library Archives at Marquette University in Milwaukee, Wisconsin. It is perhaps easiest to describe these papers in terms of stages of composition, which I shall label from A to F.

Stage A: A six-page handwritten manuscript of Chapter 1 (the opening pages are missing). This is the earliest surviving manuscript, in which the dragon is named Pryftan, and the head dwarf Gandalf, and the wizard Bladorthin.

Stage B: A mixed typescript and handwritten manuscript. The first twelve pages are typed (on Tolkien's Hammond typewriter), and the remainder of the pages are handwritten and numbered consecutively from 13 to 167. This stage of composition constitutes Chapters 1 through 12 of the published book, and Chapter 14. The name of the dragon was originally typed (in Chapter 1) Pryftan, but this is hand-corrected to Smaug. The manuscript continues with the head dwarf still named Gandalf, and the wizard Bladorthin. Beorn is called Medwed throughout this version, and the wizard does not produce the key to the back door of the Lonely Mountain — a key found in the trolls' hoard is used to open Durin's Door. Some stoppages are discernable at certain points, evidenced by a change of paper or ink, or a slight change in the handwriting, perhaps because a different pen was used. The breaks occur roughly at page 50 (near the beginning of chapter 5), page 77 (at the end of chapter 6), page 107 (the middle of chapter 8), and page 119 (the beginning of chapter 9). In the last thirty-five pages, the head dwarf becomes Thorin, and the wizard Gandalf.

An outline of six pages summarizes the tale from the Elvenking's Halls to the end of the story.[10]

Stage C: A typescript done on the Hammond typewriter (with the songs in italics), with the pages numbered from 1 to 132, covering the same material as in stage B. (The final pages were renumbered at Stage E, at the time of the insertion of the matter that became Chapter 13; see below.) This typescript uses Thorin and Gandalf throughout, and must have been prepared toward the end of stage B. Also, the character first named Medwed is now called Beorn.

Stage D: A handwritten manuscript, with pages numbered from 1 to 45, covering Chapters 13 and 15–19.

Stage E: The typescript from Stage C was reworked, with the new insert of Chapter 13 paginated 127–134, and the typescript of the former

Chapter 13, now Chapter 14, renumbered by hand 135–40. The new chapters from stage D are now typed and hand-numbered from 141–68.

Stage F: A second full typescript, first intended as a printer's typescript, was made at this point, but it seems not to have been used, as it has a significant number of typographical mistakes.

After this came the first set of page proofs, followed by the revised page proofs.

To combine the physical evidence of the manuscript with what is known of the chronology of the composition of the book is a tentative process, and it is not always possible to determine dates precisely.

Tolkien often recounted how he began the story. One hot summer afternoon he was sitting at home at his desk, correcting School Certificate examination papers on English literature. He told one interviewer, "One of the candidates had mercifully left one of the pages with no writing on it, which is the best thing that can possibly happen to an examiner, and I wrote on it: 'In a hole in the ground there lived a hobbit.' Names always generate a story in my mind: eventually I thought I'd better find out what hobbits were like." (*Biography,* p. 172) Elsewhere he added, "Later on, some months later, I thought this was just too good to leave just on the back of an examination [paper] . . . I wrote the first chapter first — then I forgot about it, then I wrote another part. I myself can still see the gaps. There is a very big gap after they reach the eyrie of the Eagles. After that I really didn't know how to go on." And further to this he said, "I just spun a yarn out of any elements in my head: I don't remember organizing the thing at all."[11]

Just when he wrote that first sentence is not precisely clear. Enough of the book was in existence by January 1933 to be shown to C. S. Lewis,

FOLKLORE OF THE NORTH OF ENGLAND.

79

pigmies, chittifaces, nixies (22), Jinny-burnt-tails, dudmen, hell-hounds, dopplé-gangers (23), boggleboes, bogies, redmen, portunes, grants, hobbits, hobgoblins, brown-men (24), cowies, dunnies (25), wirrikows (26), alholdes, mannikins, follets, korreds, lubberkins, cluricauns, kobolds, leprechauns, kors, mares, korreds, puckles, korigans, sylvans, succubuses, black-men, shadows, banshees, lian-hanshees, clabbernappers, Gabriel-hounds, mawkins, doubles (27), corpse lights or candles, scrats, mahounds, trows, gnomes, sprites, fates, fiends, sybils, nick-nevins (28), whitewomen, fairies (29), thrummy-caps (30),

When he first wrote the sentence that opens *The Hobbit*— "In a hole in the ground there lived a hobbit"—Tolkien believed that he was inventing the word *hobbit.* Many possible derivations for the word have been suggested, including combinations based on *hob* (a common word for rustic) and *rabbit.* The similarity of *hobbit* with the names of some of the creatures of British folklore has also been noted: some country sprites and brownies are called Hobs and Hob-thrusts, and in Joseph Jacobs's collection *More English Fairy Tales* (1894) there is a story of more sinister creatures called Hobyahs. In an interview, Tolkien once suggested that the word *hobbit* might have been associated with Sinclair Lewis's *Babbitt,* the 1922 satirical novel about a hopelessly middle-class businessman. In *The Lord of the Rings,* however, Tolkien offered a derivation from a hypothetical Old English word *hol-bytla,* or "hole-dweller."[12]

After Tolkien's death, it was discovered that the word *hobbit* actually appears in a long list of about two hundred kinds of supernatural creatures published in 1895. The list is in a volume called *The Denham Tracts,* a collection of folklore writings by Michael Aislabie Denham (1801?–1859), edited by Dr. James Hardy, and published in two volumes (1892 and 1895) by the Folklore Society in London. *Hobbit* appears in Volume Two (p. 79; see line 3 in the illustration above), and in the index, where the word is defined as "a class of spirit."[13]

J.R.R. Tolkien and his four children, photograph taken circa 1936 in the garden at 20 Northmoor Road. From left to right: Priscilla, Michael, John, J.R.R. Tolkien, and Christopher.

who wrote of it to Arthur Greeves on February 4, 1933: "Since term began [on January 15] I have had a delightful time reading a children's story which Tolkien has just written . . . Whether it is really good (I think it is until the end) is of course another question: still more, whether it will succeed with modern children" (*They Stand Together,* ed. Walter Hooper, No. 183). Tolkien's eldest sons, John and Michael, remembered having heard elements of the story told to them in their father's study at 22 Northmoor Road, where the Tolkien family lived from early 1926 to January 1930, when they moved from this house into the larger one next door. But what these "elements" were remains uncertain — they could have been from other impromptu tales that Tolkien told his children and then were later reused in *The Hobbit.* Michael Tolkien preserved some of his own childhood compositions that late in life he believed dated from 1929, which were written in imitation of *The Hobbit.* However, certain elements in these stories, as described by Michael Tolkien, make it clear that they compare not with the earliest phases of composition but with later stages.[14]

There are a few other important pieces of contemporary evidence to discuss. First there is a letter by Christopher Tolkien written to Father Christmas in December 1937, proposing *The Hobbit* as an idea for Christmas presents. This letter

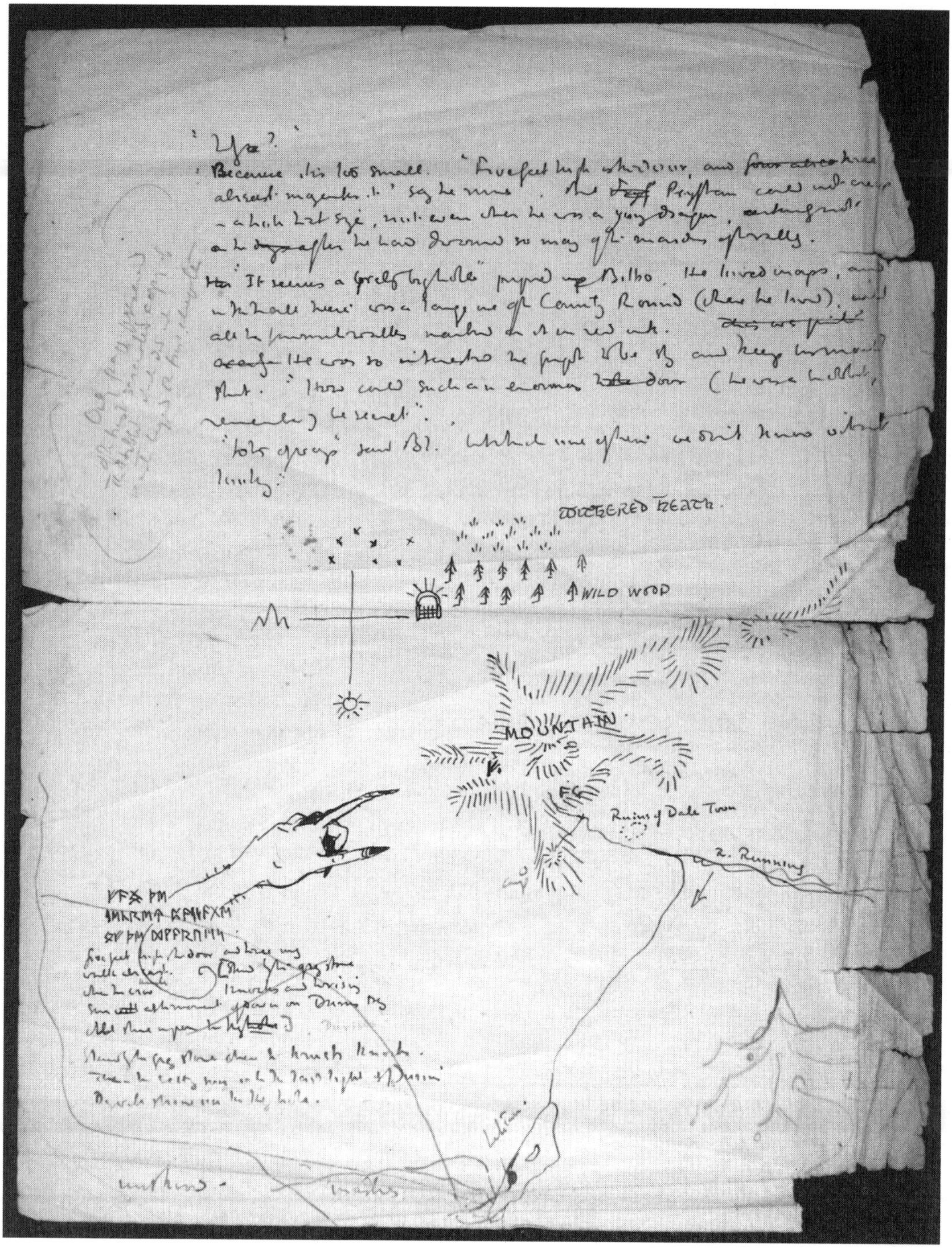

'Yes?'

'Because this is too small. "Five feet high the door, and three abreast may enter it," say the runes . The ... Professor could not creep
... a little bit ... , not even when he was a young dragon, ...
... after he had devoured so many of the maidens of the valley.

'It seems a great height to me' piped up Bilbo. He loved maps, and
in his hall there was a large one of County Round (where he lived), with
all the surrounding walks marked on it in red ink. ...
... the door so intrigued he forgot that he ... and keep his mouth
shut . "Those call such an enormous ... door (he was thinking,
remembering the secret)".

'Don't argue' said Bilbo . Whichever way you please we don't know without
family .

WITHERED HEATH.

WILD WOOD

MOUNTAIN

Ruins of Dale Town

R. Running

Opposite: A page from the original manuscript of *The Hobbit*, which did not reach beyond the first chapter.[15] The back door to the mountain is here marked with an F rune, and the runic passage next to the hand reads (with characters underlined here represented by a single rune): FA<u>NG</u> <u>THE</u> | SE-CRET PASSAGE | OF <u>THE</u> DWARVES. (The rune used for O is the one Tolkien would later use for EE.) The text underneath the runes reads: "five feet high the door and three may walk abreast." A bracketed sentence is crossed out: "Stand by the grey stone when [*or where*] the crow [*written above:* thrush] knocks and the rising sun at the moment of dawn on Durin's Day will shine upon the key hole [*"hole" crossed out*]." This sentence is reworked underneath: "Stand by the grey stone where the thrush knocks. Then the setting sun with the last light of Durin's Day will shine on the key hole."

In this early version of Thror's Map the geography around the Lonely Mountain is seen to have already taken shape. The Withered Heath and the ruins of Dale Town are marked, and the River Running, Lake Town, the nearby marshes, and Mirkwood. A sketch of the Lonely Mountain appears at the lower right. A compass in the center shows the seven stars of the Great Bear (called the Big Dipper in North America) to the north, with what is apparently the sun to the south. The symbols to the east and west may reflect elements from Tolkien's "Silmarillion" writings of the 1930s—the Gates of Morn to the east, and the Mountains of Valinor to the west. (See volume four of the *History, The Shaping of Middle-earth*.)

gives the history of the book as follows: "Daddy wrote it ages ago, and read it to John, Michael, and me in our Winter 'Reads' after tea in the evening; but the ending chapters were rather roughly done, and not typed out at all; he finished it about a year ago" (*Biography*, p. 177). And in a memorandum Stanley Unwin wrote after meeting with Tolkien in late October 1937, he recorded the fact that Tolkien "mentioned that *The Hobbit* took him 2 or 3 years to write because he works very slowly" (*George Allen & Unwin—A Rembrancer*, p. 81).

If we take the publication of *The Marvellous Land of Snergs* as necessarily antecedent to Tolkien's idea of hobbits, then the earliest he could have written that first sentence would have been the summer of 1928. Tolkien clearly had the inspiration for the first sentence while grading ex-

aminations one summer, and that seems likely to have been in one of the three years from 1928 to 1930. Tolkien returned to the idea of hobbits some indefinite time period later, writing the first version of Chapter 1 (stage A). Some unknown amount of time elapsed, and he returned to the story, typing up chapter one and continuing on by hand (with an additional gap in composition after the eagle episode), making stage B. He clearly must have reached stage C, a typescript, by January 1933, in time for C. S. Lewis to read the book and feel uncertain about the ending, which was apparently not written out beyond an outline. Stages D, E, and F probably belong to the summer of 1936, when Tolkien returned to the book in order to finish it for consideration by Allen & Unwin.

Tolkien himself dated the beginning of the writing of *The Hobbit* to 1930. In one account, he said that he wrote the first chapter "certainly after 1930 when I moved to 20 Northmoor Road" (*Biography*, p. 177). In the 1968 BBC television program "Tolkien in Oxford," Tolkien gave the following account of his writing of the first sentence, and again he specifically associates it with the house at number 20 Northmoor Road:

The actual flashpoint was — I can remember very clearly — I can still see the corner of my house in 20 Northmoor Road where it happened. I'd got an enormous pile of examinations papers there [pointing to his right], and marking school examinations in the summertime is an enormous [task], very laborious and unfortunately also very boring. I remember picking up a paper and actually finding — I nearly gave it an extra mark on it, an extra five marks — one page of the particular paper was left blank. Glorious. Nothing to read, so I scribbled on it, I can't think why, "In a hole in the ground there lived a hobbit." (*Tolkien in Oxford*, 1968)

Tolkien also wrote in a letter to Allen & Unwin of August 31, 1937, that "my eldest boy was thirteen when he heard the serial," and since John was born in November 1917, he would have turned thirteen in November 1930, which suggests that Tolkien might have read the first chapters to his sons during their "Winter Reads" in the winter of 1930–31.

The sequence of events that brought the manuscript of *The Hobbit* to the attention of George Allen & Unwin is no longer clear. Tolkien's "home manuscript" had been lent to some people outside of the family, including C. S. Lewis, Elaine Griffiths, the Reverend Mother St. Teresa Gale (the Mother Superior at Cherwell Edge, a convent of the Order of the Holy Child Jesus), and one child, a girl of twelve or thirteen, presumably Aileen Jennings, the older sister of the poet Elizabeth Jennings, whose family was friends with the Tolkiens.

Elaine Griffiths (1909–1996) was a pupil of Tolkien's who was for many years afterward a Fellow of St. Anne's College, Oxford. In the early 1930s she was tutoring undergraduates at Cherwell Edge, to which was attached a hostel (where Griffiths lived) for Catholic women in the Society of Home-Students, as St. Anne's was then called. Since 1934 Griffiths was working on a B.Litt. with Tolkien on the language of the *Ancrene Wisse*. She once recalled:

> When I was a young graduate, Professor Tolkien lent me his — not manuscript, but beautifully typed copy of *The Hobbit.* He had a fascinating typewriter with an italic script, and I thought it was wonderful and read it with enormous pleasure. And quite a time afterwards, somebody I had known when she was an undergraduate who was working for Allen & Unwin, came to me and wanted something, I've forgotten what, and I said, "Oh Susan, I don't know it or can't get it, but I'll tell you something, go along to Professor Tolkien and see if you can get out of him a work called *The Hobbit,* as I think it's frightfully good.[16]

The person from Allen & Unwin was Susan Dagnall (1910–1952), who was at Oxford at the same time as Griffiths and who went to work at Allen & Unwin in 1933. Sometime in the late spring or early summer of 1936, Dagnall visited Oxford to discuss with Griffiths the revision of a translation of *Beowulf* that was a popular undergraduate crib. Tolkien had in fact recommended Griffiths for the job, though in the end she was unable to do it. The task was completed by Tolkien's colleague C. L. Wrenn, and Allen & Unwin published it in 1940 as *Beowulf and the Finnesburgh Fragment,* with prefatory remarks by Tolkien.

Dagnall did borrow the manuscript of *The Hobbit,* and after reading it she encouraged Tolkien to finish it so that it could be considered for publication by Allen & Unwin. Tolkien set to work. In August he wrote that *The Hobbit* was nearly finished, but it was not until October 3, 1936, that he sent the typescript to Allen & Unwin.

Stanley Unwin, the firm's chairman, read the book and approved it. A second opinion was solicited from the children's writer Rose Fyleman (1877–1957), who was then working as an outside reader and translator for Allen & Unwin. But Stanley Unwin believed that children were the best judges of children's books, and intermittently he employed his own children, including his youngest son Rayner, to review the children's book submissions for the standard fee of one shilling per written report. *The Hobbit* was given to Rayner Unwin, then aged ten, who thought the book was good and judged, with the superiority of a ten-year-old, that it should appeal to all children between the ages of five and nine. *The Hobbit* was officially accepted for publication. Contracts were signed in early December.

On December 4, 1936, Susan Dagnall asked Tolkien for a short paragraph describing the book for Allen & Unwin's catalog. Tolkien evidently

A photograph of Stanley Unwin, as appeared in the January 1, 1938, issue of the *Publishers' Circular and The Publisher & Bookseller.* Tolkien's biographer, Humphrey Carpenter, described the publisher as "small, bright-eyed, and bearded," and noted that Tolkien himself said that Unwin looked "exactly like one of my dwarves" (*Biography*, p. 183).

Stanley Unwin (1884–1968) had worked in publishing before acquiring the assets of the bankrupt firm George Allen & Sons in 1914, renaming it George Allen & Unwin. His company proved very successful, and he became a leading figure in publishing. His book *The Truth About Publishing* (1926) remains one of the classic accounts of the business. In his autobiography *The Truth About a Publisher* (1960), Unwin named *The Hobbit* as "one of my favourite publications." Unwin was knighted in 1946.

supplied this before December 10. It not only appeared in the Allen & Unwin 1937 *Summer Announcements* but it was also used on the front flap of the dust jacket of the published book, where additional remarks were added by the publisher. Tolkien's paragraphs read as follows:

> If you care for journeys there and back, out of the comfortable Western world, over the edge of the Wild, and home again, and can take an interest in a humble hero (blessed with a little wisdom and a little courage and considerable good luck), here is the

record of such a journey and such a traveller. The period is the ancient time between the age of Faerie and the dominion of men, when the famous forest of Mirkwood was still standing, and the mountains were full of danger. In following the path of this humble adventurer, you will learn by the way (as he did) – if you do not already know all about these things – much about trolls, goblins, dwarves, and elves, and get some glimpses into the history and politics of a neglected but important period.

For Mr. Bilbo Baggins visited various notable persons; conversed with the dragon, Smaug the Magnificent; and was present, rather unwillingly, at the Battle of Five Armies. This is all the more remarkable, since he was a hobbit. Hobbits have hitherto been passed over in history and legend, perhaps because they as a rule preferred comfort to excitement. But this account, based on his personal memoirs, of the one exciting year in the otherwise quiet life of Mr. Baggins will give you a fair idea of this estimable people, now (it is said) becoming rather rare. They do not like noise.

There were evidently some of Tolkien's own illustrations with the "home manuscript" of *The Hobbit,* but just what these might have been remains uncertain. There were also some maps, five of which were apparently with the book when it was submitted to Allen & Unwin in October 1936.[17]

Over the years since *The Hobbit* was first published, a number of Tolkien's illustrations, eight in black and white and five in color (plus the two maps), have become what might be called the "standard" illustrations that usually appear in the book.[18] But this standard took some time to evolve, and the surviving artwork associated with *The Hobbit* numbers around seventy pieces.

The first British edition had no color illustrations, but included ten black-and-white ones, and two maps. All of Tolkien's black-and-white *Hobbit* drawings seem to have been made after the holidays of December 1936 and before the middle of

> Report on "The Hobbit"
> by
> 30 OCT 1936
>
> Bilbo Baggins was a hobbit who lived in his hobbit-hole and never went for adventures, at last Gandalf the wizard and his dwarves persuaded him to go. He had a very exiting time fighting goblins and wargs. at last they got to the lonely mountains; Smaug, the dragon who gaurds it is killed and after a terrific battle with the goblins he returned home — rich!
>
> This book, with the help of maps, does not need any illustrations it is good and should appeal to all children between the ages of 5 and 9.
>
> Rayner Unwin

Rayner Unwin's reader's report on *The Hobbit*, written when he was age ten.

Rayner Unwin (1925–2000) was, more than anyone else, Tolkien's publisher. After he went to work at his father's firm in 1951, he was responsible for seeing Tolkien's works through publication for the rest of Tolkien's life and for long afterward. Rayner Unwin succeeded his father as chairman of George Allen & Unwin on his father's death in 1968. His delightful memoir of the family firm, *George Allen & Unwin: A Remembrancer*, appeared in 1999. It contains two long chapters recounting his experiences publishing Tolkien.

January 1937. On January 4, Tolkien sent Allen & Unwin four finished drawings, including *The Elvenking's Gate, Lake Town, The Front Gate,* and *Mirkwood* (which Tolkien envisioned as the front endpaper). At the same time he sent on the redrawn versions of Thror's Map and the map of Wilderland, having decided that the other three were not necessary (though Tolkien would have to redraw Thror's Map yet again, in a horizontal framework suitable for an endpaper). Two weeks later he sent six more pictures, which he had designed so as to more evenly distribute the illustrations throughout the book. These six illustrations included *The Hill: Hobbiton-across-the Water* (a black-and-white version), *The Trolls, The Moun-tain-path, The Misty Mountains Looking West, Beorn's Hall,* and *The Hall at Bag-End.*

As of the end of March, Allen & Unwin were hopeful that Tolkien might find time to provide a dust jacket design for the book. He submitted a preliminary design in early April, and by April 25 he had turned in the final art (with elaborate instructions to the printers written in the margins).

Four of Tolkien's five color paintings for *The Hobbit* were done during a couple of weeks of university vacation in mid-July 1937. These include *Rivendell, Bilbo Woke Up with the Early Sun in His Eyes, Bilbo Comes to the Huts of the Raft-elves,* and *Conversation with Smaug.* The fifth, a colored painting to replace the ink version of *The Hill: Hobbiton-across-the Water,* was completed by August 13.

The complexities with the various maps, illustrations, and the dust jacket occupied Tolkien and Allen & Unwin for much of the first half of 1937. In his publishing memoir, Rayner Unwin described the situation as follows:

> In 1937 alone Tolkien wrote 26 letters to George Allen & Unwin and received 31 letters in return. On Tolkien's part these were all in handwriting, often up to five pages long, detailed, fluent, often pungent, but infinitely polite and exasperatingly pre-cise. The time and patience that his publishers devoted to what should have been a straightforward typesetting job is astonishing. I doubt whether any author today, however famous, would get such scrupulous attention. (*George Allen & Unwin — A Remembrancer,* p. 75)

The first announcement of the publication of *The Hobbit* came in the February 6, 1937, issue of the *Publishers' Circular and The Publisher & Bookseller.* Allen & Unwin placed an advertisement for their March and April publications, and *The Hobbit* is listed as the first book under the April heading, where it is described (in a strange comparison) as "the most delightful story of its kind since *The Crock of Gold*," a book by James Stephens originally published in 1912. *The Hobbit* was announced to be "illustrated," with the same price (7s. 6d.) as the published book would carry.

Probably in late April 1937 a proof copy of *The Hobbit* was submitted to the Boston firm Houghton Mifflin Company, who were invited to make an offer for American rights. At that time, various British publishers had working arrangements with compatible American firms, and in this context Allen & Unwin's ties were with Houghton Mifflin. Paul Brooks was then a young editor at Houghton Mifflin, and many years later he recounted in his memoir *Two Park Street* (1986) the initial reaction at Houghton Mifflin to *The Hobbit:* "Our managing editor (he then had charge of children's books) was not impressed. Nor was the children's librarian at the Boston Public Library, whom we asked for a professional opinion. Yet for some reason — though I know nothing about juveniles — I read *The Hobbit* and fell for Mr. Bilbo Baggins and his crew. No matter what age this story was written for, we must give it a try" (p. 107).[19]

Strangely, Houghton Mifflin suggested commissioning some additional color illustrations from "good American artists" to accompany Tolkien's black-and-white drawings. Tolkien consented to this in a letter of May 13, 1937, as long as it was possible "to veto anything from or influenced by the Disney studios (for all whose works I have a heartfelt loathing)"[20] (*Letters*, No. 13); but Allen & Unwin convinced him that it would be better if all illustrations were from his hand. Further confusion resulted when Tolkien sent Houghton Mifflin some sample color illustrations that were not for *The Hobbit* before he sent them five paintings for the story. Houghton Mifflin chose four of these five and, with a nudge from

Allen & Unwin, paid the artist one hundred dollars.

Tolkien received the first proofs of the text in two batches, on February 20 and 24, 1937. Tolkien returned them to Allen & Unwin on March 11. His corrections were considered somewhat heavy, and even though he had carefully calculated the length of the replacement passages, it was necessary to reset several sections. Tolkien received the revised proofs in early April and returned them on April 13.

The book was printed in June, but publication was postponed to allow for the sending out of advance copies and to aim for the Christmas market. In an advertisement in the July 3, 1937, issue of the *Publishers' Circular and The Publisher & Bookseller*, Allen & Unwin repositioned the book to the Autumn list. The description in this advertisement reads: "A book of adventures in a magic world of dwarves and dragons, by an Oxford Professor. Perhaps a new *Alice in Wonderland*."

Tolkien received his first copy of the book on August 13. A few weeks before the book's publication on September 21, Stanley Unwin took the unusual measure of purchasing a full-page advertisement in the *Publishers' Circular and The Publisher & Bookseller*, unhesitatingly calling *The Hobbit* "the children's book of the year." Allen & Unwin rarely used full-page ads for any single title, but they did so three times in promoting *The Hobbit*.

The Hobbit was finally published in England on September 21, 1937, in a first printing of 1,500 copies. Tolkien arranged for Allen & Unwin to send review copies to C. S. Lewis, the *Oxford Magazine*, the Book Society, and two of his close colleagues, professors George Gordon of Oxford and R. W. Chambers of the University of London. Of his own personal copies, Tolkien gave copies to several close members of his family. Others went to

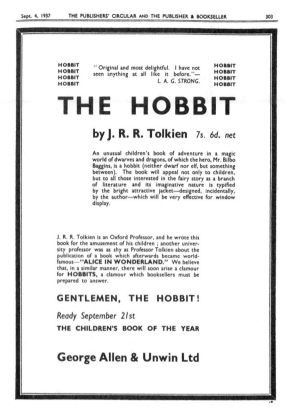

HOBBIT HOBBIT HOBBIT HOBBIT   " Original and most delightful. I have not seen anything at all like it before."— L. A. G. STRONG.   HOBBIT HOBBIT HOBBIT HOBBIT

THE HOBBIT

by J. R. R. Tolkien *7s. 6d. net*

An unusual children's book of adventure in a magic world of dwarves and dragons, of which the hero, Mr. Bilbo Baggins, is a hobbit (neither dwarf nor elf, but something between). The book will appeal not only to children, but to all those interested in the fairy story as a branch of literature and its imaginative nature is typified by the bright attractive jacket—designed, incidentally, by the author—which will be very effective for window display.

J. R. R. Tolkien is an Oxford Professor, and he wrote this book for the amusement of his children ; another university professor was as shy as Professor Tolkien about the publication of a book which afterwards became world-famous—"**ALICE IN WONDERLAND.**" We believe that, in a similar manner, there will soon arise a clamour for **HOBBITS**, a clamour which booksellers must be prepared to answer.

GENTLEMEN, THE HOBBIT!

Ready September 21st
THE CHILDREN'S BOOK OF THE YEAR

George Allen & Unwin Ltd

Allen & Unwin's full-page advertisement announcing the publication of *The Hobbit,* from the September 4, 1937, issue of the *Publishers' Circular and The Publisher & Bookseller.*

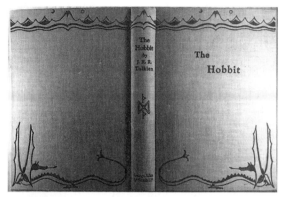

The binding case for the Allen & Unwin edition of *The Hobbit* was designed by Tolkien. (Some of his drawings for the binding can be seen in *Artist,* Nos. 140–41.) The runes on the spine, two TH runes above and below a D rune, refer to Thorin and Thror, and to the secret door of the Lonely Mountain (marked similarly with a D rune on Thror's Map).

his former students who had become colleagues and family friends, including E. V. Gordon, Elaine Griffiths, Helen Buckhurst, Simonne d'Ardenne, Stella Mills, and Katherine Kilbride. One copy went to the Jennings family.

Allen & Unwin also sent copies to some critics, including Richard Hughes and Arthur Ransome, soliciting their opinions. A selection of critic's comments became the basis of Allen & Unwin's next full-page advertisement for *The Hobbit,* which appeared in the November 6, 1937, issue of the *Publishers' Circular and The Publisher & Bookseller.* Allen & Unwin prepared additional publicity materials, including a showcard of the

mounted dust jacket and a facsimile of a letter from the novelist Richard Hughes.[21]

The National Book Fair was held in London on Saturday, November 20, and reports of the fair published in the *Publishers' Circular and The Publisher & Bookseller* noted that His Royal Highness the Duke of Kent had attended and purchased a copy of *The Hobbit.* Tolkien himself also visited the Book Fair.

At Allen & Unwin's headquarters in Museum Street, a window display was artfully arranged, exhibiting about fifty copies of *The Hobbit* faced out in rows on a bookcase. (A small photograph of the display appears in the November 20, 1937, issue of the *Publishers' Circular and The Publisher & Bookseller.*)

The first printing of *The Hobbit* sold well, and a reprint was needed before Christmas. Tolkien's five color pictures were called back to England before the publication of the American edition, and Allen & Unwin decided to use four in the second impression without raising the price of the book. Four color plates would later appear in the American edition, too, but whereas Allen & Unwin

Do you know what the critics say about

THE HOBBIT?

" All who love that kind of book which can be read and reread by adults should take note that a new star has appeared in this constellation. . . . . On the edge of a valley one of Professor Tolkien's characters can pause and say ' It smells like elves ! ' It may be years before we produce another author with such a nose for an elf." — THE TIMES

" *The Hobbit* is a glorious book . . . a lusty full-length riot of unlikely adventures with dwarfs, eagles, dragons, goblins and gold. . . . No normal child could resist it." — TIME AND TIDE

" *The Hobbit* . . . belongs to a very small class of books which have nothing in common save that each admits us to a world of its own. . . Its place is with *Alice, The Wind in the Willows*. . . . Prediction is dangerous, but *The Hobbit* may well prove a classic." — TIMES LITERARY SUPPLEMENT

" It is one of the best stories for children I have come across for a long time. The author has a natural gift for storytelling ; and at the same time he is so saturated with his mythological background that he is able to evoke it effortlessly, with a quite astonishing vividness and completeness." — RICHARD HUGHES

" Original and most delightful. I have not seen anything at all like it before." — L. A. G. STRONG

" It is a delightful and enthralling tale." — JOHN BEEVERS

It is worth your while to stock and to DISPLAY this remarkable children's book

The Publishers will be glad to supply the following publicity material :—

Attractive 3-colour showcard (18″×12″) with mounted jacket
Copies of facsimile letter from Richard Hughes
Decorative announcement sheet containing extracts from reviews
Display card with offprint of full-length review from Time and Tide

GEORGE ALLEN & UNWIN LIMITED

Allen & Unwin's second full-page advertisement for *The Hobbit*, announcing the critical reception of the book, in the November 6, 1937, issue of the *Publishers' Circular and The Publisher & Bookseller*.

The dust jacket for the Allen & Unwin edition of *The Hobbit* was also designed by Tolkien, using the colors blue and green in addition to black and white. (A fragmentary earlier design by Tolkien, along with the finished art, can be seen in *Artist,* Nos. 143–44.) Tolkien originally intended the sun and dragon to be printed in red, but this idea was rejected by Allen & Unwin because of the additional cost.

Wayne G. Hammond and Christina Scull have written perceptively of Tolkien's design as follows:

> Tolkien's *Hobbit* dust-jacket is as eye-catching today as it was in 1937. It attracts not by colour but by its graphic energy. Mountains march rhythmically across the spread, their snowcaps brightly contrasting with dark lower slopes. Jagged lines like lightning bolts pass across the mountains and pulsate at their feet. Tree trunks along the bottom of the picture flash alternately black and white. Like so many of Tolkien's pictures it is designed around a central axis, here with the long road through the forest to the Lonely Mountain. Its content is also symmetrical: on the back are night, darkness, Evil in the shape of the dragon; on the front are day, light, Good in the form of eagles that come to the rescue twice in the story (*Artist,* p. 149).

chose *Bilbo Comes to the Huts of the Raft-elves,* Houghton Mifflin chose instead *Bilbo Woke Up with the Early Sun in His Eyes.*[22]

The second Allen & Unwin impression of *The Hobbit* consisted of 2,300 copies. These were printed in early December 1937, but not all of the printed sheets were immediately bound. (423 copies of the printed sheets were destroyed in November 1940 when the publisher's stock was bombed.)

The first two published reviews of *The Hobbit* are among the most sympathetic and perceptive. They appeared anonymously in the *Times Literary Supplement* and in the parent paper, the *Times.* Both were written by Tolkien's close friend C. S. Lewis.

The first responds directly to the publisher's blurb[23] comparing the book to Lewis Carroll:

> The publisher's claim that *The Hobbit,* though very unlike *Alice,* resembles it in being the work of a professor at play. A more important truth is that both belong to a very small class of books which have nothing in common save that each admits us to a world of its own — a world that seems to have been going on before we stumbled into it but which, once found by the right reader, becomes indispensable to him. Its place is with *Alice, Flatland, Phantastes, The Wind in the Willows.*

. . . It must be understood that this is a children's book only in the sense that the first of many readings can be undertaken in the nursery. *Alice* is read gravely by children and with laughter by grown-ups; *The Hobbit,* on the other hand, will be funniest to its youngest readers, and only years later, at a tenth or twentieth reading, will they begin to realize what deft scholarship and profound reflection have gone to make everything in it so ripe, so friendly, and in its own way so true. Prediction is dangerous: but *The Hobbit* may well prove a classic. (*Times Literary Supplement,* October 2, 1937)

The second review contains more insights:

The truth is that in this book a number of good things, never before united, have come together; a fund of humour, an understanding of children, and a happy fusion of the scholar's with the poet's grasp of mythology. On the edge of a valley one of Professor Tolkien's characters can pause and say: "It smells like elves." It may be years before we produce another author with such a nose for an elf. The Professor has the air of inventing nothing. He has studied trolls and dragons at first hand and describes them with that fidelity which is worth oceans of glib "originality." (*The Times,* October 8, 1937)

Around thirty reviews of the first British edition of *The Hobbit* have been traced. Many of these are very brief, but a handful of them have something more to say than merely describing the book.[24]

The review by Alice Forrester in *Poetry Review* (November–December 1937), not surprisingly, comments on Tolkien's verse: "Not the least item to be commended in his book are the songs and poems which blend with and add to the lively and somewhat mysterious atmosphere."

In the *Junior Bookshelf,* Eleanor Graham gave *The Hobbit* one of its few unfavorable reviews. Graham wrote:

The Hobbit is a strange book. It has in it the makings of a very good story, or perhaps a book of short stories for children, but it is marred, in my opinion, by

The dust jacket for the 1938 American edition of *The Hobbit,* published by Houghton Mifflin Company, used two of Tolkien's color illustrations on the upper and lower covers.

some reflection of the author's attitude to the world. A sort of "Aunt Sally" spirit replaces the benevolence which is notable in the most loved books for children. Instead of natural obstacles in the path of achievement, the journey of the Hobbit and his companions is interrupted by obstructions which somehow give the effect of deliberately intentional setbacks and not of natural developments. . . . There is instead an uneasy sort of compulsion and the Hobbit never really resigns himself to his exile or his long journey. While making these criticisms, I must also say that there is a strong sense of reality in the writing and real distinction, and that those people who like it, will like it very much indeed. (*Junior Bookshelf,* December 1937)

L.A.G. Strong wrote in the *Spectator,* December 3, 1937: "It is dangerous to say that a book is really original, but in this case I risk it gladly. *The Hobbit* should become a classic."

An Australian publication, *All About Books,* gave the book one of its longest reviews in the January 15, 1938, issue. The reviewer was G. H. Cowling, who had been a colleague of Tolkien's at Leeds. He suggested a number of possible sources for elements in *The Hobbit,* writing: "If I were a scientist, I should speak learnedly of hobbits, and say whether they derived their name from 'hobs'

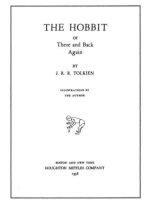 

There are at least two printings of the 1938 Houghton Mifflin edition of *The Hobbit*. The earliest printing has a bowing hobbit on the title page, while the other variants have instead the Houghton Mifflin Company colophon, a seated figure playing a flute.[25]

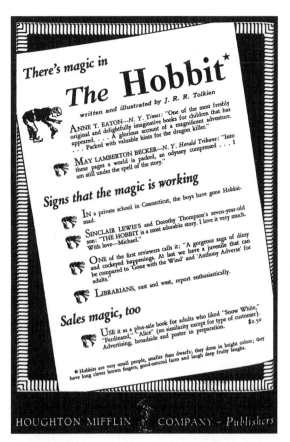

Houghton Mifflin's full-page advertisement for *The Hobbit*, from the March 26, 1938, issue of *Publishers Weekly*.

or 'rabbits.' But I am not, so I will merely enjoy the tale." Cowling concluded, "This is a real fairy story, with the undoubted apparatus of fairy land."

R. B. McCallum, one of the Inklings and a colleague of Tolkien's, wrote in the *Pembroke College Record* for 1937–38: "The whole book is remarkable for the solidity and exactitude of the narrative, a happy and reflective vein of humour and for the sanity of the underlying philosophy. Nothing could diminish the lustre which the name of Lewis Carroll brings to Christ Church, but it may well be that the fact that the author of *The Hobbit* was a fellow of Pembroke will be an additional interest to those who visit us in the future."

In the United States, *The Hobbit* was announced for publication on February 23, 1938, in the February 1938 issue of the *Retail Bookseller*, but evidently some problems with the printing or binding slightly delayed the book. It was reannounced in the March issue of the *Retail Bookseller* for publication on March 2, but finished copies were apparently ready a few days earlier.

More than twenty reviews of the first American edition of *The Hobbit* have been traced, and a selection of representative extracts follows. The first review, which slightly preceded the book's publication, was by May Lamberton Becker in the *New York Herald Tribune*:

At the time of writing, still under the spell of the story, I cannot bend my mind to ask myself whether our American children will like it. My impulse is to say if they don't so much the worse for them. Like the learned Charles Dogdson, the author is an Oxford professor, his specialty being Anglo-Saxon; like Alice, the story has unmistakable signs of having been told to intelligent children. But its style is not like Lewis Carroll's; it is much more like Dunsany's. . . . Into these pages a world is packed, an odyssey compressed, as adventures on the road to the dragon's ill-got treasure thickens. I do not know how our children will like story so close-packed, one of whose chapters would make a book elsewhere; they may think they are getting too much for their money. But dwarfs have come this year into fashion in America; perhaps these will benefit from the Disney boom. (*New York Herald Tribune,* February 20, 1938)

Sophia L. Goldsmith wrote in the *New York Post,* March 1938: "This book will be worn ragged by boys and girls alike. It has immense charm, genuine wit, and dwarfs which put Snow White's boy friends completely in the shade."

Anne T. Eaton (1881–1971), a well-known figure in children's literature and a librarian at the Lincoln School of the Teachers' College at Columbia University, wrote:

This is one of the most freshly original and delightfully imaginative books for children that have appeared in many a long day. . . . [There are] forests that suggest those of William Morris's prose romances. Like Morris's countries, Wilderland is Faerie, yet it has an earthly quality, the scent of trees, drenching rains and the smell of woodfires. . . . The songs of the dwarves and elves are real poetry, and since the author is fortunate enough to be able to make his own drawings, the illustrations are a perfect accompaniment to the text. (*New York Times Book Review,* March 13, 1938)

Eaton also wrote about the book in the *Horn Book:*

The time of the story is between the age of Faerie and the dominion of men, and the scene is laid in one of those magical countries which, like the lands of William Morris's prose romances, are unmistakably a part of England and of Faeryland at the same

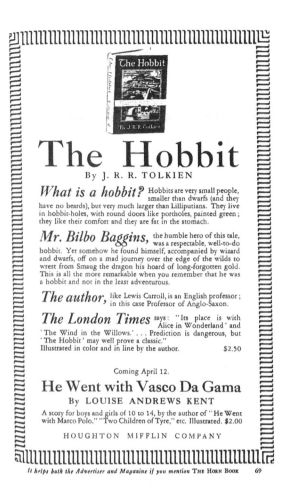

Houghton Mifflin's advertisement for *The Hobbit,* for the March–April 1938 issue of the *Horn Book.*

time. The background of the story is full of authentic bits of mythology and magic and the book has the rare quality of style. It is written with a quiet humor and the logical detail in which children take delight. . . . All those, young or old, who love a finely imagined story, beautifully told, will take *The Hobbit* to their hearts. (*Horn Book,* March–April 1938)

The *Horn Book* took considerable interest in *The Hobbit.* Anne Carroll Moore (1871–1961), the children's librarian at the New York Public Library, also wrote of the book in her column "The Three Owls' Notebook" in the March–April issue, calling it:

> a refreshingly adventurous and original tale of dwarfs, goblins, elves, dragons, trolls, etc., in the true tradition of the old sagas. I think it is a mistake to compare *The Hobbit* with *Alice* or with *The Wind in the Willows*. It is unlike either book. It is firmly rooted in *Beowulf* and authentic Saxon lore, and while appealing to younger children has something in common with W. W. Tarn's *The Treasure of the Isle of Mist,* and with certain tales by William Morris. There is sound learning behind *The Hobbit,* while a rich vein of humor connects this little being, described as smaller than a dwarf, with the strange beings of the ancient world and the world we live in today. (*Horn Book,* March–April 1938)

In the May 1938 issue, one of the magazine's founders, Bertha E. Mahony, introduced *The Hobbit* as one of a group of "certain rare books which stay in the mind like poetry, revealing always fresh joys and new meaning." And several pages of Chapter 1 of *The Hobbit* were reprinted in this issue.

Mary A. Whitney wrote in the *Christian Science Monitor* on March 31, 1938: "All who enjoy a well wrought tale of originality and imagination will revel in the adventures of the hobbit." And William Rose Benét, in the *Saturday Review,* April 2, 1938, called *The Hobbit* "as remarkable a work of imaginative literature for children to have come from a professor of Anglo-Saxon at Oxford as was *Alice in Wonderland* to have come from such a mathematician as the Reverend Dodgson. *The Hobbit* is both prose and poetry, and, above all, gorgeous fancy."

On April 25, 1938, Tolkien received a cablegram from Ferris Greenslet of Houghton Mifflin, telling him that *The Hobbit* was going to receive an award of $250. At their second annual Children's

May 7, 1938   THE PUBLISHERS' CIRCULAR AND THE PUBLISHER & BOOKSELLER   611

J. R. R. TOLKIEN'S

THE HOBBIT

Acclaimed in America as the best juvenile of the season

WESTERN UNION CABLEGRAM

American opinion is only following in the footsteps of critics here

'*The Hobbit* is pure fantasy . . . It is grand imaginative stuff . . . Mr. Baggins is well worth knowing and grows on you."—Howard Spring in *Evening Standard.*
"Its place is with *Alice, Flatland, The Wind in the Willows.*"—*Times Literary Supplement.*

"*The Hobbit* is a glorious book, a lusty full-length riot of unlikely adventures with dwarfs, eagles, dragons, goblins and gold . . . No normal child could resist it."—Phoebe Fenwick Gaye in *Time and Tide.*

With line and four-colour half-tone Illustrations by the Author

Stock and display *The Hobbit* 7s. 6d. net
LONDON: GEORGE ALLEN AND UNWIN LTD

After *The Hobbit* won the *New York Herald Tribune* award, Tolkien was notified of the award in a cablegram from Ferris Greenslet of Houghton Mifflin Company. Stanley Unwin recognized the value of publicizing the award to the book trade in England and reproduced the cablegram in a full-page advertisement in the May 7, 1938, issue of the *Publishers' Circular and The Publisher & Bookseller.*

Festival, the *New York Herald Tribune* planned to award two prizes of $250 each, one for the best book published in the spring for younger children, and the other for the best book for older children. *The Hobbit* won the award for younger children, and the winner in the category for older children was *Iron Duke,* by John R. Tunis, a college story set at Harvard.

The judges in the category for younger children

were May Lamberton Becker (chair), Elizabeth Morrow (the wife of the United States Ambassador to Mexico, Dwight W. Morrow, and the mother of the writer Anne Morrow Lindbergh), and Stephen Vincent Benét. The award was officially presented at a special luncheon on Tuesday, May 17, 1938. The luncheon, chaired by Irita Van Doren, the editor of the Books section of the *New York Herald Tribune,* was held on the final day of the American Bookseller's Association annual convention at the Hotel Pennsylvania in New York City. A member of Houghton Mifflin's sales force, LeBaron R. Barker, Jr., accepted the award on behalf of J.R.R. Tolkien.[26]

As in England, there was one dissenting view in the batch of reviews of *The Hobbit.* It was written by Mary L. Lucas, who discussed the hobbit and the dwarves as follows: "Their adventures and mishaps are numerous, too numerous in fact for really enjoyable reading. The book would be better read aloud in small doses, or the child should be advised to read it that way, himself. It will have a limited appeal unless properly introduced and even then will be best-liked by those children whose imagination is alert" (*Library Journal,* May 1, 1938).

In the *Catholic World* for July 1938, the anonymous reviewer wrote: "We guarantee that you will enjoy this stirring tale as much as your boy. Make him solve the riddles of Gollum and Bilbo. They alone are worth the price of the book." And Harry Lorin Bisse called the book, in a very short review in the *Commonweal* of December 2, 1938, "a brilliantly told modern fairy story."

The Hobbit was a success in America. By June, nearly three thousand copies of the book had been sold. Houghton Mifflin decided to reannounce the book at the head of their fall juvenile list, in hopes of spurring further sales. Their advertisement for the book in the Christmas 1938 issue of the *Horn Book* magazine (see note 6 to Chapter 1), includes a drawing of a hobbit for which Tolkien had provided further descriptive details. *The Hobbit* was displayed with about fifty other children's books in the annual November–December exhibition in the Central Children's Room of the New York Public Library and was suitably praised in a little booklet, *Children's Books 1938,* published for the occasion. The book was reprinted, and by the end of 1938 the sales of the American edition had exceeded five thousand copies.

The Hobbit lost some momentum after the outbreak of the Second World War. Owing to paper rationing, which was introduced in England in April 1940 (several months before Allen & Unwin's warehouse in north London was bombed, with the resulting loss of more than a million books), *The Hobbit* was unavailable in England for long stretches of the 1940s, despite the desire of both the publisher and author to keep it in stock. Paper rationing remained in force until 1949.

Beginning in the early 1950s (perhaps spurred on by the publication in late 1949 of *Farmer Giles of Ham*), *The Hobbit* began to be noticed again. Nearly thirteen years after the *Junior Bookshelf* had given *The Hobbit* a perplexing review, the same publication weighed in with some astute remarks by another reviewer, Marcus S. Crouch:

> *The Hobbit* had a mixed reception, as of most books of marked originality. It has been, I believe, no more than a moderate success in the bookshops, and librarians who have had the courage to buy it in suitable quantities cannot claim that it rivals the popularity of current mass-produced goods. It seems to me, however, to possess in a high degree some of the qualities which make for endurance. I know of no children's book published in the last twenty-five years of which I could more confidently predict that it will be read in the twenty-first century. (*Junior Bookshelf,* March 1950)

In the 1950s sales of *The Hobbit* picked up considerably, climbing even more dramatically after the publication of its long-awaited sequel, *The Lord of the Rings.* There have been many dramatizations of the book, both amateur and professional, since March 1953, when the first authorized adaptation was performed at St. Margaret's School in Edinburgh. These have been followed by various other reworkings, including a truly execrable 1977 television program based on the book, a graphic novel version, and, more recently, various audio versions and a performance by the Finnish National Opera in October 2001. Sales of the book long ago soared into the multimillion copy level. In Great Britain, a postage stamp honoring *The Hobbit* was released in 1998. As *The Hobbit* approaches the sixty-fifth anniversary of its first publication, it will have appeared in more than forty languages. There is no doubt that *The Hobbit* is a worldwide classic, for all ages, and all times.

On July 21, 1998, *The Hobbit* was honored by the Royal Mail of Great Britain by being made the subject of a postage stamp, one of a series "Magical Worlds: Classic Fantasy Books for Children." The series celebrated four other works besides *The Hobbit,* including *Through the Looking-Glass* (1872) by Lewis Carroll, *The Phoenix and the Carpet* (1904) by E. Nesbit, *The Lion, the Witch and the Wardrobe* (1950) by C. S. Lewis, and *The Borrowers* (1952) by Mary Norton. The stamps feature art by Peter Malone.

NOTES

1. The statement is attributed to Tolkien by Eugène Vinaver, who recalled that Tolkien made the remark to an audience in Oxford who had come to hear him lecture on philology, but to whom he instead read a poem of his own composition. This anecdote is cited (p. 80) by Richard C. West in "The Interlace Structure of *The Lord of the Rings*," published in *A Tolkien Compass* (1975), edited by Jared Lobdell.

2. An interview with Denys Gueroult, recorded on January 20, 1965. Parts of this recording were eventually broadcast on the BBC Radio show *Now Read On* in December 1970.

3. A photograph of Tolkien working at his desk can be seen on page 56 of *The Tolkien Family Album* (1992), by John and Priscilla Tolkien, who also write:

> The study was very much the centre of Ronald's home life, and the centre of his study was his desk. Over the years the top of his desk continued to show familiar landscapes: his dark brown wooden tobacco jar, a Toby jug containing pipes and a large bowl into which the ash from his pipe was regularly knocked out. We also remember vividly a row of coloured Quink and Stevenson inks, and sets of sealing-wax in different shades to match his large supply of stationery. There were also wonderful boxes of Koh-i-Noor coloured pencils, and tubes of paint with magical names like Burnt Sienna, Gamboge, and Crimson Lake.

4. In his office at Merton College, Tolkien had an impressive rolltop desk. After his death, it was bought by the novelist Iris Murdoch (1919–1999), who was an admirer of Tolkien's writings. A photograph of Murdoch sitting at the desk in her downstairs study can be seen in Peter J. Conradi's *Iris Murdoch: A Life* (2001).

5. Clyde S. Kilby quotes this in his 1976 book *Tolkien and The Silmarillion*, p. 57, where he has misread Tolkien's handwriting of the first word. For a study of the philological origins of Tolkien's Earendel myth, see "Over Middle-earth Sent unto Men," by Carl F. Hostetter, in *Mythlore*, Spring 1991 (17, no. 3; whole no. 65): 5–10.

6. "The Orgog" is described in *Artist* (p. 77), where an illustration Tolkien apparently made for the story is also reproduced. On the dating of *Mr. Bliss,* see "Origin of a Tolkien Tale" by Joan Tolkien, *Sunday Times,* October 10, 1982 (p. 25).

7. "Glip" can be found in Chapter 5, note 7; "Progress in Bimble Town," in Chapter 10, note 8; and "The Dragon's Visit," in Chapter 14, note 2. A much-revised version of another of these poems, "The Bumpus" (variantly titled "William and the Bumpus"), appears in *The Adventures of Tom Bombadil* (1962) as "Perry-the-winkle." The two other poems, "A Song of Bimble Bay" and "Poor Old Grabbler" (a later version is titled "Old Grabbler"), are unpublished.

8. *Farmer Giles of Ham* was extensively expanded in 1938, and published in 1949. The much shorter earlier version was published in the fiftieth anniversary edition, edited by Christina Scull and Wayne G. Hammond, which appeared in 1999.

9. The best assessment of Tolkien and his medieval roots can be found in T. A. Shippey's *The Road to Middle-earth* (1982; revised edition 1992).

10. This outline contains the passage, described by Humphrey Carpenter as follows: "These notes suggest that Bilbo Baggins might

creep into the dragon's lair and stab him. 'Bilbo plunges in his little magic knife,' [Tolkien] wrote. 'Throes of dragon. Smashes walls and entrance to tunnel' " (*Biography,* p. 179). This passage was struck through by Tolkien, apparently immediately after the writing of it, and the outline continues with the story as we know it in the published book.

11. Tolkien's statement beginning "Later on . . ." is quoted from a 1957 radio interview with Ruth Harshaw for her *Carnival of Books* program. The subsequent statement ("I just spun a yarn . . .") is quoted from a 1964 BBC interview with Irene Slade, for *A World of Sound.*

12. For theories on the word *hobbit,* see Donald O'Brien's "On the Origin of the Name 'Hobbit,' " in *Mythlore,* Winter 1989 (16, no. 2; whole no. 60): 32–38. And although the story "The Hobyahs" appears in Joseph Jacobs's collection *More English Fairy Tales,* its immediate source was a Scotch nursery tale, written up in the *Journal of American Folk-Lore,* volume 4 (1891), by S. V. Proudfit, who remembered hearing the story in his childhood told by a family that came from near Perth.

13. Denham, a tradesman of Piercebridge (near Darlington in the north of England), made his collection of folklore tracts between 1846 and 1859, publishing various parts in pamphlets and newspapers. The list that contains the word *hobbit* originally appeared as a letter to the London *Literary Gazette* of December 23, 1848, but *hobbit* does not appear in this early version, and must have been added by Dr. James Hardy, a correspondent of Denham's who possessed many of the tracts annotated by Denham and by himself. *Hobbit* appears in print only in the 1895 volume.

14. The interview with Michael Tolkien was done by Radio Blackburn, probably around 1975. A transcription of it was published in a dual issue of the *Minas Tirith Evening-Star* (18, no. 1) and *Ravenhill* (7, no. 4), dated Spring 1989. In it, and in his 1977 speech to the Tolkien Society, Michael Tolkien discussed some of the characters in these childhood compositions, including various dwarves with names similar to those in *The Hobbit;* the terrible froglike Ollum, clearly based on Gollum; and a wizard called Scandalf the Beanpiper, evidently modeled after Gandalf. In the earliest manuscripts of *The Hobbit,* however, the wizard was named *Bladorthin* and the chief dwarf *Gandalf,* so Michael Tolkien's compositions must date from a somewhat advanced stage of the writing of *The Hobbit.* In the same interview, Michael Tolkien suggested that these writings in exercise books dated from the time when he was ten or eleven, and since he would have turned ten in late October 1930, the idea that these writings date from after 1930, rather than from 1929, seems much more plausible.

15. At the left of this page, and evidently late in his life, Tolkien wrote in pencil: "Only page preserved of the first scrawled copy of *The Hobbit* which did not reach beyond the first chapter." Tolkien's statement is incorrect, for this leaf (actually two pages, for it has writing on both sides) was merely the only portion that remained among Tolkien's own papers subsequent to his selling, in 1957, the manuscripts of some of his writings, including *The Hobbit* and *The Lord of*

the Rings, to Marquette University in Milwaukee, Wisconsin. The two additional leaves (four more pages) of this draft held in the Marquette Archives have recently been joined by the original of this leaf, making a total of six pages of this draft held at Marquette.

The text on this page (omitting cancellations) reads as follows:

"Why?"

"Because it is too small. 'Five feet high is the door, and three abreast may enter it' say the runes. But Pryftan [an early name for Smaug] could not creep in a hole that size, not even when he was a young dragon, certainly not after he had devoured so many maidens of the valley."

"It seems a pretty big hole," piped up Bilbo. He loved maps, and in the hall there was a large one of the Country Round (where he lived), with all his favourite walks marked on it in red ink. He was so interested he forgot to be shy and keep his mouth shut. "How could such an enormous door" (he was a hobbit, remember) "be secret?"

"Lots of ways," said Bl[adorthin, an early name for the wizard], "but which one of them we don't know without looking."

In his introduction to the fiftieth anniversary edition of *The Hobbit,* Christopher Tolkien reproduced and transcribed both sides of this leaf of his father's manuscript.

16. Elaine Griffiths's reminiscence is quoted from "The Road Goes Ever On," a 1974 Radio Oxford program about Tolkien's life.

17. These were apparently early versions of Thror's Map (probably a variant of *Artist* No. 85; see also page 51 of this book) and the Wilderland Map (*Artist* No. 84), and maps of the land between the Misty Mountains and Mirkwood, of the land east of Mirkwood to the east of the River Running, and of Long Lake (combined with a view of the Lonely Mountain) (*Artist* No. 128).

18. The five color illustrations are *The Hill: Hobbiton-across-the Water, Rivendell, Bilbo Woke Up with the Early Sun in His Eyes, Bilbo Comes to the Huts of the Raft-elves,* and *Conversation with Smaug.* The eight black-and-white illustrations are *The Trolls, The Mountain-path, The Misty Mountains Looking West, Beorn's Hall, The Elvenking's Gate, Lake Town, The Front Gate,* and *The Hall at Bag-End.*

19. The managing editor was Ferris Greenslet (1875–1959), a leading figure at Houghton Mifflin for thirty-five years until his retirement in 1942. The children's librarian at the Boston Public Library was Alice M. Jordan (1870–1960), who reviewed with partial appreciation another of Tolkien's books, *Farmer Giles of Ham,* in the July 1950 issue of the *Horn Book,* noting that "those to whom *The Hobbit* brought lasting delight will open this book by the same writer with eager anticipation. . . . To enjoy this book, one must have a lively imagination, an ear for wonders, a sense of absurdity and pleasure in oddly-compounded words." Paul Brooks (1909–1998) was the editor in chief and director of Houghton Mifflin in the 1950s when the firm published *The Lord of the Rings.*

20. It may be argued that in 1938, when Tolkien made this state-

ment, the Disney Studios had only just released *Snow White and the Seven Dwarfs* (1937) and other signature works, like *Fantasia* (1940), were still in the future. However, Tolkien's opinion remained very much the same nearly thirty years later. In a letter of July 15, 1964, to Jane Louise Curry, Tolkien wrote of Walt Disney: "I recognize his talent, but it has always seemed to me hopelessly corrupted. Though in most of the 'pictures' proceeding from his studios there are admirable or charming passages, the effect of them is to me disgusting. Some have given me nausea."

21. The letter from Richard Hughes, dated October 5, 1937, reads in part:

I agree with you that it is one of the best stories for children I have come across for a very long time. The author has a gift for story-telling; and at the same time he is so saturated in his mythological background that he is able to evoke it, effortlessly, with a quite astonishing vividness and competence.

The only snag that I can see is that many parents (and still more, Child Authorities) may be afraid that certain parts of it would be too terrifying for bedside reading.

Frankly I don't agree with that point of view myself; children seem to have a natural capacity for terror which you can't do much about: I mean, if you don't give them dragons to be frightened of they will frighten themselves with an old chest-of-drawers.

Richard Hughes (1900–1976) is primarily known for his novel *A High Wind in Jamaica* (1929), but he is also remembered for several books of stories for children.

22. Houghton Mifflin also, without exception, cropped, retitled, or otherwise altered Tolkien's colored art.

23. The blurb about the author on the dust jacket of the first impression of *The Hobbit* reads as follows:

J.R.R. Tolkien is Rawlinson and Bosworth professor of Anglo-Saxon at Oxford, and fellow of Pembroke College. He has four children and *The Hobbit* was written for them, and read aloud to them in nursery days, which is of course the way in which practically all the immortal children's stories have come into being. But the fame of the story spread beyond his immediate family and the manuscript of *The Hobbit* was lent to friends in Oxford and read to their children. Though they are utterly dissimilar in character, the birth of *The Hobbit* recalls very strongly that of *Alice in Wonderland*. Here again a professor of an abstruse subject is at play; while *Alice in Wonderland* is full of crazy conundrums, *The Hobbit* has constant echoes of magic and mythology culled from a wide and exact knowledge. Dodgson [*sic*] at first did not think it worth publishing his tale of Wonderland and Professor Tolkien — but not his publishers — still remains to be convinced that anybody will want to read his most delightful history of a Hobbit's journey.

In a letter of August 31, 1937, to Charles Furth of Allen & Unwin (see *Letters,* No. 15), Tolkien sent several corrections and comments about the inaccuracies of the blurb. For the second impression, the blurb was changed to read:

J.R.R. Tolkien is Rawlinson and Bosworth professor of Anglo-Saxon at Oxford, and fellow of Pembroke College. He has four children and *The Hobbit* was written for them, and read aloud to them. It became a standing family entertainment, especially at Christmas-time. But the manuscript soon began to go visiting among older and younger friends (there are many lovers of real fairy stories); and the fame of the hobbit spread beyond the family. Though they are altogether dissimilar, the birth of *The Hobbit* recalls strongly that of *Alice and Wonderland* and *Through the Looking Glass;* and here again we have a student at play. There is as little philology in *The Hobbit* as there is mathematics in Alice; but this play is not an escape from the study – a most attractive room, as most children know who have the chance of invading it.

The Hobbit has riddles, runes, and Icelandic dwarves; and though its world of magic and mythology is its own, a new land of lore, it has the atmosphere of the ancient North. Dodgson at first did not think it worth publishing his tale of Wonderland, and it was very hard to convince Professor Tolkien that anyone would want to read his delightful book. The following few extracts chosen from a battery of favourable reviews, will show that leading critics at any rate have sided with the publishers in claiming that *The Hobbit* is a work of genius.

24. For an analysis of more of the reviews, see "Some Notes on the Reception of *The Hobbit*" by Åke Bertenstam, in *Angerthas in English* 2 (1992): 17–25.

25. All variants use the Wilderland map at the front of the book and *Thror's Map* at the rear, but in the "bowing hobbit" version, the printed list of illustrations on page 9 describes *Thror's Map* as "endpaper 1" and the *Map of Wilderland* as "endpaper 2." In the "flute player" version, the printed list is reversed.

In all copies observed of the "bowing hobbit" version, the half-title is not present (and the frontispiece is pasted onto a stub), and the leaf containing pages 309–10 has been excised, leaving only a stub onto which is pasted a replacement leaf. In the "flute player" variant, the half-title is present (and the frontispiece is not pasted to a stub), and page 309–10 is integral.

In the "bowing hobbit" variant, the heading (on page 118) for Chapter 7, "Queer Lodgings," is erroneously labeled "Chapter VI." Copies of the "flute player" variant have been observed in two states: with "Chapter VI" or with the correct "Chapter VII."

26. John and Priscilla Tolkien, in *The Tolkien Family Album*, record: "In 1938 [Tolkien] received a literary prize for the Best Children's Story of the Year. A somewhat poignant memory is of him opening the letter at the breakfast table and passing the enclosed cheque for fifty pounds – a formidable sum in those days – to Edith, so that she could pay an outstanding doctor's bill with it" (p. 69).

ᚦᛖ·ᚻᚩᛒᛒᛁᛏ
ᚩᚱ
ᚦᛖᚱᛖ·ᚪᚾᛞ·ᛒᚪᚳᚳ·ᚪᚷᚪᛁᚾ

This is a story of long ago. At that time the languages and letters were quite different from ours of today. English is used to represent the languages. But two points may be noted. (1) In English the only correct plural of *dwarf* is *dwarfs,* and the adjective is *dwarfish.* In this story *dwarves* and *dwarvish* are used,* but only when speaking of the ancient people to whom Thorin Oakenshield and his companions belonged.[1] (2) *Orc* is not an English word. It occurs in one or two places but is usually translated *goblin* (or *hobgoblin* for the larger kinds).[2] *Orc* is the hobbits' form of the name given at that time to these creatures, and it is not connected at all with our *orc, ork,* applied to sea-animals of dolphin-kind.

Runes were old letters originally used for cutting or scratching on wood, stone, or metal, and so were thin and angular. At the time of this tale only the Dwarves made regular use of them, especially for private or secret records. Their runes are in this book represented by English runes, which are known now to few people. If the runes on Thror's Map are compared with the transcriptions into modern letters (on pp. 52 and 95–96), the alphabet, adapted to modern English, can be discovered and the above runic title also read. On the Map all the normal runes are found, except ᛉ for X. I and U are used for J and V. There was no rune for Q (use CW); nor for Z (the dwarf-rune ᛦ may be used if required). It will be found, however, that some single runes stand for two modern letters: *th, ng, ee;* other runes of the same kind (ᛠ *ea* and ᛥ *st*) were also sometimes used. The secret door was marked D ᛥ. From the side a hand pointed to this, and under it was written:

ᚠᛁᚢᛖ·ᚠᛟᛏ·ᚻᛁᚷᚻ·ᚦᛖ·ᛞᚩᚱ·ᚪᚾᛞ·ᚦᚱᛟ·ᛗᚪᚣ·ᚹᚪᛚᚳ·ᚪᛒᚱᛖᚪᛋᛏ⁝ ᚦ. ᚦ.

The last two runes are the initials of Thror and Thrain.

The moon-runes read by Elrond were:

ᛋᛏᚪᚾᛞ·ᛒᚣ·ᚦᛖ·ᚷᚱᛖᚣ·ᛋᛏᚩᚾᛖ·ᚻᚹᛖᚾ·ᚦᛖ·ᚦᚱᚢᛋᚻ·ᚳᚾᚩᚳᚳᛋ·ᚪᚾ
ᛞ·ᚦᛖ·ᛋᛖᛏᛏᛁᛝ·ᛋᚢᚾ·ᚹᛁᚦ·ᚦᛖ·ᛚᚪᛋᛏ·ᛚᛁᚷᚻᛏ·ᚩᚠ·ᛞᚢᚱᛁᚾᛋ·ᛞᚪᚣ·
ᚹᛁᛚᛚ·ᛋᚻᛁᚾᛖ·ᚢᛈᚩᚾ·ᚦᛖ·ᚳᛖᚣᚻᚩᛚᛖ.

On the Map the compass points are marked in runes, with East at the top, as usual in dwarf-maps, and so read clockwise: E(ast), S(outh), W(est), N(orth).[3]

* The reason for this use is given in *The Lord of the Rings,* III, 415.

1 On October 15, 1937, soon after the publication of *The Hobbit,* Tolkien wrote to Stanley Unwin:

No reviewer (that I have seen), although all have carefully used the correct *dwarfs* themselves, has commented on the fact (which I only became conscious of through reviews) that I use throughout the "incorrect" plural *dwarves.* I am afraid it is just a piece of private bad grammar, rather shocking in a philologist. . . . The real "historical" plural of *dwarf* (like *teeth* of *tooth*) is *dwarrows,* anyway: rather a nice word, but a bit too archaic. Still I rather wish I had used the word *dwarrow.* (*Letters,* No. 17)

In an interview, Tolkien commented: "*Dwarves* was originally a mistake in grammar. I tried to cover it up, but it was just purely the fact that I have a tendency to increase the number of these vestigial plurals in which there is a change of consonant, like *leaf, leaves.* My tendency is to make more of them than are now standard. And I really thought *dwarf, dwarves; wharf, wharves* – why not?" (Interview by Denys Gueroult for BBC Radio, recorded in January 1965.)

In Section II ("On Translation") of Appendix F in *The Lord of the Rings,* Tolkien offered another explanation:

It may be observed that in this book as in *The Hobbit* the form *dwarves* is used, although the dictionaries tell us that the plural form of *dwarf* is *dwarfs.* It should be *dwarrows* (or *dwerrows*), if singular and plural had each gone its own way down the years, as have *man* and *men,* or *goose* and *geese.* But we no longer speak of a dwarf as often as we do of a man, or even of a goose, and memories have not been fresh enough among Men to keep hold of a special plural for a race now abandoned to folk-tales, where at least a shadow of truth is preserved, or at last to nonsense-stories in which they have become mere figures of fun. But in the Third Age something of their old character and power is still glimpsed . . . . It is to mark this that I have ventured to use the form *dwarves,* and so remove them a little, perhaps, from the sillier tales of these latter days. *Dwarrows* would have been better; but I have used that form only in the name *Dwarrowdelf,* to represent the name Moria in the Common Speech.

2 The statement that *hobgoblin* is used for the larger kind of goblin is the reverse of the original tradition. In fairy lore, hobgoblins are the smaller of the creatures. They are usually portrayed as mischievous house sprites.

3 The original text (*1937*) had no note, nor was one necessary until the changes (particularly in Chapter 5) that resulted in the second edition (*1951*) were made. The following note was added at that time:

In this reprint several minor inaccuracies, most of them noted by readers, have been corrected. For example, the text on pages 30 and 64 now corresponds exactly with the runes on Thror's Map. More important is the matter of Chapter Five. There the true story of the ending of the Riddle Game, as it was eventually revealed (under pressure) by Bilbo to Gandalf, is now given according to the Red

Book, in place of the version Bilbo first gave to his friends, and actually set down in his diary. This departure from truth on the part of a most honest hobbit was a portent of great significance. It does not, however, concern the present story, and those who in this edition make their first acquaintance with hobbit-lore need not trouble about it. Its explanation lies in the history of the Ring, as it is set out in the chronicles of the Red Book of Westmarch, and it must await their publication.

A final note may be added, on a point raised by several students of the lore of the period. On Thror's Map is written *Here of old was Thrain King under the Mountain;* yet Thrain was the son of Thror, the last King under the Mountain before the coming of the dragon. The Map, however, is not in error. Names are often repeated in dynasties, and the genealogies show that a distant ancestor of Thror was referred to, Thrain I, a fugitive from Moria, who first discovered the Lonely Mountain, Erebor, and ruled there for a while, before his people moved on to the remoter mountains of the North.

The 1961 Puffin Books edition includes only the second paragraph, with the opening altered to read: "It has been suggested by several students of the lore of the period that there is an error in Thror's Map on pp. 6–7. On the Map is written: *Here of old . . .*"

1966-Ball repeats the *1951* note, with the alteration of the final sentence of the first paragraph to: ". . . it was set out in the chronicles of the Red Book of Westmarch, and is now told in *The Lord of the Rings*"; and with alteration of the page references in the second sentence. *1966-Longmans/Unwin* has an entirely new note, exactly as printed here.

1

An Unexpected Party

In a hole in the ground there lived a hobbit.[1] Not a nasty, dirty, wet hole, filled with the ends of worms and an oozy smell, nor yet a dry, bare, sandy hole with nothing in it to sit down on or to eat: it was a hobbit-hole, and that means comfort.

It had a perfectly round door like a porthole, painted green, with a shiny yellow brass knob in the exact middle. The door opened on to a tube-shaped hall like a tunnel: a very comfortable tunnel without smoke, with panelled walls, and floors tiled and carpeted, provided with polished chairs, and lots and lots of pegs for hats and coats — the hobbit was fond of visitors. The tunnel wound on and on, going fairly but not quite straight into the side of the hill — The Hill, as all the people for many miles round called it — and many little round doors opened out of it, first on one side and then on another. No going upstairs for the hobbit: bedrooms, bathrooms, cellars, pantries (lots of these), wardrobes (he had whole rooms devoted to clothes), kitchens, dining-rooms, all were on the same floor, and indeed on the same passage. The best rooms were all on the left-hand side (going in), for these were the only ones to have windows, deep-set round windows looking over his garden, and meadows beyond, sloping down to the river.[2]

This hobbit was a very well-to-do hobbit, and his

1 The opening paragraph has become so widely known that in 1980 it was added to the fifteenth edition of *Bartlett's Familiar Quotations*. The first sentence is recognized in many languages, of which the following is a small selection: *Dans un trou vivait un hobbit* (French); *In einer Höhle in der Erde, da lebte ein Hobbit* (German; Scherf translation); *Volt egyszer egy földbe vájt lyuk, abban élt egy babó* (Hungarian); *In una caverna sotto terra viveva uno Hobbit* (Italian); *En un agujero en el suelo, vivía un hobbit* (Spanish; Figueroa translation); *I en håla under jorden bodde en hobbit* (Swedish; Hallqvist translation). *The Hobbit* has been translated into forty-one languages to date. A full listing can be found in Section III of the bibliography at the end of this book.

2 Bilbo's comfortable hobbit-hole inevitably recalls the similarly cozy underground homes of Badger and Mole in *The Wind in the Willows* (1908) by Kenneth Grahame. The name of Bilbo's home, Bag End, even echoes the name of Mole's, Mole End, though such a for-

X

mulation is common in British home-names. ⊃

Grahame (1859–1932) worked for many years at the Bank of England, and though he found the work not uncongenial, it was through his writings that he found success, beginning with *The Golden Age* (1895) and *Dream Days* (1898), collections of stories and sketches that delicately recapture the experience of childhood. *The Wind in the Willows* began as bedtime stories to Grahame's young son and continued in numerous letters written to the boy when Grahame was away. These letters were published posthumously in *First Whisper of "The Wind in the Willows"* (1944), edited by Grahame's widow, Elspeth. When Tolkien heard about the publication of this volume, he informed his son Christopher in a letter written on July 31 and August 1, 1944, adding: "I must get hold of a copy" (*Letters,* No. 77).

3 In *The Road to Middle-earth,* Tom Shippey notes that *baggins* probably comes from *bagging,* a term that the *Oxford English Dictionary* says is "used in the northern counties of England for food eaten between regular meals; now, especially in Lancashire, an afternoon meal, 'afternoon tea' in substantial form." It is therefore an appropriate name to be found among hobbits, who we are told have dinner twice a day, and for Bilbo, who later in Chapter 1 sits down to his second breakfast. In the Prologue to *The Lord of the Rings,* Tolkien notes that hobbits were fond of "six meals a day (when they could get them)."

Shippey states that "the *OED* prefers

name was Baggins.**3** The Bagginses had lived in the neighbourhood of The Hill for time out of mind, and people considered them very respectable, not only because most of them were rich, but also because they never had any adventures or did anything unexpected: you could tell what a Baggins would say on any question without the bother of asking him. This is a story of how a Baggins had an adventure, and found himself doing and saying things altogether unexpected. He may have lost the neighbours' respect, but he gained — well, you will see whether he gained anything in the end. ⊃

The mother of our particular hobbit — what is a hobbit? I suppose hobbits need some description nowadays, since they have become rare and shy of the Big People, as they call us. They are (or were) a little people, about half our height, and smaller than the bearded Dwarves.**4** Hobbits have no beards. There is little or no magic about them, except the ordinary everyday sort which helps them to disappear quietly and quickly when large stupid folk like you and me come blundering along, making a noise like elephants which they can hear a mile off.**5** They are inclined to be fat in the stomach; they dress in bright colours (chiefly green and yellow); wear no shoes, because their feet grow natural leathery soles and thick warm brown hair like the stuff on their heads (which is curly); have long clever brown fingers, good-natured faces, and laugh deep fruity laughs (especially after dinner, which they have twice a day when they can get it).**6** Now you know enough to go on with. As I was saying, the mother of this hobbit — of Bilbo**7** Baggins, that is — was the famous Belladonna Took, one of the three remarkable daughters of the Old Took,**8** head of the hobbits who lived across The Water, the small river that ran at the foot of The Hill. It was often said (in other families) that long ago one of the Took ancestors must have taken a fairy wife.**9** That was, of course, absurd, but certainly there was still something not entirely hobbitlike about them, and once in a while members of the Took-clan would go and have adventures. They discreetly disappeared, and the family hushed it up; but the fact remained that the Tooks were not as respectable as the Bagginses, though they were undoubtedly richer.

Not that Belladonna Took ever had any adventures after she became Mrs. Bungo Baggins. Bungo, that was Bilbo's father, built the most luxurious hobbit-hole for her (and partly with her money) that was to be found either under The Hill or over The Hill or across The Water, and there they remained to the end of their days. Still it is probable that Bilbo, her only son, although he looked and behaved exactly like a second edition of his solid and comfortable father, got something a bit queer in his make-up from the Took side, something that only waited for a chance to come out. The chance never arrived, until Bilbo Baggins was grown up, being about fifty years old or so,[10] and living in the beautiful hobbit-hole built by his father, which I have just described for you, until he had in fact apparently settled down immovably.

By some curious chance one morning long ago in the quiet of the world, when there was less noise and more green, and the hobbits were still numerous and prosperous, and Bilbo Baggins was standing at his door after breakfast smoking an enormous long wooden pipe that reached nearly down to his woolly toes (neatly brushed) — Gandalf came by. Gandalf![11] If you had heard only a quarter of what I have heard about him, and I have only heard very little of all there is to hear, you would be prepared for any sort of remarkable tale. Tales and adventures sprouted up all over the place wherever he went, in the most extraordinary fashion. He had not been down that way under The Hill for ages and ages, not since his friend the Old Took died,[12] in fact, and the hobbits had almost forgotten what he looked like. He had been away

the 'politer' form *bagging*, but Tolkien knew that people who used words like that were almost certain to drop the terminal -g" (p. 66). The word also appears in a phonetically spelled form as *bæggin* in Walter E. Haigh's *A New Glossary of the Dialect of the Huddersfield District* (1928), to which Tolkien wrote an appreciative foreword. Haigh defines *bæggin* as "a meal, now usually 'tea,' but formerly any meal; a bagging. Probably so called because workers generally carried their meals to work in a bag of some kind."

Huddersfield was probably the most isolated part of the south of Yorkshire through the end of the eighteenth century, and in its dialect there survived many words that died out elsewhere. Tolkien's foreword shows how Haigh's work sheds light on some obscure words and phrases in *Sir Gawain and the Green Knight*.

Tolkien came to know Haigh in 1923, when he joined the Yorkshire Dialect Society. Walter Edward Haigh (1856–1930) was a native of the Huddersfield district and, at the time of the publication of his glossary, Emeritus Lecturer in English at the Huddersfield Technical College.

4 *1937:* "They are (or were) small people, smaller than dwarves (and they have no beards) but very much larger than lilliputians." > *1966-Ball:* "They are (or were) a little people, about half our height, and smaller than the bearded Dwarves. Hobbits have no beards." (*1966-A&U* and *1967-HM* follow *1966-Ball,* but with "Dwarves" mistakenly not capitalized. Tolkien's 1954 check copy confirms the intended reading

"Dwarves," also found in *1966-Long-mans/Unwin.*)

Tolkien probably removed the reference to lilliputians because of the unsuitability of directly referring to elements from another work of literature. In *Gulliver's Travels* (1726) by Jonathan Swift, the people of Lilliput are about six inches tall. The association of lilliputians with fairy tales is seen in the children's version of the story (rewritten and abridged by May Kendall) that appears in Andrew Lang's *Blue Fairy Book* (1891) under the title "A Voyage to Lilliput." In his essay "On Fairy-Stories" Tolkien objected to its classification as a fairy-story, both in its original and condensed forms.

5 Tolkien did not use the word *elephant* in *The Lord of the Rings,* where he preferred the obsolete form *oliphaunt.* In Chapter 3 of Book IV of *The Lord of the Rings,* Sam recites a short poem about an oliphaunt. The poem is also included in *The Adventures of Tom Bombadil,* and Tolkien himself can be heard reciting the poem on the 1975 record *J.R.R. Tolkien Reads and Sings His "The Lord of the Rings"* (Caedmon TC 1478), based on tape recordings made in August 1952.

Tolkien published a longer poem entitled "Iumbo, or Ye Kinde of Ye Oliphaunt," one of a series of two poems headed "Adventures in Unnatural History and Medieval Metres, Being the Freaks of Fisiologus," published by Exeter College in the *Stapeldon Magazine,* June 1927 (7, no. 40). These poems are written in the manner of old bestiaries that descend from the Greek *Physiologus* of the second century.

over The Hill and across The Water on businesses of his own since they were all small hobbit-boys and hobbit-girls.

All that the unsuspecting Bilbo saw that morning was an old man with a staff.[13] He had a tall pointed blue hat, a long grey cloak, a silver scarf over which his long white beard hung down below his waist, and immense black boots.[14]

"Good Morning!" said Bilbo, and he meant it. The sun was shining, and the grass was very green. But Gandalf looked at him from under long bushy eyebrows that stuck out further than the brim of his shady hat.

"What do you mean?" he said. "Do you wish me a good morning, or mean that it is a good morning whether I want it or not; or that you feel good this morning; or that it is a morning to be good on?"

"All of them at once," said Bilbo. "And a very fine morning for a pipe of tobacco out of doors, into the bargain. If you have a pipe about you, sit down and have a fill of mine! There's no hurry, we have all the day before us!" Then Bilbo sat down on a seat by his door, crossed his legs, and blew out a beautiful grey ring of smoke that sailed up into the air without breaking and floated away over The Hill.

"Very pretty!" said Gandalf. "But I have no time to blow smoke-rings this morning. I am looking for someone to share in an adventure that I am arranging, and it's very difficult to find anyone."

"I should think so — in these parts! We are plain quiet folk and have no use for adventures. Nasty disturbing uncomfortable things! Make you late for dinner! I can't think what anybody sees in them," said our Mr. Baggins, and stuck one thumb behind his braces, and blew out another even bigger smoke-ring. Then he took out his morning letters,[15] and began to read, pretending to take no more notice of the old man. He had decided that he was not quite his sort, and wanted him to go away. But the old man did not move. He stood leaning

The

Hobbit

by J. R. R. TOLKIEN

"This book will be worn ragged by boys and girls alike. It has immense charm, genuine wit, and dwarfs which put Snow White's boy friends completely in the shade."—*Sophia L. Goldsmith in the New York Post.*

"One of the most freshly original and delightfully imaginative books for children that has appeared in many a long day . . . a glorious account of a magnificent adventure, filled with suspense and seasoned with a quiet humor that is irresistible. . . . The tale is packed with valuable hints for the dragon killer and adventurer in Faerie."—*Anne T. Eaton in the New York Times.*
$2.50

on his stick and gazing at the hobbit without saying anything, till Bilbo got quite uncomfortable and even a little cross. ⌐

"Good morning!" he said at last. "We don't want any adventures here, thank you! You might try over The Hill or across The Water." By this he meant that the conversation was at an end.

"What a lot of things you do use *Good morning* for!" said Gandalf.[16] "Now you mean that you want to get rid of me, and that it won't be good till I move off."

"Not at all, not at all, my dear sir! Let me see, I don't think I know your name?"

"Yes, yes, my dear sir — and I do know your name, Mr. Bilbo Baggins. And you do know my name, though you don't remember that I belong to it. I am Gandalf, and Gandalf means me! To think that I should have lived to be good-morninged by Belladonna Took's son, as if I was selling buttons at the door!" ⌐

"Gandalf, Gandalf! Good gracious me! Not the wandering wizard that gave Old Took a pair of magic diamond studs that fastened themselves and never came undone till ordered? Not the fellow who used to tell

6 In March 1938, Tolkien was cabled by his American publisher and asked to supply some drawings of hobbits in various attitudes for use in advertising. Tolkien responded that he did not feel competent to do so. His actual letter to Houghton Mifflin does not survive, but a typed extract was found in the publisher's files and printed in *Letters*. Tolkien wrote:

I picture a fairly human figure, not a kind of "fairy" rabbit as some of my British reviewers seem to fancy: fattish in the stomach, short-ish in the leg. A round, jovial face; ears only slightly pointed and "elvish"; hair short and curling (brown). The feet from the ankles down, covered with brown hairy fur. Clothing: green velvet breeches; red or brown waistcoat; brown or green jacket; gold (or brass) buttons; a dark green hood and cloak (belonging to a dwarf). Actual size — only important if other objects are in picture — say about three feet or three feet six inches. (*Letters*, No. 27)

Clearly Houghton Mifflin used these details in designing their advertisement for *The Hobbit* (see illustration on this page) printed in the Christmas 1938 issue of the *Horn Book* magazine.

In *Artist*, Wayne G. Hammond and Christina Scull note that Tolkien drew for himself on the telegram "a very inadequate pencil sketch of a hobbit . . . with the face left blank and with ears rather more than 'slightly' pointed" (p. 99). In the best reproductions of Tolkien's illustrations *Bilbo Woke Up with the Early Sun in His Eyes* and *The Hall at Bag-End*, such as those found in *Artist* (Nos. 113 and 139), a very close examination shows that Bilbo's ears are drawn pointed.

7 According to Thomas Wright's *Dictionary of Obsolete and Provincial*

English (1857), a bilbo was "a Spanish sword, so named from Bilbao, where choice swords were made. A swordsman was sometimes termed a bilbo-man." However, there is no evidence that Tolkien derived the name from this word.

8 In his biography of Tolkien, Humphrey Carpenter noticed the similarities between Bilbo Baggins and his creator:

In the story, Bilbo Baggins, son of the lively Belladonna Took, herself one of the three remarkable daughters of the Old Took, descended also from the respectable and solid Bagginses, is middle aged and unadventurous, dresses in sensible clothes but likes bright colours, and has a taste for plain food. . . . John Ronald Reuel Tolkien, son of the enterprising Mabel Suffield, herself one of the three remarkable daughters of John Suffield (who lived to be nearly a hundred), descended also from the respectable and solid Tolkiens, was middle aged and inclined to pessimism, dressed in sensible clothes but liked coloured waistcoats when he could afford them, and had a taste for plain food. (*Biography*, p. 175)

Tolkien probably chose the name *Belladonna* for its Italian meaning, "beautiful lady" (from Latin *bella,* the feminine of *bellus,* beauty, and *domina,* lady). The plant name *belladonna* (a variety of nightshade) is the same word, for Italian ladies formerly used a cosmetic made from the juice of the poisonous plant. In *The Lord of the Rings,* Tolkien continued using plant and flower names for female hobbits. Belladonna Took is the only female character named in *The Hobbit.* The surname *Took* should be pronounced with the same vowel sound as *tool* or *moon.*

From the Hobbit family trees in Appendix C of *The Lord of the Rings,* we learn that Belladonna's two sisters were

Bilbo. Illustration by Tamás Szecskó for the 1975 Hungarian edition. Szecskó (1925–1987) was a prolific illustrator of children's books in Hungary. He had previously teamed up with the translator of *The Hobbit,* Tibor Szobotka, to illustrate a Hungarian version of Lewis Carroll's *Alice in Wonderland* (1974). Szobotka (1913–1982) was a well-known writer of novels and plays, a literary historian of the Romantic poets (Byron, Keats, Shelley, etc.) and a translator of writings by Agatha Christie, George Eliot, and James Joyce. Four additional illustrations by Szecskó are included on pages 52, 283, 305, and 334. See also page 391 (book cover).

Bilbo and Gandalf outside Bag End. Illustration by Klaus Ensikat for the 1971 German edition. Ensikat (b. 1937) has won many awards for his illustrations, which frequently have a surrealistic quality to them. Other books he has illustrated include works by the Brothers Grimm and Charles Perrault, as well as Lewis Carroll's *Alice in Wonderland* (1993). Three more illustrations by Ensikat can be found on pages 110, 176, and 210.

such wonderful tales at parties, about dragons and goblins and giants and the rescue of princesses and the unexpected luck of widows' sons? Not the man that used to make such particularly excellent fireworks! I remember those! Old Took used to have them on Midsummer's Eve. Splendid! They used to go up like great lilies and snapdragons and laburnums of fire and hang in the twilight all evening!" You will notice already that Mr. Baggins was not quite so prosy as he liked to believe, also that he was very fond of flowers. "Dear me!" he went on. "Not the Gandalf who was responsible for so many quiet lads and lasses going off into the Blue for mad adventures?[17] Anything from climbing trees to visiting elves — or sailing in ships, sailing to other shores! Bless me, life used to be quite inter— I mean, you used to upset things badly in these parts once upon a time. I beg your pardon, but I had no idea you were still in business."

"Where else should I be?" said the wizard. "All the same I am pleased to find you remember something about me. You seem to remember my fireworks kindly, at any rate, and that is not without hope. Indeed for your old grandfather Took's sake, and for the sake of poor Belladonna, I will give you what you asked for."

Right: Bilbo and Gandalf. Illustration by Mikhail Belomlinskiy for the 1976 Russian edition. Belomlinskiy (his name is sometimes transliterated Belomlinskii or Belomlinsky) graduated from the I. E. Repin Institute for Painting, Sculpture and Architecture in 1960. He became well known as a political cartoonist and as a caricaturist of famous Russian actors, artists, and authors. He also illustrated many original Russian children's books, as well as translations of Mark Twain's *A Connecticut Yankee in King Arthur's Court* (1988), Gerald Durrell's children's fantasy, *Talking Parcel* (1990), and work by Dr. Seuss. Belomlinskiy's illustrations also appear in one American book — an English translation of a Russian folktale, *Lions and Sailing Ships* by Svyatoslav Sakharov, published in 1982. The artist now lives in the United States.

David Doughan, in his review of the Russian edition in *Amon Hen* no. 55 (April 1982), notes that "everyday Russian does not differentiate between feet and legs, and nobody seems to have told the illustrator." Hence Bilbo's entire legs are drawn as hairy, instead of his feet only. Three additional illustrations by Belomlinskiy are included on pages 213, 227, and 268. See also page 393 (book cover).

named Donnamira and Mirabella. Mirabella's grandson was Frodo Baggins, the central character of *The Lord of the Rings*. Frodo was also related to Bilbo on the Baggins side, with Bilbo's grandfather and Frodo's great-grandfather being brothers.

9 *1937:* "It had always been said that long ago one or other of the Tooks had married into a fairy family (the less friendly said a goblin family); certainly there was" > *1966-Ball:* "It was often said (in other families) that long ago one of the Took ancestors must have taken a fairy wife. That was, of course, absurd, but certainly there was"

10 In *The Lord of the Rings* we learn that Bilbo Baggins was born on the twenty-second of September in the year

2890 of the Third Age of Middle-earth. This tale begins in April of the year 2941 of the Third Age, when Bilbo was in his fifty-first year.

11 Tolkien left unfinished a sketch of Gandalf approaching Bilbo, who is smoking outside of his front door. It is labeled "One Morning Early in the Quiet of the World" and is published in *Artist* (No. 89). Another unfinished sketch titled "Gandalf" shows Gandalf standing to the right side of Bilbo's front door (see *Artist* No. 91), and the marks Gandalf made on the door — the runes for B and D, followed by a diamond — are seen next to the shrub at the right.

12 Gerontius, the Old Took, died in the year 2920 of the Third Age, aged one hundred and thirty years, about twenty-one years before the present story begins.

13 *1937:* "a little old man with a tall pointed blue hat" > *1966-Ball:* "an old man with a staff. He had a tall pointed blue hat"

The idea that Gandalf was "little" persisted into the early drafts of *The Lord of the Rings* before being abandoned. These early drafts, dating from soon after the publication of *The Hobbit,* can be read in *The Return of the Shadow* (1988), volume six of *History.*

14 In *Biography,* Humphrey Carpenter relates the story that Tolkien, during his walking tour of Switzerland in the summer of 1911, purchased some picture postcards, one of which was a reproduc-

"I beg your pardon, I haven't asked for anything!"

"Yes, you have! Twice now. My pardon. I give it you. In fact I will go so far as to send you on this adventure. Very amusing for me, very good for you — and profitable too, very likely, if you ever get over it."

"Sorry! I don't want any adventures, thank you. Not today. Good morning! But please come to tea — any time you like! Why not tomorrow? Come tomorrow! Good bye!" With that the hobbit turned and scuttled inside his round green door, and shut it as quickly as he dared, not to seem rude. Wizards after all are wizards.

"What on earth did I ask him to tea for!" he said to himself, as he went to the pantry. He had only just had breakfast, but he thought a cake or two and a drink of something would do him good after his fright.

Gandalf in the meantime was still standing outside the door, and laughing long but quietly. After a while he stepped up, and with the spike on his staff scratched a queer sign on the hobbit's beautiful green front-door. Then he strode away, just about the time when Bilbo was finishing his second cake and beginning to think that he had escaped adventures very well.

The next day he had almost forgotten about Gandalf. He did not remember things very well, unless he put them down on his Engagement Tablet: like this: *Gandalf Tea Wednesday.* Yesterday he had been too flustered to do anything of the kind.

Just before tea-time[18] there came a tremendous ring on the front-door bell, and then he remembered! He rushed and put on the kettle, and put out another cup and saucer, and an extra cake or two, and ran to the door.

"I am so sorry to keep you waiting!" he was going to say, when he saw that it was not Gandalf at all. It was a dwarf with a blue beard tucked into a golden belt, and very bright eyes under his dark-green hood. As soon as

Bilbo and Gandalf, outside Bag End. Illustration by Livia Rusz for the 1975 Romanian edition. Rusz (b. 1930) has also illustrated Hungarian translations of fairy tales by Wilhelm Hauff and Charles Perrault. An English language translation of some Romanian children's stories, written by Lucia Olteanu and illustrated by Rusz, appeared in 1978 under the title *The Adventures of Quacky and His Friends.* Three additional illustrations by Rusz can be found on pages 107, 221, and 284.

Right: Bilbo and Gandalf, outside of Bag End. Illustration by António Quadros for the 1962 Portuguese edition. Quadros (1933–1994) also illustrated Portuguese translations of Joel Chandler Harris's Uncle Remus tales (1959), George Macdonald's *The Princess and the Goblin* (1960), and Nathaniel Hawthorne's *Wonder Book* (1961). He translated works by Albert Camus (1913–1960) and André Maurois (1885–1967) from the French into Portuguese.

Quadros's illustrations to *The Hobbit* did not please Tolkien. Clyde S. Kilby, an American professor who assisted Tolkien during the summer of 1966, wrote in his memoir, *Tolkien and The Silmarillion* (1976), that Tolkien regarded the Portuguese illustrations as "horrible." Two more can be seen on pages 71 and 278.

the door was opened, he pushed inside, just as if he had been expected.

He hung his hooded cloak on the nearest peg, and "Dwalin at your service!" he said with a low bow.

"Bilbo Baggins at yours!" said the hobbit, too surprised to ask any questions for the moment. When the silence that followed had become uncomfortable, he added: "I am just about to take tea; pray come and have some with me." A little stiff perhaps, but he meant it kindly. And what would you do, if an uninvited dwarf

tion of a painting of an old man with a red cloak and a long white beard, seated under a tree and nuzzling a fawn. It is entitled *Der Berggeist* and signed J. Madelener (see illustration on page 38). Carpenter records that Tolkien "preserved this postcard carefully, and long afterwards he wrote on the paper cover in which he kept it: 'Origin of Gandalf' " (p. 51).

Carpenter is mistaken on a few points, for the artist's name is not Madelener but Madlener, and the painting dates not from 1911 (or earlier) but from the latter half of the 1920s. Josef Madlener (1881–1967) was a German artist and illustrator born near Memmingen. His work appeared in various newspapers, magazines, and a few children's Christmas books with religious themes, like *Das Christkind Kommt* (1929) and *Das Buch vom Christkind* (1938). Madlener's

Christmas art also appeared in several postcard series.

For his article "The Origin of Gandalf and Josef Madlener" in *Mythlore,* Winter 1983 (9, no. 4; whole no. 34), Manfred Zimmermann interviewed the artist's daughter Julie (born 1910), who distinctly remembered her father painting *Der Berggeist* sometime after 1925–26. She also noted that the postcard version was "published in the late twenties by Ackermann Verlag München, in a folder with three or four similar pictures with motifs drawn from German mythology: a fairy lady of the woods, a deer carrying a shining cross between its antlers, 'Rübezahl' (a fairy tale character), and possibly one more" (p. 22).

The monograph *Josef Madlener 1881 bis 1967* (1981), written by Eduard Raps and published in Memmingen for the artist's centenary, shows a good sampling of Madlener's art, which went through various phases. It is clear by

came and hung his things up in your hall without a word of explanation?

They had not been at table long, in fact they had hardly reached the third cake, when there came another even louder ring at the bell.

"Excuse me!" said the hobbit, and off he went to the door.

"So you have got here at last!"[19] That was what he was going to say to Gandalf this time. But it was not Gandalf. Instead there was a very old-looking dwarf on the step with a white beard and a scarlet hood; and he too hopped inside as soon as the door was open, just as if he had been invited.

"I see they have begun to arrive already," he said when he caught sight of Dwalin's green hood hanging up. He hung his red one next to it, and "Balin at your service!" he said with his hand on his breast.

"Thank you!" said Bilbo with a gasp. It was not the correct thing to say, but *they have begun to arrive* had flustered him badly. He liked visitors, but he liked to know them before they arrived, and he preferred to ask them himself. He had a horrible thought that the cakes might run short, and then he — as the host: he knew his duty and stuck to it however painful — he might have to go without.

"Come along in, and have some tea!" he managed to say after taking a deep breath.

"A little beer would suit me better, if it is all the same to you, my good sir," said Balin with the white beard. "But I don't mind some cake — seed-cake,[20] if you have any."

"Lots!" Bilbo found himself answering, to his own surprise; and he found himself scuttling off, too, to the cellar to fill a pint beer-mug, and then to a pantry[21] to fetch two beautiful round seed-cakes which he had baked that afternoon for his after-supper morsel.

When he got back Balin and Dwalin were talking at the table like old friends (as a matter of fact they were brothers). Bilbo plumped down the beer and the cake in front of them, when loud came a ring at the bell again, and then another ring.

"Gandalf for certain this time,"[22] he thought as he puffed along the passage. But it was not. It was two more dwarves, both with blue hoods, silver belts, and yellow beards; and each of them carried a bag of tools and a spade. In they hopped, as soon as the door began to open — Bilbo was hardly surprised at all.

"What can I do for you, my dwarves?" he said.

"Kili at your service!" said the one. "And Fili!" added the other; and they both swept off their blue hoods and bowed.

"At yours and your family's!" replied Bilbo, remembering his manners this time.

"Dwalin and Balin here already, I see," said Kili. "Let us join the throng!"

"Throng!" thought Mr. Baggins. "I don't like the sound of that. I really must sit down for a minute and collect my wits, and have a drink." He had only just had a sip — in the corner, while the four dwarves sat round the table, and talked about mines and gold and troubles with the goblins, and the depredations of dragons, and lots of other things which he did not understand, and did not want to, for they sounded much too adventurous — when, *ding-dong-a-ling-dang,* his bell rang again, as if some naughty little hobbit-boy was trying to pull the handle off.

"Someone at the door!" he said, blinking.

"Some four, I should say by the sound," said Fili. "Besides, we saw them coming along behind us in the distance."

The poor little hobbit sat down in the hall and put his head in his hands, and wondered what had happened, and what was going to happen, and whether they would all stay to supper. Then the bell rang again louder than ever, and he had to run to the door. It was not four after all, it was FIVE. Another dwarf had come[23] along while

the similarities in style that the painting *Der Berggeist* belongs to the period around 1925–30.

15 In England in the 1930s there were at least two mail deliveries per day — hence the distinction of morning letters.

The word *braces,* a few lines earlier, is the term in England for the straps or bands passed over the shoulders to support trousers. They are called suspenders in America.

16 Deirdre Greene, in her article "Tolkien's Dictionary Poetics: The Influence of the *OED*'s Defining Style on Tolkien's Fiction," notes that this exchange between Bilbo and Gandalf exhibits the lexicographer's concern with the semantic possibilities of words and phrases. It "shows Bilbo using the same phrase as both a greeting and a farewell" and calls attention to the difference between basic meaning and connotation (*Proceedings of the J.R.R. Tolkien Centenary Conference 1992,* edited by Patricia Reynolds and Glen H. Goodknight, p. 196).

17 *1937:* "mad adventures, anything from climbing trees to stowing away aboard the ships that sail to the Other Side?" > *1966-Longmans/Unwin:* "mad adventures? Anything from climbing trees to visiting elves — or sailing in ships, sailing to other shores!" (The reading in *1966-Ball* agrees with that in *1966-Longmans/Unwin* but mistakenly has a period, or full stop, instead of a question mark after *adventures.*)

The idea of hobbits sailing over "to the Other Side" is incompatible with the conception in *The Lord of the Rings* that no mortal ships could sail over seas to the Undying Lands in the West.

18 Tea-time in England is traditionally around four P.M. It is a light afternoon meal, usually consisting of tea, bread (with butter and jam), and various cakes or biscuits. On page 352, Bilbo remarks in a farewell to the dwarves: "Tea is at four; but any of you are welcome at any time!"

19 *1937:* "here at last!' what was what he was going to say" > *1961* (Puffin): "here at last!' was what he was going to say" > *1966-Ball:* "here at last!' That was what he was going to say" (The 1961 reading seems to have been an intermediate revision, rather than merely an erroneous dropped word, for the notes in Tolkien's 1954 check-copy seem to reflect two stages of change.)

20 A seed-cake is a sweetened cake flavored with caraway seeds.

21 *1937:* "and to the pantry" > *1966-Ball:* "and then to a pantry"

22 *1937:* "Gandalf for sure this time" > *1966-Ball:* "Gandalf for certain this time"

23 *1937:* "Another one had come" > *1966-Ball:* "Another dwarf had come"

24 The Dwarf Gloin is the father of Gimli, one of the nine members of the Fellowship of the Ring in *The Lord of the Rings.*

25 Porter is a dark brown beer, usually stronger than a regular beer.

he was wondering in the hall. He had hardly turned the knob, before they were all inside, bowing and saying "at your service" one after another. Dori, Nori, Ori, Oin, and Gloin[24] were their names; and very soon two purple hoods, a grey hood, a brown hood, and a white hood were hanging on the pegs, and off they marched with their broad hands stuck in their gold and silver belts to join the others. Already it had almost become a throng. Some called for ale, and some for porter,[25] and one for coffee, and all of them for cakes; so the hobbit was kept very busy for a while.

A big jug of coffee had just been set in the hearth, the seed-cakes were gone, and the dwarves were starting on a round of buttered scones, when there came — a loud knock. Not a ring, but a hard rat-tat on the hobbit's beautiful green door. Somebody was banging with a stick!

Bilbo rushed along the passage, very angry, and altogether bewildered and bewuthered — this was the most awkward Wednesday he ever remembered. He pulled open the door with a jerk, and they all fell in, one on top of the other. More dwarves, four more! And there was Gandalf behind, leaning on his staff and laughing. He had made quite a dent on the beautiful door; he had also, by the way, knocked out the secret mark that he had put there the morning before.

"Carefully! Carefully!" he said. "It is not like you, Bilbo, to keep friends waiting on the mat, and then open the door like a pop-gun! Let me introduce Bifur, Bofur, Bombur, and especially Thorin!"

"At your service!" said Bifur, Bofur, and Bombur standing in a row. Then they hung up two yellow hoods and a pale green one; and also a sky-blue one with a long silver tassel. This last belonged to Thorin, an enormously important dwarf, in fact no other than the great Thorin Oakenshield himself, who was not at all pleased at falling flat on Bilbo's mat with Bifur, Bofur, and Bombur on top of him. For one thing Bombur was immensely fat and heavy. Thorin indeed was very haughty, and said nothing about *service;* but poor Mr. Baggins said he was sorry so many times, that at last he grunted "pray don't mention it," and stopped frowning.

"Now we are all here!" said Gandalf, looking at the row of thirteen hoods — the best detachable party hoods — and his own hat hanging on the pegs. "Quite a merry gathering! I hope there is something left for the late-comers to eat and drink! What's that? Tea! No thank you! A little red wine, I think for me."

"And for me," said Thorin.

"And raspberry jam and apple-tart," said Bifur.

"And mince-pies and cheese," said Bofur.

"And pork-pie and salad," said Bombur.

"And more cakes — and ale — and coffee, if you don't mind," called the other dwarves through the door.

"Put on a few eggs, there's a good fellow!" Gandalf called after him, as the hobbit stumped off to the pantries. "And just bring out the cold chicken and pickles!"26

"Seems to know as much about the inside of my larders27 as I do myself!" thought Mr. Baggins, who was feeling positively flummoxed, and was beginning to wonder whether a most wretched adventure had not come right into his house. By the time he had got all the bottles and dishes and knives and forks and glasses and plates and spoons and things piled up on big trays, he was getting very hot, and red in the face, and annoyed.

"Confusticate28 and bebother these dwarves!" he said aloud. "Why don't they come and lend a hand?" Lo and behold! there stood Balin and Dwalin at the door of the kitchen, and Fili and Kili behind them, and before he could say *knife* they had whisked the trays and a couple of small tables into the parlour and set out everything afresh.

Gandalf sat at the head of the party with the thirteen

26 *1937:* "cold chicken and tomatoes!" > *1966-Ball:* "cold chicken and pickles!"

This revision brings up the question as to why it should matter whether Bilbo's larder was stocked with tomatoes or pickles. Tom Shippey, in *The Road to Middle-earth,* suggests that as Tolkien wrote the sequel to *The Hobbit,* and as he came to perceive the hobbits and their land as characteristically English in nature, he recognized tomatoes as foreign in origin and in name. They were imports from America, like potatoes and tobacco, which were quickly adopted in England. Though Tolkien does use the word *tobacco* in *The Hobbit* a handful of times, it is strictly avoided in *The Lord of the Rings,* where *pipeweed* is used. There, as well, potatoes are given the more rustic name *taters.* Tomatoes were thus out of place in the Shire as Tolkien came to perceive it.

27 *1937:* "the inside of my larder" > *1966-Ball:* "the inside of my larders"

28 The word *confusticate* appears in the 1989 second edition of the *Oxford English Dictionary,* where it is described as a fantastic alteration of *confound* or *confuse.* Usage of the word is cited from as early as 1891, and in another example, it is described as schoolboy slang. Tolkien's own usage from *The Hobbit* is also cited.

Confusticate is used similarly in two other instances: by Dori on page 139, and collectively by the dwarves on page 205.

29 In England biscuits are small, thin, and usually crisp flour-based items. Nonsweet biscuits are also called crackers. In North America sweet biscuits are called cookies.

The Dwarves clean up the plates while Bilbo looks on alarmed. Illustration by Chica for the 1976 French edition. The French illustrator and author known as Chica (b. 1933) has illustrated books by Enid Blyton and written and illustrated a series of children's picture books about Celestine, a mouse, and her adventures. Several of the Celestine books appeared in English translations in the early 1980s. Four additional illustrations by Chica appear on pages 247, 285, 317, and 331.

dwarves all round: and Bilbo sat on a stool at the fireside, nibbling at a biscuit[29] (his appetite was quite taken away), and trying to look as if this was all perfectly ordinary and not in the least an adventure. The dwarves ate and ate, and talked and talked, and time got on. At last they pushed their chairs back, and Bilbo made a move to collect the plates and glasses.

"I suppose you will all stay to supper?" he said in his politest unpressing tones.

"Of course!" said Thorin. "And after. We shan't get through the business till late, and we must have some music first. Now to clear up!"

Thereupon the twelve dwarves — not Thorin, he was too important, and stayed talking to Gandalf — jumped to their feet, and made tall piles of all the things. Off they went, not waiting for trays, balancing columns of plates, each with a bottle on the top, with one hand, while the hobbit ran after them almost squeaking with fright: "please be careful!" and "please, don't trouble! I can manage." But the dwarves only started to sing:

> *Chip the glasses and crack the plates!*
> *Blunt the knives and bend the forks!*
> *That's what Bilbo Baggins hates–*
> *Smash the bottles and burn the corks!*
>
> *Cut the cloth and tread on the fat!*
> *Pour the milk on the pantry floor!*
> *Leave the bones on the bedroom mat!*
> *Splash the wine on every door!*
>
> *Dump the crocks in a boiling bowl;*
> *Pound them up with a thumping pole;*
> *And when you've finished, if any are whole,*
> *Send them down the hall to roll!*
>
> *That's what Bilbo Baggins hates!*
> *So, carefully! carefully with the plates!*

And of course they did none of these dreadful things, and everything was cleaned and put away safe as quick as lightning, while the hobbit was turning round and round in the middle of the kitchen trying to see what they were doing. Then they went back, and found Thorin with his feet on the fender smoking a pipe. He was blowing the most enormous smoke-rings, and wherever he told one to go, it went — up the chimney, or behind the clock on the mantelpiece, or under the table, or round and round the ceiling; but wherever it went it was not quick enough to escape Gandalf. Pop! he sent a smaller smoke-ring from his short clay-pipe straight through each one of Thorin's. Then Gandalf's smoke-ring would go green and come back[30] to hover over the wizard's head. He had a cloud of them about him already, and in the dim light it made him look strange and sorcerous.[31] Bilbo stood still and watched — he loved smoke-rings — and then he blushed to think how proud he had been yesterday morning of the smoke-rings he had sent up the wind over The Hill.

"Now for some music!" said Thorin. "Bring out the instruments!"

Kili and Fili rushed for their bags and brought back little fiddles; Dori, Nori, and Ori brought out flutes from somewhere inside their coats; Bombur produced a drum from the hall; Bifur and Bofur went out too, and came back with clarinets that they had left among the walking-sticks. Dwalin and Balin said: "Excuse me, I left mine in the porch!"[32] "Just bring mine in with you!" said Thorin. They came back with viols as big as themselves, and with Thorin's harp wrapped in a green cloth. It was a beautiful golden harp, and when Thorin struck it the music began all at once, so sudden and sweet that Bilbo forgot everything else, and was swept away into dark lands under strange moons, far over The Water and very far from his hobbit-hole under The Hill.

The dark came into the room from the little window

30 *1937:* "Then Gandalf's smoke-ring would go green with the joke and come back" > *1966-Ball:* "Then Gandalf's smoke-ring would go green and come back"

31 *1937:* "He had quite a cloud of them about him already, and it made him look positively sorcerous." > *1966-Longmans/Unwin:* "He had a cloud of them about him already, and in the dim light it made him look strange and sorcerous." (*1966-Ball* retains the reading "quite a cloud" but otherwise matches *1966-Longmans/Unwin*.)

32 Tolkien may have intended rhyming dwarf names to denote a familial (sometimes filial) relationship. Elsewhere we learn that Fili and Kili are brothers (on page 249 Thorin describes them as "the sons of my father's daughter"), as are Dwalin and Balin (see pages 38–39). In Appendix A of *The Lord of the Rings* it is confirmed that Oin and Gloin are brothers, and it is stated there that Dori, Ori, and Nori are also of the House of Durin and remote kinsmen of Thorin, though their exact relationships to one another are not discussed. Bifur, Bofur, and Bombur, on the other hand, are of a different line than Thorin, not of the House of Durin. On page 215 we learn that Bofur and Bombur are brothers, and on page 274 Bifur describes Bombur and Bofur as his cousins. See note 20 to Chapter 2 for information on the source of Tolkien's dwarf-names.

The Dwarves make music. Illustration by Torbjörn Zetterholm for the 1947 Swedish edition. Zetterholm (b. 1921), a versatile artist whose work has been exhibited worldwide, has also illustrated the writings of Hans Christian Andersen. He is the younger brother of Tore Zetterholm (1915–2001), a well-known novelist and writer who also translated the 1947 Swedish edition of *The Hobbit*. Four additional illustrations by Zetterholm appear on pages 73, 112, 212, and 248.

that opened in the side of The Hill; the firelight flickered — it was April — and still they played on, while the shadow of Gandalf's beard wagged against the wall.

The dark filled all the room, and the fire died down, and the shadows were lost, and still they played on. And suddenly first one and then another began to sing as they played, deep-throated singing of the dwarves in the deep places of their ancient homes; and this is like a fragment of their song, if it can be like their song without their music.

Far over the misty mountains cold
To dungeons deep and caverns old
We must away ere break of day
To seek the pale enchanted gold.

The dwarves of yore made mighty spells,
While hammers fell like ringing bells
In places deep, where dark things sleep,
In hollow halls beneath the fells.

For ancient king and elvish lord
There many a gleaming golden hoard
They shaped and wrought, and light they caught
To hide in gems on hilt of sword.

On silver necklaces they strung
The flowering stars, on crowns they hung
The dragon-fire, in twisted wire
They meshed the light of moon and sun.

Far over the misty mountains cold
To dungeons deep and caverns old
We must away, ere break of day,
To claim our long-forgotten gold.

Goblets they carved there for themselves
And harps of gold; where no man delves

There lay they long, and many a song
Was sung unheard by men or elves.

The pines were roaring on the height,
The winds were moaning in the night.
The fire was red, it flaming spread;
The trees like torches blazed with light.

The bells were ringing in the dale
And men looked up with faces pale;
The dragon's ire more fierce than fire[33]
Laid low their towers and houses frail.

The mountain smoked beneath the moon;
The dwarves, they heard the tramp of doom.
They fled their hall to dying fall
Beneath his feet, beneath the moon.

Far over the misty mountains grim
To dungeons deep and caverns dim
We must away, ere break of day,
To win our harps and gold from him!

As they sang the hobbit felt the love of beautiful things made by hands and by cunning and by magic moving through him, a fierce and a jealous love, the desire of the hearts of dwarves. Then something Tookish woke up inside him, and he wished to go and see the great mountains, and hear the pine-trees and the waterfalls, and explore the caves, and wear a sword instead of a walking-stick. He looked out of the window. The stars were out in a dark sky above the trees. He thought of the jewels of the dwarves shining in dark caverns. Suddenly in the wood beyond The Water a flame leapt up — probably somebody lighting a wood-fire — and he thought of plundering dragons settling on his quiet Hill and kindling it all to flames. He shuddered; and very quickly he

33 *1937:* "*The dragon's ire more fierce then fire*" > *1966-Ball:* "*The dragon's ire more fierce than fire*" > *1966-A&U:* "*Then dragon's ire more fierce than fire*" (*1966-Longmans/Unwin* follows *1966-Ball*, which basically corrects the typographical error *then* for *than*. *1967-HM* follows *1966-A&U*, which erroneously begins with the word *Then* instead of *The*.)

34 Tolkien wrote in his guide for translators, "Nomenclature of *The Lord of the Rings,*" that Bag End, the local name for Bilbo's home, was "meant to be associated (by hobbits) with the end of a 'bag' or 'pudding-bag' = cul-de-sac." It was the local name for Tolkien's aunt's farm in Worcestershire, which was at the end of a lane that led up to it but no farther. Tolkien's aunt Jane Neave (1872–1963) was his mother's younger sister. She accompanied Tolkien on a walking tour of Switzerland in the summer of 1911 (see note 1 to Chapter 4), and it was owing to her request in 1961 for a small book with Tom Bombadil at the heart of it that Tolkien compiled *The Adventures of Tom Bombadil and Other Verses from the Red Book* (1962).

Tolkien's early sketch "Bag End Underhill" is reproduced at right, showing (as the text on page 29 relates) the "best rooms on the left-hand side (going in)," with "deepset round windows" looking over Bilbo's garden and the meadows beyond. In later illustrations, Tolkien moved the tree further away from Bilbo's front door, to the top of the hill.

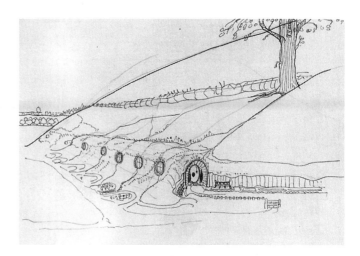

was plain Mr. Baggins of Bag-End, Under-Hill, again.**34**

He got up trembling. He had less than half a mind to fetch the lamp, and more than half a mind to pretend to, and go and hide behind the beer-barrels in the cellar, and not come out again until all the dwarves had gone away. Suddenly he found that the music and the singing had stopped, and they were all looking at him with eyes shining in the dark.

"Where are you going?" said Thorin, in a tone that seemed to show that he guessed both halves of the hobbit's mind.

"What about a little light?" said Bilbo apologetically.

"We like the dark," said all the dwarves. "Dark for dark business! There are many hours before dawn."

"Of course!" said Bilbo, and sat down in a hurry. He missed the stool and sat in the fender, knocking over the poker and shovel with a crash.

"Hush!" said Gandalf. "Let Thorin speak!" And this is how Thorin began.

"Gandalf, dwarves and Mr. Baggins! We are met together in the house of our friend and fellow conspirator, this most excellent and audacious hobbit — may the hair on his toes never fall out! all praise to his wine and ale! —" He paused for breath and for a polite remark from the hobbit, but the compliments were quite lost on poor Bilbo Baggins, who was wagging his mouth in protest at being called *audacious* and worst of all *fellow conspirator,* though no noise came out, he was so flummoxed. So Thorin went on:

"We are met to discuss our plans, our ways, means, policy and devices. We shall soon before the break of day start on our long journey, a journey from which some of us, or perhaps all of us (except our friend and counsellor, the ingenious wizard Gandalf) may never return. It is a solemn moment. Our object is, I take it, well known to us all. To the estimable Mr. Baggins, and perhaps to one or two of the younger dwarves (I think I should be right in naming Kili and Fili, for instance), the exact situation at the moment may require a little brief explanation —"

This was Thorin's style. He was an important dwarf. If he had been allowed, he would probably have gone on like this until he was out of breath, without telling any one there anything that was not known already. But he was rudely interrupted. Poor Bilbo couldn't bear it any longer. At *may never return* he began to feel a shriek coming up inside, and very soon it burst out like the whistle of an engine coming out of a tunnel.[35] All the dwarves sprang up, knocking over the table. Gandalf struck a blue light on the end of his magic staff, and in its firework glare the poor little hobbit could be seen kneeling on the hearth-rug, shaking like a jelly that was melting. Then he fell flat on the floor, and kept on calling out "struck by lightning, struck by lightning!" over and over again; and that was all they could get out of him for a long time. So they took him and laid him out of the way on the drawing-room sofa with a drink at his elbow, and they went back to their dark business.

"Excitable little fellow,"[36] said Gandalf, as they sat down again. "Gets funny queer fits, but he is one of the best, one of the best — as fierce as a dragon in a pinch."

If you have ever seen a dragon in a pinch, you will realize that this was only poetical exaggeration applied to

Bilbo listens to the Dwarves. Illustration by Nada Rappensbergerová for the 1973 Slovak edition. Rappensbergerová (b. 1936) has illustrated many books by Slovak writers. The artist's name is sometimes given as Nada Rappensbergerová-Jankovičová. Four additional illustrations by Rappensbergerová can be found on pages 72, 203, 309, and 341.

35 *1937:* "like the whistle of an engine coming out of a tunnel"

Tolkien was certainly aware of the narrator's possible anachronism in using a metaphor involving the noise of a railway train in a story that takes place in what is otherwise a pre-industrialized world. For the 1966 revision of the text, Tolkien carefully considered the spacing of a possible replacement line here — "like the whee of a rocket going up into the sky" — but in the end rejected it. This usage need not be viewed as an anachronism, for Tolkien as narrator was telling this story to his children in the early 1930s, and they lived in a world where railway trains were a very important feature of life.

A similar usage occurs in the first chapter of *The Lord of the Rings*, describing one of Gandalf's fireworks: "The dragon passed like an express train."

36 *1937: "Excitable little man" > 1951: "Excitable little fellow"*

This revision came about because of a suggestion by Arthur Ransome (1884–1967), whose books were much admired by Tolkien's children. Soon after its publication, Allen & Unwin had sent a copy of *The Hobbit* to Ransome, then convalescing in a nursing home. Ransome, describing himself as "a humble hobbit-fancier (and one certain that your book will be many times reprinted)," wrote to Tolkien on December 13, 1937, wondering if it was perhaps an error of the human scribe in attributing to Gandalf the use of the word *man* when describing Bilbo. Tolkien agreed that the word was wrong and suggested the change in a letter to Allen & Unwin of December 19, 1937, but the revision did not appear until 1951.

Ransome suggested two other possible corrections. See note 11 to Chapter 6 and note 2 to Chapter 18.

37 The reference to Bullroarer Took as the great-grand-uncle of the Old Took is original to the 1937 edition of *The Hobbit*, but this does not agree with the Took family tree in Appendix C of *The Lord of the Rings*, where Bullroarer is merely the grand-uncle of the Old Took. In *The Peoples of Middle-earth*,

any hobbit, even to Old Took's great-grand-uncle Bullroarer,[37] who was so huge (for a hobbit) that he could ride a horse. He charged the ranks of the goblins of Mount Gram in the Battle of the Green Fields, and knocked their king Golfimbul's head clean off with a wooden club. It sailed a hundred yards through the air and went down a rabbit-hole, and in this way the battle was won and the game of Golf invented at the same moment.

In the meanwhile, however, Bullroarer's gentler descendant was reviving in the drawing-room. After a while and a drink he crept nervously to the door of the parlour. This is what he heard, Gloin speaking: "Humph!" (or some snort more or less like that). "Will he do, do you think? It is all very well for Gandalf to talk about this hobbit being fierce, but one shriek like that in a moment of excitement would be enough to wake the dragon and all his relatives, and kill the lot of us. I think it sounded more like fright than excitement! In fact, if it had not been for the sign on the door, I should have been sure we had come to the wrong house. As soon as I clapped eyes on the little fellow bobbing and puffing on the mat, I had my doubts. He looks more like a grocer than a burglar!"

Then Mr. Baggins turned the handle and went in. The Took side had won. He suddenly felt he would go without bed and breakfast to be thought fierce. As for *little fellow bobbing on the mat* it almost made him really fierce. Many a time afterwards the Baggins part regretted what he did now, and he said to himself: "Bilbo, you were a fool; you walked right in and put your foot in it."

"Pardon me," he said, "if I have overheard words that you were saying. I don't pretend to understand what you are talking about, or your reference to burglars, but I think I am right in believing" (this is what he called being on his dignity) "that you think I am no good. I will show you. I have no signs on my door — it was painted a week ago −, and I am quite sure you have come to the wrong house. As soon as I saw your funny faces on the door-step, I had my doubts. But treat it as the right one. Tell me what you want done, and I will try it, if I have to walk from here to the East of East and fight the wild Were-worms in the Last Desert. I had a great-great-great-grand-uncle once, Bullroarer Took, and −"**38**

"Yes, yes, but that was long ago," said Gloin. "I was talking about *you*. And I assure you there is a mark on this door − the usual one in the trade, or used to be. *Burglar wants a good job, plenty of Excitement and reasonable Reward,* that's how it is usually read. You can say *Expert Treasure-hunter* instead of *Burglar* if you like. Some of them do. It's all the same to us. Gandalf told us that there was a man of the sort in these parts looking for a Job at once, and that he had arranged for a meeting here this Wednesday tea-time."

"Of course there is a mark," said Gandalf. "I put it there myself. For very good reasons. You asked me to find the fourteenth man for your expedition, and I chose Mr. Baggins. Just let any one say I chose the wrong man or the wrong house, and you can stop at thirteen and have all the bad luck you like, or go back to digging coal."

He scowled so angrily at Gloin that the dwarf huddled back in his chair; and when Bilbo tried to open his mouth to ask a question, he turned and frowned at him and stuck out his bushy eyebrows, till Bilbo shut his mouth tight with a snap. "That's right," said Gandalf. "Let's have no more argument. I have chosen Mr. Baggins and that ought to be enough for all of you. If I say he is a Burglar, a Burglar he is, or will be when the time comes. There is a lot more in him than you guess, and a deal more than he has any idea of himself. You may (possibly) all live to thank me yet. Now Bilbo, my boy, fetch the lamp, and let's have a little light on this!"

On the table in the light of a big lamp with a red shade he spread a piece of parchment rather like a map.

volume twelve of *History,* two earlier versions (labeled T2 and T3) of the Took family tree are shown, and they correspond with the relationship as given in *The Hobbit.* Evidently when Tolkien reworked the relationships between the Tooks for *The Lord of the Rings,* he neglected to account for it in *The Hobbit.*

According to Appendix B ("The Tale of Years") in *The Lord of the Rings,* Bandobras Took defeated an Orc-band in the Northfarthing of the Shire in 2747.

38 Tolkien commented in his guide for translators, "Nomenclature of *The Lord of the Rings,*" that he believed when he wrote it "that *bullroarer* was a word used by anthropologists for instruments that made a roaring sound, used by uncivilised peoples; but I cannot find it in any dictionaries."

The word does in fact appear in the *Oxford English Dictionary,* under the entry *bull* (sb[1] meaning 11), where the following usage from 1881 is cited: "A flat slip of wood a few inches long, narrowing to one or both ends, and fastened by one end to a thong for whirling it round, when it gives an intermittent whirring or roaring noise; heard a long way off. It is . . . called in England a 'whizzer' or 'bull-roarer.' "

In his short article "Possible Sources of Tolkien's Bullroarer" in the December 2000 issue of *Mythprint* (37, no. 12; whole no. 225), Arden R. Smith notes that *bullroarer* occurs a number of times in the twelve-volume edition of James G. Frazer's *The Golden Bough: A Study in Magic and Religion* (1911-15), while Andrew Lang, in his *Custom and Myth* (1884), devotes an entire chapter

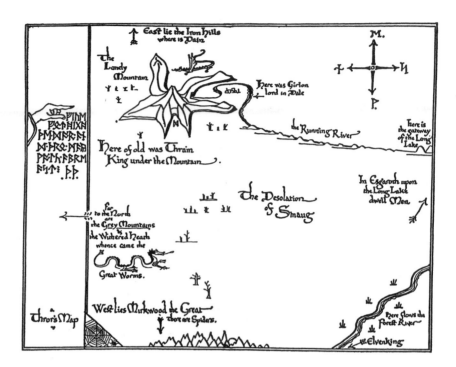

to the bullroarer, calling it "familiar to English country lads." Lang continues:

The common bull-roarer is an inexpensive toy which anyone can make. I do not, however, recommend it to families, for two reasons. In the first place, it produces a most horrible and unexampled din, which endears it to the very young, but renders it detested by persons of mature age. In the second place, the character of the toy is such that it will almost infallibly break all that is fragile in the house where it is used, and will probably put out the eyes of some of the inhabitants. . . . The bull-roarer has, of all toys, the widest diffusion and the most extraordinary history. To study the bull-roarer is to take a lesson in folklore. The instrument is found among the most widely severed peoples, savage and civilised, and is used in the celebration of savage and civilised mysteries. (pp. 29–31)

The reference here to Bullroarer Took as Bilbo's great-great-great-grand-uncle is original to the 1937 edition of

Thror's Map by J.R.R. Tolkien. Transcribed (with the underlined pairs of letters represented by one character in the runes), the runes in the left column read: FIVE I FEET HIGH I THE DOR AN I D THREE MAY I WOLK ABRE I AST. TH. TH. In the introductory note to The Hobbit on page 27, Tolkien gives these runes with the correction of an A-rune for an O-rune in WOLK and states that the last two runes are the initials of Thror and Thrain. In the same note Tolkien remarks that "on the Map the compass points are marked in runes, with East at the top, as usual in dwarf-maps, and so read clockwise: E(ast), S(outh), W(est), N(orth)." See also page 97.

An earlier version of Thror's Map (opposite) was done in a vertical rather than a horizontal format, for Tolkien wished it to be inserted in the Chapter 1 at the first mention of it in the text. The legend clearly states that the map was to be considered a copy of Thror's Map made by Bilbo, rather than the original. For this version Tolkien drew the special moon-runes, which will be discovered by Elrond in Chapter 3, in reverse on the back of the illustration, where he hoped they could be printed so that the moon-runes would become visible only when the map was held up to a light. In faint pencil at the top and bottom are versions of the rune text in Elvish and in Old English, respectively (for transcriptions, see Artist, p. 150 n. 6).

The earliest version of Thror's Map was not on a separate page but is drawn in the manuscript of the first chapter of The Hobbit (see page 10).

The regular illustration of Thror's Map was colored by H. E. Riddett (together with the map of "Wilderland") and issued as a poster by Allen & Unwin in 1979. The moon-runes for Thror's Map were printed on the verso of the poster so they would be visible through the paper only when it was held up to a light.

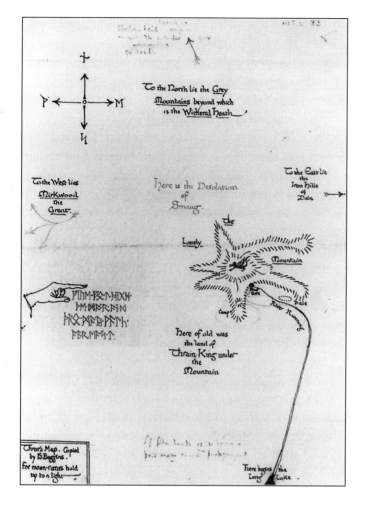

The Hobbit, and as with Bullroarer's relationship to the Old Took discussed in the previous note, this does not agree with the Took family tree in Appendix C of *The Lord of the Rings*. There Bullroarer is Bilbo's great-great-grand-uncle, whereas in earlier versions (T2 and T3) of the Took family tree, printed in *The Peoples of Middle-earth,* the relationship as given corresponds with that in *The Hobbit.* Additionally, in the Prologue to *The Lord of the Rings,* Bullroarer is said to be the son of Isengrim the Second, while in the Took family tree in Appendix C, Bullroarer is listed as the grandson of Isengrim II. (The earlier Took family trees list Bullroarer as the son of Isengrim I.)

39 *1937:* "made by your grandfather, Thorin" > *1966-Ball:* "made by Thror, your grandfather, Thorin"

"This was made by Thror, your grandfather, Thorin,"[39] he said in answer to the dwarves' excited questions. "It is a plan of the Mountain."

"I don't see that this will help us much," said Thorin disappointedly after a glance. "I remember the Mountain well enough and the lands about it. And I know where Mirkwood is, and the Withered Heath where the great dragons bred."

"There is a dragon marked in red on the Mountain," said Balin, "but it will be easy enough to find him without that, if ever we arrive there."

40 This sentence has been changed in various editions, according to where (and in what colors) Thror's Map is printed. The original *1937* reading is: "(Look at the map at the beginning of this book, and you will see there the runes in red.)" The 1937 Allen & Unwin edition uses Thror's Map as the front endpaper. Mistakenly, the 1938 Houghton Mifflin edition retains this reading but uses Thror's Map as the rear endpaper.

41 *1937:* "Five feet high is the door and three abreast may enter it" > *1951:* "Five feet high the door and three may walk abreast"

The revision was made to bring the text exactly in line with the runes on Thror's Map.

42 *1937:* "devouring so many of the maidens of the valley" > *1966-Ball:* "devouring so many of the dwarves and men of Dale"

The idea of a dragon devouring maidens of the valley is a conventional fairy-tale one, and Tolkien replaced it with a reference more relevant to his story.

"There is one point that you haven't noticed," said the wizard, "and that is the secret entrance. You see that rune on the West side, and the hand pointing to it from the other runes? That marks a hidden passage to the Lower Halls." (Look at the map on page 50 of this book, and you will see there the runes.)**40**

"It may have been secret once," said Thorin, "but how do we know that it is secret any longer? Old Smaug has lived there long enough now to find out anything there is to know about those caves."

"He may — but he can't have used it for years and years."

"Why?"

"Because it is too small. 'Five feet high the door and three may walk abreast'**41** say the runes, but Smaug could not creep into a hole that size, not even when he was a young dragon, certainly not after devouring so many of the dwarves and men of Dale."**42**

"It seems a great big hole to me," squeaked Bilbo (who had no experience of dragons and only of hobbit-holes). He was getting excited and interested again, so that he forgot to keep his mouth shut. He loved maps, and in his hall there hung a large one of the Country Round with all his favourite walks marked on it in red

Thorin, Gandalf and Bilbo reading Thror's Map. Illustration by Tamás Szecskó for the 1975 Hungarian edition.

ink. "How could such a large door be kept secret from everybody outside, apart from the dragon?" he asked. He was only a little hobbit you must remember.

"In lots of ways," said Gandalf. "But in what way this one has been hidden we don't know without going to see. From what it says on the map I should guess there is a closed door which has been made to look exactly like the side of the Mountain. That is the usual dwarves' method — I think that is right, isn't it?"

"Quite right," said Thorin.

"Also," went on Gandalf, "I forgot to mention that with the map went a key, a small and curious key. Here it is!" he said, and handed to Thorin a key with a long barrel and intricate wards, made of silver. "Keep it safe!"

"Indeed I will," said Thorin, and he fastened it upon a fine chain that hung about his neck and under his jacket. "Now things begin to look more hopeful. This news alters them much for the better. So far we have had no clear idea what to do. We thought of going East, as quiet and careful as we could, as far as the Long Lake. After that the trouble would begin —."

"A long time before that, if I know anything about the roads East," interrupted Gandalf.

"We might go from there up along the River Running," went on Thorin taking no notice, "and so to the ruins of Dale — the old town in the valley there, under the shadow of the Mountain. But we none of us liked the idea of the Front Gate. The river runs right out of it through the great cliff at the South of the Mountain, and out of it comes the dragon too — far too often, unless he has changed his habits."

"That would be no good," said the wizard, "not without a mighty Warrior, even a Hero. I tried to find one; but warriors are busy fighting one another in distant lands, and in this neighbourhood heroes are scarce, or simply not to be found. Swords in these parts are mostly blunt, and axes are used for trees, and shields as cradles

43 *1937:* "Long ago in my grandfather's time some dwarves were driven out of the far North, and came with all their wealth and their tools to this Mountain on the map. There they mined and they tunnelled and they made huge halls and great workshops" > *1966-Ball:* "Long ago in my grandfather Thror's time our family was driven out of the far North, and came back with all their wealth and their tools to this Mountain on the map. It had been discovered by my far ancestor, Thrain the Old, but now they mined and they tunnelled and they made huger halls and greater workshops"

This revision was made to introduce into the text Thrain the Old, and thereby explain the note on Thror's Map that "Here of old was Thrain King under the Mountain," making the distinction that there were two dwarves named Thrain, one being Thorin's father (and Thror's son), the other being the much earlier dwarf who founded the Kingdom under the Mountain. This explanation first appeared in the introductory note added to the 1951 second edition (see note 3 to page 27); the revision here made that part of the 1951 introductory note no longer necessary.

44 In Appendix B of *The Lord of the Rings,* "The Tale of Years," we learn that Thrain I (the Old) founded the kingdom under the Lonely Mountain in the year 1999 of the Third Age, but in 2210 the son of Thrain I, Thorin I, left Erebor and gathered his people in the Grey Mountains in the north.

Thrain I's descendant, Thror, re-established the kingdom under the Mountain in 2590.

or dish-covers; and dragons are comfortably far-off (and therefore legendary). That is why I settled on *burglary* — especially when I remembered the existence of a Side-door. And here is our little Bilbo Baggins, *the* burglar, the chosen and selected burglar. So now let's get on and make some plans."

"Very well then," said Thorin, "supposing the burglar-expert gives us some ideas or suggestions." He turned with mock-politeness to Bilbo.

"First I should like to know a bit more about things," said he, feeling all confused and a bit shaky inside, but so far still Tookishly determined to go on with things. "I mean about the gold and the dragon, and all that, and how it got there, and who it belongs to, and so on and further."

"Bless me!" said Thorin, "haven't you got a map? and didn't you hear our song? and haven't we been talking about all this for hours?"

"All the same, I should like it all plain and clear," said he obstinately, putting on his business manner (usually reserved for people who tried to borrow money off him), and doing his best to appear wise and prudent and professional and live up to Gandalf's recommendation. "Also I should like to know about risks, out-of-pocket expenses, time required and remuneration, and so forth" — by which he meant: "What am I going to get out of it? and am I going to come back alive?"

"O very well," said Thorin.**43** "Long ago in my grandfather Thror's time our family was driven out of the far North, and came back with all their wealth and their tools to this Mountain on the map. It had been discovered by my far ancestor, Thrain the Old,**44** but now they mined and they tunnelled and they made huger halls and greater workshops — and in addition I believe they found a good deal of gold and a great many jewels too. Anyway they grew immensely rich and famous, and my grandfather was King under the Mountain again,**45** and treated with great reverence by the mortal men, who lived to the South, and were gradually spreading up the Running River as far as the valley overshadowed by the Mountain. They built the merry town of Dale there in those days. Kings used to send for our smiths, and reward even the least skillful most richly. Fathers would beg us to take their sons as apprentices, and pay us handsomely, especially in food-supplies, which we never bothered to grow or find for ourselves. Altogether those were good days for us, and the poorest of us had money to spend and to lend, and leisure to make beautiful things just for the fun of it, not to speak of the most marvellous and magical toys, the like of which is not to be found in the world now-a-days. So my grandfather's halls became full of armour and jewels and carvings and cups,[46] and the toy market of Dale was the wonder of the North.

"Undoubtedly that was what brought the dragon. Dragons steal gold and jewels, you know, from men and elves and dwarves, wherever they can find them; and they guard their plunder as long as they live (which is practically for ever, unless they are killed), and never enjoy a brass ring of it. Indeed they hardly know a good bit of work from a bad, though they usually have a good notion of the current market value; and they can't make a thing for themselves, not even mend a little loose scale of their armour. There were lots of dragons in the North in those days, and gold was probably getting scarce up there, with the dwarves flying south or getting killed, and all the general waste and destruction that dragons make going from bad to worse. There was a most specially greedy, strong and wicked worm called Smaug. One day he flew up into the air and came south.[47] The first we heard of it was a noise like a hurricane coming from the North, and the pine-trees on the Mountain creaking and cracking in the wind. Some of the dwarves who happened to be outside (I was one luckily — a fine

45 *1937:* "King under the Mountain" > *1966-Ball:* "King under the Mountain again"

46 *1937:* "full of wonderful jewels and carvings and cups, and the toyshops of Dale were a sight to behold" > *1966-Longmans/Unwin:* "full of armour and jewels and carvings and cups, and the toy market of Dale was the wonder of the North" (*1966-Ball* has the same reading as *1966-Longmans/Unwin* but uses the American spelling *armor*.)

47 Smaug descended on Erebor in the year 2770 of the Third Age, one hundred and eighty years after Thror had reestablished the kingdom under the Mountain and one hundred and seventy-one years before the time in which *The Hobbit* is set.

48 *1937:* "Your grandfather was killed, you remember, in the mines of Moria by a goblin – " > *1966-Longmans/Unwin:* "Your grandfather Thror was killed, you remember, in the mines of Moria by Azog the Goblin." (*1966-Ball* matches *1966-Longmans/Unwin,* but ends with a dash, as in *1937.*)

⟡ The story of Thror's death is told in Section III of Appendix A in *The Lord of the Rings.* In brief, Thror was killed in the year 2790 of the Third Age, after he had entered Moria alone. His head was severed and tossed outside the Gate of Moria along with his body. The name of his slayer, Azog, was written on his face. This was the beginning of the war of the Dwarves and the Goblins, named in *The Lord of the Rings* as the War of the Dwarves and the Orcs.

The Mines of Moria are not visible on the map of "Wilderland" in *The Hobbit,* but they would be located further to the south, among the Misty Mountains. ⟡

49 *1937:* "Curse the goblin, yes" > *1966-Ball:* "Curse his name, yes"

50 *1937:* "And your father went away on the third of March" > *1951:* "And your father went away on the twenty-first of April" > *1966-Ball:* "And Thrain your father went away on the twenty-first of April"

The statement that Thrain "went away on the twenty-first of April, a hundred years ago last Thursday" provides one of the few firm dates within *The Hobbit* for the chronology of the story. From what Bilbo should have put down in his Engagement Tablet, Gandalf and the dwarves came to tea on a Wednes-

adventurous lad in those days, always wandering about, and it saved my life that day) – well, from a good way off we saw the dragon settle on our mountain in a spout of flame. Then he came down the slopes and when he reached the woods they all went up in fire. By that time all the bells were ringing in Dale and the warriors were arming. The dwarves rushed out of their great gate; but there was the dragon waiting for them. None escaped that way. The river rushed up in steam and a fog fell on Dale, and in the fog the dragon came on them and destroyed most of the warriors – the usual unhappy story, it was only too common in those days. Then he went back and crept in through the Front Gate and routed out all the halls, and lanes, and tunnels, alleys, cellars, mansions and passages. After that there were no dwarves left alive inside, and he took all their wealth for himself. Probably, for that is the dragons' way, he has piled it all up in a great heap far inside, and sleeps on it for a bed. Later he used to crawl out of the great gate and come by night to Dale, and carry away people, especially maidens, to eat, until Dale was ruined, and all the people dead or gone. What goes on there now I don't know for certain, but I don't suppose any one lives nearer to the Mountain than the far edge of the Long Lake now-a-days.

"The few of us that were well outside sat and wept in hiding, and cursed Smaug; and there we were unexpectedly joined by my father and my grandfather with singed beards. They looked very grim but they said very little. When I asked how they had got away, they told me to hold my tongue, and said that one day in the proper time I should know. After that we went away, and we have had to earn our livings as best we could up and down the lands, often enough sinking as low as blacksmith-work or even coalmining. But we have never forgotten our stolen treasure. And even now, when I will allow we have a good bit laid by and are not so badly off" – here Thorin stroked the gold chain round his neck – "we still mean to get it back, and to bring our curses home to Smaug – if we can.

"I have often wondered about my father's and my grandfather's escape. I see now they must have had a private Side-door which only they knew about. But apparently they made a map, and I should like to know how Gandalf got hold of it, and why it did not come down to me, the rightful heir."

"I did not 'get hold of it,' I was given it," said the wizard. "Your grandfather Thror was killed, you remember, in the mines of Moria by Azog the Goblin."[48]

"Curse his name, yes,"[49] said Thorin.

"And Thrain your father went away on the twenty-first of April, a hundred years ago last Thursday,[50] and has never been seen by you since –"

"True, true," said Thorin.

"Well, your father gave me this to give to you; and if I have chosen my own time and way for handing it over, you can hardly blame me, considering the trouble I had to find you. Your father could not remember his own name when he gave me the paper, and he never told me yours; so on the whole I think I ought to be praised and thanked! Here it is," said he handing the map to Thorin.

"I don't understand," said Thorin, and Bilbo felt he would have liked to say the same. The explanation did not seem to explain.

"Your grandfather," said the wizard slowly and grimly,[51] "gave the map to his son for safety before he went to the mines of Moria. Your father went away to try his luck with the map after your grandfather was killed; and lots of adventures of a most unpleasant sort he had, but he never got near the Mountain. How he got there I don't know, but I found him a prisoner in the dungeons of the Necromancer."[52]

"Whatever were you doing there?" asked Thorin with a shudder, and all the dwarves shivered.

day (see page 36). Thus, if the previous Thursday was April 21, Wednesday would be April 27. (However, in "The Quest of Erebor," which was originally written to be part of an appendix to *The Lord of the Rings* and which tells Gandalf's account of how he came to arrange Bilbo's journey, the date of Thorin and his companions arriving at Bag End is given precisely as Wednesday, April 26, with Gandalf's visit of the previous day specified to be Tuesday, April 25. These dates cannot be reconciled with the text as given in *The Hobbit*. See "The Quest of Erebor" in Appendix A of this book.)

The two other exact dates given in *The Hobbit* occur near the end of the book. On page 355, when Bilbo reaches Rivendell again on his journey home, it is May 1 of the following year. And on page 360, Bilbo arrives home in the middle of an auction on June 22.

51 *1937:* "said the wizard slowly and crossly" > *1966-Ball:* "said the wizard slowly and grimly"

52 Thorin's father Thrain was imprisoned in the dungeons of the Necromancer in 2845. Gandalf entered and received from Thrain the map and key in 2850, ninety-one years before the start of *The Hobbit*. Thrain died soon after giving Gandalf the map and key.

In *The Lord of the Rings*, we learn that the Necromancer of *The Hobbit* is also the Dark Lord, or Sauron, of *The Lord of the Rings*.

53 *1937:* "That is a job quite beyond the
powers" > *1966-Ball:* "He is an enemy
quite beyond the powers" > *1966-Long-
mans/Unwin:* "He is an enemy far beyond the powers"

54 *1937:* "was for you to read the
map" > *1966-Ball:* "was for his son to
read the map"

"Never you mind. I was finding things out, as usual;
and a nasty dangerous business it was. Even I, Gandalf,
only just escaped. I tried to save your father, but it was
too late. He was witless and wandering, and had forgotten almost everything except the map and the key."

"We have long ago paid the goblins of Moria," said
Thorin; "we must give a thought to the Necromancer."

"Don't be absurd! He is an enemy far beyond the
powers[53] of all the dwarves put together, if they could all
be collected again from the four corners of the world.
The one thing your father wished was for his son to read
the map[54] and use the key. The dragon and the Mountain are more than big enough tasks for you!"

"Hear, hear!" said Bilbo, and accidentally said it
aloud.

"Hear what?" they all said turning suddenly towards
him, and he was so flustered that he answered "Hear
what I have got to say!"

"What's that?" they asked.

"Well, I should say that you ought to go East and have
a look round. After all there is the Side-door, and dragons must sleep sometimes, I suppose. If you sit on the
door-step long enough, I daresay you will think of something. And well, don't you know, I think we have talked
long enough for one night, if you see what I mean. What
about bed, and an early start, and all that? I will give you
a good breakfast before you go."

"Before *we* go, I suppose you mean," said Thorin.
"Aren't you the burglar? And isn't sitting on the doorstep your job, not to speak of getting inside the door?
But I agree about bed and breakfast. I like six eggs with
my ham, when starting on a journey: fried not poached,
and mind you don't break 'em."

After all the others had ordered their breakfasts without so much as a please (which annoyed Bilbo very
much), they all got up. The hobbit had to find room for
them all, and filled all his spare-rooms and made beds

on chairs and sofas, before he got them all stowed and went to his own little bed very tired and not altogether happy. One thing he did make his mind up about was not to bother to get up very early and cook everybody else's wretched breakfast. The Tookishness was wearing off, and he was not now quite so sure that he was going on any journey in the morning.

As he lay in bed he could hear Thorin still humming to himself in the best bedroom next to him:

> *Far over the misty mountains cold*
> *To dungeons deep and caverns old*
> *We must away, ere break of day,*
> *To find our long-forgotten gold.*

Bilbo went to sleep with that in his ears, and it gave him very uncomfortable dreams. It was long after the break of day, when he woke up.

2

Roast Mutton

UP JUMPED BILBO, and putting on his dressing-gown went into the dining-room. There he saw nobody, but all the signs of a large and hurried breakfast. There was a fearful mess in the room, and piles of unwashed crocks in the kitchen. Nearly every pot and pan he possessed seemed to have been used. The washing-up was so dismally real that Bilbo was forced to believe the party of the night before had not been part of his bad dreams, as he had rather hoped. Indeed he was really relieved after all to think that they had all gone without him, and without bothering to wake him up ("but with never a thank-you" he thought); and yet in a way he could not help feeling just a trifle disappointed. The feeling surprised him.

"Don't be a fool, Bilbo Baggins!" he said to himself, "thinking of dragons and all that outlandish nonsense at your age!" So he put on an apron, lit fires, boiled water, and washed up. Then he had a nice little breakfast in the kitchen before turning out the dining-room. By that time the sun was shining; and the front door was open, letting in a warm spring breeze. Bilbo began to whistle loudly and to forget about the night before. In fact he was just sitting down to a nice little second breakfast in the dining-room by the open window, when in walked Gandalf.

"My dear fellow," said he, "whenever *are* you going to come? What about *an early start?* — and here you are having breakfast, or whatever you call it, at half past ten! They left you the message, because they could not wait."

"What message?" said poor Mr. Baggins all in a fluster.

"Great Elephants!" said Gandalf, "you are not at all yourself this morning — you have never dusted the mantelpiece!"

"What's that got to do with it? I have had enough to do with washing up for fourteen!"

"If you had dusted the mantelpiece, you would have found this just under the clock," said Gandalf, handing Bilbo a note (written, of course, on his own note-paper).

This is what he read:

"Thorin and Company to Burglar Bilbo greeting! For your hospitality our sincerest thanks, and for your offer of professional assistance our grateful acceptance. Terms: cash on delivery, up to and not exceeding one fourteenth of total profits (if any); all travelling expenses guaranteed in any event; funeral expenses to be defrayed by us or our representatives, if occasion arises and the matter is not otherwise arranged for.

"Thinking it unnecessary to disturb your esteemed repose, we have proceeded in advance to make requisite preparations, and shall await your respected person at the Green Dragon Inn,[1] Bywater, at 11 a.m. sharp. Trusting that you will be *punctual,*

"*We have the honour to remain*
"*Yours deeply*
"*Thorin & Co.*"

"That leaves you just ten minutes. You will have to run," said Gandalf.

"But —," said Bilbo.

"No time for it," said the wizard.

[1] From a very early age, Tolkien had a fondness for green dragons. He wrote to W. H. Auden on June 7, 1955: "I first tried to write a story when I was about seven. It was about a dragon. I remember nothing about it except a philological fact. My mother said nothing about the dragon, but pointed out that one could not say 'a green great dragon,' but had to say, 'a great green dragon.' I wondered why, and still do" (*Letters,* No. 163).

Tolkien's poem "The Dragon's Visit" (see note 2 to Chapter 14) is about a green dragon, and in some of his drawings the dragons are green as well (see *Artist,* Nos. 48, 49, and *Pictures,* No. 40, which includes both of the dragons in *Artist* plus an additional green one).

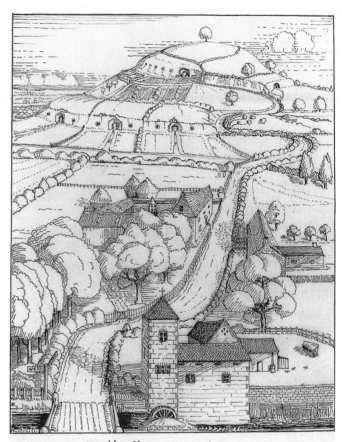

The Hill: Hobbiton across the Water.

The Hill: Hobbiton across the Water by J.R.R. Tolkien. This line drawing first appeared as the frontispiece to the 1937 first edition, after which it was replaced by the colored version. It was supposed to be reprinted in the 1979 edition of *Pictures* (No. 1, left), but an earlier pencil drawing was erroneously substituted and appears instead. The finished drawing correctly appears in the 1992 second edition of *Pictures* (No. 1, left), and in *Artist* (No. 97).

Tolkien made several attempts to draw this scene before he achieved the proper balance in the S-curve in the road and in the design of the Mill in the foreground (including various details such as the shapes of the windows and whether the weather vane appears or not). One such attempt is *The Hill: Hobbiton* (left), which also appears in *Artist* (No. 92). Four additional unfinished sketches can be seen in *Artist* (Nos. 93–96), along with a discussion of the evolution of the pictures (pp. 101–7).

The Hill: Hobbiton-across-the Water by J.R.R. Tolkien, one of the standard color illustrations for *The Hobbit.* This drawing was first published as the frontispiece to the 1937 second impression of the first English edition and as the frontispiece to the 1938 American edition (where Tolkien's monogram and lettered title were removed). For both appearances the illustration was given the printed caption "The Hill: Hobbiton across the Water" (the second *the* is capitalized in the American edition). This illustration appears in *Artist* (No. 98) and *Pictures* (No. 1, right). Various aspects of the buildings that can be seen in this picture are discussed by Pat Reynolds in her article " 'The Hill at Hobbiton': Vernacular Architecture in the Shire," in *Mallorn,* September 1997 (no. 35).

2 *1937:* "and so for a whole mile or more" > *1966-Ball:* "and then on for a whole mile or more" > *1966-Longmans/ Unwin:* "and then on for a mile or more"

3 Following from note 50 to Chapter 1, the "fine morning just before May" on which Bilbo's journey began would be Thursday, April 28.

"But —," said Bilbo again.

"No time for that either! Off you go!"

To the end of his days Bilbo could never remember how he found himself outside, without a hat, a walking-stick or any money, or anything that he usually took when he went out; leaving his second breakfast half-finished and quite unwashed-up, pushing his keys into Gandalf's hands, and running as fast as his furry feet could carry him down the lane, past the great Mill, across The Water, and then on for a mile or more.[2]

Very puffed he was, when he got to Bywater just on the stroke of eleven, and found he had come without a pocket-handkerchief!

"Bravo!" said Balin who was standing at the inn door looking out for him.

Just then all the others came round the corner of the road from the village. They were on ponies, and each pony was slung about with all kinds of baggages, packages, parcels, and paraphernalia. There was a very small pony, apparently for Bilbo.

"Up you two get, and off we go!" said Thorin.

"I'm awfully sorry," said Bilbo, "but I have come without my hat, and I have left my pocket-handkerchief behind, and I haven't got any money. I didn't get your note until after 10.45 to be precise."

"Don't be precise," said Dwalin, "and don't worry! You will have to manage without pocket-handkerchiefs, and a good many other things, before you get to the journey's end. As for a hat, I have got a spare hood and cloak in my luggage."

That's how they all came to start, jogging off from the inn one fine morning just before May,[3] on laden ponies; and Bilbo was wearing a dark-green hood (a little weather-stained) and a dark-green cloak borrowed from Dwalin. They were too large for him, and he looked rather comic. What his father Bungo would have thought of him, I daren't think. His only comfort was

A sketch of Dwarves marching by J.R.R. Tolkien. This sketch comes from a page reproduced in *Artist* (No. 103) on which also appears a sketch of Smaug. This visual depiction of the dwarves is the best there is from Tolkien's own hand. ·

he couldn't be mistaken for a dwarf, as he had no beard.

They had not been riding[4] very long, when up came Gandalf very splendid on a white horse. He had brought a lot of pocket-handkerchiefs, and Bilbo's pipe and tobacco. So after that the party went along very merrily, and they told stories or sang songs as they rode forward all day, except of course when they stopped for meals. These didn't come quite as often as Bilbo would have liked them, but still he began to feel that adventures were not so bad after all.

At first they had passed through hobbit-lands, a wide respectable country inhabited by decent folk, with good roads, an inn or two, and now and then a dwarf or a farmer ambling by on business. Then they came to lands where people spoke strangely, and sang songs Bilbo had never heard before.[5] Now they had gone on far into the Lone-lands, where there were no people left, no inns, and the roads grew steadily worse. Not far ahead were dreary hills, rising higher and higher, dark with trees. On some of them were old castles with an evil look, as if they had been built by wicked people. Everything seemed gloomy, for the weather that day had taken a nasty turn. Mostly it had been as good as May can be, even in merry tales, but now it was cold and wet. In the

4 *1937:* "They hadn't been riding" > *1966-Ball:* "They had not been riding"

5 *1937:* "Things went on like this for quite a long while. There was a good deal of wide respectable country to pass through, inhabited by decent respectable folk, men or hobbits or elves or what not, with good roads, an inn or two, and every now and then a dwarf, or a tinker, or a farmer ambling by on business. But after a time they came to places where people spoke strangely, and sang songs Bilbo had never heard before." > *1966-Longmans/Unwin:* "At first they had passed through hobbit-lands, a wide respectable country inhabited by decent folk, with good roads, an inn or two, and now and then a dwarf or a farmer ambling by on business. Then they came to lands where people spoke strangely, and sang songs Bilbo had never heard before." (*1966-Ball* and *1967-HM* follow *1966-Longmans/Unwin* but have the erroneous reading "wild respectable country" in the first sentence.)

6 *1937:* "Inns were rare and not good, the roads were worse, and there were hills in the distance rising higher and higher. There were castles on some of the hills, and many looked as if they had not been built for any good purpose. Also the weather which had often been as good as May can be, even in tales and legends, took a nasty turn." > *1966-Longmans/Unwin:* "Now they had gone on far into the Lone-lands, where there were no people left, no inns, and the roads grew steadily worse. Not far ahead were dreary hills, rising higher and higher, dark with trees. On some of them were old castles with an evil look, as if they had been built by wicked people. Everything seemed gloomy, for the weather that day had taken a nasty turn. Mostly it had been as good as May can be, even in merry tales, but now it was cold and wet. In the Lone-lands they had been obliged to camp when they could, but at least it had been dry." (*1966-Ball* matches the reading of *1966-Longmans/Unwin,* but omits *been obliged* from the last sentence.)

In introducing the name *Lone-lands* into the 1966 edition of *The Hobbit,* Tolkien was providing a linguistic equivalent of the Sindarin Elvish name *Eriador* ("wilderness"), which in *The Lord of the Rings* refers to the vast lands between the Blue Mountains to the west and the Misty Mountains to the east. The Shire, where the Hobbits dwell, lies near its center.

7 *1937:* "To think it is June the first tomorrow," > *1966-Longmans/Unwin:* "To think it will soon be June!" (*1966-Ball, 1966-A&U* and *1967-HM* erroneously have a comma instead of an exclamation mark.)

Lone-lands they had been obliged to camp when they could, but at least it had been dry.[6]

"To think it will soon be June!"[7] grumbled Bilbo, as he splashed along behind the others in a very muddy track. It was after tea-time; it was pouring with rain, and had been all day; his hood was dripping into his eyes, his cloak was full of water; the pony was tired and stumbled on stones; the others were too grumpy to talk. "And I'm sure the rain has got into the dry clothes and into the food-bags," thought Bilbo. "Bother burgling and everything to do with it! I wish I was at home in my nice hole by the fire, with the kettle just beginning to sing!" It was not the last time that he wished that!

Still the dwarves jogged on, never turning round or taking any notice of the hobbit. Somewhere behind the grey clouds the sun must have gone down, for it began to get dark as they went down into a deep valley with a river at the bottom. Wind got up, and willows along its banks bent and sighed.[8] Fortunately the road went over an ancient stone bridge, for the river, swollen with the rains, came rushing down from the hills and mountains in the north.[9]

It was nearly night when they had crossed over. The wind broke up the grey clouds, and a wandering moon appeared[10] above the hills between the flying rags. Then they stopped, and Thorin muttered something about supper, "and where shall we get a dry patch to sleep on?"

Not until then did they notice that Gandalf was missing. So far he had come all the way with them, never saying if he was in the adventure or merely keeping them company for a while. He had eaten most, talked most, and laughed most. But now he simply was not there at all!

"Just when a wizard would have been most useful, too," groaned Dori and Nori (who shared the hobbit's views about regular meals, plenty and often).

They decided in the end that they would have to

Bilbo and the Dwarves cross the stone bridge with their ponies. Illustration by Tove Jansson for the 1962 Swedish and 1973 Finnish editions. Tove Jansson (1914–2001) was a native of Finland, born to a Swedish-speaking family. Out of all of the foreign illustrators of *The Hobbit*, Jansson is without question the most well known and acclaimed, both as an artist and as a writer. Her illustrated children's stories about the Moomins, a family of eccentric trolls who resemble hippopotamuses, came out between 1945 and 1970 and have been translated worldwide. She also illustrated translations of Lewis Carroll's *The Hunting of the Snark* (1959) and *Alice in Wonderland* (1966). An English edition of the latter with Jansson's illustrations was published in 1977. She also published fiction for adults.

On illustrating Tolkien, Jansson wrote to Mikael Ahlström of the Finnish Tolkien Society in 1992 that "for me, illustrating *The Hobbit* was an adventure," and one wishes that she would have elaborated further. The Moominvalley Museum in Tampere, Finland, is devoted to Jansson's fictional characters, but it also holds her original artwork for *The Hobbit*. Three more illustrations by Jansson can be found on pages 153, 291, and 342. See also page 395 (book cover).

8 *1937:* "it began to get dark. Wind got up, and the willows along the river-bank bent and sighed." > *1966-Longmans/Unwin:* "it began to get dark as they went down into a deep valley with a river at the bottom. Wind got up, and willows along its banks bent and sighed." (*1966-Ball* matches the reading of the *1937* text.)

9 *1937:* "I don't know what river it was, a rushing red one, swollen with the rains of the last few days, that came down from the hills and mountains in front of them." > *1966-Longmans/Unwin:* "Fortunately the road went over an ancient stone bridge, for the river, swollen with the rains, came rushing down from the hills and mountains in the north." (*1966-Ball* follows *1937*. *1966-A&U* and *1967-HM* do not have a comma after the word *river*.)

This revision was made to bring the geography of *The Hobbit* more in line with that in *The Lord of the Rings*, and specifically to introduce the "ancient stone bridge," called "the Last Bridge," or "the Bridge of Mitheithel" in *The Fellowship of the Ring*. It was a three-arched bridge, the easternmost on the Road, crossing over the River Hoarwell, which the Elves call Mitheithel (Sindarin "grey-spring").

10 *1937:* "Soon it was nearly dark. The winds broke up the grey clouds, and a waning moon appeared" > *1966-Longmans/Unwin:* "It was nearly night when they had crossed over. The wind broke up the grey clouds, and a wandering moon appeared" (*1966-Ball* follows *1937*.)

11 *1937:* "camp where they were. So far they had not camped before on this journey, and though they knew that they soon would have to camp regularly, when they were among the Misty Mountains and far from the lands of respectable people, it seemed a bad wet evening to begin on. They moved to a clump of trees" > *1966-Longmans/ Unwin:* "camp where they were. They moved to a clump of trees." (*1966-Ball* follows *1937.*)

The middle sentence was removed because, in terms of the geography of *The Lord of the Rings,* they had long passed out of the lands of respectable people.

Trolls' Hill, drawn by J.R.R. Tolkien. In the original drawing, red ink is used to focus attention to the firelight near the crest of the hill in the left foreground. The sketch is clearly meant to illustrate the following passage: "There was a hill some way off with trees on it, pretty thick in parts. Out of the dark mass of the trees they could now see a light shining, a reddish comfortable-looking light, as it might be a fire or torches twinkling." A color reproduction of the original can be seen in *Artist* (No. 99).

camp where they were.[11] They moved to a clump of trees, and though it was drier under them, the wind shook the rain off the leaves, and the drip, drip, was most annoying. Also the mischief seemed to have got into the fire. Dwarves can make a fire almost anywhere out of almost anything, wind or no wind; but they could not do it that night, not even Oin and Gloin, who were specially good at it.

Then one of the ponies took fright at nothing and

bolted. He got into the river before they could catch him; and before they could get him out again, Fili and Kili were nearly drowned, and all the baggage that he carried was washed away off him. Of course it was mostly food, and there was mighty little left for supper, and less for breakfast.

There they all sat glum and wet and muttering, while Oin and Gloin went on trying to light the fire, and quarrelling about it. Bilbo was sadly reflecting that adventures are not all pony-rides in May-sunshine, when Balin, who was always their look-out man, said: "There's a light over there!"[12] There was a hill some way off with trees on it, pretty thick in parts. Out of the dark mass of the trees they could now see a light shining, a reddish comfortable-looking light, as it might be a fire or torches twinkling.

When they had looked at it for some while, they fell to arguing. Some said "no" and some said "yes". Some said they could but go and see, and anything was better than little supper, less breakfast, and wet clothes all the night.

Others said: "These parts are none too well known, and are too near the mountains. Travellers seldom come this way now. The old maps are no use: things have changed for the worse and the road is unguarded.[13] They have seldom even heard of the king[14] round here, and the less inquisitive you are as you go along, the less trouble you are likely to find." Some said: "After all there are fourteen of us." Others said: "Where has Gandalf got to?" This remark was repeated by everybody. Then the rain began to pour down worse than ever, and Oin and Gloin began to fight.

That settled it. "After all we have got a burglar with us," they said; and so they made off, leading their ponies (with all due and proper caution) in the direction of the light. They came to the hill and were soon in the wood. Up the hill they went; but there was no proper path to

12 Here the dwarves have just crossed the River Hoarwell, and they see the light of the trolls' fire "some way off," surely a very small distance. This brings up a major discrepancy in the geography of *The Hobbit* as compared with that of *The Lord of the Rings*. In the latter book, Aragorn and the hobbits take almost six days from the time they cross the Hoarwell to the time they reach the Trolls' clearing. Tolkien was aware of this discrepancy, and in his aborted 1960 rewriting of the early chapters of *The Hobbit*, he tried to reconcile the matter. However, when he came to revise the book for the third edition of 1966, he made only minor changes, like the addition of the crossing of the stone bridge (see note 9 to this chapter), and did not attempt to account for the difference in geography.

13 *1937:* "Policemen never come so far, and the map-makers have not reached this country yet." > *1966-Ball:* "Travellers seldom come this way now. The old maps are no use: things have changed for the worse and the road is unguarded."

The reference to "policemen" was removed because of its unsuitability.

14 The mention here of the king is probably not meant to refer to an actual personage but instead to invoke the idea of the king as the theoretical source of justice, law, and order.

15 Tolkien presents the Trolls' speech in a comic, lower-class dialect. This linguistic joke shows a perception for language similar to that which Tolkien ascribed to Geoffrey Chaucer in a long paper presented to the Philological Society in Oxford on May 16, 1931. This paper, entitled "Chaucer as a Philologist: *The Reeve's Tale*," shows how Chaucer used the northern dialect of Middle English as a source of humor for his southern (London) audience. Many of the views expressed about Chaucer could be said about Tolkien as well:

Chaucer deliberately relies on the easy laughter that is roused by "dialect" in the ignorant or the unphilological. But he gives not mere popular ideas of dialect: he gives the genuine thing, even if he is careful to give his audience certain obvious features that they were accustomed to regard as funny. He certainly was inspired here to use this easy joke for the purpose of dramatic realism—and he saved *The Reeve's Tale* by the touch. Yet he certainly would not have done these things, let alone done them so well, if he had not possessed a private philological interest, and a knowledge, too, of "dialect" spoken and written, greater than was usual in his day.

   Such elaborate jests, so fully carried out, are those only of a man interested in language and consciously observant of it. It is universal to notice oddities in the speech of others, and to laugh at them. . . . Many may laugh, but few can analyse or record. (*Transactions of the Philological Society 1934*, pp. 3-4)

   In August 1938, Tolkien, wearing fourteenth-century robes, impersonated Chaucer and recited *The Nonnes Preestes Tale* from memory at the Summer Diversions in Oxford, organized by John Masefield and Nevill Coghill. The following year, Tolkien did the same for *The Reeves Tale,* and his text

be seen, such as might lead to a house or a farm; and do what they could they made a deal of rustling and crackling and creaking (and a good deal of grumbling and dratting), as they went through the trees in the pitch dark.

Suddenly the red light shone out very bright through the tree-trunks not far ahead.

"Now it is the burglar's turn," they said, meaning Bilbo. "You must go on and find out all about that light, and what it is for, and if all is perfectly safe and canny," said Thorin to the hobbit. "Now scuttle off, and come back quick, if all is well. If not, come back if you can! If you can't, hoot twice like a barn-owl and once like a screech-owl, and we will do what we can."

Off Bilbo had to go, before he could explain that he could not hoot even once like any kind of owl any more than fly like a bat. But at any rate hobbits can move quietly in woods, absolutely quietly. They take a pride in it, and Bilbo had sniffed more than once at what he called "all this dwarvish racket," as they went along, though I don't suppose you or I would have noticed anything at all on a windy night, not if the whole cavalcade had passed two feet off. As for Bilbo walking primly towards the red light, I don't suppose even a weasel would have stirred a whisker at it. So, naturally, he got right up to the fire — for fire it was — without disturbing anyone. And this is what he saw.

Three very large persons sitting round a very large fire of beech-logs. They were toasting mutton on long spits of wood, and licking the gravy off their fingers. There was a fine toothsome smell. Also there was a barrel of good drink at hand, and they were drinking out of jugs. But they were trolls. Obviously trolls. Even Bilbo, in spite of his sheltered life, could see that: from the great heavy faces of them, and their size, and the shape of their legs, not to mention their language, which was not drawing-room fashion at all, at all.**15**

Bilbo and the Trolls. Illustration by António Quadros
for the 1962 Portuguese edition.

was printed in a small booklet so that
members of the audience could follow
his recitation.

"Mutton yesterday, mutton today, and blimey, if it
don't look like mutton again tomorrer," said one of the
trolls.

"Never a blinking bit of manflesh have we had for
long enough," said a second. "What the 'ell William was
a-thinkin' of to bring us into these parts at all, beats
me — and the drink runnin' short, what's more," he said
jogging the elbow of William, who was taking a pull at
his jug.

William choked. "Shut yer mouth!" he said as soon as
he could. "Yer can't expect folk to stop here for ever just
to be et by you and Bert. You've et a village and a half between yer, since we come down from the mountains.
How much more d'yer want? And time's been up our
way, when yer'd have said 'thank yer Bill' for a nice bit o'
fat valley mutton like what this is." He took a big bite off

16 Often in fairy stories, trolls are depicted as having many heads. The illustration above, by Lancelot Speed
(1860–1931), is of the troll in the story
"Soria Moria Castle" in *The Red Fairy
Book* (1890), edited by Andrew Lang.
The Red Fairy Book also contains one of
Tolkien's favorite childhood stories, that
of Sigurd and the dragon Fafnir.

꓿ Bilbo's approach to the three trolls,
who are roasting meat on their fire, is
strongly reminiscent of a scene in the
Grimms' tale "The Expert Huntsman"
in which the young hunter enters a forest and, seeing the glimmer of a fire in
the distance, approaches three uncouth
giants who are roasting an ox. "The Expert Huntsman" ("Der gelernte Jäger")
was published in volume two of the
first edition of *Die Kinder– und Hausmärchen* (1815).

Bilbo stealing the Troll's purse. Illustration by Nada Rappensbergerová for the 1973 Slovak edition.

a sheep's leg he was roasting, and wiped his lips on his
sleeve.

Yes, I am afraid trolls do behave like that, even those
with only one head each.**16** After hearing all this Bilbo
ought to have done something at once. Either he should
have gone back quietly and warned his friends that there
were three fair-sized trolls at hand in a nasty mood, quite
likely to try roasted dwarf, or even pony, for a change; or
else he should have done a bit of good quick burgling. A
really first-class and legendary burglar would at this
point have picked the trolls' pockets — it is nearly always
worth while, if you can manage it —, pinched the very

mutton off the spits, purloined the beer, and walked off without their noticing him. Others more practical but with less professional pride would perhaps have stuck a dagger into each of them before they observed it. Then the night could have been spent cheerily.

Bilbo knew it. He had read of a good many things he had never seen or done. He was very much alarmed, as well as disgusted; he wished himself a hundred miles away, and yet — and yet somehow he could not go straight back to Thorin and Company emptyhanded. So he stood and hesitated in the shadows. Of the various burglarious proceedings he had heard of picking the trolls' pockets seemed the least difficult, so at last he crept behind a tree just behind William.

Bert and Tom went off to the barrel. William was having another drink. Then Bilbo plucked up courage and put his little hand in William's enormous pocket. There was a purse in it, as big as a bag to Bilbo. "Ha!" thought he, warming to his new work as he lifted it carefully out, "this is a beginning!"

It was! Trolls' purses are the mischief, and this was no exception. "'Ere, 'oo are you?" it squeaked, as it left the pocket; and William turned round at once and grabbed Bilbo by the neck, before he could duck behind the tree.

"Blimey, Bert, look what I've copped!" said William.

"What is it?" said the others coming up.

"Lumme, if I knows! What are yer?"

"Bilbo Baggins, a bur — a hobbit," said poor Bilbo, shaking all over, and wondering how to make owl-noises before they throttled him.

"A burrahobbit?" said they a bit startled. Trolls are slow in the uptake, and mighty suspicious about anything new to them.[17]

"What's a burrahobbit got to do with my pocket, anyways?" said William.

"And can yer cook 'em?" said Tom.

"Yer can try," said Bert, picking up a skewer.

The Trolls. Illustration by Torbjörn Zetterholm for the 1947 Swedish edition.

[17] In 1926 Tolkien wrote a long poem about a troll, intended to be sung to the tune of the traditional English folk song "The Fox Went Out." (The American version of the folk song is rather different, both in terms of story and in tune.) The first version of Tolkien's poem is titled "Pēro & Pōdex" ("Boot and Bottom") and the next version, "The Root of the Boot." This version (given below) was printed under unusual circumstances in 1936 in a booklet entitled *Songs for the Philologists*. (For further information, see *The Return of the Shadow*, volume six of the *History*, pp. 142–45, where the printed text of the poem includes some additional revisions.) A later and less sophisticated version of this poem appears in Chap-

ter 12 of Book I of *The Lord of the Rings* and is reprinted under the title of "The Stone Troll" in *The Adventures of Tom Bombadil*.

Tolkien himself can be heard singing another version of this poem on the 1975 record *J.R.R. Tolkien Reads and Sings His "The Hobbit" and "The Fellowship of the Ring"* (Caedmon TC 1477), based on tape recordings made in August 1952.

THE ROOT OF THE BOOT

A troll sat alone on his seat of stone,
And munched and mumbled a bare old bone;
And long and long he had sat there lone
    And seen no man nor mortal –
      Ortal! Portal!
And long and long he had sat there lone
    And seen no man nor mortal.

Up came Tom with his big boots on;
"Hallo!" says he, "pray what is yon?
It looks like the leg of me nuncle John
    As should be lying in the churchyard.
      Searchyard, Birchyard!
It looks like the leg of me nuncle John
    As should be lying in the churchyard."

"Young man," says the troll, "that bone I stole;
But what be bones, when mayhap the soul
In heaven on high hath an aureole
    As big and as bright as a bonfire?
      On fire, yon fire!
In heaven on high hath an aureole
    As big and as bright as a bonfire?"

Says Tom: "Oddsteeth! 'tis my belief,
If bonfire there be, 'tis underneath;
For old man John was as proper a thief
    As ever wore black on a Sunday –
      Grundy, Monday!
For old man John was as proper a thief
    As ever wore black on a Sunday.

But I still doan't see what that is to thee,
With me kith and me kin a-makin' free:
So get to hell and ax leave o' he,
    Afore thou gnaws me nuncle!

.The Trolls.

The Trolls by J.R.R. Tolkien, one of the standard black-and-white illustrations that has appeared in *The Hobbit* since 1937. This illustration appears in *Artist* (No. 102) and in *Pictures* (No. 2, left). A version colored by H. E. Riddett first appeared in *The Hobbit Calendar 1976* (1975), and in *Pictures* (No. 2, right).

Tolkien's drawing was clearly modeled on the illustration *Hansel and Grethel Sat Down by the Fire* by Jennie Harbour (opposite), which has a slightly complicated history. It first appeared in Edric Vredenburg's *My Book of Favourite Fairy Tales* (1921), published by the London firm Raphael Tuck and illustrated by Harbour in color and black and white. Vredenburg (1860–c. 1943) was for many years an editor at Tuck, a firm that predominately published children's books, including the popular *Father Tuck's Annual*. Tuck frequently recycled content from its own previously published books into new forms. Priscilla Tolkien recalls having several Raphael Tuck books as a child.

Tolkien encountered Harbour's illustration in *The Fairy Tale Book*, published by Tuck in May 1934. *The Fairy Tale Book* contains eight of the fifteen stories in *My Book of Favourite Fairy Tales*, but the texts have been rewritten, the illustrations rearranged, and, in the case of the story "Hansel and Grethel," its color plate omitted. No editor is credited.

Uncle, Buncle!
So get to hell and ax leave o' he,
Afore thou gnaws me nuncle!"

In the proper place upon the base
Tom boots him right — but, alas!, that race
Hath a stonier seat than its stony face;
So he rued that root on the rumpo,
Lumpo, Bumpo!
Hath a stonier seat than its stony face;
So he rued that root on the rumpo.

Now Tom goes lame since home he came,
And his bootless foot is grievous game;
But troll's old seat is much the same,
And the bone he boned from its owner!
Donor, Boner!
But troll's old seat is much the same,
And the bone he boned from its owner!

In the final stanza, *boned* is from the verb *bone,* to steal, to make off with.

(American reprints done in the 1990s complicate the matter further. *My Book of Favorite Fairy Tales,* published by Derrydale Books in 1993, does not credit Vredenburg and contains only ten tales, the texts of which are rewritten yet again, and Harbour's illustrations are reformatted when included and sometimes cropped and even added to. The 1998 Derrydale edition is the same as the 1993 edition but is in a smaller format.)

In comparing the two illustrations, Wayne G. Hammond and Christina Scull write that Tolkien's picture "is more structured than Harbour's, his woods more menacing, his flames and smoke more animated. Also his drawing is more distinctly Art Nouveau, especially in its sinuous, stylized smoke and sharp contrasts of black and white. It is a technically brilliant illustration" (*Artist,* 109).

Almost nothing is known of Jennie Harbour, save that she illustrated a small number of books, nearly all for the firm Raphael Tuck, including *My Book of Mother Goose Nursery Rhymes* (1926) and *Hans Andersen's Stories* (1932), the latter perhaps her supreme achievement with twelve striking color plates and about fifty black-and-white drawings. Harbour's work is highly valued by those who know it, but otherwise it remains little known and underappreciated.

18 *1937:* "said William (I told you he had already had as much supper as he could hold; also he had had lots of beer)." > *1966-Ball:* "said William. He had already had as much supper as he could hold; also he had had lots of beer."

Here Tolkien removed one of the direct addresses to the reader. To an interviewer in 1967 Tolkien commented: "*The Hobbit* was written in what I should now regard as bad style, as if one were talking to children. There's nothing my children loathed more. They taught me a lesson. Anything that in any way marked out *The Hobbit* as for children instead of just for people, they disliked – instinctively. I did too, now I think about it. All this 'I won't tell you any more; you think about it' stuff. Oh no, they loathe it; it's awful. Children aren't a class. They are merely human beings, at differing stages of maturity." (Philip Norman, "The Hobbit Man," *Sunday Times Magazine,* London, January 15, 1967; also published on the same date in the *New York Times Magazine* under the title "The Prevalence of Hobbits.")

The *Oxford English Dictionary* notes that *blighter* is slang for "a contemptible or unpleasant person; often [used] merely as an extravagant substitute for *fellow.*"

19 *1937:* "when they dropped him" > *1966-Ball:* "when Bert dropped him"

"He wouldn't make above a mouthful," said William, who had already had a fine supper, "not when he was skinned and boned."

"P'raps there are more like him round about, and we might make a pie," said Bert. "Here you, are there any more of your sort a-sneakin' in these here woods, yer nassty little rabbit," said he looking at the hobbit's furry feet; and he picked him up by the toes and shook him.

"Yes, lots," said Bilbo, before he remembered not to give his friends away. "No none at all, not one," he said immediately afterwards.

"What d'yer mean?" said Bert, holding him right way up, by the hair this time.

"What I say," said Bilbo gasping. "And please don't cook me, kind sirs! I am a good cook myself, and cook better than I cook, if you see what I mean. I'll cook beautifully for you, a perfectly beautiful breakfast for you, if only you won't have me for supper."

"Poor little blighter," said William. He had already had as much supper as he could hold; also he had had lots of beer.**18** "Poor little blighter! Let him go!"

"Not till he says what he means by *lots* and *none at all,*" said Bert. "I don't want to have me throat cut in me sleep! Hold his toes in the fire, till he talks!"

"I won't have it," said William. "I caught him anyway."

"You're a fat fool, William," said Bert, "as I've said afore this evening."

"And you're a lout!"

"And I won't take that from you, Bill Huggins," says Bert, and puts his fist in William's eye.

Then there was a gorgeous row. Bilbo had just enough wits left, when Bert dropped him**19** on the ground, to scramble out of the way of their feet, before they were fighting like dogs, and calling one another all sorts of perfectly true and applicable names in very loud voices. Soon they were locked in one another's arms, and rolling nearly into the fire kicking and thumping, while Tom whacked at them both with a branch to bring them to their senses — and that of course only made them madder than ever.

That would have been the time for Bilbo to have left. But his poor little feet had been very squashed in Bert's big paw, and he had no breath in his body, and his head was going round; so there he lay for a while panting, just outside the circle of firelight.

Right in the middle of the fight up came Balin. The dwarves had heard noises from a distance, and after waiting for some time for Bilbo to come back, or to hoot like an owl, they started off one by one to creep towards the light as quietly as they could. No sooner did Tom see Balin come into the light than he gave an awful howl. Trolls simply detest the very sight of dwarves (uncooked). Bert and Bill stopped fighting immediately, and "a sack, Tom, quick!" they said. Before Balin, who was wondering where in all this commotion Bilbo was, knew what was happening, a sack was over his head, and he was down.

"There's more to come yet," said Tom, "or I'm mighty mistook. Lots and none at all, it is," said he. "No burrahobbits, but lots of these here dwarves. That's about the shape of it!"

"I reckon you're right," said Bert, "and we'd best get out of the light."

And so they did. With sacks in their hands, that they used for carrying off mutton and other plunder, they waited in the shadows. As each dwarf came up and looked at the fire, and the spilled jugs, and the gnawed mutton, in surprise, pop! went a nasty smelly sack over his head, and he was down. Soon Dwalin lay by Balin, and Fili and Kili together, and Dori and Nori and Ori all in a heap, and Oin and Gloin and Bifur and Bofur and Bombur[20] piled uncomfortably near the fire.

20 Nearly all of the dwarf names in *The Hobbit* were derived from a list of dwarf names in the Old Norse poem "Voluspá" (The Prophecy of the Seeress), which is part of a collection of ancient Norse mythological and heroic poems generally known as the *Elder* (or Poetic) *Edda*. The versions of the poem that survive provided Tolkien with the following names: Durin, Dwalin, Nain, Dain, Bifur, Bofur, Bombur, Nori, Thrain, Thorin, Thror, Fili, Kili, Fundin, Gloin, Dori, Nori, and Ori. Thorin's epithet Oakenshield is a translation of the dwarf name Eikinskjaldi. The name Gandalf also appears and would be translated as "wand-elf" or "sorcerer-elf" — hence "wizard." Bombur can be translated as "tubby." The only dwarf names used by Tolkien that are not precisely found in "Voluspá" are Oin and Balin, but each of these can be seen as rhyming with names like Gloin and Dwalin.

The list of dwarf names, or "Dvergatal" (The Tally of Dwarfs), is generally considered to be an interpolated section in the manuscript. In the Henry Adams Bellows translation, *The Poetic Edda* (1923), it reads as follows:

Then sought the gods   their assembly-seats,
The holy-ones,   and council held,
To find who should raise   the race of dwarfs
Out of Brimir's blood   and the legs of Blain.

There was Motsognir   the mightiest made
Of all the dwarfs,   and Durin next;
Many a likeness   of men they made,
The dwarfs in the earth,   as Durin said.

Nyi and Nithi,   Northri and Suthri,
Austri and Vestri,   Althjof, Dvalin,
Nar and Nain,   Niping, Dain,
Bifur, Bofur,   Bombur, Nori,
An and Onar,   Ai, Mjothvitnir.

Vigg and Gandalf,   Vindalf, Thrain,
Thekk and Thorin,   Thror, Vit and Lit,
Nyr and Nyrath, —   now have I told —
Regin and Rathsvith —   the list aright.

Fili, Kili,   Fundin, Nali,
Heptifili,   Hannar, Sviur,
Frar, Hornbori,   Fræg and Loni,
Aurvang, Jari,   Eikinskjaldi.

The race of the dwarfs   in Dvalin's throng
Down to Lofar   the list I must tell;
The rocks they left,   and through wet lands
They sought a home   in the fields of sand.

There were Draupnir   and Dolgthrasir,
Hor, Haugspori,   Hlevang, Gloin,
Dori, Ori,   Duf, Andvari,
Skirfir, Virfir,   Skafith, Ai.

Alf and Yngvi,   Eikinskjaldi,
Fjalar and Frosti,   Fith and Ginnar;
So for all time   shall the tale be known,
The list of all   the forbears of Lofar.
                   (stanzas 9–16; pp. 6–8)

Most of the dwarf names mentioned
above are unique to the "Dvergatal,"
and some of the names presumably had
some significance (e.g., Northri, Suthri,
Austri and Vestri translate merely as
the directions North, South, East and
West), but for many of the names any in-
terpretations are problematical.

The names of the dwarves may come
from the Old Norse tradition, but elements of their behavior come right
out of fairy tales like "Snow White"
("Schneewittchen"), from the first edition of *Die Kinder– und Hausmärchen*
(1812) of the Brothers Grimm (more fa-
miliarly known today as *Grimms' Fairy
Tales*), and "Snow White and Rose
Red" ("Schneeweisschen und Rosen-
rot"), from the third edition of 1837.
"Snow White," which tells the familiar
tale of Snow White and the seven
dwarfs, can also be found in *The Red*

"That'll teach 'em," said Tom; for Bifur and Bombur
had given a lot of trouble, and fought like mad, as
dwarves will when cornered.

Thorin came last — and he was not caught unawares.
He came expecting mischief, and didn't need to see his
friends' legs sticking out of sacks to tell him that things
were not all well. He stood outside in the shadows some
way off, and said: "What's all this trouble? Who has
been knocking my people about?"

"It's trolls!" said Bilbo from behind a tree. They had
forgotten all about him. "They're hiding in the bushes
with sacks," said he.

"O! are they?" said Thorin, and he jumped forward
to the fire, before they could leap on him. He caught up
a big branch all on fire at one end; and Bert got that
end in his eye before he could step aside. That put him
out of the battle for a bit. Bilbo did his best. He caught
hold of Tom's leg — as well as he could, it was thick as a
young tree-trunk — but he was sent spinning up into the
top of some bushes, when Tom kicked the sparks up in
Thorin's face.

Tom got the branch in his teeth for that, and lost one
of the front ones. It made him howl, I can tell you. But
just at that moment William came up behind and
popped a sack right over Thorin's head and down to his
toes. And so the fight ended. A nice pickle they were all
in now: all neatly tied up in sacks, with three angry trolls
(and two with burns and bashes to remember) sitting by
them, arguing whether they should roast them slowly, or
mince them fine and boil them, or just sit on them one
by one and squash them into jelly; and Bilbo, up in a
bush, with his clothes and his skin torn, not daring to
move for fear they should hear him.

It was just then that Gandalf came back. But no one saw
him. The trolls had just decided to roast the dwarves
now and eat them later — that was Bert's idea, and after
a lot of argument they had all agreed to it.

"No good roasting 'em now, it'd take all night," said a voice. Bert thought it was William's.

"Don't start the argument all over again, Bill," he said, "or it *will* take all night."

"Who's a-arguing?" said William, who thought it was Bert that had spoken.

"You are," said Bert.

"You're a liar," said William; and so the argument began all over again. In the end they decided to mince them fine and boil them. So they got a great black pot, and they took out their knives.

"No good boiling 'em! We ain't got no water, and it's a long way to the well and all," said a voice. Bert and William thought it was Tom's.

"Shut up!" said they, "or we'll never have done. And yer can fetch the water yerself, if yer say any more."

"Shut up yerself!" said Tom, who thought it was William's voice. "Who's arguing but you, I'd like to know."

"You're a booby," said William.

"Booby yerself!" said Tom.

And so the argument began all over again, and went on hotter than ever, until at last they decided to sit on the sacks one by one and squash them, and boil them next time.

"Who shall we sit on first?" said the voice.

"Better sit on the last fellow first," said Bert, whose eye had been damaged by Thorin. He thought Tom was talking.

"Don't talk to yerself!" said Tom. "But if you wants to sit on the last one, sit on him. Which is he?"

"The one with the yellow stockings," said Bert.

"Nonsense, the one with the grey stockings," said a voice like William's.

"I made sure it was yellow," said Bert.

"Yellow it was," said William.

"Then what did yer say it was grey for?" said Bert.

"I never did. Tom said it."

"That I never did!" said Tom. "It was you."

Fairy Book (1890), edited by Andrew Lang, where it appears under the title "Snowdrop." "Snow White and Rose Red" can also be found in Lang's *Blue Fairy Book* (1889). Interestingly, this story includes a bear-man, slightly reminiscent of Beorn, who turns out to be a young prince cursed by a dwarf to roam the woods as a wild bear.

In Section I ("The Languages and Peoples of the Third Age") of Appendix F of *The Lord of the Rings,* Tolkien wrote of dwarves: "They are a tough, thrawn race for the most part, secretive, laborious, retentive of the memory of injuries (and of benefits), lovers of stone, of gems, of things that take shape under the hands of craftsmen rather than things that live by their own life. But they are not evil by nature, and few ever served the Enemy of free will, whatever the tales of Men may have alleged."

In *The Hobbit,* none of the dwarf names are accented, and I have followed that usage throughout this book. In *The Lord of the Rings,* however, Tolkien accented some of the dwarf names as follows: Fíli, Kíli, Óin, Glóin, Thrór, Thráin, Dáin, and Náin. The accents serve as an aid to pronunciation. Following the "pronouncing index" for Old Norse in Bellows's translation of *The Poetic Edda,* an *í* (as in Fíli and Kíli) sounds like the *i* in *machine;* the *ó* as in *old* (hence *Oʹ-in* and *Gloʹ-in*), and the *á* as in *father* (thus *Thraʹ-in,* etc.).

21 On February 16, 1926, Tolkien's friend and colleague Helen Buckhurst (1894–1963), a Fellow and Tutor at St. Hugh's College, Oxford, from 1926 to 1930, read a paper titled "Icelandic Folklore" to the Viking Society for Northern Research. The paper was later published in the organization's proceedings, the *Saga-Book,* vol. 10 (covering the years 1919–27; published in 1928–29). Buckhurst's paper relates in full some interesting stories from Icelandic folklore, including some tales of trolls, which she describes as follows:

The Icelandic Trolls, as depicted both in the Sagas and in more recent tales, are huge, misshapen creatures, bearing some resemblance to human form, but always hideously ugly. They make their homes among the mountains, living generally in caves among the rocks or in the lava. They are almost always malignant in disposition, and frequently descend at night upon outlying farms in order to carry off sheep and horses, children, or even grown men and women, to devour in their mountain homes.

(pp. 222–23)

She also notes that "some kinds of trolls have no power except during the hours of darkness; during the day they must remain hidden in their caves, for the rays of the sun turn them into stone" (229). Buckhurst gives one short example of this type of troll:

THE NIGHT TROLL

At a certain farm it befell that whoever had to keep watch over the house on Yule night, while the rest of the household was at Midnight Mass, was found either dead or mad next morning. Folk were troubled about this, and few were willing to sit at home on Yule night. One year a girl volunteered to look after the house, whereat the others were glad, and went to church. The girl sat down on the bench in

"Two to one, so shut yer mouth!" said Bert.

"Who are you a-talkin' to?" said William.

"Now stop it!" said Tom and Bert together. "The night's gettin' on, and dawn comes early. Let's get on with it!"

"Dawn take you all, and be stone to you!" said a voice that sounded like William's. But it wasn't. For just at that moment the light came over the hill, and there was a mighty twitter in the branches. William never spoke for he stood turned to stone as he stooped; and Bert and Tom were stuck like rocks as they looked at him. And there they stand to this day, all alone, unless the birds perch on them; for trolls, as you probably know, must be underground before dawn, or they go back to the stuff of the mountains they are made of, and never move again.21 That is what had happened to Bert and Tom and William.

"Excellent!" said Gandalf, as he stepped from behind a tree, and helped Bilbo to climb down out of a thornbush.22 Then Bilbo understood. It was the wizard's voice that had kept the trolls bickering and quarrelling, until the light came and made an end of them.23

The next thing was to untie the sacks and let out the dwarves. They were nearly suffocated, and very annoyed: they had not at all enjoyed lying there listening to the trolls making plans for roasting them and squashing them and mincing them. They had to hear Bilbo's account of what had happened to him twice over, before they were satisfied.

"Silly time to go practising pinching24 and pocket-picking," said Bombur, "when what we wanted was fire and food!"

"And that's just what you wouldn't have got of those fellows without a struggle, in any case," said Gandalf. "Anyhow you are wasting time now. Don't you realize that the trolls must have a cave or a hole dug somewhere near to hide from the sun in? We must look into it!"

The Three Trolls are turned to Stone

The Three Trolls are turned to Stone by J.R.R. Tolkien. This illustration was not used in the original edition of *The Hobbit,* probably because the ink wash that Tolkien had applied to the trolls (and to Gandalf's cloak) would not have reproduced well by line block (see *Artist,* p. 108). Otherwise it is the only finished drawing by Tolkien to depict Gandalf and to show Bilbo's face from the front. Of the trolls, the figure at right, stooping from his knees, is apparently William, with Bert and Tom looking at him. The "great black pot" in the foreground does not look as if it would hold many dwarves for the boiling.

This illustration was first published in its original form in 1979 in *Pictures* (No. 3, left); it also appears in *Artist* (No. 100). A version of this illustration colored by H. E. Riddett first appeared in *The J.R.R. Tolkien Calendar 1979* (1978) and in *Pictures* (No. 3, right).

They searched about, and soon found the marks of trolls' stony boots going away through the trees. They followed the tracks up the hill, until hidden by bushes they came on a big door of stone leading to a cave. But they could not open it, not though they all pushed while Gandalf tried various incantations.

"Would this be any good?" asked Bilbo, when they were getting tired and angry. "I found it on the ground where the trolls had their fight." He held out a largish key, though no doubt William had thought it very small

the living-room, talking and crooning to a child she had on her knee. During the night there came a Thing to the window, and said:

> *"Fair in my sight is that hand of thing —*
> *My brisk one, my brave one, sing dillido!"*

Then she sang:
> *"Filth has it never swept from the floor*
> *Foul fiend Kári, sing korriro!"*

Then the Thing at the window:
> *"Fair in my sight is that eye of thing —*
> *My brisk one, my brave one, sing dillido!"*

Then sang she:
　　"Evil it has never lookéd upon,
　　Foul fiend Kári, sing korriro!"

Then said the Thing at the window:
　　"Fair in my sight is that foot of thing,
　　My brisk one, my brave one, sing dillido!"

Then sang she:
　　"Nought unclean has it trodden upon,
　　Foul fiend Kári, sing korriro!"

Then said the Thing at the window:
　　"Day now dawns in the eastern sky,
　　My brisk one, my brave one, sing dillido!"

Then she sang:
　　"Dawn now hath caught thee, a stone shalt
　　　　thou be,
　　And no man henceforth shall be harméd
　　　　by thee,
　　Foul fiend Kári, sing korriro!"

Then the spectre vanished from the window; and when the people of the house came in the morning, they saw a great stone standing between the ridges of the roof; and there it has stood ever since. The girl told them what she had heard; but of what the troll was like she could say nothing, for she had never looked towards the window. (pp. 229–31)

Buckhurst did not cite it, but her source for the tale was Jón Árnason's *Islenzkar Þjódsögur og Æfintyri*, volume one (1862). A selection from Árnason's two-volume collection was translated by George E. J. Powell and Eiríkur Magnússon and published under the title *Iceland Legends* (1864), but this volume does not include this story.

In Norwegian folk tales, trolls caught in the sunlight burst into pieces.

22 *1937:* "he stepped from behind the bushes, and helped Bilbo to climb down out of a thorn-tree." > *1966-Ball:* "he stepped from behind a tree, and helped

and secret. It must have fallen out of his pocket, very luckily, before he was turned to stone.

"Why on earth didn't you mention it before?" they cried. Gandalf grabbed it and fitted it into the key-hole. Then the stone door swung back with one big push, and they all went inside. There were bones on the floor and a nasty smell was in the air; but there was a good deal of food jumbled carelessly on shelves and on the ground, among an untidy litter of plunder, of all sorts from brass buttons to pots full of gold coins standing in a corner. There were lots of clothes, too, hanging on the walls — too small for trolls, I am afraid they belonged to victims — and ᶜamong them were several swords of various makes, shapes, and sizes. Two caught their eyes particularly, because of their beautiful scabbards and jewelled hilts.

Gandalf and Thorin each took one of these; and Bilbo took a knife in a leather sheath. It would have made only a tiny pocket-knife for a troll, but it was as good as a short sword for the hobbit.ᐦ

"These look like good blades," said the wizard, half drawing them and looking at them curiously. "They were not made by any troll, nor by any smith among men in these parts and days; but when we can read the runes[25] on them, we shall know more about them."

"Let's get out of this horrible smell!" said Fili. So they carried out the pots of coins, and such food as was untouched and looked fit to eat, also one barrel of ale which was still full. By that time they felt like breakfast, and being very hungry they did not turn their noses up at what they had got from the trolls' larder. Their own provisions were very scanty. Now they had bread and cheese, and plenty of ale, and bacon to toast in the embers of the fire.

After that they slept, for their night had been disturbed; and they did nothing more till the afternoon. Then they brought up their ponies, and carried away the pots of gold, and buried them very secretly not far from the track by the river, putting a great many spells over them, just in case they ever had the chance to come back and recover them. When that was done, they all mounted once more, and jogged along again on the path towards the East.

"Where did you go to, if I may ask?" said Thorin to Gandalf as they rode along.

"To look ahead," said he.

"And what brought you back in the nick of time?"

"Looking behind," said he.

"Exactly!" said Thorin; "but could you be more plain?"

"I went on to spy out our road. It will soon become dangerous and difficult. Also I was anxious about re-plenishing our small stock of provisions. I had not gone very far, however, when I met a couple of friends of mine from Rivendell."**26**

"Where's that?" asked Bilbo.

"Don't interrupt!" said Gandalf. "You will get there in a few days now, if we're lucky, and find out all about it. As I was saying I met two of Elrond's people. They were hurrying along for fear of the trolls. It was they who told me that three of them had come down from the moun-tains and settled in the woods not far from the road: they had frightened everyone away from the district, and they waylaid strangers.

"I immediately had a feeling that I was wanted back. Looking behind I saw a fire in the distance and made for it. So now you know. Please be more careful, next time, or we shall never get anywhere!"

"Thank you!" said Thorin.**27**

Bilbo to climb down out of a thorn-bush."

This passage may have been revised in order to bring the text in line with the statement on page 78 that Bilbo was "up in a bush." Also, this revision matches the text with the details of Tolkien's drawing *The Three Trolls are turned to Stone.*

23 Gandalf's trickery in keeping the trolls quarrelling is reminiscent of the Grimms' tale "The Brave Little Tailor," in which the title character keeps two gi-ants fighting by secretly lobbing stones at them in such a way that each giant thinks the other is doing it. "The Brave Little Tailor" (*"Das tapfere Schneider-lein"*) was published in the first edition of *Die Kinder– und Hausmärchen* (1812). In addition to the numerous English editions of the Grimms' tales, a translation of "The Brave Little Tailor" appears in *The Blue Fairy Book* (1889), edited by Andrew Lang.

A similarly analogous passage occurs in "Puss-cat Mew" by E. H. Knatchbull-Hugessen. In a letter from January 8, 1971, Tolkien commented that before 1900 he used to be read to from an old collection that "contained one story I was then very fond of called 'Puss Cat Mew'" (*Letters,* No. 319). The book is certainly *Stories for My Children* (1869), a collection by E. H. Knatchbull-Hugesson. In the story "Puss-cat Mew," a young man named Joe Brown journeys into a large and gloomy forest, where ogres, dwarfs, and fairies dwell. The dwarfs (with names like Juff, Jumper, and Gandleperry) are allied with the sinister and giant ogres (with names like Munchemup, Mumblechumps, and Grindbones) in wishing to capture Joe and other mortals in order to eat them. The fairies are their enemies, and so a fairy, in the form of an enchanted cat called Puss-cat Mew, helps Joe.

At one point in his adventure, when looking to rescue Puss-cat Mew, Joe uses a glove on his left hand that makes him invisible:

He had not gone far before he heard footsteps, and looking round, having first put on his glove, he perceived the Dwarf Juff, with two of the Ogres, talking eagerly.

"Why don't he eat her?" said the Dwarf.

"You little hop-o'-my-thumb!" growled one of the Giants, "you can't eat a Fairy, you know, or he'd have made but a mouthful of her. But if he catches that lout of a Mortal whom she is so sweet on, he can eat *him,* and then he has the right to marry her. But I know one thing — I wouldn't marry such a squalling Cat for ninepence-halfpenny. The row she makes after that Joe! I wish I had him here! I'd Joe him! Wouldn't you, Mumblechumps?"

"Yes," returned the other Ogre, to whom he had spoken; "yes, brother Munchemup, I think we could show him a trick or two worth mentioning."

"Why don't you do it, then?" said a loud voice close to them; and Joe, with his glove on, hit Juff such a crack on the head that the little wretch rolled over like a nine-pin.

"Help, oh, help me!" he roared in agony, as Joe dealt him another blow; but the Ogres could see nobody, and therefore did nothing, while Juff lay there bellowing.

However, Joe, finding how well he was concealed by his glove, and being highly indignant with the Ogre Munchemup, who had spoken so disrespectfully of Puss-cat Mew, dealt him a blow across the shins with his staff, which made him jump.

"What do you mean by kicking me, Mumblechumps?"

"I didn't touch you," answered the other,

to whom Joe at the same time administered a like blow.

"But I'm not going to stand being kicked by you!" and as Joe dealt them another blow apiece, the two monsters furiously attacked each other, each believing that his friend had assaulted him.

Joe stepped back and watched the fight with interest, until a blow from Mumblechumps felled Munchemup to the ground where he lay senseless. (pp. 50–51)

With his steel dagger, Joe then puts an end to the two ogres and the dwarf.

Edward Hugessen Knatchbull-Hugessen (1829–1893), a grandnephew of Jane Austen, was a member of Parliament for twenty-three years. In 1880 he was raised to the House of Lords as the first Baron Brabourne. Between 1869 and 1886, he published thirteen collections of fairy stories, of which *Stories for My Children* was the first.

There are a few other similarities to Tolkien found in "Puss-cat Mew." At one point, when an ogre feels he has been tricked by the fairies, he says, "Spiflicate those Fairies!" which resembles Bilbo's remark of annoyance on page 41: "Confusticate and bebother these dwarves!"

More significantly there is an unsigned illustration (opposite) to this story showing an ogre waiting in his oak dress in order to catch a Mortal, which foreshadows Tolkien's Ents, the tree-creatures in *The Lord of the Rings.* The text accompanying this illustration reads as follows, with Joe Brown having just entered the wood:

At last, however, he came to a rather open space, when he saw immediately before him, some thirty or forty yards off, an old dead Oak, with two great branches, with scarce a leaf upon them, spreading out right and left. Al-

most as soon as he noticed the Tree, he perceived, to his intense surprise, that it was visibly agitated, and trembled all over. Gradually, as he stood stock-still with amazement, this trembling rapidly increased, the bark of the tree appeared to become the skin of a living body, the two dead limbs became the gigantic arms of a man, a head popped up from the trunk, and an enormous Ogre stood before the astonished traveller. Stood, but only for an instant; for, brandishing a stick as big as a young tree, he took a step forward, uttering at the same moment such a tremendous roar as overpowered the singing of all the birds, and made the whole forest re-echo with the awful sound. (pp. 15–16)

Joe is saved by the Fairies, who turn him temporarily into a Hawthorn tree.

"Puss-cat Mew" may have inspired Tolkien in another way too, for it tells the story behind the nursery rhyme of the same title, an exercise that Tolkien also did in his two "Man in the Moon"

poems, collected in *The Adventures of Tom Bombadil* as "The Man in the Moon Stayed Up Too Late" and "The Man in the Moon Came Down Too Soon." Both of these poems date from the mid- to late 1910s.

"The Man in the Moon Stayed Up Too Late," which tells the story behind the nursery rhyme "Hey diddle diddle, the cat and the fiddle," was (according to a note on the earliest manuscript) written in "Oxford 1919–20." It was first published in *Yorkshire Poetry,* October–November 1923 (2, no. 19), under the title "The Cat and the Fiddle: A Nursery-Rhyme Undone and Its Scandalous Secret Unlocked." Tolkien revised the poem and used it as Frodo's song at Bree in *The Lord of the Rings.* A closely related version of the poem (the text coming from an early manuscript) appears in volume six of the *History, The Return of the Shadow,* pp. 145–47.

"The Man in the Moon Came Down Too Soon" (which tells the story behind the nursery rhyme of the same name) was written on March 10–11, 1915, and an early version of it, entitled "Why the Man in the Moon Came Down Too Soon," appears in the small book *A Northern Venture: Verses by Members of the Leeds University English School Association,* published in Leeds in June 1923. This early version, with slight differences, appears in the first volume of the *History, The Book of Lost Tales, Part One,* pp. 204–6.

The Man in the Moon also appears as a character in "The Tale of the Sun and Moon" in *The Book of Lost Tales, Part One;* in *Roverandom,* written around 1927 but not published until 1998; and in the Father Christmas letter for 1927, published in the expanded *Letters from Father Christmas* (1999) but not in the original *Father Christmas Letters* (1976). Thomas Honegger's "The Man in the Moon: Structural Depth in Tolkien," published in *Root and Branch: Approaches Towards Understanding Tolkien* (1999), edited by Honegger, is a very interesting study of the Man in the Moon traditions in western Europe and Tolkien's use of the character.

24 *1937:* "practising burglary" > *1966-Ball:* "practising pinching"

25 *1937:* "if we can read the runes" > *1966-Ball:* "when we can read the runes"

26 In his guide for translators, "Nomenclature of *The Lord of the Rings*," Tolkien noted that Rivendell, or "Cloven-dell," is "a Common Speech translation of *Imladris(t)* 'deep dale of the cleft.'" Imladris is Sindarin Elvish, but the name is not used in *The Hobbit,* first appearing in *The Lord of the Rings.*

27 In a 1977 speech to the Tolkien Society in England, Tolkien's second son, Michael, said that as children, he, his two brothers, and his sister had each, at some point in their development, thought that the Troll chapter was the best chapter in the book. He continued, "We thought there was something rather nice about Trolls, and it was a pity they had to be turned to stone at all."

3

A Short Rest

THEY DID NOT SING or tell stories that day, even though the weather improved; nor the next day, nor the day after. They had begun to feel that danger was not far away on either side. They camped under the stars, and their horses had more to eat than they had; for there was plenty of grass, but there was not much in their bags, even with what they had got from the trolls. One morning they forded a river[1] at a wide shallow place full of the noise of stones and foam. The far bank was steep and slippery. When they got to the top of it, leading their ponies, they saw that the great mountains had marched down very near to them. Already they seemed only a day's easy journey from the feet of the nearest. Dark and drear it looked, though there were patches of sunlight on its brown sides, and behind its shoulders the tips of snow-peaks gleamed.

"Is that *The* Mountain?" asked Bilbo in a solemn voice, looking at it with round eyes. He had never seen a thing that looked so big before.

"Of course not!" said Balin. "That is only the beginning of the Misty Mountains, and we have got to get through, or over, or under those somehow, before we can come into Wilderland[2] beyond. And it is a deal of a way even from the other side of them to the Lonely Mountain in the East where Smaug lies on our treasure."

"O!" said Bilbo, and just at that moment he felt more

1 *1937:* "One afternoon they forded the river" > *1966-Ball:* "One morning they forded a river"

This slight change brings the geography of *The Hobbit* in line with that of *The Lord of the Rings,* making this river the second one crossed instead of the only one. This river is called the Loudwater (a translation of the Elvish name *Bruinen*). It does not have a bridge here at the Road but is crossed at the Ford of Bruinen, also called the Ford of Rivendell.

2 In his guide for translators, "Nomenclature of *The Lord of the Rings*," Tolkien described the word *Wilderland* as "an invention (not actually found in English), based on *wilderness* (originally meaning country of wild creatures, not inhabited by Men), but with a side-reference to the verbs *wilder* 'wander astray' and *bewilder.*"

Bilbo thinks once again of home. Illustration by Mirna Pavlovec for the 1986 Slovenian edition. Pavlovec (b. 1953) also illustrated the Slovenian translation of *Watership Down* (1987) by Richard Adams. One additional Pavlovec illustration appears on page 100.

3 The Edge of the Wild is clearly drawn on Tolkien's map of "Wilderland." Tolkien also carefully noted this Edge when Bilbo crosses it again on his return journey (see page 358: "they came to the river that marked the very edge of the borderland of the Wild").

4 *1937:* "That sounded nice and comforting, and I daresay you think it ought to have been easy to make straight for the Last Homely House" > *1966-Ball:* "That sounded nice and comforting, but they had not got there yet, and it was not so easy as it sounds to find the Last Homely House"

In describing Elrond's house as *homely,* Tolkien refers to what the *Ox-*

tired than he ever remembered feeling before. He was thinking once again of his comfortable chair before the fire in his favourite sitting-room in his hobbit-hole, and of the kettle singing. Not for the last time!

Now Gandalf led the way. "We must not miss the road, or we shall be done for," he said. "We need food, for one thing, *and* rest in reasonable safety — also it is very necessary to tackle the Misty Mountains by the proper path, or else you will get lost in them, and have to come back and start at the beginning again (if you ever get back at all)."

They asked him where he was making for, and he answered: "You are come to the very edge of the Wild,[3] as some of you may know. Hidden somewhere ahead of us is the fair valley of Rivendell where Elrond lives in the Last Homely House. I sent a message by my friends, and we are expected."

That sounded nice and comforting, but they had not got there yet, and it was not so easy as it sounds to find the Last Homely House[4] west of the Mountains. There seemed to be no trees and no valleys and no hills to break the ground in front of them, only one vast slope going slowly up and up to meet the feet of the nearest mountain, a wide land the colour of heather and crumbling rock, with patches and slashes of grass-green and moss-green showing where water might be.

Morning passed, afternoon came; but in all the silent waste there was no sign of any dwelling. They were growing anxious, for they saw now that the house might be hidden[5] almost anywhere between them and the mountains. They came on unexpected valleys, narrow with steep sides, that opened suddenly at their feet, and they looked down surprised to see trees below them and running water at the bottom. There were gullies that they could almost leap over, but very deep with waterfalls in them. There were dark ravines that one could neither jump over nor climb into. There were bogs,

Rivendell by J.R.R. Tolkien, one of the standard color illustrations for *The Hobbit*. This illustration was first published in the 1937 second impression of the first English edition and in the 1938 American edition (where Tolkien's decorated border and title were removed). For both appearances the illustration was given the printed caption "The Fair Valley of Rivendell." This illustration appears in *Artist* (No. 108) and *Pictures* (No. 6).

In the text of *The Hobbit* (as well as in *The Lord of the Rings*), there is very little description of the shape and style of Elrond's house. This illustration gives the only clues to its outward appearance.

Marie Barnfield, in her article "The Roots of Rivendell; or, Elrond's House Now Open as a Museum" in *Þe Lyfe ant þe Auncestrye,* Spring 1996 (no. 3), discusses the close similarities between the *Rivendell* painting and the area around Lauterbrunnen in Switzerland, where Tolkien had visited during his walking tour in the summer of 1911. The article includes photographs of the area, and the author concludes that the position of Elrond's House in relation to the valley and the mountains corresponds similarly with the position of the Old Mill in Lauterbrunnen and the area surrounding it. The Old Mill is now the town museum.

ford English Dictonary describes as "characteristic of home as the place where one receives kind treatment; kind, kindly."

5 *1937:* "The afternoon sun shone down; but in all the silent waste there was no sign of any dwelling. They rode on for a while, and they soon saw that that the house might be hidden" > *1966-Longmans/Unwin:* "Morning passed, afternoon came; but in all the silent waste there was no sign of any dwelling. They were growing anxious, for they saw now that the house might be hidden" (*1966-Ball* follows *1966-Longmans/Unwin,* but with the erroneous reading "for they now saw" instead of "for they saw now." Tolkien's 1954 check-copy has an additional phrase: "They rode on for a while, *but soon they had to dismount and lead their ponies;* for they . . ." This phrase was probably discarded with the removal of the reference to riding and the change of the sentence opening to "They were growing anxious.")

6 *1937:* "They still seemed to have gone only a little way, carefully following the wizard, whose head and beard wagged this way and that as he searched for the path, when the day began to fail." > *1966-Longmans/Unwin:* "His head and beard wagged this way and that as he looked for the stones, and they followed his lead, but they seemed no nearer to the end of the search when the day began to fail." (*1966-Ball* follows *1966-Longmans/Unwin,* save for the erroneous reading "followed his head.")

some of them green pleasant places to look at, with flowers growing bright and tall; but a pony that walked there with a pack on its back would never have come out again.

It was indeed a much wider land from the ford to the mountains than ever you would have guessed. Bilbo was astonished. The only path was marked with white stones, some of which were small, and others were half covered with moss or heather. Altogether it was a very slow business following the track, even guided by Gandalf, who seemed to know his way about pretty well.

His head and beard wagged this way and that as he looked for the stones, and they followed his lead, but they seemed no nearer to the end of the search when the day began to fail.[6] Tea-time had long gone by, and it seemed supper-time would soon do the same. There were moths fluttering about, and the light became very dim, for the moon had not risen. Bilbo's pony began to stumble over roots and stones. They came to the edge of a steep fall in the ground so suddenly that Gandalf's horse nearly slipped down the slope.

"Here it is at last!" he called, and the others gathered round him and looked over the edge. They saw a valley far below. They could hear the voice of hurrying water in a rocky bed at the bottom; the scent of trees was in the air; and there was a light on the valley-side across the water.

Bilbo never forgot the way they slithered and slipped in the dusk down the steep zig-zag path into the secret valley of Rivendell. The air grew warmer as they got lower, and the smell of the pine-trees made him drowsy, so that every now and again he nodded and nearly fell off, or bumped his nose on the pony's neck. Their spirits rose as they went down and down. The trees changed to beech and oak, and there was a comfortable feeling in the twilight. The last green had almost faded out of the grass, when they came at length to an open glade not far above the banks of the stream.

"Hmmm! it smells like elves!" thought Bilbo, and he looked up at the stars. They were burning bright and blue. Just then there came a burst of song like laughter in the trees:

> O! What are you doing,
> And where are you going?
> Your ponies need shoeing!
> The river is flowing!
> O! tra-la-la-lally
> here down in the valley!

> O! What are you seeking,
> And where are you making?
> The faggots are reeking,
> The bannocks are baking![7]
> O! tril-lil-lil-lolly
> the valley is jolly,
> ha! ha!

> O! Where are you going
> With beards all a-wagging?
> No knowing, no knowing
> What brings Mister Baggins
> And Balin and Dwalin
> down into the valley
> in June
> ha! ha!

> O! Will you be staying,
> Or will you be flying?
> Your ponies are straying!
> The daylight is dying!
> To fly would be folly,
> To stay would be jolly
> And listen and hark
> Till the end of the dark
> to our tune
> ha! ha!

7 A faggot is a bundle of sticks or twigs. *Bannock,* according to the *Oxford English Dictionary,* is "the name, in Scotland and north of England, of a form in which home-made bread is made; usually unleavened, of large size, round or oval in form, and flattish."

8 Virtually all of the poems in *The Hobbit* were apparently written in sequence with the manuscript of the book. Thus, in the context of the statement here that the elves "went into another song as ridiculous as the one I have written down in full," it is highly interesting to discover an unpublished poem labeled, at the top of one of the two manuscripts, "Elvish Song in Rivendell." The untitled version is probably the earliest, and it is the later version (on which the title is a late addition) that is printed below.

The manuscript of the early version is written on a page that also contains a version (likewise untitled) of the poem "Shadow-Bride," eventually published in *The Adventures of Tom Bombadil*. Both "Shadow-Bride" and "Elvish Song in Rivendell" seem to date from the very early 1930s, contemporaneous with the writing of *The Hobbit*. (A version of "Shadow-Bride" was apparently published in the early 1930s in something called the "Abingdon Chronicle," but this publication has so far eluded researchers.)

ELVISH SONG IN RIVENDELL

Come home, come home, ye merry folk!
The sun is sinking, and the oak
*   In gloom has wrapped his feet.*
Come home! The shades of evening loom
Beneath the hills, and palely bloom
*   Night-flowers white and sweet.*

Come home! The birds have fled the dark,
And in the sky with silver spark
*   The early stars now spring.*
Come home! The bats begin to flit,
And by the hearth 'tis time to sit.
*   Come home, come home and sing!*

Sing merrily, sing merrily, sing all together!
*   Let the song go! Let the sound ring!*

So they laughed and sang in the trees; and pretty fair nonsense I daresay you think it. Not that they would care; they would only laugh all the more if you told them so. They were elves of course. Soon Bilbo caught glimpses of them as the darkness deepened. He loved elves, though he seldom met them; but he was a little frightened of them too. Dwarves don't get on well with them. Even decent enough dwarves like Thorin and his friends think them foolish (which is a very foolish thing to think), or get annoyed with them. For some elves tease them and laugh at them, and most of all at their beards.

"Well, well!" said a voice. "Just look! Bilbo the hobbit on a pony, my dear! Isn't it delicious!"

"Most astonishing wonderful!"

Then off they went into another song as ridiculous as the one I have written down in full.**8** At last one, a tall young fellow, came out from the trees and bowed to Gandalf and to Thorin.

"Welcome to the valley!" he said.

"Thank you!" said Thorin a bit gruffly; but Gandalf was already off his horse and among the elves, talking merrily with them.

"You are a little out of your way," said the elf: "that is, if you are making for the only path across the water and to the house beyond. We will set you right, but you had best get on foot, until you are over the bridge. Are you going to stay a bit and sing with us, or will you go straight on? Supper is preparing over there," he said. "I can smell the wood-fires for the cooking."

Tired as he was, Bilbo would have liked to stay a while. Elvish singing is not a thing to miss, in June under the stars, not if you care for such things. Also he would have liked to have a few private words with these people that seemed to know his names and all about him, although he had never seen them before. He thought their opinion of his adventure might be interesting. Elves know a lot and are wondrous folk for news, and know what is going on among the peoples of the land, as quick as water flows, or quicker.

But the dwarves were all for supper as soon as possible just then, and would not stay. On they all went, leading their ponies, till they were brought to a good path and so at last to the very brink of the river. It was flowing fast and noisily, as mountain-streams do of a summer evening, when sun has been all day on the snow far up above. There was only a narrow bridge of stone without a parapet, as narrow as a pony could well walk on; and over that they had to go, slow and careful, one by one, each leading his pony by the bridle. The elves had brought bright lanterns to the shore, and they sang a merry song as the party went across.

"Don't dip your beard in the foam, father!" they cried to Thorin, who was bent almost on to his hands and knees. "It is long enough without watering it."

"Mind Bilbo doesn't eat all the cakes!" they called. "He is too fat to get through key-holes yet!"

"Hush, hush! Good People! and good night!" said Gandalf, who came last. "Valleys have ears, and some elves have over merry tongues. Good night!"

And so at last they all came to the Last Homely House, and found its doors flung wide.

Now it is a strange thing, but things that are good to have and days that are good to spend are soon told about, and not much to listen to; while things that are uncomfortable, palpitating, and even gruesome, may make a good tale, and take a deal of telling anyway. They stayed long in that good house, fourteen days at least, and they found it hard to leave. Bilbo would gladly have stopped there for ever and ever – even supposing a wish would have taken him right back to his hobbit-hole without trouble. Yet there is little to tell about their stay.

The master of the house was an elf-friend – one of those people whose fathers came into the strange stories

The moon with his light, the bird with his
  feather:
  Let the moon sail, let the bird wing!
The flower with her honey, the tree with his
  weather:
  Let the flower blow, let the tree swing!
Sing merrily, sing merrily, sing all together!

The third line of the second stanza originally read "The earliest star doth swing." This was corrected to the reading given above at the same time the title "Elvish Song in Rivendell" was added.

9 Of Elrond and of the further development of his character in *The Lord of the Rings,* Tolkien wrote to Christopher Bretherton in a letter of July 16, 1964, "The passage in Ch. 3 relating him to the Half-elven of the mythology was a fortunate accident, due to the difficulty of constantly inventing good names for new characters. I gave him the name Elrond casually, but as this came from the mythology . . . I made him half-elven" (*Letters,* No. 257).

Elrond first appeared in the legendarium in Tolkien's 1926 "Sketch of the Mythology," which is the earliest "Silmarillion." It is published in volume four of the *History*, *The Shaping of Middle-earth.* Elrond is introduced as the son of Eärendel (himself half-elven) and Elwing (of mixed ancestry, including elf, human, and divine blood): "Their son (Elrond) who is half-mortal and half-elfin [*sic*], a child, was saved however by Maidros. When later the Elves return to the West, bound by his mortal half he elects to stay on earth. Through him the blood of Húrin (his great-uncle) and of the Elves is yet among Men, and is seen yet in valour and in beauty and in poetry" (p. 38).

10 *1937:* "their bruises their tempers and their hopes." > *1966-Ball:* "their bruises, their tempers and their hopes." (*1966-A&U* and *1967-HM* follow *1937.*)

11 *1937:* "swords of the elves that are now called Gnomes" > *1966-Ball:* "swords of the High Elves of the West, my kin"

The name *gnomes* was originally used for one of the peoples of the *elves,* the Noldor (Quenya, "knowledgeable"). In

before the beginning of History, the wars of the evil goblins and the elves and the first men in the North. In those days of our tale there were still some people who had both elves and heroes of the North for ancestors, and Elrond[9] the master of the house was their chief.

He was as noble and as fair in face as an elf-lord, as strong as a warrior, as wise as a wizard, as venerable as a king of dwarves, and as kind as summer. He comes into many tales, but his part in the story of Bilbo's great adventure is only a small one, though important, as you will see, if we ever get to the end of it. His house was perfect, whether you liked food, or sleep, or work, or storytelling, or singing, or just sitting and thinking best, or a pleasant mixture of them all. Evil things did not come into that valley.

I wish I had time to tell you even a few of the tales or one or two of the songs that they heard in that house. All of them, the ponies as well, grew refreshed and strong in a few days there. Their clothes were mended as well as their bruises, their tempers and their hopes.[10] Their bags were filled with food and provisions light to carry but strong to bring them over the mountain passes. Their plans were improved with the best advice. So the time came to midsummer eve, and they were to go on again with the early sun on midsummer morning.

Elrond knew all about runes of every kind. That day he looked at the swords they had brought from the trolls' lair, and he said: "These are not troll-make. They are old swords, very old swords of the High Elves of the West, my kin.[11] They were made in Gondolin for the Goblin-wars. They must have come from a dragon's hoard or goblin plunder, for dragons and goblins destroyed that city many ages ago. This, Thorin, the runes name Orcrist, the Goblin-cleaver in the ancient tongue of Gondolin; it was a famous blade. This, Gandalf, was Glamdring, Foe-hammer that the king of Gondolin once wore.[12] Keep them well!"

"Whence did the trolls get them, I wonder?" said Thorin looking at his sword with new interest.

"I could not say," said Elrond, "but one may guess that your trolls had plundered other plunderers, or come on the remnants of old robberies in some hold in the mountains. I have heard that there are still forgotten treasures of old to be found[13] in the deserted caverns of the mines of Moria, since the dwarf and goblin war."

Thorin pondered these words. "I will keep this sword in honour," he said. "May it soon cleave goblins once again!"

"A wish that is likely to be granted soon enough in the mountains!" said Elrond. "But show me now your map!"

He took it and gazed long at it, and he shook his head; for if he did not altogether approve of dwarves and their love of gold, he hated dragons and their cruel wickedness, and he grieved to remember the ruin of the town of Dale and its merry bells, and the burned banks of the bright River Running. The moon was shining in a broad silver crescent. He held up the map and the white light shone through it. "What is this?" he said. "There are moon-letters here, beside the plain runes which say 'five feet high the door and three may walk abreast.' "

"What are moon-letters?" asked the hobbit full of excitement. He loved maps, as I have told you before; and he also liked runes and letters and cunning handwriting, though when he wrote himself it was a bit thin and spidery.

"Moon-letters are rune-letters, but you cannot see them," said Elrond, "not when you look straight at them. They can only be seen when the moon shines behind them, and what is more, with the more cunning sort it must be a moon of the same shape and season as the day when they were written. The dwarves invented them and wrote them with silver pens, as your friends could tell you. These must have been written on a midsummer's eve in a crescent moon, a long while ago."

Elrond discovers the moon-letters. Illustration by Maret Kernumees for the 1977 Estonian edition. Kernumees (1934–1997) was a prolific illustrator of Estonian children's books. She also illustrated Estonian translations of works by Hans Christian Andersen and the Brothers Grimm. Her illustrations for *The Hobbit* truly capture the fairy-tale charm of the story. Eight other illustrations by Kernumees can be found on pages 110, 119, 166, 197, 303, 330, 347, and 359.

a letter to Allen & Unwin dated July 20, 1962, Tolkien wrote that "the word was used as a translation of the real name, according to my mythology, of the High-elven people of the West. Pedantically, associating it with the Greek *gnome* 'thought, intelligence.' But I have abandoned it, since it is quite impossible to dissociate the name from the popular associations of Paracelsan *gnomus = pygmaeus*" (*Letters*, No. 239). Gnomes, according to Paracelsus (1493–1531), were elemental creatures of the earth, living underground and able to move through earth as freely as if it were air. In popular tradition, gnomes have often been equated with dwarfs or goblins.

12 The sword names are both Sindarin Elvish: *Orcrist*, meaning "Goblin-cleaver," and *Glamdring,* meaning "Foe-hammer."

The story of the fall of the Elvish stronghold Gondolin was first written around 1916–17 and is one of the earliest stories in Tolkien's legendarium. The essential tale appears in several other forms but is probably best known from Chapter 23, "Of Tuor and the Fall of Gondolin," in *The Silmarillion.*

13 *1937:* "in some hold in the mountains of the North. I have heard that there are still forgotten treasures to be found" > *1966-Longmans/Unwin:* "in some hold in the mountains. I have heard that there are still forgotten treasures of old to be found" (*1966-Ball* follows *1937,* with the slight change to "treasures of old." *1966-A&U* erroneously reads: "in some hole [*sic,* for *hold*] in the mountains of old. I have heard that there are forgotten treasures to be found" *1967-HM* erroneously

"What do they say?" asked Gandalf and Thorin together, a bit vexed perhaps that even Elrond should have found this out first, though really there had not been a chance before, and there would not have been another until goodness knows when.

"Stand by the grey stone when the thrush knocks,"**14** read Elrond, "and the setting sun with the last light of Durin's Day will shine upon the key-hole."

"Durin, Durin!" said Thorin. "He was the father of the fathers of the eldest race of Dwarves,**15** the Long-beards, and my first ancestor: I am his heir."**16**

"Then what is Durin's Day?" asked Elrond.

"The first day of the dwarves' New Year," said Thorin, "is as all should know**17** the first day of the last moon of Autumn on the threshold of Winter. We still call it Durin's Day when the last moon of Autumn and the sun are in the sky together. But this will not help us much, I fear, for it passes our skill in these days to guess when such a time will come again."

"That remains to be seen," said Gandalf. "Is there any more writing?"

"None to be seen by this moon," said Elrond, and he gave the map back to Thorin; and then they went down

Left: Elrond discovers the moon-letters. Illustration by Ryûichi Terashima for the 1965 Japanese edition. Terashima (1918–2001) also illustrated the Japanese translation of *The Lord of the Rings* (1972), which, like *The Hobbit,* was translated by Teiji Seta (1916–1979), a well-known translator, editor, and writer of children's books. Seta and Terashima worked together on a few other projects besides Tolkien. Terashima also painted portraits, specializing in those of exotic women. The many children's books he illustrated include translations of *Kidnapped* (1972) and *Treasure Island* (1976) by Robert Louis Stevenson, *The Weirdstone of Brisingamen* (1969) and *The Moon of Gomrath* (1969) by Alan Garner, and works by Kenneth Grahame, Arthur Ransome, and John Masefield. He also illustrated many original Japanese children's books.

Terashima's illustrations to *The Hobbit* show that he studied Tolkien's own illustrations very closely, letting Tolkien's conceptions inform his own drawings. Clyde S. Kilby wrote in his memoir, *Tolkien and The Silmarillion* (1976), that Tolkien "was pleased with the Japanese translation of *The Hobbit* and showed me with particular satisfaction the frontispiece which portrayed Smaug falling convulsively" over Lake-town. Seven more illustrations by Terashima can be found on pages 105, 121, 176, 202, 234, 265, and 297.

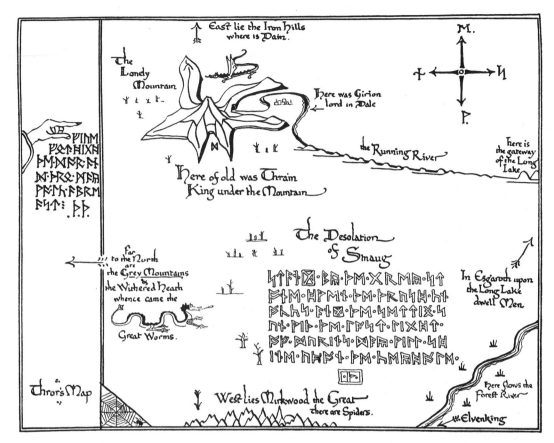

Thror's Map by J.R.R. Tolkien, with moon-runes visible. Transcribed (with the underlined pairs of letters represented by one character in the runes), the runes read: STAND BY <u>TH</u>E GREY ST | ONE HWEN <u>TH</u>E <u>TH</u>RUSH KN | OCKS AND <u>TH</u>E SETTING S | UN WI<u>TH</u> <u>TH</u>E LAST LIGHT | OF DURINS DAY WILL SH | INE UPON <u>TH</u>E KEYHOLE | <u>TH</u>. The spelling *hwen* for *when* in the second line reflects Anglo-Saxon usage.

to the water to see the elves dance and sing upon the midsummer's eve.

The next morning was a midsummer's[18] morning as fair and fresh as could be dreamed: blue sky and never a cloud, and the sun dancing on the water. Now they rode away amid songs of farewell and good speed, with their hearts ready for more adventure, and with a knowledge of the road they must follow over the Misty Mountains to the land beyond.

reads: "in some hole [*sic,* for *hold*] in the mountains of old. I have heard that there are still forgotten treasures of old to be found" In the 1988 edition of *The Annotated Hobbit,* the reading was suggested to be: "in some hold in the mountains of old. I have heard that there are still forgotten treasures to be found." The correct reading, clearly entered in Tolkien's 1954 check-copy, is that published in the *1966-Longmans/ Unwin* text: "in some hold in the mountains. I have heard that there are still forgotten treasures of old to be found.")

14 *1937:* "Stand by the grey stone where the thrush knocks" > *1951:*

"Stand by the grey stone when the thrush knocks"

Tolkien wrote to his former student G. E. Selby on December 14, 1937, "W*here* for *when* p. 64 is just an error, and I will correct it, gratefully."

15 Durin is the name of the eldest of the Seven Fathers of the race of Dwarves. In *The Peoples of Middle-earth,* volume twelve of the *History,* in some writings originally intended to be part of Appendix A of *The Lord of the Rings,* we learn that the seven houses of the Dwarves are the Longbeards, Firebeards, Broadbeams, Ironfists, Stiffbeards, Blacklocks, and Stonefoots (p. 301). In *The Hobbit* we are told that Bifur, Bofur, and Bombur are of a different line than Durin's, but which line is unspecified.

The distinction of Seven Houses is a later conception, first mentioned in Appendix A in the first edition of *The Lord of the Rings.* In the original edition of *The Hobbit,* Durin's line represents one of only two races of Dwarves. This statement remained unchanged until Tolkien's revisions of 1966.

For the story of the creation of the Dwarves by Aulë, see Chapter 2 of *The Silmarillion.* In calling the Dwarves Longbeards, Tolkien is probably recalling the Lombards ("Long-beards," Old English *Longbeardan*), a Germanic people renowned for their ferocity. (See volume five of the *History, The Lost Road,* p. 53.)

16 *1937:* "He was the father of the fathers of one of the two races of dwarves, the Longbeards, and my grandfather's ancestor" > *1966-Ball:* "He was the father of the fathers of the eldest race of Dwarves, the Longbeards, and my first ancestor: I am his heir"

17 *1937:* "as everyone knows" > *1966-Ball:* "as all should know"

18 The reference here to midsummer is ambiguous. It could mean the summer solstice, about June 21, or it could mean June 24, which is traditionally Midsummer Day, the feast of St. John the Baptist. Both dates are supported by the *Oxford English Dictionary.*

Karen Wynn Fonstad, in her chronology of *The Hobbit* as printed in the revised edition of *The Atlas of Middle-earth* (1991), interpreted the midsummer reference as synonymous with the summer solstice and also as equivalent with Mid-year's Day from the Shire Calendar in Appendix D of *The Lord of the Rings.* This latter correspondence is supported by the statement in Appendix A that Aragorn and Arwen were married "at Midsummer in the year of the Fall of Sauron," and in Appendix B, "The Tale of Years," where the wedding is specified as having taken place on "Mid-year's Day." Yet in Appendix D, it is written that "it appears, however, that Mid-year's Day was intended to correspond as nearly as possible to the summer solstice" — which suggests that it may not necessarily have been on the actual solstice.

Rivendell looking East by J.R.R. Tolkien. This color sketch was first published in *The Lord of the Rings 1977 Calendar* (1976) and appears in *Pictures* (No. 5) and *Artist* (No. 106). Elrond's house here appears slightly different than in the color *Rivendell* picture (see page 89) that usually appears with the book, and the bridge in the foreground has three spans, unlike in the finished picture, which has a single span. The text itself describes it only as "a narrow bridge of stone without a parapet" (page 93).

A few of Tolkien's other attempts at illustrating Rivendell have also been published. *Riding Down into Rivendell* (see *Artist*, No. 104) is probably the earliest, for the valley is not as deep as is described in the text and as appears in all other illustrations. Gandalf is seen riding a pony and sporting a red cloak (whereas in the text on page 32 he is described as wearing "a long grey cloak"). The appearance of the red cloak may reflect Gandalf's origin in the postcard painting *Der Berggeist* by Josef Madlener (see note 14 to Chapter 1), in which the wizardlike figure has a long red cloak.

Another unfinished illustration is titled *Rivendell looking West* and was first published in *The Lord of the Rings 1977 Calendar* (1976). It can be viewed in *Pictures* (No. 4) and *Artist* (No. 105). In this illustration the words in the title *looking West* can be seen to be an addition, written in sometime later than the much larger word *Rivendell*. The perspective in the drawing is also confused, for sketched outlines of Elrond's House appear in two places, on each side of the river. Moreover, the river is depicted as descending from the mountains, so the perspective of the illustration must be looking to the east, not the west, and the addition of the direction in the title is therefore incorrect. A third unfinished sketch titled simply *Rivendell* appears only in *Artist* (No. 107).

4

Over Hill and Under Hill

THERE WERE MANY PATHS that led up into those mountains, and many passes over them. But most of the
paths were cheats and deceptions and led nowhere or to
bad ends; and most of the passes were infested by evil
things and dreadful dangers. The dwarves and the hobbit, helped by the wise advice of Elrond and the knowledge and memory of Gandalf, took the right road to the
right pass.

Long days after they had climbed out of the valley

Bilbo climbs out of the valley, leaving Rivendell behind. Illustration by
Mirna Pavlovec for the 1986 Slovenian edition.

and left the Last Homely House miles behind, they were still going up and up and up. It was a hard path and a dangerous path, a crooked way and a lonely and a long. Now they could look back over the lands they had left, laid out behind them far below. Far, far away in the West, where things were blue and faint, Bilbo knew there lay his own country of safe and comfortable things, and his little hobbit-hole. He shivered. It was getting bitter cold up here, and the wind came shrill among the rocks. Boulders, too, at times came galloping down the mountain-sides, let loose by mid-day sun upon the snow, and passed among them (which was lucky), or over their heads (which was alarming).[1] The nights were comfortless and chill, and they did not dare to sing or talk too loud, for the echoes were uncanny, and the silence seemed to dislike being broken — except by the noise of water and the wail of wind and the crack of stone.

"The summer is getting on down below," thought Bilbo, "and haymaking is going on and picnics. They will be harvesting and blackberrying, before we even begin to go down the other side at this rate." And the others were thinking equally gloomy thoughts, although when they had said good-bye to Elrond in the high hope of a midsummer morning, they had spoken gaily of the passage of the mountains, and of riding swift across the lands beyond. They had thought of coming to the secret door in the Lonely Mountain, perhaps that very next last moon of Autumn[2] "and perhaps it will be Durin's Day" they had said. Only Gandalf had shaken his head and said nothing. Dwarves had not passed that way for many years, but Gandalf had, and he knew how evil and danger had grown and thriven in the Wild, since the dragons had driven men from the lands, and the goblins had spread in secret after the battle of the Mines of Moria.[3] Even the good plans of wise wizards like Gandalf and of good friends like Elrond go astray sometimes when you are off on dangerous adventures over the Edge of

[1] In a letter begun in 1967 but misplaced during a move and not completed until late 1968, Tolkien wrote to his son Michael:

The hobbit's (Bilbo's) journey from Rivendell to the other side of the Misty Mountains, including the glissade down the slithering stones into the pine woods, is based on my adventures [in Switzerland] in 1911 . . . Our wanderings mainly on foot in a party of 12 are not now clear in sequence, but leave many vivid pictures as clear as yesterday . . . We went on foot carrying great packs . . . We slept rough — the men-folk — often in hayloft or cowbyre, since we were walking by map and avoided roads and never booked, and after a meagre breakfast fed ourselves in the open . . . One day we went on a long march with guides up the Aletsch glacier — when I came near to perishing. We had guides, but either the effects of the hot summer were beyond their experience, or they did not much care, or we were late in starting. Any way at noon we were strung out in file along a narrow track with a snow-slope on the right going up to the horizon, and on the left a plunge down into a ravine. The summer of that year had melted away much of the snow, and stones and boulders were exposed that (I suppose) were normally covered. The heat of the day continued the melting and we were alarmed to see many of them starting to roll down the slope at gathering speed: anything from the size of oranges to large footballs, and a few much larger. They were whizzing across our path and plunging into the ravine. "Hard pounding," ladies and gentlemen. They started slowly, and then usually held a straight line of descent, but the path was rough and one had also to keep an eye on one's feet. I remember the member of the party just in front of me (an elderly schoolmistress) gave a sudden squeak and jumped forward as a large lump of rock shot between us. About a foot at most from my unmanly knees. (*Letters*, No. 306)

Tolkien's walking tour of Switzerland was during August and early September of 1911. It consisted of a party of around a dozen people, including Tolkien, his younger brother Hilary, and their aunt Jane Neave. It began in Interlaken and went south to Lauterbrunnen and Mürren, then northeast to Grindelwald and Meiringen, southeast through the Grimsel Pass, and finally southwest along the Aletsch glacier and toward the Matterhorn, eventually reaching Sion.

In his drawings, Tolkien's mountains are usually Alpine in appearance and shape. The picture below of Grindelwald and the Wetterhorn was taken by E. Elliot Stock and published in his *Scrambles in Storm and Sunshine* (1910), an account of Stock's own journeys in the Swiss Alps, published the year before Tolkien's expedition.

2 *1937:* "that very next first moon of Autumn" > *1995:* "that very next last moon of Autumn"

This change has no authorial authority and is the correction of what seems to be an error that Tolkien never caught. On page 96, Durin's Day is defined as the first day of the dwarves' New Year, and more specifically as "the first day of the last moon of Autumn on the threshold of Winter . . . when the last moon of Autumn and the sun are in the sky together." On page 263, with the dwarves

The Mountain-path

The Mountain-path by J.R.R. Tolkien, one of the standard black-and-white illustrations that has appeared in *The Hobbit* since 1937.
This illustration appears in *Artist* (No. 109) and *Pictures* (No. 7, left). A version of it colored by H. E. Riddett first appeared in *The Hobbit Calendar 1976* (1975) and in *Pictures* (No. 7, right). The colored version was also used on the front cover of the first American edition of *The Silmarillion* (1977).

the Wild; and Gandalf was a wise enough wizard to know it.

He knew that something unexpected might happen, and he hardly dared to hope that they would pass without

Pauline Baynes depicted the party's climb into the mountains in the cover illustration for the 1961 Puffin Books edition of *The Hobbit.* Her original painting is displayed at the Marion E. Wade Center, Wheaton College, in Wheaton, Illinois. The Wade Center has also published it as a postcard. In a letter to his publisher dated March 13, 1961, Tolkien wrote of it, "Personally I like it very much."

Pauline Baynes (b. 1922) is a very well known and much-admired illustrator. She has long been associated with Tolkien, having illustrated his *Farmer Giles of Ham* (1949), *The Adventures of Tom Bombadil* (1962), *Smith of Wootton Major* (1967), *Poems and Stories* (1980), and *Bilbo's Last Song* (1990), the latter being a picture book based on a twenty-four-line poem. For this book Baynes provided color illustrations to each couplet of the poem, as well as a series of running illustrations that show Bilbo sleepily recalling his life, and thus depict the story of *The Hobbit.* Baynes also provided cover illustrations to various editions of Tolkien's books, and decorated some posters and maps. Her illustrations to the seven volumes of *The Chronicles of Narnia* (1950–56) by Tolkien's friend C. S. Lewis are also very popular. Baynes won the Kate Greenaway Medal for her illustrations to Grant Uden's *A Dictionary of Chivalry* (1968).

on the back doorstep to the Lonely Mountain, Thorin remarks: "Tomorrow begins the last week of autumn." On the following evening, with a thin new moon above the rim of the earth, the light of the setting sun discloses the keyhole, the combination of which occurs only on Durin's Day. Thus the above change seems to be correct, even if Tolkien himself never noticed the discrepancy.

3 *1937:* "after the sack of the mines of Moria" > *1966-Ball:* "after the battle of the Mines of Moria"

This change became necessary when Tolkien expanded his conception of the dwarf and goblin war (mentioned by Elrond on page 95 and by Bilbo on page 330). The word *sack* implies devastation and a plundering of Moria, while *battle* is a much more general term for the conflict.

4 Tolkien wrote to Joyce Reeves on November 4, 1961 that the thunder-battle in *The Hobbit* had been based on a bad night during his 1911 walking tour in the mountains of Switzerland, as described in note 1 to this chapter. He added, "We lost our way and slept in a cattle-shed" (*Letters*, No. 232).

fearful adventure over those great tall mountains with lonely peaks and valleys where no king ruled. They did not. All was well, until one day they met a thunderstorm — more than a thunderstorm, a thunder-battle.⁴ You know how terrific a really big thunderstorm can be down in the land and in a river-valley; especially at times when two great thunderstorms meet and clash. More terrible still are thunder and lightning in the mountains at night, when storms come up from East and West and

5 The stone-giants are mentioned only in *The Hobbit*. It seems probable that they can be interpreted as a type of troll. Both are large and apparently malicious beings, and in Appendix F of *The Lord of the Rings*, Tolkien mentions as a type of troll the Stone-trolls of the Westlands, who spoke a debased form of Common Speech, and this description certainly applies to Bert, Tom, and William Huggins. It is perhaps relevant to note that the trolls come from a place to the north of Rivendell that is called the Ettenmoors, or the Ettendales. In his "Nomenclature of *The Lord of the Rings*," Tolkien notes in the entry for Ettendales that it is "meant to be a Common Speech (not Elvish) name, though it contains an obsolete element *eten* 'troll, ogre.' " Old English *eoten,* Middle English *eten,* is usually translated as "giant, monster." And the form *etayn* appears twice (lines 140, 723) in *Sir Gawain and the Green Knight;* in the 1925 Tolkien and Gordon edition it is glossed "ogre, giant." In *Beowulf,* the monster Grendel clearly derives from a tradition of waterfall-trolls, but is also referred to as an *eoten* (line 761).

make war. The lightning splinters on the peaks, and rocks shiver, and great crashes split the air and go rolling and tumbling into every cave and hollow; and the darkness is filled with overwhelming noise and sudden light.**7**

Bilbo had never seen or imagined anything of the kind. They were high up in a narrow place, with a dreadful fall into a dim valley at one side of them. There they were sheltering under a hanging rock for the night, and he lay beneath a blanket and shook from head to toe. When he peeped out in the lightning-flashes, he saw that across the valley the stone-giants**5** were out, and were hurling rocks at one another for a game, and catching them, and tossing them down into the darkness where they smashed among the trees far below, or splintered into little bits with a bang. Then came a wind and a rain, and the wind whipped the rain and the hail about in every direction, so that an overhanging rock was no protection at all. Soon they were getting drenched and their ponies were standing with their heads down and their tails between their legs, and some of them were whinnying with fright. They could hear the giants guffawing and shouting all over the mountainsides.

"This won't do at all!" said Thorin. "If we don't get blown off, or drowned, or struck by lightning, we shall be picked up by some giant and kicked sky-high for a football."

"Well, if you know of anywhere better, take us there!" said Gandalf, who was feeling very grumpy, and was far from happy about the giants himself.

The end of their argument was that they sent Fili and Kili to look for a better shelter. They had very sharp eyes, and being the youngest of the dwarves by some fifty years they usually got these sort of jobs (when everybody could see that it was absolutely no use sending Bilbo). There is nothing like looking, if you want to find something (or so Thorin said to the young dwarves). You certainly usually find something, if you look, but it is not always quite the something you were after. So it proved on this occasion.

Soon Fili and Kili came crawling back, holding on to the rocks in the wind. "We have found a dry cave," they said, "not far round the next corner; and ponies and all could get inside."

"Have you *thoroughly* explored it?" said the wizard, who knew that caves up in the mountains were seldom unoccupied.

"Yes, yes!" they said, though everybody knew they could not have been long about it; they had come back too quick. "It isn't all that big, and it does not go far back."

That, of course, is the dangerous part about caves: you don't know how far they go back, sometimes, or where a passage behind may lead to, or what is waiting for you inside. But now Fili and Kili's news seemed good enough. So they all got up and prepared to move. The wind was howling and the thunder still growling, and they had a business getting themselves and their ponies along. Still it was not very far to go, and before long they came to a big rock standing out into the path. If you stepped behind, you found a low arch in the side of the mountain. There was just room to get the ponies through with a squeeze, when they had been unpacked and unsaddled. As they passed under the arch, it was good to hear the wind and the rain outside instead of all about them, and to feel safe from the giants and their rocks. But the wizard was taking no risks. He lit up his wand — as he did that day in Bilbo's dining-room that seemed so long ago, if you remember —, and by its light they explored the cave from end to end.

It seemed quite a fair size, but not too large and mysterious. It had a dry floor and some comfortable nooks. At one end there was room for the ponies; and there they stood (mighty glad of the change) steaming, and champing in their nosebags. Oin and Gloin wanted to light a fire at the door to dry their clothes, but Gan-

The Mountain-path. Illustration by Ryûichi Tera-shima for the 1965 Japanese edition

6 The idea of goblins coming through a crack may owe its inspiration to the children's play *Through the Crack* by Algernon Blackwood and Violet Pearn, first performed in December 1920 and published in an acting edition in 1925. It was a regular favorite of amateur and repertory companies in England through the 1920s. The play was based on sections from two of Blackwood's novels, *The Education of Uncle Paul* (1909) and *The Extra Day* (1915), but neither of these contains the goblin element, which was probably introduced into the play by Pearn. In the play, some children pass through The Crack between yesterday and tomorrow, and they must be wary of the chanting goblins who try to catch people and drag them underground to be made into a goblins' dinner party.

Blackwood (1869–1951) was a prolific writer of supernatural fiction, and several of his works involve children and their adventures in various spirit worlds or fairylands. Tolkien apparently knew some of Blackwood's work, for in a note to the entry "Crack of Doom" (omitted from the published version) in his "Nomenclature of *The Lord of the Rings*," Tolkien wrote of the usage of *crack* meaning *fissure:* "I think that this usage is ultimately derived from Algernon Blackwood, which [*sic,* for *who*] as my memory seems to recall used it in this way in one of his books read many years ago." This usage in Blackwood, however, has so far eluded researchers.

A goblin-crack is also mentioned in the 1932 Father Christmas letter that Tolkien wrote for his children. This letter introduces goblins into Tolkien's Father Christmas mythology, as Father Christmas must journey through some

dalf would not hear of it. So they spread out their wet things on the floor, and got dry ones out of their bundles; then they made their blankets comfortable, got out their pipes and blew smoke rings, which Gandalf turned into different colours and set dancing up by the roof to amuse them. They talked and talked, and forgot about the storm, and discussed what each would do with his share of the treasure (when they got it, which at the moment did not seem so impossible); and so they dropped off to sleep one by one. And that was the last time that they used the ponies, packages, baggages, tools and paraphernalia that they had brought with them.

It turned out a good thing that night that they had brought little Bilbo with them, after all. For, somehow, he could not go to sleep for a long while; and when he did sleep, he had very nasty dreams. He dreamed that a crack in the wall at the back of the cave got bigger and bigger, and opened wider and wider, and he was very afraid but could not call out or do anything but lie and look. Then he dreamed that the floor of the cave was giving way, and he was slipping – beginning to fall down, down, goodness knows where to.

At that he woke up with a horrible start, and found that part of his dream was true. A crack had opened at the back of the cave, and was already a wide passage. He was just in time to see the last of the ponies' tails disappearing into it. Of course he gave a very loud yell, as loud a yell as a hobbit can give, which is surprising for their size.

Out jumped the goblins, big goblins, great ugly-looking goblins, lots of goblins, before you could say *rocks and blocks.* There were six to each dwarf, at least, and two even for Bilbo; and they were all grabbed and carried through the crack,**6** before you could say *tinder and flint.* But not Gandalf. Bilbo's yell had done that much good. It had wakened him up wide in a splintered second, and when goblins came to grab him, there was a terrific flash like lightning in the cave, a smell like gunpowder, and several of them fell dead.

The crack closed with a snap, and Bilbo and the dwarves were on the wrong side of it! Where was Gandalf? Of that neither they nor the goblins had any idea, and the goblins did not wait to find out. They seized Bilbo and the dwarves and hurried them along. It was deep, deep, dark, such as only goblins that have taken to living in the heart of the mountains can see through. The passages there were crossed and tangled in all directions, but the goblins knew their way, as well as you do to the nearest post-office; and the way went down and down, and it was most horribly stuffy. The goblins were very rough, and pinched unmercifully, and chuckled and laughed in their horrible stony voices; and Bilbo was more unhappy even than when the troll had picked him up by his toes. He wished again and again for his nice bright hobbit-hole. Not for the last time.

Now there came a glimmer of a red light before them. The goblins began to sing, or croak, keeping time with the flap of their flat feet on the stone, and shaking their prisoners as well.

> *Clap! Snap! the black crack!*
> *Grip, grab! Pinch, nab!*
> *And down down to Goblin-town*
> *You go, my lad!*
>
> *Clash, crash! Crush, smash!*
> *Hammer and tongs! Knocker and gongs!*
> *Pound, pound, far underground!*
> *Ho, ho! my lad!*
>
> *Swish, smack! Whip crack!*
> *Batter and beat! Yammer and bleat!*
> *Work, work! Nor dare to shirk,*
> *While Goblins quaff, and Goblins laugh,*
> *Round and round far underground*
> *Below, my lad!*

goblin caves in order to find the North Polar Bear, who has become lost in them. The 1933 letter continues with an account of the worst goblin attack in centuries. Subsequent to his adventures in the caves, the Polar Bear invented an alphabet using the Goblin marks on the walls. He sent a short letter in it, and later sent the alphabet itself. Parts of these letters, along with their marvelous accompanying illustrations, were first published in *The Father Christmas Letters* (1976), edited by Baillie Tolkien.

The Goblins come through the crack. Illustration by Livia Rusz for the 1975 Romanian edition.

7 Tolkien's goblins resemble those in George Macdonald's *The Princess and the Goblin* (1872), with some notable differences. Macdonald's goblins have soft and very vulnerable feet. In a letter to Naomi Mitchison of April 25, 1954, Tolkien wrote that his goblins "owe, I suppose, a good deal to the goblin tradition . . . especially as it appears in George Macdonald, except for the soft feet which I never believed in" (*Letters* No. 144). And whereas Macdonald's goblins flee at the sound of poetry, Tolkien's goblins sing poetry of the very same rhythmic and exclamatory sort that Macdonald's goblins so detested.

George Macdonald (1824–1905) was a clergyman of Scottish descent and a prolific writer of novels and children's stories, like *At the Back of the North Wind* (1871), *The Princess and the Goblin* (1872), and its sequel, *The Princess and Curdie* (1883). His fairy tales, including the well-known "The Golden Key," were first collected in *Dealings with the Fairies* (1867). His fantasy novels for adults include *Phantastes* (1858) and *Lilith* (1895).

Tolkien's feelings about George Macdonald changed over the years. In the essay "On Fairy-Stories," first given as a lecture on March 8, 1939, and greatly expanded about four years later, Tolkien, in referring to how a fairy tale could be made into a vehicle for Mystery, stated: "This at least is what George Macdonald attempted, achieving stories of power and beauty when he succeeded, as in *The Golden Key* (which he called a fairy-tale); and even when he partly failed, as in *Lilith* (which he called a romance)." However, in January 1965, after Tolkien had agreed to write a preface to an illustrated edition of *The*

It sounded truly terrifying. The walls echoed to the *clap, snap!* and the *crush, smash!* and to the ugly laughter of their *ho, ho! my lad!* The general meaning of the song was only too plain; for now the goblins took out whips and whipped them with a *swish, smack!,* and set them running as fast as they could in front of them; and more than one of the dwarves were already yammering and bleating like anything, when they stumbled into a big cavern.

It was lit by a great red fire in the middle, and by torches along the walls, and it was full of goblins. They all laughed and stamped and clapped their hands, when the dwarves (with poor little Bilbo at the back and nearest to the whips) came running in, while the goblin-drivers whooped and cracked their whips behind. The ponies were already there huddled in a corner; and there were all the baggages and packages lying broken open, and being rummaged by goblins, and smelt by goblins, and fingered by goblins, and quarrelled over by goblins.

5 I am afraid that was the last they ever saw of those excellent little ponies, including a jolly sturdy little white fellow that Elrond had lent to Gandalf, since his horse was not suitable for the mountain-paths. For goblins eat horses and ponies and donkeys (and other much more dreadful things), and they are always hungry. Just now however the prisoners were thinking only of themselves. The goblins chained their hands behind their backs and linked them all together in a line, and dragged them to the far end of the cavern with little Bilbo tugging at the end of the row. ⊃

There in the shadows on a large flat stone sat a tremendous goblin with a huge head, and armed goblins were standing round him carrying the axes and the bent swords that they use. ⵣNow goblins are cruel, wicked, and bad-hearted. They make no beautiful things, but they make many clever ones. They can tunnel and mine as well as any but the most skilled dwarves, when they take the trouble, though they are usually untidy and dirty. Hammers, axes, swords, daggers, pickaxes, tongs, and also instruments of torture, they make very well, or get other people to make to their design, prisoners and slaves that have to work till they die for want of air and light. It is not unlikely that they invented some of the machines that have since troubled the world, especially the ingenious devices for killing large numbers of people at once, for wheels and engines and explosions always delighted them, and also not working with their own hands more than they could help; but in those days and those wild parts they had not advanced (as it is called) so far. They did not hate dwarves especially, no more than they hated everybody and everything, and particularly the orderly and prosperous; in some parts wicked dwarves had even made alliances with them. But they had a special grudge against Thorin's people, because of the war which you have heard mentioned, but which does not come into this tale; and anyway goblins don't care who they catch, as long as it is done smart and secret, and the prisoners are not able to defend themselves.

"Who are these miserable persons?" said the Great Goblin.

"Dwarves, and this!" said one of the drivers, pulling at Bilbo's chain so that he fell forward onto his knees. "We found them sheltering in our Front Porch."

"What do you mean by it?" said the Great Goblin turning to Thorin. "Up to no good, I'll warrant! Spying on the private business of my people, I guess! Thieves, I shouldn't be surprised to learn! Murderers and friends of Elves, not unlikely! Come! What have you got to say?"

"Thorin the dwarf at your service!" he replied — it was merely a polite nothing. "Of the things which you suspect and imagine we had no idea at all. We sheltered from a storm in what seemed a convenient cave and unused; nothing was further from our thoughts than in-

Golden Key for an American publisher, Tolkien reread the story and found it "ill-written, incoherent, and bad, in spite of a few memorable passages" (*Biography*, p. 242). Tolkien began to write the preface but became inspired instead by an idea for a fairy story, which he had started to use as an example in the preface. In the end, the preface was abandoned, but Tolkien's fairy story grew to be *Smith of Wootton Major* (1967). In an interview for BBC Radio recorded in late January 1965, Tolkien commented: "I now find that I can't stand George Macdonald's books at any price at all." And Clyde S. Kilby, who assisted Tolkien in the summer of 1966, recalled in his memoir *Tolkien and The Silmarillion* (1976) that "though elsewhere he had spoken of George Macdonald with real appreciation, at the time I visited Tolkien he was making frequent wholesale attacks on him. He called him an 'old grandmother' who preached instead of writing" (p. 31).

Above is an illustration of a goblin family by Arthur Hughes (1832–1915), from the original edition of *The Princess and the Goblin*. Hughes illustrated many books by George Macdonald.

The Great Goblin. Illustration by Klaus Ensikat for the 1971 German edition.

Thorin and the Great Goblin. Illustration by Maret Kernumees for the 1977 Estonian edition.

8 *1937:* "and rushed himself at Thorin" > *1966-Ball:* "and himself rushed at Thorin"

conveniencing goblins in any way whatever." That was true enough!

"Um!" said the Great Goblin. "So you say! Might I ask what you were doing up in the mountains at all, and where you were coming from, and where you were going to? In fact I should like to know all about you. Not that it will do you much good, Thorin Oakenshield, I know too much about your folk already; but let's have the truth, or I will prepare something particularly uncomfortable for you!"

"We were on a journey to visit our relatives, our nephews and nieces, and first, second, and third cousins, and the other descendants of our grandfathers, who live on the East side of these truly hospitable mountains," said Thorin, not quite knowing what to say all at once in a moment, when obviously the exact truth would not do at all.

"He is a liar, O truly tremendous one!" said one of the drivers. "Several of our people were struck by lightning in the cave, when we invited these creatures to come below; and they are as dead as stones. Also he has not explained this!" He held out the sword which Thorin had worn, the sword which came from the Trolls' lair.

The Great Goblin gave a truly awful howl of rage when he looked at it, and all his soldiers gnashed their teeth, clashed their shields, and stamped. They knew the sword at once. It had killed hundreds of goblins in its time, when the fair elves of Gondolin hunted them in the hills or did battle before their walls. They had called it Orcrist, Goblin-cleaver, but the goblins called it simply Biter. They hated it and hated worse any one that carried it.

"Murderers and elf-friends!" the Great Goblin shouted. "Slash them! Beat them! Bite them! Gnash them! Take them away to dark holes full of snakes, and never let them see the light again!" He was in such a rage that he jumped off his seat and himself rushed at Thorin8 with his mouth open.

Just at that moment all the lights in the cavern went out, and the great fire went off poof! into a tower of blue glowing smoke, right up to the roof, that scattered piercing white sparks all among the goblins.

The yells and yammering, croaking, jibbering and jabbering; howls, growls and curses; shrieking and skriking,[9] that followed were beyond description. Several hundred wild cats and wolves being roasted slowly alive together would not have compared with it. The sparks were burning holes in the goblins, and the smoke that now fell from the roof made the air too thick for even their eyes to see through. Soon they were falling over one another and rolling in heaps on the floor, biting and kicking and fighting as if they had all gone mad.

⸲ Suddenly a sword flashed in its own light. Bilbo saw it go right through the Great Goblin as he stood dumbfounded in the middle of his rage. He fell dead, and the goblin soldiers fled before the sword shrieking into the darkness.

The sword went back into its sheath. "Follow me quick!" said a voice fierce and quiet; and before Bilbo understood what had happened he was trotting along again, as fast as he could trot, at the end of the line, down more dark passages with the yells of the goblin-hall growing fainter behind him. A pale light was leading them on.⸴

"Quicker, quicker!" said the voice. "The torches will soon be relit."

"Half a minute!" said Dori, who was at the back next to Bilbo, and a decent fellow. He made the hobbit scramble on his shoulders as best he could with his tied hands, and then off they all went at a run, with a clink-clink of chains, and many a stumble, since they had no hands to steady themselves with. Not for a long while did they stop, and by that time they must have been right down in the very mountain's heart.

Then Gandalf lit up his wand. Of course it was Gandalf; but just then they were too busy to ask how he got

9 The term *skriking* comes from *skrike,* "a shrill cry, a screeching." Its usage is now chiefly dialectal, but the second edition (1989) of the *Oxford English Dictionary* cites as an example of usage Tolkien's words given here. Walter E. Haigh's *A New Glossary of the Dialect of the Huddersfield District* does list the word under *skrāūk, skrīk,* "to screech, shriek," which Hague relates to Middle English *scrīken* and Old Norse *skrækja, skrīkja,* "to shriek."

Tolkien uses a similar list of noises to describe various kinds of barking in *Roverandom:* "yaps and yelps, and yammers and yowls, growling and grizzling, whickering and whining, snickering and snarling, mumping and moaning, and the most enormous baying" (p. 20).

10 In his undergraduate years, Tolkien held very different views on the nature of goblins and the feelings stirred in one's heart by the padding of goblin feet. Goblins were tiny elfin creatures, and the sound of their song and dance was magical. Tolkien wrote of such creatures in a poem called "Goblin Feet," which was his first published work of note. It was written on April 27–28, 1915, and appeared in the annual volume of *Oxford Poetry* published in December 1915. The poem was reprinted in Dora Owen's *Book of Fairy Poetry* (1920), a comprehensive and sumptuous collection with sixteen color plates and a number of pen drawings by Warwick Goble (1862–1943), who is mostly remembered for his watercolor illustrations for gift books like *Green Willow and Other Japanese Fairy Tales* (1910) by Grace James. Tolkien's poem was accompanied by a delightfully bizarre il-

The Goblins capture the Dwarves. Illustration by Torbjörn Zetterholm for the 1947 Swedish edition.

there. He took out his sword again, and again it flashed in the dark by itself. It burned with a rage that made it gleam if goblins were about; now it was bright as blue flame for delight in the killing of the great lord of the cave. It made no trouble whatever of cutting through the goblin-chains and setting all the prisoners free as quickly as possible. This sword's name was Glamdring the Foe-hammer, if you remember. The goblins just called it Beater, and hated it worse than Biter if possible. Orcrist, too, had been saved; for Gandalf had brought it along as well, snatching it from one of the terrified guards. Gandalf thought of most things; and though he could not do everything, he could do a great deal for friends in a tight corner.

"Are we all here?" said he, handing his sword back to Thorin with a bow. "Let me see: one — that's Thorin; two, three, four, five, six, seven, eight, nine, ten, eleven; where are Fili and Kili? Here they are! twelve, thirteen — and here's Mr. Baggins: fourteen! Well, well! it might be worse, and then again it might be a good deal better. No ponies, and no food, and no knowing quite where we are, and hordes of angry goblins just behind! On we go!"

On they went. Gandalf was quite right: they began to

hear goblin noises and horrible cries far behind in the passages they had come through. That sent them on faster than ever, and as poor Bilbo could not possibly go half as fast — for dwarves can roll along at a tremendous pace, I can tell you, when they have to — they took it in turn to carry him on their backs.

Still goblins go faster than dwarves, and these goblins knew the way better (they had made the paths themselves), and were madly angry; so that do what they could the dwarves heard the cries and howls getting closer and closer. Soon they could hear even the flap of the goblin feet, many many feet which seemed only just round the last corner.[10] The blink of red torches could be seen behind them in the tunnel they were following; and they were getting deadly tired.

⊂ "Why, O why did I ever leave my hobbit-hole!" said poor Mr. Baggins bumping up and down on Bombur's back.

"Why, O why did I ever bring a wretched little hobbit on a treasure hunt!" said poor Bombur, who was fat, and staggered along with the sweat dripping down his nose in his heat and terror. ⊃

At this point Gandalf fell behind, and Thorin with him. They turned a sharp corner. "About turn!" he shouted. "Draw your sword Thorin!"

There was nothing else to be done; and the goblins did not like it. They came scurrying round the corner in full cry, and found Goblin-cleaver, and Foe-hammer shining cold and bright right in their astonished eyes. The ones in front dropped their torches and gave one yell before they were killed. The ones behind yelled still more, and leaped back knocking over those that were running after them. "Biter and Beater!" they shrieked; and soon they were all in confusion, and most of them were hustling back the way they had come.

It was quite a long while before any of them dared to turn that corner. By that time the dwarves had gone on

lustration by Goble (opposite), which apparently is the first artwork (from an artist other than Tolkien himself) to be based on his writings.

GOBLIN FEET

I am off down the road
Where the fairy lanterns glowed
And the pretty little flittermice are flying:
A slender band of grey
It runs creepily away
And the hedges and the grasses are a-sighing.
The air is full of wings,
And of blundering beetle-things
That warn you with their whirring and their
humming.
O! I hear the tiny horns
Of enchanted leprechauns
And the padding feet of many gnomes a-coming!

O! the lights: O! the gleams: O! the little
tinkly sounds:
O! the rustle of their noiseless little robes:
O! the echo of their feet — of their little happy
feet:
O! their swinging lamps in little starlit
globes.

I must follow in their train
Down the crooked fairy lane
Where the coney-rabbits long ago have gone,
And where silverly they sing
In a moving moonlit ring
All a-twinkle with the jewels they have on.
They are fading round the turn
Where the glow-worms palely burn
And the echo of their padding feet is dying!
O! it's knocking at my heart —
Let me go! O! let me start!
For the little magic hours are all a-flying.

O! the warmth! O! the hum! O! the colours
in the dark!
O! the gauzy wings of golden honey-flies!
O! the music of their feet — of their dancing
goblin feet!
O! the magic! O! the sorrow when it dies!

The flittermice referred to in line three are bats. The leprechauns, gnomes, and goblins in this poem seem to be familiar types of nursery fairies.

In volume one of the *History, The Book of Lost Tales Part One,* Christopher Tolkien notes that in 1971 his father said of "Goblin Feet," "I wish the unhappy little thing, representing all that I came (so soon after) to fervently dislike, could be buried forever" (p. 32). Yet Tolkien's phrase "so soon after" needs to be carefully considered, for as late as the mid-1930s Tolkien did include the poem in a planned collection of his poetry (the collection did not achieve publication), and elements showing the whimsy of the dancing elves do appear in *The Hobbit.* It seems that Tolkien's dislike of this poem and of the type of beings it describes probably dates to the mid- to late 1930s, around the time of the first publication of *The Hobbit* and when he was beginning to work on *The Lord of the Rings.*

again, a long, long, way on into the dark tunnels of the goblins' realm. When the goblins discovered that, they put out their torches and they slipped on soft shoes, and they chose out their very quickest runners with the sharpest ears and eyes. These ran forward, as swift as weasels in the dark, and with hardly any more noise than bats.

That is why neither Bilbo, nor the dwarves, nor even Gandalf heard them coming. Nor did they see them. But they were seen by the goblins that ran silently up behind, for Gandalf was letting his wand give out a faint light to help the dwarves as they went along.

⊂ Quite suddenly Dori, now at the back again carrying Bilbo, was grabbed from behind in the dark. He shouted and fell; and the hobbit rolled off his shoulders into the blackness, bumped his head on hard rock, and remembered nothing more. ⊃

5

Riddles in the Dark

WHEN BILBO OPENED HIS EYES, he wondered if he had; for it was just as dark as with them shut. No one was anywhere near him. Just imagine his fright! He could hear nothing, see nothing, and he could feel nothing except the stone of the floor.

Very slowly he got up and groped about on all fours, till he touched the wall of the tunnel; but neither up nor down it could he find anything: nothing at all, no sign of goblins, no sign of dwarves. His head was swimming, and he was far from certain even of the direction they had been going in when he had his fall. He guessed as well as he could, and crawled along for a good way, till suddenly his hand met what felt like a tiny ring of cold metal lying on the floor of the tunnel. It was a turning point in his career, but he did not know it. He put the ring in his pocket almost without thinking; certainly it did not seem of any particular use at the moment. He did not go much further, but sat down on the cold floor and gave himself up to complete miserableness, for a long while. He thought of himself frying bacon and eggs in his own kitchen at home — for he could feel inside that it was high time for some meal or other; but that only made him miserabler.

He could not think what to do; nor could he think what had happened; or why he had been left behind; or why, if he had been left behind, the goblins had not

1 Bilbo's matches seem anachronistic to most readers. The Dwarves, we are told on page 159, have never taken to using matches, but use tinder-boxes instead. In "The Old Forest," Chapter 6 in Book I of *The Lord of the Rings,* Sam starts a fire with a tinder-box, and later in *The Two Towers* he is mentioned again as carrying with his gear a small tinder-box. Anders Stenström's study of Tolkien's use of matches and tinder-boxes, "Striking Matches," appears in *Arda 1985,* vol. 5 (1988).

2 *1937:* "nor do the goblins seem to have noticed it" > *1966 Longmans/ Unwin:* "nor fortunately had the goblins noticed it" (*1966-Ball* follows *1937.*)

caught him; or even why his head was so sore. The truth was he had been lying quiet, out of sight and out of mind, in a very dark corner for a long while.

After some time he felt for his pipe. It was not broken, and that was something. Then he felt for his pouch, and there was some tobacco in it, and that was something more. Then he felt for matches[1] and he could not find any at all, and that shattered his hopes completely. Just as well for him, as he agreed when he came to his senses. Goodness knows what the striking of matches and the smell of tobacco would have brought on him out of dark holes in that horrible place. Still at the moment he felt very crushed. But in slapping all his pockets and feeling all round himself for matches his hand came on the hilt of his little sword — the little dagger that he got from the trolls, and that he had quite forgotten; nor fortunately had the goblins noticed it,[2] as he wore it inside his breeches.

Now he drew it out. It shone pale and dim before his eyes. "So it is an elvish blade, too," he thought; "and goblins are not very near, and yet not far enough."

But somehow he was comforted. It was rather splendid to be wearing a blade made in Gondolin for the goblin-wars of which so many songs had sung; and also he had noticed that such weapons made a great impression on goblins that came upon them suddenly.

"Go back?" he thought. "No good at all! Go sideways? Impossible! Go forward? Only thing to do! On we go!" So up he got, and trotted along with his little sword held in front of him and one hand feeling the wall, and his heart all of a patter and a pitter.

Now certainly Bilbo was in what is called a tight place. But you must remember it was not quite so tight for him as it would have been for me or for you. Hobbits are not quite like ordinary people; and after all if their holes are nice cheery places and properly aired, quite different from the tunnels of the goblins, still they are more used to tunnelling than we are, and they do not easily lose their sense of direction underground — not when their heads have recovered from being bumped. Also they can move very quietly, and hide easily, and recover wonderfully from falls and bruises, and they have a fund of wisdom and wise sayings that men have mostly never heard or have forgotten long ago.

I should not have liked to have been in Mr. Baggins' place, all the same. The tunnel seemed to have no end. All he knew was that it was still going down pretty steadily and keeping in the same direction in spite of a twist and a turn or two. There were passages leading off to the side every now and then, as he knew by the glimmer of his sword, or could feel with his hand on the wall. Of these he took no notice, except to hurry past for fear of goblins or half-imagined dark things coming out of them. On and on he went, and down and down; and still he heard no sound of anything except the occasional whirr of a bat by his ears, which startled him at first, till it became too frequent to bother about. I do not know how long he kept on like this, hating to go on, not daring to stop, on, on, until he was tireder than tired. It seemed like all the way to tomorrow and over it to the days beyond.[3]

Suddenly without any warning he trotted splash into water! Ugh! it was icy cold. That pulled him up sharp and short. He did not know whether it was just a pool in the path, or the edge of an underground stream that crossed the passage, or the brink of a deep dark subterranean lake. The sword was hardly shining at all. He stopped, and he could hear, when he listened hard, drops drip-drip-dripping from an unseen roof into the water below; but there seemed no other sort of sound.

"So it is a pool or a lake, and not an underground river," he thought. Still he did not dare to wade out into the darkness. He could not swim; and he thought, too, of nasty slimy things, with big bulging blind eyes, wriggling in the water. There are strange things living in the

3 The view of the inside of a mountain as expressed here is very dark. Compare it with that of George Macdonald in his *The Princess and Curdie,* sequel to *The Princess and the Goblin.* The first chapter, "The Mountain," begins with a very long and mythopoeic description of a mountain, first from the outside and then from the inside:

But the inside, who shall tell what lies there? Caverns of the awfullest solitude, their walls miles thick, sparkling with ores of gold or silver, copper or iron, tin or mercury, studded perhaps with precious stones — perhaps a brook, with eyeless fish in it, running, running ceaselessly, cold and babbling, through banks crusted with carbuncles and golden topazes, or over a gravel of which some of the stones are rubies and emeralds, perhaps diamonds and sapphires — who can tell?

4 In August 1952, Tolkien visited his friend George Sayer in Malvern, where he made a tape recording of a large portion of this chapter, starting with the sentence beginning, "Deep down there by the dark water . . ." In 1975, this recording was released as *J.R.R. Tolkien Reads and Sings His "The Hobbit" and "The Fellowship of the Ring"* (Caedmon TC 1477). Tolkien's performance is marvelous, and his nasty, high, hissing voice for Gollum is very effective.

5 *1937:* "lived old Gollum. I don't know where" > *1966-Ball:* "lived old Gollum, a small slimy creature. I don't know where"

This revision was probably made in direct response to the illustrated foreign editions of *The Hobbit* that had appeared before 1966. In most of these, Gollum is depicted as a very large creature. In the 1947 Swedish edition, he is drawn as a large, dark rock about four times the size of Bilbo, and in the 1957 German edition he is several times larger than Bilbo (his legs, dangling over his boat, are themselves longer than Bilbo is tall). In the 1962 Portuguese edition, he appears as a bearded and alarming-looking figure, twice the size of Bilbo, while in the 1965 Japanese edition he is like a large reptile, probably three times Bilbo's size.

pools and lakes in the hearts of mountains: fish whose fathers swam in, goodness only knows how many years ago, and never swam out again, while their eyes grew bigger and bigger and bigger from trying to see in the blackness; also there are other things more slimy than fish. Even in the tunnels and caves the goblins have made for themselves there are other things living unbeknown to them that have sneaked in from outside to lie up in the dark. Some of these caves, too, go back in their beginnings to ages before the goblins, who only widened them and joined them up with passages, and the original owners are still there in odd corners, slinking and nosing about.

Deep down here by the dark water[4] lived old Gollum, a small slimy creature. I don't know where[5] he came from, nor who or what he was. He was Gollum — as

Gollum. Pencil sketch by Alan Lee, for his 1997 illustrated edition of *The Hobbit*. Lee (b. 1947) was born in Middlesex, England, and educated at the Ealing School of Art. He has illustrated several books, including *Faeries* (with Brian Froud; 1978), *The Mabinogion* (1982), *Castles* (1984), *Merlin Dreams* (1988), and Rosemary Sutcliff's retellings of *The Iliad* and *The Odyssey, Black Ships Before Troy* (1993) and *The Wanderings of Odysseus* (1995).

His edition of *The Hobbit*, published for the book's sixtieth anniversary, contains twenty-six full-page color paintings and more than three dozen sketches. Lee also illustrated the centenary edition of *The Lord of the Rings* with fifty full-page color illustrations. He served as conceptual artist and set decorator for Peter Jackson's three films *The Lord of the Rings*. Two additional pencil sketches by Lee appear on pages 134 and 315.

dark as darkness, except for two big round pale eyes in his thin face.[6] He had a little boat,[7] and he rowed about quite quietly on the lake; for lake it was, wide and deep and deadly cold. He paddled it with large feet dangling over the side, but never a ripple did he make. Not he. He was looking out of his pale lamp-like eyes for blind fish, which he grabbed with his long fingers as quick as thinking. He liked meat too. Goblin he thought good, when he could get it; but he took care they never found him out. He just throttled them from behind, if they ever came down alone anywhere near the edge of the water, while he was prowling about. They very seldom did, for they had a feeling that something unpleasant was lurking down there, down at the very roots of the mountain. They had come on the lake, when they were tunnelling down long ago, and they found they could go no further; so there their road ended in that direction, and there was no reason to go that way — unless the Great Goblin sent them. Sometimes he took a fancy for fish from the lake, and sometimes neither goblin nor fish came back.

Actually Gollum lived on a slimy island of rock in the middle of the lake. He was watching Bilbo now from the distance with his pale eyes like telescopes. Bilbo could not see him, but he was wondering a lot about Bilbo, for he could see that he was no goblin at all.

Gollum. Illustration by Maret Kernumees for the 1977 Estonian edition.

6 Within Tolkien's writings, Gollum's antecedent was a slimy little creature named Glip, who appears in a poem of that name. "Glip" is one in a series of poems called "Tales and Songs of Bimble Bay," and though it is undated it was probably written around 1928. It survives in two nearly identical versions, both fair copy manuscripts written in green ink.

GLIP

Under the cliffs of Bimble Bay
Is a little cave of stone
With wet walls of shining grey;
And on the floor a bone,
A white bone that is gnawed quite clean
With sharp white teeth.
But inside nobody can be seen —
He lives far underneath,
Under the floor, down a long hole
Where the sea gurgles and sighs.
Glip is his name, as blind as a mole
In his two round eyes
While daylight lasts; but when night falls
With a pale gleam they shine
Like green jelly, and out he crawls
All long and wet with slime.
He slinks through weeds at highwater mark
To where the mermaid sings,
The wicked mermaid singing in the dark
And threading golden rings
On wet hair; for many ships
She draws to the rock to die.
And Glip listens, and quietly slips
And lies in shadow by.
It is there that Glip steals his bones.
He is a slimy little thing
Sneaking and crawling under fishy stones,
And slinking home to sing
A gurgling song in his damp hole;
But after the last light
There are darker and wickeder things that
*   prowl*
On Bimble rocks at night.

7 *1937:* "round pale eyes. He had a boat" > *1966-Ball:* "round pale eyes in his thin face. He had a little boat"

8 In the first edition of *The Hobbit* (1937), Gollum uses the phrase "my precious" to refer only to himself. In the second edition (1951), in which Gollum's role was significantly altered (see note 25 to this chapter), the phrase might be taken to refer to the ring, as is often the case in *The Lord of the Rings.*

The Old Norse word *gull* means "gold." In the oldest manuscripts it is spelled *goll.* One inflected form would be *gollum,* "gold, treasure, something precious." It can also mean "ring," as is found in the compound word *fingr-gull,* "finger-ring" — points that may have occurred to Tolkien.

9 *1937:* "It likes riddles" > *1951:* "It like riddles"

Tolkien noted this error in a letter to Rayner Unwin of December 30, 1961: "This crept in in the 6th imp. I think. Not that Gollum would miss the chance of a sibilant!" (*Letters,* No. 236). However, the error remained in *1966-Ball, 1966-Longmans/Unwin, 1966-A&U, 1967-HM,* and in the 1978 fourth edition by Allen & Unwin.

10 In a letter published in the London newspaper *The Observer* on February 20, 1938, Tolkien wrote of the riddles used in *The Hobbit,* "There is work to be done here on the sources and analogues. I should not be at all surprised to learn that both the hobbit and Gollum will find their claim to have invented any of them disallowed" (*Letters,* No. 25).

Gollum got into his boat and shot off from the island, while Bilbo was sitting on the brink altogether flummoxed and at the end of his way and his wits. Suddenly up came Gollum and whispered and hissed:

"Bless us and splash us, my precioussss! I guess it's a choice feast; at least a tasty morsel it'd make us, gollum!" And when he said *gollum* he made a horrible swallowing noise in his throat. That is how he got his name, though he always called himself 'my precious'.8

The hobbit jumped nearly out of his skin when the hiss came in his ears, and he suddenly saw the pale eyes sticking out at him.

"Who are you?" he said, thrusting his dagger in front of him.

"What iss he, my preciouss?" whispered Gollum (who always spoke to himself through never having anyone else to speak to). This is what he had come to find out, for he was not really very hungry at the moment, only curious; otherwise he would have grabbed first and whispered afterwards.

"I am Mr. Bilbo Baggins. I have lost the dwarves and I have lost the wizard, and I don't know where I am; and I don't want to know, if only I can get away."

"What's he got in his handses?" said Gollum, looking at the sword, which he did not quite like.

"A sword, a blade which came out of Gondolin!"

"Sssss" said Gollum, and became quite polite. "Praps ye sits here and chats with it a bitsy, my preciousss. It likes riddles,9 praps it does, does it?"10 He was anxious to appear friendly, at any rate for the moment, and until he found out more about the sword and the hobbit, whether he was quite alone really, whether he was good to eat, and whether Gollum was really hungry. Riddles were all he could think of. Asking them, and sometimes guessing them, had been the only game he had ever played with other funny creatures sitting in their holes in the long, long ago, before he lost all his friends and was driven away, alone, and crept down, down, into the dark under the mountains.[11]

"Very well," said Bilbo, who was anxious to agree, until he found out more about the creature, whether he was quite alone, whether he was fierce or hungry, and whether he was a friend of the goblins.

"You ask first," he said, because he had not had time to think of a riddle.

So Gollum hissed:

> *What has roots as nobody sees,*
> *Is taller than trees,*
> *Up, up it goes,*
> *And yet never grows?*

"Easy!" said Bilbo. "Mountain, I suppose."

"Does it guess easy? It must have a competition with us, my preciouss! If precious asks, and it doesn't answer, we eats it, my preciousss. If it asks us, and we doesn't answer, then we does what it wants, eh? We shows it the way out, yes!"[12]

"All right!" said Bilbo, not daring to disagree, and nearly bursting his brain to think of riddles that could save him from being eaten.

> *Thirty white horses on a red hill,*
> *First they champ,*
> *Then they stamp,*
> *Then they stand still.*[13]

That was all he could think of to ask — the idea of eating was rather on his mind. It was rather an old one, too, and Gollum knew the answer as well as you do.

"Chestnuts, chestnuts,"[14] he hissed. "Teeth! teeth! my preciousss; but we has only six!" Then he asked his second:

> *Voiceless it cries,*
> *Wingless flutters,*

The Riddles. Illustration by Ryûichi Terashima for the 1965 Japanese edition.

11 *1937:* "before the goblins came, and he was cut off from his friends far under under [*sic*] the mountains" > *1951:* "before he lost all his friends and was driven away, alone, and crept down, down, into the dark under the mountains"

12 *1937:* "and we doesn't answer, we gives it a present, gollum!" > *1951:* "and we doesn't answer, then we does what it wants, eh? We shows it the way out, yes!"

13 Tolkien here has touched up a very common riddle, No. 229 in Iona and

Peter Opie's *Oxford Dictionary of Nursery Rhymes* (1951):

Thirty white horses
Upon a red hill,
Now they tramp,
Now they champ,
Now they stand still.

14 Gollum's usage of *chestnut* is slang, meaning an old, well-known joke or tale, which this particular riddle is.

15 I can find no single comparable analogue to this riddle. However, traditional wind riddles often contain variations of phrase on the elements of "flying without wings" and "speaking without a mouth."

16 This riddle cleverly expresses the etymology of the word *daisy* in riddle form. The flower name comes from the Anglo-Saxon *dæges éage* ("day's eye"), which alludes to the flower's petals opening in the morning (revealing the yellow center) and closing in the evening. Hence it is the "eye of day" or "day's eye" — the modern *daisy*.

Tolkien used this phrase similarly in "The Lay of the Children of Húrin," an unfinished poem in Anglo-Saxon alliterative verse on which he worked in the early 1920s. It was published in *The Lays of Beleriand,* volume three of the *History:*

but Beleg yet breathed   in blood drenchéd
aswoon, till the sun   to the South hastened,
and the eye of day   was opened wide.
      (lines 716–18, p. 33)

17 *1937:* "Bilbo was beginning to wonder what Gollum's present would be like" > *1961* (Puffin): "Bilbo was begin-

Toothless bites,
Mouthless mutters.[15]

"Half a moment!" cried Bilbo, who was still thinking uncomfortably about eating. Fortunately he had once heard something rather like this before, and getting his wits back he thought of the answer. "Wind, wind of course," he said, and he was so pleased that he made up one on the spot. "This'll puzzle the nasty little underground creature," he thought:

> *An eye in a blue face*
> *Saw an eye in a green face.*
> *"That eye is like to this eye"*
> *Said the first eye,*
> *"But in low place*
> *Not in high place."*[16]

"Ss, ss, ss," said Gollum. He had been underground a long long time, and was forgetting this sort of thing. But just as Bilbo was beginning to hope that the wretch would not be able to answer,[17] Gollum brought up memories of ages and ages and ages before, when he lived with his grandmother in a hole in a bank by a river, "Sss, sss, my preciouss," he said. "Sun on the daisies it means, it does."

But these ordinary above ground everyday sort of riddles were tiring for him. Also they reminded him of days when he had been less lonely and sneaky and nasty, and that put him out of temper. What is more they made him hungry; so this time he tried something a bit more difficult and more unpleasant:

> *It cannot be seen, cannot be felt,*
> *Cannot be heard, cannot be smelt.*
> *It lies behind stars and under hills,*
> *And empty holes it fills.*
> *It comes first and follows after,*
> *Ends life, kills laughter.*[18]

Unfortunately for Gollum Bilbo had heard that sort of thing before; and the answer was all round him any way. "Dark!" he said without even scratching his head or putting on his thinking cap.

> *A box without hinges, key, or lid,*
> *Yet golden treasure inside is hid,*[19]

he asked to gain time, until he could think of a really hard one. This he thought a dreadfully easy chestnut, though he had not asked it in the usual words. But it proved a nasty poser for Gollum. He hissed to himself, and still he did not answer; he whispered and spluttered.

After some while Bilbo became impatient. "Well, what is it?" he said. "The answer's not a kettle boiling over, as you seem to think from the noise you are making."

"Give us a chance; let it give us a chance, my preciouss — ss — ss."

"Well," said Bilbo after giving him a long chance, "what about your guess?"[20]

But suddenly Gollum remembered thieving from nests long ago, and sitting under the river bank teaching his grandmother, teaching his grandmother to suck — "Eggses!"[21] he hissed. "Eggses it is!" Then he asked:

> *Alive without breath,*
> *As cold as death;*
> *Never thirsty, ever drinking,*
> *All in mail never clinking.*[22]

He also in his turn thought this was a dreadfully easy one, because he was always thinking of the answer. But he could not remember anything better at the moment, he was so flustered by the egg-question. All the same it was a poser for poor Bilbo, who never had anything to do with the water if he could help it. I imagine you know the answer, of course, or can guess it as easy as winking,

ning to hope that he would not be able to answer" > *1966-Ball:* "Bilbo was beginning to hope that the wretch would not be able to answer" (*1951* follows *1937*. The intermediate revision in the 1961 Puffin edition was communicated to that publisher directly by Tolkien in a letter of April 1961.)

This passage had been overlooked when, in 1951, Tolkien published a major revision of the chapter "Riddles in the Dark," altering Gollum's promise of a present if Bilbo won the riddle contest to Gollum showing Bilbo the way out. This alteration brings the passage in line with the revised version of the story.

18 In his copy of the first edition of *The Annotated Hobbit* (now with the Tolkien collection at Marquette University), the late Tolkien scholar Taum Santoski noted a riddle analogue from Jón Árnason's *Íslenzkar Gátur* (1887), a collection of about twelve hundred Icelandic riddles:

It will soon cover the roof of a high house.
It flies higher than the mountains
and causes the fall of many a man.
Everyone can see it, but no one can fetter it.
It can stand both blows and the wind,
and it is not harmful.
[No. 352, p. 52. Answer: darkness]

19 In a letter to his publisher dated September 20, 1947, Tolkien called this riddle "a reduction to a couplet (my own) of a longer literary riddle which appears in some 'Nursery Rhyme' books" (*Letters,* No. 110). The longer literary riddle is certainly this one:

In marble halls as white as milk,
Lined with a skin as soft as silk,

Within a fountain crystal-clear,
A golden apple doth appear.
No doors there are to this stronghold,
Yet thieves break in and steal the gold.

At Leeds, Tolkien reworked this riddle into Anglo Saxon. On June 26, 1922, he sent it in a postcard to Henry Bradley, who had been in charge of the *Oxford English Dictionary* when Tolkien was on the staff in 1918–20. Tolkien published it, together with another riddle similarly refashioned, in *A Northern Venture: Verses by Members of the Leeds University English School Association* (1923). The title under which both riddles appear translates as "Two Saxon Riddles Recently Discovered." Tolkien's versions are not simply translations but original compositions based on traditional riddles.

"Enigmata Saxonica Nuper Inventa Duo"

I.

Meolchwitum sind marmanstane
wagas mine wundrum frætwede;
is hrægl ahongen hnesce on-innan,
seolce gelicost; siththan on-middan
is wylla geworht, waeter glaes-hluttor;
Thær glisnath gold-hladen on gytestreamum
æppla scienost. Infær nænig
nah min burg-fæsten; berstath hwæthre
thriste theofas on thrythærn min,
ond thæt sinc reafiath — saga hwæt ic hatte!

II.

Hæfth Hild Hunecan hwite tunecan,
ond swa read rose hæfth rudige nose;
the leng heo bideth, the læss heo wrideth;
hire tearas hate on tan blate
biernende dreaosath ond bearhtme freosath;
hwæt heo sie saga, searothancla maga. (p. 20)

The second riddle, translated back into modern English, would be:

Hild Hunic has a white tunic
And like a red rose, a ruddy nose.

since you are sitting comfortably at home and have not the danger of being eaten to disturb your thinking. Bilbo sat and cleared his throat once or twice, but no answer came.

After a while Gollum began to hiss with pleasure to himself: "Is it nice, my preciousss? Is it juicy? Is it scrumptiously crunchable?" He began to peer at Bilbo out of the darkness.

"Half a moment," said the hobbit shivering. "I gave you a good long chance just now."

"It must make haste, haste!" said Gollum, beginning to climb out of his boat on to the shore to get at Bilbo. But when he put his long webby foot in the water, a fish jumped out in a fright and fell on Bilbo's toes.

"Ugh!" he said, "it is cold and clammy!" — and so he guessed. "Fish! fish!" he cried. "It is fish!"

Gollum was dreadfully disappointed; but Bilbo asked another riddle as quick as ever he could, so that Gollum had to get back into his boat and think.

No-legs lay on one-leg, two-legs sat near on three-legs,
four-legs got some.[23]

It was not really the right time for this riddle, but Bilbo was in a hurry. Gollum might have had some trouble guessing it, if he had asked it at another time. As it was, talking of fish, "no-legs" was not so very difficult, and after that the rest was easy. "Fish on a little table, man at table sitting on a stool, the cat has the bones" that of course is the answer, and Gollum soon gave it. Then he thought the time had come to ask something hard and horrible. This is what he said:

This thing all things devours:
Birds, beasts, trees, flowers;
Gnaws iron, bites steel;
Grinds hard stones to meal;
Slays king, ruins town,
And beats high mountain down.[24]

Poor Bilbo sat in the dark thinking of all the horrible names of all the giants and ogres he had ever heard told of in tales, but not one of them had done all these things. He had a feeling that the answer was quite different and that he ought to know it, but he could not think of it. He began to get frightened, and that is bad for thinking. Gollum began to get out of his boat. He flapped into the water and paddled to the bank; Bilbo could see his eyes coming towards him. His tongue seemed to stick in his mouth; he wanted to shout out: "Give me more time! Give me time!" But all that came out with a sudden squeal was:

"Time! Time!"

Bilbo was saved by pure luck. For that of course was the answer.

Gollum was disappointed once more; and now he was getting angry, and also tired of the game. It had made him very hungry indeed. This time he did not go back to the boat. He sat down in the dark by Bilbo. That made the hobbit most dreadfully uncomfortable and scattered his wits.

"It's got to ask uss a quesstion, my preciouss, yes, yess, yesss. Jusst one more question to guess, yes, yess," said Gollum.

But Bilbo simply could not think of any question with that nasty wet cold thing sitting next to him, and pawing and poking him. He scratched himself, he pinched himself; still he could not think of anything.

"Ask us! ask us!" said Gollum.

Bilbo pinched himself and slapped himself; he gripped on his little sword; he even felt in his pocket with his other hand. There he found the ring he had picked up in the passage and forgotten about.

"What have I got in my pocket?" he said aloud. He was talking to himself, but Gollum thought it was a riddle, and he was frightfully upset.

The longer she bides, the less she thrives.
On the pale branch her tears blanch,
Their heat leaves as they freeze.
What she may be say, wise lad if you may.

Tolkien's version is an imaginative expansion of a familiar riddle that survives in many variations:

Little Nancy Etticoat
In a white petticoat
And a red nose;
The longer she stands
The shorter she grows.

The answer is a candle.

20 *1937:* "what about your present?" > after *1951:* "what about your guess?" (The *1951* second edition "fifth impression" retains the *1937* reading. The correction was made in *1955* in the seventh impression.)

This reason for this revision is the same as that given above for note 17 to this chapter.

21 Gollum's train of thought in answering this riddle, by recalling that he once taught his grandmother to suck eggs, provides an amusingly literal usage of this old phrase. Francis Grose, in his *Classical Dictionary of the Vulgar Tongue* (1785), recorded under the entry *granny* (an abbreviation for grandmother) that the phrase "go teach your granny to suck eggs" was said to anyone who would try to instruct others "in a matter he knows better than themselves" — that is, the phrase is said derisively to someone who tries to teach his elders or those more experienced than himself.

22 There is a slight analogue to this riddle in the Old Norse *Saga of King Hei-*

drek the Wise, in a contest of wisdom
between King Heidrek and Gestumblindi, who is the Norse god Odin in
disguise. I give here the translation by
Christopher Tolkien, published in 1960:

What lives on high fells?
What falls in deep dales?
What lives without breath?
What is never silent?
This riddle ponder,
O prince Heidrek!

"Your riddle is good, Gestumblindi," said the
king; "I have guessed it. The raven lives ever
on the high fells, the dew falls ever in the deep
dales, the fish lives without breath, and the
rushing waterfall is never silent." (p. 80)

In Chapter 2 of Book IV of *The Lord of
the Rings,* Gollum gives a longer variant
of this riddle:

Alive without breath;
as cold as death;
never thirsting, ever drinking;
clad in mail, never clinking.
Drowns on dry land,
thinks an island
is a mountain;
thinks a fountain
is a puff of air.
So sleek, so fair!
   What a joy to meet!
We only wish
to catch a fish,
   so juicy-sweet!

23 Leg riddles are traditional, going
back to the riddle the Sphinx posed to
Oedipus. (What animal walks on four
legs in the morning, two at noon, and
three in the evening? The answer, as
given by Oedipus, is man: Man walked
on his hands and feet in the morning of
life, strode erect on his two feet in his
prime at noon, and in the evening of life
supported his infirmities with a cane.)

"Not fair! not fair!" he hissed. "It isn't fair, my precious, is it, to ask us what it's got in its nassty little pocketses?"

Bilbo seeing what had happened and having nothing
better to ask stuck to his question, "What have I got in
my pocket?" he said louder.

"S-s-s-s-s," hissed Gollum. "It must give us three
guesseses, my preciouss, three guesseses."

"Very well! Guess away!" said Bilbo.

"Handses!" said Gollum.

"Wrong," said Bilbo, who had luckily just taken his
hand out again. "Guess again!"

"S-s-s-s-s," said Gollum more upset than ever. He
thought of all the things he kept in his own pockets: fish-
bones, goblins' teeth, wet shells, a bit of bat-wing, a
sharp stone to sharpen his fangs on, and other nasty
things. He tried to think what other people kept in their
pockets.

"Knife!" he said at last.

"Wrong!" said Bilbo, who had lost his some time ago.
"Last guess!"

Now Gollum was in a much worse state than when
Bilbo had asked him the egg-question. He hissed and
spluttered and rocked himself backwards and forwards,
and slapped his feet on the floor, and wriggled and
squirmed; but still he did not dare to waste his last
guess.

"Come on!" said Bilbo. "I am waiting!" He tried to
sound bold and cheerful, but he did not feel at all sure
how the game was going to end, whether Gollum
guessed right or not.

"Time's up!" he said.

"String, or nothing!" shrieked Gollum, which was
not quite fair — working in two guesses at once.

"Both wrong," cried Bilbo very much relieved; and
he jumped at once to his feet, put his back to the nearest
wall, and held out his little sword.**25** He knew, of course,
that the riddle-game was sacred and of immense antiq-

uity,[26] and even wicked creatures were afraid to cheat when they played at it. But he felt he could not trust this slimy thing to keep any promise at a pinch. Any excuse would do for him to slide out of it. And after all that last question had not been a genuine riddle according to the ancient laws.[27]

But at any rate Gollum did not at once attack him. He could see the sword in Bilbo's hand. He sat still, shivering and whispering. At last Bilbo could wait no longer.

"Well?" he said. "What about your promise? I want to go. You must show me the way."

"Did we say so, precious? Show the nassty little Baggins the way out, yes, yes. But what has it got in its pocketses, eh? Not string, precious, but not nothing. Oh no! gollum!"

"Never you mind," said Bilbo. "A promise is a promise."

"Cross it is, impatient, precious," hissed Gollum. "But it must wait, yes it must. We can't go up the tunnels so hasty. We must go and get some things first, yes, things to help us."

"Well, hurry up!" said Bilbo, relieved to think of Gollum going away. He thought he was just making an excuse and did not mean to come back. What was Gollum talking about? What useful thing could he keep out on the dark lake? But he was wrong. Gollum did mean to come back. He was angry now and hungry. And he was a miserable wicked creature, and already he had a plan.

Not far away was his island, of which Bilbo knew nothing, and there in his hiding-place he kept a few wretched oddments, and one very beautiful thing, very beautiful, very wonderful. He had a ring, a golden ring, a precious ring.

"My birthday-present!" he whispered to himself, as he had often done in the endless dark days. "That's what we wants now, yes; we wants it!"

He wanted it because it was a ring of power, and if you slipped that ring on your finger, you were invisible;

The Oxford Dictionary of Nursery Rhymes includes a very common riddle similar to Tolkien's:

Two legs sat upon three legs
With one leg in his lap;
In comes four legs
And runs away with one leg;
Up jumps two legs,
Catches up three legs,
Throws it after four legs,
And makes him bring back one leg.(No. 302)

The solution is a man sitting on a stool, with a leg of mutton in his lap. A dog comes in and steals the mutton; the man picks up the stool, throws it at the dog, and makes him bring back the mutton.

24 There is an analogue to this riddle in the Old English "Second Dialogue of Solomon and Saturn." I give here the translation by Tom Shippey, from his *Poems of Wisdom and Learning in Old English* (1976):

Saturn said: But what is that strange thing that travels through this world, goes on inexorably, beats at foundations, causes tears of sorrow, and often comes here? Neither star nor stone nor eye-catching jewel, neither water nor wild beast can deceive it at all, but into its hands go hard and soft, small and great. . . .

Solomon said: Old age has power over everything on earth. . . . She smashes trees and breaks their branches, in her progress she uproots the standing trunk and fells it to the ground. After that she eats the wild bird. She fights better than a wolf, she waits longer than a stone, she proves stronger than steel, she bites iron with rust; she does the same to us.

(pp. 91, 93)

Another time riddle was noted by Taum Santoski in Jón Árnason's *Íslenzkar Gátur*:

I am without beginning, yet I am born. I am also without end, and yet I die. I have neither eyes nor ears, yet I see and hear. I am never seen, and yet my works are visible. I am long conquered, I am never conquered, and yet I am vanquished. I labor ever, but am never tired. I am wise but dwell among the foolish. I am a lover of Providence, and yet it may appear to me that it hates me. Often I die before I am born, and yet I am immortal. Without being aware of it, I often take by surprise. I live with Christians, I dwell among the heathen; among the cursed in Hell I am cursed, and I reign in the Kingdom of Glory.

[No. 105, p. 25–6. Answer: time]

25 The first edition of *The Hobbit* (1937) contains a significantly different version of this chapter. As Tolkien wrote the sequel, *The Lord of the Rings,* he found it necessary to revise *The Hobbit* in order to bring it in line with the sequel. The portrayal of Gollum has been substantially altered; in the first edition, he is not nearly as wretched a creature. And the stakes of the riddle contest are slightly different: It was still Bilbo's life if he lost, but if he won, Gollum would give him a present. The riddle contest is pretty much the same in both versions, but the conclusion in the earlier version is about half as long as that in later editions. The ending of the early version is given in here and in note 32 to this chapter.

1937: But funnily enough he need not have been alarmed. For one thing Gollum had learned long long ago was never, never, to cheat at the riddle-game, which is a sacred one and of immense antiquity. Also there was the sword. He simply sat and whispered.

"What about the present?" asked Bilbo, not that he cared very much, still he felt that he had won it, pretty fairly, and in very difficult circumstances too.

"Must we give it the thing, preciouss? Yess, we must! We must fetch it, preciouss, and give it the present we promised." So Gollum pad-

only in the full sunlight could you be seen, and then only by your shadow, and that would be shaky and faint.

"My birthday-present! It came to me on my birthday, my precious." So he had always said to himself. But who knows how Gollum came by that present, ages ago in the old days when such rings were still at large in the world? Perhaps even the Master[28] who ruled them could not have said. Gollum used to wear it at first, till it tired him; and then he kept it in a pouch next his skin, till it galled him; and now usually he hid it in a hole in the rock on his island, and was always going back to look at it. And still sometimes he put it on, when he could not bear to be parted from it any longer, or when he was very, very, hungry, and tired of fish. Then he would creep along dark passages looking for stray goblins. He might even venture into places where the torches were lit and made his eyes blink and smart; for he would be safe. Oh yes, quite safe. No one would see him, no one would notice him, till he had his fingers on their throat. Only a few hours ago he had worn it, and caught a small goblin-imp. How it squeaked! He still had a bone or two left to gnaw, but he wanted something softer.

"Quite safe, yes," he whispered to himself. "It won't see us, will it, my precious? No. It won't see us, and its nasty little sword will be useless, yes quite."

That is what was in his wicked little mind, as he slipped suddenly from Bilbo's side, and flapped back to his boat, and went off into the dark. Bilbo thought he had heard the last of him. Still he waited a while; for he had no idea how to find his way out alone.

Suddenly he heard a screech. It sent a shiver down his back. Gollum was cursing and wailing away in the gloom, not very far off by the sound of it. He was on his island, scrabbling here and there, searching and seeking in vain.

"Where iss it? Where iss it?" Bilbo heard him crying. "Losst it is, my precious, lost, lost! Curse us and crush us, my precious is lost!"

"What's the matter?" Bilbo called. "What have you lost?"

"It mustn't ask us," shrieked Gollum. "Not its business, no, gollum! It's losst, gollum, gollum, gollum."

"Well, so am I," cried Bilbo, "and I want to get unlost. And I won the game, and you promised. So come along! Come and let me out, and then go on with your looking!" Utterly miserable as Gollum sounded, Bilbo could not find much pity in his heart, and he had a feeling that anything Gollum wanted so much could hardly be something good. "Come along!" he shouted.

"No, not yet, precious!" Gollum answered. "We must search for it, it's lost, gollum."

"But you never guessed my last question, and you promised," said Bilbo.

"Never guessed!" said Gollum. Then suddenly out of the gloom came a sharp hiss. "What has it got in its pocketses? Tell us that. It must tell first."

As far as Bilbo knew, there was no particular reason why he should not tell. Gollum's mind had jumped to a guess quicker than his; naturally, for Gollum had brooded for ages on this one thing, and he was always afraid of its being stolen. But Bilbo was annoyed at the delay. After all, he had won the game, pretty fairly, at a horrible risk. "Answers were to be guessed not given," he said.

"But it wasn't a fair question," said Gollum. "Not a riddle, precious, no."

"Oh well, if it's a matter of ordinary questions," Bilbo replied, "then I asked one first. What have you lost? Tell me that!"

"What has it got in its pocketses?" The sound came hissing louder and sharper, and as he looked towards it, to his alarm Bilbo now saw two small points of light peering at him. As suspicion grew in Gollum's mind, the light of his eyes burned with a pale flame.[29]

"What have you lost?" Bilbo persisted.

But now the light in Gollum's eyes had become a

dled back to his boat, and Bilbo thought he had heard the last of him. But he had not. The hobbit was just thinking of going back up the passage — having had quite enough of Gollum and the dark water's edge — when he heard him wailing and squeaking away in the gloom. He was on his island (of which, of course, Bilbo knew nothing), scrabbling here and there, searching and seeking in vain, and turning out his pockets.

"Where iss it? Where iss it?" Bilbo heard him squeaking. "Lost, lost, my preciouss, lost, lost! Bless us and splash us! We haven't the present we promised, and we haven't even got it for ourselves."

Bilbo turned round and waited, wondering what it could be that the creature was making such a fuss about. This proved very fortunate afterwards. For Gollum came back and made a tremendous spluttering and whispering and croaking; and in the end Bilbo gathered that Gollum had had a ring — a wonderful, beautiful ring, a ring that he had been given for a birthday present, ages and ages before in old days when such rings were less uncommon. Sometimes he had it in his pocket; usually he kept it in a little hole in the rock on his island; sometimes he wore it — when he was very, very hungry, and tired of fish, and crept along dark passages looking for stray goblins. Then he might venture even into places where the torches were lit and made his eyes blink and smart; but he would be safe. O yes! very nearly safe; for if you slipped that ring on your finger, you were invisible; only in the sunlight could you be seen, and then only by your shadow, and that was a faint and shaky sort of shadow.

I don't know how many times Gollum begged Bilbo's pardon. He kept on saying: "We are ssorry; we didn't mean to cheat, we meant to give it our only only pressent, if it won the competition." He even offered to catch Bilbo some nice juicy fish to eat as a consolation.

Bilbo shuddered at the thought of it. "No thank you!" he said as politely as he could.

He was thinking hard, and the idea came to him that Gollum must have dropped that ring sometime and that he must have found it, and that he had that very ring in his pocket. But he had the wits not to tell Gollum.

"Finding's keeping!" he said to himself; and being in a very tight place, I daresay, he was right. Anyway the ring belonged to him now.

"Never mind!" he said. "The ring would have been mine now, if you had found it; so you would have lost it anyway. And I will let you off on one condition."

"Yes, what iss it? What does it wish us to do, my precious?"

"Help me to get out of these places," said Bilbo.

Now Gollum had to agree to this, if he was not to cheat. He still very much wanted just to try what the stranger tasted like; but now he had to give up all idea of it. Still there was the little sword; and the stranger was wide awake and on the look out, not unsuspecting as Gollum liked to have the things which he attacked. So perhaps it was best after all.

That is how Bilbo got to know that the tunnel ended at the water and went no further on the other side where the mountain wall was dark and solid. He also learned that he ought to have turned down one of the side passages to the right before he came to the bottom; but he could not follow Gollum's directions for finding it again on the way up, and he made the wretched creature come and show him the way.

As they went along up the tunnel together, Gollum flip-flapping at his side, Bilbo going very softly, he thought he would try the ring. He slipped it on his finger.

"Where iss it? Where iss it gone to?" said Gollum at once, peering about with his long eyes.

"Here I am, following behind!" said Bilbo slipping off the ring again, and feeling very pleased to have it and to find that it really did what Gollum said.

Now on they went again, while Gollum counted the passages to left and right: "One left, one right, two right, three right, two left," and so on. He began to get very shaky and afraid as they left the water further and further

green fire, and it was coming swiftly nearer. Gollum was in his boat again, paddling wildly back to the dark shore; and such a rage of loss and suspicion was in his heart that no sword had any more terror for him.

Bilbo could not guess what had maddened the wretched creature, but he saw that all was up, and that Gollum meant to murder him at any rate. Just in time he turned and ran blindly back up the dark passage down which he had come, keeping close to the wall and feeling it with his left hand.

"What has it got in its pocketses?" he heard the hiss loud behind him, and the splash as Gollum leapt from his boat. "What have I, I wonder?" he said to himself, as he panted and stumbled along. He put his left hand in his pocket. The ring felt very cold as it quietly slipped on to his groping forefinger.

The hiss was close behind him. He turned now and saw Gollum's eyes like small green lamps coming up the slope.[30] Terrified he tried to run faster, but suddenly he struck his toes on a snag in the floor, and fell flat with his little sword under him.

In a moment Gollum was on him. But before Bilbo could do anything, recover his breath, pick himself up, or wave his sword, Gollum passed by, taking no notice of him, cursing and whispering as he ran.

What could it mean? Gollum could see in the dark. Bilbo could see the light of his eyes palely shining even from behind. Painfully he got up, and sheathed his sword, which was now glowing faintly again, then very cautiously he followed. There seemed nothing else to do. It was no good crawling back down to Gollum's water. Perhaps if he followed him, Gollum might lead him to some way of escape without meaning to.

"Curse it! curse it! curse it!" hissed Gollum. "Curse the Baggins! It's gone! What has it got in its pocketses? Oh we guess, we guess, my precious. He's found it, yes he must have. My birthday-present."

Bilbo pricked up his ears. He was at last beginning to

guess himself. He hurried a little, getting as close as he dared behind Gollum, who was still going quickly, not looking back, but turning his head from side to side, as Bilbo could see from the faint glimmer on the walls.

"My birthday-present! Curse it! How did we lose it, my precious? Yes, that's it. When we came this way last, when we twisted that nassty young squeaker. That's it. Curse it! It slipped from us, after all these ages and ages! It's gone, gollum."

Suddenly Gollum sat down and began to weep, a whistling and gurgling sound horrible to listen to. Bilbo halted and flattened himself against the tunnel-wall. After a while Gollum stopped weeping and began to talk. He seemed to be having an argument with himself.

"It's no good going back there to search, no. We doesn't remember all the places we've visited. And it's no use. The Baggins has got it in its pocketses; the nassty noser has found it, we says."

"We guesses, precious, only guesses. We can't know till we find the nassty creature and squeezes it. But it doesn't know what the present can do, does it? It'll just keep it in its pocketses. It doesn't know, and it can't go far. It's lost itself, the nassty nosey thing. It doesn't know the way out. It said so."

"It said so, yes; but it's tricksy. It doesn't say what it means. It won't say what it's got in its pocketses. It knows. It knows a way in, it must know a way out, yes. It's off to the back-door. To the back-door, that's it."

"The goblinses will catch it then. It can't get out that way, precious."

"Ssss, sss, gollum! Goblinses! Yes, but if it's got the present, our precious present, then goblinses will get it, gollum! They'll find it, they'll find out what it does. We shan't ever be safe again, never, gollum! One of the goblinses will put it on, and then no one will see him. He'll be there but not seen. Not even our clever eyeses will notice him; and he'll come creepsy and tricksy and catch us, gollum, gollum!"

behind; but at last he stopped by a low opening on their left (going up) – "six right, four left."

"Here'ss the passage," he whispered. "It musst squeeze in and sneak down. We durstn't go with it, my preciouss, no we durstn't, gollum!"

So Bilbo slipped under the arch, and said good-bye to the nasty miserable creature; and very glad he was. He did not feel comfortable until he felt quite sure it was gone, and he kept his head out in the main tunnel listening until the flip-flap of Gollum going back to his boat died away in the darkness. Then he went down the new passage.

It was a low narrow one roughly made. It was all right for the hobbit, except when he stubbed his toes in the dark on nasty jags in the floor; but it must have been a bit low for goblins. Perhaps it was not knowing that goblins are used to this sort of thing, and go along quite fast stooping low with their hands almost on the floor, that made Bilbo forget the danger of meeting them and hurry forward recklessly.

As the text that replaced the above in 1951 is exactly that given in the main text of this book, I do not repeat it here. See page 126, beginning, "He knew, of course, that the riddle-game was sacred," through page 134, ending, "stooping low with their hands almost on the ground."

26 The riddling tradition is attested to in Anglo-Saxon times by the appearance of nearly one hundred Anglo-Saxon riddles in *The Exeter Book,* one of the four great surviving collections of Anglo-Saxon poetry. It was compiled by Leofric, the bishop of Exeter, sometime before his death in 1072. Tolkien's riddles are generally much shorter than those in the Exeter book, and many of them rhyme, while the Exeter riddles do not.

27 The two greatest riddle contests in Old Norse literature both end on the same sort of questionable nonriddle. In the "Vafthrúdismal" (The Lay of Vafthrúdnir) in the *Elder Edda,* when Odin hears of the great wisdom of the giant Vafthrúdnir, he resolves to match his own lore against the giant's. Disguised, he wins the contest by asking the question, "What did Odin whisper in the ear of his son, before Baldur was carried to the pyre?" Only Odin could know the answer, and thus his identity is revealed. In *The Saga of King Heidrek the Wise,* another riddle contest involves Odin in disguise, and the contest ends with the exact same question.

In the prologue to *The Lord of the Rings* (Section 4, "Of the Finding of the Ring"), Tolkien commented, "The Authorities, it is true, differ whether this last question was a mere 'question' and not a 'riddle' according to the strict rules of the Game; but all agree that, after accepting it and trying to guess the answer, Gollum was bound by his promise."

28 The story of how Gollum came by his ring is told by Gandalf in the second chapter of *The Lord of the Rings,* "The Shadow of the Past." The mention of the Master who rules the rings introduces the sinister nature of Gollum's ring. The Master is Sauron, the Dark Lord, who is called the Necromancer in *The Hobbit.*

29 The light in Gollum's eyes burning with a pale flame recalls Grendel in *Beowulf,* as he enters the dark hall Heorot for the last time. The passage reads as follows, from *Beowulf and the Finnesburg Fragment* (1940), translated by

"Then let's stop talking, precious, and make haste. If the Baggins has gone that way, we must go quick and see. Go! Not far now. Make haste!"

With a spring Gollum got up and started shambling off at a great pace. Bilbo hurried after him, still cautiously, though his chief fear now was of tripping on another snag and falling with a noise. His head was in a whirl of hope and wonder. It seemed that the ring he had was a magic ring: it made you invisible![31] He had heard of such things, of course, in old old tales; but it was hard to believe that he really had found one, by accident. Still there it was: Gollum with his bright eyes had passed him by, only a yard to one side.

On they went, Gollum flip-flapping ahead, hissing and cursing; Bilbo behind going as softly as a hobbit can. Soon they came to places where, as Bilbo had noticed on the way down, side-passages opened, this way and that. Gollum began at once to count them.

"One left, yes. One right, yes. Two right, yes, yes. Two left, yes, yes." And so on and on.

As the count grew he slowed down, and he began to get shaky and weepy; for he was leaving the water further and further behind, and he was getting afraid. Goblins might be about, and he had lost his ring. At last he stopped by a low opening, on their left as they went up.

"Seven right, yes. Six left, yes!" he whispered. "This is it. This is the way to the back-door, yes. Here's the passage!"

He peered in, and shrank back. "But we dursn't go in, precious, no we dursn't. Goblinses down there. Lots of goblinses. We smells them. Ssss!"

"What shall we do? Curse them and crush them! We must wait here, precious, wait a bit and see."

So they came to a dead stop. Gollum had brought Bilbo to the way out after all, but Bilbo could not get in! There was Gollum sitting humped up right in the opening, and his eyes gleamed cold in his head, as he swayed it from side to side between his knees.

Bilbo crept away from the wall more quietly than a mouse; but Gollum stiffened at once, and sniffed, and his eyes went green. He hissed softly but menacingly. He could not see the hobbit, but now he was on the alert, and he had other senses that the darkness had sharpened: hearing and smell. He seemed to be crouched right down with his flat hands splayed on the floor, and his head thrust out, nose almost to the stone. Though he was only a black shadow in the gleam of his own eyes, Bilbo could see or feel that he was tense as a bowstring, gathered for a spring.

Bilbo almost stopped breathing, and went stiff himself. He was desperate. He must get away, out of this horrible darkness, while he had any strength left. He must fight. He must stab the foul thing, put its eyes out, kill it. It meant to kill him. No, not a fair fight. He was invisible now. Gollum had no sword. Gollum had not actually threatened to kill him, or tried to yet. And he was miserable, alone, lost. A sudden understanding, a pity mixed with horror, welled up in Bilbo's heart: a glimpse of endless unmarked days without light or hope of betterment, hard stone, cold fish, sneaking and whispering. All these thoughts passed in a flash of a second. He trembled. And then quite suddenly in another flash, as if lifted by a new strength and resolve, he leaped.

No great leap for a man, but a leap in the dark. Straight over Gollum's head he jumped, seven feet forward and three in the air; indeed, had he known it, he only just missed cracking his skull on the low arch of the passage.

Gollum threw himself backwards, and grabbed as the hobbit flew over him, but too late: his hands snapped on thin air, and Bilbo, falling fair on his sturdy feet, sped off down the new tunnel. He did not turn to see what Gollum was doing. There was a hissing and cursing almost at his heels at first, then it stopped. All at once there came a blood-curdling shriek, filled with hatred and despair. Gollum was defeated. He dared go no further. He

John R. Clark Hall, revised by C. L. Wrenn: "The fiend stepped on to the many-coloured paving of the floor, — advanced in angry mood; from his eyes there came a horrible light, most like a flame" (lines 724–27).

30 It is in attempting to draw Gollum that most illustrators of *The Hobbit* fail. Tolkien himself observed this in the illustrations to the translations of the book. In a letter of December 12, 1963, to Allen & Unwin, he wrote that "Gollum should not be made a monster, as he is by practically all other illustrators in disregard of the text."

What should Gollum look like? Based on various descriptions by Tolkien, he should be a slimy little creature not larger than Bilbo: thin, with a large head for his size; large, protuberant eyes; a long, skinny neck; and thin, lank hair. His skin was white, and evidently he wore black garments. (He was never naked.) His hands were long and his feet were webby, with prehensile toes.

31 Rings of invisibility are often traced back to the story of Gyges in Book II of *The Republic* by Plato (c.429–347 B.C.). The story is little more than an anecdote, in which the wearing of a golden ring brings invisibility when the bezel is turned inward from the hand, with visibility restored when the bezel is turned outward. Talismans of invisibility are very common in fairy tales, and rings conferring invisibility can be found in two stories in the collections edited by Andrew Lang, including "The Enchanted Ring" in *The Green Fairy Book* (1892) and "The Dragon of the North" in *The Yellow Fairy Book* (1894).

32 *1937:*

Soon the passage began to go up again, and after a while it climbed steeply. That slowed him down. But at last after some time the slope stopped, the passage turned a corner and dipped down again, and at the bottom of a short incline he saw filtering round another corner — a glimmer of light. Not red light as of fire or lantern, but pale ordinary out-of-doors sort of light. The he began to run. Scuttling along as fast as his little legs would carry him he turned the corner and came suddenly right into an open place where the light, after all that time in the dark, seemed dazzlingly bright. Really it was only a leak of sunshine in through a doorway, where a great door, a stone door, was left a little open.

Bilbo blinked, and then he suddenly saw the goblins: goblins in full armour with drawn swords sitting just inside the door, and watching it with wide eyes, and the passage that led to it! They saw him sooner than he saw them, and with yells of delight they rushed upon him.

Whether it was accident or presence of mind, I don't know. Accident, I think, because the hobbit was not used yet to his new treasure. Anyway he slipped the ring on his left hand — and the goblins stopped short. They could not see a sign of him. Then they yelled twice as loud as before, but not so delightedly.

> *1951:*

Soon the passage that had been sloping down began to go up again, and after a while it climbed steeply. That slowed Bilbo down. But at last the slope stopped, the passage turned a corner, and dipped down again, and there, at the bottom of a short incline, he saw, filtering around another corner — a glimpse of light. Not red light, as of fire or lantern, but a pale out-of-doors sort of light. Then Bilbo began to run.

Scuttling as fast as his legs would carry him he turned the last corner and came suddenly right into an open space, where the light, after

had lost: lost his prey, and lost, too, the only thing he had ever cared for, his precious. The cry brought Bilbo's heart to his mouth, but still he held on. Now faint as an echo, but menacing, the voice came behind:

"Thief, thief, thief! Baggins! We hates it, we hates it, we hates it for ever!"

Then there was a silence. But that too seemed menacing to Bilbo. "If goblins are so near that he smelt them," he thought, "then they'll have heard his shrieking and cursing. Careful now, or this way will lead you to worse things."

The passage was low and roughly made. It was not too difficult for the hobbit, except when, in spite of all care, he stubbed his poor toes again, several times, on nasty jagged stones in the floor. "A bit low for goblins, at least for the big ones," thought Bilbo, not knowing that even the big ones, the orcs of the mountains, go along at a great speed stooping low with their hands almost on the ground.

Soon the passage that had been sloping down began to go up again, and after a while it climbed steeply.[32] That slowed Bilbo down. But at last the slope stopped, the passage turned a corner and dipped down again,

Goblin-guards. Pencil sketch by Alan Lee, for his 1997 illustrated edition of *The Hobbit*.

and there, at the bottom of a short incline, he saw, filtering round another corner — a glimpse of light. Not red light, as of fire or lantern, but a pale out-of-doors sort of light. Then Bilbo began to run.

Scuttling as fast as his legs would carry him he turned the last corner and came suddenly right into an open space, where the light, after all that time in the dark, seemed dazzlingly bright. Really it was only a leak of sunshine in through a doorway, where a great door, a stone door, was left standing open.

Bilbo blinked, and then suddenly he saw the goblins: goblins in full armour with drawn swords sitting just inside the door, and watching it with wide eyes, and watching the passage that led to it. They were aroused, alert, ready for anything.

They saw him sooner than he saw them. Yes, they saw him. Whether it was an accident, or a last trick of the ring before it took a new master, it was not on his finger. With yells of delight the goblins rushed upon him.

A pang of fear and loss, like an echo of Gollum's misery, smote Bilbo, and forgetting even to draw his sword he struck his hands into his pockets. And there was the ring still, in his left pocket, and it slipped on his finger. The goblins stopped short. They could not see a sign of him. He had vanished. They yelled twice as loud as before, but not so delightedly.

"Where is it?" they cried.

"Go back up the passage!" some shouted.

"This way!" some yelled. "That way!" others yelled.

"Look out for the door," bellowed the captain.

Whistles blew, armour clashed, swords rattled, goblins cursed and swore and ran hither and thither, falling over one another and getting very angry. There was a terrible outcry, to-do, and disturbance.

Bilbo was dreadfully frightened, but he had the sense to understand what had happened and to sneak behind a big barrel which held drink for the goblin-guards, and so get out of the way and avoid being bumped into, trampled to death, or caught by feel.

"I must get to the door, I must get to the door!" he kept on saying to himself, but it was a long time before he ventured to try. Then it was like a horrible game of blind-man's-buff. The place was full of goblins running about, and the poor little hobbit dodged this way and that, was knocked over by a goblin who could not make out what he had bumped into, scrambled away on all fours, slipped between the legs of the captain just in time, got up, and ran for the door.

It was still ajar, but a goblin had pushed it nearly to. Bilbo struggled but he could not move it. He tried to squeeze through the crack. He squeezed and squeezed, and he stuck! It was awful. His buttons had got wedged on the edge of the door and the door-post. He could see outside into the open air: there were a few steps running down into a narrow valley between tall mountains; the sun came out from behind a cloud and shone bright on the outside of the door — but he could not get through.

Suddenly one of the goblins inside shouted: "There is a shadow by the door. Something is outside!"

Bilbo's heart jumped into his mouth. He gave a terrific squirm. Buttons burst off in all directions. He was through, with a torn coat and waistcoat, leaping down the steps like a goat, while bewildered goblins were still picking up his nice brass buttons on the doorstep.

Of course they soon came down after him, hooting and hallooing, and hunting among the trees. But they don't like the sun: it makes their legs wobble and their heads giddy. They could not find Bilbo with the ring on, slipping in and out of the shadow of the trees, running quick and quiet, and keeping out of the sun; so soon they went back grumbling and cursing to guard the door. Bilbo had escaped.

6

Out of the Frying-Pan into the Fire

BILBO HAD ESCAPED THE GOBLINS, but he did not know where he was. He had lost hood, cloak, food, pony, his buttons and his friends. He wandered on and on, till the sun began to sink westwards — *behind the mountains.* Their shadows fell across Bilbo's path, and he looked back. Then he looked forward and could see before him only ridges and slopes falling towards lowlands and plains glimpsed occasionally between the trees.

"Good heavens!" he exclaimed. "I seem to have got right to the other side of the Misty Mountains,[1] right to the edge of the Land Beyond! Where and O where can Gandalf and the dwarves have got to? I only hope to goodness they are not still back there in the power of the goblins!"

He still wandered on, out of the little high valley, over its edge, and down the slopes beyond; but all the while a very uncomfortable thought was growing inside him. He wondered whether he ought not, now he had the magic ring, to go back into the horrible, horrible, tunnels and look for his friends. He had just made up his mind that it was his duty, that he must turn back — and very miserable he felt about it — when he heard voices.

[1] Tom Shippey traces Tolkien's use of the name *Misty Mountains* to the poem "Skírnismál" (The Lay of Skírnir), from the Old Norse *Elder Edda.*

Skírnir, who has been sent to abduct a giant's daughter, makes a speech to his horse; Shippey translates part of it as follows: "The mirk is outside, I call it our business to fare over the misty mountains, over the tribes of orcs; we will both come back, or else he will take us both, he the mighty giant" (*The Road to Middle-earth,* second edition, p. 65).

Tolkien had imagined the Misty Mountains in some form long before he began *The Hobbit.* A small watercolor, in an early style and titled *The Misty Mountains,* shows a row of mountains with a road and bridge leading toward them (see *Artist,* No. 200).

He stopped and listened. It did not sound like goblins; so he crept forward carefully. He was on a stony path winding downwards with a rocky wall on the left hand; on the other side the ground sloped away and there were dells below the level of the path overhung with bushes and low trees. In one of these dells under the bushes people were talking.

He crept still nearer, and suddenly he saw peering between two big boulders a head with a red hood on: it was Balin doing look-out. He could have clapped and shouted for joy, but he did not. He had still got the ring on, for fear of meeting something unexpected and unpleasant, and he saw that Balin was looking straight at him without noticing him.

"I will give them all a surprise," he thought, as he crawled into the bushes at the edge of the dell. Gandalf was arguing with the dwarves. They were discussing all that had happened to them in the tunnels, and wondering and debating what they were to do now. The dwarves were grumbling, and Gandalf was saying that they could not possibly go on with their journey leaving Mr. Baggins in the hands of the goblins, without trying to find out if he was alive or dead, and without trying to rescue him.

"After all he is my friend," said the wizard, "and not a bad little chap. I feel responsible for him. I wish to goodness you had not lost him."

The dwarves wanted to know why he had ever been brought at all, why he could not stick to his friends and come along with them, and why the wizard had not chosen someone with more sense. "He has been more trouble than use so far," said one. "If we have got to go back now into those abominable tunnels to look for him, then drat him, I say."

Gandalf answered angrily: "I brought him, and I don't bring things that are of no use. Either you help me to look for him, or I go and leave you here to get out of the mess as best you can yourselves. If we can only find him again, you will thank me before all is over. Whatever did you want to go and drop him for, Dori?"

"You would have dropped him," said Dori, "if a goblin had suddenly grabbed your legs from behind in the dark, tripped up your feet, and kicked you in the back!"

"Then why didn't you pick him up again?"

"Good heavens! Can you ask! Goblins fighting and biting in the dark, everybody falling over bodies and hitting one another! You nearly chopped off my head with Glamdring, and Thorin was stabbing here there and everywhere with Orcrist. All of a sudden you gave one of your blinding flashes, and we saw the goblins running back yelping. You shouted 'follow me everybody!' and everybody ought to have followed. We thought everybody had. There was no time to count, as you know quite well, till we had dashed through the gate-guards, out of the lower door, and helter-skelter down here. And here we are — without the burglar, confusticate him!"

"And here's the burglar!" said Bilbo stepping down into the middle of them, and slipping off the ring.

Bless me, how they jumped! Then they shouted with surprise and delight. Gandalf was as astonished as any of them, but probably more pleased than all the others. He called to Balin and told him what he thought of a look-out man who let people walk right into them like that without warning. It is a fact that Bilbo's reputation went up a very great deal with the dwarves after this. If they had still doubted that he was really a first-class burglar, in spite of Gandalf's words, they doubted no longer. Balin was the most puzzled of all; but everyone said it was a very clever bit of work.

Indeed Bilbo was so pleased with their praise that he just chuckled inside and said nothing whatever about the ring; and when they asked him how he did it, he said: "Oh, just crept along, you know — very carefully and quietly."

2 In the prologue to *The Lord of the Rings* (Section 4, "Of the Finding of the Ring"), Tolkien briefly retells the story of Bilbo's encounter with Gollum and of his finding the ring, as it is given in the second and later editions of *The Hobbit.* He continues:

Now it is a curious fact that this is not the story as Bilbo first told it to his companions. To them his account was that Gollum had promised to give him a *present,* if he won the game; but when Gollum went to fetch it from his island he found the treasure was gone: a magic ring, which had been given to him long ago on his birthday. Bilbo guessed that this was the very ring he had found, and as he had won the game, it was already his by right. But being in a tight place, he said nothing about it, and made Gollum show him the way out, as a reward instead of a present. This account Bilbo set down in his memoirs . . .

What Tolkien has described is the scenario for the first edition of *The Hobbit,* and the statement that "this is not the story as Bilbo first told it to his companions" contradicts the statement given here, that Bilbo "sat down and told them everything, except the finding of the ring" and the statement given later (in the spiders episode) that the dwarves, after hearing about the ring, insist on "having the Gollum story, riddles and all, told all over again, with the ring in its proper place." Bilbo's dishonesty, of great importance in *The Lord of the Rings,* is nowhere explicitly present in *The Hobbit.*

3 *1937:* "So I asked for my present, and he went to look for it, and couldn't find it. So I said, 'very well, help me to get out of this nasty place!' and he showed me the passage to the door. 'Good-bye' I said, and I went on down" > *1951:* "So I

"Well, it is the first time that even a mouse has crept along carefully and quietly under my very nose and not been spotted," said Balin, "and I take off my hood to you." Which he did.

"Balin at your service," said he.

"Your servant, Mr. Baggins," said Bilbo.

Then they wanted to know all about his adventures after they had lost him, and he sat down and told them everything — except about the finding of the ring ("not just now" he thought).**2** They were particularly interested in the riddle-competition, and shuddered most appreciatively at his description of Gollum.

"And then I couldn't think of any other question with him sitting beside me," ended Bilbo; "so I said 'what's in my pocket?' And he couldn't guess in three goes. So I said: 'what about your promise? Show me the way out!' But he came at me to kill me, and I ran, and fell over, and he missed me in the dark. Then I followed him, because I heard him talking to himself. He thought I really knew the way out, and so he was making for it. And then he sat down in the entrance, and I could not get by. So I jumped over him and escaped, and ran down to the gate."**3**

"What about the guards?" they asked. "Weren't there any?"

"O yes! lots of them; but I dodged 'em. I got stuck in the door, which was only open a crack, and I lost lots of buttons," he said sadly looking at his torn clothes. "But I squeezed through all right — and here I am."

The dwarves looked at him with quite a new respect, when he talked about dodging guards, jumping over Gollum, and squeezing through,**4** as if it was not very difficult or very alarming.

"What did I tell you?" said Gandalf laughing. "Mr. Baggins has more about him than you guess." He gave Bilbo a queer look from under his bushy eyebrows, as he said this, and the hobbit wondered if he guessed at the part of his tale that he had left out.

Then he had questions of his own to ask, for if Gandalf had explained it all by now to the dwarves, Bilbo had not heard it. He wanted to know how the wizard had turned up again, and where they had all got to now.

The wizard, to tell the truth, never minded explaining his cleverness more than once, so now he told Bilbo that both he and Elrond had been well aware of the presence of evil goblins in that part of the mountains. But their main gate used to come out on a different pass, one more easy to travel by, so that they often caught people benighted near their gates. Evidently people had given up going that way, and the goblins must have opened their new entrance at the top of the pass the dwarves had taken, quite recently, because it had been found quite safe up to now.

"I must see if I can't find a more or less decent giant to block it up again," said Gandalf, "or soon there will be no getting over the mountains at all."

As soon as Gandalf had heard Bilbo's yell he realized what had happened. In the flash which killed the goblins that were grabbing him he had nipped inside the crack, just as it snapped to. He followed after the drivers and prisoners right to the edge of the great hall, and there he sat down and worked up the best magic he could in the shadows.

"A very ticklish business, it was," he said. "Touch and go!"

But, of course, Gandalf had made a special study of bewitchments with fire and lights (even the hobbit had never forgotten the magic fireworks at Old Took's midsummer-eve parties, as you remember). The rest we all know — except that Gandalf knew all about the backdoor, as the goblins called the lower gate, where Bilbo lost his buttons.[5] As a matter of fact it was well known to anybody who was acquainted with this part of the mountains; but it took a wizard to keep his head in the tunnels and guide them in the right direction.

"They made that gate ages ago," he said, "partly for a

said: 'what about your promise? Show me the way out!' But he came at me to kill me, and I ran, and fell over, and he missed me in the dark. Then I followed him, because I heard him talking to himself. He thought I really knew the way out, and so he was making for it. And then he sat down in the entrance, and I could not get by. So I jumped over him and escaped, and ran down to the gate."

4 *1937:* "dodging guards, and squeezing through" > *1951:* "dodging guards, jumping over Gollum, and squeezing through"

5 *1937:* "Gandalf knew all about the back-gate, as he called it, the lower door where Bilbo lost his buttons" > *1951:* "Gandalf knew all about the back-door, as the goblins called the lower gate, where Bilbo lost his buttons"

way of escape, if they needed one; partly as a way out into the lands beyond, where they still come in the dark and do great damage. They guard it always and no one has ever managed to block it up. They will guard it doubly after this," he laughed.

All the others laughed too. After all they had lost a good deal, but they had killed the Great Goblin and a great many others besides, and they had all escaped, so they might be said to have had the best of it so far.

But the wizard called them to their senses. "We must be getting on at once, now we are a little rested," he said. "They will be out after us in hundreds when night comes on; and already shadows are lengthening. They can smell our footsteps for hours and hours after we have passed. We must be miles on before dusk. There will be a bit of moon, if it keeps fine, and that is lucky. Not that they mind the moon much, but it will give us a little light to steer by."

"O yes!" he said in answer to more questions from the hobbit. "You lose track of time inside goblin-tunnels. Today's Thursday, and it was Monday night or Tuesday morning that we were captured. We have gone miles and miles, and come right down through the heart of the mountains, and are now on the other side – quite a short cut. But we are not at the point to which our pass would have brought us; we are too far to the North, and have some awkward country ahead. And we are still pretty high up. Let's get on!"

"I am dreadfully hungry," groaned Bilbo, who was suddenly aware that he had not had a meal since the night before the night before last. Just think of that for a hobbit! His stomach felt all empty and loose and his legs all wobbly, now that the excitement was over.

"Can't help it," said Gandalf, "unless you like to go back and ask the goblins nicely to let you have your pony back and your luggage."

"No thank you!" said Bilbo.

"Very well then, we must just tighten our belts and trudge on — or we shall be made into supper, and that will be much worse than having none ourselves."

As they went on Bilbo looked from side to side for something to eat; but the blackberries were still only in flower, and of course there were no nuts, not even hawthorn-berries. He nibbled a bit of sorrel, and he drank from a small mountain-stream that crossed the path, and he ate three wild strawberries that he found on its bank, but it was not much good.

They still went on and on. The rough path disappeared. The bushes, and the long grasses between the boulders, the patches of rabbit-cropped turf, the thyme and the sage and the marjoram, and the yellow rockroses all vanished, and they found themselves at the top of a wide steep slope of fallen stones, the remains of a landslide. When they began to go down this, rubbish and small pebbles rolled away from their feet; soon larger bits of split stone went clattering down and started other pieces below them slithering and rolling; then lumps of rock were disturbed and bounded off, crashing down with a dust and a noise. Before long the whole slope above them and below them seemed on the move, and they were sliding away, huddled all together, in a fearful confusion of slipping, rattling, cracking slabs and stones.[6]

It was the trees at the bottom that saved them. They slid into the edge of a climbing wood of pines that here stood right up the mountain slope from the deeper darker forests of the valleys below. Some caught hold of the trunks and swung themselves into lower branches, some (like the little hobbit) got behind a tree to shelter from the onslaught of the rocks. Soon the danger was over, the slide had stopped, and the last faint crashes could be heard as the largest of the disturbed stones went bounding and spinning among the bracken and the pine-roots far below.

[6] This passage again recalls Tolkien's 1911 walking tour in Switzerland (see note 1 to Chapter 4).

"Well! that has got us on a bit," said Gandalf; "and even goblins tracking us will have a job to come down here quietly."

"I daresay," grumbled Bombur; "but they won't find it difficult to send stones bouncing down on our heads." The dwarves (and Bilbo) were feeling far from happy, and were rubbing their bruised and damaged legs and feet.

"Nonsense! We are going to turn aside here out of the path of the slide. We must be quick! Look at the light!"

The sun had long gone behind the mountains. Already the shadows were deepening about them, though far away through the trees and over the black tops of those growing lower down they could still see the evening lights on the plains beyond. They limped along now as fast as they were able down the gentle slopes of a pine forest in a slanting path leading steadily southwards. At times they were pushing through a sea of bracken with tall fronds rising right above the hobbit's head; at times they were marching along quiet as quiet over a floor of pine-needles; and all the while the forest-gloom got heavier and the forest-silence deeper. There was no wind that evening to bring even a sea-sighing into the branches of the trees.

"Must we go any further?" asked Bilbo, when it was so dark that he could only just see Thorin's beard wagging beside him, and so quiet that he could hear the dwarves' breathing like a loud noise. "My toes are all bruised and bent, and my legs ache, and my stomach is wagging like an empty sack."

"A bit further," said Gandalf.

After what seemed ages further they came suddenly to an opening where no trees grew. The moon was up and was shining into the clearing. Somehow it struck all of them as not at all a nice place, although there was nothing wrong to see.

All of a sudden they heard a howl away down hill, a long shuddering howl. It was answered by another away to the right and a good deal nearer to them; then by another not far away to the left. It was wolves howling at the moon, wolves gathering together!

There were no wolves living near Mr. Baggins' hole at home, but he knew that noise. He had had it described to him often enough in tales. One of his elder cousins (on the Took side), who had been a great traveller, used to imitate it to frighten him. To hear it out in the forest under the moon was too much for Bilbo. Even magic rings are not much use against wolves — especially against the evil packs that lived under the shadow of the goblin-infested mountains, over the Edge of the Wild on the borders of the unknown. Wolves of that sort smell keener than goblins, and do not need to see you to catch you!

"What shall we do, what shall we do!" he cried. "Escaping goblins to be caught by wolves!" he said, and it became a proverb, though we now say "out of the frying-pan into the fire"[7] in the same sort of uncomfortable situations.

"Up the trees quick!" cried Gandalf; and they ran to the trees at the edge of the glade, hunting for those that had branches fairly low, or were slender enough to swarm up. They found them as quick as ever they could, you can guess; and up they went as high as ever they could trust the branches. You would have laughed (from a safe distance), if you had seen the dwarves sitting up in the trees with their beards dangling down, like old gentlemen gone cracked and playing at being boys. Fili and Kili were at the top of a tall larch like an enormous Christmas tree. Dori, Nori, Ori, Oin, and Gloin were more comfortable in a huge pine with regular branches sticking out at intervals like the spokes of a wheel. Bifur, Bofur, Bombur, and Thorin were in another. Dwalin and Balin had swarmed up a tall slender fir with few

7 "Out of the frying-pan into the fire" is a traditional proverb. In the second edition of *The Oxford Dictionary of English Proverbs* (1948), compiled by William George Smith and revised by Sir Paul Harvey, examples of usage are given as far back as the early sixteenth century. ꝫ

8 Tolkien usually refuted any association between his invented word *hobbit* and *rabbit.* But internal evidence suggests otherwise. One of the trolls calls Bilbo a "nassty little rabbit" (page 76). Here he is likened to "a rabbit that has lost its hole and has a dog after it." In the eagle's eyrie he worries about "being torn up for supper like a rabbit" (page 156). One of the eagles says to him, "You need not be frightened like a rabbit, even if you look rather like one" (page 161). Beorn chides him, "Little bunny is getting nice and fat" (page 181), and Thorin in his fury shakes "poor Bilbo like a rabbit" (page 334).

In discussing the origin of the word *hobbit,* Tolkien said: "I don't know where the word came from. You can't catch your mind out. It might have been associated with Sinclair Lewis's *Babbitt.* Certainly not *rabbit,* as some people think" ("The Man Who Understands Hobbits," by Charlotte and Denis Plimmer, *Daily Telegraph Magazine,* March 22, 1968).

Yet in drafting Appendix F of *The Lord of the Rings,* Tolkien wrote of the word: "I must admit that its faint suggestion of *rabbit* appealed to me. Not that hobbits at all resemble rabbits, unless it be in burrowing." This note was struck out in the draft and is published in volume twelve of the *History, The Peoples of Middle-earth* (p. 49).

9 Tolkien described his use of *warg* in a letter to Gene Wolfe of November 7, 1966: "It is an old word for wolf, which also had the sense of an outlaw or hunted criminal. This is its usual sense in surviving texts. I adopted the word, which had a good sound for the meaning, as a name for this particular brand

branches and were trying to find a place to sit in the greenery of the topmost boughs. Gandalf, who was a good deal taller than the others, had found a tree into which they could not climb, a large pine standing at the very edge of the glade. He was quite hidden in its boughs, but you could see his eyes gleaming in the moon as he peeped out.

And Bilbo? He could not get into any tree, and was scuttling about from trunk to trunk, like a rabbit that has lost its hole and has a dog after it.**8**

"You've left the burglar behind again!" said Nori to Dori looking down.

"I can't be always carrying burglars on my back," said Dori, "down tunnels and up trees! What do you think I am? A porter?"

"He'll be eaten if we don't do something," said Thorin, for there were howls all round them now, getting nearer and nearer. "Dori!" he called, for Dori was lowest down in the easiest tree, "be quick, and give Mr. Baggins a hand up!"

Dori was really a decent fellow in spite of his grumbling. Poor Bilbo could not reach his hand even when he climbed down to the bottom branch and hung his arm down as far as ever he could. So Dori actually climbed out of the tree and let Bilbo scramble up and stand on his back.

Just at that moment the wolves trotted howling into the clearing. All of a sudden there were hundreds of eyes looking at them. Still Dori did not let Bilbo down. He waited till he had clambered off his shoulders into the branches, and then he jumped for the branches himself. Only just in time! A wolf snapped at his cloak as he swung up, and nearly got him. In a minute there was a whole pack of them yelping all round the tree and leaping up at the trunk, with eyes blazing and tongues hanging out.

But even the wild Wargs (for so the evil wolves over the Edge of the Wild were named)**9** cannot climb trees.

For a time they were safe. Luckily it was warm and not windy. Trees are not very comfortable to sit in for long at any time; but in the cold and the wind, with wolves all round below waiting for you, they can be perfectly miserable places.

This glade in the ring of trees was evidently a meeting-place of the wolves. More and more kept coming in. They left guards at the foot of the tree in which Dori and Bilbo were, and then went snuffling about till they had smelt out every tree that had anyone in it. These they guarded too, while all the rest (hundreds and hundreds it seemed) went and sat in a great circle in the glade; and in the middle of the circle was a great grey wolf. He spoke to them in the dreadful language of the Wargs. Gandalf understood it. Bilbo did not, but it sounded terrible to him, and as if all their talk was about cruel and wicked things, as it was. Every now and then all the Wargs in the circle would answer their grey chief all together, and their dreadful clamour almost made the hobbit fall out of his pine-tree.

I will tell you what Gandalf heard, though Bilbo did not understand it. The Wargs and the goblins often helped one another in wicked deeds. Goblins do not usually venture very far from their mountains, unless they are driven out and are looking for new homes, or are marching to war (which I am glad to say has not happened for a long while). But in those days they sometimes used to go on raids, especially to get food or slaves to work for them. Then they often got the Wargs to help and shared the plunder with them. Sometimes they rode on wolves like men do on horses. Now it seemed that a great goblin-raid had been planned for that very night. The Wargs had come to meet the goblins and the goblins were late. The reason, no doubt, was the death of the Great Goblin, and all the excitement caused by the dwarves and Bilbo and the wizard, for whom they were probably still hunting.

In spite of the dangers of this far land bold men had

of demonic wolf in the story." Tolkien derived the word from Old English *wearg-*, Old High German *warg-*, Old Norse *varg*-r (also = "wolf," especially of a legendary kind).

At the time of his correspondence with Tolkien, Gene Wolfe (b. 1931) was at the very beginning of what would become a long and acclaimed career as a writer of fantasy and science fiction (his first published story had appeared in 1965). Wolfe has published two meditations on Tolkien's work, "The Tolkien Toll-Free Fifties Freeway to Mordor and Points Beyond Hurray!" in *Vector*, Spring 1974 (no. 67/68) and "The Best Introduction to the Mountains" in *Interzone* (December 2001). That Wolfe should have written to Tolkien about the usage of a variant form of his own name is almost typical. Wolfe's writings are very linguistically textured and allusive, and Wolfe frequently inserts himself as a character in his fictional writings with a variant form of his lupine name.

of late been making their way back into it from the South, cutting down trees, and building themselves places to live in among the more pleasant woods in the valleys and along the river-shores. There were many of them, and they were brave and well-armed, and even the Wargs dared not attack them if there were many together, or in the bright day. But now they had planned with the goblins' help to come by night upon some of the villages nearest the mountains. If their plan had been carried out, there would have been none left there next day; all would have been killed except the few the goblins kept from the wolves and carried back as prisoners to their caves.

This was dreadful talk to listen to, not only because of the brave woodmen and their wives and children, but also because of the danger which now threatened Gandalf and his friends. The Wargs were angry and puzzled at finding them here in their very meeting-place. They thought they were friends of the woodmen, and were come to spy on them, and would take news of their plans down into the valleys, and then the goblins and the wolves would have to fight a terrible battle instead of capturing prisoners and devouring people waked suddenly from their sleep. So the Wargs had no intention of going away and letting the people up the trees escape, at any rate not until morning. And long before that, they said, goblin soldiers would be coming down from the mountains; and goblins can climb trees, or cut them down.

Now you can understand why Gandalf, listening to their growling and yelping, began to be dreadfully afraid, wizard though he was, and to feel that they were in a very bad place, and had not yet escaped at all. All the same he was not going to let them have it all their own way, though he could not do very much stuck up in a tall tree with wolves all round on the ground below. He gathered the huge pine-cones from the branches of the tree. Then he set one alight with bright blue fire, and threw it whizzing down among the circle of the wolves. It struck one on the back, and immediately his shaggy coat caught fire, and he was leaping to and fro yelping horribly. Then another came and another, one in blue flames, one in red, another in green. They burst on the ground in the middle of the circle and went off in coloured sparks and smoke. A specially large one hit the chief wolf on the nose, and he leaped in the air ten feet, and then rushed round and round the circle biting and snapping even at the other wolves in his anger and fright.

The dwarves and Bilbo shouted and cheered. The rage of the wolves was terrible to see, and the commotion they made filled all the forest. Wolves are afraid of fire at all times, but this was a most horrible and uncanny fire. If a spark got in their coats it stuck and burned into them, and unless they rolled over quick they were soon all in flames. Very soon all about the glade wolves were rolling over and over to put out the sparks on their backs, while those that were burning were running about howling and setting others alight, till their own friends chased them away and they fled off down the slopes crying and yammering and looking for water.10

"What is all this uproar in the forest tonight?" said the Lord of the Eagles. He was sitting, black in the moonlight, on the top of a lonely pinnacle of rock at the eastern edge of the mountains. "I hear wolves' voices! Are the goblins at mischief in the woods?"

He swept up into the air, and immediately two of his guards from the rocks at either hand leaped up to follow him. They circled up in the sky and looked down upon the ring of the Wargs, a tiny spot far far below. But eagles have keen eyes and can see small things at a great distance. The Lord of the Eagles of the Misty Mountains

10 Tolkien recounted his experiences in the Swiss Alps in 1911 in a long letter to his son Michael, quoted in note 1 to Chapter 4. In this letter Tolkien also remarked that "the episode of the 'wargs' (I believe) is in part derived from a scene in S. R. Crockett's *The Black Douglas,* probably his best romance and anyway one that deeply impressed me in school-days, though I have never looked at it again" (*Letters,* No. 306).

The scene is without doubt "The Battle of the Were-Wolves" (Chapter 49 of *The Black Douglas*), in which three men (James Douglas, Sholto McKim, and his father, Malise McKim), having just escaped from the house of the witch woman La Meffraye, are beset by a pack of werewolves in a clearing in a pine woods:

Yells and howls as of triumphant fiends were borne to their ears upon the western wind. The noises approached nearer, and presently out of the dark of the woods shadowy forms glided . . . Gleaming eyes glared upon them as the wolves trotted out and sat down in a wide circle to wait for the full muster of the pack before rushing their prey . . . Sholto noted in especial one gigantic she-wolf, which appeared at every point of the circle and seemed to muster and encourage the pack to attack.

The wild-fire flickered behind the jet black silhouettes of the dense trees so that their tops stood out against the pale sky as if carved of ivory. Then the night shut down darker than before. As the soundless lightning wavered and brightened, the shadows of the wolves appeared simultaneously to start forward and then retreat, while the noise of their howling carried with it some diabolic suggestion of discordant human voices.

"La Meffraye! La Meffraye! Meffraye!" . . .

"It were better to find a tree that we could

"All the wild beasts appeared to be obeying the summons of the witch woman." Illustration by Frank Richards from *The Black Douglas.*

climb," growled Malise with a practical suggestiveness, which, however, came too late. For they dared not move out of the open space, and the great trunk of the blasted pine rose behind them bare of branches almost to the top.

The werewolves finally attack. After a long battle, illumined in the night by occasional flashes of wildfire, the werewolves retreat before the line of corpses of their brethren, and the three men are victorious. The ending of the scene (and chapter) is similar to the ending of the chapter "The Siege of Gondor" in *The Lord of the Rings,* with the appearance at daybreak of a symbol of hope after a long and dark night:

The howling stopped and there fell a silence. Lord James would have spoken.

"Hush!" said Malise, yet more solemnly.

And far off, like an echo from another world, thin and sweet and silver clear, a cock crew.

had eyes that could look at the sun unblinking, and could see a rabbit moving on the ground a mile below even in the moonlight. So though he could not see the people in the trees, he could make out the commotion among the wolves and see the tiny flashes of fire, and hear the howling and yelping come up faint from far beneath him. Also he could see the glint of the moon on goblin spears and helmets, as long lines of the wicked folk crept down the hillsides from their gate and wound into the wood.

Eagles are not kindly birds. Some are cowardly and cruel. But the ancient race of the northern mountains were the greatest of all birds; they were proud and strong and noble-hearted. They did not love goblins, or fear them. When they took any notice of them at all (which was seldom, for they did not eat such creatures), they swooped on them and drove them shrieking back to their caves, and stopped whatever wickedness they were doing. The goblins hated the eagles and feared them, but could not reach their lofty seats, or drive them from the mountains.

Tonight the Lord of the Eagles was filled with curiosity to know what was afoot; so he summoned many other eagles to him, and they flew away from the mountains, and slowly circling ever round and round they came down, down, down towards the ring of the wolves and the meeting-place of the goblins.

A very good thing too! Dreadful things had been going on down there. The wolves that had caught fire and fled into the forest had set it alight in several places. It was high summer, and on this eastern side of the mountains there had been little rain for some time. Yellowing bracken, fallen branches, deep-piled pine-needles, and here and there dead trees, were soon in flames. All round the clearing of the Wargs fire was leaping. But the wolf-guards did not leave the trees. Maddened and angry they were leaping and howling round the trunks, and cursing the dwarves in their horrible language, with their tongues hanging out, and their eyes shining as red and fierce as the flames.

Then suddenly goblins came running up yelling. They thought a battle with the woodmen was going on; but they soon learned what had really happened. Some of them actually sat down and laughed. Others waved their spears and clashed the shafts against their shields. Goblins are not afraid of fire, and they soon had a plan which seemed to them most amusing.

Some got all the wolves together in a pack. Some stacked fern and brushwood round the tree-trunks. Others rushed round and stamped and beat, and beat and stamped, until nearly all the flames were put out — but they did not put out the fire nearest to the trees where the dwarves were. That fire they fed with leaves and dead branches and bracken. Soon they had a ring of smoke and flame all round the dwarves, a ring which they kept from spreading outwards; but it closed slowly in, till the running fire was licking the fuel piled under the trees. Smoke was in Bilbo's eyes, he could feel the heat of the flames; and through the reek he could see the goblins dancing round and round in a circle like people round a midsummer bonfire. Outside the ring of dancing warriors with spears and axes stood the wolves at a respectful distance, watching and waiting.

He could hear the goblins beginning a horrible song:

Fifteen birds in five fir-trees,
their feathers were fanned in a fiery breeze!
But, funny little birds, they had no wings!
O what shall we do with the funny little things?
Roast 'em alive, or stew them in a pot;
fry them, boil them and eat them hot?

Then they stopped and shouted out: "Fly away little birds! Fly away if you can! Come down little birds, or you will get roasted in your nests! Sing, sing little birds! Why don't you sing?"

"Go away! little boys!" shouted Gandalf in answer. "It

The blue leaping flame of the wild-fire abruptly ceased. The dawn arose red and broad in the east. The piles of dead beasts shone out black on the grey plain of the forest glade, and on the topmost bough of a pine tree a thrush began to sing.

Samuel Rutherford Crockett (1859–1914) was an extremely prolific writer of Scottish sentimental fiction, children's books (some retelling Crockett's favorite novels by Sir Walter Scott), and historical romances. *The Black Douglas* (1899) was the thirteenth out of his fifty novels. A sequel, *Maid Margaret of Galloway*, appeared in 1904.

11 Arthur Ransome wrote to Tolkien on December 13, 1937 (see note 36 to Chapter 1), questioning the suitability of using the phrase *little boys* for the non-human goblins. In a letter to Allen & Unwin of December 19, 1937, Tolkien agreed that the insult was "rather silly and not quite up to form" and wondered if *oaves* might be better. But in his later revisions of the text, he let *boys* remain (*Letters,* No. 20).

Incidentally, the *Oxford English Dictionary* records two plurals for the word *oaf: oafs* and *oaves. Oaf* is defined as "an elf's child, a goblin child, a supposed changeling left by the elves or fairies; hence, a misbegotten, deformed, or idiot child; a half-wit, fool, dolt, booby, as being by inference a changeling."

12 The goblin shouts of "Ya-harri-hey! Ya hoy!" may sound like gibberish, but Tolkien used closely similar phrases in "The Choices of Master Samwise," the final chapter of *The Two Towers,* when Sam overhears some Orcs "hooting and laughing, as something was lifted up from the ground. 'Ya hoi! Ya harri hoi! Up! Up!'"

It may be that Tolkien intended the phrases to be Common Speech renderings of Orkish curses. In Section I of Appendix F ("The Languages and Peoples of the Third Age") of *The Lord of the Rings,* Tolkien wrote of the Orcs: "It is said that they had no language of their own, but took what they could of other tongues and perverted it to their own liking; yet they made only brutal jargons, scarcely sufficient even to their own needs, unless it were for curses and abuse."

isn't bird-nesting time. Also naughty little boys that play with fire get punished."[11] He said it to make them angry, and to show them he was not frightened of them — though of course he was, wizard though he was. But they took no notice, and they went on singing.

> *Burn, burn tree and fern!*
> *Shrivel and scorch! A fizzling torch*
> *To light the night for our delight,*
>   *Ya hey!*
>
> *Bake and toast 'em, fry and roast 'em!*
> *till beards blaze, and eyes glaze;*
> *till hair smells and skins crack,*
> *fat melts, and bones black*
>   *in cinders lie*
>   *beneath the sky!*
>   *So dwarves shall die,*
> *and light the night for our delight,*
>   *Ya hey!*
>   *Ya-harri-hey!*
>   *Ya hoy!*[12]

And with that *Ya hoy!* the flames were under Gandalf's tree. In a moment it spread to the others. The bark caught fire, the lower branches cracked.

Then Gandalf climbed to the top of his tree. The sudden splendour flashed from his wand like lightning, as he got ready to spring down from on high right among the spears of the goblins. That would have been the end of him, though he would probably have killed many of them as he came hurtling down like a thunderbolt. But he never leaped.

Just at that moment the Lord of the Eagles swept down from above, seized him in his talons, and was gone.

There was a howl of anger and surprise from the goblins. Loud cried the Lord of the Eagles, to whom Gan-

dalf had now spoken. Back swept the great birds that
were with him, and down they came like huge black
shadows. The wolves yammered and gnashed their
teeth; the goblins yelled and stamped with rage, and
flung their heavy spears in the air in vain. Over them
swooped the eagles; the dark rush of their beating wings
smote them to the floor or drove them far away; their
talons tore at goblin faces. Other birds flew to the tree-
tops and seized the dwarves, who were scrambling up
now as far as they ever dared to go.

Poor little Bilbo was very nearly left behind again! He
just managed to catch hold of Dori's legs, as Dori was
borne off last of all; and up they went together above the
tumult and the burning, Bilbo swinging in the air with
his arms nearly breaking.

The Goblins and Wolves dance. Illustration by
Tove Jansson for the 1962 Swedish and 1973
Finnish editions.

Now far below the goblins and the wolves were scat-
tering far and wide in the woods. A few eagles were still
circling and sweeping above the battle-ground. The
flames about the trees sprang suddenly up above the
highest branches. They went up in crackling fire. There
was a sudden flurry of sparks and smoke. Bilbo had escaped only just in time!

Soon the light of the burning was faint below, a red
twinkle on the black floor; and they were high up in the
sky, rising all the time in strong sweeping circles. Bilbo
never forgot that flight, clinging onto Dori's ankles. He
moaned "my arms, my arms!"; but Dori groaned "my
poor legs, my poor legs!"

At the best of times heights made Bilbo giddy. He
used to turn queer if he looked over the edge of quite a
little cliff; and he had never liked ladders, let alone trees
(never having had to escape from wolves before). So you
can imagine how his head swam now, when he looked
down between his dangling toes and saw the dark lands
opening wide underneath him, touched here and there
with the light of the moon on a hill-side rock or a stream
in the plains.

The pale peaks of the mountains were coming nearer,

Rescue by the eagles. Illustration by Virgil Finlay. Beginning in January 1963, Tolkien's American publisher, Houghton Mifflin, solicited sample illustrations for *The Hobbit* from some prominent American artists in hope of producing a sumptuous illustrated edition. Virgil Finlay (1914–1971) had begun his career in 1935 by illustrating stories in the legendary magazine *Weird Tales* and soon thereafter was illustrating for many of the prominent science fiction magazines, until the bust in magazine publishing in the mid-1950s limited his market. Finlay's sample illustration for *The Hobbit* was sent to Tolkien via his British publisher, to whom he replied on October 11, 1963:

> Though it gives prospects of a general treatment rather heavier and more violent and airless than I should like, I thought it was good, and actually I thought Bilbo's rather rotund and babyish (but anxious) face was in keeping with his character up to that point. After the horrors of the "illustrations" to the translations [of *The Hobbit*] Mr. Finlay is a welcome relief. As long (as seems likely) he will leave humour to the text and pay reasonable attention to what the text says, I expect I shall be quite happy.

Unfortunately Finlay was not called on to illustrate *The Hobbit*. His sample illustration was first published posthumously in Gerry de la Ree's *The Book of Virgil Finlay* (1975).

Rescue by the eagles. Illustration by Eric Fraser for the 1979 Folio Society edition. Fraser (1902–1983) began his career as an illustrator in the advertising field and later turned to both magazine and book illustration. He worked mainly in black ink, with white overlaid to give something of the quality of wood engraving. His striking illustrations can be found in many books, including *English Legends* (1950) and *Folklore, Myths and Legends of Britain* (1973). For the 1977 Folio Society edition of *The Lord of the Rings,* he redrew illustrations by Queen Margrethe II of Denmark (b. 1940), resizing them to work as chapter headings. The Queen's work is credited to her pseudonym, Ingahild Grathmer. She had discovered *The Lord of the Rings* around 1969, and this rekindled her interest in drawing. Her illustrations were sent to Tolkien and found among his papers after his death. Fraser's edition of *The Hobbit* similarly includes illustrations as headings to each chapter, along with two full-page drawings. A fine monograph on the artist is *Eric Fraser: Designer and Illustrator* (1998) by Sylvia Backemeyer. One additional illustration by Fraser can be found on page 264.

13 Bilbo's rescue by the eagle recalls a scene in Chaucer's unfinished poem "The House of Fame," which was probably written between 1378 and 1381. In it, the poet (Chaucer himself) relates a dream in which an eagle has seized him and carried him up into the sky to the House of Fame. The talkative eagle serves as Chaucer's guide. I give here two short scenes in Middle English from *The Student's Chaucer* (1895), edited by Walter W. Skeat, followed by prose translations by John S. P. Tatlock and Percy MacKaye from *The Complete Poetical Works of Geoffrey Chaucer* (1912):

This egle, of which I have yow told,
That shoon with fethres as of gold,
Which that so hyë gan to sore,
I gan beholde more and more,
To see hir beautee and the wonder;
But never was ther dint of thonder,
Ne that thing that men calle foudre,
That smoot somtyme a tour to poudre,
And in his swifte coming brende,
That so swythe gan descende,
As this foul, whan hit behelde
That I a-roume was in the felde;
And with his grimme pawes stronge,
Within his sharpe nayles longe,
Me, fleinge, at a swappe he hente,
And with his sours agayn up wente,
Me caryinge in his clawes starke
As lightly as I were a larke,
How high, I can not telle yow,
For I cam up, I niste how,
For so astonied and a-sweved
Was every vertu in my heved,
What with his sours and with my drede,
That al my feling gan to dede;
For-why hit was to greet affray.
			(Book II, lines 529–53)

And I adoun gan loken tho,
And beheld feldes and plaines,

moonlit spikes of rock sticking out of black shadows.**13** Summer or not, it seemed very cold. He shut his eyes and wondered if he could hold on any longer. Then he imagined what would happen if he did not. He felt sick.

The flight ended only just in time for him, just before his arms gave way. He loosed Dori's ankles with a gasp and fell onto the rough platform of an eagle's eyrie. There he lay without speaking, and his thoughts were a mixture of surprise at being saved from the fire, and fear lest he fall off that narrow place into the deep shadows on either side. He was feeling very queer indeed in his head by this time after the dreadful adventures of the last three days with next to nothing to eat, and he found himself saying aloud: "Now I know what a piece of bacon feels like when it is suddenly picked out of the pan on a fork and put back on the shelf!"

"No you don't!" he heard Dori answering, "because the bacon knows that it will get back in the pan sooner or later; and it is to be hoped we shan't. Also eagles aren't forks!"

"O no! Not a bit like storks – forks, I mean," said Bilbo sitting up and looking anxiously at the eagle who was perched close by. He wondered what other nonsense he had been saying, and if the eagle would think it rude. You ought not to be rude to an eagle, when you are only the size of a hobbit, and are up in his eyrie at night!

The eagle only sharpened his beak on a stone and trimmed his feathers and took no notice.

Soon another eagle flew up. "The Lord of the Eagles bids you to bring your prisoners to the Great Shelf," he cried and was off again. The other seized Dori in his claws and flew away with him into the night leaving Bilbo all alone. He had just strength to wonder what the messenger had meant by 'prisoners,' and to begin to think of being torn up for supper like a rabbit, when his own turn came.

The eagle came back, seized him in his talons by the

The Lord of the Eagles speaks with Gandalf. Illustration by Évelyne Drouhin for the 1983 French edition. Drouhin (b. 1955) has illustrated other French children's books and French translations of works by the Brothers Grimm. The artist's last name is sometimes given as Faivre-Drouhin. Two additional illustrations by Drouhin can be found on pages 189 and 270.

And now hilles, and now mountaines,
Now valeys, and now forestes,
And now, unethes, grete bestes;
Now riveres, now citees,
Now tounes, and now grete trees,
Now shippes sailinge in the see.
But thus sone in a whyle he
Was flowen fro the grounde so hyë,
That al the world, as to myn yë,
No more semed than a prikke;
Or elles was the air so thikke
That I ne mighte not discerne.
(Book II, lines 896–909)

This eagle that I have spoken of, that soared so far on high and shone as with feathers of gold, I began to behold more and more, and to see its beauty and the marvel of it all. But never was lightning-stroke, or that thing which men call thunderbolt — which sometimes has smitten a tower to powder and burned it by its swift onslaught — that so swiftly descended as this bird, when it beheld me abroad in the field. And with his grim mighty feet, within his long sharp claws, he caught me at a swoop as I fled, and soared up again, carrying me in his strong claws as easily as if I were a lark, — how high I cannot tell you, for how I came up I knew not. For every faculty in my head was so astonied and stunned, what with his swift ascent and mine own fear, that all my sense of feeling died away, so great was mine affright.
(p. 523)

And then I looked down and beheld fields and plains, and now hills, now mountains, now valleys, now forests, and now (but scarce I saw them) great beasts; now rivers, now cities, now towns, now great trees, now ships sailing on the sea. But soon, after a while, he had flown so high from the ground that all the world seemed no more than a point to mine eyes; or else the air was so thick that I could discern naught. (p. 528)

back of his coat, and swooped off. This time he flew only a short way. Very soon Bilbo was laid down, trembling with fear, on a wide shelf of rock on the mountainside. There was no path down on to it save by flying; and no path down off it except by jumping over a precipice. There he found all the others sitting with their backs to the mountain wall. The Lord of the Eagles also was there and was speaking to Gandalf.

It seemed that Bilbo was not going to be eaten after all. The wizard and the eagle-lord appeared to know one another slightly, and even to be on friendly terms. As a matter of fact Gandalf, who had often been in the mountains, had once rendered a service to the eagles and healed their lord from an arrow-wound. So you see 'prisoners' had meant 'prisoners rescued from the gob-

The Misty Mountains looking West from the Eyrie towards Goblin Gate

The Misty Mountains looking West from the Eyrie towards Goblin Gate by J.R.R. Tolkien, one of the standard black-and-white illustrations that has appeared in *The Hobbit* since 1937.
   An earlier version, which differs slightly, can be seen in *Artist* (No. 110). In both versions, Goblin Gate (through which Bilbo escaped) can be seen as a shaded spot in the mountains at the upper right. This illustration appears in *Artist* (No. 111) and *Pictures* (No. 8, left). A version of it colored by H. E. Riddett first appeared in *The Hobbit Calendar 1976* (1975) and in *Pictures* (No. 8, right).

lins' only, and not captives of the eagles. As Bilbo listened to the talk of Gandalf he realized that at last they were going to escape really and truly from the dreadful mountains. He was discussing plans with the Great Eagle for carrying the dwarves and himself and Bilbo far away and setting them down well on their journey across the plains below.

   The Lord of the Eagles would not take them anywhere near where men lived. "They would shoot at us with their great bows of yew," he said, "for they would think we were after their sheep. And at other times they would be right. No! we are glad to cheat the goblins of their sport, and glad to repay our thanks to you, but we will not risk ourselves for dwarves in the southward plains."

"Very well," said Gandalf. "Take us where and as far as you will! We are already deeply obliged to you. But in the meantime we are famished with hunger."

"I am nearly dead of it," said Bilbo in a weak little voice that nobody heard.

"That can perhaps be mended," said the Lord of the Eagles.

Later on you might have seen a bright fire on the shelf of rock and the figures of the dwarves round it cooking and making a fine roasting smell. The eagles had brought up dry boughs for fuel, and they had brought rabbits, hares, and a small sheep. The dwarves managed all the preparations. Bilbo was too weak to help, and anyway he was not much good at skinning rabbits or cutting up meat, being used to having it delivered by the butcher all ready to cook. Gandalf, too, was lying down after doing his part in setting the fire going, since Oin and Gloin had lost their tinder-boxes. (Dwarves have never taken to matches even yet.)

So ended the adventures of the Misty Mountains. Soon Bilbo's stomach was feeling full and comfortable again, and he felt he could sleep contentedly, though really he would have liked a loaf and butter better than bits of meat toasted on sticks. He slept curled up on the hard rock more soundly than ever he had done on his feather-bed in his own little hole at home. But all night he dreamed of his own house and wandered in his sleep into all his different rooms looking for something that he could not find nor remember what it looked like.

Bilbo Woke Up with the Early Sun in His Eyes by J.R.R. Tolkien, one of the standard color illustrations for *The Hobbit*, first published in the 1938 American edition (where it was slightly cropped), but not included in the English edition.

In painting the eagle, Tolkien's interest in the smallest details of the natural world is apparent, as is his perfectionism, which led him to model the bird on an illustration of a golden eagle by Archibald Thorburn. Christopher Tolkien remembers finding the picture for his father in T. A. Coward's *Birds of the British Isles and Their Eggs* (1919). Thorburn's illustration (left) is of an immature bird, and the young of this species have a white base to the tail. Wayne G. Hammond and Christina Scull have determined that Thorburn's illustration (reproduced as a chromolithograph) originally appeared in Lord Lilford's *Birds of the British Islands* (1891), from which Coward reprinted it in his volume (*Artist,* p. 124). Thorburn (1860–1935) was one of the great bird artists of the late nineteenth and early twentieth centuries.Tolkien's illustration appears in *Artist* (No. 113) and *Pictures* (No. 9), in the latter under the title *Bilbo Woke with the Early Sun in his Eyes.*

7

Queer Lodgings

⟨ THE NEXT MORNING BILBO WOKE UP with the early sun in his eyes. He jumped up to look at the time and to go and put his kettle on — and found he was not home at all. So he sat down and wished in vain for a wash and a brush. He did not get either, nor tea nor toast nor bacon for his breakfast, only cold mutton and rabbit. And after that he had to get ready for a fresh start. ⟩

This time he was allowed to climb on to an eagle's back and cling between his wings. The air rushed over him and he shut his eyes. The dwarves were crying farewells and promising to repay the Lord of the Eagles[1] if ever they could, as off rose fifteen great birds from the mountain's side. The sun was still close to the eastern edge of things. The morning was cool, and mists were in the valleys and hollows and twined here and there about the peaks and pinnacles of the hills. Bilbo opened an eye to peep and saw that the birds were already high up and the world was far away, and the mountains were falling back behind them into the distance. He shut his eyes again and held on tighter.

"Don't pinch!" said his eagle. "You need not be frightened like a rabbit, even if you look rather like one. It is a fair morning with little wind. What is finer than flying?"

Bilbo would have liked to say: "A warm bath and late

[1] The reading "lord of the eagles," with lowercase initial letters, is original to the *1937* text in this instance and on the following page. The *1951, 1966-Ball,* and *1966-Longmans/ Unwin* texts retain the lowercase initials. However, the *1966-A&U,* the *1967-HM,* and the 1978 fourth edition published by Allen & Unwin use "Lord of the Eagles." The change may have been made for editorial convention; yet Tolkien himself used the uppercase initial letters (in *1937* and onward) when introducing the Lord of the Eagles in the previous chapter.

⨯

2 Some Tolkien commentators, including Robert Foster in his *Complete Guide to Middle-earth*, have been tempted to equate the Lord of the Eagles in *The Hobbit* with Gwaihir the Windlord, the eagle who rescues Gandalf in *The Lord of the Rings*. However, this cannot be the case, for in Chapter 4 of Book V of *The Return of the King*, "The Field of Cormallen," Gandalf says to Gwaihir: "Twice you have borne me, Gwaihir my friend." The two previous times were demonstrably Gandalf's escape from Orthanc and when Gwaihir bore Gandalf to Lorien after finding him on the peak of Zirak-zigil subsequent to his fight with the Balrog. These two instances exclude the possibility of Gwaihir being the eagle who rescued Gandalf in *The Hobbit*.

breakfast on the lawn afterwards;" but he thought it better to say nothing at all, and to let go his clutch just a tiny bit.

After a good while the eagles must have seen the point they were making for, even from their great height, for they began to go down circling round in great spirals. They did this for a long while, and at last the hobbit opened his eyes again. The earth was much nearer, and below them were trees that looked like oaks and elms, and wide grass lands, and a river running through it all. But cropping out of the ground, right in the path of the stream which looped itself about it, was a great rock, almost a hill of stone, like a last outpost of the distant mountains, or a huge piece cast miles into the plain by some giant among giants.

Quickly now to the top of this rock the eagles swooped one by one and set down their passengers.

"Farewell!" they cried, "wherever you fare, till your eyries receive you at the journey's end!" That is the polite thing to say among eagles.

"May the wind under your wings bear you where the sun sails and the moon walks," answered Gandalf, who knew the correct reply.

And so they parted. And though the Lord of the Eagles became in after days the King of All Birds and wore a golden crown,[2] and his fifteen chieftains golden collars (made of the gold that the dwarves gave them), Bilbo never saw them again — except high and far off in the battle of Five Armies. But as that comes in at the end of this tale we will say no more about it just now.

There was a flat space on the top of the hill of stone and a well worn path with many steps leading down it to the river, across which a ford of huge flat stones led to the grass-land beyond the stream. There was a little cave (a wholesome one with a pebbly floor) at the foot of the steps and near the end of the stony ford. Here the party gathered and discussed what was to be done.

"I always meant to see you all safe (if possible) over the mountains," said the wizard, "and now by good management *and* good luck I have done it. Indeed we are now a good deal further east than I ever meant to come with you, for after all this is not my adventure. I may look in on it again before it is all over, but in the meanwhile I have some other pressing business to attend to."

The dwarves groaned and looked most distressed, and Bilbo wept. They had begun to think Gandalf was going to come all the way and would always be there to help them out of difficulties. "I am not going to disappear this very instant," said he. "I can give you a day or two more. Probably I can help you out of your present plight, and I need a little help myself. We have no food, and no baggage, and no ponies to ride; and you don't know where you are. Now I can tell you that. You are still some miles north of the path which we should have been following, if we had not left the mountain pass in a hurry. Very few people live in these parts, unless they have come here since I was last down this way, which is some years ago. But there is *somebody* that I know of, who lives not far away. That Somebody made the steps on the great rock – the Carrock I believe he calls it. He does not come here often, certainly not in the daytime, and it is no good waiting for him. In fact it would be very dangerous. We must go and find him; and if all goes well at our meeting, I think I shall be off and wish you like the eagles 'farewell wherever you fare!' "

They begged him not to leave them. They offered him dragon-gold and silver and jewels, but he would not change his mind. "We shall see, we shall see!" he said, "and I think I have earned already some of your dragon-gold – when you have got it."

After that they stopped pleading. Then they took off their clothes and bathed in the river, which was shallow

3 Tolkien described the Carrock as "a great rock, almost a hill of stone," about which is looped a stream. The word *carrock* seems to contain Old English *carr,* "a stone, rock." *Carrock* also appears in volume one of *The English Dialect Dictionary* (1898) compiled by Joseph Wright, where it is found as a variant spelling of *currick,* "a cairn, a heap of stones, used as a boundary mark, burial place, or guide for travellers."

Tom Shippey has also observed that *carrecc* is Old Welsh for "rock." And Mark Hooker, in "And Why Is It Called the Carrock? – Bilbo Baggins" in *Beyond Bree,* November 2001, has suggested similarities between Tolkien's Carrock and Carreg Cennen, the limestone carreg in the Black Mountains in Carmarthenshire in Wales.

4 The name *Beorn* is actually an Old English word for "man, warrior," but originally meant "bear"; it is cognate with the Old Norse *björn,* "bear."

and clear and stony at the ford. When they had dried in the sun, which was now strong and warm, they were refreshed, if still sore and a little hungry. Soon they crossed the ford (carrying the hobbit), and then began to march through the long green grass and down the lines of the wide-armed oaks and the tall elms.

"And why is it called the Carrock?" asked Bilbo as he went along at the wizard's side.

"He called it the Carrock, because carrock is his word for it. He calls things like that carrocks, and this one is *the* Carrock because it is the only one near his home and he knows it well."**3**

"Who calls it? Who knows it?"

"The Somebody I spoke of – a very great person. You must all be very polite when I introduce you. I shall introduce you slowly, two by two, I think; and you *must* be careful not to annoy him, or heaven knows what will happen. He can be appalling when he is angry, though he is kind enough if humoured. Still I warn you he gets angry easily."

The dwarves all gathered round when they heard the wizard talking like this to Bilbo. "Is that the person you are taking us to now?" they asked. "Couldn't you find someone more easy-tempered? Hadn't you better explain it all a bit clearer?" – and so on.

"Yes it certainly is! No I could not! And I was explaining very carefully," answered the wizard crossly. "If you must know more, his name is Beorn.**4** He is very strong, and he is a skin-changer."

"What! a furrier, a man that calls rabbits conies, when he doesn't turn their skins into squirrels?" asked Bilbo.

"Good gracious heavens, no, no, NO, NO!" said Gandalf. "Don't be a fool Mr. Baggins if you can help it; and in the name of all wonder don't mention the word furrier again as long as you are within a hundred miles of his house, nor rug, cape, tippet, muff, nor any other such unfortunate word! He is a skin-changer. He changes his skin: sometimes he is a huge black bear, sometimes he is a great strong black-haired man with huge arms and a great beard. I cannot tell you much more, though that ought to be enough. Some say that he is a bear descended from the great and ancient bears of the mountains that lived there before the giants came. Others say that he is a man descended from the first men who lived before Smaug or the other dragons came into this part of the world, and before the goblins came into the hills out of the North. I cannot say, though I fancy the last is the true tale. He is not the sort of person to ask questions of.

"At any rate he is under no enchantment but his own. He lives in an oak-wood and has a great wooden house; and as a man he keeps cattle and horses which are nearly as marvellous as himself. They work for him and talk to him. He does not eat them; neither does he hunt or eat wild animals. He keeps hives and hives of great fierce bees, and lives most on cream and honey. As a bear he ranges far and wide.[5] I once saw him sitting all alone on the top of the Carrock at night watching the moon sinking towards the Misty Mountains, and I heard him growl in the tongue of bears: 'The day will come when they will perish and I shall go back!' That is why I believe he once came from the mountains himself."

Bilbo and the dwarves had now plenty to think about, and they asked no more questions. They still had a long way to walk before them. Up slope and down dale they plodded. It grew very hot. Sometimes they rested under the trees, and then Bilbo felt so hungry that he would have eaten acorns, if any had been ripe enough yet to have fallen to the ground.

It was the middle of the afternoon before they noticed that great patches of flowers had begun to spring up, all the same kinds growing together as if they had been planted. Especially there was clover, waving patches of

[5] Tom Shippey has observed that Beorn has "a very close analogue in Bǫthvarr Bjarki (= 'little bear'), a hero from the Norse *Saga of Hrólfr Kraki,* and another in Beowulf himself, whose name is commonly explained as Beowulf = 'bees' wolf' = honey-eater = bear, and who breaks swords, rips off arms and cracks ribs with ursine power and clumsiness" (*The Road to Middle-earth,* second edition, p. 73).

In Chapter 33 of *The Saga of Hrolf Kraki,* Bothvar Bjarki sits idle and removed from a battle while his fetch, a great bear, defends King Hrolf. When Bothvar is roused, the bear disappears, and Hrolf and his men, including Bothvar, are killed.

What is perhaps a closer analogue is found in Bothvar's father, Bjorn, whose story is told in Chapters 19–20. When Bjorn has spurned the advances of King Hring's queen, she curses him to become a bear during the daytime and revert to being a man during the night.

Tolkien knew *The Saga of Hrolf Kraki* very well. One of his students at Leeds, Stella Mills, translated it under the supervision of Tolkien's colleague and close friend E. V. Gordon. Several years later, Mills's translation was published as *The Saga of Hrolf Kraki* (1933), with an introduction by Gordon. This edition is dedicated to Gordon, Tolkien, and C. T. Onions, the lexicographer of the *Oxford English Dictionary.* Stella Mills received her B.A. at Leeds in 1924. She was a close friend of the Tolkien family for many years.

cockscomb clover, and purple clover, and wide stretches of short white sweet honey-smelling clover. There was a buzzing and a whirring and a droning in the air. Bees were busy everywhere. And such bees! Bilbo had never seen anything like them.

"If one was to sting me," he thought, "I should swell up as big again as I am!"

They were bigger than hornets. The drones were bigger than your thumb, a good deal, and the bands of yellow on their deep black bodies shone like fiery gold.

"We are getting near," said Gandalf. "We are on the edge of his bee-pastures."

After a while they came to a belt of tall and very ancient oaks, and beyond these to a high thorn-hedge through which you could neither see nor scramble.

"You had better wait here," said the wizard to the dwarves; "and when I call or whistle begin to come after me — you will see the way I go — but only in pairs, mind, about five minutes between each pair of you. Bombur is fattest and will do for two, he had better come alone and last. Come on Mr. Baggins! There is a gate somewhere round this way." And with that he went off along the hedge taking the frightened hobbit with him.

They soon came to a wooden gate, high and broad, beyond which they could see gardens and a cluster of low wooden buildings, some thatched and made of un-shaped logs: barns, stables, sheds, and a long low wooden house. Inside on the southward side of the great hedge were rows and rows of hives with bell-shaped tops made of straw. The noise of the giant bees flying to and fro and crawling in and out filled all the air.

The wizard and the hobbit pushed open the heavy creaking gate and went down a wide track towards the house. Some horses, very sleek and well-groomed, trotted up across the grass and looked at them intently

Gandalf and Bilbo speak with Beorn. Illustration by Maret Kernumees for the 1977 Estonian edition.

with very intelligent faces; then off they galloped to the buildings.

"They have gone to tell him of the arrival of strangers," said Gandalf.

Soon they reached a courtyard, three walls of which were formed by the wooden house and its two long wings. In the middle there was lying a great oak-trunk with many lopped branches beside it. Standing near was a huge man with a thick black beard and hair, and great bare arms and legs with knotted muscles. He was clothed in a tunic of wool down to his knees, and was leaning on a large axe. The horses were standing by him with their noses at his shoulder.

"Ugh! here they are!" he said to the horses. "They don't look dangerous. You can be off!" He laughed a great rolling laugh, put down his axe and came forward.

"Who are you and what do you want?" he asked gruffly, standing in front of them and towering tall above Gandalf. As for Bilbo he could easily have trotted through his legs without ducking his head to miss the fringe of the man's brown tunic.

"I am Gandalf," said the wizard.

"Never heard of him," growled the man. "And what's this little fellow?" he said, stooping down to frown at the hobbit with his bushy black eyebrows.

"That is Mr. Baggins, a hobbit of good family and unimpeachable reputation," said Gandalf. Bilbo bowed. He had no hat to take off, and was painfully conscious of his many missing buttons. "I am a wizard," continued Gandalf. "I have heard of you, if you have not heard of me; but perhaps you have heard of my good cousin Radagast[6] who lives near the Southern borders of Mirkwood?"

"Yes; not a bad fellow as wizards go, I believe. I used to see him now and again," said Beorn. "Well, now I know who you are, or who you say you are. What do you want?"

6 In referring to Radagast as "my good cousin," Gandalf is probably not suggesting actual close kinship. The *Oxford English Dictionary* supports three variant meanings of *cousin* that could apply here. First, as a term "applied to people of kindred races or nations (e.g. British and Americans)"; second, as "a person or thing having affinity of nature to another"; and, last, as "a term of intimacy, friendship or familiarity." Since Radagast and Gandalf are both wizards, the first meaning is probably intended.

Tolkien does not discuss the nature of wizards in *The Hobbit*, though in *The Lord of the Rings* we learn that they are called the Istari and they are five in number. Some highly interesting notes by Tolkien about the wizards are included in the section "The Istari" published in *Unfinished Tales*. A further short but important note appears in volume twelve of the *History, The Peoples of Middle-earth*.

The name *Radagast* is not easily decipherable, nor are its origins clear. Edward Gibbon's *The History of the Decline and Fall of the Roman Empire* (seven volumes, 1776–1788) tells of a Gothic leader named Radagaisus who invaded Italy in the early years of the fifth century. Other sources, including the eleventh-century German historian Adam of Bremen, tell of a possible Slavic deity called *Redigast*. Yet these similarities in name reveal nothing about Tolkien's wizard Radagast the Brown.

7 Beorn's Hall is a typical example of a
Germanic hall, an example of which is
also found in the poem *Beowulf*. It is an
oblong hall built of timber, with rows of
wooden pillars dividing the inside into a
central nave and side aisles. Such halls
usually had doors at both ends, but windows in the modern sense were unknown. A hearth-fire would burn in the
middle, and the smoke would escape
through shutters in the roof, which were
also used to provide light in the day.
The raised floor in the side aisles served
as a sitting place during the day and at
night as a place for beds.

"To tell you the truth, we have lost our luggage and
nearly lost our way, and are rather in need of help, or at
least of advice. I may say we have had rather a bad time
with goblins in the mountains."

"Goblins?" said the big man less gruffly. "O ho, so
you've been having trouble with *them* have you? What
did you go near them for?"

"We did not mean to. They surprised us at night in a
pass which we had to cross; we were coming out of the
Lands over West into these countries — it is a long tale."

"Then you had better come inside and tell me some
of it, if it won't take all day," said the man leading the way
through a dark door that opened out of the courtyard
into the house.

Following him they found themselves in a wide hall
with a fire-place in the middle.**7** Though it was summer
there was a wood-fire burning and the smoke was rising
to the blackened rafters in search of the way out through
an opening in the roof. They passed through this dim
hall, lit only by the fire and the hole above it, and came
through another smaller door into a sort of veranda
propped on wooden posts made of single tree-trunks. It
faced south and was still warm and filled with the light
of the westering sun which slanted into it, and fell
golden on the garden full of flowers that came right up
to the steps.

Here they sat on wooden benches while Gandalf
began his tale, and Bilbo swung his dangling legs and
looked at the flowers in the garden, wondering what
their names could be, as he had never seen half of them
before.

"I was coming over the mountains with a friend or
two. . ." said the wizard.

"Or two? I can only see one, and a little one at that,"
said Beorn.

"Well to tell you the truth, I did not like to bother you
with a lot of us, until I found out if you were busy. I will
give a call, if I may."

"Go on, call away!"

So Gandalf gave a long shrill whistle, and presently Thorin and Dori came round the house by the garden path and stood bowing low before them.

"One or three you meant, I see!" said Beorn. "But these aren't hobbits, they are dwarves!"

"Thorin Oakenshield, at your service! Dori at your service!" said the two dwarves bowing again.

"I don't need your service, thank you," said Beorn, "but I expect you need mine. I am not over fond of dwarves; but if it is true you are Thorin (son of Thrain, son of Thror, I believe), and that your companion is respectable, and that you are enemies of goblins and are not up to any mischief in my lands — what are you up to, by the way?"

"They are on their way to visit the land of their fathers, away east beyond Mirkwood," put in Gandalf, "and it is entirely an accident that we are in your lands at all. We were crossing by the High Pass that should have brought us to the road that lies to the south of your country, when we were attacked by the evil goblins — as I was about to tell you."

"Go on telling, then!" said Beorn, who was never very polite.

"There was a terrible storm; the stone-giants were out hurling rocks, and at the head of the pass we took refuge in a cave, the hobbit and I and several of our companions. . ."

"Do you call two several?"

"Well, no. As a matter of fact there were more than two."

"Where are they? Killed, eaten, gone home?"

"Well, no. They don't seem all to have come when I whistled. Shy, I expect. You see, we are very much afraid that we are rather a lot for you to entertain."

"Go on, whistle again! I am in for a party, it seems, and one or two more won't make much difference," growled Beorn.

Beorn's Hall by J.R.R. Tolkien, one of the standard black-and-white illustrations that has appeared in *The Hobbit* since 1937. This illustration appears in *Artist* (No. 116) and in *Pictures* (No. 10, left). A version of this illustration colored by H. E. Riddett first appeared in *The Hobbit Calendar 1976* (1975), and in *Pictures* (No. 10, right).

Firelight in Beorn's House by J.R.R. Tolkien (left), an earlier version with an angled perspective of the hall, which also appears in *Artist* (No. 114), shares the perspective of a drawing of the interior of a Norse hall in E. V. Gordon's *An Introduction to Old Norse* (1927). Gordon (1896–1938) was a former student of Tolkien's who became his colleague at Leeds and a close friend. They collaborated on the 1925 edition of the Middle English poem *Sir Gawain and the Green Knight* and worked together on other projects until Gordon's untimely death at the age of forty-two. For more on Gordon, see my own essay " 'An Industrious Little Devil': E. V. Gordon as Friend and Collaborator with Tolkien" in *Tolkien the Medievalist* (2002), edited by Jane Chance.

The illustration (left) in Gordon's book is uncredited, but it is a close copy of one that appears in a number of sources, including Andreas Heusler's *Die Altergermanische Dichtung* (1924), Axel Olrik's *Nordisches Geistesleben in Heidnischer und Frühchristlicher Zeit* (1908), and some translations of *Beowulf*. The ultimate source is an essay *Den Islanske Bolig i Fristatstiden* (1894) by Valtýr Guðmundsson, published as a small booklet. This essay includes an illustration dated 1894 and drawn by the painter E. Rondahl after a model then found in the National Museum in Copenhagen. The model was made in the year 1892 and exhibited at the Columbian Exposition in Spain. It depicted a fully furnished Icelandic room from around the year 1000, showing the high-seats nearest the fire, the tables with drinking horns, and burning long-fires on the lower clay floor.

Gandalf whistled again; but Nori and Ori were there almost before he had stopped, for, if you remember, Gandalf had told them to come in pairs every five minutes.

"Hullo!" said Beorn. "You came pretty quick — where were you hiding? Come on my jack-in-the-boxes!"

"Nori at your service, Ori at . . ." they began; but Beorn interrupted them.

"Thank you! When I want your help I will ask for it. Sit down, and let's get on with this tale, or it will be supper-time before it is ended."

"As soon as we were asleep," went on Gandalf, "a crack at the back of the cave opened; goblins came out and grabbed the hobbit and the dwarves and our troop of ponies —"

"Troop of ponies? What were you — a travelling circus? Or were you carrying lots of goods? Or do you always call six a troop?"

"O no! As a matter of fact there were more than six ponies, for there were more than six of us — and well, here are two more!" Just at that moment Balin and Dwalin appeared and bowed so low that their beards swept the stone floor. The big man was frowning at first, but they did their best to be frightfully polite, and kept on nodding and bending and bowing and waving their hoods before their knees (in proper dwarf-fashion), till he stopped frowning and burst into a chuckling laugh: they looked so comical.

"Troop, was right," he said. "A fine comic one. Come in my merry men, and what are *your* names? I don't want your service just now, only your names; and then sit down and stop wagging!"

"Balin and Dwalin," they said not daring to be offended, and sat flop on the floor looking rather surprised.

"Now go on again!" said Beorn to the wizard.

"Where was I? O yes — I was *not* grabbed. I killed a goblin or two with a flash —"

"Good!" growled Beorn. "It is some good being a wizard, then."

"— and slipped inside the crack before it closed. I followed down into the main hall, which was crowded with goblins. The Great Goblin was there with thirty or forty armed guards. I thought to myself 'even if they were not all chained together, what can a dozen do against so many?' "

"A dozen! That's the first time I've heard eight called a dozen. Or have you still got some more jacks that haven't yet come out of their boxes?"

"Well, yes, there seem to be a couple more here now — Fili and Kili, I believe," said Gandalf, as these two now appeared and stood smiling and bowing.

"That's enough!" said Beorn. "Sit down and be quiet! Now go on, Gandalf!"

So Gandalf went on with the tale, until he came to the fight in the dark, the discovery of the lower gate, and their horror when they found that Mr. Baggins had been mislaid. "We counted ourselves and found that there was no hobbit. There were only fourteen of us left!"

"Fourteen! That's the first time I've heard one from ten leave fourteen. You mean nine, or else you haven't told me yet all the names of your party."

"Well, of course you haven't seen Oin and Gloin yet. And, bless me! here they are. I hope you will forgive them for bothering you."

"O let 'em all come! Hurry up! Come along, you two, and sit down! But look here, Gandalf, even now we have only got yourself and ten dwarves and the hobbit that was lost. That only makes eleven (plus one mislaid) and not fourteen, unless wizards count differently to other people. But now please get on with the tale." Beorn did not show it more than he could help, but really he had begun to get very interested. You see, in the old days he

8 This is the reverse of the ploy that Gandalf successfully worked on Bilbo in Chapter 1. There Gandalf made an appointment to tea for himself and sent the dwarves ahead unannounced, arriving with the last of them, only to demand some red wine, eggs, cold chicken, and pickles.

had known the very part of the mountains that Gandalf was describing. He nodded and he growled, when he heard of the hobbit's reappearance and of their scramble down the stone-slide and of the wolf-ring in the woods.

When Gandalf came to their climbing into trees with the wolves all underneath, he got up and strode about and muttered: "I wish I had been there! I would have given them more than fireworks!"

"Well," said Gandalf very glad to see that his tale was making a good impression, "I did the best I could. There we were with the wolves going mad underneath us and the forest beginning to blaze in places, when the goblins came down from the hills and discovered us. They yelled with delight and sang songs making fun of us. *Fifteen birds in five fir-trees. . . .*"

"Good heavens!" growled Beorn. "Don't pretend that goblins can't count. They can. Twelve isn't fifteen and they know it."

"And so do I. There were Bifur and Bofur as well. I haven't ventured to introduce them before, but here they are."

In came Bifur and Bofur. "And me!" gasped Bombur puffing up behind. He was fat, and also angry at being left till last. He refused to wait five minutes, and followed immediately after the other two.

"Well, now there *are* fifteen of you; and since goblins can count, I suppose that is all that there were up the trees. Now perhaps we can finish this story without any more interruptions." Mr. Baggins saw then how clever Gandalf had been. The interruptions had really made Beorn more interested in the story, and the story had kept him from sending the dwarves off at once like suspicious beggars.**8** He never invited people into his house, if he could help it. He had very few friends and they lived a good way away; and he never invited more than a couple of these to his house at a time. Now he had got fifteen strangers sitting in his porch!

By the time the wizard had finished his tale and had told of the eagles' rescue and of how they had all been brought to the Carrock, the sun had fallen behind the peaks of the Misty Mountains and the shadows were long in Beorn's garden.

"A very good tale!" said he. "The best I have heard for a long while. If all beggars could tell such a good one, they might find me kinder. You may be making it all up, of course, but you deserve a supper for the story all the same. Let's have something to eat!"

"Yes please!" they all said together. "Thank you very much!"

Inside the hall it was now quite dark. Beorn clapped his hands, and in trotted four beautiful white ponies and several large long-bodied grey dogs. Beorn said something to them in a queer language like animal noises turned into talk. They went out again and soon came back carrying torches in their mouths, which they lit at the fire and stuck in low brackets on the pillars of the hall about the central hearth. The dogs could stand on their hind-legs when they wished, and carry things with their fore-feet. Quickly they got out boards and trestles from the side walls and set them up near the fire.

Then baa — baa — baa! was heard, and in came some snow-white sheep led by a large coal-black ram. One bore a white cloth embroidered at the edges with figures of animals; others bore on their broad backs trays with bowls and platters and knives and wooden spoons, which the dogs took and quickly laid on the trestle-tables. These were very low, low enough even for Bilbo to sit at comfortably. Beside them a pony pushed two low-seated benches with wide rush-bottoms and little short thick legs for Gandalf and Thorin, while at the far end he put Beorn's big black chair of the same sort (in which he sat with his great legs stuck far out under the table). These were all the chairs he had in his hall, and he prob-

Beorn's animal servants. Illustration by Horus Engels for the 1957 German edition. Engels had hopes of illustrating *The Hobbit* as early as the mid-1940s. On November 1, 1946, he sent Tolkien a letter illustrated with color illustrations of the Trolls, Gollum, and Gandalf. The original is now on display at the Department of Special Collections, Marquette University, Milwaukee, Wisconsin. On December 7, 1946, Tolkien wrote to his British publisher, Sir Stanley Unwin: "I continue to receive letters from poor Horus Engels about a German translation. . . . He has sent me some illustrations (of the Trolls and Gollum) which despite certain merits, such as one would expect of a German, are I fear too 'Disnified' for my taste: Bilbo with a dribbling nose, and Gandalf as a figure of vulgar fun rather than the Odinic wanderer that I think of" (*Letters*, No. 107).

Little is known of Engels. In 1946 he was living in Wolfsburg, Germany. From 1951 through 1963 he illustrated seven books, mainly by German authors (including one by Walter Scherf, the translator of *The Hobbit*). Among these is another translation from the English, *The Rolling Season* (1963) by William Mayne.

Engels's colored work is both more expressive and interesting than his black-and-white work, and it is a pity that his illustrated edition of *The Hobbit* contains only the latter. Two additional illustrations by Engels can be found on pages 223 and 232.

Beorn's animal servants. Illustration by Klaus Ensikat for the 1971 German edition.

ably had them low like the tables for the convenience of the wonderful animals that waited on him. What did the rest sit on? They were not forgotten. The other ponies came in rolling round drum-shaped sections of logs, smoothed and polished, and low enough even for Bilbo; so soon they were all seated at Beorn's table, and the hall had not seen such a gathering for many a year.

There they had a supper, or a dinner, such as they had not had since they left the Last Homely House in the West and said good-bye to Elrond. The light of the torches and the fire flickered about them, and on the table were two tall red beeswax candles. All the time they ate, Beorn in his deep rolling voice told tales of the wild lands on this side of the mountains, and especially of the dark and dangerous wood, that lay outstretched

Beorn's Hall. Illustration by Ryûichi Terashima for the 1965 Japanese edition.

far to North and South a day's ride before them, barring their way to the East, the terrible forest of Mirkwood.

The dwarves listened and shook their beards, for they knew that they must soon venture into that forest and that after the mountains it was the worst of the perils they had to pass before they came to the dragon's stronghold. When dinner was over they began to tell tales of their own, but Beorn seemed to be growing drowsy and paid little heed to them. They spoke most of gold and silver and jewels and the making of things by smith-craft, and Beorn did not appear to care for such things: there were no things of gold or silver in his hall, and few save the knives were made of metal at all.

They sat long at the table with their wooden drinking-bowls filled with mead.[9] The dark night came on outside. The fires in the middle of the hall were built with fresh logs and the torches were put out, and still they sat in the light of the dancing flames with the pillars of the house standing tall behind them, and dark at the top like trees of the forest. Whether it was magic or not, it seemed to Bilbo that he heard a sound like wind in the branches stirring in the rafters, and the hoot of owls. Soon he began to nod with sleep and the voices seemed to grow far away, until he woke with a start.

The great door had creaked and slammed. Beorn was gone. The dwarves were sitting cross-legged on the floor round the fire, and presently they began to sing. Some of the verses were like this, but there were many more, and their singing went on for a long while:

> *The wind was on the withered heath,*
> *but in the forest stirred no leaf:*
> *there shadows lay by night and day,*
> *and dark things silent crept beneath.*
>
> *The wind came down from mountains cold,*
> *and like a tide it roared and rolled;*

[9] Mead is an alcoholic beverage made from fermented honey and water. The drink was very popular in Anglo-Saxon times.

the branches groaned, the forest moaned,
and leaves were laid upon the mould.

The wind went on from West to East;
all movement in the forest ceased,
but shrill and harsh across the marsh
its whistling voices were released.

The grasses hissed, their tassels bent,
the reeds were rattling — on it went
o'er shaken pool under heavens cool
where racing clouds were torn and rent.

It passed the lonely Mountain bare
and swept above the dragon's lair:
there black and dark lay boulders stark
and flying smoke was in the air.

It left the world and took its flight
over the wide seas of the night.
The moon set sail upon the gale,
and stars were fanned to leaping light.

Bilbo began to nod again. Suddenly up stood Gandalf.

"It is time for us to sleep," he said, " — for us, but not I think for Beorn. In this hall we can rest sound and safe, but I warn you all not to forget what Beorn said before he left us: you must not stray outside until the sun is up, on your peril."

Bilbo found that beds had already been laid at the side of the hall, on a sort of raised platform between the pillars and the outer wall. For him there was a little mattress of straw and woollen blankets. He snuggled into them very gladly, summertime though it was. The fire burned low and he fell asleep. Yet in the night he woke: the fire had now sunk to a few embers; the dwarves and

The Hill: Hobbiton-across-the Water by J.R.R. Tolkien.

Rivendell by J.R.R. Tolkien.

Bilbo Woke Up with the Early Sun in His Eyes by J.R.R. Tolkien.

Bilbo Comes to the Huts of the Raft-elves by J.R.R. Tolkien.

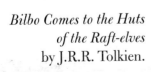

Conversation with Smaug
by J.R.R. Tolkien.

Dust jacket art for the 1937
British edition of *The Hobbit,*
by J.R.R. Tolkien.

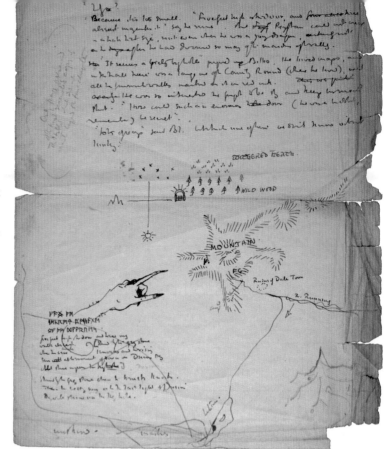

A page from the earliest
manuscript of *The Hobbit*,
including Thror's Map,
by J.R.R. Tolkien.

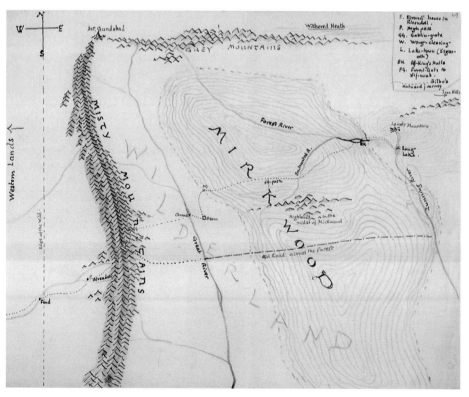

An early version
of the map of
Wilderland by
J.R.R. Tolkien.

A sketch labeled "Death of Smaug" by J.R.R. Tolkien.

The origin of Gandalf: a postcard, *Der Berggeist,* by Josef Madlener.

Gandalf Being Rescued by the Eagles
by Michael Hague, from his
1984 illustrated edition
of *The Hobbit*.

An illustrated letter, dated November 1, 1946, sent
to J.R.R. Tolkien by the German artist Horus Engels.

The Carrock by Alan Lee,
from his 1997 illustrated edition
of *The Hobbit.*

The Burial of Thorin by Alan Lee,
from his 1997 illustrated edition
of *The Hobbit.*

Rivendell by
Ted Nasmith, from
*Tolkien's World:
Paintings of Middle-
earth* (1992).

(Originally published in
The Tolkien Calendar 1988.)

Smaug over Esgaroth
by John Howe, from
*Tolkien's World:
Paintings of Middle-
earth* (1992).

(Originally published
as *The Death of Smaug*, in
The Tolkien Calendar 1988.)

Gandalf were all asleep, to judge by their breathing; a splash of white on the floor came from the high moon, which was peering down through the smoke-hole in the roof.

There was a growling sound outside, and a noise as of some great animal scuffling at the door. Bilbo wondered what it was, and whether it could be Beorn in enchanted shape, and if he would come in as a bear and kill them. He dived under the blankets and hid his head, and fell asleep again at last in spite of his fears.

It was full morning when he awoke. One of the dwarves had fallen over him in the shadows where he lay, and had rolled down with a bump from the platform on to the floor. It was Bofur, and he was grumbling about it, when Bilbo opened his eyes.

"Get up lazybones," he said, "or there will be no breakfast left for you."

Up jumped Bilbo. "Breakfast!" he cried. "Where is breakfast?"

"Mostly inside us," answered the other dwarves who were moving about the hall; "but what is left is out on the veranda. We have been about looking for Beorn ever since the sun got up; but there is no sign of him any-where, though we found breakfast laid as soon as we went out."

"Where is Gandalf?" asked Bilbo, moving off to find something to eat as quick as he could.

"O! out and about somewhere," they told him. But he saw no sign of the wizard all that day until the evening. Just before sunset he walked into the hall, where the hobbit and the dwarves were having supper, waited on by Beorn's wonderful animals, as they had been all day. Of Beorn they had seen and heard nothing since the night before, and they were getting puzzled.

"Where is our host, and where have *you* been all day yourself?" they all cried.

"One question at a time — and none till after supper!
I haven't had a bite since breakfast."

At last Gandalf pushed away his plate and jug — he
had eaten two whole loaves (with masses of butter and
honey and clotted cream) and drunk at least a quart of
mead — and he took out his pipe. "I will answer the second question first," he said, " — but bless me! this is a
splendid place for smoke rings!" Indeed for a long time
they could get nothing more out of him, he was so busy
sending smoke rings dodging round the pillars of the
hall, changing them into all sorts of different shapes and
colours, and setting them at last chasing one another out
of the hole in the roof. They must have looked very
queer from outside, popping out into the air one after
another, green, blue, red, silver-grey, yellow, white; big
ones, little ones; little ones dodging through big ones
and joining into figure-eights, and going off like a flock
of birds into the distance.

"I have been picking out bear-tracks," he said at last.
"There must have been a regular bears' meeting outside
here last night. I soon saw that Beorn could not have
made them all: there were far too many of them, and
they were of various sizes too. I should say there were little bears, large bears, ordinary bears, and gigantic big
bears, all dancing outside from dark to nearly dawn.
They came from almost every direction, except from the
west over the river, from the Mountains. In that direction
only one set of footprints led — none coming, only ones
going away from here. I followed these as far as the Carrock. There they disappeared into the river, but the
water was too deep and strong beyond the rock for me
to cross. It is easy enough, as you remember, to get from
this bank to the Carrock by the ford, but on the other
side is a cliff standing up from a swirling channel. I had
to walk miles before I found a place where the river was
wide and shallow enough for me to wade and swim, and
then miles back again to pick up the tracks again. By that

time it was too late for me to follow them far. They went straight off in the direction of the pine-woods on the east side of the Misty Mountains, where we had our pleasant little party with the Wargs the night before last. And now I think I have answered your first question, too," ended Gandalf, and he sat a long while silent.

Bilbo thought he knew what the wizard meant. "What shall we do," he cried, "if he leads all the Wargs and the goblins down here? We shall all be caught and killed! I thought you said he was not a friend of theirs."

"So I did. And don't be silly! You had better go to bed, your wits are sleepy."

The hobbit felt quite crushed, and as there seemed nothing else to do he did go to bed; and while the dwarves were still singing songs he dropped asleep, still puzzling his little head about Beorn, till he dreamed a dream of hundreds of black bears dancing slow heavy dances round and round in the moonlight in the court-yard. Then he woke up when everyone else was asleep, and he heard the same scraping, scuffling, snuffling, and growling as before.

Next morning they were all wakened by Beorn himself. "So here you all are still!" he said. He picked up the hobbit and laughed: "Not eaten up by Wargs or goblins or wicked bears yet I see"; and he poked Mr. Baggins' waistcoat most disrespectfully. "Little bunny is getting nice and fat again on bread and honey," he chuckled. "Come and have some more!"

So they all went to breakfast with him. Beorn was most jolly for a change; indeed he seemed to be in a splendidly good humour and set them all laughing with his funny stories; nor did they have to wonder long where he had been or why he was so nice to them, for he told them himself. He had been over the river and right back up into the mountains — from which you can guess that he could travel quickly, in bear's shape at any rate. From the burnt wolf-glade he had soon found out that part of their story was true; but he had found more than that: he had caught a Warg and a goblin wandering in the woods. From these he had got news: the goblin patrols were still hunting with Wargs for the dwarves, and they were fiercely angry because of the death of the Great Goblin, and also because of the burning of the chief wolf's nose and the death from the wizard's fire of many of his chief servants. So much they told him when he forced them, but he guessed there was more wickedness than this afoot, and that a great raid of the whole goblin army with their wolf-allies into the lands shadowed by the mountains might soon be made to find the dwarves, or to take vengeance on the men and creatures that lived there, and who they thought must be sheltering them.

"It was a good story, that of yours," said Beorn, "but I like it still better now I am sure it is true. You must forgive my not taking your word. If you lived near the edge of Mirkwood, you would take the word of no one that you did not know as well as your brother or better. As it is, I can only say that I have hurried home as fast as I could to see that you were safe, and to offer you any help that I can. I shall think more kindly of dwarves after this. Killed the Great Goblin, killed the Great Goblin!" he chuckled fiercely to himself.

"What did you do with the goblin and the Warg?" asked Bilbo suddenly.

"Come and see!" said Beorn, and they followed round the house. A goblin's head was stuck outside the gate and a warg-skin was nailed to a tree just beyond. Beorn was a fierce enemy. But now he was their friend, and Gandalf thought it wise to tell him their whole story and the reason of their journey, so that they could get the most help he could offer.

This is what he promised to do for them. He would provide ponies for each of them, and a horse for Gandalf, for their journey to the forest, and he would lade them with food to last them for weeks with care, and packed so as to be as easy as possible to carry — nuts, flour, sealed jars of dried fruits, and red earthenware pots of honey, and twice-baked cakes that would keep good a long time, and on a little of which they could march far. The making of these was one of his secrets; but honey was in them, as in most of his foods, and they were good to eat, though they made one thirsty. Water, he said, they would not need to carry this side of the forest, for there were streams and springs along the road. "But your way through Mirkwood is dark, dangerous and difficult,"[10] he said. "Water is not easy to find there, nor food. The time is not yet come for nuts (though it may be past and gone indeed before you get to the other side), and nuts are about all that grows there fit for food; in there the wild things are dark, queer, and savage. I will provide you with skins for carrying water, and I will give you some bows and arrows. But I doubt very much whether anything you find in Mirkwood will be wholesome to eat or to drink. There is one stream there, I know, black and strong which crosses the path. That you should neither drink of, nor bathe in; for I have heard that it carries enchantment and a great drowsiness and forgetfulness. And in the dim shadows of that place I don't think you will shoot anything, wholesome or unwholesome, without straying from the path. That you MUST NOT do, for any reason.

"That is all the advice I can give you. Beyond the edge of the forest I cannot help you much; you must depend on your luck and your courage and the food I send with you. At the gate of the forest I must ask you to send back my horse and my ponies. But I wish you all speed, and my house is open to you, if ever you come back this way again."

They thanked him, of course, with many bows and sweepings of their hoods and with many an "at your

10 On July 29, 1966, Tolkien wrote to his grandson:

Mirkwood is not an invention of mine, but a very ancient name, weighted with legendary associations. It was probably the Primitive Germanic name for the great mountainous forest regions that anciently formed a barrier to the south of the lands of Germanic expansion. In some traditions it became used especially of the boundary between Goths and Huns. I speak now from memory: its ancientness seems indicated by its appearance in very early German (11th c.?) as *mirkiwidu* although the **merkw-* stem "dark" is not otherwise found in German at all (only in O[ld] E[nglish], O[ld] S[axon], and O[ld] N[orse]), and the stem **widu- > witu* was in German (I think) limited to the sense of "timber," not very common, and did not survive into mod[ern] G[erman]. In O.E. *mirce* only survives in poetry, and in the sense "dark," or rather "gloomy," only in *Beowulf* [line] 1405 *ofer myrcan mor:* elsewhere only with the sense "murky" > wicked, hellish. It was never, I think, a mere "colour" word: "black," and was from the beginning weighted down with the sense of "gloom" . . . It seemed to me too good a fortune that Mirkwood remained intelligible (with exactly the right tone) in modern English to pass over: whether *mirk* is a Norse loan or a freshment of the obsolete O.E. word." (*Letters,* No. 289)

The name *Mirkwood,* as a great forest with similar associations, was used earlier in a novel that Tolkien knew well: *A Tale of the House of the Wolfings* (1888) by William Morris.

service, O master of the wide wooden halls!" But their spirits sank at his grave words, and they all felt that the adventure was far more dangerous than they had thought, while all the time, even if they passed all the perils of the road, the dragon was waiting at the end.

All that morning they were busy with preparations. Soon after midday they ate with Beorn for the last time, and after the meal they mounted the steeds he was lending them, and bidding him many farewells they rode off through his gate at a good pace.

As soon as they left his high hedges at the east of his fenced lands they turned north and then bore to the north-west. By his advice they were no longer making for the main forest-road to the south of his land. Had they followed the pass, their path would have led them down a stream from the mountains that joined the great river miles south of the Carrock. At that point there was a deep ford which they might have passed, if they had still had their ponies, and beyond that a track led to the skirts of the wood and to the entrance of the old forest road. But Beorn had warned them that that way was now often used by the goblins, while the forest-road itself, he had heard, was overgrown and disused at the eastern end and led to impassable marshes where the paths had long been lost. Its eastern opening had also always been far to the south of the Lonely Mountain, and would have left them still with a long and difficult northward march when they got to the other side. North of the Carrock the edge of Mirkwood drew closer to the borders of the Great River, and though here the Mountains too drew down nearer, Beorn advised them to take this way; for at a place a few days' ride due north of the Carrock was the gate of a little-known pathway through Mirkwood that led almost straight towards the Lonely Mountain.

"The goblins," Beorn had said, "will not dare to cross the Great River for a hundred miles north of the Carrock

nor to come near my house — it is well protected at
night! — but I should ride fast; for if they make their raid
soon they will cross the river to the south and scour all
the edge of the forest so as to cut you off, and Wargs run
swifter than ponies. Still you are safer going north, even
though you seem to be going back nearer to their strongholds; for that is what they will least expect, and they
will have the longer ride to catch you. Be off now as
quick as you may!"

That is why they were now riding in silence, galloping wherever the ground was grassy and smooth, with
the mountains dark on their left, and in the distance the
line of the river with its trees drawing ever closer. The
sun had only just turned west when they started, and till
evening it lay golden on the land about them. It was difficult to think of pursuing goblins behind, and when
they had put many miles between them and Beorn's
house they began to talk and to sing again and to forget
the dark forest-path that lay in front. But in the evening
when the dusk came on and the peaks of the mountains
glowered against the sunset they made a camp and set a
guard, and most of them slept uneasily with dreams in
which there came the howl of hunting wolves and the
cries of goblins.

Still the next morning dawned bright and fair again.
There was an autumn-like mist white upon the ground
and the air was chill, but soon the sun rose red in the
East and the mists vanished, and while the shadows
were still long they were off again. So they rode now for
two more days, and all the while they saw nothing save
grass and flowers and birds and scattered trees, and occasionally small herds of red deer browsing or sitting at
noon in the shade. Sometimes Bilbo saw the horns of
the harts sticking up out of the long grass, and at first he
thought they were the dead branches of trees. That third
evening they were so eager to press on, for Beorn had
said that they should reach the forest-gate early on the

fourth-day, that they rode still forward after dusk and into the night beneath the moon. As the light faded Bilbo thought he saw away to the right, or to the left, the shadowy form of a great bear prowling along in the same direction. But if he dared to mention it to Gandalf, the wizard only said: "Hush! Take no notice!"

Next day they started before dawn, though their night had been short. As soon as it was light they could see the forest coming as it were to meet them, or waiting for them like a black and frowning wall before them. The land began to slope up and up, and it seemed to the hobbit that a silence began to draw in upon them. Birds began to sing less. There were no more deer; not even rabbits were to be seen. By the afternoon they had reached the eaves of Mirkwood, and were resting almost beneath the great overhanging boughs of its outer trees. Their trunks were huge and gnarled, their branches twisted, their leaves were dark and long. Ivy grew on them and trailed along the ground.

"Well, here is Mirkwood!" said Gandalf. "The greatest of the forests of the Northern world. I hope you like the look of it. Now you must send back these excellent ponies you have borrowed."

The dwarves were inclined to grumble at this, but the wizard told them they were fools. "Beorn is not as far off as you seem to think, and you had better keep your promises anyway, for he is a bad enemy. Mr. Baggins' eyes are sharper than yours, if you have not seen each night after dark a great bear going along with us or sitting far off in the moon watching our camps. Not only to guard you and guide you, but to keep an eye on the ponies too. Beorn may be your friend, but he loves his animals as his children. You do not guess what kindness he has shown you in letting dwarves ride them so far and so fast, nor what would happen to you, if you tried to take them into the forest."

"What about the horse, then?" said Thorin. "You don't mention sending that back."

"I don't, because I am not sending it."

"What about *your* promise then?"

"I will look after that. I am not sending the horse back, I am riding it!"

Then they knew that Gandalf was going to leave them at the very edge of Mirkwood, and they were in despair. But nothing they could say would change his mind.

"Now we had this all out before, when we landed on the Carrock," he said. "It is no use arguing. I have, as I told you, some pressing business away south; and I am already late through bothering with you people. We may meet again before all is over, and then again of course we may not. That depends on your luck and on your courage and sense; and I am sending Mr. Baggins with you. I have told you before that he has more about him than you guess, and you will find that out before long. So cheer up Bilbo and don't look so glum. Cheer up Thorin and Company! This is your expedition after all. Think of the treasure at the end, and forget the forest and the dragon, at any rate until tomorrow morning!"

When tomorrow morning came he still said the same. So now there was nothing left to do but to fill their water-skins at a clear spring they found close to the forest-gate, and unpack the ponies. They distributed the packages as fairly as they could, though Bilbo thought his lot was wearisomely heavy, and did not at all like the idea of trudging for miles and miles with all that on his back.

"Don't you worry!" said Thorin. "It will get lighter all too soon. Before long I expect we shall all wish our packs heavier, when the food begins to run short."

Then at last they said good-bye to their ponies and turned their heads for home. Off they trotted gaily, seeming very glad to put their tails towards the shadow of Mirkwood. As they went away Bilbo could have sworn that a thing like a bear left the shadow of the trees and shambled off quickly after them.

Now Gandalf too said farewell. Bilbo sat on the

11 This is the only appearance of the word *orc* (other than in the sword name Orcrist) original to the first edition of *The Hobbit* (1937). (There is a second instance in the present text, in a portion of Chapter 5 that was rewritten for the 1951 second edition; see page 134.)

In his guide for translators, "Nomenclature of *The Lord of the Rings*," Tolkien wrote, "I originally took the word from Old English *orc* (*Beowulf* [line] 112 *orc-neas*) and the gloss *orc* = þyrs ('ogre'), *heldeofol* ('hell-devil'). This is supposed not to be connected with modern English *orc, ork*, a name applied to various sea-beasts of the dolphin order."

In *The Lord of the Rings* Tolkien virtually abandoned the use of *goblin* (it occurs less than ten times, and only in *The Fellowship of the Ring* and *The Two Towers*) and used *orc* throughout.

12 The reintroduction of the Necromancer here was originally quite casual; his function, as Tolkien wrote in a letter to Christopher Bretherton on July 16, 1964, was "hardly more than to provide a reason for Gandalf going away and leaving Bilbo and the Dwarves to fend for themselves, which was necessary for the tale" (*Letters*, No. 257).

A *necromancer* is (generally) a wizard or conjurer who communicates and has dealings with the dead. In the essay "Laws and Customs Among the Eldar," published in *Morgoth's Ring*, volume ten of the *History*, we see an explanation as to why Sauron is called a necromancer. In discussing what happens to the Elvish spirit (or *fëa*) after the death of the body, a wicked *fëa* may seek friendship with the living and attempt to

ground feeling very unhappy and wishing he was beside the wizard on his tall horse. He had gone just inside the forest after breakfast (a very poor one), and it had seemed as dark in there in the morning as at night, and very secret: "a sort of watching and waiting feeling," he said to himself.

"Good-bye!" said Gandalf to Thorin. "And good-bye to you all, good-bye! Straight through the forest is your way now. Don't stray off the track! – if you do, it is a thousand to one you will never find it again and never get out of Mirkwood; and then I don't suppose I, or any one else, will ever see you again."

"Do we really have to go through?" groaned the hobbit.

"Yes, you do!" said the wizard, "if you want to get to the other side. You must either go through or give up your quest. And I am not going to allow you to back out now, Mr. Baggins. I am ashamed of you for thinking of it. You have got to look after all these dwarves for me," he laughed.

"No! no!" said Bilbo. "I didn't mean that. I meant, is there no way round?"

"There is, if you care to go two hundred miles or so out of your way north, and twice that south. But you wouldn't get a safe path even then. There are no safe paths in this part of the world. Remember you are over the Edge of the Wild now, and in for all sorts of fun wherever you go. Before you could get round Mirkwood in the North you would be right among the slopes of the Grey Mountains, and they are simply stiff with goblins, hobgoblins, and orcs[11] of the worst description. Before you could get round it in the South, you would get into the land of the Necromancer;[12] and even you, Bilbo, won't need me to tell you tales of that black sorcerer. I don't advise you to go anywhere near the places overlooked by his dark tower! Stick to the forest-track, keep your spirits up, hope for the best, and with a tremen-

Mirkwood. Illustration by Évelyne Drouhin for the 1983 French edition.

dous slice of luck you *may* come out one day and see the Long Marshes lying below you, and beyond them, high in the East, the Lonely Mountain where dear old Smaug lives, though I hope he is not expecting you."

"Very comforting you are to be sure," growled Thorin. "Good-bye! If you won't come with us, you had better get off without any more talk!"

"Good-bye then, and really good-bye!" said Gandalf, and he turned his horse and rode down into the West.[13] But he could not resist the temptation to have the last word. Before he had passed quite out of hearing he turned and put his hands to his mouth and called to them. They heard his voice come faintly: "Good-bye! Be good, take care of yourselves — and DON'T LEAVE THE PATH!"

house itself in a living body, either to enslave its host or to wrest from the other *fëa* its rightful body. Tolkien continues: "It is said that Sauron did these things, and taught his followers how to achieve them" (p. 224).

13 Gandalf's actions in *The Hobbit* are similar to those attributed to a legendary mountain spirit of the Riesengebirge (the mountain range in central Europe between Bohemia and Silesia) called the Rübezahl. In tales, the Rübezahl appears in various forms — as a guide, a messenger, or a farmer. He delights in leading travelers astray. There is a considerable Rübezahl tradition, and while much of this has not appeared in English, some tales from the eight-volume series of fairy tales *Volksmärchen der Deutschen* (1782–86) by Johann Karl August Musäus have been translated, including one entitled "Rübezahl" in *The Brown Fairy Book* (1904), edited by Andrew Lang.

In illustrations, the Rübezahl often appears as a bearded man with a staff. The two examples shown here (overleaf) both come from postcards from the late nineteenth or early twentieth century, a prolific time for Rübezahl artwork. In fact, the postcard illustration *Der Berggeist* by Josef Madlener, which Tolkien stated to be the origin of Gandalf (see note 14 to Chapter 1), could be a interpreted as the Rübezahl (*berggeist* literally means "mountain spirit") and thus may be the origin of some of Gandalf's behavior as well as his outward appearance.

It is Gandalf's role through most of *The Hobbit* to serve as guide. He disappears from the party before it was caught by the Trolls; he disappears as the party is caught by the goblins; and having just led them over the Edge of the Wild to the borders of Mirkwood, he deserts them again. But in all cases, he reappears to help when he is most needed.

Then he galloped away and was soon lost to sight. "O good-bye and go away!" grunted the dwarves, all the more angry because they were really filled with dismay at losing him. Now began the most dangerous part of all the journey. They each shouldered the heavy pack and the water-skin which was their share, and turned from the light that lay on the lands outside and plunged into the forest.

8

Flies and Spiders

THEY WALKED IN SINGLE FILE. The entrance to the path was like a sort of arch leading into a gloomy tunnel made by two great trees that leant together, too old and strangled with ivy and hung with lichen to bear more than a few blackened leaves. The path itself was narrow and wound in and out among the trunks. Soon the light at the gate was like a little bright hole far behind, and the quiet was so deep that their feet seemed to thump along while all the trees leaned over them and listened.

As their eyes became used to the dimness they could see a little way to either side in a sort of darkened green glimmer. Occasionally a slender beam of sun that had the luck to slip in through some opening in the leaves far above, and still more luck in not being caught in the tangled boughs and matted twigs beneath, stabbed down thin and bright before them. But this was seldom, and it soon ceased altogether.

There were black squirrels in the wood. As Bilbo's sharp inquisitive eyes got used to seeing things he could catch glimpses of them whisking off the path and scuttling behind tree-trunks. There were queer noises too, grunts, scufflings, and hurryings in the undergrowth, and among the leaves that lay piled endlessly thick in places on the forest-floor; but what made the noises he could not see. The nastiest things they saw were the

Mirkwood by J.R.R. Tolkien. This drawing has perhaps the most curious history of any in *The Hob-bit*. It was the only printed plate in the first British edition of *The Hobbit*, where it appears facing the first page of Chapter 8, though Tolkien had originally wanted it to be used as an endpaper. A border at the top of the picture was cut off in making the halftone block, which Tolkien noted with regret, and, since Tolkien gave the original to a student, it has not been possible to restore it.

The illustration is based on a color drawing by Tolkien that illustrates a scene in the "Silmarillion" tale of Túrin, when the elf Beleg meets another elf Flindor (later renamed Gwindor) in the forest of Taur-na-Fúin. This watercolor was originally painted in July 1928 and appears in *Artist* (No. 54). Many years later Tolkien retitled it *Fangorn Forest* and allowed it to appear in *The J.R.R. Tolkien Calendar 1974* (1973). The two tall figures in the drawing, both very unhobbitlike and one of which is seen carrying a very long sword, were thus allowed to pass for Merry and Pippin in Fangorn For-est. The true context of this painting was first revealed by Christopher Tolkien in the notes to its ap-pearance in *The Silmarillion Calendar 1978* (1977) and in *Pictures* (No. 37, right).

cobwebs: dark dense cobwebs with threads extraordi-narily thick, often stretched from tree to tree, or tangled in the lower branches on either side of them. There were none stretched across the path, but whether because some magic kept it clear, or for what other reason they could not guess.

It was not long before they grew to hate the forest as heartily as they had hated the tunnels of the goblins, and it seemed to offer even less hope of any ending. But they had to go on and on, long after they were sick for a sight of the sun and of the sky, and longed for the feel of wind on their faces. There was no movement of air down

In the 1938 American edition of *The Hobbit, Mirkwood* appears not as a halftone plate but as a line drawing. The small amount of surviving correspondence gives no clue as to what happened here, but probably the American publisher felt that the cost of redrawing the illustration as a line drawing would be much less than printing the original as a halftone plate that would have to be inserted into the book. But whether Tolkien himself did the redrawing or Houghton Mifflin had it done without mentioning it to him remains uncertain. It seems unlikely, though, that Tolkien did it himself, even though it was redone very expertly, for Tolkien's monogram appears in the lower right corner of the halftone illustration but not in the line drawing. There are other very slight differences, particularly in the border design (and one would suspect that if Tolkien had been given the chance to redraw the illustration, he would have restored the upper border). After the 1937 second printing of the British edition of *The Hobbit, Mirkwood* was dropped from the book. It appears in *Artist* (No. 88) and *Pictures* (No. 37, left). After the 1938 American edition of *The Hobbit*, the *Mirkwood* line drawing was dropped and until now has never been reprinted.

under the forest-roof, and it was everlastingly still and dark and stuffy. Even the dwarves felt it, who were used to tunnelling, and lived at times for long whiles without the light of the sun; but the hobbit, who liked holes to make a house in but not to spend summer days in, felt that he was being slowly suffocated.

The nights were the worst. It then became pitch-dark — not what you call pitch-dark,[1] but really pitch: so black that you really could see nothing. Bilbo tried flapping his hand in front of his nose, but he could not see it at all. Well, perhaps it is not true to say that they could see nothing: they could see eyes. They slept all closely

1 1937: "nor what you call pitch-dark" > 1966-Ball: "not what you call pitch-dark"

2 As can be seen on the map of Wilderland, this stream is named the Enchanted River, and it runs northward from the Mountains of Mirkwood in the south to the Forest River, into which it flows to the west of the Elvenking's Halls.

huddled together, and took it in turns to watch; and when it was Bilbo's turn he would see gleams in the darkness round them, and sometimes pairs of yellow or red or green eyes would stare at him from a little distance, and then slowly fade and disappear and slowly shine out again in another place. And sometimes they would gleam down from the branches just above him; and that was most terrifying. But the eyes that he liked the least were horrible pale bulbous sort of eyes. "Insect eyes," he thought, "not animal eyes, only they are much too big."

Although it was not yet very cold, they tried lighting watch-fires at night, but they soon gave that up. It seemed to bring hundreds and hundreds of eyes all round them, though the creatures, whatever they were, were careful never to let their bodies show in the little flicker of the flames. Worse still it brought thousands of dark-grey and black moths, some nearly as big as your hand, flapping and whirring round their ears. They could not stand that, nor the huge bats, black as a top-hat, either; so they gave up fires and sat at night and dozed in the enormous uncanny darkness.

All this went on for what seemed to the hobbit ages upon ages; and he was always hungry, for they were extremely careful with their provisions. Even so, as days followed days, and still the forest seemed just the same, they began to get anxious. The food would not last for ever: it was in fact already beginning to get low. They tried shooting at the squirrels, and they wasted many arrows before they managed to bring one down on the path. But when they roasted it, it proved horrible to taste, and they shot no more squirrels.

They were thirsty too, for they had none too much water, and in all the time they had seen neither spring nor stream. This was their state when one day they found their path blocked by a running water.**2** It flowed fast and strong but not very wide right across the way, and it was black, or looked it in the gloom. It was well that Beorn had warned them against it, or they would have drunk from it, whatever its colour, and filled some of their emptied skins at its bank. As it was they only thought of how to cross it without wetting themselves in its water. There had been a bridge of wood across, but it had rotted and fallen leaving only the broken posts near the bank.

Bilbo kneeling on the brink and peering forward cried: "There is a boat against the far bank! Now why couldn't it have been this side!"

"How far away do you think it is?" asked Thorin, for by now they knew Bilbo had the sharpest eyes among them.

"Not at all far. I shouldn't think above twelve yards."

"Twelve yards! I should have thought it was thirty at least, but my eyes don't see as well as they used a hundred years ago. Still twelve yards is as good as a mile. We can't jump it, and we daren't try to wade or swim."

"Can any of you throw a rope?"

"What's the good of that? The boat is sure to be tied up, even if we could hook it, which I doubt."

"I don't believe it is tied," said Bilbo, "though of course I can't be sure in this light; but it looks to me as if it was just drawn up on the bank, which is low just there where the path goes down into the water."

"Dori is the strongest, but Fili is the youngest and still has the best sight," said Thorin. "Come here Fili, and see if you can see the boat Mr. Baggins is talking about."

Fili thought he could; so when he had stared a long while to get an idea of the direction, the others brought him a rope. They had several with them, and on the end of the longest they fastened one of the large iron hooks they had used for catching their packs to the straps about their shoulders. Fili took this in his hand, balanced it for a moment, and then flung it across the stream.

Splash it fell in the water! "Not far enough!" said Bilbo who was peering forward. "A couple of feet and

3 A painter is a rope attached to the bow of a boat, used for fastening it or securing it to a ship, a stake, or another object.

you would have dropped it on to the boat. Try again. I don't suppose the magic is strong enough to hurt you, if you just touch a bit of wet rope."

Fili picked up the hook when he had drawn it back, rather doubtfully all the same. This time he threw it with great strength.

"Steady!" said Bilbo, "you have thrown it right into the wood on the other side now. Draw it back gently." Fili hauled the rope back slowly, and after a while Bilbo said: "Carefully! It is lying on the boat; let's hope the hook will catch."

It did. The rope went taut, and Fili pulled in vain. Kili came to his help, and then Oin and Gloin. They tugged and tugged, and suddenly they all fell over on their backs. Bilbo was on the look out, however, caught the rope, and with a piece of stick fended off the little black boat as it came rushing across the stream. "Help!" he shouted, and Balin was just in time to seize the boat before it floated off down the current.

"It was tied after all," said he, looking at the snapped painter[3] that was still dangling from it. "That was a good pull, my lads; and a good job that our rope was the stronger."

"Who'll cross first?" asked Bilbo.

"I shall," said Thorin, "and you will come with me, and Fili and Balin. That's as many as the boat will hold at a time. After that Kili and Oin and Gloin and Dori; next Ori and Nori, Bifur and Bofur; and last Dwalin and Bombur."

"I'm always last and I don't like it," said Bombur. "It's somebody else's turn today."

"You should not be so fat. As you are, you must be with the last and lightest boatload. Don't start grumbling against orders, or something bad will happen to you."

"There aren't any oars. How are you going to push the boat back to the far bank?" asked the hobbit.

"Give me another length of rope and another hook,"

said Fili, and when they had got it ready, he cast it into the darkness ahead and as high as he could throw it. Since it did not fall down again, they saw that it must have stuck in the branches. "Get in now," said Fili, "and one of you haul on the rope that is stuck in a tree on the other side. One of the others must keep hold of the hook we used at first, and when we are safe on the other side he can hook it on, and you can draw the boat back."

In this way they were all soon on the far bank safe across the enchanted stream. Dwalin had just scrambled out with the coiled rope on his arm, and Bombur (still grumbling) was getting ready to follow, when something bad did happen. There was a flying sound of hooves on the path ahead. Out of the gloom came suddenly the shape of a flying deer. It charged into the dwarves and bowled them over, then gathered itself for a leap. High it sprang and cleared the water with a mighty jump. But it did not reach the other side in safety. Thorin was the only one who had kept his feet and his wits. As soon as they had landed he had bent his bow and fitted an arrow in case any hidden guardian of the boat appeared. Now he sent a swift and sure shot into the leaping beast. As it reached the further bank it stumbled. The shadows swallowed it up, but they heard the sound of hooves quickly falter and then go still.

Before they could shout in praise of the shot, however, a dreadful wail from Bilbo put all thoughts of venison out of their minds. "Bombur has fallen in! Bombur is drowning!" he cried. It was only too true. Bombur had only one foot on the land when the hart bore down on him, and sprang over him. He had stumbled, thrusting the boat away from the bank, and then toppled back into the dark water, his hands slipping off the slimy roots at the edge, while the boat span slowly off and disappeared.

They could still see his hood above the water when they ran to the bank. Quickly, they flung a rope with a

The enchanted stream. Illustration by Maret Kernumees for the 1977 Estonian edition.

Bombur in the enchanted stream. Illustration by Peter Chuklev from the 1979 version of the 1975 Bulgarian edition. Chuklev is a professor at the National Academy of Fine Arts, Sofia, Bulgaria. In 1974 he illustrated an English translation of a Bulgarian folktale, *Is Fried Fish Good?* by Luchezar Stanchev. Three additional illustrations by Chuklev can be found on pages 214, 316, and 358.

4 An enchanted stream is a familiar motif in Celtic legends. In a similar episode
in the Irish accounts of the life of Saint
Brendan (c. 483–577), Brendan and his
brethren land on an island and find a
stream from which all save Brendan
drink. Those who have drunk the water
fall into fits of sleep and torpor, with
those who have drunk the most suffer-
ing the longest. The following excerpt is
from the "Life of Brendan of Clonfert"
in volume two of Charles Plummer's
*Bethada náem nÉrenn: Lives of Irish
Saints* (1922):

They landed on an island, and found a clear
bright fountain there . . . and many kinds of
fish swimming to and fro in the stream that
flowed down from the fountain towards the
sea. . . . Brenden said to them: "Take heed,
brethren, that ye drink not much of the water,
lest ye be upset thereby more than ye are at
present." But the brethren did not abide by
the command of their father, but drank abun-
dantly, some drinking two draughts, some
three, while the third part drank one draught.
And thus were they affected by the drink; some
of them fell into a sleep and torpor of three
days and three nights, and a sleep of two days
and nights fell on others of them, and sleep
and torpor of a day and a night on the third
part of them. (p. 58)

Sometime around 1945, Tolkien
wrote a poem about Saint Brendan, who
before his death contemplates the most
memorable events of his many voyages.
Tolkien called the poem "The Death
of Saint Brendan," and it is a part of his
unfinished future history of an imaginary Oxford literary club, "The Notion
Club Papers." About ten years later,
he revised the poem and retitled it
"Imram," which is Irish for "sailing,
voyaging." It was published in the
December 3, 1955, issue of *Time and*

hook towards him. His hand caught it, and they pulled
him to the shore. He was drenched from hair to boots,
of course, but that was not the worst. When they laid
him on the bank he was already fast asleep, with one
hand clutching the rope so tight that they could not get
it from his grasp; and fast asleep he remained in spite of
all they could do.**4**

They were still standing over him, cursing their ill
luck, and Bombur's clumsiness, and lamenting the loss
of the boat which made it impossible for them to go back
and look for the hart, when they became aware of the
dim blowing of horns in the wood and the sound as of
dogs baying far off. Then they all fell silent; and as they
sat it seemed they could hear the noise of a great hunt**5**
going by to the north of the path, though they saw no
sign of it.

There they sat for a long while and did not dare to
make a move. Bombur slept on with a smile on his fat
face, as if he no longer cared for all the troubles that
vexed them. Suddenly on the path ahead appeared some
white deer, a hind and fawns as snowy white as the hart
had been dark. They glimmered in the shadows. Before
Thorin could cry out three of the dwarves had leaped to
their feet and loosed off arrows from their bows. None
seemed to find their mark. The deer turned and vanished in the trees as silently as they had come, and in
vain the dwarves shot their arrows after them.

"Stop! stop!" shouted Thorin; but it was too late, the
excited dwarves had wasted their last arrows, and now
the bows that Beorn had given them were useless.

They were a gloomy party that night, and the gloom
gathered still deeper on them in the following days.
They had crossed the enchanted stream; but beyond it
the path seemed to straggle on just as before, and in the
forest they could see no change. Yet if they had known
more about it and considered the meaning of the hunt
and the white deer**6** that had appeared upon their path,

they would have known that they were at last drawing towards the eastern edge, and would soon have come, if they could have kept up their courage and their hope, to thinner trees and places where the sunlight came again.

But they did not know this, and they were burdened with the heavy body of Bombur, which they had to carry along with them as best they could, taking the wearisome task in turns of four each while the others shared their packs. If these had not become all too light in the last few days, they would never have managed it; but a slumbering and smiling Bombur was a poor exchange for packs filled with food however heavy. In a few days a time came when there was practically nothing left to eat or to drink. Nothing wholesome could they see growing in the wood, only funguses and herbs with pale leaves and unpleasant smell.

About four days from the enchanted stream they came to a part where most of the trees were beeches. They were at first inclined to be cheered by the change, for here there was no undergrowth and the shadow was not so deep. There was a greenish light about them, and in places they could see some distance to either side of the path. Yet the light only showed them endless lines of straight grey trunks like the pillars of some huge twilight hall. There was a breath of air and a noise of wind, but it had a sad sound. A few leaves came rustling down to remind them that outside autumn was coming on. Their feet ruffled among the dead leaves of countless other autumns that drifted over the banks of the path from the deep red carpets of the forest.

Still Bombur slept and they grew very weary. At times they heard disquieting laughter. Sometimes there was singing in the distance too. The laughter was the laughter of fair voices not of goblins, and the singing was beautiful, but it sounded eerie and strange, and they were not comforted, rather they hurried on from those parts with what strength they had left.

Tide. Both versions are included in volume nine of the *History, Sauron Defeated.*

5 The fairy hunt is another traditional motif. (Fairy sports are mostly ones that were popular with the medieval court.) It seems certain that when writing this passage Tolkien had in mind a scene from the fourteenth-century Middle English verse romance "Sir Orfeo" (a version of the legend of Orpheus and Eurydice in Greek mythology). I quote from Tolkien's own translation, which was published posthumously in 1975 but had been completed many years before. This scene takes place after Orfeo has wandered as a beggar for ten years, searching for his Lady Heurodis, who had been stolen by the fairies:

There often by him would he see,
when noon was hot on leaf and tree,
the king of Faërie with his rout
came hunting in the woods about
with blowing far and crying dim,
and barking hounds that were with him;
yet never a beast they took or slew,
and where they went he never knew.
                    (lines 281–88)

Tolkien had a very long association with the poem. He studied "Sir Orfeo" as an undergraduate at Oxford, for it was a specified topic of his degree course and was also part of his final public examinations in the summer of 1915. He came to know literally every word of it when compiling his *Middle English Vocabulary* (1922), which was designed for use with Kenneth Sisam's anthology *Fourteenth Century Verse & Prose* (1921). Sisam's anthology contains the whole of the 604-line poem.

In 1944, Tolkien's own edition of the poem (containing the text in Middle English only, without any notes or commentary) was published as a booklet for use in an English course for Naval Cadets at Oxford. In Tolkien's edition of the original, the lines given above read:

Hi miȝte se him bisides
oft in hote vndertides
the king o Faierie with his route
comen hunten him al aboute,
with dim cri and blowinge,
and houndes also berkinge;
ac no best thai neuer nome,
no neuer he niste whider thai become.
                (lines 281–88)

The definitive scholarly edition of *Sir Orfeo* is that by A. J. Bliss, who studied under Tolkien from 1946 to 1948. It was first published in 1954 as part of the Oxford English Monographs, a series of books from Oxford University Press for which Tolkien was one of the three general editors. After Tolkien's death, Bliss (1921–1985) edited Tolkien's lecture notes *Finn and Hengest: The Fragment and the Episode* (1982), reconstructing the stories of two fifth-century Germanic heroes as partially survive in *Beowulf* and the Old English fragment "The Fight at Finnesburgh."

6 In Celtic tradition, encounters with white animals (especially white deer) usually prefigure an encounter with beings from the Otherworld (Faërie). The meaning of the hunt and the white deer (in this instance) should have been understood to be that Bilbo and the dwarves were approaching the dwellings of the Elves, who lived at the eastern

Two days later they found their path going downwards, and before long they were in a valley filled almost entirely with a mighty growth of oaks.

"Is there no end to this accursed forest?" said Thorin. "Somebody must climb a tree and see if he can get his head above the roof and have a look round. The only way is to choose the tallest tree that overhangs the path."

Of course "somebody" meant Bilbo. They chose him, because to be of any use the climber must get his head above the topmost leaves, and so he must be light enough for the highest and slenderest branches to bear him. Poor Mr. Baggins had never had much practice in climbing trees, but they hoisted him up into the lowest branches of an enormous oak that grew right out into the path, and up he had to go as best he could. He pushed his way through the tangled twigs with many a slap in the eye; he was greened and grimed from the old bark of the greater boughs; more than once he slipped and caught himself just in time; and at last, after a dreadful struggle in a difficult place where there seemed to be no convenient branches at all, he got near the top. All the time he was wondering whether there were spiders in the tree, and how he was going to get down again (except by falling).

In the end he poked his head above the roof of leaves, and then he found spiders all right. But they were only small ones of ordinary size, and they were after the butterflies. Bilbo's eyes were nearly blinded by the light. He could hear the dwarves shouting up at him from far below, but he could not answer, only hold on and blink. The sun was shining brilliantly, and it was a long while before he could bear it. When he could, he saw all round him a sea of dark green, ruffled here and there by the breeze; and there were everywhere hundreds of butterflies. I expect they were a kind of 'purple emperor', a butterfly that loves the tops of oak-woods, but these were not purple at all, they were a dark dark velvety black without any markings to be seen.

He looked at the 'black emperors' for a long time, and enjoyed the feel of the breeze in his hair and on his face; but at length the cries of the dwarves, who were now simply stamping with impatience down below, re-minded him of his real business. It was no good. Gaze as much as he might, he could see no end to the trees and the leaves in any direction. His heart, that had been lightened by the sight of the sun and the feel of the wind, sank back into his toes: there was no food to go back to down below.

Actually, as I have told you, they were not far off the edge of the forest; and if Bilbo had had the sense to see it, the tree that he had climbed, though it was tall in it-self, was standing near the bottom of a wide valley, so that from its top the trees seemed to swell up all round like the edges of a great bowl, and he could not expect to see how far the forest lasted. Still he did not see this, and he climbed down full of despair. He got to the bot-tom again at last, scratched, hot, and miserable, and he could not see anything in the gloom below when he got there. His report soon made the others as miserable as he was.

"The forest goes on for ever and ever and ever in all directions! Whatever shall we do? And what is the use of sending a hobbit!" they cried, as if it was his fault. They did not care tuppence about the butterflies, and were only made more angry when he told them of the beautiful breeze, which they were too heavy to climb up and feel.[7]

That night they ate their very last scraps and crumbs of food; and next morning when they woke the first thing they noticed was that they were still gnawingly hungry, and the next thing was that it was raining and that here and there the drip of it was dropping heavily on the for-

edge of the forest. A similar encounter with a white doe occurs in Tolkien's poem "The Lay of Aotrou and Itroun," just before Aotrou meets a witch. (See note 9 to Chapter 15.)

The Purple Emperor (*Apatura iris*) is one of the largest and most elusive species of butterflies in England. They dwell in the canopy of leaves at the top of oak trees in woodlands, where they live off a sugary solution secreted by aphids. Today they are very scarce and found only in central southern England. The illustra-tion comes from *A History of British Butterflies* (1890) by Rev. F. O. Morris.

7 Bilbo's early travels in Mirkwood have a slightly analogous passage in E. A. Wyke-Smith's *The Marvellous Land of Snergs,* where Joe, Sylvia, and Gorbo become lost among the Twisted Trees:

It was getting dark; the sky was now hidden by a roof of matted leaves, and on all sides and above them the thick and smooth branches twisted and locked together. The air was damp and smelt of mould and old moss, and there was a horrid silence. A great leather-skinned bat flickered past them, almost brushing against Sylvia's hair, so that she ducked and gave a little squeal.

Gorbo at last swarmed up one of the bigger trees and, after a lot of struggling, managed to force his way out through the leaves, disturbing numbers of bats that came flopping and wheeling about . . . A minute or two later, Gorbo came sliding down.

"It's all right," he said. "I couldn't see much else but leaves, but I saw the sun so I know which way to go now. The sun is just over" — here he stopped and thought and scratched his head. "Yes, I *think* it's over that way. You see I got twisted round a bit coming down."

They followed him again, working their way over and under the branches. After a time he stopped and thought again, and then began climbing and creeping in another direction — it was all climbing and creeping now. Then he stopped and looked at them in dismay. The horrible writhing grey trunks surrounded them on all sides like an ugly giant net, in a gloom so deep that their shapes were lost to an eye a dozen yards away. Gorbo, the clever one, the woodsman, had done this thing. They were lost. (pp. 51–52)

Joe, Sylvia, and Gorbo among the Twisted Trees, drawn by George Morrow, in *The Marvellous Land of Snergs*.

Bilbo watches the black emperors. Illustration by Ryûichi Terashima for the 1965 Japanese edition.

est floor. That only reminded them that they were also parchingly thirsty, without doing anything to relieve them: you cannot quench a terrible thirst by standing under giant oaks and waiting for a chance drip to fall on your tongue. The only scrap of comfort there was came unexpectedly from Bombur.

He woke up suddenly and sat up scratching his head. He could not make out where he was at all, nor why he felt so hungry; for he had forgotten everything that had happened since they started their journey that May morning long ago.[8] The last thing that he remembered was the party at the hobbit's house, and they had great difficulty in making him believe their tale of all the many adventures they had had since.

When he heard that there was nothing to eat, he sat down and wept, for he felt very weak and wobbly in the legs. "Why ever did I wake up!" he cried. "I was having such beautiful dreams. I dreamed I was walking in a forest rather like this one, only lit with torches on the trees and lamps swinging from the branches and fires burning on the ground; and there was a great feast going on, going on for ever. A woodland king was there with a crown of leaves, and there was a merry singing, and I could not count or describe the things there were to eat and drink."

"You need not try," said Thorin. "In fact if you can't talk about something else, you had better be silent. We are quite annoyed enough with you as it is. If you hadn't waked up, we should have left you to your idiotic dreams in the forest; you are no joke to carry even after weeks of short commons."

There was nothing now to be done but to tighten the belts round their empty stomachs, and hoist their empty sacks and packs, and trudge along the track without any great hope of ever getting to the end before they lay down and died of starvation. This they did all that day, going very slowly and wearily; while Bombur kept on wailing that his legs would not carry him and that he wanted to lie down and sleep. >

"No you don't!" they said. "Let your legs take their share, we have carried you far enough."

All the same he suddenly refused to go a step further and flung himself on the ground. "Go on, if you must," he said. "I'm just going to lie here and sleep and dream of food, if I can't get it any other way. I hope I never wake up again."

At that very moment Balin, who was a little way ahead, called out: "What was that? I thought I saw a twinkle of light in the forest."

They all looked, and a longish way off, it seemed, they saw a red twinkle in the dark; then another and another sprang out beside it. Even Bombur got up, and they hurried along then, not caring if it was trolls or goblins. The light was in front of them and to the left of the path, and when at last they had drawn level with it, it seemed plain that torches and fires were burning under the trees, but a good way off their track.

"It looks as if my dreams were coming true," gasped Bombur puffing up behind. He wanted to rush straight off into the wood after the lights. But the others re-

8 The mention that the journey was started "that May morning long ago" is not precisely correct. On page 64, Tolkien wrote that Bilbo and the dwarves started "one fine morning just before May." See note 3 to Chapter 2, where it is determined that the date was April 28.

The Elves. Illustration by Nada Rappensberg-erová for the 1973 Slovak edition

9 This scene contains a distant echo from an early part of Francis Thompson's poem *Sister Songs: An Offering to Two Sisters* (1895), where the poet sees first a single elf in a glade and then "elfin swarms" singing and dancing, but when the poet moves and rustles about, they flee from the glade. This episode is spread out over many lines; the following are selected excerpts:

Now at that music and that mirth
Rose, as 'twere veils from earth;
 And I spied
 How beside
Bud, bell, bloom, an elf
Stood, or was the flower itself;
 'Mid radiant air
 All the fair
Frequence swayed in irised wavers.
  (lines 74–82)

Others, not yet extricate,
On their hands leaned their weight,
And writhed them free with mickle toil,
Still folded in their veiny vans:
And all with an unsought accord
Sang together from the sward;
Whence had come, and from sprites
Yet unseen, those delights,
As of tempered musics blent,
Which had given me such content.
For haply our best instrument,
Pipe or cithern, stopped or strung,
Mimics but some spirit tongue.
  (lines 99–111)

Next I saw, wonder-whist,
How from the atmosphere a mist,
So it seemed, slow uprist;
And, looking from those elfin swarms,
 I was 'ware
 How the air
Was all populous with forms
Of the Hours, floating down,
Like Nereids through a watery town.
  (lines 120–28)

membered only too well the warnings of the wizard and of Beorn.

"A feast would be no good, if we never got back alive from it," said Thorin.

"But without a feast we shan't remain alive much longer anyway," said Bombur, and Bilbo heartily agreed with him. They argued about it backwards and forwards for a long while, until they agreed at length to send out a couple of spies, to creep near the lights and find out more about them. But then they could not agree on who was to be sent: no one seemed anxious to run the chance of being lost and never finding his friends again. In the end, in spite of warnings, hunger decided them, because Bombur kept on describing all the good things that were being eaten, according to his dream, in the woodland feast; so they all left the path and plunged into the forest together.

After a good deal of creeping and crawling they peered round the trunks and looked into a clearing where some trees had been felled and the ground levelled. There were many people there, elvish-looking folk, all dressed in green and brown and sitting on sawn rings of the felled trees in a great circle. There was a fire in their midst and there were torches fastened to some of the trees round about; but most splendid sight of all: they were eating and drinking and laughing merrily.

The smell of the roast meats was so enchanting that, without waiting to consult one another, every one of them got up and scrambled forwards into the ring with the one idea of begging for some food. No sooner had the first stepped into the clearing than all the lights went out as if by magic.**9** Somebody kicked the fire and it went up in rockets of glittering sparks and vanished. They were lost in a completely lightless dark and they could not even find one another, not for a long time at any rate. After blundering frantically in the gloom, falling over logs, bumping crash into trees, and shouting and calling till they must have waked everything in the forest for miles, at last they managed to gather themselves in a bundle and count themselves by touch. By that time they had, of course, quite forgotten in what direction the path lay, and they were all hopelessly lost, at least till morning.

There was nothing for it but to settle down for the night where they were; they did not even dare to search on the ground for scraps of food for fear of becoming separated again. But they had not been lying long, and Bilbo was only just getting drowsy, when Dori, whose turn it was to watch first, said in a loud whisper:

"The lights are coming out again over there, and there are more than ever of them."

Up they all jumped. There, sure enough, not far away were scores of twinkling lights, and they heard the voices and the laughter quite plainly. They crept slowly towards them, in a single line, each touching the back of the one in front. When they got near Thorin said: "No rushing forward this time! No one is to stir from hiding till I say. I shall send Mr. Baggins alone first to talk to them. They won't be frightened of him — ('What about me of them?' thought Bilbo) — and any way I hope they won't do anything nasty to him."

When they got to the edge of the circle of lights they pushed Bilbo suddenly from behind. Before he had time to slip on his ring, he stumbled forward into the full blaze of the fire and torches. It was no good. Out went all the lights again and complete darkness fell.

If it had been difficult collecting themselves before, it was far worse this time. And they simply could not find the hobbit. Every time they counted themselves it only made thirteen. They shouted and called: "Bilbo Baggins! Hobbit! You dratted hobbit! Hi! hobbit, confusticate you, where are you?" and other things of that sort, but there was no answer.

They were just giving up hope, when Dori stumbled across him by sheer luck. In the dark he fell over what he thought was a log, and he found it was the hobbit curled

Every step was a tinkling sound,
As they glanced in their dancing-ground.
Clouds in cluster with such a sailing
Float o'er the light of the wasting moon,
As the cloud of their gliding veiling
Swung in the sway of the dancing-tune.
(lines 191–96)

I stirred, I rustled more than meet;
Whereat they broke to the left and right,
With eddying robes like aconite
  Blue of helm;
And I beheld to the foot o' the elm.
(lines 201–5)

Francis Thompson (1859–1907) is remembered mostly for his religious poetry. He was a devout Roman Catholic, and he frequently presents in his poems mystical visions of heaven. In everyday life, Thompson was an extremely impractical person and was saved from a life on the streets by the sympathetic magazine editor to whom he submitted his first poems.

Tolkien had a great admiration for Thompson's poetry during his student days at Oxford. On March 4, 1914, he presented a paper, "Francis Thompson," to the Exeter College Essay Club. In it he contended that Thompson should rank among the very greatest of all poets because of his metrical powers, the greatness of his language, and the immensity of his imagery, together with the faith underlying it. Tolkien concluded the paper (according to the club's secretary) with the observation, "One must begin with the elfin and delicate and progress to the profound: listed first to the violin and the flute, and then learn to hearken to the organ of being's harmony."

10 The golden hair of the Elvenking is unusual. In Appendix F of *The Lord of the Rings,* Tolkien wrote of the Elves that "they were tall, fair of skin and grey-eyed, though their locks were dark, save in the golden house of Finarfin." (In early editions of *The Lord of the Rings* this phrase reads "golden house of Finrod" but was subsequently altered to reflect the changed genealogy of the "Silmarillion.") Finarfin was a Noldorin elf, and in Appendix B ("The Tale of Years") of *The Lord of the Rings* we learn that the Elvenking of Mirkwood was a Sindarin elf, so he was not of the house of Finarfin, and thus his having golden hair is unusual.

However, the passage cited from Appendix F has a curious history, and when originally written it was meant to refer to the Noldor, not to all of the Elves. Christopher Tolkien has noted that the Vanyar, one of the Three Kindreds of the High Elves, had golden hair, and it was from the Vanya Indis (the mother of Fingolfin and Finarfin) that the golden-haired Noldor descended. (See *The Book of Lost Tales, Part One,* pp. 43–44; and *The Peoples of Middle-earth,* p. 77).

11 In neither *The Hobbit* nor *The Lord of the Rings* does Tolkien give any clue to the answer to a question that has been fiercely debated among his readership: Did his Elves have pointed ears?

The nearest thing to an answer that one can give is founded on the linguistic elements in Tolkien's invented languages. In the "Etymologies," a kind of dictionary of Elvish word relationships that Tolkien maintained for his personal use in the 1930s, which is now pub-

up fast asleep. It took a deal of shaking to wake him, and when he was awake he was not pleased at all.

"I was having such a lovely dream," he grumbled, "all about having a most gorgeous dinner."

"Good heavens! he has gone like Bombur," they said. "Don't tell us about dreams. Dream-dinners aren't any good, and we can't share them."

"They are the best I am likely to get in this beastly place," he muttered, as he lay down beside the dwarves and tried to go back to sleep and find his dream again.

But that was not the last of the lights in the forest. Later when the night must have been getting old, Kili who was watching then, came and roused them all again, saying:

"There's a regular blaze of light begun not far away — hundreds of torches and many fires must have been lit suddenly and by magic. And hark to the singing and the harps!"

After lying and listening for a while, they found they could not resist the desire to go nearer and try once more to get help. Up they got again; and this time the result was disastrous. The feast that they now saw was greater and more magnificent than before; and at the head of a long line of feasters sat a woodland king with a crown of leaves upon his golden hair,**10** very much as Bombur had described the figure in his dream. The elvish folk were passing bowls from hand to hand and across the fires, and some were harping and many were singing. Their gleaming hair was twined with flowers; green and white gems glinted on their collars and their belts; and their faces and their songs were filled with mirth.**11** Loud and clear and fair were those songs, and out stepped Thorin in to their midst.

Dead silence fell in the middle of a word. Out went all light. The fires leaped up in black smokes. Ashes and cinders were in the eyes of the dwarves, and the wood was filled again with their clamour and their cries.

Bilbo found himself running round and round (as he thought) and calling and calling: "Dori, Nori, Ori, Oin, Gloin, Fili, Kili, Bombur, Bifur, Bofur, Dwalin, Balin, Thorin Oakenshield," while people he could not see or feel were doing the same all round him (with an occasional "Bilbo!" thrown in). But the cries of the others got steadily further and fainter, and though after a while it seemed to him they changed to yells and cries for help in the far distance, all noise at last died right away, and he was left alone in complete silence and darkness.

That was one of his most miserable moments. But he soon made up his mind that it was no good trying to do anything till day came with some little light, and quite useless to go blundering about tiring himself out with no hope of any breakfast to revive him. So he sat himself down with his back to a tree, and not for the last time fell to thinking of his far-distant hobbit-hole with its beautiful pantries. He was deep in thoughts of bacon and eggs and toast and butter when he felt something touch him. Something like a strong sticky string was against his left hand, and when he tried to move he found that his legs were already wrapped in the same stuff, so that when he got up he fell over.

Then the great spider, who had been busy tying him up while he dozed, came from behind him and came at him. He could only see the thing's eyes, but he could feel its hairy legs as it struggled to wind its abominable threads round and round him. It was lucky that he had come to his senses in time. Soon he would not have been able to move at all. As it was, he had a desperate fight before he got free. He beat the creature off with his hands — it was trying to poison him to keep him quiet, as small spiders do to flies — until he remembered his sword and drew it out. Then the spider jumped back, and he had time to cut his legs loose. After that it was his turn to attack. The spider evidently was not used to things that

lished in volume five of the *History, The Lost Road,* he notes in regard to the stems LAS{1} from *lassē* = "leaf" and LAS{2} "listen" (*lassē* = "ear") that there is a possible relationship between the two in that Elven "ears were more pointed and leaf-shaped" than human ones. All that can be said, then, is that certainly at one time (probably in the mid-1930s) Tolkien held this view.

Tolkien's own artwork does not provide any further clues, for in the only drawing in which he depicts elves, they appear as very small figures, and features such as ears are not visible. See the drawing *Taur-na-Fúin* in *Artist* (No. 54).

carried such stings at their sides, or it would have hurried away quicker. Bilbo came at it before it could disappear and stuck it with his sword right in the eyes. Then it went mad and leaped and danced and flung out its legs in horrible jerks, until he killed it with another stroke; and then he fell down and remembered nothing more for a long while.

There was the usual dim grey light of the forest-day about him when he came to his senses. The spider lay dead beside him, and his sword-blade was stained black. Somehow the killing of the giant spider, all alone by himself in the dark without the help of the wizard or the dwarves or of anyone else, made a great difference to Mr. Baggins. He felt a different person, and much fiercer and bolder in spite of an empty stomach, as he wiped his sword on the grass and put it back into its sheath.

"I will give you a name," he said to it, "and I shall call you *Sting.*"

After that he set out to explore. The forest was grim and silent, but obviously he had first of all to look for his friends, who were not likely to be very far off, unless they had been made prisoners by the elves (or worse things). Bilbo felt that it was unsafe to shout, and he stood a long while wondering in what direction the path lay, and in what direction he should go first to look for the dwarves.

"O! why did we not remember Beorn's advice, and Gandalf's!" he lamented. "What a mess we are in now! We! I only wish it was *we:* it is horrible being all alone."

In the end he made as good a guess as he could at the direction from which the cries for help had come in the night — and by luck (he was born with a good share of it) he guessed more or less right, as you will see. Having made up his mind he crept along as cleverly as he could. Hobbits are clever at quietness, especially in woods, as I have already told you; also Bilbo had slipped on his ring before he started. That is why the spiders neither saw nor heard him coming.

He had picked his way stealthily for some distance,

when he noticed a place of dense black shadow ahead of him, black even for that forest, like a patch of midnight that had never been cleared away. As he drew nearer, he saw that it was made by spider-webs one behind and over and tangled with another. Suddenly he saw, too, that there were spiders huge and horrible sitting in the branches above him, and ring or no ring he trembled with fear lest they should discover him. Standing behind a tree he watched a group of them for some time, and then in the silence and stillness of the wood he realised that these loathsome creatures were speaking one to another. Their voices were a sort of thin creaking and hissing, but he could make out many of the words that they said. They were talking about the dwarves!

"It was a sharp struggle, but worth it," said one. "What nasty thick skins they have to be sure, but I'll wager there is good juice inside."

"Aye, they'll make fine eating, when they've hung a bit," said another.

"Don't hang 'em too long," said a third. "They're not as fat as they might be. Been feeding none too well of late, I should guess."

"Kill 'em, I say," hissed a fourth; "kill 'em now and hang 'em dead for a while."

"They're dead now, I'll warrant," said the first.

"That they are not. I saw one a-struggling just now. Just coming round again, I should say, after a bee-autiful sleep. I'll show you."

With that one of the fat spiders ran along a rope till it came to a dozen bundles hanging in a row from a high branch. Bilbo was horrified, now that he noticed them for the first time dangling in the shadows, to see a dwarvish foot sticking out of the bottoms of some of the bundles, or here and there the tip of a nose, or a bit of beard or of a hood.

To the fattest of these bundles the spider went — "It is poor old Bombur, I'll bet," thought Bilbo — and nipped hard at the nose that stuck out. There was a muf-

12 On January 15, 1957, Tolkien was interviewed by Ruth Harshaw for an American radio show called "Carnival of Books." He said, "I put in the spiders largely because this was, you remember, primarily written for my children (at least I had them in mind), and one of my sons in particular dislikes spiders with a great intensity. I did it to thoroughly frighten him and it did!" Throughout his life, Tolkien's son Michael had what he called "a deep-rooted abhorrence of spiders."

13 Of the various activities listed here, quoits is a game in which flat rings are pitched at a stake, the object being to get the ring around the stake. Shooting at the Wand is a game in which a narrow slat is used as an archery target. Bowls is an old game played on a smooth lawn

Bilbo and the spiders. Illustration by Klaus Ensikat for the 1971 German edition.

fled yelp inside, and a toe shot up and kicked the spider straight and hard. There was life in Bombur still. There was a noise like the kicking of a flabby football, and the enraged spider fell off the branch, only catching itself with its own thread just in time.

The others laughed. "You were quite right," they said, "the meat's alive and kicking!"

"I'll soon put an end to that," hissed the angry spider climbing back onto the branch.[12]

Bilbo saw that the moment had come when he must do something. He could not get up at the brutes and he had nothing to shoot with; but looking about he saw that in this place there were many stones lying in what appeared to be a now dry little watercourse. Bilbo was a pretty fair shot with a stone, and it did not take him long to find a nice smooth egg-shaped one that fitted his hand cosily. As a boy he used to practise throwing stones at things, until rabbits and squirrels, and even birds, got out of his way as quick as lightning if they saw him stoop; and even grown-up he had still spent a deal of his time at quoits, dart-throwing, shooting at the wand, bowls, ninepins and other quiet games of the aiming and throwing sort[13] – indeed he could do lots of things, besides blowing smoke-rings, asking riddles and cooking, that I haven't had time to tell you about. There is no time now. While he was picking up stones, the spider had reached Bombur, and soon he would have been dead. At that moment Bilbo threw. The stone struck the spider plunk on the head, and it dropped senseless off the tree, flop to the ground, with all its legs curled up.

The next stone went whizzing through a big web, snapping its cords, and taking off the spider sitting in the middle of it, whack, dead. After that there was a deal of commotion in the spider-colony, and they forgot the dwarves for a bit, I can tell you. They could not see Bilbo, but they could make a good guess at the direction

from which the stones were coming. As quick as lightning they came running and swinging towards the hobbit, flinging out their long threads in all directions, till
the air seemed full of waving snares.

Bilbo, however, soon slipped away to a different
place. The idea came to him to lead the furious spiders
further and further away from the dwarves, if he could;
to make them curious, excited and angry all at once.
When about fifty had gone off to the place where he had
stood before, he threw some more stones at these, and at
others that had stopped behind; then dancing among
the trees he began to sing a song to infuriate them and
bring them all after him, and also to let the dwarves hear
his voice.

This is what he sang:

> *Old fat spider spinning in a tree!*
> *Old fat spider can't see me!*
>   *Attercop! Attercop!*[14]
>   *Won't you stop,*
> *Stop your spinning and look for me?*
>
> *Old Tomnoddy,*[15] *all big body,*
> *Old Tomnoddy can't spy me!*
>   *Attercop! Attercop!*
>   *Down you drop!*
> *You'll never catch me up your tree!*

Not very good perhaps, but then you must remember that he had to make it up himself, on the spur of a
very awkward moment. It did what he wanted any way.
As he sang he threw some more stones and stamped.
Practically all the spiders in the place came after him:
some dropped to the ground, others raced along the
branches, swung from tree to tree, or cast new ropes
across the dark spaces. They made for his noise far
quicker than he had expected. They were frightfully
angry. Quite apart from the stones no spider has ever

with weighted wooden balls. Ninepins,
sometimes also called skittles, is like ten-
pin bowling but with only nine pins set
up at the end of an alley and bowled at.

14 *Attercop* is from Old English *at(t)or-
coppa*, Middle English *atter-cop(pe)*,
"spider." In Chapter 5 ("Archaic Literary Words in the Dialects") of her *Rustic Speech and Folk-lore* (1913), Elizabeth
Mary Wright notes that "many a delightful old word which ran away from a
public career a century or two ago, and
left no address, may thus be discovered
in its country retreat, hale and hearty
yet, though hoary with age" (p. 36–37).
In this context she discusses *attercop:*
"This was in Old English *attorcoppe*, a
spider, from *ātor, attor,* poison, and
coppe, which probably means head, the
old idea being that spiders were poisonous insects" (p. 37). She cites as an example of literary usage a line in the thir-
teenth-century Middle English poem
"The Owl and the Nightingale" (which
Tolkien knew well), where the owl
taunts the nightingale with eating "nothing but attercops, and foul flies, and
worms" (lines 600–601).

Elizabeth Mary Wright (1863–1958)
was a philologist, teacher, and the wife
of Tolkien's teacher Joseph Wright
(1855–1930), editor of the six-volume
English Dialect Dictionary and professor of comparative philology at Oxford.
Tolkien and the Wrights were close
friends, and Tolkien served as Joseph
Wright's executor.

15 The *Oxford English Dictionary* defines *tomnoddy* as "a foolish or stupid
person."

16 Both *lob* and *cob* are words for "spider." *Lob* comes from Old English *loppe, lobbe;* Middle English *loppe, lop(þ), lob. Cob* is rare as a separate word and is probably taken from *cobweb* (Middle English *coppe-web*). In *The Princess and the Goblin,* however, George Macdonald used *cob* as a word for *goblin.*

liked being called Attercop, and Tomnoddy of course is insulting to anybody.

Off Bilbo scuttled to a fresh place, but several of the spiders had run now to different points in the glade where they lived, and were busy spinning webs across all the spaces between the tree-stems. Very soon the hobbit would be caught in a thick fence of them all round him — that at least was the spiders' idea. Standing now in the middle of the hunting and spinning insects Bilbo plucked up his courage and began a new song:

> *Lazy Lob and crazy Cob*[16]
> *are weaving webs to wind me.*
> *I am far more sweet than other meat,*
> *but still they cannot find me!*
>
> *Here am I, naughty little fly;*
> *you are fat and lazy.*
> *You cannot trap me, though you try,*
> *in your cobwebs crazy.*

With that he turned and found that the last space between two tall trees had been closed with a web — but luckily not a proper web, only great strands of double-thick spider-rope run hastily backwards and forwards from trunk to trunk. Out came his little sword. He slashed the threads to pieces and went off singing.

The spiders saw the sword, though I don't suppose they knew what it was, and at once the whole lot of them came hurrying after the hobbit along the ground and the branches, hairy legs waving, nippers and spinners snapping, eyes popping, full of froth and rage. They followed him into the forest until Bilbo had gone as far as he dared. Then quieter than a mouse he stole back.

He had precious little time, he knew, before the spiders were disgusted and came back to their trees where the dwarves were hung. In the meanwhile he had to rescue them. The worst part of the job was getting up on to

Bilbo fights a spider. Illustration by Torbjörn Zetterholm for the 1947 Swedish edition.

the long branch where the bundles were dangling. I
don't suppose he would have managed it, if a spider had
not luckily left a rope hanging down; with its help,
though it stuck to his hand and hurt him, he scrambled
up — only to meet an old slow wicked fat-bodied spider
who had remained behind to guard the prisoners, and
had been busy pinching them to see which was the juici-
est to eat. It had thought of starting the feast while the
others were away, but Mr. Baggins was in a hurry, and
before the spider knew what was happening it felt his
sting and rolled off the branch dead.

Bilbo's next job was to loose a dwarf. What was he to
do? If he cut the string which hung him up, the
wretched dwarf would tumble thump to the ground a
good way below. Wriggling along the branch (which
made all the poor dwarves dance and dangle like ripe
fruit) he reached the first bundle.

"Fili or Kili," he thought by the tip of a blue hood
sticking out at the top. "Most likely Fili," he thought by
the tip of a long nose poking out of the winding threads.
He managed by leaning over to cut most of the strong
sticky threads that bound him round, and then, sure
enough, with a kick and a struggle most of Fili emerged.
I am afraid Bilbo actually laughed at the sight of him
jerking his stiff arms and legs as he danced on the spi-
der-string under his armpits, just like one of those funny
toys bobbing on a wire.

Somehow or other Fili was got on to the branch, and
then he did his best to help the hobbit, although he was
feeling very sick and ill from spider-poison, and from
hanging most of the night and the next day wound
round and round with only his nose to breathe through.
It took him ages to get the beastly stuff out of his eyes
and eyebrows, and as for his beard, he had to cut most
of it off. Well, between them they started to haul up first
one dwarf and then another and slash them free. None
of them were better off than Fili, and some of them were

Bilbo rescuing the Dwarves from a spider. Illustration by Mikhail Belomlinskiy for the 1976
Russian edition.

A spider. Illustration by Peter Chuklev from the 1979 version of the 1975 Bulgarian edition.

worse. Some had hardly been able to breathe at all (long noses are sometimes useful you see) and some had been more poisoned.

In this way they rescued Kili, Bifur, Bofur, Dori and Nori. Poor old Bombur was so exhausted — he was the fattest and had been constantly pinched and poked — that he just rolled off the branch and fell plop on to the ground, fortunately on to leaves, and lay there. But there were still five dwarves hanging at the end of the branch when the spiders began to come back, more full of rage than ever.

Bilbo immediately went to the end of the branch nearest the tree-trunk and kept back those that crawled up. He had taken off his ring when he rescued Fili and forgotten to put it on again, so now they all began to splutter and hiss:

"Now we see you, you nasty little creature! We will eat you and leave your bones and skin hanging on a tree. Ugh! he's got a sting has he? Well, we'll get him all the same, and then we'll hang him head downwards for a day or two."

While this was going on, the other dwarves were working at the rest of the captives, and cutting at the threads with their knives. Soon all would be free, though it was not clear what would happen after that. The spiders had caught them pretty easily the night before, but that had been unawares and in the dark. This time there looked like being a horrible battle.

Suddenly Bilbo noticed that some of the spiders had gathered round old Bombur on the floor, and had tied him up again and were dragging him away. He gave a shout and slashed at the spiders in front of him. They quickly gave way, and he scrambled and fell down the tree right into the middle of those on the ground. His little sword was something new in the way of stings for them. How it darted to and fro! It shone with delight as he stabbed at them. Half a dozen were killed before the rest drew off and left Bombur to Bilbo.

"Come down! Come down!" he shouted to the dwarves on the branch. "Don't stay up there and be netted!" For he saw spiders swarming up all the neighbouring trees, and crawling along the boughs above the heads of the dwarves.

Down the dwarves scrambled or jumped or dropped, eleven all in a heap, most of them very shaky and little use on their legs. There they were at last, twelve of them counting poor old Bombur, who was being propped up on either side by his cousin Bifur, and his brother Bofur; and Bilbo was dancing about and waving his Sting; and hundreds of angry spiders were goggling at them all round and about and above. It looked pretty hopeless.

Then the battle began. Some of the dwarves had knives, and some had sticks, and all of them could get at stones; and Bilbo had his elvish dagger. Again and again the spiders were beaten off, and many of them were killed. But it could not go on for long. Bilbo was nearly tired out; only four of the dwarves were able to stand firmly, and soon they would all be overpowered like weary flies. Already the spiders were beginning to weave their webs all round them again from tree to tree.[17]

In the end Bilbo could think of no plan except to let the dwarves into the secret of his ring. He was rather sorry about it, but it could not be helped.

"I am going to disappear," he said. "I shall draw the spiders off, if I can; and you must keep together and make in the opposite direction. To the left there, that is more or less the way towards the place where we last saw the elf-fires."

It was difficult to get them to understand, what with their dizzy heads, and the shouts, and the whacking of sticks and the throwing of stones; but at last Bilbo felt he could delay no longer — the spiders were drawing their circle ever closer. He suddenly slipped on his ring, and to the great astonishment of the dwarves he vanished.

17 Kelley M. Wickham-Crowley has pointed out to me a possible pun here on the word *dvergs-nät*. In *Anglo-Saxon Magic and Medicine* (1952), J. H. G. Grattan and Charles Singer mention the Anglo-Saxon peoples' fear of both elves and dwarfs, and in their text of the Old English semi-pagan "Lacnunga" they include a charm to be spoken for protection against a dwarf. Grattan and Singer also note that "Swedish *dverg* means not only dwarf but also spider, and *dvergs-nät* means cobweb," and "in Breton, Welsh, and Cornish, the word *cor* also means both dwarf and spider" (p. 61). The pun is in the situation: the dwarves were caught in dwarf-nets, which are also spider webs.

Soon there came the sound of "Lazy Lob" and "Attercop" from among the trees away on the right. That upset the spiders greatly. They stopped advancing, and some went off in the direction of the voice. "Attercop" made them so angry that they lost their wits. Then Balin, who had grasped Bilbo's plan better than the rest, led an attack. The dwarves huddled together in a knot, and sending a shower of stones they drove at the spiders on the left, and burst through the ring. Away behind them now the shouting and singing suddenly stopped.

Hoping desperately that Bilbo had not been caught the dwarves went on. Not fast enough, though. They were sick and weary, and they could not go much better than a hobble and a wobble, though many of the spiders were close behind. Every now and then they had to turn and fight the creatures that were overtaking them; and already some spiders were in the trees above them and throwing down their long clinging threads.

Things were looking pretty bad again, when suddenly Bilbo reappeared, and charged into the astonished spiders unexpectedly from the side.

"Go on! Go on!" he shouted. "I will do the stinging!"

And he did. He darted backwards and forwards, slashing at spider-threads, hacking at their legs, and stabbing at their fat bodies if they came too near. The spiders swelled with rage, and spluttered and frothed, and hissed out horrible curses; but they had become mortally afraid of Sting, and dared not come very near, now that it had come back. So curse as they would, their prey moved slowly but steadily away. It was a most terrible business, and seemed to take hours. But at last, just when Bilbo felt that he could not lift his hand for a single stroke more, the spiders suddenly gave it up, and followed them no more, but went back disappointed to their dark colony.

The dwarves then noticed that they had come to the edge of a ring where elf-fires had been. Whether it was one of those they had seen the night before, they could not tell. But it seemed that some good magic lingered in such spots, which the spiders did not like. At any rate here the light was greener, and the boughs less thick and threatening, and they had a chance to rest and draw breath.

There they lay for some time, puffing and panting. But very soon they began to ask questions. They had to have the whole vanishing business carefully explained, and the finding of the ring interested them so much that for a while they forgot their own troubles. Balin in particular insisted on having the Gollum story, riddles and all, told all over again, with the ring in its proper place.[18] But after a time the light began to fail, and then other questions were asked. Where were they, and where was their path, and where was there any food, and what were they going to do next? These questions they asked over and over again, and it was from little Bilbo that they seemed to expect to get the answers. From which you can see that they had changed their opinion of Mr. Baggins very much, and had begun to have a great respect for him (as Gandalf had said they would). Indeed they really expected him to think of some wonderful plan for helping them, and were not merely grumbling. They knew only too well that they would soon all have been dead, if it had not been for the hobbit; and they thanked him many times. Some of them even got up and bowed right to the ground before him, though they fell over with the effort, and could not get on their legs again for some time. Knowing the truth about the vanishing did not lessen their opinion of Bilbo at all; for they saw that he had some wits, as well as luck and a magic ring — and all three are very useful possessions.[19] In fact they praised him so much that Bilbo began to feel there really was something of a bold adventurer about himself after all, though he would have felt a lot bolder still, if there had been anything to eat.

But there was nothing, nothing at all; and none of them were fit to go and look for anything, or to search

18 Here Bilbo retells the story of his encounter with Gollum, including the parts related to the ring, which he had omitted previously. See note 2 to Chapter 6.

19 Tom Shippey sees Bilbo's magic ring as an equalizer, lifting Bilbo's status to that of the dwarves. Bilbo begins the journey as merely a piece of baggage to be carried along, but with the ring he can take an active part in the adventure. (See the second edition of *The Road to Middle-earth,* pp. 70–72).

20 This is the only occurrence of the word *faerie* in *The Hobbit.* Here the "Faerie in the West" refers to the Elven-home (Eldamar) over the sea.

21 The Light-elves, Deep-elves, and Sea-elves refer to the Three Kindred of the High Elves. In *The Silmarillion,* these are named the Vanyar, the Noldor, and the Teleri. However, the Vanyar had been called the Lindar in earlier writings, including those contemporary with the writing of *The Hobbit,* now published in volume five of the *History, The Lost Road.*

Over time, Tolkien's names of the divisions of the Elves went through very complicated changes, with shifting meanings assigned to the same names. In one very minor example, Tolkien sometimes used Light-elves to refer to all Three Kindreds, who passed over the sea and saw the light of the Two Trees in Valinor. They were thus distinguished from the Dark-elves, who (like the Elvenking and his people) never left Middle-earth.

On the usage of *Gnomes,* see note 11 Chapter 3.

22 *1937:* "the Deep-elves (or Gnomes) and the Sea-elves lived for ages" > *1966-Ball:* "the Deep-elves and the Sea-elves went and lived for ages"

23 *1937:* "before they came back into the Wide World. In the Wide World the Wood-elves lingered in the twilight before the raising of the Sun and Moon; and afterwards they wandered in the forests that grew beneath the sunrise. They loved best the edges of the woods," > *1966-Longmans/Unwin:*

for the lost path. The lost path! No other idea would come into Bilbo's tired head. He just sat staring in front of him at the endless trees; and after a while they all fell silent again. All except Balin. Long after the others had stopped talking and shut their eyes, he kept on muttering and chuckling to himself.

"Gollum! Well I'm blest! So that's how he sneaked past me, is it? Now I know! Just crept quietly along did you, Mr. Baggins? Buttons all over the doorstep! Good old Bilbo — Bilbo — Bilbo — bo — bo — bo — " And then he fell asleep, and there was complete silence for a long while.

All of a sudden Dwalin opened an eye, and looked round at them. "Where is Thorin?" he asked.

It was a terrible shock. Of course there were only thirteen of them, twelve dwarves and the hobbit. Where indeed was Thorin? They wondered what evil fate had befallen him, magic or dark monsters; and shuddered as they lay lost in the forest. There they dropped off one by one into uncomfortable sleep full of horrible dreams, as evening wore to black night; and there we must leave them for the present, too sick and weary to set guards or to take turns at watching.

Thorin had been caught much faster than they had. You remember Bilbo falling like a log into sleep, as he stepped into a circle of light? The next time it had been Thorin who stepped forward, and as the lights went out he fell like a stone enchanted. All the noise of the dwarves lost in the night, their cries as the spiders caught them and bound them, and all the sounds of the battle next day, had passed over him unheard. Then the Wood-elves had come to him, and bound him, and carried him away.

The feasting people were Wood-elves, of course. These are not wicked folk. If they have a fault it is distrust of strangers. Though their magic was strong, even in those days they were wary. They differed from the

High Elves of the West, and were more dangerous and less wise. For most of them (together with their scattered relations in the hills and mountains) were descended from the ancient tribes that never went to Faerie[20] in the West. There the Light-elves and the Deep-elves and the Sea-elves[21] went and lived for ages,[22] and grew fairer and wiser and more learned, and invented their magic and their cunning craft in the making of beautiful and marvellous things, before some came back into the Wide World.[23] In the Wide World the Wood-elves lingered in the twilight of our Sun and Moon, but loved best the stars; and they wandered in the great forests that grew tall in lands that are now lost. They dwelt most often by the edges of the woods, from which they could escape at times to hunt, or to ride and run over the open lands by moonlight or starlight; and after the coming of Men they took ever more and more to the gloaming and the dusk. Still elves they were and remain, and that is Good People.

In a great cave some miles within the edge of Mirkwood on its eastern side there lived at this time their greatest king. Before his huge doors of stone a river ran out of the heights of the forest and flowed on and out into the marshes at the feet of the high wooded lands. This great cave, from which countless smaller ones opened out on every side, wound far underground and had many passages and wide halls; but it was lighter and more wholesome than any goblin-dwelling, and neither so deep nor so dangerous. In fact the subjects of the king mostly lived and hunted in the open woods, and had houses or huts on the ground and in the branches. The beeches were their favourite trees. The king's cave was his palace, and the strong place of his treasure, and the fortress of his people against their enemies.

It was also the dungeon of his prisoners. So to the cave they dragged Thorin — not too gently, for they did not love dwarves, and thought he was an enemy. In an-

"before some came back into the Wide World. In the Wide World the Wood-elves lingered in the twilight of our Sun and Moon, but loved best the stars; and they wandered in the great forests that grew tall in lands that are now lost. They dwelt most often by the edges of the woods," (*1966-Ball* follows *1966-Longmans/Unwin* but erroneously has no comma after *Moon*.)

The change from "they came back" to "some came back" was made because it was only the Deep-elves or Noldor who "came back into the Wide World."

The 1937 version of this passage is in full accord with both the early history of the Elves and the story of the making of the Sun and Moon from the last fruits of the Two Trees in Valinor, as is told in Chapter 11 of the published version of *The Silmarillion*. The revised reading seems to reflect Tolkien's decision late in life to abandon this idea and accept that Middle-earth was illuminated by the Sun and Moon from its very beginning. Tolkien's various written considerations of this idea are published in the section "Myths Transformed" in volume ten of the *History, Morgoth's Ring*.

24 This account of an elf-king of "ancient days" (not to be confused with the Elvenking) is the story of King Thingol of Doriath, who was murdered by the dwarves after refusing to give them their pay. The elements of this story go back to the earliest writings of Tolkien's legendarium, and in its earliest form this tale can be read in "The Nauglafring: The Necklace of the Dwarves," published in volume two of the *History, The Book of Lost Tales, Part Two.* Various reworkings of the story can be found in the versions of the "Silmarillion" as given in the *History.* In the published *Silmarillion,* the story is related in Chapter 22, "Of the Ruin of Doriath."

cient days they had had wars with some of the dwarves, whom they accused of stealing their treasure. It is only fair to say that the dwarves gave a different account, and said that they only took what was their due, for the elf-king had bargained with them to shape his raw gold and silver, and had afterwards refused to give them their pay.**24** If the elf-king had a weakness it was for treasure, especially for silver and white gems; and though his hoard was rich, he was ever eager for more, since he had not yet as great a treasure as other elf-lords of old. His people neither mined nor worked metals or jewels, nor did they bother much with trade or with tilling the earth. All this was well known to every dwarf, though Thorin's family had had nothing to do with the old quarrel I have spoken of. Consequently Thorin was angry at their treatment of him, when they took their spell off him and he came to his senses; and also he was determined that no word of gold or jewels should be dragged out of him.

The king looked sternly on Thorin, when he was brought before him, and asked him many questions. But Thorin would only say that he was starving.

"Why did you and your folk three times try to attack my people at their merrymaking?" asked the king.

"We did not attack them," answered Thorin; "we came to beg, because we were starving."

"Where are your friends now, and what are they doing?"

"I don't know, but I expect starving in the forest."

"What were you doing in the forest?"

"Looking for food and drink, because we were starving."

"But what brought you into the forest at all?" asked the king angrily.

At that Thorin shut his mouth and would not say another word.

"Very well!" said the king. "Take him away and keep

him safe, until he feels inclined to tell the truth, even if he waits a hundred years."

Then the elves put thongs[25] on him, and shut him in one of the inmost caves with strong wooden doors, and left him. They gave him food and drink, plenty of both, if not very fine; for Wood-elves were not goblins, and were reasonably well-behaved even to their worst enemies, when they captured them. The giant spiders were the only living things that they had no mercy upon.

There in the king's dungeon poor Thorin lay; and after he had got over his thankfulness for bread and meat and water, he began to wonder what had become of his unfortunate friends. It was not very long before he discovered; but that belongs to the next chapter and the beginning of another adventure in which the hobbit again showed his usefulness.

25 Thongs are narrow strips of hide or leather, here used to bind Thorin.

Thorin and the Elvenking. Illustration by Livia Rusz for the 1975 Romanian edition.

9

Barrels Out of Bond

1 Elves and arrows have a strong association in fairy lore. *Elf-shot* was a name given to flint arrowheads that were supposed to pierce the skin without leaving a mark, causing disease in humans. Various afflictions like rheumatism, cramps, and bruising were attributed to elf-shot.

THE DAY AFTER THE BATTLE with the spiders Bilbo and the dwarves made one last despairing effort to find a way out before they died of hunger and thirst. They got up and staggered on in the direction which eight out of the thirteen of them guessed to be the one in which the path lay; but they never found out if they were right. Such day as there ever was in the forest was fading once more into the blackness of night, when suddenly out sprang the light of many torches all round them, like hundreds of red stars. Out leaped Wood-elves with their bows and spears and called the dwarves to halt.

There was no thought of a fight. Even if the dwarves had not been in such a state that they were actually glad to be captured, their small knives, the only weapons they had, would have been of no use against the arrows of the elves that could hit a bird's eye in the dark.[1] So they simply stopped dead and sat down and waited — all except Bilbo, who popped on his ring and slipped quickly to one side. That is why, when the elves bound the dwarves in a long line, one behind the other, and counted them, they never found or counted the hobbit.

Nor did they hear or feel him trotting along well behind their torch-light as they led off their prisoners into the forest. Each dwarf was blindfold, but that did not make much difference, for even Bilbo with the use of his eyes could not see where they were going, and neither he nor the others knew where they had started from anyway. Bilbo had all he could do to keep up with the torches, for the elves were making the dwarves go as fast as ever they could, sick and weary as they were. The king had ordered them to make haste. Suddenly the torches stopped, and the hobbit had just time to catch them up before they began to cross the bridge. This was the bridge that led across the river to the king's doors. The water flowed dark and swift and strong beneath; and at the far end were gates before the mouth of a huge cave that ran into the side of a steep slope covered with trees. There the great beeches came right down to the bank, till their feet were in the stream.

Across the bridge the elves thrust their prisoners, but Bilbo hesitated in the rear. He did not at all like the look of the cavern-mouth, and he only made up his mind not to desert his friends just in time to scuttle over at the heels of the last elves, before the great gates of the king closed behind them with a clang.

Inside the passages were lit with red torch-light, and the elf-guards sang as they marched along the twisting, crossing, and echoing paths. These were not like those of the goblin-cities; they were smaller, less deep underground, and filled with a cleaner air. In a great hall with pillars hewn out of the living stone sat the Elvenking[2] on a chair of carven wood. On his head was a crown of berries and red leaves, for the autumn was come again. In the spring he wore a crown of woodland flowers. In his hand he held a carven staff of oak.[3]

The prisoners were brought before him; and though he looked grimly at them, he told his men to unbind them, for they were ragged and weary. "Besides they need no ropes in here," said he. "There is no escape from my magic doors for those who are once brought inside."

Long and searchingly he questioned the dwarves

2 The Elvenking remained unnamed in *The Hobbit*. In *The Lord of the Rings* we learn that his name is Thranduil. His son, Legolas, is one of the nine members of the Fellowship of the Ring in *The Lord of the Rings*.

3 Oak is traditionally a sacred tree. It was associated with the Druids and their sacred groves of worship. In fairy lore, it has stronger magical associations when growing near ash and thorn trees, two other of the most sacred fairy trees.

The three types of trees are referred to together by the Elves in the final lines of the poem on page 357: "*Hush! Hush! Oak, Ash, and Thorn! | Hushed be all water, till dawn is at hand!*"

The Elvenking. Illustration by Horus Engels for the 1957 German edition.

.The Elvenking's Gate.

Gate of the Elvenking's Halls

The Elvenking's Gate by J.R.R. Tolkien, one of the standard black-and-white illustrations that has appeared in *The Hobbit* since 1937. This illustration appears in *Artist* (No. 121) and *Pictures* (No. 12, left). A version of this illustration colored by H. E. Riddett first appeared in *The Hobbit Calendar 1976* (1975) and in *Pictures* (No. 12, right).

Tolkien made several attempts to draw this scene. What is perhaps the earliest is a straight-on view from the bridge, showing a somewhat simple gate at the front of a tunnel (see *Artist*, No. 117). From there, Tolkien moved the perspective farther back and shifted it left to view the entrance from an angle. Three drawings from this perspective use trees to frame the scene. One is titled *Entrance to the Elvenking's Halls* (*Artist*, No. 118) and the second is an untitled but slightly closer view (*Artist*, No. 119). The third is Tolkien's only color version, with a striking blue river and a dark night sky. Unfortunately it was never finished. It appears here in black-and-white (left, top), but a color reproduction was published in *The J.R.R. Tolkien Calendar 1979* (1978) and in *Pictures* (No. 11).

The trilithon doorway (*pi*-shaped, with slanted sides) entered in the next drawing (left, bottom), *Gate of the Elvenking's Halls* (*Artist* No. 120), which closely resembles a few drawings of the underground Elven realm of Nargothrond in the "Silmarillion" legends, whose entrance has three stone doorways. Tolkien drew one of these in ink (see *Artist*, No. 57) and the other in watercolor (see *Pictures*, No. 33), the latter unfinished.

For the final version Tolkien returned to the straight-on perspective and included a larger number of trees to frame the view.

about their doings, and where they were going to, and where they were coming from; but he got little more news out of them than out of Thorin. They were surly and angry and did not even pretend to be polite.

"What have we done, O king?" said Balin, who was the eldest left. "Is it a crime to be lost in the forest, to be hungry and thirsty, to be trapped by spiders? Are the spiders your tame beasts or your pets, if killing them makes you angry?"

Such a question of course made the king angrier than ever, and he answered: "It is a crime to wander in my realm without leave. Do you forget that you were in my kingdom, using the road that my people made? Did you not three times pursue and trouble my people in the forest and rouse the spiders with your riot and clamour? After all the disturbance you have made I have a right to know what brings you here, and if you will not tell me now, I will keep you all in prison until you have learned sense and manners!"

Then he ordered the dwarves each to be put in a separate cell and to be given food and drink, but not to be allowed to pass the doors of their little prisons, until one at least of them was willing to tell him all he wanted to know. But he did not tell them that Thorin was also a prisoner with him. It was Bilbo who found that out.

Poor Mr. Baggins — it was a weary long time that he lived in that place all alone, and always in hiding, never daring to take off his ring, hardly daring to sleep, even tucked away in the darkest and remotest corners he could find. For something to do he took to wandering about the Elvenking's palace. Magic shut the gates, but he could sometimes get out, if he was quick. Companies of the Wood-elves, sometimes with the king at their head, would from time to time ride out to hunt, or to other business in the woods and in the lands to the East. Then if Bilbo was very nimble, he could slip out just behind them; though it was a dangerous thing to do. More than once he was nearly caught in the doors, as they clashed together when the last elf passed; yet he did not dare to march among them because of his shadow (altogether thin and wobbly as it was in torchlight), or for fear of being bumped into and discovered. And when he did go out, which was not very often, he did no good. He did not wish to desert the dwarves, and indeed he did not know where in the world to go without them. He could not keep up with the hunting elves all the time they were out, so he never discovered the ways out of the wood, and was left to wander miserably in the forest, terrified of losing himself, until a chance came of returning. He was hungry too outside, for he was no hunter; but inside the caves he could pick up a living of some sort by stealing food from store or table when no one was at hand.

"I am like a burglar that can't get away, but must go on miserably burgling the same house day after day," he thought. "This is the dreariest and dullest part of all this wretched, tiresome, uncomfortable adventure! I wish I was back in my hobbit-hole by my own warm fireside with the lamp shining!" He often wished, too, that he could get a message for help sent to the wizard, but that of course was quite impossible; and he soon realized that if anything was to be done, it would have to be done by Mr. Baggins, alone and unaided.

Eventually, after a week or two of this sneaking sort of life, by watching and following the guards and taking what chances he could, he managed to find out where each dwarf was kept. He found all their twelve cells in different parts of the palace, and after a time he got to know his way about very well. What was his surprise one day to overhear some of the guards talking and to learn that there was another dwarf in prison too, in a specially deep dark place. He guessed at once, of course, that that was Thorin; and after a while he found that his guess was right. At last after many difficulties he managed to find the place when no one was about, and to have a word with the chief of the dwarves.

Thorin was too wretched to be angry any longer at his misfortunes, and was even beginning to think of telling the king all about his treasure and his quest (which shows how low-spirited he had become), when he heard Bilbo's little voice at his keyhole. He could hardly believe his ears. Soon however he made up his mind that he could not be mistaken, and he came to the door and had a long whispered talk with the hobbit on the other side.

Thorin in the Elvenking's dungeon. Illustration by Mikhail Belomlinskiy for the 1976 Russian edition.

So it was that Bilbo was able to take secretly Thorin's message to each of the other imprisoned dwarves, telling them that Thorin their chief was also in prison close at hand, and that no one was to reveal their errand to the king, not yet, nor before Thorin gave the word. For Thorin had taken heart again hearing how the hobbit had rescued his companions from the spiders, and was determined once more not to ransom himself with promises to the king of a share in the treasure, until all hope of escaping in any other way had disappeared; until in fact the remarkable Mr. Invisible Baggins (of whom he began to have a very high opinion indeed) had altogether failed to think of something clever.

The other dwarves quite agreed when they got the message. They all thought their own shares in the treasure (which they quite regarded as theirs, in spite of their plight and the still unconquered dragon) would suffer seriously if the Wood-elves claimed part of it, and they all trusted Bilbo. Just what Gandalf had said would happen, you see. Perhaps that was part of his reason for going off and leaving them.

Bilbo, however, did not feel nearly so hopeful as they did. He did not like being depended on by everyone, and he wished he had the wizard at hand. But that was no use: probably all the dark distance of Mirkwood lay between them. He sat and thought and thought, until his head nearly burst, but no bright idea would come. One invisible ring was a very fine thing, but it was not much good among fourteen. But of course, as you have guessed, he did rescue his friends in the end, and this is how it happened.

One day, nosing and wandering about, Bilbo discovered a very interesting thing: the great gates were *not* the only entrance to the caves. A stream flowed under part of the lowest regions of the palace, and joined the Forest River some way further to the east, beyond the steep slope out of which the main mouth opened. Where this underground watercourse came forth from the hillside there was a water-gate. There the rocky roof came down close to the surface of the stream, and from it a portcullis could be dropped right to the bed of the river to prevent anyone coming in or out that way. But the portcullis was often open, for a good deal of traffic went out and in by the water-gate. If anyone had come in that way, he would have found himself in a dark rough tunnel leading deep into the heart of the hill; but at one point where it passed under the caves the roof had been cut away and covered with great oaken trapdoors. These opened upwards into the king's cellars. There stood barrels, and barrels, and barrels; for the Wood-elves, and especially their king, were very fond of wine, though no vines grew in those parts. The wine, and other goods, were brought from far away, from their kinsfolk in the South, or from the vineyards of Men in distant lands.

Hiding behind one of the largest barrels Bilbo discovered the trapdoors and their use, and lurking there, listening to the talk of the king's servants, he learned how the wine and other goods came up the rivers, or over land, to the Long Lake. It seemed a town of Men still throve there, built out on bridges far into the water as a protection against enemies of all sorts, and especially against the dragon of the Mountain. From Laketown the barrels were brought up the Forest River. Often they were just tied together like big rafts and poled or rowed up the stream; sometimes they were loaded on to flat boats.

When the barrels were empty the elves cast them through the trapdoors, opened the water-gate, and out the barrels floated on the stream, bobbing along, until they were carried by the current to a place far down the river where the bank jutted out, near to the very eastern edge of Mirkwood. There they were collected and tied together and floated back to Lake-town, which stood close to the point where the Forest River flowed into the Long Lake.

For some time Bilbo sat and thought about this water-gate, and wondered if it could be used for the escape of his friends, and at last he had the desperate beginnings of a plan.

The evening meal had been taken to the prisoners. The guards were tramping away down the passages taking the torchlight with them and leaving everything in darkness. Then Bilbo heard the king's butler bidding the chief of the guards good-night.

"Now come with me," he said, "and taste the new wine that has just come in. I shall be hard at work tonight clearing the cellars of the empty wood, so let us have a drink first to help the labour."

"Very good," laughed the chief of the guards. "I'll taste with you, and see if it is fit for the king's table. There is a feast tonight and it would not do to send up poor stuff!"

When he heard this Bilbo was all in a flutter, for he saw that luck was with him and he had a chance at once to try his desperate plan. He followed the two elves, until they entered a small cellar and sat down at a table on which two large flagons were set. Soon they began to drink and laugh merrily. Luck of an unusual kind was

4 The name *Dorwinion* is clearly of Elvish origin, and it appears in Tolkien's earlier writings. In "The Lay of the Children of Húrin," a long unfinished alliterative poem written in the early to mid 1920s, the especially potent wine of Dor-Winion [*sic*] is described as coming from the burning South, which implies that Dor-Winion is located in Beleriand (Part I, lines 230, 425; Part II, lines 553, 806; see volume three of the *History, The Lays of Beleriand*).

Dorwinion also appears in a text probably dating from the mid-1930s, just before Tolkien began writing *The Lord of the Rings* in December 1937. This text is the conclusion to the *Quenta Silmarillion* (published in volume five of the *History, The Lost Road*), and "the undying flowers in the meads of Dorwinion" are mentioned in the final paragraph, implying that Dorwinion is overseas in Tol Eressëa (p. 334).

Finally, on Pauline Baynes's *Map of Middle-earth* (1970), which was compiled with Tolkien's assistance, Dorwinion is placed on the northwest shores of the inland Sea of Rhûn, far down the banks of the River Running in the East. The placement here certainly accords with the mentions of Dorwinion in *The Hobbit* but does not account for the appearance of the name in earlier texts.

with Bilbo then. It must be potent wine to make a wood-elf drowsy; but this wine, it would seem, was the heady vintage of the great gardens of Dorwinion,4 not meant for his soldiers or his servants, but for the king's feasts only, and for smaller bowls not for the butler's great flagons.

Very soon the chief guard nodded his head, then he laid it on the table and fell fast asleep. The butler went on talking and laughing to himself for a while without seeming to notice, but soon his head too nodded to the table, and he fell asleep and snored beside his friend. Then in crept the hobbit. Very soon the chief guard had no keys, but Bilbo was trotting as fast as he could along the passages towards the cells. The great bunch seemed very heavy to his arms, and his heart was often in his mouth, in spite of his ring, for he could not prevent the keys from making every now and then a loud clink and clank, which put him all in a tremble.

First he unlocked Balin's door, and locked it again carefully as soon as the dwarf was outside. Balin was most surprised, as you can imagine; but glad as he was to get out of his wearisome little stone room, he wanted to stop and ask questions, and know what Bilbo was going to do, and all about it.

"No time now!" said the hobbit. "You just follow me! We must all keep together and not risk getting separated. All of us must escape or none, and this is our last chance. If this is found out, goodness knows where the king will put you next, with chains on your hands and feet too, I expect. Don't argue, there's a good fellow!"

Then off he went from door to door, until his following had grown to twelve — none of them any too nimble, what with the dark, and what with their long imprisonment. Bilbo's heart thumped every time one of them bumped into another, or grunted or whispered in the dark. "Drat this dwarvish racket!" he said to himself. But all went well, and they met no guards. As a matter of fact there was a great autumn feast in the woods that night, and in the halls above. Nearly all the king's folk were merrymaking.

At last after much blundering they came to Thorin's dungeon, far down in a deep place and fortunately not far from the cellars.

"Upon my word!" said Thorin, when Bilbo whispered to him to come out and join his friends, "Gandalf spoke true, as usual! A pretty fine burglar you make, it seems, when the time comes. I am sure we are all for ever at your service, whatever happens after this. But what comes next?"

Bilbo saw that the time had come to explain his idea, as far as he could; but he did not feel at all sure how the dwarves would take it. His fears were quite justified, for they did not like it a bit, and started grumbling loudly in spite of their danger.

"We shall be bruised and battered to pieces, and drowned too, for certain!" they muttered. "We thought you had got some sensible notion, when you managed to get hold of the keys. This is a mad idea!"

"Very well!" said Bilbo very downcast, and also rather annoyed. "Come along back to your nice cells, and I will lock you all in again, and you can sit there comfortably and think of a better plan — but I don't suppose I shall ever get hold of the keys again, even if I feel inclined to try."

That was too much for them, and they calmed down. In the end, of course, they had to do just what Bilbo suggested, because it was obviously impossible for them to try and find their way into the upper halls, or to fight their way out of gates that closed by magic; and it was no good grumbling in the passages until they were caught again. So following the hobbit, down into the lowest cellars they crept. They passed a door through which the chief guard and the butler could be seen still happily snoring with smiles upon their faces. The wine of Dorwinion brings deep and pleasant dreams. There would be a different expression on the face of the chief guard next day, even though Bilbo, before they went on, stole in and kindheartedly put the keys back on his belt.

"That will save him some of the trouble he is in for," said Mr. Baggins to himself. "He wasn't a bad fellow, and quite decent to the prisoners. It will puzzle them all too. They will think we had a very strong magic to pass through all those locked doors and disappear. Disappear! We have got to get busy very quick, if that is to happen!"

Balin was told off to watch the guard and the butler and give warning if they stirred. The rest went into the adjoining cellar with the trapdoors. There was little time to lose. Before long, as Bilbo knew, some elves were under orders to come down and help the butler get the empty barrels through the doors into the stream. These were in fact already standing in rows in the middle of the floor waiting to be pushed off. Some of them were wine-barrels, and these were not much use, as they could not easily be opened at the end without a deal of noise, nor could they easily be secured again. But among them were several others, which had been used for bringing other stuffs, butter, apples, and all sorts of things, to the king's palace.

They soon found thirteen with room enough for a dwarf in each. In fact some were too roomy, and as they climbed in the dwarves thought anxiously of the shaking and the bumping they would get inside, though Bilbo did his best to find straw and other stuff to pack them in as cosily as could be managed in a short time. At last twelve dwarves were stowed. Thorin had given a lot of trouble, and turned and twisted in his tub and grumbled like a large dog in a small kennel; while Balin, who came last, made a great fuss about his air-holes and said he was stifling, even before his lid was on. Bilbo had done

Bilbo puts the dwarves in barrels. Illustration by Horus Engels for the 1957 German edition.

what he could to close holes in the sides of the barrels, and to fix on all the lids as safely as could be managed, and now he was left alone again, running round putting the finishing touches to the packing, and hoping against hope that his plan would come off.

It had not been done a bit too soon. Only a minute or two after Balin's lid had been fitted on there came the sound of voices and the flicker of lights. A number of elves came laughing and talking into the cellars and singing snatches of song. They had left a merry feast in one of the halls and were bent on returning as soon as they could.

"Where's old Galion,[5] the butler?" said one. "I haven't seen him at the tables tonight. He ought to be here now to show us what is to be done."

"I shall be angry if the old slowcoach[6] is late," said another. "I have no wish to waste time down here while the song is up!"

"Ha, ha!" came a cry. "Here's the old villain with his head on a jug! He's been having a little feast all to himself and his friend the captain."[7]

"Shake him! Wake him!" shouted the others impatiently.

Galion was not at all pleased at being shaken or wakened, and still less at being laughed at. "You're all late," he grumbled. "Here am I waiting and waiting down here, while you fellows drink and make merry and forget your tasks. Small wonder if I fall asleep from weariness!"

"Small wonder," said they, "when the explanation stands close at hand in a jug! Come give us a taste of your sleeping-draught before we fall to! No need to wake the turnkey[8] yonder. He has had his share by the looks of it."

Then they drank once round and became mighty merry all of a sudden. But they did not quite lose their wits. "Save us, Galion!" cried some, "you began your feasting early and muddled your wits! You have stacked

5 The elf-name *Galion* appears to be of Sindarin Elvish origin, but its meaning is uncertain. The name could derive from GAL- "shine" or GALA- "thrive (prosper, be in health — be glad)." The ending *-ion* could be related to YŌ, YON- "son."

6 A slowcoach is someone who acts, works, or moves slowly. In America the more common term is *slowpoke.*

7 The behavior of the Elvenking's butler is similar to that of the king's butler in Chapter 17, "The Wine Cellar," in George Macdonald's *The Princess and Curdie:* Both like to drink the king's best wines in the king's own cellar.

8 A turnkey is the person who has the charge of the keys of a prison, hence a jailer or warden.

9 A toss-pot is a heavy drinker or a drunkard.

10 In Chapter 12 of *The Wind in the Willows,* a trapdoor to the butler's pantry at Toad Hall and a secret passage that runs underground to the river provide the means for Mole, Rat, Badger, and Toad to retake Toad Hall from the weasels, which is the opposite of the use Bilbo finds for the trapdoor here.

some full casks here instead of the empty ones, if there is anything in weight."

"Get on with the work!" growled the butler. "There is nothing in the feeling of weight in an idle toss-pot's[9] arms. These are the ones to go and no others. Do as I say!"

"Very well, very well," they answered rolling the barrels to the opening. "On your head be it, if the king's full buttertubs and his best wine is pushed into the river for the Lake-men to feast on for nothing!"

Roll — roll — roll — roll,
roll-roll-rolling down the hole!
Heave ho! Splash plump!
Down they go, down they bump!

So they sang as first one barrel and then another rumbled to the dark opening and was pushed over into the cold water some feet below. Some were barrels really empty, some were tubs neatly packed with a dwarf each; but down they all went, one after another, with many a clash and a bump, thudding on top of ones below, smacking into the water, jostling against the walls of the tunnel, knocking into one another, and bobbing away down the current.

It was just at this moment that Bilbo suddenly discovered the weak point in his plan. Most likely you saw it some time ago and have been laughing at him; but I don't suppose you would have done half as well yourselves in his place. Of course he was not in a barrel himself, nor was there anyone to pack him in, even if there had been a chance! It looked as if he would certainly lose his friends this time (nearly all of them had already disappeared through the dark trapdoor[10]), and get utterly left behind and have to stay lurking as a permanent burglar in the elf-caves for ever. For even if he could have escaped through the upper gates at once, he had precious small chance of ever finding the dwarves again. He did

The barrels are emptied from the Elvenking's cellars. Illustration by Ryûichi Terashima for the 1965 Japanese edition.

not know the way by land to the place where the barrels were collected. He wondered what on earth would happen to them without him; for he had not had time to tell the dwarves all that he had learned, or what he had meant to do, once they were out of the wood.

While all these thoughts were passing through his mind, the elves being very merry began to sing a song round the river-door. Some had already gone to haul on the ropes which pulled up the portcullis at the water-gate so as to let out the barrels as soon as they were all afloat below.

> *Down the swift dark stream you go*
> *Back to lands you once did know!*
> *Leave the halls and caverns deep,*
> *Leave the northern mountains steep,*
> *Where the forest wide and dim*
> *Stoops in shadow grey and grim!*
> *Float beyond the world of trees*
> *Out into the whispering breeze,*
> *Past the rushes, past the reeds,*
> *Past the marsh's waving weeds,*
> *Through the mist that riseth white*
> *Up from mere and pool at night!*
> *Follow, follow stars that leap*
> *Up the heavens cold and steep;*
> *Turn when dawn comes over land,*
> *Over rapid, over sand,*
> *South away! and South away!*
> *Seek the sunlight and the day,*
> *Back to pasture, back to mead,*
> *Where the kine[11] and oxen feed!*
> *Back to gardens on the hills*
> *Where the berry swells and fills*
> *Under sunlight, under day!*
> *South away! and South away!*
> *Down the swift dark stream you go*
> *Back to lands you once did know!*

11 *Kine* is the archaic double plural of *cow,* from the Old English *cy,* the plural of *cu,* cow, plus -(*e*)*n*.

Now the very last barrel was being rolled to the doors! In despair and not knowing what else to do, poor little Bilbo caught hold of it and was pushed over the edge with it. Down into the water he fell, splash! into the cold dark water with the barrel on top of him.

He came up again spluttering and clinging to the wood like a rat, but for all his efforts he could not scramble on top. Every time he tried, the barrel rolled round and ducked him under again. It was really empty, and floated light as a cork. Though his ears were full of water, he could hear the elves still singing in the cellar above. Then suddenly the trapdoors fell to with a boom and their voices faded away. He was in the dark tunnel floating in icy water, all alone – for you cannot count friends that are all packed up in barrels.

Very soon a grey patch came in the darkness ahead. He heard the creak of the water-gate being hauled up, and he found that he was in the midst of a bobbing and bumping mass of casks and tubs all pressing together to pass under the arch and get out into the open stream. He had as much as he could do to prevent himself from being hustled and battered to bits; but at last the jostling crowd began to break up and swing off, one by one, under the stony arch and away. Then he saw that it would have been no good even if he had managed to get astride his barrel, for there was no room to spare, not even for a hobbit, between its top and the suddenly stooping roof where the gate was.

Out they went under the overhanging branches of the trees on either bank. Bilbo wondered what the dwarves were feeling and whether a lot of water was getting into their tubs. Some of those that bobbed along by him in the gloom seemed pretty low in the water, and he guessed that these had dwarves inside.

"I do hope I put the lids on tight enough!" he thought, but before long he was worrying too much about himself to remember the dwarves. He managed to keep his head above the water, but he was shivering with the cold, and he wondered if he would die of it before the luck turned, and how much longer he would be able to hang on, and whether he should risk the chance of letting go and trying to swim to the bank.

The luck turned all right before long: the eddying current carried several barrels close ashore at one point and there for a while they stuck against some hidden root. Then Bilbo took the opportunity of scrambling up the side of his barrel while it was held steady against another. Up he crawled like a drowned rat, and lay on the top spread out to keep the balance as best he could. The breeze was cold but better than the water, and he hoped he would not suddenly roll off again when they started off once more.

Before long the barrels broke free again and turned and twisted off down the stream, and out into the main current. Then he found it quite as difficult to stick on as he had feared; but he managed it somehow, though it was miserably uncomfortable. Luckily he was very light, and the barrel was a good big one and being rather leaky had now shipped a small amount of water. All the same it was like trying to ride, without bridle or stirrups, a round-bellied pony that was always thinking of rolling on the grass.

In this way at last Mr. Baggins came to a place where the trees on either hand grew thinner. He could see the paler sky between them. The dark river opened suddenly wide, and there it was joined to the main water of the Forest River flowing down in haste from the king's great doors. There was a dim sheet of water no longer overshadowed, and on its sliding surface there were dancing and broken reflections of clouds and of stars. Then the hurrying water of the Forest River swept all the company of casks and tubs away to the north bank, in which it had eaten out a wide bay. This had a shingly shore under hanging banks and was walled at the eastern end by a little jutting cape of hard rock. On the shal-

Sketch for The Forest River by J.R.R. Tolkien. This illustration was first published in *The J.R.R. Tolkien Calendar 1979* (1978). It also appears in *Artist* (No. 122) and *Pictures* (No. 13).

According to the text, Bilbo and the barrels containing the dwarves arrive at the huts of the Raft-elves while it is dark. Tolkien's version of this scene depicted in the picture at right is therefore accurate in this detail, while the finer and more striking illustration usually published with the book, *Bilbo comes to the Huts of the Raft-elves,* is incorrect, showing a freshly risen sun.

But there remain some other problems of perspective with the *Sketch for The Forest River.* The text describes Bilbo and the barrels as being on the northern branch of the Forest River as they merge with the stronger main branch from the south, with the current pushing the barrels to the north bank where a wide bay has formed. In the picture at right, Bilbo seems to be on the main branch, with the northern branch entering at the left and the wide bay in the distance at the right. If the wide bay is supposed to be on the north side of the river, then the moon (unmentioned in the text) is rising impossibly in the north. Tolkien's final version matches all of these points in the text save for having the sun rising, while the text says that on the surface of the river can be seen the "broken reflections of clouds and stars."

low shore most of the barrels ran aground, though a few went on to bump against the stony pier.

There were people on the look-out on the banks. They quickly poled and pushed all the barrels together into the shallows, and when they had counted them they roped them together and left them till the morning. Poor dwarves! Bilbo was not badly off now. He slipped from his barrel and waded ashore, and then sneaked along to some huts that he could see near the water's edge. He no longer thought twice about picking up a supper uninvited if he got the chance, he had been obliged to do it for so long, and he knew now only too well what it was to be really hungry, not merely politely interested in the dainties of a well-filled larder. Also he had caught a

Bilbo comes to the Huts of the Raft-elves

glimpse of a fire through the trees, and that appealed to him with his dripping and ragged clothes clinging to him cold and clammy.

There is no need to tell you much of his adventures that night, for now we are drawing near the end of the eastward journey and coming to the last and greatest adventure, so we must hurry on. Of course helped by his magic ring he got on very well at first, but he was given away in the end by his wet footsteps and the trail of drippings that he left wherever he went or sat; and also he began to snivel, and wherever he tried to hide he was

Bilbo comes to the Huts of the Raft-elves by J.R.R. Tolkien, one of the standard color illustrations for *The Hobbit,* first published in the 1937 second impression of the first English edition (where it was given a printed caption "The dark river opened suddenly wide") but not included in the 1938 American edition. This illustration appears in *Artist* (No. 124) and *Pictures* (No. 14). John and Priscilla Tolkien, in *The Tolkien Family Album* (1992), refer to this illustration as their father's favorite painting (p. 57). An unfinished sketch in colored pencil also appears in *Artist* (No. 123).

found out by the terrific explosions of his suppressed
sneezes. Very soon there was a fine commotion in the
village by the riverside; but Bilbo escaped into the
woods carrying a loaf and a leather bottle of wine and a
pie that did not belong to him. The rest of the night he
had to pass wet as he was and far from a fire, but the bottle helped him to do that, and he actually dozed a little
on some dry leaves, even though the year was getting
late and the air was chilly.

He woke again with a specially loud sneeze. It was already grey morning, and there was a merry racket down
by the river. They were making up a raft of barrels, and
the raft-elves would soon be steering it off down the
stream to Lake-town. Bilbo sneezed again. He was no
longer dripping but he felt cold all over. He scrambled
down as fast as his stiff legs would take him and managed just in time to get on to the mass of casks without
being noticed in the general bustle. Luckily there was no
sun at the time to cast an awkward shadow, and for a
mercy he did not sneeze again for a good while.

There was a mighty pushing of poles. The elves that
were standing in the shallow water heaved and shoved.
The barrels now all lashed together creaked and fretted.

"This is a heavy load!" some grumbled. "They float
too deep — some of these are never empty. If they had
come ashore in the daylight, we might have had a look
inside," they said.

"No time now!" cried the raftman. "Shove off!"

And off they went at last, slowly at first, until they had
passed the point of rock where other elves stood to fend
them off with poles, and then quicker and quicker as
they caught the main stream and went sailing away
down, down towards the Lake.

They had escaped the dungeons of the king and were
through the wood, but whether alive or dead still remains to be seen.

10

A Warm Welcome

THE DAY GREW LIGHTER AND WARMER as they floated along.[1] After a while the river rounded a steep shoulder of land that came down upon their left. Under its rocky feet like an inland cliff the deepest stream had flowed lapping and bubbling. Suddenly the cliff fell away. The shores sank. The trees ended. Then Bilbo saw a sight:

The lands opened wide about him, filled with the waters of the river which broke up and wandered in a hundred winding courses, or halted in marshes and pools dotted with isles on every side; but still a strong water flowed on steadily through the midst. And far away, its dark head in a torn cloud, there loomed the Mountain! Its nearest neighbours to the North-East and the tumbled land that joined it to them could not be seen. All alone it rose and looked across the marshes to the forest. The Lonely Mountain! Bilbo had come far and through many adventures to see it, and now he did not like the look of it in the least.

As he listened to the talk of the raftmen and pieced together the scraps of information they let fall, he soon realized that he was very fortunate ever to have seen it at all, even from this distance. Dreary as had been his imprisonment and unpleasant as was his position (to say nothing of the poor dwarves underneath him) still, he had been more lucky than he had guessed. The talk was

1 From Bilbo's speech at his birthday party in the first chapter of *The Lord of the Rings* we learn that Bilbo's birthday, September 22, is "the anniversary of my arrival by barrel at Esgaroth on the Long Lake; though the fact that it was my birthday slipped my memory on that occasion. I was only fifty-one then, and birthdays did not seem so important. The banquet was very splendid, however, though I had a bad cold at the time, I remember, and could only say 'thag you very buch.' "

However, on page 252 it states that Bilbo was too sick to attend banquets immediately: "for three days he sneezed and coughed, and he could not go out, and even after that his speeches at banquets were limited to 'Thag you very buch.' "

all of the trade that came and went on the waterways and the growth of the traffic on the river, as the roads out of the East towards Mirkwood vanished or fell into disuse; and of the bickerings of the Lake-men and the Wood-elves about the upkeep of the Forest River and the care of the banks. Those lands had changed much since the days when dwarves dwelt in the Mountain, days which most people now remembered only as a very shadowy tradition. They had changed even in recent years, and since the last news that Gandalf had had of them. Great floods and rains had swollen the waters that flowed east; and there had been an earthquake or two (which some were inclined to attribute to the dragon—alluding to him chiefly with a curse and an ominous nod in the direction of the Mountain). The marshes and bogs had spread wider and wider on either side. Paths had vanished, and many a rider and wanderer too, if they had tried to find the lost ways across. The elf-road through the wood which the dwarves had followed on the advice of Beorn now came to a doubtful and little used end at the eastern edge of the forest; only the river offered any longer a safe way from the skirts of Mirkwood in the North to the mountain-shadowed plains beyond, and the river was guarded by the Wood-elves' king.

So you see Bilbo had come in the end by the only road that was any good. It might have been some comfort to Mr. Baggins shivering on the barrels, if he had known that news of this had reached Gandalf far away and given him great anxiety, and that he was in fact finishing his other business (which does not come into this tale) and getting ready to come in search of Thorin's company. But Bilbo did not know it.

All he knew was that the river seemed to go on and on and on for ever, and he was hungry, and had a nasty cold in the nose, and did not like the way the Mountain seemed to frown at him and threaten him as it drew ever nearer. After a while, however, the river took a more southerly course and the Mountain receded again, and at last, late in the day the shores grew rocky, the river gathered all its wandering waters together into a deep and rapid flood, and they swept along at great speed.

The sun had set when turning with another sweep towards the East the forest-river rushed into the Long Lake. There it had a wide mouth with stony clifflike gates at either side whose feet were piled with shingles. The Long Lake! Bilbo had never imagined that any water that was not the sea could look so big. It was so wide that the opposite shores looked small and far, but it was so long that its northerly end, which pointed towards the Mountain, could not be seen at all. Only from the map[2] did Bilbo know that away up there, where the stars of the Wain[3] were already twinkling, the Running River came down into the lake from Dale[4] and with the Forest River filled with deep waters what must once have been a great deep rocky valley. At the southern end the doubled waters poured out again over high waterfalls and ran away hurriedly to unknown lands. In the still evening air the noise of the falls could be heard like a distant roar.

Not far from the mouth of the Forest River was the strange town he heard the elves speak of in the king's cellars. It was not built on the shore, though there were a few huts and buildings there, but right out on the surface of the lake, protected from the swirl of the entering river by a promontory of rock which formed a calm bay. A great bridge made of wood ran out to where on huge piles made of forest trees was built a busy wooden town, not a town of elves but of Men, who still dared to dwell here under the shadow of the distant dragon-mountain. They still throve on the trade that came up the great river from the South and was carted past the falls to their town; but in the great days of old, when Dale in the North was rich and prosperous, they had been wealthy and powerful, and there had been fleets of boats on the waters, and some were filled with gold and some with warriors in armour, and there had been wars and deeds

2 The map referred to by Bilbo must be Thror's Map. In the original "home manuscript" of *The Hobbit*, Tolkien did have some additional maps he had drawn for the story. One of these, published in *Artist* (No. 128), shows the Lonely Mountain and a map of Long Lake.

3 The Wain is a name for the seven main stars of the constellation Ursa Major, the Great Bear. These stars are more commonly known in England as the Plough and in America as the Big Dipper.

4 The extent of William Morris's influence on Tolkien is often underrated. Morris was a poet who translated some of the great literature of the medieval North. He also wrote prose romances that are tinged with a medieval flavor and written with great precision in the details of the imagined landscapes. Tolkien, in his literary endeavors, followed Morris's example.

Additionally, as Richard Matthews has aptly expressed it, "Tolkien was clearly influenced by Morris's sensibilities for landscape and geography—wood, mountain, waste, etc.—and his obvious pleasure in naming. Tolkien carried it further and developed the linguistics of the game to a considerably advanced state, but the seeds are to be found in Morris." For example, in Morris's prosaically titled *The Roots of the Mountain: Wherein is Told Somewhat of the Lives of the Men of Burgdale, Their Friends, Their Neighbours, Their Foemen, and Their Fellows in Arms* (1890), we find a river named the Weltering Water, which runs through the Dale, and one called the Wildlake, which run

Lake Town by J.R.R. Tolkien, one of the standard black-and-white illustrations that has appeared in *The Hobbit* since 1937. This illustration appears in *Artist* (No. 127) and in *Pictures* (No. 15, left). A version of this illustration colored by H. E. Riddett first appeared in *The Hobbit Calendar 1976* (1975), and in *Pictures* (No. 15, right).

An earlier version entitled *Esgaroth,* closely similar but showing two dwarves emerging from the barrels at the left, is published in *Artist* (No. 126).

The conception of "Lake Town" recalls the various prehistoric lake villages of Europe, many of which were in Switzerland, though evidence has been found for similar settlements all around Europe as well as in Scotland and England, including the Holderness peninsula, Yorkshire, where Tolkien was posted for almost a year during World War I beginning in April 1917. Much of the scholarship on lake dwellings dates from the mid- to late nineteenth century, and some of the archeological monographs include artistic reconstructions of lake dwellings.

One such reconstruction (opposite, top) is from *Les Stations Lacustres d'Europe aux Ages de la Pierre et du Bronze* (1908) by Robert Munro. The printed illustration is credited as being based on one by A. de Mortillet.

A more curious reconstruction (opposite, center), with some very odd roofs on the structures, comes from *Die Keltische Pfahlbauten in den Schweizerseen* (1854) by Ferdinand Keller.

The *Ideal Sketch of a Swiss Lake Dwelling* (opposite, bottom) is the frontispiece to the English edition of volume one of the "greatly enlarged" second edition of Ferdinand Keller's *The Lake Dwellings of Switzerland and Other Parts of Europe* (1878), translated by John Edward Lee. It differs from the illustration in other editions of this work but was made under Keller's direction and received his approval.

A lake village on Lake Prasias, near Mt. Pangaeum (in present-day Greece, near the Aegean Sea and to the south of Bulgaria), is described by the Greek historian Herodotus (c. 480–c. 425 B.C.) as follows:

> The houses of these lake-dwellers are actually in the water, and stand on platforms supported by long piles and approached from the land by a single narrow bridge. . . . Each member of the tribe has his own hut on one of the platforms, with a trap-door opening to the water underneath. . . . Their horses and other pack-animals they feed on fish, which are so abundant in the lake that, when they open the trap-door and let down an empty basket on a rope, they have only a minute to wait before they pull it up again, full. (Book V, *The Histories*, translation by Aubrey de Sélincourt, revised by A. R. Burn, published in 1972)

away to the Plain-country. The similarity to Tolkien's Running River, Dale, and Forest River is easily apparent.

Although the phrase "roots of the mountain" considerably predates Morris, Tolkien uses it twice in *The Hobbit,* on page 119, describing where Gollum lives, and on page 287, describing where the Dwarves had found the Arkenstone. Another phrase that seems a more deliberate echo of Morris occurs on page 45, "the wood beyond The Water," which recalls the titles of his later novels *The Wood Beyond the World* (1894), and *The Water of the Wondrous Isles* (1897).

IDEAL SKETCH ᴏꜰᴀ SWISS LAKE-DWELLING.

5 The history of this "greater town" was not chronicled by J.R.R. Tolkien.

which were now only a legend. The rotting piles of a greater town could still be seen along the shores when the waters sank in a drought.[5]

But men remembered little of all that, though some still sang old songs of the dwarf-kings of the Mountain, Thror and Thrain of the race of Durin, and of the coming of the Dragon, and the fall of the lords of Dale. Some sang too that Thror and Thrain would come back one day and gold would flow in rivers, through the mountain-gates, and all that land would be filled with new song and new laughter. But this pleasant legend did not much affect their daily business.

As soon as the raft of barrels came in sight boats rowed out from the piles of the town, and voices hailed the raft-steerers. Then ropes were cast and oars were pulled, and soon the raft was drawn out of the current of the Forest River and towed away round the high shoulder of rock into the little bay of Lake-town. There it was moored not far from the shoreward head of the great bridge. Soon men would come up from the South and take some of the casks away, and others they would fill with goods they had brought to be taken back up the stream to the Wood-elves' home. In the meanwhile the barrels were left afloat while the elves of the raft and the boatmen went to feast in Lake-town.

They would have been surprised, if they could have seen what happened down by the shore, after they had gone and the shades of night had fallen. First of all a barrel was cut loose by Bilbo and pushed to the shore and opened. Groans came from inside, and out crept a most unhappy dwarf. Wet straw was in his draggled beard; he was so sore and stiff, so bruised and buffeted he could hardly stand or stumble through the shallow water to lie groaning on the shore. He had a famished and a savage look like a dog that has been chained and forgotten in a kennel for a week. It was Thorin, but you could only have told it by his golden chain, and by the colour of his now dirty and tattered sky-blue hood with its tarnished silver tassel. It was some time before he would be even polite to the hobbit.

"Well, are you alive or are you dead?" asked Bilbo quite crossly. Perhaps he had forgotten that he had had at least one good meal more than the dwarves, and also the use of his arms and legs, not to speak of a greater allowance of air. "Are you still in prison, or are you free? If you want food, and if you want to go on with this silly adventure — it's yours after all and not mine — you had better slap your arms and rub your legs and try and help me get the others out while there is a chance!"

Bilbo releases a Dwarf from a barrel. Illustration by Chica for the 1976 French edition

Thorin of course saw the sense of this, so after a few more groans he got up and helped the hobbit as well as he could. In the darkness floundering in the cold water they had a difficult and very nasty job finding which were the right barrels. Knocking outside and calling only discovered about six dwarves that could answer. These were unpacked and helped ashore where they sat or lay muttering and moaning; they were so soaked and bruised and cramped that they could hardly yet realize their release or be properly thankful for it.

Dwalin and Balin were two of the most unhappy, and it was no good asking them to help. Bifur and Bofur were less knocked about and drier, but they lay down and would do nothing. Fili and Kili, however, who were young (for dwarves) and had also been packed more neatly with plenty of straw into smaller casks, came out more or less smiling, with only a bruise or two and a stiffness that soon wore off.

"I hope I never smell the smell of apples again!" said Fili. "My tub was full of it. To smell apples everlastingly when you can scarcely move and are cold and sick with hunger is maddening. I could eat anything in the wide world now, for hours on end — but not an apple!"

With the willing help of Fili and Kili, Thorin and Bilbo at last discovered the remainder of the company and got them out. Poor fat Bombur was asleep or sense-

Bilbo frees the Dwarves from their barrels. Illustration by Torbjörn Zetterholm for the 1947 Swedish edition.

6 A gammer is an old woman. The term is often used contemptuously or humorously. In origin it is apparently a contraction of *grandmother*. *Gaffer* is the corresponding term for an old man.

less; Dori, Nori, Ori, Oin and Gloin were waterlogged and seemed only half alive; they all had to be carried one by one and laid helpless on the shore.

"Well! Here we are!" said Thorin. "And I suppose we ought to thank our stars and Mr. Baggins. I am sure he has a right to expect it, though I wish he could have arranged a more comfortable journey. Still — all very much at your service once more, Mr. Baggins. No doubt we shall feel properly grateful, when we are fed and recovered. In the meanwhile what next?"

"I suggest Lake-town," said Bilbo. "What else is there?"

Nothing else could, of course, be suggested; so leaving the others Thorin and Fili and Kili and the hobbit went along the shore to the great bridge. There were guards at the head of it, but they were not keeping very careful watch, for it was so long since there had been any real need. Except for occasional squabbles about river-tolls they were friends with the Wood-elves. Other folk were far away; and some of the younger people in the town openly doubted the existence of any dragon in the mountain, and laughed at the greybeards and gammers**6** who said that they had seen him flying in the sky in their young days. That being so it is not surprising that the guards were drinking and laughing by a fire in their hut, and did not hear the noise of the unpacking of the dwarves or the footsteps of the four scouts. Their astonishment was enormous when Thorin Oakenshield stepped in through the door.

"Who are you and what do you want?" they shouted leaping to their feet and groping for weapons.

"Thorin son of Thrain son of Thror King under the Mountain!" said the dwarf in a loud voice, and he looked it, in spite of his torn clothes and draggled hood. The gold gleamed on his neck and waist; his eyes were dark and deep. "I have come back. I wish to see the Master of your town!"

Then there was tremendous excitement. Some of the more foolish ran out of the hut as if they expected the Mountain to go golden in the night and all the waters of the lake turn yellow right away. The captain of the guard came forward.

"And who are these?" he asked, pointing to Fili and Kili and Bilbo.

"The sons of my father's daughter," answered Thorin, "Fili and Kili of the race of Durin, and Mr. Baggins who has travelled with us out of the West."

"If you come in peace lay down your arms!" said the captain.

"We have none," said Thorin, and it was true enough: their knives had been taken from them by the wood-elves, and the great sword Orcrist too. Bilbo had his short sword, hidden as usual, but he said nothing about that. "We have no need of weapons, who return at last to our own as spoken of old. Nor could we fight against so many. Take us to your master!"

"He is at feast," said the captain.

"Then all the more reason for taking us to him," burst in Fili, who was getting impatient at these solemnities. "We are worn and famished after our long road and we have sick comrades. Now make haste and let us have no more words, or your master may have something to say to you."

"Follow me then," said the captain, and with six men about them he led them over the bridge through the gates and into the market-place of the town. This was a wide circle of quiet water surrounded by the tall piles on which were built the greater houses, and by long wooden quays with many steps and ladders going down to the surface of the lake. From one great hall shone many lights and there came the sound of many voices. They passed its doors and stood blinking in the light looking at long tables filled with folk.

"I am Thorin son of Thrain son of Thror King under

the Mountain! I return!" cried Thorin in a loud voice from the door, before the captain could say anything.

All leaped to their feet. The Master of the town sprang from his great chair. But none rose in greater surprise than the raft-men of the elves who were sitting at the lower end of the hall. Pressing forward before the Master's table they cried:

"These are prisoners of our king that have escaped, wandering vagabond dwarves that could not give any good account of themselves, sneaking through the woods and molesting our people!"

"Is this true?" asked the Master. As a matter of fact he thought it far more likely than the return of the King under the Mountain, if any such person had ever existed.

"It is true that we were wrongfully waylaid by the Elvenking and imprisoned without cause as we journeyed back to our own land," answered Thorin. "But lock nor bar may hinder the homecoming spoken of old. Nor is this town in the Wood-elves' realm. I speak to the Master of the town of the Men of the Lake, not to the raft-men of the king."

Then the Master hesitated and looked from one to the other. The Elvenking was very powerful in those parts and the Master wished for no enmity with him, nor did he think much of old songs, giving his mind to trade and tolls, to cargoes and gold, to which habit he owed his position. Others were of different mind, however, and quickly the matter was settled without him. The news had spread from the doors of the hall like fire through all the town. People were shouting inside the hall and outside it. The quays were thronged with hurrying feet. Some began to sing snatches of old songs concerning the return of the King under the Mountain; that it was Thror's grandson not Thror himself that had come back did not bother them at all. Others took up the song and it rolled loud and high over the lake.

The King beneath the mountains,
The King of carven stone,
The lord of silver fountains
Shall come into his own!

His crown shall be upholden,
His harp shall be restrung,
His halls shall echo golden
To songs of yore re-sung.

The woods shall wave on mountains
And grass beneath the sun;
His wealth shall flow in fountains
And the rivers golden run.

The streams shall run in gladness,
The lakes shall shine and burn,
All sorrow fail and sadness
At the Mountain-king's return!

So they sang, or very like that, only there was a great deal more of it, and there was much shouting as well as the music of harps and of fiddles mixed up with it. Indeed such excitement had not been known in the town in the memory of the oldest grandfather. The Wood-elves themselves began to wonder greatly and even to be afraid. They did not know of course how Thorin had escaped, and they began to think their king might have made a serious mistake. As for the Master he saw there was nothing else for it but to obey the general clamour, for the moment at any rate, and to pretend to believe that Thorin was what he said. So he gave up to him his own great chair and set Fili and Kili beside him in places of honour. Even Bilbo was given a seat at the high table, and no explanation of where he came in — no songs had alluded to him even in the obscurest way — was asked for in the general bustle.

Soon afterwards the other dwarves were brought into

7 *1937:* "the dwarves good feeling" >
1966-Ball: "the dwarves' good feeling"
   A typographical error that escaped
detection until 1966.

the town amid scenes of astonishing enthusiasm. They were all doctored and fed and housed and pampered in the most delightful and satisfactory fashion. A large house was given up to Thorin and his company; boats and rowers were put at their service; and crowds sat outside and sang songs all day, or cheered if any dwarf showed so much as his nose.

Some of the songs were old ones; but some of them were quite new and spoke confidently of the sudden death of the dragon and of cargoes of rich presents coming down the river to Lake-town. These were inspired largely by the Master and they did not particularly please the dwarves, but in the meantime they were well contented and they quickly grew fat and strong again. Indeed within a week they were quite recovered, fitted out in fine cloth of their proper colours, with beards combed and trimmed, and proud steps. Thorin looked and walked as if his kingdom was already regained and Smaug chopped up into little pieces.

Then, as he had said, the dwarves' good feeling[7] towards the little hobbit grew stronger every day. There were no more groans or grumbles. They drank his health, and they patted him on the back, and they made a great fuss of him; which was just as well, for he was not feeling particularly cheerful. He had not forgotten the look of the Mountain, nor the thought of the dragon, and he had besides a shocking cold. For three days he sneezed and coughed, and he could not go out, and even after that his speeches at banquets were limited to "Thag you very buch."

In the meanwhile the Wood-elves had gone back up the Forest River with their cargoes, and there was great excitement in the king's palace. I have never heard what happened to the chief of the guards and the butler. Nothing of course was ever said about keys or barrels while the dwarves stayed in Lake-town, and Bilbo was careful never to become invisible. Still, I daresay, more was guessed than was known, though doubtless Mr. Baggins remained a bit of a mystery. In any case the king knew now the dwarves' errand, or thought he did, and he said to himself:

"Very well! We'll see! No treasure will come back through Mirkwood without my having something to say in the matter. But I expect they will all come to a bad end, and serve them right!" He at any rate did not believe in dwarves fighting and killing dragons like Smaug, and he strongly suspected attempted burglary or something like it—which shows he was a wise elf and wiser than the men of the town, though not quite right, as we shall see in the end. He sent out his spies about the shores of the lake and as far northward towards the Mountain as they would go, and waited.

At the end of a fortnight Thorin began to think of departure. While the enthusiasm still lasted in the town was the time to get help. It would not do to let everything cool down with delay. So he spoke to the Master and his councillors[8] and said that soon he and his company must go on towards the Mountain.

Then for the first time the Master was surprised and a little frightened; and he wondered if Thorin was after all really a descendant of the old kings. He had never thought that the dwarves would actually dare to approach Smaug, but believed they were frauds who would sooner or later be discovered and be turned out. He was wrong. Thorin, of course, was really the grandson of the King under the Mountain, and there is no knowing what a dwarf will not dare and do for revenge or the recovery of his own.

But the Master was not sorry at all to let them go. They were expensive to keep, and their arrival had turned things into a long holiday in which business was at a standstill. "Let them go and bother Smaug, and see how he welcomes them!" he thought. "Certainly, O Thorin Thrain's son Thror's son!" was what he said. "You must claim your own. The hour is at hand, spoken

8 The Master and his councillors may owe their inspiration to the Mayor and Corporation who rule the city of Hamelin in Robert Browning's poem "The Pied Piper of Hamelin" (1842). Both the master of Lake-town and the Mayor of Hamelin are niggardly, selfish, and aware of their townsmen's interests in only the most self-serving manner.

Tolkien knew the Browning poem well—in fact, he loathed it, calling it, in a letter to his aunt Jane Neave of November 22, 1961, a "terrible presage of the most vulgar elements in Disney . . . It failed with me, even as a child, when I could not yet distinguish the shallow vulgarity of Browning from the general grown-uppishness of things that I was expected to like" (*Letters,* No. 234). That it was on his mind around the time *The Hobbit* was being written is confirmed in his satirical poem "Progress in Bimble Town," published in the *Oxford Magazine* on October 15, 1931; it appears below. The poem, dedicated to the Mayor and Corporation, was published under the pseudonym K. Bagpuize, which was short for Kingston Bagpuize, a village some miles west of Oxford.

The poem is one of Tolkien's series of "Tales and Songs of Bimble Bay" and was probably written in the few years just prior to its publication. The poem as published contains only forty-four lines, but the earliest surviving manuscript, a clear copy with very few emendations entitled "The Progress of Bimble," is a full one hundred and twenty-two lines long. On this manuscript, at a stanza break following line 44, Tolkien penciled a note that says "end here," and all of the subsequent versions do. The remaining seventy-eight lines, continuing on in the same manner, are unpublished. One other Bimble Bay poem, the unpublished "Old Grabbler" (the earlier version is titled "Poor Old Grabbler"), continues in this satirical mode, showing Tolkien's concerns over pollution and the effects of industrialization (these concerns are also apparent in *Roverandom*).

The seaside setting may have been inspired by the family's summer holidays in Filey in North Yorkshire in 1923 and 1925.

PROGRESS IN BIMBLE TOWN

(Dedicated to the Mayor and Corporation.)

Bimble-bay has a steep street:
it runs down with many houses,
tall ones, short ones; shops with meat,
shops with cabbages, shops with blouses,
jersies, jumpers and umbrellas;
a post-office (new and squalid);
a library filled with best-sellers
in yellow jackets; an old, solid,
manywindowed inn where motors
make strong smells, and no horse goes
in cobbled yard; a place where bloaters
from wooden boxes lie in rows
(brought by train for sea-side air);
a pharmacy with sunburn-lotion
and picture-cards (of Godknowswhere,
and fat women dipped in ocean);
a toy bazaar with things of tin,
and bits of crock, and all the news;
windows, windows with chocolates in,
cigarettes, and gum one chews
(wrapped in paper, cased in card,
for folk to strew on grass and shore);
loud garages, where toiling hard
grimy people bang and roar,
and engines buzz, and the lights flare,
all night long — a merry noise!
Sometimes through it (this is rare)
one can hear the shouts of boys;
sometimes late, when motor-bikes
are not passing with a screech,

of old. What help we can offer shall be yours, and we trust to your gratitude when your kingdom is regained."

So one day, although autumn was now getting far on, and winds were cold, and leaves were falling fast, three large boats left Lake-town, laden with rowers, dwarves, Mr. Baggins, and many provisions. Horses and ponies had been sent round by circuitous paths to meet them at their appointed landing-place. The Master and his councillors bade them farewell from the great steps of the town-hall that went down to the lake. People sang on the quays and out of windows. The white oars dipped and splashed, and off they went north up the lake on the last stage of their long journey. The only person thoroughly unhappy was Bilbo.

one hears faintly (if one likes)
the sea still at it on the beach.
at what? At churning orange-rind,
piling up banana-skins,
gnawing paper, trying to grind
a broth of bottles, packets, tins,
before a new day comes with more,
before next morning's charabangs,
stopping at the old inn-door
with reek and rumble, hoots and clangs,
bring more folk to Godknowswhere
and Theydontcare, to Bimble Town
where the steep street, that once was fair,
with many houses staggers down,
    See Britain First!
    K. Bagpuize

The mention in lines 7–8 of "best sellers in yellow jackets" probably refers to the publications of the firm Victor Gollancz Limited, founded in 1927, whose books for many years sported bright yellow dust jackets, without any illustrations but with advertising hooks and reviewer's comments printed on the front covers. "See Britain First" was a contemporary tourism slogan.

11

On the Doorstep

IN TWO DAYS GOING THEY ROWED right up the Long Lake and passed out into the River Running, and now they could all see the Lonely Mountain towering grim and tall before them. The stream was strong and their going slow. At the end of the third day, some miles up the river, they drew in to the left or western bank and disembarked. Here they were joined by the horses with other provisions and necessaries and the ponies for their own use that had been sent to meet them. They packed what they could on the ponies and the rest was made into a store under a tent, but none of the men of the town would stay with them even for the night so near the shadow of the Mountain.

"Not at any rate until the songs have come true!" said they. It was easier to believe in the Dragon and less easy to believe in Thorin in these wild parts. Indeed their stores had no need of any guard, for all the land was desolate and empty. So their escort left them, making off swiftly down the river and the shoreward paths, although the night was already drawing on.

They spent a cold and lonely night and their spirits fell. The next day they set out again. Balin and Bilbo rode behind, each leading another pony heavily laden beside him; the others were some way ahead picking out a slow road, for there were no paths. They made north-

As with the Misty Mountains, Tolkien's Lonely Mountain is Alpine in shape and form. The above photograph is of the Matterhorn, viewed from the northeast. It was taken by E. Elliot Stock and published in his *Scrambles in Storm and Sunshine* (1910). In his walking tour of Switzerland in the summer of 1911, Tolkien and his companions would have had some spectacular views of the Matterhorn as they approached it from the northeast and passed by it to the north.

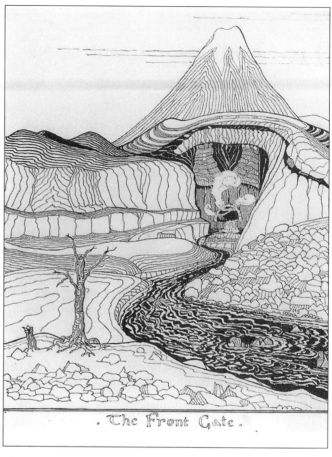

. The Front Gate .

The Front Gate by J.R.R. Tolkien, one of the standard black-and-white illustrations that has appeared in *The Hobbit* since 1937. This drawing appears in *Artist* (No. 130) and *Pictures* (No. 16, left). A version of this illustration colored by H. E. Riddett first appeared in *The Hobbit Calendar 1976* (1975) and in *Pictures* (No. 16, right). The gnarled and anthropomorphic tree in the foreground is a close copy of an ink sketch Tolkien made in July 1928 (see *Artist,* No. 129).

west, slanting away from the River Running, and drawing ever nearer and nearer to a great spur of the Mountain that was flung out southwards towards them.

It was a weary journey, and a quiet and stealthy one. There was no laughter or song or sound of harps, and the pride and hopes which had stirred in their hearts at the singing of old songs by the lake died away to a plodding gloom. They knew that they were drawing near to the end of their journey, and that it might be a very horrible end. The land about them grew bleak and barren, though once, as Thorin told them, it had been green and fair. There was little grass, and before long there was neither bush nor tree, and only broken and blackened stumps to speak of ones long vanished. They were come to the Desolation of the Dragon,[1] and they were come at the waning of the year.

They reached the skirts of the Mountain all the same without meeting any danger or any sign of the Dragon other than the wilderness he had made about his lair. The Mountain lay dark and silent before them and ever higher above them. They made their first camp on the western side of the great southern spur, which ended in a height called Ravenhill. On this there had been an old watch-post; but they dared not climb it yet, it was too exposed.

Before setting out to search the western spurs of the Mountain for the hidden door, on which all their hopes rested, Thorin sent out a scouting expedition to spy out the land to the South where the Front Gate stood. For this purpose he chose Balin and Fili and Kili, and with them went Bilbo. They marched under the grey and silent cliffs to the feet of Ravenhill. There the river, after winding a wide loop over the valley of Dale, turned from the Mountain on its road to the Lake, flowing swift and noisily. Its bank was bare and rocky, tall and steep above the stream; and gazing out from it over the narrow water, foaming and splashing among many boulders, they could see in the wide valley shadowed by the Mountain's arms the grey ruins of ancient houses, towers, and walls.

"There lies all that is left of Dale," said Balin. "The mountain's sides were green with woods and all the

1 The extent of the Desolation of Smaug is marked on both Thror's Map and on the map of Wilderland.

sheltered valley rich and pleasant in the days when the bells rang in that town." He looked both sad and grim as he said this: he had been one of Thorin's companions on the day the Dragon came.

They did not dare to follow the river much further towards the Gate; but they went on beyond the end of the southern spur, until lying hidden behind a rock they could look out and see the dark cavernous opening in a great cliff-wall between the arms of the Mountain. Out of it the waters of the Running River sprang; and out of it too there came a steam and a dark smoke. Nothing moved in the waste, save the vapour and the water, and every now and again a black and ominous crow. The only sound was the sound of the stony water, and every now and again the harsh croak of a bird. Balin shuddered.

"Let us return!" he said. "We can do no good here! And I don't like these dark birds, they look like spies of evil."

"The dragon is still alive and in the halls under the Mountain then — or I imagine so from the smoke," said the hobbit.

"That does not prove it," said Balin, "though I don't doubt you are right. But he might be gone away some time, or he might be lying out on the mountain-side keeping watch, and still I expect smokes and steams would come out of the gates: all the halls within must be filled with his foul reek."

With such gloomy thoughts, followed ever by croaking crows above them, they made their weary way back to the camp. Only in June they had been guests in the fair house of Elrond, and though autumn was now crawling towards winter that pleasant time now seemed years ago. They were alone in the perilous waste without hope of further help. They were at the end of their journey, but as far as ever, it seemed, from the end of their quest. None of them had much spirit left.

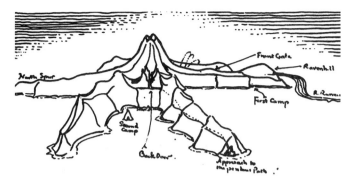

A schematic drawing by J.R.R. Tolkien of the Lonely Mountain as seen from the west. Tolkien has noted the positions of the First Camp by the southeast spur, and the Second Camp near the northwest spur. The note near the southwest spur reads, "Approach to the perilous Path." The Back Door is marked between the two western spurs.

A pencil sketch entitled *The Back Door* (below) gives a much closer look at that area, with the door itself open and several Dwarves visible, a few hauling up ropes, and Bilbo seen sitting near the trapezoid-shaped door. *The Back Door* also appears in *Artist* (No. 131), with another less complete sketch labeled *View from Back Door* (No. 132).

Now strange to say Mr. Baggins had more than the others. He would often borrow Thorin's map and gaze at it, pondering over the runes and the message of the moon-letters Elrond had read. It was he that made the dwarves begin the dangerous search on the western slopes for the secret door. They moved their camp then to a long valley, narrower than the great dale in the South where the Gates of the river stood, and walled with lower spurs of the Mountain. Two of these here thrust forward west from the main mass in long steep-sided ridges that fell ever downwards towards the plain. On this western side there were fewer signs of the dragon's marauding feet, and there was some grass for their ponies. From this western camp, shadowed all day by cliff and wall until the sun began to sink towards the forest, day by day they toiled in parties searching for paths up the mountain-side. If the map was true, somewhere high above the cliff at the valley's head must stand the secret door. Day by day they came back to their camp without success.

But at last unexpectedly they found what they were seeking. Fili and Kili and the hobbit went back one day down the valley and scrambled among the tumbled rocks at its southern corner. About midday, creeping behind a great stone that stood alone like a pillar, Bilbo came on what looked like rough steps going upwards. Following these excitedly he and the dwarves found traces of a narrow track, often lost, often rediscovered, that wandered on to the top of the southern ridge and brought them at last to a still narrower ledge, which turned north across the face of the Mountain. Looking down they saw that they were at the top of the cliff at the valley's head and were gazing down on to their own camp below. Silently, clinging to the rocky wall on their right, they went in single file along the ledge, till the wall opened and they turned into a little steep-walled bay, grassy-floored, still and quiet. Its entrance which they had found could not be seen from below because of the overhang of the cliff, nor from further off because it was so small that it looked like a dark crack and no more. It was not a cave and was open to the sky above; but at its inner end a flat wall rose up that in the lower part, close to the ground, was as smooth and upright as masons' work, but without a joint or crevice to be seen.[2] No sign was there of post or lintel or threshold, nor any sign of bar or bolt or key-hole; yet they did not doubt that they had found the door at last.

They beat on it, they thrust and pushed at it, they implored it to move, they spoke fragments of broken spells of opening, and nothing stirred. At last tired out they rested on the grass at its feet, and then at evening began their long climb down.

There was excitement in the camp that night. In the morning they prepared to move once more. Only Bofur and Bombur were left behind to guard the ponies and such stores as they had brought with them from the river. The others went down the valley and up the newly found path, and so to the narrow ledge. Along this they could carry no bundles or packs, so narrow and breathless was it, with a fall of a hundred and fifty feet beside them on to sharp rocks below; but each of them took a good coil of rope wound tight about his waist, and so at last without mishap they reached the little grassy bay.

There they made their third camp, hauling up what they needed from below with their ropes. Down the same way they were able occasionally to lower one of the more active dwarves, such as Kili, to exchange such news as there was, or to take a share in the guard below, while Bofur was hauled up to the higher camp. Bombur would not come up either the rope or the path.

"I am too fat for such fly-walks," he said. "I should turn dizzy and tread on my beard, and then you would be thirteen again. And the knotted ropes are too slender

2 In *1937, 1951, 1966-Ball,* and *1966-Longmans/Unwin* there is no break here to form a new paragraph. An erroneous paragraph break here has appeared in the *1966-A&U,* the *1967-HM,* and the 1978 fourth edition by Allen & Unwin.

for my weight." Luckily for him that was not true, as you will see.

In the meanwhile some of them explored the ledge beyond the opening and found a path that led higher and higher on to the mountain; but they did not dare to venture very far that way, nor was there much use in it. Out up there a silence reigned, broken by no bird or sound except that of the wind in the crannies of stone. They spoke low and never called or sang, for danger brooded in every rock. The others who were busy with the secret of the door had no more success. They were too eager to trouble about the runes or the moon-letters, but tried without resting to discover where exactly in the smooth face of the rock the door was hidden. They had brought picks and tools of many sorts from Lake-town, and at first they tried to use these. But when they struck the stone the handles splintered and jarred their arms cruelly, and the steel heads broke or bent like lead. Mining work, they saw clearly, was no good against the magic that had shut this door; and they grew terrified, too, of the echoing noise.

Bilbo found sitting on the doorstep lonesome and wearisome — there was not a doorstep, of course, really, but they used to call the little grassy space between the wall and the opening the "doorstep" in fun, remembering Bilbo's words long ago at the unexpected party in his hobbit-hole, when he said they could sit on the doorstep till they thought of something. And sit and think they did, or wandered aimlessly about, and glummer and glummer they became.

Their spirits had risen a little at the discovery of the path, but now they sank into their boots; and yet they would not give it up and go away. The hobbit was no longer much brighter than the dwarves. He would do nothing but sit with his back to the rock-face and stare away west through the opening, over the cliff, over the wide lands to the black wall of Mirkwood, and to the distances beyond, in which he sometimes thought he could catch glimpses of the Misty Mountains small and far. If the dwarves asked him what he was doing he answered:

"You said sitting on the doorstep and thinking would be my job, not to mention getting inside, so I am sitting and thinking." But I am afraid he was not thinking much of the job, but of what lay beyond the blue distance, the quiet Western Land and the Hill and his hobbit-hole under it.

A large grey stone lay in the centre of the grass and he stared moodily at it or watched the great snails. They seemed to love the little shut-in bay with its walls of cool rock, and there were many of them of huge size crawling slowly and stickily along its sides.

"Tomorrow begins the last week of autumn," said Thorin one day.

"And winter comes after autumn," said Bifur.

"And next year after that," said Dwalin, "and our beards will grow till they hang down the cliff to the valley before anything happens here. What is our burglar doing for us? Since he has got an invisible ring, and ought to be a specially excellent performer now, I am beginning to think he might go through the Front Gate and spy things out a bit!"

Bilbo heard this — the dwarves were on the rocks just above the enclosure where he was sitting — and "Good Gracious!" he thought, "so that is what they are beginning to think, is it? It is always poor me that has to get them out of their difficulties, at least since the wizard left. Whatever am I going to do? I might have known that something dreadful would happen to me in the end. I don't think I could bear to see the unhappy valley of Dale again, and as for that steaming gate! ! !"

That night he was very miserable and hardly slept. Next day the dwarves all went wandering off in various

Durin's Day. Illustration by Eric Fraser for the 1979 Folio Society edition.

directions; some were exercising the ponies down below, some were roving about the mountain-side. All day Bilbo sat gloomily in the grassy bay gazing at the stone, or out west through the narrow opening. He had a queer feeling that he was waiting for something. "Perhaps the wizard will suddenly come back today," he thought.

If he lifted his head he could see a glimpse of the distant forest. As the sun turned west there was a gleam of yellow upon its far roof, as if the light caught the last pale leaves. Soon he saw the orange ball of the sun sinking towards the level of his eyes. He went to the opening and there pale and faint was a thin new moon above the rim of Earth.

At that very moment he heard a sharp crack behind him. There on the grey stone in the grass was an enormous thrush, nearly coal black, its pale yellow breast freckled with dark spots. Crack! It had caught a snail and was knocking it on the stone. Crack! Crack!

Suddenly Bilbo understood. Forgetting all danger he stood on the ledge and hailed the dwarves, shouting and waving. Those that were nearest came tumbling over the rocks and as fast as they could along the ledge to him, wondering what on earth was the matter; the others shouted to be hauled up the ropes (except Bombur, of course: he was asleep).

Quickly Bilbo explained. They all fell silent: the hobbit standing by the grey stone, and the dwarves with wagging beards watching impatiently. The sun sank lower and lower, and their hopes fell. It sank into a belt of reddened cloud and disappeared. The dwarves groaned, but still Bilbo stood almost without moving. The little moon was dipping to the horizon. Evening was coming on. Then suddenly when their hope was lowest a red ray of the sun escaped like a finger through a rent in the cloud. A gleam of light came straight through the opening into the bay and fell on the smooth rock-face. The old thrush, who had been watching from a high perch with beady eyes and head cocked on one

Durin's Day. Illustration by Ryûichi Terashima for the 1965 Japanese edition.

side, gave a sudden trill. There was a loud crack. A flake of rock split from the wall and fell. A hole appeared suddenly about three feet from the ground.

Quickly, trembling lest the chance should fade, the dwarves rushed to the rock and pushed — in vain.

"The key! The key!" cried Bilbo. "Where is Thorin?"

Thorin hurried up.

"The key!" shouted Bilbo. "The key that went with the map! Try it now while there is still time!"

Then Thorin stepped up and drew the key on its chain from round his neck. He put it to the hole. It fitted and it turned! Snap! The gleam went out, the sun sank, the moon was gone, and evening sprang into the sky.

Now they all pushed together, and slowly a part of the rock-wall gave way. Long straight cracks appeared and widened. A door five feet high and three broad was outlined, and slowly without a sound swung inwards. It seemed as if darkness flowed out like a vapour from the hole in the mountain-side, and deep darkness in which nothing could be seen lay before their eyes, a yawning mouth leading in and down.

12

Inside Information

FOR A LONG TIME the dwarves stood in the dark before the door and debated, until at last Thorin spoke:

"Now is the time for our esteemed Mr. Baggins, who has proved himself a good companion on our long road, and a hobbit full of courage and resource far exceeding his size, and if I may say so possessed of good luck far exceeding the usual allowance — now is the time for him to perform the service for which he was included in our Company; now is the time for him to earn his Reward."

You are familiar with Thorin's style on important occasions, so I will not give you any more of it, though he went on a good deal longer than this. It certainly was an important occasion, but Bilbo felt impatient. By now he was quite familiar with Thorin too, and he knew what he was driving at.

"If you mean you think it is my job to go into the secret passage first, O Thorin Thrain's son Oakenshield, may your beard grow ever longer," he said crossly, "say so at once and have done! I might refuse. I have got you out of two messes already, which were hardly in the original bargain, so that I am, I think, already owed some reward. But 'third time pays for all'[1] as my father used to say, and somehow I don't think I shall refuse. Perhaps I have begun to trust my luck more than I used to in the old days" — he meant last spring before he left his own

[1] "Third time pays for all" is a medieval proverb, a notable use of which occurs in *Sir Gawain and the Green Knight*, where the lord of the house in which Gawain is staying says to him:

> *For I haf fraysted þe twys, and faythful I fynde þe.*
> *Now "þrid tyme þrowe best" þenk on þe morne.*
>   (lines 1679–80 of the 1925 Tolkien and Gordon edition)

Tolkien himself translated these lines as follows:

> *For I have tested thee twice, and trusty I find thee.*
> *Now "third time pays for all", bethink thee tomorrow!*
>   (p. 66 of the 1975 translation)

Bilbo uses the same proverb again on page 290.

Jared Lobdell, in his short article "A Medieval Proverb in *The Lord of the Rings*" from *American Notes and Queries Supplement* 1 (1978), notes three appearances of the proverb (two in variant form) in *The Lord of the Rings* and quotes a letter from Tolkien to Lobdell dated July 31, 1964, on the usage: "It is an old alliterative saying using the word *throw:* time, period (unrelated to the verb *throw*); sc. this third occasion is the best time — the time for special effort and/or luck. It is used when a third try is needed to rectify two poor efforts, or when a third occurrence may surpass the others and finally prove a man's worth, or a thing's."

Bilbo entering the back door to the Lonely Mountain, as the Dwarves look on. Illustration by Mikhail Belomlinskiy for the 1976 Russian edition.

house, but it seemed centuries ago — "but anyway I think I will go and have a peep at once and get it over. Now who is coming with me?"

He did not expect a chorus of volunteers, so he was not disappointed. Fili and Kili looked uncomfortable and stood on one leg, but the others made no pretence of offering — except old Balin, the look-out man, who was rather fond of the hobbit. He said he would come inside at least and perhaps a bit of the way too, ready to call for help if necessary.

The most that can be said for the dwarves is this: they intended to pay Bilbo really handsomely for his services; they had brought him to do a nasty job for them, and they did not mind the poor little fellow doing it if he would; but they would all have done their best to get him out of trouble, if he got into it, as they did in the case of the trolls at the beginning of their adventures before they had any particular reasons for being grateful to him. There it is: dwarves are not heroes, but calculating folk with a great idea of the value of money; some are tricky and treacherous and pretty bad lots; some are not, but are decent enough people like Thorin and Company, if you don't expect too much.

*

The stars were coming out behind him in a pale sky barred with black when the hobbit crept through the enchanted door and stole into the Mountain. It was far easier going than he expected. This was no goblin entrance, or rough wood-elves' cave. It was a passage made by dwarves, at the height of their wealth and skill: straight as a ruler, smooth-floored and smooth-sided, going with a gentle never-varying slope direct — to some distant end in the blackness below.

After a while Balin bade Bilbo "Good luck!" and stopped where he could still see the faint outline of the door, and by a trick of the echoes of the tunnel hear the rustle of the whispering voices of the others just outside. Then the hobbit slipped on his ring, and warned by the echoes to take more than hobbit's care to make no sound, he crept noiselessly down, down, down into the dark. He was trembling with fear, but his little face was set and grim. Already he was a very different hobbit from the one that had run out without a pocket-handkerchief from Bag-End long ago. He had not had a pocket-handkerchief for ages. He loosened his dagger in its sheath, tightened his belt, and went on.

"Now you are in for it at last, Bilbo Baggins," he said to himself. "You went and put your foot right in it that night of the party, and now you have got to pull it out and pay for it! Dear me, what a fool I was and am!" said the least Tookish part of him. "I have absolutely no use for dragon-guarded treasures, and the whole lot could stay here for ever, if only I could wake up and find this beastly tunnel was my own front-hall at home!"

He did not wake up of course, but went still on and on, till all sign of the door behind had faded away. He was altogether alone. Soon he thought it was beginning to feel warm. "Is that a kind of a glow I seem to see coming right ahead down there?" he thought.

It was. As he went forward it grew and grew, till there was no doubt about it. It was a red light steadily getting redder and redder. Also it was now undoubtedly hot in the tunnel. Wisps of vapour floated up and past him and he began to sweat. A sound, too, began to throb in his ears, a sort of bubbling like the noise of a large pot galloping on the fire, mixed with a rumble as of a gigantic tom-cat purring. This grew to the unmistakable gurgling noise of some vast animal snoring in its sleep down there in the red glow in front of him.

It was at this point that Bilbo stopped. Going on from there was the bravest thing he ever did. The tremendous things that happened afterwards were as nothing compared to it. He fought the real battle in the tunnel alone, before he ever saw the vast danger that lay in wait. At any rate after a short halt go on he did; and you can picture him coming to the end of the tunnel, an opening of much the same size and shape as the door above. Through it peeps the hobbit's little head. Before him lies the great bottommost cellar or dungeon-hall of the ancient dwarves right at the Mountain's root. It is almost dark so that its vastness can only be dimly guessed, but rising from the near side of the rocky floor there is a great glow. The glow of Smaug!

Bilbo steals a cup. Illustration by Évelyne Drouhin for the 1983 French edition.

There he lay, a vast red-golden dragon, fast asleep; a thrumming came from his jaws and nostrils, and wisps of smoke, but his fires were low in slumber. Beneath him, under all his limbs and his huge coiled tail, and about him on all sides stretching away across the unseen floors, lay countless piles of precious things, gold wrought and unwrought, gems and jewels, and silver red-stained in the ruddy light.

Smaug lay, with wings folded like an immeasurable bat, turned partly on one side, so that the hobbit could see his underparts and his long pale belly crusted with gems and fragments of gold from his long lying on his costly bed. Behind him where the walls were nearest could dimly be seen coats of mail, helms and axes, swords and spears hanging; and there in rows stood great jars and vessels filled with a wealth that could not be guessed.

To say that Bilbo's breath was taken away is no description at all. There are no words left to express his staggerment, since Men changed the language that they learned of elves in the days when all the world was wonderful.[2] Bilbo had heard tell and sing of dragon-hoards before, but the splendour, the lust, the glory of such treasure had never yet come home to him. His heart was filled and pierced with enchantment and with the desire of dwarves; and he gazed motionless, almost forgetting the frightful guardian, at the gold beyond price and count.

He gazed for what seemed an age, before drawn almost against his will, he stole from the shadow of the doorway, across the floor to the nearest edge of the mounds of treasure. Above him the sleeping dragon lay, a dire menace even in his sleep. He grasped a great two-handled cup, as heavy as he could carry, and cast one fearful eye upwards. Smaug stirred a wing, opened a claw, the rumble of his snoring changed its note.

Then Bilbo fled. But the dragon did not wake — not yet — but shifted into other dreams of greed and violence, lying there in his stolen hall while the little hobbit toiled back up the long tunnel. His heart was beating and a more fevered shaking was in his legs than when he was going down, but still he clutched the cup, and his chief thought was: "I've done it! This will show them. 'More like a grocer than a burglar' indeed! Well, we'll hear no more of that."[3]

Nor did he. Balin was overjoyed to see the hobbit again, and as delighted as he was surprised. He picked Bilbo up and carried him out into the open air. It was midnight and clouds had covered the stars, but Bilbo lay with his eyes shut, gasping and taking pleasure in the feel of the fresh air again, and hardly noticing the excite-

2 Tolkien wrote to Allen & Unwin on August 31, 1937, that these two sentences contain the only philological remark in *The Hobbit*, being "an odd mythological way of referring to linguistic philosophy, and a point that will (happily) be missed by any who have not read Barfield (few have), and probably by those who have" (*Letters*, No. 15).

Owen Barfield (1898–1997) was a close friend of C. S. Lewis's, and Tolkien came to know Barfield by way of Lewis. Barfield also attended meetings of the Inklings in the 1930s and 1940s, but, as he worked primarily in London as a solicitor, his attendance was infrequent. Barfield's book of linguistic philosophy, *Poetic Diction* (1928), deeply influenced both Tolkien and Lewis. Barfield's children's book, *The Silver Trumpet* (1925), was especially enjoyed by Tolkien's children in 1936 when Lewis loaned his copy to the Tolkien family.

The Tolkien scholar Verlyn Flieger suggests that Tolkien's letter refers to Barfield's thesis that language in its original state was premetaphoric — that there was once an ancient semantic unity of word and thing, and words therefore referred to realities. Language is now, however, no longer concrete and literal. Hence in referring to this passage in *The Hobbit*, Tolkien meant that Bilbo's breath was actually taken away, in a literal sense, not a metaphoric one.

Flieger's book *Splintered Light: Logos and Language in Tolkien's World* (1983; revised 2002) explores the influence of Barfield on Tolkien in much greater detail, and her explication of Barfield ideas is masterly:

Barfield suggests that myth, language, and man's perception of his world are inseparable. Words are expressed myth, the embodiment of mythic concepts and a mythic world view. The word *myth,* in this context, must be taken to mean that which describes man's perception of his relationship to the natural and supernatural world. Barfield's theory postulates that language, in its beginnings, made no distinction between the literal and the metaphoric meaning of a word, as it does today. Indeed, the very concept of metaphor, of one thing described in terms of another, was non-existent. All diction was literal, directly giving voice to man's perception of phenomena and his intuitive mythic participation in them. The modern distinction between the literal and the metaphoric use of a word suggests a separation of the abstract from the concrete which did not exist in earlier times. Man in his beginnings had a vision of the cosmos as a whole, and of himself as a part of it, a vision which he has long since left behind. We now perceive the cosmos as particularized, fragmented, and wholly separate from ourselves. Our consciousness and the language with which we express it have changed and splintered. In that earlier, primal world-view, every word would have had its own unified meaning, embodying what we now can understand only as a multiplicity of concepts, concepts for which we (no longer able to participate in the original world and world view) must use many different words. (p. 39)

3 On January 16, 1938, the London newspaper the *Observer* published a letter (signed "Habit") asking several questions about *The Hobbit,* including: "Is the hobbit's stealing of the dragon's cup based on the cup-stealing episode in *Beowulf?*" Tolkien's reply was printed in the February 20 issue of the newspaper: "*Beowulf* is among my most valued sources; though it was not consciously present to the mind in the process of writing, in which the episode of the theft arose naturally (and almost

ment of the dwarves, or how they praised him and patted him on the back and put themselves and all their families for generations to come at his service.

The dwarves were still passing the cup from hand to hand and talking delightedly of the recovery of their treasure, when suddenly a vast rumbling woke in the mountain underneath as if it was an old volcano that had made up its mind to start eruptions once again. The door behind them was pulled nearly to, and blocked from closing with a stone, but up the long tunnel came the dreadful echoes, from far down in the depths, of a bellowing and a trampling that made the ground beneath them tremble.

Then the dwarves forgot their joy and their confident boasts of a moment before and cowered down in fright. Smaug was still to be reckoned with. It does not do to leave a live dragon out of your calculations, if you live near him. Dragons may not have much real use for all their wealth, but they know it to an ounce as a rule, especially after long possession; and Smaug was no exception. He had passed from an uneasy dream (in which a warrior, altogether insignificant in size but provided with a bitter sword and great courage, figured most unpleasantly) to a doze, and from a doze to wide waking. There was a breath of strange air in his cave. Could there be a draught from that little hole? He had never felt quite happy about it, though it was so small, and now he glared at it in suspicion and wondered why he had never blocked it up. Of late he had half fancied he had caught the dim echoes of a knocking sound from far above that came down through it to his lair. He stirred and stretched forth his neck to sniff. Then he missed the cup!

Thieves! Fire! Murder! Such a thing had not happened since first he came to the Mountain! His rage passes description — the sort of rage that is only seen when rich folk that have more than they can enjoy sud-

The Lonely Mountain by J.R.R. Tolkien. This drawing was not used in *The Hobbit*, probably because its large area of solid black would have been difficult to print by letterpress as a line-block (see *Artist*, p. 141).

The Lonely Mountain was first published as a poster in 1974 by the Science Fiction Shop in New York. In September 1960, Tolkien had sent the original of this drawing to an American correspondent, who later gave it to Baird Searles, the owner of the Science Fiction Shop. (The original is now at the Bodleian Library in Oxford.)

This drawing also appears in *Artist* (No. 136). Three other published drawings are closely related to it. The earliest appears to be the untitled pencil-and-ink drawing published as No. 134 in *Artist*. This was probably followed by the watercolor *Smaug flies round the Mountain*, published in *Pictures* (No. 18). Neither of the early versions have the pronounced S-curve in the river (though it is lightly penciled on No. 134 in *Artist*), the description of which was a last-minute addition to the page proofs of *The Hobbit* (see *Artist*, pp. 139, 141). The third drawing, in pencil and ink, is titled *The Front Door*, and it shows the pronounced S-curve and is overall very similar to *The Lonely Mountain*, though the shadings in the sky and on the mountain slopes are made of lines, rather than being solid black. *The Front Door* is published in *Artist* (No. 135).

denly lose something that they have long had but have never before used or wanted. His fire belched forth, the hall smoked, he shook the mountain-roots. He thrust his head in vain at the little hole, and then coiling his length together, roaring like thunder underground, he sped from his deep lair through its great door, out into the huge passages of the mountain-palace and up towards the Front Gate.

To hunt the whole mountain till he had caught the

inevitably) from the circumstances. It is difficult to think of any other way of conducting the story at that point. I fancy the author of *Beowulf* would say much the same" (*Letters*, No. 25).

The cup-stealing episode in *Beowulf* is fairly brief. It takes place after the dragon has guarded its treasure for three hundred years, when a man seeking the favor of his lord steals a golden cup to present to him. When the dragon awakes, it discovers the theft and is enraged. After night falls, the dragon goes forth in flames and destroys the lord and his people, hastening back to its hall before daytime (section 32, lines 2278 ff.).

thief and had torn and trampled him was his one thought. He issued from the Gate, the waters rose in fierce whistling steam, and up he soared blazing into the air and settled on the mountain-top in a spout of green and scarlet flame. The dwarves heard the awful rumour of his flight, and they crouched against the walls of the grassy terrace cringing under boulders, hoping somehow to escape the frightful eyes of the hunting dragon.

There they would have all been killed, if it had not been for Bilbo once again. "Quick! Quick!" he gasped. "The door! The tunnel! It's no good here."

Roused by these words they were just about to creep inside the tunnel when Bifur gave a cry: "My cousins! Bombur and Bofur — we have forgotten them, they are down in the valley!"

"They will be slain, and all our ponies too, and all our stores lost," moaned the others. "We can do nothing."

"Nonsense!" said Thorin, recovering his dignity. "We cannot leave them. Get inside Mr. Baggins and Balin, and you two Fili and Kili — the dragon shan't have all of us. Now you others, where are the ropes? Be quick!"

Those were perhaps the worst moments they had been through yet. The horrible sounds of Smaug's anger were echoing in the stony hollows far above; at any moment he might come blazing down or fly whirling round and find them there, near the perilous cliff's edge hauling madly on the ropes. Up came Bofur, and still all was safe. Up came Bombur, puffing and blowing while the ropes creaked, and still all was safe. Up came some tools and bundles of stores, and then danger was upon them.

A whirring noise was heard. A red light touched the points of standing rocks. The dragon came.

They had barely time to fly back to the tunnel, pulling and dragging in their bundles, when Smaug came hurtling from the North, licking the mountain-sides with flame, beating his great wings with a noise like a roaring wind. His hot breath shrivelled the grass before the door, and drove in through the crack they had left and scorched them as they lay hid. Flickering fires leaped up and black rock-shadows danced. Then darkness fell as he passed again. The ponies screamed with terror, burst their ropes and galloped wildly off. The dragon swooped and turned to pursue them, and was gone.

"That'll be the end of our poor beasts!" said Thorin. "Nothing can escape Smaug once he sees it. Here we are and here we shall have to stay, unless any one fancies tramping the long open miles back to the river with Smaug on the watch!"

It was not a pleasant thought! They crept further down the tunnel, and there they lay and shivered though it was warm and stuffy, until dawn came pale through the crack of the door. Every now and again through the night they could hear the roar of the flying dragon grow and then pass and fade, as he hunted round and round the mountain-sides.

He guessed from the ponies, and from the traces of the camps he had discovered, that men had come up from the river and the lake and had scaled the mountain-side from the valley where the ponies had been standing; but the door withstood his searching eye, and the little high-walled bay had kept out his fiercest flames. Long he had hunted in vain till the dawn chilled his wrath and he went back to his golden couch to sleep — and to gather new strength. He would not forget or forgive the theft, not if a thousand years turned him to smouldering stone, but he could afford to wait. Slow and silent he crept back to his lair and half closed his eyes.

When morning came the terror of the dwarves grew less. They realized that dangers of this kind were inevitable in dealing with such a guardian, and that it was no good giving up their quest yet. Nor could they get away just now, as Thorin had pointed out. Their ponies were lost or killed, and they would have to wait some time before Smaug relaxed his watch sufficiently for them to dare the long way on foot. Luckily they had saved enough of their stores to last them still for some time.

They debated long on what was to be done, but they could think of no way of getting rid of Smaug — which had always been a weak point in their plans, as Bilbo felt inclined to point out. Then as is the nature of folk that are thoroughly perplexed, they began to grumble at the hobbit, blaming him for what had at first so pleased them: for bringing away a cup and stirring up Smaug's wrath so soon.

"What else do you suppose a burglar is to do?" asked Bilbo angrily. "I was not engaged to kill dragons, that is warrior's work, but to steal treasure. I made the best beginning I could. Did you expect me to trot back with the whole hoard of Thror on my back? If there is any grumbling to be done, I think I might have a say. You ought to have brought five hundred burglars not one. I am sure it reflects great credit on your grandfather, but you cannot pretend that you ever made the vast extent of his wealth clear to me. I should want hundreds of years to bring it all up, if I was fifty times as big, and Smaug as tame as a rabbit."

After that of course the dwarves begged his pardon. "What then do you propose we should do, Mr. Baggins?" asked Thorin politely.

"I have no idea at the moment — if you mean about removing the treasure. That obviously depends entirely on some new turn of luck and the getting rid of Smaug. Getting rid of dragons is not at all in my line, but I will do my best to think about it. Personally I have no hopes at all, and wish I was safe back at home."

"Never mind that for the moment! What are we to do now, to-day?"

"Well, if you really want my advice, I should say we

Left: *Conversation with Smaug* by J.R.R. Tolkien, one of the standard color illustrations for *The Hobbit*, first published in the 1937 second impression of the first English edition, and in the 1938 American edition (where Tolkien's monogram and bannered title were removed). For both appearances the illustration was given the printed caption "O Smaug the Chiefest and Greatest of Calamities."

Presumably in March 1938, Tolkien wrote to his American publisher:

> The hobbit in the picture of the gold-hoard, Chapter XII, is of course (apart from being fat in the wrong places) enormously too large. But (as my children, at any rate, understand) he is really in a separate picture or "plane"—being invisible to the dragon. There is in the text no mention of his acquiring boots. There should be! It has dropped out somehow or other in the various revisions—the bootings occurred at Rivendell; and he was again bootless after leaving Rivendell on the way home. (*Letters*, No. 27)

The gem shining from the top of the pile of treasure at the rear is probably the Arkenstone, and to the left of the end of the dragon's tail, there is visible a strand of green gems, possibly representing the necklace of Girion, described on page 287 as "made of five hundred emeralds green as grass."

An example of Tolkien's Elvish script, the Tengwar (or Fëanorian alphabet), appears on the pot of gold in the foreground. The inscription reads: *gold th*[portion obscured by ladder] *Thrain / accursed be the thief*. Further details on the Tengwar can be found in Section II ("Writing") of Appendix E in *The Lord of the Rings*. This illustration also appears in *Artist* (No. 133) and *Pictures* (No. 17).

can do nothing but stay where we are. By day we can no doubt creep out safely enough to take the air. Perhaps before long one or two could be chosen to go back to the store by the river and replenish our supplies. But in the meanwhile everyone ought to be well inside the tunnel by night.

"Now I will make you an offer. I have got my ring and will creep down this very noon — then if ever Smaug ought to be napping — and see what he is up to. Perhaps something will turn up. 'Every worm has his weak spot,' as my father used to say, though I am sure it was not from personal experience."

Naturally the dwarves accepted the offer eagerly. Al-

Smaug and Bilbo. Illustration by António Quadros for the 1962 Portuguese edition.

ready they had come to respect little Bilbo. Now he had become the real leader in their adventure. He had begun to have ideas and plans of his own. When midday came he got ready for another journey down into the Mountain. He did not like it of course, but it was not so bad now he knew, more or less, what was in front of him. Had he known more about dragons and their wily ways, he might have been more frightened and less hopeful of catching this one napping.

The sun was shining when he started, but it was as dark as night in the tunnel. The light from the door, almost closed, soon faded as he went down. So silent was his going that smoke on a gentle wind could hardly have surpassed it, and he was inclined to feel a bit proud of himself as he drew near the lower door. There was only the very faintest glow to be seen.

"Old Smaug is weary and asleep," he thought. "He can't see me and he won't hear me. Cheer up Bilbo!" He had forgotten or had never heard about dragons' sense of smell. It is also an awkward fact that they can keep half an eye open watching while they sleep, if they are suspicious.

᚜ Smaug certainly looked fast asleep, almost dead and dark, with scarcely a snore more than a whiff of unseen steam, when Bilbo peeped once more from the entrance. He was just about to step out on to the floor when he caught a sudden thin and piercing ray of red from under the drooping lid of Smaug's left eye. He was only pretending to sleep! He was watching the tunnel entrance! Hurriedly Bilbo stepped back and blessed the luck of his ring. Then Smaug spoke.

"Well, thief! I smell you and I feel your air. I hear your breath. Come along! Help yourself again, there is plenty and to spare!"

But Bilbo was not quite so unlearned in dragon-lore as all that, and if Smaug hoped to get him to come nearer so easily he was disappointed. "No thank you, O Smaug the Tremendous!" he replied. "I did not come for presents. I only wished to have a look at you and see if you were truly as great as tales say. I did not believe them."

"Do you now?" said the dragon somewhat flattered, even though he did not believe a word of it.

"Truly songs and tales fall utterly short of the reality, O Smaug the Chiefest and Greatest of Calamities," replied Bilbo.

"You have nice manners for a thief and a liar," said the dragon. "You seem familiar with my name,[4] but I don't seem to remember smelling you before. Who are you and where do you come from, may I ask?"

"You may indeed! I come from under the hill, and under the hills and over the hills my paths led. And through the air. I am he that walks unseen."

"So I can well believe," said Smaug, "but that is hardly your usual name."

"I am the clue-finder, the web-cutter, the stinging fly. I was chosen for the lucky number."

"Lovely titles!" sneered the dragon. "But lucky numbers don't always come off."

"I am he that buries his friends alive and drowns them and draws them alive again from the water. I came from the end of a bag, but no bag went over me."

"These don't sound so creditable," scoffed Smaug.

"I am the friend of bears and the guest of eagles. I am Ringwinner and Luckwearer; and I am Barrel-rider," went on Bilbo beginning to be pleased with his riddling.

"That's better!" said Smaug. "But don't let your imagination run away with you!"

This of course is the way to talk to dragons, if you don't want to reveal your proper name (which is wise), and don't want to infuriate them by a flat refusal (which is also very wise). No dragon can resist the fascination of riddling talk and of wasting time trying to understand it.[5] There was a lot here which Smaug did not understand at all (though I expect you do, since you know all

4 In a letter published in the *Observer* on February 20, 1938, Tolkien noted that "the dragon bears as a name — a pseudonym — the past tense of the primitive Germanic verb *Smugan,* to squeeze through a hole: a low philological jest" (*Letters,* No. 25).

5 In *The Road to Middle-earth,* Tom Shippey noted that Bilbo's conversation with Smaug has a model in the poem "Fáfnismál" (The Lay of Fáfnir) in the *Elder Edda.* There the hero, Sigurthr, and the dragon Fáfnir talk while the dragon dies of the wound he has just been given. Shippey notes: "Like Bilbo, Sigurthr refuses to tell the dragon his name but replies riddingly (for fear of being cursed); like Smaug, Fáfnir sows dissension between partners by remarking on the greed that gold excites" (second edition, p. 82).

In Henry Adams Bellows's translation of "Fáfnismál" in *The Poetic Edda* (1923), the conversation begins as follows, with Fáfnir's words first, followed by those of Sigurthr:

"Youth, oh, youth! of whom then, youth, art
*   thou born?*
*   Say whose son thou art*
Who in Fafnir's blood thy bright blade
*   reddened,*
*   And struck thy sword to my heart."*

"The Noble Hart my name, and I go
*   A motherless man abroad;*
Father I had not, as others have,
*   And lonely ever I live."*
*   (stanzas 1–2)*

There is another slight analogue to Bilbo's speech with Smaug, as well as Bilbo's encounter with Gollum, in the story "Ernest" by E. H. Knatchbull-Hugessen, in his *Stories for My Children*

(1869), a book that Tolkien had as a child. In this story, a young boy named Ernest loses his ball in the well in a garden, and he journeys down the well to find his ball:

Down he went for some distance, and at last got to what he supposed was the bottom of the well. He wasn't far wrong, either; but the well was much larger at the bottom than the top, and all the water in it seemed to come up like a wall from the ground, leaving a large dry space all round it, into which Ernest crept out of the water, and began to look about him. It wasn't so *very* dry, either, but rather moist, and he could see no ball anywhere; but all round the sides of the kind of cave in which he was there was a bright substance like crystal, which lighted up the place, and on the floor sat an enormous Toad, smoking a very bad cigar, and evidently thinking himself every body. He turned upon Ernest directly, and cried out to him in an angry tone,

"You presumptuous fool, how dare you come down here?"

Now Ernest, having been carefully brought up, was well aware that no one loses any thing by politeness. Far from being angry, therefore, he replied, with the lowest bow which circumstances enabled him to make,

"Presumptuous, sir, I may possibly be, but it can hardly be the act of a fool which has brought me into the presence of so noble and handsome a Toad as yourself."

"Not so bad," replied the Toad; "I see you have been taught manners. But what do you want?"

"My ball, sir," said Ernest; when instantly a low silvery laugh echoed through the cave, and the Toad, after swelling till Ernest thought he must certainly burst, went into a fit of laughter which rather puzzled the boy.

"Your ball!" at length shouted the Toad. "If you mean that india rubber affair that came crashing down here some time ago, I should hope it was long since cut up into gaiters for the tame Mice." (pp. 71–72)

about Bilbo's adventures to which he was referring), but he thought he understood enough, and he chuckled in his wicked inside.

"I thought so last night," he smiled to himself. "Lake-men, some nasty scheme of those miserable tub-trading Lake-men, or I'm a lizard. I haven't been down that way for an age and an age; but I will soon alter that!"

"Very well, O Barrel-rider!" he said aloud. "Maybe Barrel was your pony's name; and maybe not, though it was fat enough. You may walk unseen, but you did not walk all the way. Let me tell you I ate six ponies last night and I shall catch and eat all the others before long.[6] In return for the excellent meal I will give you one piece of advice for your good: don't have more to do with dwarves than you can help!"

"Dwarves!" said Bilbo in pretended surprise.

"Don't talk to me!" said Smaug. "I know the smell (and taste) of dwarf — no one better. Don't tell me that I can eat a dwarf-ridden pony and not know it! You'll come to a bad end, if you go with such friends, Thief Barrel-rider. I don't mind if you go back and tell them so from me." But he did not tell Bilbo that there was one smell he could not make out at all, hobbit-smell; it was quite outside his experience and puzzled him mightily.

"I suppose you got a fair price for that cup last night?" he went on. "Come now, did you? Nothing at all! Well, that's just like them. And I suppose they are skulking outside, and your job is to do all the dangerous work and get what you can when I'm not looking — for them? And you will get a fair share? Don't you believe it! If you get off alive, you will be lucky."

Bilbo was now beginning to feel really uncomfortable. Whenever Smaug's roving eye, seeking for him in the shadows, flashed across him, he trembled, and an unaccountable desire seized hold of him to rush out and reveal himself and tell all the truth to Smaug. In fact he was in grievous danger of coming under the dragon-spell. But plucking up courage he spoke again.

"You don't know everything, O Smaug the Mighty," said he. "Not gold alone brought us hither."

"Ha! Ha! You admit the 'us'?" laughed Smaug. "Why not say 'us fourteen' and be done with it, Mr. Lucky Number? I am pleased to hear that you had other business in these parts besides my gold. In that case you may, perhaps, not altogether waste your time.

"I don't know if it has occurred to you that, even if you could steal the gold bit by bit — a matter of a hundred years or so — you could not get it very far? Not much use on the mountain-side? Not much use in the forest? Bless me! Had you never thought of the catch? A fourteenth share, I suppose, or something like it, those were the terms, eh? But what about delivery? What about cartage? What about armed guards and tolls?" And Smaug laughed aloud. He had a wicked and a wily heart, and he knew his guesses were not far out, though he suspected that the Lake-men were at the back of the plans, and that most of the plunder was meant to stop there in the town by the shore that in his young days had been called Esgaroth.[7]

You will hardly believe it, but poor Bilbo was really very taken aback. So far all his thoughts and energies had been concentrated on getting to the Mountain and finding the entrance. He had never bothered to wonder how the treasure was to be removed, certainly never how any part of it that might fall to his share was to be brought back all the way to Bag-End Under-Hill.

Now a nasty suspicion began to grow in his mind — had the dwarves forgotten this important point too, or were they laughing in their sleeves at him all the time? That is the effect that dragon-talk has on the inexperienced. Bilbo of course ought to have been on his guard; but Smaug had rather an overwhelming personality.

"I tell you," he said, in an effort to remain loyal to his

A drawing (below), *Ernest and the Toad*, accompanies this story in Knatchbull-Hugessen's book. The artwork is uncredited.

6 *1937:* "I shall catch and eat the eight others before long" > *1966-Ball:* "I shall catch and eat all the others before long"

7 In the "Etymologies," Tolkien's personal dictionary of Elvish word relationships now published in volume five of the *History, The Lost Road* (1987), Tolkien defined *Esgaroth* as meaning "Reedlake," noting that the place was so named because of the reed banks in the west (p. 356).

8 Both of the greatest dragons in north-ern literature, Fáfnir, the dragon of the Völsungs, and the dragon in *Beowulf,* were given their death strokes by being stabbed in their lower parts.

In the *Völsunga Saga,* translated by Jesse L. Byock as *The Saga of the Volsungs* (1990), Sigurd digs some ditches in the path where the dragon crawls and hides in one of the ditches:

When the worm crawled to the water the earth quaked mightily, so that all the ground nearby shook. He blew poison over all the path before him, but Sigurd was neither afraid of nor concerned by the din. And when the serpent crawled over the pit, Sigurd plunged the sword up under the left shoulder, so that it sank to the hilt. Then Sigurd leapt up out of the ditch, and drew the sword out of the serpent. His arms were bloody to the shoulder. And when the huge worm felt his mortal wound he

Fafnir the dragon. Illustration by Lancelot Speed to accompany "The Story of Sigurd," as retold by Andrew Lang, in *The Red Fairy Book* (1890).

friends and to keep his end up, "that gold was only an af-terthought with us. We came over hill and under hill, by wave and wind, for *Revenge.* Surely, O Smaug the unassessably wealthy, you must realize that your success has made you some bitter enemies?"

Then Smaug really did laugh — a devastating sound which shook Bilbo to the floor, while far up in the tunnel the dwarves huddled together and imagined that the hobbit had come to a sudden and a nasty end.

"Revenge!" he snorted, and the light of his eyes lit the hall from floor to ceiling like scarlet lightning. "Revenge! The King under the Mountain is dead and where are his kin that dare seek revenge? Girion Lord of Dale is dead, and I have eaten his people like a wolf among sheep, and where are his sons' sons that dare approach me? I kill where I wish and none dare resist. I laid low the warriors of old and their like is not in the world today. Then I was but young and tender. Now I am old and strong, strong, strong, Thief in the Shadows!" he gloated. "My armour is like tenfold shields, my teeth are swords, my claws spears, the shock of my tail a thunderbolt, my wings a hurricane, and my breath death!"

"I have always understood," said Bilbo in a frightened squeak, "that dragons were softer underneath,**8** especially in the region of the — er — chest; but doubtless one so fortified has thought of that."

The dragon stopped short in his boasting. "Your information is antiquated," he snapped. "I am armoured above and below with iron scales and hard gems. No blade can pierce me."

"I might have guessed it," said Bilbo. "Truly there can nowhere be found the equal of Lord Smaug the Impenetrable. What magnificence to possess a waistcoat of fine diamonds!"

"Yes, it is rare and wonderful, indeed," said Smaug absurdly pleased. He did not know that the hobbit had already caught a glimpse of his peculiar under-covering on his previous visit, and was itching for a closer view for reasons of his own. The dragon rolled over. "Look!" he said. "What do you say to that?"

"Dazzlingly marvellous! Perfect! Flawless! Staggering!" exclaimed Bilbo aloud, but what he thought inside was: "Old fool! Why, there is a large patch in the hollow of his left breast as bare as a snail out of its shell!"

After he had seen that Mr. Baggins' one idea was to get away. "Well, I really must not detain Your Magnificence any longer," he said, "or keep you from much needed rest. Ponies take some catching, I believe, after a long start. And so do burglars," he added as a parting shot, as he darted back and fled up the tunnel.

It was an unfortunate remark, for the dragon spouted terrific flames after him, and fast though he sped up the slope, he had not gone nearly far enough to be comfortable before the ghastly head of Smaug was thrust against the opening behind. Luckily the whole head and jaws could not squeeze in, but the nostrils sent forth fire and vapour to pursue him, and he was nearly overcome, and stumbled blindly on in great pain and fear. He had been feeling rather pleased with the cleverness of his conversation with Smaug, but his mistake at the end shook him into better sense.

"Never laugh at live dragons, Bilbo you fool!" he said to himself, and it became a favourite saying of his later, and passed into a proverb. "You aren't nearly through this adventure yet," he added, and that was pretty true as well.

The afternoon was turning into evening when he came out again and stumbled and fell in a faint on the 'doorstep'. The dwarves revived him, and doctored his scorches as well as they could; but it was a long time before the hair on the back of his head and his heels grew properly again: it had all been singed and frizzled right down to the skin. In the meanwhile his friends did their

thrashed his head and his tail, destroying everything that got in his way. (p. 63)

In the 1982 revised translation of *Beowulf* by Constance B. Hieatt, included in her *Beowulf and Other Old English Poems,* Beowulf receives aid from the young warrior Wiglaf after his own sword fails him against the dragon: "the noble warrior at the king's side showed his valor, the skill and boldness which was his nature. The brave man paid no attention to the dragon's head, although his hand burned as he helped his kinsman, and he struck the hostile creature lower down; the shining sword sank in so that the fire began to die down at once" (section 37, lines 2695–702).

Smaug. Illustration by Tamás Szecskó for the 1975 Hungarian edition.

Smaug. Illustration by Livia Rusz for the 1975 Romanian edition.

best to cheer him up; and they were eager for his story, especially wanting to know why the dragon had made such an awful noise, and how Bilbo had escaped.

But the hobbit was worried and uncomfortable, and they had difficulty in getting anything out of him. On thinking things over he was now regretting some of the things he had said to the dragon, and was not eager to repeat them. The old thrush was sitting on a rock near by with his head cocked on one side, listening to all that was said. It shows what an ill temper Bilbo was in: he picked up a stone and threw it at the thrush, which merely fluttered aside and came back.

"Drat the bird!" said Bilbo crossly. "I believe he is listening, and I don't like the look of him."

"Leave him alone!" said Thorin. "The thrushes are good and friendly — this is a very old bird indeed, and is maybe the last left of the ancient breed that used to live about here, tame to the hands of my father and grandfather. They were a long-lived and magical race, and this might even be one of those that were alive then, a couple of hundreds of years or more ago. The Men of Dale used to have the trick of understanding their language, and used them for messengers to fly to the Men of the Lake and elsewhere."

"Well, he'll have news to take to Lake-town all right, if that is what he is after," said Bilbo; "though I don't suppose there are any people left there that trouble with thrush-language."

"Why what has happened?" cried the dwarves. "Do get on with your tale!"

So Bilbo told them all he could remember, and he confessed that he had a nasty feeling that the dragon guessed too much from his riddles added to the camps and the ponies. "I am sure he knows we came from Lake-town and had help from there; and I have a horrible feeling that his next move may be in that direction. I wish to goodness I had never said that about Barrel-rider; it would make even a blind rabbit in these parts think of the Lake-men."

"Well, well! It cannot be helped, and it is difficult not to slip in talking to a dragon, or so I have always heard," said Balin anxious to comfort him. "I think you did very well, if you ask me — you found out one very useful thing at any rate, and got home alive, and that is more than most can say who have had words with the likes of Smaug. It may be a mercy and a blessing yet to know of the bare patch in the old Worm's diamond waistcoat."

That turned the conversation, and they all began discussing dragon-slayings historical, dubious, and mythical, and the various sorts of stabs and jabs and undercuts, and the different arts devices and stratagems by which they had been accomplished. The general opinion was that catching a dragon napping was not as easy as it sounded, and the attempt to stick one or prod one asleep was more likely to end in disaster than a bold frontal attack. All the while they talked the thrush listened, till at last when the stars began to peep forth, it silently spread its wings and flew away. And all the while they talked and the shadows lengthened Bilbo became more and more unhappy and his foreboding grew.

At last he interrupted them. "I am sure we are very unsafe here," he said, "and I don't see the point of sitting here. The dragon has withered all the pleasant green, and anyway the night has come and it is cold. But I feel it in my bones that this place will be attacked again. Smaug knows now how I came down to his hall, and you can trust him to guess where the other end of the tunnel is. He will break all this side of the Mountain to bits, if necessary, to stop up our entrance, and if we are smashed with it the better he will like it."

"You are very gloomy, Mr. Baggins!" said Thorin. "Why has not Smaug blocked the lower end, then, if he is so eager to keep us out? He has not, or we should have heard him."

Bilbo escapes from Smaug's fire. Illustration by Chica for the 1976 French edition

"I don't know, I don't know — because at first he wanted to try and lure me in again, I suppose, and now perhaps because he is waiting till after tonight's hunt, or because he does not want to damage his bedroom if he can help it — but I wish you would not argue. Smaug will be coming out at any minute now, and our only hope is to get well in the tunnel and shut the door."

He seemed so much in earnest that the dwarves at last did as he said, though they delayed shutting the door — it seemed a desperate plan, for no one knew whether or how they could get it open again from the inside, and the thought of being shut in a place from which the only way out led through the dragon's lair was not one they liked. Also everything seemed quite quiet, both outside and down the tunnel. So for a longish while they sat inside not far down from the half-open door and went on talking.

The talk turned to the dragon's wicked words about the dwarves. Bilbo wished he had never heard them, or at least that he could feel quite certain that the dwarves now were absolutely honest when they declared that they had never thought at all about what would happen after the treasure had been won. "We knew it would be a desperate venture," said Thorin, "and we know that still; and I still think that when we have won it will be time enough to think what to do about it. As for your share, Mr. Baggins, I assure you we are more than grateful and you shall choose your own fourteenth, as soon as we have anything to divide. I am sorry if you are worried about transport, and I admit the difficulties are great — the lands have not become less wild with the passing of time, rather the reverse — but we will do whatever we can for you, and take our share of the cost when the time comes. Believe me or not as you like!"

From that the talk turned to the great hoard itself and to the things that Thorin and Balin remembered. They wondered if they were still lying there unharmed in the hall below: the spears that were made for the armies of the great King Bladorthin[9] (long since dead), each had a thrice-forged head and their shafts were inlaid with cunning gold, but they were never delivered or paid for; shields made for warriors long dead; the great golden cup of Thror, two-handed, hammered and carven with birds and flowers whose eyes and petals were of jewels; coats of mail gilded and silvered and impenetrable; the necklace of Girion, Lord of Dale, made of five hundred emeralds green as grass, which he gave for the arming of his eldest son in a coat of dwarf-linked rings the like of which had never been made before, for it was wrought of pure silver to the power and strength of triple steel. But fairest of all was the great white gem, which the dwarves had found beneath the roots of the Mountain, the Heart of the Mountain, the Arkenstone of Thrain.

"The Arkenstone! The Arkenstone!" murmured Thorin in the dark, half dreaming with his chin upon his knees. "It was like a globe with a thousand facets; it shone like silver in the firelight, like water in the sun, like snow under the stars, like rain upon the Moon!"

But the enchanted desire of the hoard had fallen from Bilbo. All through their talk he was only half listening to them. He sat nearest to the door with one ear cocked for any beginnings of a sound without, his other was alert for echoes beyond the murmurs of the dwarves, for any whisper of a movement from far below.

Darkness grew deeper and he grew ever more uneasy. "Shut the door!" he begged them, "I fear that dragon in my marrow. I like this silence far less than the uproar of last night. Shut the door before it is too late!"

Something in his voice gave the dwarves an uncomfortable feeling. Slowly Thorin shook off his dreams and getting up he kicked away the stone that wedged the door. Then they thrust upon it, and it closed with a snap and a clang. No trace of a keyhole was there left on the inside. They were shut in the Mountain!

9 The history of King Bladorthin is referred to nowhere else in Tolkien's writings. In the context here, with the description of Bladorthin as "long since dead," it seems that he may have been a man rather than an elf. The name *Bladorthin,* however, appears to be of Elvish construction. The Sindarin element *-thin* = "grey" is easily deciphered, while *Blador-* is elsewhere present in the name Bladorwen, from the earliest phases of Tolkien's legendarium, now published in volume one of the *History, The Book of Lost Tales, Part One. Bladorwen* is glossed "the wide earth" (p. 264), and in Tolkien's earliest lexicon there are the related words *bladwen,* "a plain"; *blath,* "a floor"; and *blant,* "flat, open." Christopher Gilson, in a letter to *Vinyar Tengwar,* May 1991 (No. 17), suggested that *blador-* might be an agent noun "wanderer, ranger, pilgrim," for in the manuscript of *The Hobbit* the original name of the wizard was *Bladorthin,* which was later changed to *Gandalf.* In *The Lord of the Rings* we learn that Gandalf is called by the Elves Mithrandir, which is Sindarin for "grey pilgrim." *Bladorthin* may have been an earlier form with the same meaning.

And not a moment too soon. They had hardly gone any distance down the tunnel when a blow smote the side of the Mountain like the crash of battering-rams made of forest oaks and swung by giants. The rock boomed, the walls cracked and stones fell from the roof on their heads. What would have happened if the door had still been open I don't like to think. They fled further down the tunnel glad to be still alive, while behind them outside they heard the roar and rumble of Smaug's fury. He was breaking rocks to pieces, smashing wall and cliff with the lashings of his huge tail, till their little lofty camping ground, the scorched grass, the thrush's stone, the snail-covered walls, the narrow ledge, and all disappeared in a jumble of smithereens, and an avalanche of splintered stones fell over the cliff into the valley below.

Smaug had left his lair in silent stealth, quietly soared into the air, and then floated heavy and slow in the dark like a monstrous crow, down the wind towards the west of the Mountain, in the hopes of catching unawares something or somebody there, and of spying the outlet to the passage which the thief had used. This was the outburst of his wrath when he could find nobody and see nothing, even where he guessed the outlet must actually be.

After he had let off his rage in this way he felt better and he thought in his heart that he would not be troubled again from that direction. In the meanwhile he had further vengeance to take. "Barrel-rider!" he snorted. "Your feet came from the waterside and up the water you came without a doubt. I don't know your smell, but if you are not one of those men of the Lake, you had their help. They shall see me and remember who is the real King under the Mountain!"

He rose in fire and went away south towards the Running River.

13

Not at Home

IN THE MEANWHILE, the dwarves sat in darkness, and utter silence fell about them. Little they ate and little they spoke. They could not count the passing of time; and they scarcely dared to move, for the whisper of their voices echoed and rustled in the tunnel. If they dozed, they woke still to darkness and to silence going on unbroken. At last after days and days of waiting, as it seemed, when they were becoming choked and dazed for want of air, they could bear it no longer. They would almost have welcomed sounds from below of the dragon's return. In the silence they feared some cunning devilry of his, but they could not sit there for ever.

Thorin spoke: "Let us try the door!" he said. "I must feel the wind on my face soon or die. I think I would rather be smashed by Smaug in the open than suffocate in here!" So several of the dwarves got up and groped back to where the door had been. But they found that the upper end of the tunnel had been shattered and blocked with broken rock. Neither key nor the magic it had once obeyed would ever open that door again.

"We are trapped!" they groaned. "This is the end. We shall die here."

But somehow, just when the dwarves were most despairing, Bilbo felt a strange lightening of the heart, as if a heavy weight had gone from under his waistcoat.

"Come, come!" he said. " 'While there's life there's hope!' as my father used to say, and 'Third time pays for all.' I am going *down* the tunnel once again. I have been that way twice, when I knew there was a dragon at the other end, so I will risk a third visit when I am no longer sure. Anyway the only way out is down. And I think this time you had better all come with me."

In desperation they agreed, and Thorin was the first to go forward by Bilbo's side.

"Now do be careful!" whispered the hobbit, "and as quiet as you can be! There may be no Smaug at the bottom, but then again there may be. Don't let us take any unnecessary risks!"

Down, down they went. The dwarves could not, of course, compare with the hobbit in real stealth, and they made a deal of puffing and shuffling which echoes magnified alarmingly; but though every now and again Bilbo in fear stopped and listened, not a sound stirred below. Near the bottom, as well as he could judge, Bilbo slipped on his ring and went ahead. But he did not need it: the darkness was complete, and they were all invisible, ring or no ring. In fact so black was it that the hobbit came to the opening unexpectedly, put his hand on air, stumbled forward, and rolled headlong into the hall!

There he lay face downwards on the floor and did not dare to get up, or hardly even to breathe. But nothing moved. There was not a gleam of light — unless, as it seemed to him, when at last he slowly raised his head, there was a pale white glint, above him and far off in the gloom. But certainly it was not a spark of dragon-fire, though the worm-stench was heavy in the place, and the taste of vapour was on his tongue.

At length Mr. Baggins could bear it no longer. "Confound you, Smaug, you worm!" he squeaked aloud. "Stop playing hide-and-seek! Give me a light, and then eat me, if you can catch me!"

Bilbo explores while Smaug is away. Illustration by Tove Jansson for the 1962 Swedish and 1973 Finnish editions.

Faint echoes ran round the unseen hall, but there was no answer.

Bilbo got up, and found that he did not know in what direction to turn.

"Now I wonder what on earth Smaug is playing at," he said. "He is not at home today (or tonight, or whatever it is), I do believe. If Oin and Gloin have not lost their tinder-boxes, perhaps we can make a little light, and have a look round before the luck turns."

"Light!" he cried. "Can anybody make a light?"

*

The dwarves, of course, were very alarmed when Bilbo fell forward down the step with a bump into the hall, and they sat huddled just where he had left them at the end of the tunnel.

"Sh! sh!" they hissed, when they heard his voice; and though that helped the hobbit to find out where they were, it was some time before he could get anything else out of them. But in the end, when Bilbo actually began to stamp on the floor, and screamed out "light!" at the top of his shrill voice, Thorin gave way, and Oin and Gloin were sent back to their bundles at the top of the tunnel.

After a while a twinkling gleam showed them returning, Oin with a small pine-torch alight in his hand, and Gloin with a bundle of others under his arm. Quickly Bilbo trotted to the door and took the torch; but he could not persuade the dwarves to light the others or to come and join him yet. As Thorin carefully explained, Mr. Baggins was still officially their expert burglar and investigator. If he liked to risk a light, that was his affair. They would wait in the tunnel for his report. So they sat near the door and watched.

They saw the little dark shape of the hobbit start across the floor holding his tiny light aloft. Every now and again, while he was still near enough, they caught a glint and a tinkle as he stumbled on some golden thing. The light grew smaller as he wandered away into the vast hall; then it began to rise dancing into the air. Bilbo was climbing the great mound of treasure. Soon he stood upon the top, and still went on. Then they saw him halt and stoop for a moment; but they did not know the reason.

It was the Arkenstone, the Heart of the Mountain. So Bilbo guessed from Thorin's description; but indeed there could not be two such gems, even in so marvellous a hoard, even in all the world. Ever as he climbed, the same white gleam had shone before him and drawn his feet towards it. Slowly it grew to a little globe of pallid light. Now as he came near, it was tinged with a flickering sparkle of many colours at the surface, reflected and splintered from the wavering light of his torch. At last he looked down upon it, and he caught his breath. The great jewel shone before his feet of its own inner light, and yet, cut and fashioned by the dwarves, who had dug it from the heart of the mountain long ago, it took all light that fell upon it and changed it into ten thousand sparks of white radiance shot with glints of the rainbow.[1]

Suddenly Bilbo's arm went towards it drawn by its enchantment. His small hand would not close about it, for it was a large and heavy gem; but he lifted it, shut his eyes, and put it in his deepest pocket.

"Now I am a burglar indeed!" thought he. "But I suppose I must tell the dwarves about it — some time. They did say I could pick and choose my own share; and I think I would choose this, if they took all the rest!" All the same he had an uncomfortable feeling that the picking and choosing had not really been meant to include this marvellous gem, and that trouble would yet come of it.

Now he went on again. Down the other side of the great mound he climbed, and the spark of his torch vanished from the sight of the watching dwarves. But soon they saw it far away in the distance again. Bilbo was crossing the floor of the hall.

He went on, until he came to the great doors at the further side, and there a draught of air refreshed him, but it almost puffed out his light. He peeped timidly through, and caught a glimpse of great passages and of the dim beginnings of wide stairs going up into the gloom. And still there was no sight nor sound of Smaug. He was just going to turn and go back, when a black shape swooped at him, and brushed his face. He squeaked and started, stumbled backwards and fell. His torch dropped head downwards and went out!

"Only a bat, I suppose and hope!" he said miserably.

[1] The name *Arkenstone* comes from the Anglo-Saxon *eorclanstān*, "precious stone." The word, found also in slightly varying forms beginning *eorcnan-*, *eorcan-*, or *earcnan-*, appears once in *Beowulf*, in the context of the death of Hygelac, king of the Geats:

> hyne wyrd fornam,
> syþðan hē for wlenco wēan āhsode,
> fæhðe tō Frÿsum. Hē þā fætwe wæg,
> eorclan-stānas ofer ÿða ful,
> rīce þēoden; hē under rande gecranc.
> (lines 1205–09)

This is translated by R. M. Liuzza in his *Beowulf* (2000) as follows:

> Fate struck him down
> when in his pride he went looking for woe,
> a feud with the Frisians. He wore that finery,
> those precious stones, over the cup of the sea,
> that powerful lord, and collapsed under his shield.
> (p. 90)

(The origin of the name *Théoden*, King of Rohan in *The Lord of the Rings*, is seen in line 1209, where in *þēoden* the Anglo-Saxon character þ (thorn) represents *th*. It is an Anglo-Saxon word meaning "prince" or "king," here translated *lord*.)

An Old Norse cognate form of *eorclanstān* appears in *Volundarkviða* (The Lay of Volund), one of the poems in the *Elder Edda*, after the smith Volund (who is identical to the Wayland of English folklore) has killed two young brothers who were coveting his treasure. Volund cut off their heads, and from their eyes he made gems (*iarknasteina*) to send to their mother (stanza 25).

In the third volume of Jacob Grimm's four-volume *Teutonic Mythology* (1844), translated by James Steven Stallybrass in 1883, Grimm noted that corresponding forms in Gothic *aírkna-stáins* (*aírknis* meaning "holy") and Old High German *erchan-stein* could be safely assumed, and he suggested that the precious stone referred to might be "the oval, milk-white opal" (p. 1217).

The description of the Arkenstone given here in *The Hobbit* is very similar to that given in *The Silmarillion* of those three great jewels of light, the Silmarils: ". . . even in the darkness of the deepest treasury the Silmarils of their own radiance shone like the stars of Varda; and yet, as were they indeed living things, they rejoiced in light and received it and gave it back in hues more marvelous than before" (p. 67). When (probably in the 1930s) Tolkien translated some of the "Annals of Valinor" from his legendarium into Anglo-Saxon, he used *eorclanstánas* specifically to refer to the Silmarils (see volume four of the *History, The Shaping of Middle-earth*, p. 283).

"But now what am I to do? Which is East, South, North, or West?"

"Thorin! Balin! Oin! Gloin! Fili! Kili!" he cried as loud as he could — it seemed a thin little noise in the wide blackness. "The light's gone out! Someone come and find me and help me!" For the moment his courage had failed altogether.

Faintly the dwarves heard his small cries, though the only word they could catch was "help!"

"Now what on earth or under it has happened?" said Thorin. "Certainly not the dragon, or he would not go on squeaking."

They waited a moment or two, and still there were no dragon-noises, no sound at all in fact but Bilbo's distant voice. "Come, one of you, get another light or two!" Thorin ordered. "It seems we have got to go and help our burglar."

"It is about our turn to help," said Balin, "and I am quite willing to go. Anyway I expect it is safe for the moment."

Gloin lit several more torches, and then they all crept out, one by one, and went along the wall as hurriedly as they could. It was not long before they met Bilbo himself coming back towards them. His wits had quickly returned as soon as he saw the twinkle of their lights.

"Only a bat and a dropped torch, nothing worse!" he said in answer to their questions. Though they were much relieved, they were inclined to be grumpy at being frightened for nothing; but what they would have said, if he had told them at that moment about the Arkenstone, I don't know. The mere fleeting glimpses of treasure which they had caught as they went along had rekindled all the fire of their dwarvish hearts; and when the heart of a dwarf, even the most respectable, is wakened by gold and by jewels, he grows suddenly bold, and he may become fierce.

The dwarves indeed no longer needed any urging.

All were now eager to explore the hall while they had the chance, and willing to believe that, for the present, Smaug was away from home. Each now gripped a lighted torch; and as they gazed, first on one side and then on another, they forgot fear and even caution. They spoke aloud, and cried out to one another, as they lifted old treasures from the mound or from the wall and held them in the light, caressing and fingering them.

Fili and Kili were almost in merry mood, and finding still hanging there many golden harps strung with silver they took them and struck them; and being magical (and also untouched by the dragon, who had small interest in music) they were still in tune. The dark hall was filled with a melody that had long been silent. But most of the dwarves were more practical: they gathered gems and stuffed their pockets, and let what they could not carry fall back through their fingers with a sigh. Thorin was not least among these; but always he searched from side to side for something which he could not find. It was the Arkenstone; but he spoke of it yet to no one.

Now the dwarves took down mail and weapons from the walls, and armed themselves. Royal indeed did Thorin look, clad in a coat of gold-plated rings, with a silver-hafted axe in a belt crusted with scarlet stones.

"Mr. Baggins!" he cried. "Here is the first payment of your reward! Cast off your old coat and put on this!"

With that he put on Bilbo a small coat of mail, wrought for some young elf-prince long ago. It was of silver-steel,[2] which the elves call *mithril,* and with it went a belt of pearls and crystals. A light helm of figured leather, strengthened beneath with hoops of steel, and studded about the brim with white gems, was set upon the hobbit's head.

"I feel magnificent," he thought; "but I expect I look rather absurd. How they would laugh on the Hill at home! Still I wish there was a looking-glass handy!"

All the same Mr. Baggins kept his head more clear of

2 *1937:* "It was of silvered steel and ornamented with pearls, and with it went a belt of pearls and crystals" > *1966-Ball:* "It was of silver-steel, which the elves call *mithril,* and with it went a belt of pearls and crystals"

This revision introduces the name *mithril* into *The Hobbit* and brings the description of Bilbo's mail-coat into accord with that in *The Lord of the Rings.*

Mithril is a Sindarin Elvish word, which translates as "grey glitter." This silver-steel is also called Moria-silver and true-silver. In Middle-earth it was found only in Moria.

the bewitchment of the hoard than the dwarves did. Long before the dwarves were tired of examining the treasures, he became weary of it and sat down on the floor; and he began to wonder nervously what the end of it all would be. "I would give a good many of these precious goblets," he thought, "for a drink of something cheering out of one of Beorn's wooden bowls!"

"Thorin!" he cried aloud. "What next? We are armed, but what good has any armour ever been before against Smaug the Dreadful? This treasure is not yet won back. We are not looking for gold yet, but for a way of escape; and we have tempted luck too long!"

"You speak the truth!" answered Thorin, recovering his wits. "Let us go! I will guide you. Not in a thousand years should I forget the ways of this palace." Then he hailed the others, and they gathered together, and holding their torches above their heads they passed through the gaping doors, not without many a backward glance of longing.

Their glittering mail they had covered again with their old cloaks and their bright helms with their tattered hoods, and one by one they walked behind Thorin, a line of little lights in the darkness that halted often, listening in fear once more for any rumour of the dragon's coming.

Though all the old adornments were long mouldered or destroyed, and though all was befouled and blasted with the comings and goings of the monster, Thorin knew every passage and every turn. They climbed long stairs, and turned and went down wide echoing ways, and turned again and climbed yet more stairs, and yet more stairs again. These were smooth, cut out of the living rock broad and fair; and up, up, the dwarves went, and they met no sign of any living thing, only furtive shadows that fled from the approach of their torches fluttering in the draughts.

The steps were not made, all the same, for hobbit-

Looking out the Front Gate. Illustration by Ryûichi Terashima
for the 1965 Japanese edition.

legs, and Bilbo was just feeling that he could go on no
longer, when suddenly the roof sprang high and far beyond the reach of their torch-light. A white glimmer
could be seen coming through some opening far above,
and the air smelt sweeter. Before them light came dimly
through great doors, that hung twisted on their hinges
and half burnt.

"This is the great chamber of Thror," said Thorin;
"the hall of feasting and of council. Not far off now is the
Front Gate."

They passed through the ruined chamber. Tables
were rotting there; chairs and benches were lying there
overturned, charred and decaying. Skulls and bones
were upon the floor among flagons and bowls and broken drinking-horns and dust. As they came through yet
more doors at the further end, a sound of water fell upon
their ears, and the grey light grew suddenly more full.

"There is the birth of the Running River," said

Thorin. "From here it hastens to the Gate. Let us follow it!"

Out of a dark opening in a wall of rock there issued a boiling water, and it flowed swirling in a narrow channel, carved and made straight and deep by the cunning of ancient hands. Beside it ran a stone-paved road, wide enough for many men abreast. Swiftly along this they ran, and round a wide-sweeping turn — and behold! before them stood the broad light of day. In front there rose a tall arch, still showing the fragments of old carven work within, worn and splintered and blackened though it was. A misty sun sent its pale light between the arms of the Mountain, and beams of gold fell on the pavement at the threshold.

A whirl of bats frightened from slumber by their smoking torches flurried over them; as they sprang forward their feet slithered on stones rubbed smooth and slimed by the passing of the dragon. Now before them the water fell noisily outward and foamed down towards the valley. They flung their pale torches to the ground, and stood gazing out with dazzled eyes. They were come to the Front Gate, and were looking out upon Dale.

"Well!" said Bilbo, "I never expected to be looking out of this door. And I never expected to be so pleased to see the sun again, and to feel the wind on my face. But, ow! this wind is cold!"

It was. A bitter easterly breeze blew with a threat of oncoming winter. It swirled over and round the arms of the Mountain into the valley, and sighed among the rocks. After their long time in the stewing depths of the dragon-haunted caverns, they shivered in the sun.

Suddenly Bilbo realized that he was not only tired but also very hungry indeed. "It seems to be late morning," he said, "and so I suppose it is more or less breakfast-time — if there is any breakfast to have. But I don't feel that Smaug's front doorstep is the safest place for a meal. Do let's go somewhere where we can sit quiet for a bit!"

"Quite right!" said Balin. "And I think I know which way we should go: we ought to make for the old look-out post at the South-West corner of the Mountain."

"How far is that?" asked the hobbit.

"Five hours march, I should think. It will be rough going. The road from the Gate along the left edge of the stream seems all broken up. But look down there! The river loops suddenly east across Dale in front of the ruined town. At that point there was once a bridge, leading to steep stairs that climbed up the right bank, and so to a road running towards Ravenhill. There is (or was) a path that left the road and climbed up to the post. A hard climb, too, even if the old steps are still there."

"Dear me!" grumbled the hobbit. "More walking and more climbing without breakfast! I wonder how many breakfasts, and other meals, we have missed inside that nasty clockless, timeless hole?"

As a matter of fact two nights and the day between had gone by (and not altogether without food) since the dragon smashed the magic door, but Bilbo had quite lost count, and it might have been one night or a week of nights for all he could tell.

"Come, come!" said Thorin laughing – his spirits had begun to rise again, and he rattled the precious stones in his pockets. "Don't call my palace a nasty hole! You wait till it has been cleaned and redecorated!"

"That won't be till Smaug's dead," said Bilbo glumly. "In the meanwhile where is he? I would give a good breakfast to know. I hope he is not up on the Mountain looking down at us!"

That idea disturbed the dwarves mightily, and they quickly decided that Bilbo and Balin were right.

"We must move away from here," said Dori. "I feel as if his eyes were on the back of my head."

3 *1937:* "So on they trudged among the stones on the left side of the river—to the right the rocky wall above the water was sheer and pathless—and the emptiness and desolation" > *1966-Ball:* "Under the rocky wall to the right there was no path, so on they trudged among the stones on the left side of the river, and the emptiness and desolation"

4 *Cram* is an Elvish word. In the "Etymologies," Tolkien's list of Elvish word relationships published in volume five of the *History, The Lost Road,* he derived *cram* from the stem *KRAB-* "press." He also noted that it is a "cake of compressed flour or meal (often containing honey and milk), used on long journeys" (p. 365).

"It's a cold lonesome place," said Bombur. "There may be drink, but I see no sign of food. A dragon would always be hungry in such parts."

"Come on! Come on!" cried the others. "Let us follow Balin's path!"

Under the rocky wall to the right there was no path, so on they trudged among the stones on the left side of the river, and the emptiness and desolation[3] soon sobered even Thorin again. The bridge that Balin had spoken of they found long fallen, and most of its stones were now only boulders in the shallow noisy stream; but they forded the water without much difficulty, and found the ancient steps, and climbed the high bank. After going a short way they struck the old road, and before long came to a deep dell sheltered among the rocks; there they rested for a while and had such a breakfast as they could, chiefly *cram* and water. (If you want to know what *cram* is, I can only say that I don't know the recipe; but it is biscuitish, keeps good indefinitely, is supposed to be sustaining, and is certainly not entertaining, being in fact very uninteresting except as a chewing exercise. It was made by the Lake-men for long journeys.[4])

After that they went on again; and now the road struck westwards and left the river, and the great shoulder of the south-pointing mountain-spur drew ever nearer. At length they reached the hill path. It scrambled steeply up, and they plodded slowly one behind the other, till at last in the late afternoon they came to the top of the ridge and saw the wintry sun going downwards to the West.

Here they found a flat place without a wall on three sides, but backed to the North by a rocky face in which there was an opening like a door. From that door there was a wide view East and South and West.

"Here," said Balin, "in the old days we used always to keep watchmen, and that door behind leads into a rock-hewn chamber that was made here as a guardroom. There were several places like it round the Mountain. But there seemed small need for watching in the days of our prosperity, and the guards were made over comfortable, perhaps — otherwise we might have had longer warning of the coming of the dragon, and things might have been different. Still, here we can now lie hid and sheltered for a while, and can see much without being seen."

"Not much use, if we have been seen coming here," said Dori, who was always looking up towards the Mountain's peak, as if he expected to see Smaug perched there like a bird on a steeple.

"We must take our chance of that," said Thorin. "We can go no further to-day."

"Hear, hear!" cried Bilbo, and flung himself on the ground.

In the rock-chamber there would have been room for a hundred, and there was a small chamber further in, more removed from the cold outside. It was quite deserted; not even wild animals seemed to have used it in all the days of Smaug's dominion. There they laid their burdens; and some threw themselves down at once and slept, but the others sat near the outer door and discussed their plans. In all their talk they came perpetually back to one thing: where was Smaug? They looked West and there was nothing, and East there was nothing, and in the South there was no sign of the dragon, but there was a gathering of very many birds. At that they gazed and wondered; but they were no nearer understanding it, when the first cold stars came out.

14

Fire and Water

NOW IF YOU WISH, like the dwarves, to hear news of Smaug, you must go back again to the evening when he smashed the door and flew off in rage, two days before.

The men of the lake-town Esgaroth were mostly indoors, for the breeze was from the black East and chill, but a few were walking on the quays, and watching, as they were fond of doing, the stars shine out from the smooth patches of the lake as they opened in the sky. From their town the Lonely Mountain was mostly screened by the low hills at the far end of the lake, through a gap in which the Running River came down from the North. Only its high peak could they see in clear weather, and they looked seldom at it, for it was ominous and drear even in the light of morning. Now it was lost and gone, blotted in the dark.

Suddenly it flickered back to view; a brief glow touched it and faded.

"Look!" said one. "The lights again! Last night the watchmen saw them start and fade from midnight until dawn. Something is happening up there."

"Perhaps the King under the Mountain is forging gold," said another. "It is long since he went North. It is time the songs began to prove themselves again."

"Which king?" said another with a grim voice. "As

Smaug over Lake-town. Illustration by Maret
Kernumees for the 1977 Estonian edition.

like as not it is the marauding fire of the Dragon, the only
king under the Mountain we have ever known."

"You are always foreboding gloomy things!" said the
others. "Anything from floods to poisoned fish. Think
of something cheerful!"

Then suddenly a great light appeared in the low place
in the hills and the northern end of the lake turned
golden. "The King beneath the Mountain!" they
shouted. "His wealth is like the Sun, his silver like a
fountain, his rivers golden run! The river is running gold
from the Mountain!" they cried, and everywhere windows were opening and feet were hurrying.

There was once more a tremendous excitement and
enthusiasm. But the grim-voiced fellow ran hotfoot to
the Master. "The dragon is coming or I am a fool!" he
cried. "Cut the bridges! To arms! To arms!"

Then warning trumpets were suddenly sounded, and echoed along the rocky shores. The cheering stopped and the joy was turned to dread. So it was that the dragon did not find them quite unprepared.

Before long, so great was his speed, they could see him as a spark of fire rushing towards them and growing ever huger and more bright, and not the most foolish doubted that the prophecies had gone rather wrong. Still they had a little time. Every vessel in the town was filled with water, every warrior was armed, every arrow and dart was ready, and the bridge to the land was thrown down and destroyed, before the roar of Smaug's terrible approach grew loud, and the lake rippled red as fire beneath the awful beating of his wings.

Amid shrieks and wailing and the shouts of men he came over them, swept towards the bridges and was foiled! The bridge was gone, and his enemies were on an island in deep water — too deep and dark and cool for his liking. If he plunged into it, a vapour and a steam would arise enough to cover all the land with a mist for days; but the lake was mightier than he, it would quench him before he could pass through.

Roaring he swept back over the town. A hail of dark arrows leaped up and snapped and rattled on his scales and jewels, and their shafts fell back kindled by his breath burning and hissing into the lake. No fireworks you ever imagined equalled the sights that night. At the twanging of the bows and the shrilling of the trumpets the dragon's wrath blazed to its height, till he was blind and mad with it. No one had dared to give battle to him for many an age; nor would they have dared now, if it had not been for the grim-voiced man (Bard was his name), who ran to and fro cheering on the archers and urging the Master to order them to fight to the last arrow.

⊂ Fire leaped from the dragon's jaws. He circled for a while high in the air above them lighting all the lake; the

Smaug in flight. Illustration by Tamás Szecskó for the
1975 Hungarian edition.

trees by the shores shone like copper and like blood
with leaping shadows of dense black at their feet. Then
down he swooped straight through the arrow-storm,
reckless in his rage, taking no heed to turn his scaly sides
towards his foes, seeking only to set their town ablaze.

Fire leaped from thatched roofs and wooden beam-
ends as he hurtled down and past and round again,
though all had been drenched with water before he
came. Once more water was flung by a hundred hands
wherever a spark appeared. Back swirled the dragon. A
sweep of his tail and the roof of the Great House crum-
bled and smashed down. Flames unquenchable sprang
high into the night. Another swoop and another, and another house and then another sprang afire and fell; and
still no arrow hindered Smaug or hurt him more than a
fly from the marshes.

Already men were jumping into the water on every side.
Women and children were being huddled into laden
boats in the market-pool. Weapons were flung down.
There was mourning and weeping, where but a little
time ago the old songs of mirth to come had been sung
about the dwarves. Now men cursed their names. The
Master himself was turning to his great gilded boat, hoping to row away in the confusion and save himself. Soon
all the town would be deserted and burned down to the
surface of the lake.

Death of Smaug by J.R.R. Tolkien. This unfinished sketch was first published as the cover illustration for the 1966 Unwin Books paperback edition of *The Hobbit.* When this edition was in preparation, Tolkien expressed his doubts about using it as a cover in a letter to Rayner Unwin dated December 15, 1965: "I do not recollect when the rough sketch of the Death of Smaug was made; but I think it must have been before the first publication, and 1936 must be near the mark. I am in your hands, but I am still not very happy about the use of this scrawl as a cover. It seems too much in the modern mode in which those who can draw try to conceal it. But perhaps there is a distinction between their productions and one by a man who obviously cannot draw what he sees" (*Letters,* No. 281).

The writing in the left margin reads, "The moon should be a *crescent:* it was only a few nights after the *New Moon* on Durin's Day"; in the bottom left corner, "Dragon should have a white *naked* spot where the arrow enters"; and at the bottom, "Bard the Bowman should be standing after release of arrow at extreme left point of the piles." This illustration appears in *Artist* (No. 137) and *Pictures* (No. 19).

That was the dragon's hope. They could all get into boats for all he cared. There he could have fine sport hunting them, or they could stop till they starved. Let them try to get to land and he would be ready. Soon he would set all the shoreland woods ablaze and wither every field and pasture. Just now he was enjoying the

sport of town-baiting more than he had enjoyed anything for years.

But there was still a company of archers that held
their ground among the burning houses. Their captain
was Bard, grim-voiced and grim-faced, whose friends
had accused him of prophesying floods and poisoned
fish, though they knew his worth and courage. He was a
descendant in long line of Girion, Lord of Dale, whose
wife and child had escaped down the Running River
from the ruin long ago. Now he shot with a great yew
bow, till all his arrows but one were spent. The flames
were near him. His companions were leaving him. He
bent his bow for the last time.

Suddenly out of the dark something fluttered to his
shoulder. He started — but it was only an old thrush.
Unafraid it perched by his ear and it brought him news.
Marvelling he found he could understand its tongue, for
he was of the race of Dale.

"Wait! Wait!" it said to him. "The moon is rising.
Look for the hollow of the left breast as he flies and turns
above you!" And while Bard paused in wonder it told
him of tidings up in the Mountain and of all that it had
heard.

Then Bard drew his bow-string to his ear. The
dragon was circling back, flying low, and as he came the
moon rose above the eastern shore and silvered his great
wings.

"Arrow!" said the bowman. "Black arrow! I have
saved you to the last. You have never failed me and always I have recovered you. I had you from my father
and he from of old. If ever you came from the forges
of the true king under the Mountain, go now and speed
well!"

The dragon swooped once more lower than ever, and
as he turned and dived down his belly glittered white
with sparkling fires of gems in the moon — but not in
one place. The great bow twanged. The black arrow

1 Tolkien's use of the word *glede* here is archaic. It comes from Old English *glēde,* "burning coal, ember, fire, flames." This word does survive in modern English but is spelled as gleed, and its usage is rare. It appears a number of times in *Beowulf,* as in this description of an attack by the dragon: *Ðā se gǣst ongan glēdum spīwan / beorht hofu bærnan* (section 33, lines 2312–13): "Then the invader began to spew forth gledes to burn the bright dwellings." It also appears in line 3040 (section 41), "The fiery dragon, terribly bright, was scorched with glowing embers," which is quoted more extensively in note 1 to Chapter 17.

Glede appears twice in the Middle English poem *Sir Gawain and the Green Knight,* in lines 891 and 1609 of the 1925 Tolkien and Gordon edition. Tolkien's posthumously published translation, *Sir Gawain and the Green Knight, Pearl, and Sir Orfeo,* gives the second occurrence as follows, in a scene following a successful hunt where the quarry, a boar, is carved up by one of the huntsmen and the dogs are rewarded:

> *First he hewed off his head and on high set it,*
> *then he rent him roughly down the ridge of*
> * the back,*
> *brought out the bowels, burned them on gledes,*
> *and with them, blended with blood, the blood*
> * hounds rewarded.*
>
> (section 64; p. 65)

The modern word *glede* (now chiefly dialectal) is an entirely different word, used for kites and other birds of prey; it derives from the Old English *glīda,* a word related to the verb *glide.*

2 In his essay "On Fairy-Stories," Tolkien wrote that as a child he had

sped straight from the string, straight for the hollow by the left breast where the foreleg was flung wide. In it smote and vanished, barb, shaft and feather, so fierce was its flight. With a shriek that deafened men, felled trees and split stone, Smaug shot spouting into the air, turned over and crashed down from on high in ruin.

Full on the town he fell. His last throes splintered it to sparks and gledes.[1] The lake roared in. A vast steam leaped up, white in the sudden dark under the moon. There was a hiss, a gushing whirl, and then silence. And that was the end of Smaug and Esgaroth, but not of Bard.[2]

The waxing moon rose higher[3] and higher and the wind grew loud and cold. It twisted the white fog into bending pillars and hurrying clouds and drove it off to the West to scatter in tattered shreds over the marshes before Mirkwood. Then the many boats could be seen dotted dark on the surface of the lake, and down the wind came the voices of the people of Esgaroth lamenting their lost town and goods and ruined houses. But they had really much to be thankful for, had they thought of it, though it could hardly be expected that they should just then: three quarters of the people of the town had at least escaped alive; their woods and fields and pastures and cattle and most of their boats remained undamaged; and the dragon was dead. What that meant they had not yet realized.

They gathered in mournful crowds upon the western shores, shivering in the cold wind, and their first complaints and anger were against the Master, who had left the town so soon, while some were still willing to defend it.

"He may have a good head for business — especially his own business," some murmured, "but he is no good when anything serious happens!" And they praised the courage of Bard and his last mighty shot. "If only he had not been killed," they all said, "we would make him a

Bard and the dragon. Illustration by Nada Rappensbergerová for the 1973 Slovak edition.

king. Bard the Dragon-shooter of the line of Girion! Alas that he is lost!"

And in the very midst of their talk a tall figure stepped from the shadows. He was drenched with water, his black hair hung wet over his face and shoulders, and a fierce light was in his eyes.

"Bard is not lost!" he cried. "He dived from Esgaroth, when the enemy was slain. I am Bard, of the line of Girion; I am the slayer of the dragon!"

"King Bard! King Bard!" they shouted; but the Master ground his chattering teeth.

"Girion was lord of Dale, not king of Esgaroth," he said. "In the Lake-town we have always elected masters from among the old and wise, and have not endured the rule of mere fighting men. Let 'King Bard' go back to his own kingdom — Dale is now freed by his valour, and nothing hinders his return. And any that wish can go with him, if they prefer the cold stones under the

"desired dragons with a profound desire. Of course, I in my timid body did not wish to have them in the neighbourhood, intruding into my relatively safe world. . . . But the world that contained even the imagination of Fáfnir was richer and more beautiful, at whatever cost of peril." In an interview for BBC Radio recorded in January 1965, Tolkien added, "Dragons always attracted me as a mythological element. They seemed to be able to comprise human malice and bestiality together so extraordinarily well, and also a sort of malicious wisdom and shrewdness — terrifying creatures!" (see note 1 to Chapter 2).

In a more playful mood, and with more sympathy for the dragon, Tolkien published the following poem, one of his series of "Tales and Songs of Bimble Bay," in the February 4, 1937, issue of the *Oxford Magazine*.

THE DRAGON'S VISIT

The dragon lay on the cherry trees
a-simmering and a-dreaming:
Green was he, and the blossom white,
and the yellow sun gleaming.
He came from the land of Finis-Terre,
from over the Blue Mountains,
Where dragons live, and the moon shines
on high white fountains.

"Please, Mister Higgins, do you know
What's a-laying in your garden?
There's a dragon in your cherry trees!"
"Eh, what? I beg your pardon?"
Mister Higgins fetched the garden hose,
and the dragon woke from dreaming;
He blinked, and cocked his long green ears
when he felt the water streaming.

"How cool," he said, "delightfully cool
are Mister Higgins' fountains!
I'll sit and sing till the moon comes,
as they sing beyond the mountains;

And Higgins, and his neighbours, Box,
    Miss Biggins and old Tupper,
Will be enchanted by my voice:
    they will enjoy their supper!"

Mister Higgins sent for the fire brigade
    with a long red ladder.
And men with golden helmets on.
    The dragon's heart grew sadder:
"It reminds me of the bad old days
    when warriors unfeeling
Used to hunt dragons in their dens,
    their bright gold stealing."

Captain George, he up the ladder came.
    The dragon said: "Good people,
Why all this fuss? Please go away!
    Or your church-steeple
I shall throw down, and blast your trees,
    and kill and eat for supper
You, Cap'n George, and Higgins, Box,
    and Biggins and old Tupper!"

"Turn on the hose!" said Captain George,
    and down the ladder tumbled.
The dragon's eyes from green went red,
    and his belly rumbled.
He steamed, he smoked, he threshed his tail,
    and down the blossom fluttered;
Like snow upon the lawn it lay,
    and the dragon growled and muttered.

They poked with poles from underneath
    (where he was rather tender):
The dragon gave a dreadful cry
    and rose like thunder.
He smashed the town to smithereens,
    and over the Bay of Bimble
Sailors could see the burning red
    from Bumpus Head to Trimble.

Mister Higgins was tough; and as for Box
    just like his name he tasted.
The dragon munching his supper said:
    "So all my trouble's wasted!"
And he buried Tupper and Captain George,
    and the remains of old Miss Biggins,
On a cliff above the long white shore;
    and he sang a dirge for Higgins.

shadow of the Mountain to the green shores of the lake. The wise will stay here and hope to rebuild our town, and enjoy again in time its peace and riches."

"We will have King Bard!" the people near at hand shouted in reply. "We have had enough of the old men and the money-counters!" And people further off took up the cry: "Up the Bowman, and down with Money-bags," till the clamour echoed along the shore.

"I am the last man to undervalue Bard the Bowman," said the Master warily (for Bard now stood close beside him). "He has tonight earned an eminent place in the roll of the benefactors of our town; and he is worthy of many imperishable songs. But, why O People?" — and here the Master rose to his feet and spoke very loud and clear — "Why do I get all your blame? For what fault am I to be deposed? Who aroused the dragon from his slumber, I might ask? Who obtained of us rich gifts and ample help, and led us to believe that old songs could come true? Who played on our soft hearts and our pleasant fancies? What sort of gold have they sent down the river to reward us? Dragon-fire and ruin! From whom should we claim the recompense of our damage, and aid for our widows and orphans?"

As you see, the Master had not got his position for nothing. The result of his words was that for the moment the people quite forgot their idea of a new king, and turned their angry thoughts towards Thorin and his company. Wild and bitter words were shouted from many sides; and some of those who had before sung the old songs loudest, were now heard as loudly crying that the dwarves had stirred the dragon up against them deliberately!

"Fools!" said Bard. "Why waste words and wrath on those unhappy creatures? Doubtless they perished first in fire, before Smaug came to us." Then even as he was speaking, the thought came into his heart of the fabled treasure of the Mountain lying without guard or owner, and he fell suddenly silent. He thought of the Master's words, and of Dale rebuilt, and filled with golden bells, if he could but find the men.

At length he spoke again: "This is no time for angry words, Master, or for considering weighty plans of change. There is work to do. I serve you still – though after a while I may think again of your words and go North with any that will follow me."

Then he strode off to help in the ordering of the camps and in the care of the sick and the wounded. But the Master scowled at his back as he went, and remained sitting on the ground. He thought much but said little, unless it was to call loudly for men to bring him fire and food.

Now everywhere Bard went he found talk running like fire among the people concerning the vast treasure that was now unguarded. Men spoke of the recompense for all their harm that they would soon get from it, and wealth over and to spare with which to buy rich things from the South; and it cheered them greatly in their plight. That was as well, for the night was bitter and miserable. Shelters could be contrived for few (the Master had one) and there was little food (even the Master went short). Many took ill of wet and cold and sorrow that night, and afterwards died, who had escaped uninjured from the ruin of the town; and in the days that followed there was much sickness and great hunger.

Meanwhile Bard took the lead, and ordered things as he wished, though always in the Master's name, and he had a hard task to govern the people and direct the preparations for their protection and housing. Probably most of them would have perished in the winter that now hurried after autumn, if help had not been to hand. But help came swiftly; for Bard at once had speedy messengers sent up the river to the Forest to ask the aid of the King of the Elves of the Wood, and these messengers had found a host already on the move, although it was then only the third day after the fall of Smaug.

The Elvenking had received news from his own mes-

A sad song, while the moon rose,
  with the sea below sighing
On the grey rocks of Bimble Bay,
  and the red blaze dying.
Far over the sea he saw the peaks
  round his own land ranging;
And he mused on the folk of Bimble Bay
  and the old order changing:

"They have not got the wit to admire
  a dragon's song or colour,
Nor heart to kill him brave and quick –
  the world is getting duller!"
And the moon shone through his green wings
  the night winds beating,
And he flew back over the dappled sea
  to a green dragon's meeting.

On the first typescript of this poem (it is preceded by two fair-copy manuscripts, with various differences in text), Tolkien wrote long afterward "Oxford 1928? rev[ised] 1937."

Years later, probably in the final months of 1961, Tolkien revised the poem, changing the ending and adding another verse, intending to include it in *The Adventures of Tom Bombadil*, which was published in November 1962. But the poem was not included in the book, both because Tolkien found it deficient and because he found it impossible to remodel and bring it into the world of *The Hobbit* and *The Lord of the Rings*. Tolkien reworked it again in December 1964. This final version was published, along with another errant Tom Bombadil poem entitled "Once upon a Time," in *Winter's Tales for Children 1* (1965), edited by Caroline Hillier. Both poems were reprinted in *The Young Magicians* (1969), edited by Lin Carter, but are otherwise unavailable. In the revised version of the poem, the dragon neglects to kill Miss Biggins. The poem ends:

"None of them now have the wit to admire
  a dragon's song or colour,
Nor the nerve with steel to meet his fire —
  the world is getting duller!"
He spread his wide wings to depart;
  but just as he was rising
Miss Biggins stabbed him to the heart,
  and that he found surprising.

"I regret this very much," she said.
  "You're a very splendid creature,
And your voice is quite remarkable
  for one who has had no teacher;
But wanton damage I will not have,
  I really had to end it."
The dragon sighed before he died:
  "At least she called me splendid."

3 *1937:* "The moon rose higher" > *1966-*
Ball: "The waxing moon rose higher"

sengers and from the birds that loved his folk, and already knew much of what had happened. Very great indeed was the commotion among all things with wings that dwelt on the borders of the Desolation of the Dragon. The air was filled with circling flocks, and their swift-flying messengers flew here and there across the sky. Above the borders of the Forest there was whistling, crying and piping. Far over Mirkwood tidings spread: "Smaug is dead!" Leaves rustled and startled ears were lifted. Even before the Elvenking rode forth the news had passed west right to the pinewoods of the Misty Mountains; Beorn had heard it in his wooden house, and the goblins were at council in their caves.

"That will be the last we shall hear of Thorin Oakenshield, I fear," said the king. "He would have done better to have remained my guest. It is an ill wind, all the same," he added, "that blows no one any good." For he too had not forgotten the legend of the wealth of Thror. So it was that Bard's messengers found him now marching with many spearmen and bowmen; and crows were gathered thick above him, for they thought that war was awakening again, such as had not been in those parts for a long age.

But the king, when he received the prayers of Bard, had pity, for he was the lord of a good and kindly people; so turning his march, which had at first been direct towards the Mountain, he hastened now down the river to the Long Lake. He had not boats or rafts enough for his host, and they were forced to go the slower way by foot; but great store of goods he sent ahead by water. Still elves are lightfooted, and though they were not in these days much used to the marches and the treacherous lands between the Forest and the Lake, their going was swift. Only five days after the death of the dragon they came upon the shores and looked on the ruins of the town. Their welcome was good, as may be expected, and the men and their Master were ready to make any bargain for the future in return for the Elvenking's aid.

Their plans were soon made. With the women and the children, the old and the unfit, the Master remained behind; and with him were some men of crafts and many skilled elves; and they busied themselves felling trees, and collecting the timber sent down from the Forest. Then they set about raising many huts by the shore against the oncoming winter; and also under the Master's direction they began the planning of a new town, designed more fair and large even than before, but not in the same place. They removed northward higher up the shore; for ever after they had a dread of the water where the dragon lay. He would never again return to his golden bed, but was stretched cold as stone, twisted upon the floor of the shallows. There for ages his huge bones could be seen in calm weather amid the ruined piles of the old town. But few dared to cross the cursed spot, and none dared to dive into the shivering water or recover the precious stones that fell from his rotting carcase.

But all the men of arms who were still able, and the most of the Elvenking's array, got ready to march north to the Mountain. It was thus that in eleven days from the ruin of the town the head of their host passed the rock-gates at the end of the lake and came into the desolate lands.

15

The Gathering of the Clouds

NOW WE WILL RETURN TO BILBO and the dwarves. All night one of them had watched, but when morning came they had not heard or seen any sign of danger. But ever more thickly the birds were gathering. Their companies came flying from the South; and the crows that still lived about the Mountain were wheeling and crying unceasingly above.

"Something strange is happening," said Thorin. "The time has gone for the autumn wanderings; and these are birds that dwell always in the land; there are starlings and flocks of finches; and far off there are many carrion birds as if a battle were afoot!"

Suddenly Bilbo pointed: "There is that old thrush again!" he cried. "He seems to have escaped, when Smaug smashed the mountain-side, but I don't suppose the snails have!"

Sure enough the old thrush was there, and as Bilbo pointed, he flew towards them and perched on a stone near by. Then he fluttered his wings and sang; then he cocked his head on one side, as if to listen; and again he sang, and again he listened.

"I believe he is trying to tell us something," said Balin; "but I cannot follow the speech of such birds, it is very quick and difficult. Can you make it out Baggins?"

"Not very well," said Bilbo (as a matter of fact, he

could make nothing of it at all); "but the old fellow seems very excited."

"I only wish he was a raven!" said Balin.

"I thought you did not like them! You seemed very shy of them, when we came this way before."

"Those were crows! And nasty suspicious-looking creatures at that, and rude as well. You must have heard the ugly names they were calling after us. But the ravens are different. There used to be great friendship between them and the people of Thror; and they often brought us secret news, and were rewarded with such bright things as they coveted to hide in their dwellings.

"They live many a year,[1] and their memories are long, and they hand on their wisdom to their children. I knew many among the ravens of the rocks when I was a dwarf-lad. This very height was once named Ravenhill, because there was a wise and famous pair, old Carc and his wife, that lived here above the guard-chamber. But I don't suppose that any of that ancient breed linger here now."

No sooner had he finished speaking than the old thrush gave a loud call, and immediately flew away.

"We may not understand him, but that old bird un-

fIn traditional English folklore, ravens are usually considered unlucky birds. However, Tolkien's use of ravens as messengers recalls the two ravens in Norse mythology, Hugin and Munin, who bring Odin intelligence. In *Gylfaginning,* the first part of Snorri Sturluson's *Edda,* "Two ravens sit on his shoulders and speak into his ear all the news they see or hear. Their names are Hugin and Munin. He sends them out at dawn to fly over all the world, and they return at dinner-time. As a result he gets to find out about many events. From this he gets the name raven-god" (p. 33 of the 1987 translation, *Edda,* by Anthony Faulkes).

Ravens in the wild usually have life spans of around thirty years. Roäc, introduced below as one hundred and fifty-three years old, is a fantastically long-lived raven.

The thrush and the raven Roäc. Pencil sketch by Alan Lee, for his 1997 illustrated edition of *The Hobbit.*

2 *Fundin* is another dwarf name from the "Voluspá"; see note 20 to Chapter 2.

3 *Roäc* and *Carc* are marvelously onomatopoeic invented names for birds in bird-speech.

derstands us, I am sure," said Balin. "Keep watch now, and see what happens!"

Before long there was a fluttering of wings, and back came the thrush; and with him came a most decrepit old bird. He was getting blind, he could hardly fly, and the top of his head was bald. He was an aged raven of great size. He alighted stiffly on the ground before them, slowly flapped his wings, and bobbed towards Thorin.

"O Thorin son of Thrain, and Balin son of Fundin,"**2** he croaked (and Bilbo could understand what he said, for he used ordinary language and not bird-speech). "I am Roäc son of Carc.**3** Carc is dead, but he was well known to you once. It is a hundred years and three and fifty since I came out of the egg, but I do not forget what

Roäc speaks to Thorin. Illustration by Peter Chuklev from the 1979 version of the 1975 Bulgarian edition.

my father told me. Now I am the chief of the great ravens of the Mountain. We are few, but we remember still the king that was of old. Most of my people are abroad, for there are great tidings in the South — some are tidings of joy to you, and some you will not think so good.

"Behold! the birds are gathering back again to the Mountain and to Dale from South and East and West, for word has gone out that Smaug is dead!"

"Dead! Dead?" shouted the dwarves. "Dead! Then we have been in needless fear — and the treasure is ours!" They all sprang up and began to caper about for joy.

"Yes, dead," said Roäc. "The thrush, may his feathers never fall, saw him die, and we may trust his words. He saw him fall in battle with the men of Esgaroth the third night back from now at the rising of the moon."

It was some time before Thorin could bring the dwarves to be silent and listen to the raven's news. At length when he had told all the tale of the battle he went on:

"So much for joy, Thorin Oakenshield. You may go back to your halls in safety; all the treasure is yours — for the moment. But many are gathering hither beside the birds. The news of the death of the guardian has already gone far and wide, and the legend of the wealth of Thror has not lost in the telling during many years; many are eager for a share of the spoil. Already a host of the elves is on the way, and carrion birds are with them hoping for battle and slaughter. By the lake men murmur that their sorrows are due to the dwarves; for they are homeless and many have died, and Smaug has destroyed their town. They too think to find amends from your treasure, whether you are alive or dead.

"Your own wisdom must decide your course; but thirteen is small remnant of the great folk of Durin that once dwelt here, and now are scattered far. If you will listen to my counsel, you will not trust the Master of the

Roäc speaks to Thorin and Bilbo. Illustration by Chica for the 1976 French edition.

4 An arrow pointing eastward from the Lonely Mountain to the Iron Hills is visible at the eastern edge of the map of Wilderland. According to Appendix B, "The Tale of Years," in *The Lord of the Rings,* the Iron Hills were settled around the year 2590 by Dwarves led by Gror, a brother of Thror.

Lake-men, but rather him that shot the dragon with his bow. Bard is he, of the race of Dale, of the line of Girion; he is a grim man but true. We would see peace once more among dwarves and men and elves after the long desolation; but it may cost you dear in gold. I have spoken."

Then Thorin burst forth in anger: "Our thanks, Roäc Carc's son. You and your people shall not be forgotten. But none of our gold shall thieves take or the violent carry off while we are alive. If you would earn our thanks still more, bring us news of any that draw near. Also I would beg of you, if any of you are still young and strong of wing, that you would send messengers to our kin in the mountains of the North, both west from here and east, and tell them of our plight. But go specially to my cousin Dain in the Iron Hills,**4** for he has many people well-armed, and dwells nearest to this place. Bid him hasten!"

"I will not say if this counsel be good or bad," croaked Roäc, "but I will do what can be done." Then off he slowly flew.

"Back now to the Mountain!" cried Thorin. "We have little time to lose."

"And little food to use!" cried Bilbo, always practical on such points. In any case he felt that the adventure was, properly speaking, over with the death of the dragon – in which he was much mistaken – and he would have given most of his share of the profits for the peaceful winding up of these affairs.

"Back to the Mountain!" cried the dwarves as if they had not heard him; so back he had to go with them.

As you have heard some of the events already, you will see that the dwarves still had some days before them. They explored the caverns once more, and found, as they expected, that only the Front Gate remained open; all the other gates (except, of course, the small secret door) had long ago been broken and blocked by Smaug, and no sign of them remained. So now they began to labour hard in fortifying the main entrance, and in making a new path that led from it.[5] Tools were to be found in plenty that the miners and quarriers and builders of old had used; and at such work the dwarves were still very skilled.

As they worked the ravens brought them constant tidings. In this way they learned that the Elvenking had turned aside to the Lake, and they still had a breathing space. Better still, they heard that three of their ponies had escaped and were wandering wild far down the banks of the Running River, not far from where the rest of their stores had been left. So while the others went on with their work, Fili and Kili were sent, guided by a raven, to find the ponies and bring back all they could.

They were four days gone, and by that time they knew that the joined armies of the Lake-men and the Elves were hurrying toward the Mountain. But now their hopes were higher; for they had food for some weeks with care – chiefly *cram,* of course, and they were very tired of it; but *cram* is much better than nothing – and already the gate was blocked with a wall of squared stones laid dry, but very thick and high, across the opening. There were holes in the wall through which they could see (or shoot), but no entrance. They climbed in or out with ladders, and hauled stuff up with ropes. For the issuing of the stream they had contrived a small low arch under the new wall; but near the entrance they had so altered the narrow bed that a wide pool stretched from the mountain-wall to the head of the fall over which the stream went towards Dale. Approach to the Gate was now only possible, without swimming, along a narrow ledge of the cliff, to the right as one looked outwards from the wall.[6] The ponies they had brought only to the head of the steps above the old

5 *1937:* "and in remaking the road that led from it" > *1966-Longmans/Unwin:* "and in making a new path that led from it"

This change was probably made to bring the phrasing into accord with that on page 328, where (as it reads from 1937 on) Bilbo leaves "the newly made path."

6 *1937:* "along a narrow path close to the cliff on the right (as you looked towards the gate from the outside)" > *1966-Ball:* "along a narrow ledge of the cliff, to the right as one looked outwards from the wall"

This change moves the path from one side of the river to the other.

7 *1937:* "That day the camp was moved and was brought right between the arms of the Mountain" > *1966-Longmans/ Unwin:* "That day the camp was moved to the east of the river, right between the arms of the Mountain"

bridge, and unloading them there had bidden them return to their masters and sent them back riderless to the South.

There came a night when suddenly there were many lights as of fires and torches away south in Dale before them.

"They have come!" called Balin. "And their camp is very great. They must have come into the valley under the cover of dusk along both banks of the river."

That night the dwarves slept little. The morning was still pale when they saw a company approaching. From behind their wall they watched them come up to the valley's head and climb slowly up. Before long they could see that both men of the lake armed as if for war and elvish bowmen were among them. At length the foremost of these climbed the tumbled rocks and appeared at the top of the falls; and very great was their surprise to see the pool before them and the Gate blocked with a wall of new-hewn stone.

As they stood pointing and speaking to one another Thorin hailed them: "Who are you," he called in a very loud voice, "that come as if in war to the gates of Thorin son of Thrain, King under the Mountain, and what do you desire?"

But they answered nothing. Some turned swiftly back, and the others after gazing for a while at the Gate and its defences soon followed them. That day the camp was moved to the east of the river, right between the arms of the Mountain.7 The rocks echoed then with voices and with song, as they had not done for many a day. There was the sound, too, of elven-harps and of sweet music; and as it echoed up towards them it seemed that the chill of the air was warmed, and they caught faintly the fragrance of woodland flowers blossoming in spring.

Then Bilbo longed to escape from the dark fortress and to go down and join in the mirth and feasting by the fires. Some of the younger dwarves were moved in their hearts, too, and they muttered that they wished things had fallen out otherwise and that they might welcome such folk as friends; but Thorin scowled.

Then the dwarves themselves brought forth harps and instruments regained from the hoard, and made music to soften his mood; but their song was not as elvish song, and was much like the song they had sung long before in Bilbo's little hobbit-hole.

> *Under the Mountain dark and tall*
> *The King has come unto his hall!*
> *His foe is dead, the Worm of Dread,*
> *And ever so his foes shall fall.*
>
> *The sword is sharp, the spear is long,*
> *The arrow swift, the Gate is strong;*
> *The heart is bold that looks on gold;*
> *The dwarves no more shall suffer wrong.*
>
> *The dwarves of yore made mighty spells,*
> *While hammers fell like ringing bells*
> *In places deep, where dark things sleep,*
> *In hollow halls beneath the fells.*
>
> *On silver necklaces they strung*
> *The light of stars, on crowns they hung*
> *The dragon-fire, from twisted wire*
> *The melody of harps they wrung.*
>
> *The mountain throne once more is freed!*
> *O! wandering folk, the summons heed!*
> *Come haste! Come haste! across the waste!*
> *The king of friend and kin has need.*
>
> *Now call we over mountains cold,*
> *'Come back unto the caverns old'!*
> *Here at the Gates the king awaits,*
> *His hands are rich with gems and gold.*

8 A parley is a discussion or conference, usually as an attempt to settle a dispute. In military situations a parley is usually accompanied by a temporary truce, for the purpose of discussing terms.

The king is come unto his hall
Under the Mountain dark and tall.
The Worm of Dread is slain and dead,
And ever so our foes shall fall!

This song appeared to please Thorin, and he smiled again and grew merry; and he began reckoning the distance to the Iron Hills and how long it would be before Dain could reach the Lonely Mountain, if he had set out as soon as the message reached him. But Bilbo's heart fell, both at the song and the talk: they sounded much too warlike.

The next morning early a company of spearmen was seen crossing the river, and marching up the valley. They bore with them the green banner of the Elvenking and the blue banner of the Lake, and they advanced until they stood right before the wall at the Gate.

Again Thorin hailed them in a loud voice: "Who are you that come armed for war to the gates of Thorin son of Thrain, King under the Mountain?" This time he was answered.

A tall man stood forward, dark of hair and grim of face, and he cried: "Hail Thorin! Why do you fence yourself like a robber in his hold? We are not yet foes, and we rejoice that you are alive beyond our hope. We came expecting to find none living here; yet now that we are met there is matter for a parley[8] and a council."

"Who are you, and of what would you parley?"

"I am Bard, and by my hand was the dragon slain and your treasure delivered. Is that not a matter that concerns you? Moreover I am by right descent the heir of Girion of Dale, and in your hoard is mingled much of the wealth of his halls and towns, which of old Smaug stole. Is not that a matter of which we may speak? Further in his last battle Smaug destroyed the dwellings of the men of Esgaroth, and I am yet the servant of their Master. I would speak for him and ask whether you have no thought for the sorrow and misery of his people. They aided you in your distress, and in recompense you have thus far brought ruin only, though doubtless undesigned."

Now these were fair words and true, if proudly and grimly spoken; and Bilbo thought that Thorin would at once admit what justice was in them. He did not, of course, expect that any one would remember that it was he who discovered all by himself the dragon's weak spot; and that was just as well, for no one ever did. But also he did not reckon with the power that gold has upon which a dragon has long brooded, nor with dwarvish hearts. Long hours in the past days Thorin had spent in the treasury, and the lust of it was heavy on him. Though he had hunted chiefly for the Arkenstone, yet he had an eye for many another wonderful thing that was lying there, about which were wound old memories of the labours and the sorrows of his race.

"You put your worst cause last and in the chief place," Thorin answered. "To the treasure of my people no man has a claim, because Smaug who stole it from us also robbed him of life or home. The treasure was not his that his evil deeds should be amended with a share of it. The price of the goods and the assistance that we received of the Lake-men we will fairly pay — in due time. But *nothing* will we give, not even a loaf's worth, under threat of force. While an armed host lies before our doors, we look on you as foes and thieves.

"It is in my mind to ask what share of their inheritance you would have paid to our kindred, had you found the hoard unguarded and us slain."

"A just question," replied Bard. "But you are not dead, and we are not robbers. Moreover the wealthy may have pity beyond right on the needy that befriended them when they were in want. And still my other claims remain unanswered."

"I will not parley, as I have said, with armed men at

9 The stiff formality and stern legalism of the dialogue between Thorin, Bard, and the messengers come straight out of the Icelandic Sagas. Tom Shippey, in *The Road to Middle-earth*, suggests that "one thinks of the hero of *The Saga of Hrafnkell* ticking off the appropriate compensations for the murders he has committed" (second edition, p. 77).

In the translation of this saga by Gwyn Jones, published as "Hrafnkel the Priest of Frey" in *Eirik the Red and Other Icelandic Sagas* (1961), this passage reads:

Hrafnkel retorted that he had killed more men than this one. "And it can be no news to you that I am unwilling to make anyone reparation, and folk have to put up with it just the same. Even so, I admit that this deed of mine strikes me as among the very worst killings I have committed. You have been my neighbor a long while now, I have liked you, and each of us the other. No small matter would have made trouble between me and Einar, had he not ridden the stallion. Well, we must often regret opening our mouths too wide — and seldom repent speaking too little rather than too much. I am now going to make it clear that I regard this deed of mine as worse than anything else I have done. I shall provide your household with milch cows in summer and with meat in the autumn, and I shall do this for you season by season as long as you want to keep on your farm. . . . I will look after you to the day of your death; and we shall then be atoned. . . ."

"I'll not take this offer," said Thorbjorn.

"What do you want then?" Hrafnkel asked him.

"I want us to appoint men to arbitrate between us.""Then you consider yourself my equal," replied Hrafnkel, "and we shall never be atoned on those terms." (pp. 96–97)

Gwyn Jones (1907–1999) was a friend and colleague of Tolkien's, as well as a

my gate. Nor at all with the people of the Elvenking, whom I remember with small kindness. In this debate they have no place. Begone now ere our arrows fly! And if you would speak with me again, first dismiss the elvish host to the woods where it belongs, and then return, laying down your arms before you approach the threshold."

"The Elvenking is my friend, and he has succoured the people of the Lake in their need, though they had no claim but friendship on him," answered Bard. "We will give you time to repent your words. Gather your wisdom ere we return!" Then he departed and went back to the camp.

Ere many hours were past, the banner-bearers returned, and trumpeters stood forth and blew a blast:

"In the name of Esgaroth and the Forest," one cried, "we speak unto Thorin Thrain's son Oakenshield, calling himself the King under the Mountain, and we bid him consider well the claims that have been urged, or be declared our foe. At the least he shall deliver one twelfth portion of the treasure unto Bard, as the dragon-slayer, and as the heir of Girion. From that portion Bard will himself contribute to the aid of Esgaroth; but if Thorin would have the friendship and honour of the lands about, as his sires had of old, then he will give also somewhat of his own for the comfort of the men of the Lake."

Then Thorin seized a bow of horn and shot an arrow at the speaker. It smote into his shield and stuck there quivering.

"Since such is your answer," he called in return, "I declare the Mountain besieged. You shall not depart from it, until you call on your side for a truce and a parley. We will bear no weapons against you, but we leave you to your gold. You may eat that, if you will!"

With that the messengers departed swiftly, and the dwarves were left to consider their case.9 So grim had

Thorin become, that even if they had wished, the others would not have dared to find fault with him; but indeed most of them seemed to share his mind — except perhaps old fat Bombur and Fili and Kili. Bilbo, of course, disapproved of the whole turn of affairs. He had by now had more than enough of the Mountain, and being besieged inside it was not at all to his taste.

"The whole place still stinks of dragon," he grumbled to himself, "and it makes me sick. And *cram* is beginning simply to stick in my throat."

prolific scholar, editor, translator, and writer of fiction. For many years he was Professor of English Language and Literature in the University College of Wales, Aberystwyth. In December 1945 he published in the *Welsh Review,* a magazine he had founded in 1939, one of Tolkien's finest poems, "The Lay of Aoutrou and Itroun." It is a rhyming poem of five hundred and eight lines in octosyllabic couplets done in the manner of a Breton lay, and the earliest version dates from September 1930. The poem tells of a childless lord (*aotrou* and *itroun* are the Breton words for *lord* and *lady*) who obtains a fertility potion from a witch, with tragic results. Unfortunately the poem has not been reprinted.

Jones had also planned to publish Tolkien's "Sellic Spell," a reworking of the folktale underlying *Beowulf,* but the *Welsh Review* folded in 1948, and Jones returned the manuscript to Tolkien with regret. "Sellic Spell" remains unpublished.

16

A Thief in the Night

1 A slight confusion remains evident in the text here. In the first edition of *The Hobbit,* Thorin's father Thrain was the only character of that name. However, on Thror's Map it states "Here of old was Thrain King under the Mountain." Thorin's father Thrain was not the King under the Mountain when the dragon came; Thrain's father, Thror, was then the King under the Mountain. In the 1951 second edition of *The Hobbit,* Tolkien added an introductory note including the statement "on a point raised by several students of the lore of the period" that "the Map, however, is not in error. Names are often repeated in dynasties, and the genealogies show that a distant ancestor of Thror was referred to, Thrain I, a fugitive from Moria, who first discovered the Lonely Mountain, Erebor, and ruled there for a while, before his people moved on to remoter mountains of the North." This part of the introductory note was made unnecessary in 1966 by some revisions to the text, including the introduction of Thorin's far ancestor Thrain the Old on page 54.

In Section III ("Durin's Folk") in Ap-

NOW THE DAYS PASSED SLOWLY and wearily. Many of the dwarves spent their time piling and ordering the treasure; and now Thorin spoke of the Arkenstone of Thrain, and bade them eagerly to look for it in every corner.

"For the Arkenstone of my father,"[1] he said, "is worth more than a river of gold in itself, and to me it is beyond price. That stone of all the treasure I name unto myself, and I will be avenged on anyone who finds it and withholds it."

Bilbo heard these words and he grew afraid, wondering what would happen, if the stone was found — wrapped in an old bundle of tattered oddments that he used as a pillow. All the same he did not speak of it, for as the weariness of the days grew heavier, the beginnings of a plan had come into his little head.

Things had gone on like this for some time, when the ravens brought news that Dain and more than five hundred dwarves, hurrying from the Iron Hills, were now within about two days' march of Dale, coming from the North-East.

"But they cannot reach the Mountain unmarked," said Roäc, "and I fear lest there be battle in the valley. I do not call this counsel good. Though they are a grim folk, they are not likely to overcome the host that besets you; and even if they did so, what will you gain? Winter and snow is hastening behind them. How shall you be fed without the friendship and goodwill of the lands about you? The treasure is likely to be your death, though the dragon is no more!"

But Thorin was not moved. "Winter and snow will bite both men and elves," he said, "and they may find their dwelling in the waste grievous to bear. With my friends behind them and winter upon them, they will perhaps be in softer mood to parley with."

That night Bilbo made up his mind. The sky was black and moonless. As soon as it was full dark, he went to a corner of an inner chamber just within the gate and drew from his bundle a rope, and also the Arkenstone wrapped in a rag. Then he climbed to the top of the wall. Only Bombur was there, for it was his turn to watch, and the dwarves kept only one watchman at a time.

"It is mighty cold!" said Bombur. "I wish we could have a fire up here as they have in the camp!"

"It is warm enough inside," said Bilbo.

"I daresay; but I am bound here till midnight," grumbled the fat dwarf. "A sorry business altogether. Not that I venture to disagree with Thorin, may his beard grow ever longer; yet he was ever a dwarf with a stiff neck."

"Not as stiff as my legs," said Bilbo. "I am tired of stairs and stone passages. I would give a good deal for the feel of grass at my toes."

"I would give a good deal for the feel of a strong drink in my throat, and for a soft bed after a good supper!"

"I can't give you those, while the siege is going on. But it is long since I watched, and I will take your turn for you, if you like. There is no sleep in me tonight."

"You are a good fellow, Mr. Baggins, and I will take your offer kindly. If there should be anything to note, rouse me first, mind you! I will lie in the inner chamber to the left, not far away."

pendix A of *The Lord of the Rings,* Tolkien wrote of Thrain the Old (Thrain I): "In Erebor he found the great jewel, the Arkenstone, Heart of the Mountain." On page 287 of *The Hobbit,* the Arkenstone is referred to as "the Heart of the Mountain, the Arkenstone of Thrain." Here, Thorin speaks of "the Arkenstone of Thrain" and "the Arkenstone of my father," and on page 334 Thorin says "that stone was my father's." Surely in naming the stone "the Arkenstone of Thrain," Tolkien would have meant the Thrain who discovered it. Originally, the discoverer was Thorin's father, but when Tolkien came to expand the Dwarvish ancestry he seems to have missed the significance here of Thorin describing the stone as being his father's. By rights, at the time of the coming of the dragon, the stone belonged not to Thrain but to Thror, Thrain's father, then the King under the Mountain.

"Off you go!" said Bilbo. "I will wake you at midnight, and you can wake the next watchman."

As soon as Bombur had gone, Bilbo put on his ring, fastened his rope, slipped down over the wall, and was gone. He had about five hours before him. Bombur would sleep (he could sleep at any time, and ever since the adventure in the forest he was always trying to recapture the beautiful dreams he had then); and all the others were busy with Thorin. It was unlikely that any, even Fili or Kili, would come out on the wall until it was their turn.

It was very dark, and the road after a while, when he left the newly made path and climbed down towards the lower course of the stream, was strange to him. At last he came to the bend where he had to cross the water, if he was to make for the camp, as he wished. The bed of the stream was there shallow but already broad, and fording it in the dark was not easy for the little hobbit. He was nearly across when he missed his footing on a round stone and fell into the cold water with a splash. He had barely scrambled out on the far bank, shivering and spluttering, when up came elves in the gloom with bright lanterns and searched for the cause of the noise.

"That was no fish!" one said. "There is a spy about. Hide your lights! They will help him more than us, if it is that queer little creature that is said to be their servant."

"Servant, indeed!" snorted Bilbo; and in the middle of his snort he sneezed loudly, and the elves immediately gathered towards the sound.

"Let's have a light!" he said. "I am here, if you want me!" and he slipped off his ring, and popped from behind a rock.

They seized him quickly, in spite of their surprise. "Who are you? Are you the dwarves' hobbit? What are you doing? How did you get so far past our sentinels?" they asked one after another.

"I am Mr. Bilbo Baggins," he answered, "companion of Thorin, if you want to know. I know your king well by sight, though perhaps he doesn't know me to look at. But Bard will remember me, and it is Bard I particularly want to see."

"Indeed!" said they, "and what may be your business?"

"Whatever it is, it's my own, my good elves. But if you wish ever to get back to your own woods from this cold cheerless place," he answered shivering, "you will take me along quick to a fire, where I can dry — and then you will let me speak to your chiefs as quick as may be. I have only an hour or two to spare."

That is how it came about that some two hours after his escape from the Gate, Bilbo was sitting beside a warm fire in front of a large tent, and there sat too, gazing curiously at him, both the Elvenking and Bard. A hobbit in elvish armour, partly wrapped in an old blanket, was something new to them.

"Really you know," Bilbo was saying in his best business manner, "things are impossible. Personally I am tired of the whole affair. I wish I was back in the West in my own home, where folk are more reasonable. But I have an interest in this matter — one fourteenth share, to be precise, according to a letter, which fortunately I believe I have kept." He drew from a pocket in his old jacket (which he still wore over his mail), crumpled and much folded, Thorin's letter that had been put under the clock on his mantelpiece in May!²

"A share in the *profits*, mind you," he went on. "I am aware of that. Personally I am only too ready to consider all your claims carefully, and deduct what is right from the total before putting in my own claim. However you don't know Thorin Oakenshield as well as I do now. I assure you, he is quite ready to sit on a heap of gold and starve, as long as you sit here."

2 The statement here that Thorin's letter had been put under Bilbo's mantelpiece in May is incorrect. It was done on April 28. See note 3 to Chapter 2, where the "fine morning just before May" is cited. Tolkien also mistakenly refers to "that May morning" on page 202.

3 The Dwarf and Goblin wars referred to here are named in *The Lord of the Rings* as the War of the Dwarves and Orcs, fought between the years 2793 and 2799 of the Third Age. The war was caused by the murder and defilement of Thorin's grandfather, Thror, by Azog the Goblin, in 2790. In 2793, after mustering their forces, the Dwarves assailed various Orc strongholds in the Misty Mountains. In 2799, the decisive Battle of Azanulbizar was fought at Moria. There Azog was slain by Dain, who then returned to the Iron Hills. Dain was born in the year 2767 of the Third Age, and therefore was 174 years old in 2941, when the story of *The Hobbit* begins. Dwarves lived about 250 years, so Bilbo's suggestion that a good many of Dain's warriors had experience in the War of the Dwarves and Orcs is probably accurate.

Bilbo shows the Arkenstone to Bard and the Elven-king. Illustration by Maret Kernumees for the 1977 Estonian edition.

"Well, let him!" said Bard. "Such a fool deserves to starve."

"Quite so," said Bilbo. "I see your point of view. At the same time winter is coming on fast. Before long you will be having snow and what not, and supplies will be difficult – even for elves I imagine. Also there will be other difficulties. You have not heard of Dain and the dwarves of the Iron Hills?"

"We have, a long time ago; but what has he got to do with us?" asked the king.

"I thought as much. I see I have some information you have not got. Dain, I may tell you, is now less than two days' march off, and has at least five hundred grim dwarves with him — a good many of them have had experience in the dreadful dwarf and goblin wars,[3] of which you have no doubt heard. When they arrive there may be serious trouble."

"Why do you tell us this? Are you betraying your friends, or are you threatening us?" asked Bard grimly.

"My dear Bard!" squeaked Bilbo. "Don't be so hasty! I never met such suspicious folk! I am merely trying to avoid trouble for all concerned. Now I will make you an offer! !"

"Let us hear it!" they said.

"You may see it!" said he. "It is this!" and he drew forth the Arkenstone, and threw away the wrapping.

The Elvenking himself, whose eyes were used to things of wonder and beauty, stood up in amazement. Even Bard gazed marvelling at it in silence. It was as if a globe had been filled with moonlight and hung before them in a net woven of the glint of frosty stars.

"This is the Arkenstone of Thrain," said Bilbo, "the Heart of the Mountain; and it is also the heart of Thorin. He values it above a river of gold. I give it to you. It will aid you in your bargaining." Then Bilbo, not without a shudder, not without a glance of longing, handed the marvellous stone to Bard, and he held it in his hand, as though dazed.

"But how is it yours to give?" he asked at last with an effort.

"O well!" said the hobbit uncomfortably. "It isn't exactly; but, well, I am willing to let it stand against all my claim, don't you know. I may be a burglar — or so they say: personally I never really felt like one — but I am an honest one, I hope, more or less. Anyway I am going back now, and the dwarves can do what they like to me. I hope you will find it useful."

The Elvenking looked at Bilbo with a new wonder. "Bilbo Baggins!" he said. "You are more worthy to wear the armour of elf-princes than many that have looked more comely in it. But I wonder if Thorin Oakenshield will see it so. I have more knowledge of dwarves in general than you have perhaps. I advise you to remain with us, and here you shall be honoured and thrice welcome."

"Thank you very much I am sure," said Bilbo with a bow. "But I don't think I ought to leave my friends like this, after all we have gone through together. And I promised to wake old Bombur at midnight, too! Really I must be going, and quickly."

Bilbo and the Arkenstone. Illustration by Chica for the 1976 French edition.

Nothing they could say would stop him; so an escort was provided for him, and as he went both the king and Bard saluted him with honour. As they passed through the camp an old man, wrapped in a dark cloak, rose from a tent door where he was sitting and came towards them.

"Well done! Mr. Baggins!" he said, clapping Bilbo on the back. "There is always more about you than anyone expects!" It was Gandalf.

For the first time for many a day Bilbo was really delighted. But there was no time for all the questions that he immediately wished to ask.

"All in good time!" said Gandalf. "Things are drawing towards the end now, unless I am mistaken. There is an unpleasant time just in front of you; but keep your heart up! You *may* come through all right. There is news brewing that even the ravens have not heard. Good night!"

Puzzled but cheered, Bilbo hurried on. He was guided to a safe ford and set across dry, and then he said farewell to the elves and climbed carefully back towards the Gate. Great weariness began to come over him; but it was well before midnight when he clambered up the rope again — it was still where he had left it. He untied it and hid it, and then he sat down on the wall and wondered anxiously what would happen next.

At midnight he woke up Bombur; and then in turn rolled himself up in his corner, without listening to the old dwarf's thanks (which he felt he had hardly earned). He was soon fast asleep forgetting all his worries till the morning. As a matter of fact he was dreaming of eggs and bacon.

17

The Clouds Burst

NEXT DAY THE TRUMPETS RANG early in the camp. Soon a single runner was seen hurrying along the narrow path. At a distance he stood and hailed them, asking whether Thorin would now listen to another embassy, since new tidings had come to hand, and matters were changed.

"That will be Dain!" said Thorin when he heard. "They will have got wind of his coming. I thought that would alter their mood! Bid them come few in number and weaponless, and I will hear," he called to the messenger.

About midday the banners of the Forest and the Lake were seen to be borne forth again. A company of twenty was approaching. At the beginning of the narrow way they laid aside sword and spear, and came on towards the Gate. Wondering, the dwarves saw that among them were both Bard and the Elvenking, before whom an old man wrapped in cloak and hood bore a strong casket of iron-bound wood.

"Hail Thorin!" said Bard. "Are you still of the same mind?"

"My mind does not change with the rising and setting of a few suns," answered Thorin. "Did you come to ask me idle questions? Still the elf-host has not departed as I bade! Till then you come in vain to bargain with me."

Bilbo and Thorin. Illustration by Tamás Szecskó for the 1975 Hungarian edition.

"Is there then nothing for which you would yield any of your gold?"

"Nothing that you or your friends have to offer."

"What of the Arkenstone of Thrain?" said he, and at the same moment the old man opened the casket and held aloft the jewel. The light leapt from his hand, bright and white in the morning.

Then Thorin was stricken dumb with amazement and confusion. No one spoke for a long while.

Thorin at length broke the silence, and his voice was thick with wrath. "That stone was my father's, and is mine," he said. "Why should I purchase my own?" But wonder overcame him and he added: "But how came you by the heirloom of my house — if there is need to ask such a question of thieves?"

"We are not thieves," Bard answered. "Your own we will give back in return for our own."

"How came you by it?" shouted Thorin in gathering rage.

"I gave it to them!" squeaked Bilbo, who was peering over the wall, by now in a dreadful fright.

"You! You!" cried Thorin, turning upon him and grasping him with both hands. "You miserable hobbit! You undersized — burglar!" he shouted at a loss for words, and he shook poor Bilbo like a rabbit.

"By the beard of Durin! I wish I had Gandalf here! Curse him for his choice of you! May his beard wither! As for you I will throw you to the rocks!" he cried and lifted Bilbo in his arms.

"Stay! Your wish is granted!" said a voice. The old man with the casket threw aside his hood and cloak. "Here is Gandalf! And none too soon it seems. If you don't like my Burglar, please don't damage him. Put him down, and listen first to what he has to say!"

"You all seem in league!" said Thorin dropping Bilbo on the top of the wall. "Never again will I have dealings with any wizard or his friends. What have you to say, you descendant of rats?"

"Dear me! Dear me!" said Bilbo. "I am sure this is all very uncomfortable. You may remember saying that I might choose my own fourteenth share? Perhaps I took it too literally — I have been told that dwarves are sometimes politer in word than in deed. The time was, all the same, when you seemed to think that I had been of some service. Descendant of rats, indeed! Is this all the service of you and your family that I was promised, Thorin? Take it that I have disposed of my share as I wished, and let it go at that!"

"I will," said Thorin grimly. "And I will let you go at that — and may we never meet again!" Then he turned and spoke over the wall. "I am betrayed," he said. "It was rightly guessed that I could not forbear to redeem the Arkenstone, the treasure of my house. For it I will give one fourteenth share of the hoard in silver and gold, setting aside the gems; but that shall be accounted the promised share of this traitor, and with that reward he shall depart, and you can divide it as you will. He will get little enough, I doubt not. Take him, if you wish him to live; and no friendship of mine goes with him.

"Get down now to your friends!" he said to Bilbo, "or I will throw you down."

"What about the gold and silver?" asked Bilbo.

"That shall follow after, as can be arranged," said he. "Get down!"

"Until then we keep the stone," cried Bard.

"You are not making a very splendid figure as King under the Mountain," said Gandalf. "But things may change yet."

"They may indeed," said Thorin. And already, so strong was the bewilderment of the treasure[1] upon him, he was pondering whether by the help of Dain he might not recapture the Arkenstone and withhold the share of the reward.

And so Bilbo was swung down from the wall, and departed with nothing for all his trouble, except the armour which Thorin had given him already. More than

[1] Probably in 1922, Tolkien wrote about the power (and bewilderment) of treasure in a poem entitled "Iúmonna Gold Galdre Bewunden" published in the January 1923 issue of a Leeds University magazine called the *Gryphon*. The title is taken from *Beowulf*, line 3052, which Tolkien translated (in a letter of December 6, 1961, to Pauline Baynes) as "the gold of men of long ago, enmeshed in enchantment" (*Letters*, No. 235). Tolkien published a revised version of the poem in 1937, which was reprinted (with further revisions) as "The Hoard" in *The Adventures of Tom Bombadil* (1962), with illustrations by Pauline Baynes. Tolkien can be heard reading the poem in a recording released in 1967, *Poems and Songs of Middle-earth* (Caedmon, TC 1231). I give here the poem in its earliest form.

IÚMONNA GOLD GALDRE BEWUNDEN

There were elves olden and strong spells
Under green hills in hollow dells
They sang o'er the gold they wrought with
*   mirth,*
In the deeps of time in the young earth,
Ere Hell was digged, ere the dragon's brood
Or the dwarves were spawned in dungeons rude;
And men there were in a few lands
That caught some cunning of their mouths and
*   hands.*
Yet the doom came and their songs failed,
And greed that made them not to its holes haled
Their gems and gold and their loveliness,
And the shadows fell on Elfinesse.

There was an old dwarf in a deep grot
That counted the gold things he had got,
That the dwarves had stolen from men and elves
And kept in the dark to their gloomy selves.
His eyes grew dim and his ears dull.
And the skin was yellow on his old skull;
There ran unseen through his bony claw
The faint glimmer of gems without a flaw.

He heard not the feet that shook the earth,
Nor the rush of wings, not the brazen mirth
Of dragons young in their fiery lust:
His hope was in gold and in jewels his trust.
Yet a dragon found his dark cold hole,
And he lost the earth and the things he stole.

There was an old dragon under an old stone
Blinking with red eyes all alone.
The flames of his fiery heart burnt dim;
He was knobbed and wrinkled and bent of
*   limb;*
His joy was dead and his cruel youth,
But his lust still smouldered and he had no
*   ruth.*
To the slime of his belly the gems stuck thick
And his things of gold he would snuff and lick
As he lay thereon and dreamed of the woe
And grinding anguish thieves would know
That ever set a finger on one small ring;
And dreaming uneasy he stirred a wing.
He heard not the step nor the harness clink
Till the fearless warrior at his cavern's brink
Called him come out and fight for his gold,
Yet iron rent his heart with anguish cold.

There was an old king on a high throne:
His white beard was laid on his knees of bone,
And his mouth savoured not meat nor drink,
Nor his ears song, he could only think
Of his huge chest with carven lid
Where the gold and jewels unseen lay hid
In a secret treasury in the dark ground,
Whose mighty doors were iron-bound.
The swords of his warriors did dull and rust,
His glory was tarnished and his rule unjust,
His halls hollow and his bowers cold,
But he was king of elfin gold.
He heard not the horns in the mountain pass,
He smelt not the blood on the trodden grass,
Yet his halls were burned and his kingdom lost,
In a grave unhonoured his bones were tossed.

There is an old hoard in a dark rock
Forgotten behind doors none can unlock.
The keys are lost and the path gone,
The mound unheeded that the grass grows on;

one of the dwarves in their hearts felt shame and pity at his going.

"Farewell!" he cried to them. "We may meet again as friends."

"Be off!" called Thorin. "You have mail upon you, which was made by my folk, and is too good for you. It cannot be pierced by arrows; but if you do not hasten, I will sting your miserable feet. So be swift!"

"Not so hasty!" said Bard. "We will give you until to-morrow. At noon we will return, and see if you have brought from the hoard the portion that is to be set against the stone. If that is done without deceit, then we will depart, and the elf-host will go back to the Forest. In the meanwhile farewell!"

With that they went back to the camp; but Thorin sent messengers by Roäc telling Dain of what had passed, and bidding him come with wary speed.

That day passed and the night. The next day the wind shifted west, and the air was dark and gloomy. The morning was still early when a cry was heard in the camp. Runners came in to report that a host of dwarves had appeared round the eastern spur of the Mountain and was now hastening to Dale. Dain had come. He had hurried on through the night, and so had come upon them sooner than they had expected. Each one of his folk was clad in a hauberk[2] of steel mail that hung to his knees, and his legs were covered with hose of a fine and flexible metal mesh, the secret of whose making was possessed by Dain's people. The dwarves are exceedingly strong for their height, but most of these were strong even for dwarves. In battle they wielded heavy two-handed mattocks[3]; but each of them had also a short broad sword at his side and a roundshield slung at his back. Their beards were forked and plaited and thrust into their belts. Their caps were of iron and they were shod with iron, and their faces were grim.

Trumpets called men and elves to arms. Before long the dwarves could be seen coming up the valley at a great pace. They halted between the river and the eastern spur; but a few held on their way, and crossing the river drew near the camp; and there they laid down their weapons and held up their hands in sign of peace. Bard went out to meet them, and with him went Bilbo.

"We are sent from Dain son of Nain,⁴" they said when questioned. "We are hastening to our kinsmen in the Mountain, since we learn that the kingdom of old is renewed. But who are you that sit in the plain as foes before defended walls?" This, of course, in the polite and rather old-fashioned language of such occasions, meant simply: "You have no business here. We are going on, so make way or we shall fight you!" They meant to push on between the Mountain and the loop of the river; for the narrow land there did not seem to be strongly guarded.

Bard, of course, refused to allow the dwarves to go straight on to the Mountain. He was determined to wait until the gold and silver had been brought out in exchange for the Arkenstone; for he did not believe that this would be done, if once the fortress was manned with so large and warlike a company. They had brought with them a great store of supplies; for the dwarves can carry very heavy burdens, and nearly all of Dain's folk, in spite of their rapid march, bore huge packs on their backs in addition to their weapons. They would stand a siege for weeks, and by that time yet more dwarves might come, and yet more, for Thorin had many relatives. Also they would be able to reopen and guard some other gate, so that the besiegers would have to encircle the whole mountain; and for that they had not sufficient numbers.

These were, in fact, precisely their plans (for the raven-messengers had been busy between Thorin and Dain); but for the moment the way was barred, so after

The sheep crop it and the larks rise
From its green mantle, and no man's eyes
Shall find its secret, till those return
Who wrought the treasure, till again burn
The lights of Faery, and the woods shake,
And songs long silent once more awake.

In context, line 3052 of *Beowulf* shows the inspiration of Tolkien's poem. Here is a prose translation by John R. Clark Hall, revised by Tolkien's friend and colleague C. L. Wrenn. Wrenn's *Beowulf and the Finnesburg Fragment* was first published in 1940; the book includes prefatory remarks by Tolkien:

The fiery dragon, terribly bright, was scorched with glowing embers. Fifty measured feet long was it as it lay. Sometimes by night it used to dwell in the joyous air; then it came down again to seek its den; — and there it was, rigid in death. It had inhabited the last of its earth-caves. Goblets and flagons stood by it, dishes lay there and precious swords, rusty and eaten through, as if they had lodged there a thousand winter's in earth's bosom. At that time the mighty heritage, the gold store of men of old, was hedged round with a spell, that no man might touch the treasure-chamber, had not God himself, true king of victories (he is the shield of men), granted to whom he would to open the hoard, even to such a man as seemed meet to him. (section 41, lines 3040–57)

Tom Shippey's article "The Versions of 'The Hoard,' " published in *Lembas*, no. 100 (2001), the newsletter of the Dutch Tolkien Society (Unquendor), compares the changes in the published versions of the poem and says some highly interesting things about the meter as it relates to that of *Beowulf*:

It is probably a better description of this poem to say that (as with old English poetry) each line consists of two half-lines, with a strongly marked break or caesura, each half-line consisting of four or five syllables (rarely, three), but each half-line also containing two strong stresses, often in consecutive syllables. It is in short based on counting stresses rather than syllables, and is in that way more like the native tradition of poetry than the tradition learned from the French. . . . Tolkien was writing an Old English theme with an Old English vocabulary, with something quite close to Old English metre, as if to show it could still be done.

Shippey also notes another work strikingly similar to Tolkien's in theme and concept: the story "The King's Ankus" in *The Jungle Book* (1894) by Rudyard Kipling. In this tale a serpentlike white cobra guards a huge underground hoard of gold, which is death to all who covet it.

Tolkien's poem was also reprinted in *A Book of Dragons* (1970), edited by Roger Lancelyn Green. Green (1918–1987) was a student of Tolkien's and also a close friend of C. S. Lewis's. His 1944 B.Litt. thesis, "Andrew Lang and the Fairy Tale," was supervised by Tolkien; it was published in 1946 as *Andrew Lang: A Critical Biography. A Book of Dragons* is dedicated to Tolkien.

2 A hauberk is a shirt of mail (interwoven, flexible metal).

3 A mattock is a digging tool, similar to a pickaxe but with a blade perpendicular to the handle (like an adze) on one side and often a kind of pick on the other.

The miner boy Curdie in George Macdonald's *The Princess and Curdie* was rarely without his mattock. It served him in his mining duties and as a weapon as well.

angry words the dwarf-messengers retired muttering in their beards. Bard then sent messengers at once to the Gate; but they found no gold or payment. Arrows came forth as soon as they were within shot, and they hastened back in dismay. In the camp all was now astir, as if for battle; for the dwarves of Dain were advancing along the eastern bank.

"Fools!" laughed Bard, "to come thus beneath the Mountain's arm! They do not understand war above ground, whatever they may know of battle in the mines. There are many of our archers and spearmen now hidden in the rocks upon their right flank. Dwarf-mail may be good, but they will soon be hard put to it. Let us set on them now from both sides, before they are fully rested!"

But the Elvenking said: "Long will I tarry, ere I begin this war for gold. The dwarves cannot pass us, unless we will, or do anything that we cannot mark. Let us hope still for something that will bring reconciliation. Our advantage in numbers will be enough, if in the end it must come to unhappy blows."

But he reckoned without the dwarves. The knowledge that the Arkenstone was in the hands of the besiegers burned in their thoughts; also they guessed the hesitation of Bard and his friends, and resolved to strike while they debated.

Suddenly without a signal they sprang silently forward to attack. Bows twanged and arrows whistled; battle was about to be joined.

Still more suddenly a darkness came on with dreadful swiftness! A black cloud hurried over the sky. Winter thunder on a wild wind rolled roaring up and rumbled in the Mountain, and lightning lit its peak. And beneath the thunder another blackness could be seen whirling forward; but it did not come with the wind, it came from the North, like a vast cloud of birds, so dense that no light could be seen between their wings.

"Halt!" cried Gandalf, who appeared suddenly, and stood alone, with arms uplifted, between the advancing dwarves and the ranks awaiting them. "Halt!" he called in a voice like thunder, and his staff blazed forth with a flash like the lightning. "Dread has come upon you all! Alas! it has come more swiftly than I guessed. The Goblins are upon you! Bolg*[5] of the North is coming, O Dain! whose father you slew in Moria.[6] Behold! the bats are above his army like a sea of locusts. They ride upon wolves and Wargs are in their train!"

Amazement and confusion fell upon them all. Even as Gandalf had been speaking the darkness grew. The dwarves halted and gazed at the sky. The elves cried out with many voices.

"Come!" called Gandalf. "There is yet time for council. Let Dain son of Nain come swiftly to us!"

So began a battle that none had expected; and it was called the Battle of Five Armies,[7] and it was very terrible. Upon one side were the Goblins and the Wild Wolves, and upon the other were Elves and Men and Dwarves. This is how it fell out. Ever since the fall of the Great Goblin of the Misty Mountains the hatred of their race for the dwarves had been rekindled to fury. Messengers had passed to and fro between all their cities, colonies and strongholds; for they resolved now to win the dominion of the North. Tidings they had gathered in secret ways; and in all the mountains there was a forging and an arming. Then they marched and gathered by hill and valley, going ever by tunnel or under dark, until around and beneath the great mountain Gundabad[8] of the North, where was their capital, a vast host was assembled ready to sweep down in time of storm unawares upon the South. Then they learned of the death of Smaug, and joy was in their hearts; and they hastened

* Son of Azog. See p. 57

4 *Dain* and *Nain* are dwarf names from the "Voluspá"; see note 20 to Chapter 2.

5 This footnote first appeared in *1966-Ball*. (The page reference has changed in various editions.)

6 The great importance of maintaining the distinction between the etymology of names within Tolkien's story and the sources from which Tolkien as an author derived them is shown in the following statements Tolkien made about the source of the name *Moria* in the drafts for a letter written in August 1967:

The name Moria appears as a casual "echo" of *Soria Moria Castle* in one of the Scandinavian tales translated by Dasent. (The tale had no interest for me: I had already forgotten it and have never since looked at it. It was thus merely the source of the sound-sequence *moria*, which might have been found or composed elsewhere.) I liked the sound-sequence; it alliterated with "mines," and it connected itself with the MOR ["dark, black"] element in my linguistic construction. (*Letters*, No. 297)

Earlier in the same letter, Tolkien gave the Sindarin Elvish etymology of *Moria*, explaining that it means "Black Chasm," adding, "As for the 'land of Morīah' (note stress): that has no connexion (even 'externally') whatsoever. Internally there is no conceivable connexion between the mining of Dwarves, and the story of Abraham. I utterly repudiate any such significances and symbolisms. My mind does not work that way" (ibid.).

The story "Soria Moria Castle" appears in the collection *Popular Tales from the Norse* (1858), translated by

George Webbe Dasent from the second edition of the collection *Norske Folke-eventyr* (1852) by Peter Christen Asbjørnsen and Jørgen Moe. It also appears in *The Red Fairy Book* (1890), edited by Andrew Lang.

7 Here the Five Armies are specified as the Elves, Men, and Dwarves on the one side and the Goblins and Wolves on the other. Strangely, in the 1977 Rankin/ Bass animated television program of *The Hobbit,* the Five Armies specifically include the Eagles instead of the Wolves. This lapse is a very minor transgression compared to the major failings of that production. ✑

8 This is the only appearance of the name *Gundabad* in the text of *The Hobbit.* It also appears on the map of Wilderland, in the northwest corner, where the Grey Mountains meet the Misty Mountains.

In some writings originally intended for Appendix A of *The Lord of the Rings,* now published in volume twelve of the *History, The Peoples of Middle-earth,* we learn that Mount Gundabad was the place where Durin, one of the Seven Ancestors of the Dwarves, first awakened. Durin was the father of the eldest race of Dwarves, the Longbeards. For this reason the Dwarves revered Gundabad, and its occupation by Orcs during the Third Age was one of the chief reasons for the enmity between Dwarves and Orcs (p. 301).

night after night through the mountains, and came thus at last on a sudden from the North hard on the heels of Dain. Not even the ravens knew of their coming until they came out in the broken lands which divided the Lonely Mountain from the hills behind. How much Gandalf knew cannot be said, but it is plain that he had not expected this sudden assault.

This is the plan that he made in council with the Elvenking and with Bard; and with Dain, for the dwarf-lord now joined them: the Goblins were the foes of all, and at their coming all other quarrels were forgotten. Their only hope was to lure the goblins into the valley between the arms of the Mountain; and themselves to man the great spurs that struck south and east. Yet this would be perilous, if the goblins were in sufficient numbers to overrun the Mountain itself, and so attack them also from behind and above; but there was no time to make any other plan, or to summon any help.

Soon the thunder passed, rolling away to the South-East; but the bat-cloud came, flying lower, over the shoulder of the Mountain, and whirled above them shutting out the light and filling them with dread.

"To the Mountain!" called Bard. "To the Mountain! Let us take our places while there is yet time!"

On the Southern spur, in its lower slopes and in the rocks at its feet, the Elves were set; on the Eastern spur were men and dwarves. But Bard and some of the nimblest of men and elves climbed to the height of the Eastern shoulder to gain a view to the North. Soon they could see the lands before the Mountain's feet black with a hurrying multitude. Ere long the vanguard swirled round the spur's end and came rushing into Dale. These were the swiftest wolf-riders, and already their cries and howls rent the air afar. A few brave men were strung before them to make a feint of resistance, and many there fell before the rest drew back and fled to either side. As Gandalf had hoped, the goblin army had

gathered behind the resisted vanguard, and poured now
in rage into the valley, driving wildly up between the
arms of the Mountain, seeking for the foe. Their banners
were countless, black and red, and they came on like a
tide in fury and disorder.

It was a terrible battle. The most dreadful of all
Bilbo's experiences, and the one which at the time he
hated most — which is to say it was the one he was most
proud of, and most fond of recalling long afterwards, although he was quite unimportant in it. Actually I may
say he put on his ring early in the business, and vanished
from sight, if not from all danger. A magic ring of that
sort is not a complete protection in a goblin charge, nor
does it stop flying arrows and wild spears; but it does
help in getting out of the way, and it prevents your head
from being specially chosen for a sweeping stroke by a
goblin swordsman.

The elves were the first to charge. Their hatred for
the goblins is cold and bitter. Their spears and swords
shone in the gloom with a gleam of chill flame, so deadly
was the wrath of the hands that held them. As soon as
the host of their enemies was dense in the valley, they
sent against it a shower of arrows, and each flickered as
it fled as if with stinging fire. Behind the arrows a thousand of their spearmen leapt down and charged. The
yells were deafening. The rocks were stained black with
goblin blood.

Just as the goblins were recovering from the onslaught and the elf-charge was halted, there rose from
across the valley a deep-throated roar. With cries of
"Moria!" and "Dain, Dain!" the dwarves of the Iron
Hills plunged in, wielding their mattocks, upon the
other side; and beside them came the men of the Lake
with long swords.

Panic came upon the Goblins; and even as they
turned to meet this new attack, the elves charged again
with renewed numbers. Already many of the goblins

The Battle of Five Armies. Illustration by Nada
Rappensbergerová for the 1973 Slovak edition.

Thorin cries: "To me!" Illustration by Tove Jansson for the 1962 Swedish and 1973 Finnish editions.

were flying back down the river to escape from the trap; and many of their own wolves were turning upon them and rending the dead and the wounded. Victory seemed at hand, when a cry rang out on the heights above.

Goblins had scaled the Mountain from the other side and already many were on the slopes above the Gate, and others were streaming down recklessly, heedless of those that fell screaming from cliff and precipice, to attack the spurs from above. Each of these could be reached by paths that ran down from the main mass of the Mountain in the centre; and the defenders had too few to bar the way for long. Victory now vanished from hope. They had only stemmed the first onslaught of the black tide.

Day drew on. The goblins gathered again in the valley. There a host of Wargs came ravening and with them came the bodyguard of Bolg, goblins of huge size with scimitars[9] of steel. Soon actual darkness was coming into a stormy sky; while still the great bats swirled about the heads and ears of elves and men, or fastened vampire-like on the stricken. Now Bard was fighting to defend the Eastern spur, and yet giving slowly back; and the elf-lords were at bay about their king upon the southern arm, near to the watch-post on Ravenhill.

Suddenly there was a great shout, and from the Gate came a trumpet call. They had forgotten Thorin! Part of the wall, moved by levers, fell outward with a crash into the pool. Out leapt the King under the Mountain, and his companions followed him. Hood and cloak were gone; they were in shining armour, and red light leapt from their eyes. In the gloom the great dwarf gleamed like gold in a dying fire.

Rocks were hurled down from on high by the goblins above; but they held on, leapt down to the falls' foot, and rushed forward to battle. Wolf and rider fell or fled before them. Thorin wielded his axe with mighty strokes, and nothing seemed to harm him.

"To me! To me! Elves and Men! To me! O my kinsfolk!" he cried, and his voice shook like a horn in the valley.

Down, heedless of order, rushed all the dwarves of Dain to his help. Down too came many of the Lake-men, for Bard could not restrain them; and out upon the other side came many of the spearmen of the elves. Once

9 A scimitar is a sword with a short, curved, one-edged blade. Historically scimitars were used by East Asians, Turks, and Persians.

10 Tom Shippey has suggested to me that Bilbo's statement that "defeat may be glorious" may be a covert reference to stanza three of the chorus of the King Edward's School's song, which reads: "Oftentimes defeat is splendid, victory may still be shame; Luck is good, the prize is pleasant, but the glory's in the game." The song was composed in Victorian times by Alfred Hayes (1857–1936), and Tolkien would have known it well, having attended King Edward's School in Birmingham for almost ten years, leaving for Oxford in 1911. Shippey was also at King Edward's School almost fifty years after Tolkien, departing in 1960.

again the goblins were stricken in the valley; and they were piled in heaps till Dale was dark and hideous with their corpses. The Wargs were scattered and Thorin drove right against the bodyguard of Bolg. But he could not pierce their ranks.

Already behind him among the goblin dead lay many men and many dwarves, and many a fair elf that should have lived yet long ages merrily in the wood. And as the valley widened his onset grew ever slower. His numbers were too few. His flanks were unguarded. Soon the attackers were attacked, and they were forced into a great ring, facing every way, hemmed all about with goblins and wolves returning to the assault. The bodyguard of Bolg came howling against them, and drove in upon their ranks like waves upon cliffs of sand. Their friends could not help them, for the assault from the Mountain was renewed with redoubled force, and upon either side men and elves were being slowly beaten down.

On all this Bilbo looked with misery. He had taken his stand on Ravenhill among the Elves — partly because there was more chance of escape from that point, and partly (with the more Tookish part of his mind) because if he was going to be in a last desperate stand, he preferred on the whole to defend the Elvenking. Gandalf, too, I may say, was there, sitting on the ground as if in deep thought, preparing, I suppose, some last blast of magic before the end.

That did not seem far off. "It will not be long now," thought Bilbo, "before the goblins win the Gate, and we are all slaughtered or driven down and captured. Really it is enough to make one weep, after all one has gone through. I would rather old Smaug had been left with all the wretched treasure, than that these vile creatures should get it, and poor old Bombur, and Balin and Fili and Kili and all the rest come to a bad end; and Bard too, and the Lake-men and the merry elves. Misery me! I have heard songs of many battles, and I have always understood that defeat may be glorious.[10] It seems very uncomfortable, not to say distressing. I wish I was well out of it."

The clouds were torn by the wind, and a red sunset slashed the West. Seeing the sudden gleam in the gloom Bilbo looked round. He gave a great cry: he had seen a sight that made his heart leap, dark shapes small yet majestic against the distant glow.

"The Eagles! The Eagles!" he shouted. "The Eagles are coming!"[11]

Bilbo's eyes were seldom wrong. The eagles were coming down the wind, line after line, in such a host as must have gathered from all the eyries of the North.

"The Eagles! the Eagles!" Bilbo cried, dancing and waving his arms. If the elves could not see him they could hear him. Soon they too took up the cry, and it echoed across the valley. Many wondering eyes looked up, though as yet nothing could be seen except from the southern shoulders of the Mountain.

"The Eagles!"[12] cried Bilbo once more, but at that moment a stone hurtling from above smote heavily on his helm, and he fell with a crash and knew no more.

[11] On November 7–8, 1944, Tolkien wrote to his son Christopher, "I knew I had written a story of worth in 'The Hobbit' when reading it (after it was old enough to be detached from me) I had suddenly in a fairly strong measure the 'eucatastrophic' emotion at Bilbo's exclamation: 'The Eagles! The Eagles are coming!' " (*Letters*, No. 89).

Eucatastrophe is Tolkien's own term, from his essay "On Fairy-Stories," for the sudden, joyous turn of events (the "good catastrophe") that provides the happy ending to a fairy story. Tolkien's essay was originally delivered as the Andrew Lang memorial lecture at the University of St. Andrews on March 9, 1939; it was greatly expanded for publication in *Essays Presented to Charles Williams* (1947), edited by C. S. Lewis. The essay also appears in *Tree and Leaf* (1964) and *The Tolkien Reader* (1966).

[12] An unfinished sketch by Tolkien, *The Coming of the Eagles,* is published in *Artist* (No. 138).

18

The Return Journey

WHEN BILBO CAME TO HIMSELF, he was literally by himself. He was lying on the flat stones of Ravenhill, and no one was near. A cloudless day, but cold, was broad above him. He was shaking, and as chilled as stone, but his head burned with fire.

"Now I wonder what has happened?" he said to himself. "At any rate I am not yet one of the fallen heroes; but I suppose there is still time enough for that!"

He sat up painfully. Looking into the valley he could see no living goblins. After a while as his head cleared a little, he thought he could see elves moving in the rocks below. He rubbed his eyes. Surely there was a camp still in the plain some distance off; and there was a coming and going about the Gate? Dwarves seemed to be busy removing the wall. But all was deadly still. There was no call and no echo of a song. Sorrow seemed to be in the air.

"Victory after all, I suppose!" he said, feeling his aching head. "Well, it seems a very gloomy business."

Suddenly he was aware of a man climbing up and coming towards him.

"Hullo there!" he called with a shaky voice. "Hullo there! What news?"

"What voice is it that speaks among the stones?" said the man halting and peering about him not far from where Bilbo sat.

Thorin's death bed. Illustration by Maret Kernumees for the 1977 Estonian edition.

Then Bilbo remembered his ring! "Well I'm blessed!" said he. "This invisibility has its drawbacks after all. Otherwise I suppose I might have spent a warm and comfortable night in bed!"

"It's me, Bilbo Baggins, companion of Thorin!" he cried, hurriedly taking off the ring.

"It is well that I have found you!" said the man striding forward. "You are needed and we have looked for you long. You would have been numbered among the dead, who are many, if Gandalf the wizard had not said that your voice was last heard in this place. I have been sent to look here for the last time. Are you much hurt?"

"A nasty knock on the head, I think," said Bilbo. "But I have a helm and a hard skull. All the same I feel sick and my legs are like straws."

"I will carry you down to the camp in the valley," said the man, and picked him lightly up.

The man was swift and sure-footed. It was not long before Bilbo was set down before a tent in Dale; and there stood Gandalf, with his arm in a sling. Even the wizard had not escaped without a wound; and there were few unharmed in all the host.

When Gandalf saw Bilbo, he was delighted. "Bag-

1 In Tolkien's eschatology of Middle-earth — itself a complex and changing conception — the spirits of dead elves go to a place of waiting, where they remain until the end of the world; for their fates are bound with that of the world. The spirits of dead men go also to the place of waiting, where they are released from the bondage of the world to an unknown destiny. This special fate was the gift of God (Ilúvatar) to men.

The fate of dwarves after death remained for Tolkien an especially uncertain thing. Thorin's comment, echoing the dwarves' own beliefs, is not easily reconciled with other statements in the writings of J.R.R. Tolkien. (See *The Silmarillion*, p. 44; *The Book of Lost Tales, Part Two*, p. 247; *The Shaping of Middle-earth*, pp. 103–4; *The Lost Road*, pp. 129, 146n, 178, 372; *Morgoth's Ring*, pp. 220–25.)

2 *1937:* "If more men" > *1951:* "If more of us"

This change was suggested by Arthur Ransome in his letter to Tolkien of December 13, 1937. Ransome felt that *men* referred to humankind alone, and thus misrepresented Thorin's concerns. Tolkien discussed the change in his letter to Allen & Unwin of December 19, 1937, and it was adopted in the second edition of 1951.

gins!" he exclaimed. "Well I never! Alive after all — I *am* glad! I began to wonder if even your luck would see you through! A terrible business, and it nearly was disastrous. But other news can wait. Come!" he said more gravely. "You are called for;" and leading the hobbit he took him within the tent.

"Hail! Thorin," he said as he entered. "I have brought him."

There indeed lay ⸌Thorin⸍ Oakenshield, wounded with many wounds, and his rent armour and notched axe were cast upon the floor. He looked up as Bilbo came beside him.

"Farewell, good thief," he said. "I go now to the halls of waiting to sit beside my fathers, until the world is renewed.[1] Since I leave now all gold and silver, and go where it is of little worth, I wish to part in friendship from you, and I would take back my words and deeds at the Gate."[2]

Bilbo knelt on one knee filled with sorrow. "Farewell, King under the Mountain!" he said. "This is a bitter adventure, if it must end so; and not a mountain of gold can amend it. Yet I am glad that I have shared in your perils — that has been more than any Baggins deserves."

"No!" said Thorin. "There is more in you of good than you know, child of the kindly West. Some courage and some wisdom, blended in measure. If more of us[2] valued food and cheer and song above hoarded gold, it would be a merrier world. But sad or merry, I must leave it now. Farewell!"

Then Bilbo turned away, and he went by himself, and sat alone wrapped in a blanket, and, whether you believe it or not, he wept until his eyes were red and his voice was hoarse. He was a kindly little soul. Indeed it was long before he had the heart to make a joke again. "A mercy it is," he said at last to himself, "that I woke up when I did. I wish Thorin were living, but I am glad that we parted in kindness. You are a fool, Bilbo Baggins, and you made a great mess of that business with the stone; and there was a battle, in spite of all your efforts to buy peace and quiet, but I suppose you can hardly be blamed for that."

All that had happened after he was stunned, Bilbo learned later; but it gave him more sorrow than joy, and he was now weary of his adventure. He was aching in his bones for the homeward journey. That, however, was a little delayed, so in the meantime I will tell something of events. The Eagles had long had suspicion of the goblins' mustering; from their watchfulness the movements in the mountains could not be altogether hid. So they too had gathered in great numbers, under the great Eagle of the Misty Mountains; and at length smelling battle from afar they had come speeding down the gale in the nick of time. They it was who dislodged the goblins from the mountain-slopes, casting them over precipices, or driving them down shrieking and bewildered among their foes. It was not long before they had freed the Lonely Mountain, and elves and men on either side of the valley could come at last to the help of the battle below.

But even with the Eagles they were still outnumbered. In that last hour Beorn himself had appeared — no one knew how or from where. He came alone, and in bear's shape; and he seemed to have grown almost to giant-size in his wrath.[3]

The roar of his voice was like drums and guns; and he tossed wolves and goblins from his path like straws and feathers. He fell upon their rear, and broke like a clap of thunder through the ring. The dwarves were making a stand still about their lords upon a low rounded hill. Then Beorn stooped and lifted Thorin, who had fallen pierced with spears, and bore him out of the fray.

Swiftly he returned and his wrath was redoubled, so that nothing could withstand him, and no weapon seemed to bite upon him. He scattered the bodyguard, and pulled down Bolg himself and crushed him. Then

3 Here Beorn exhibits some of the qualities of the legendary Old Norse berserker, which Christopher Tolkien defined in the glossary to his edition of *The Saga of King Heidrek the Wise* as follows:

a man capable of fits of frenzied rage, or running amok. Berserks were said to fight without corselets, raging like wolves with the strength of bears, and might be regarded almost as shape-changers, who acquired the strength and ferocity of beasts. During pagan times, berserks were highly prized as warriors, but under Christian law those who "went berserk" were liable to heavy penalties. The word *berserkr,* "bear-shirted," implies perhaps that berserks sometimes disguised themselves as bears. (p. 93)

dismay fell on the Goblins and they fled in all directions. But weariness left their enemies with the coming of new hope, and they pursued them closely, and prevented most of them from escaping where they could. They drove many of them into the Running River, and such as fled south or west they hunted into the marshes about the Forest River; and there the greater part of the last fugitives perished, while those that came hardly to the Wood-elves' realm were there slain, or drawn in to die deep in the trackless dark of Mirkwood. Songs have said that three parts of the goblin warriors of the North perished on that day, and the mountains had peace for many a year.

Victory had been assured before the fall of night; but the pursuit was still on foot, when Bilbo returned to the camp; and not many were in the valley save the more grievously wounded.

"Where are the Eagles?" he asked Gandalf that evening, as he lay wrapped in many warm blankets.

"Some are in the hunt," said the wizard, "but most have gone back to their eyries. They would not stay here, and departed with the first light of morning. Dain has crowned their chief with gold, and sworn friendship with them for ever."

"I am sorry. I mean, I should have liked to see them again," said Bilbo sleepily; "perhaps I shall see them on the way home. I suppose I shall be going home soon?"

"As soon as you like," said the wizard.

Actually it was some days before Bilbo really set out. They buried Thorin deep beneath the Mountain, and Bard laid the Arkenstone upon his breast.

"There let it lie till the Mountain falls!" he said. "May it bring good fortune to all his folk that dwell here after!"

Upon his tomb the Elvenking then laid Orcrist, the elvish sword that had been taken from Thorin in captivity. It is said in songs that it gleamed ever in the dark if foes approached, and the fortress of the dwarves could not be taken by surprise. There now Dain son of Nain took up his abode, and he became King under the Mountain, and in time many other dwarves gathered to his throne in the ancient halls. Of the twelve companions of Thorin, ten remained. Fili and Kili had fallen defending him with shield and body, for he was their mother's elder brother. The others remained with Dain; for Dain dealt his treasure well.

There was, of course, no longer any question of dividing the hoard in such shares as had been planned, to Balin and Dwalin, and Dori and Nori and Ori, and Oin and Gloin, and Bifur and Bofur and Bombur — or to Bilbo. Yet a fourteenth share of all the silver and gold, wrought and unwrought, was given up to Bard; for Dain said: "We will honour the agreement of the dead, and he has now the Arkenstone in his keeping."

Even a fourteenth share was wealth exceedingly great, greater than that of many mortal kings. From that treasure Bard sent much gold to the Master of Lake-town; and he rewarded his followers and friends freely. To the Elvenking he gave the emeralds of Girion, such jewels as he most loved, which Dain had restored to him.

To Bilbo he said: "This treasure is as much yours as it is mine; though old agreements cannot stand, since so many have a claim in its winning and defence. Yet even though you were willing to lay aside all your claim, I should wish that the words of Thorin, of which he repented, should not prove true: that we should give you little. I would reward you most richly of all."

"Very kind of you," said Bilbo. "But really it is a relief to me. How on earth should I have got all that treasure home without war and murder all along the way, I don't know. And I don't know what I should have done with it when I got home. I am sure it is better in your hands."

In the end he would only take two small chests, one filled with silver, and the other with gold, such as one strong pony could carry. "That will be quite as much as I can manage," said he.

At last the time came for him to say good-bye to his

4 In *The Road to Middle-earth,* Tom
Shippey singles out this exchange between Balin and Bilbo as a contrast of
styles between Balin's elevated language
and Bilbo's commonplace speech:
"There is not much in common between the language of these two speak-
ers; nevertheless it is perfectly clear that
they are saying the same thing" (second
edition, p. 79).

friends. "Farewell, Balin!" he said; "and farewell, Dwa-
lin; and farewell Dori, Nori, Ori, Oin, Gloin, Bifur,
Bofur, and Bombur! May your beards never grow thin!"
And turning towards the Mountain he added: "Farewell
Thorin Oakenshield! And Fili and Kili! May your mem-
ory never fade!"

Then the dwarves bowed low before their Gate, but
words stuck in their throats. "Good-bye and good luck,
wherever you fare!" said Balin at last. "If ever you visit us
again, when our halls are made fair once more, then the
feast shall indeed be splendid!"

"If ever you are passing my way," said Bilbo, "don't
wait to knock! Tea is at four; but any of you are welcome
at any time!"[4]

Then he turned away.

The elf-host was on the march; and if it was sadly less-
ened, yet many were glad, for now the northern world
would be merrier for many a long day. The dragon was
dead, and the goblins overthrown, and their hearts
looked forward after winter to a spring of joy.

Gandalf and Bilbo rode behind the Elvenking, and
beside them strode Beorn, once again in man's shape,
and he laughed and sang in a loud voice upon the road.
So they went on until they drew near to the borders of
Mirkwood, to the north of the place where the Forest
River ran out. Then they halted, for the wizard and
Bilbo would not enter the wood, even though the king
bade them stay a while in his halls. They intended to go
along the edge of the forest, and round its northern end
in the waste that lay between it and the beginning of the
Grey Mountains. It was a long and cheerless road, but
now that the goblins were crushed, it seemed safer to
them than the dreadful pathways under the trees. Moreover Beorn was going that way too.

"Farewell! O Elvenking!" said Gandalf. "Merry be the
greenwood, while the world is yet young! And merry be
all your folk!"

"Farewell! O Gandalf!" said the king. "May you ever appear where you are most needed and least expected! The oftener you appear in my halls the better shall I be pleased!"

"I beg of you," said Bilbo stammering and standing on one foot, "to accept this gift!" and he brought out a necklace of silver and pearls that Dain had given him at their parting.

"In what way have I earned such a gift, O hobbit?" said the king.

"Well, er, I thought, don't you know," said Bilbo rather confused, "that, er, some little return should be made for your, er, hospitality. I mean even a burglar has his feelings. I have drunk much of your wine and eaten much of your bread."

"I will take your gift, O Bilbo the Magnificent!" said the king gravely. "And I name you elf-friend and blessed. May your shadow never grow less (or stealing would be too easy)! Farewell!"

Then the elves turned towards the Forest, and Bilbo started on his long road home.

He had many hardships and adventures before he got back. The Wild was still the Wild, and there were many other things in it in those days beside goblins; but he was well guided and well guarded — the wizard was with him, and Beorn for much of the way — and he was never in great danger again. Anyway by mid-winter Gandalf and Bilbo had come all the way back, along both edges of the Forest, to the doors of Beorn's house; and there for a while they both stayed. Yule-tide[5] was warm and merry there; and men came from far and wide to feast at Beorn's bidding. The goblins of the Misty Mountains were now few and terrified, and hidden in the deepest holes they could find; and the Wargs had vanished from the woods, so that men went abroad without fear. Beorn indeed became a great chief afterwards in those regions and ruled a wide land between the mountains and the

5 In Appendix D ("The Shire Calendar") to *The Lord of the Rings,* the Calendar in the Shire is shown to have two Yuledays, the last day of the year and the first of the next year. Yuletide is described as six days long, including the last three and first three days of each year.

While this illustration by George Morrow could certainly pass for being one of Gandalf riding a pony, it is actually a drawing of the witch, Mother Meldrum, from *The Marvellous Land of Snergs.* She is shown here in the disguise she used to kidnap Joe and Sylvia, who are in the baskets.

wood; and it is said that for many generations the men of his line had the power of taking bear's shape, and some were grim men and bad, but most were in heart like Beorn, if less in size and strength. In their day the last goblins were hunted from the Misty Mountains and a new peace came over the edge of the Wild.

It was spring, and a fair one with mild weathers and a bright sun, before Bilbo and Gandalf took their leave at last of Beorn, and though he longed for home, Bilbo left with regret, for the flowers of the gardens of Beorn were in springtime no less marvellous than in high summer.

At last they came up the long road, and reached the very pass where the goblins had captured them before. But they came to that high point at morning, and looking backward they saw a white sun shining over the outstretched lands. There behind lay Mirkwood, blue in the distance, and darkly green at the nearer edge even in the spring. There far away was the Lonely Mountain on the edge of eyesight. On its highest peak snow yet unmelted was gleaming pale.

"So comes snow after fire, and even dragons have their ending!" said Bilbo, and he turned his back on his adventure. The Tookish part was getting very tired, and the Baggins was daily getting stronger. "I wish now only to be in my own arm-chair!" he said.

19

The Last Stage

IT WAS ON MAY THE FIRST that the two came back at last to the brink of the valley of Rivendell, where stood the Last (or the First)[1] Homely House. Again it was evening, their ponies were tired, especially the one that carried the baggage; and they all felt in need of rest. As they rode down the steep path, Bilbo heard the elves still singing in the trees, as if they had not stopped since he left; and as soon as the riders came down into the lower glades of the wood they burst into a song of much the same kind as before. This is something like it:

> *The dragon is withered,*
> *His bones are now crumbled;*
> *His armour is shivered,*
> *His splendour is humbled!*
> *Though sword shall be rusted,*
> *And throne and crown perish*
> *With strength that men trusted*
> *And wealth that they cherish,*
> *Here grass is still growing,*
> *And leaves are yet swinging,*
> *The white water flowing,*
> *And elves are yet singing*
> > *Come! Tra-la-la-lally!*
> > *Come back to the valley!*

1 Elrond's House, being near the Edge of the Wild, could be called the Last or First Homely House, depending on the direction from which it is approached.

The stars are far brighter
Than gems without measure,
The moon is far whiter
Than silver in treasure;
The fire is more shining
On hearth in the gloaming
Than gold won by mining,
So why go a-roaming?
O! Tra-la-la-lally
Come back to the Valley.

O! Where are you going,
So late in returning?
The river is flowing,
The stars are all burning!
O! Whither so laden,
So sad and so dreary?
Here elf and elf-maiden
Now welcome the weary
With Tra-la-la-lally
Come back to the Valley,
Tra-la-la-lally
Fa-la-la-lally
Fa-la!

Then the elves of the valley came out and greeted
them and led them across the water to the house of Elrond. There a warm welcome was made them, and there
were many eager ears that evening to hear the tale of
their adventures. Gandalf it was who spoke, for Bilbo
was fallen quiet and drowsy. Most of the tale he knew, for
he had been in it, and had himself told much of it to the
wizard on their homeward way or in the house of Beorn;
but every now and again he would open one eye, and listen, when a part of the story which he did not yet know
came in.

It was in this way that he learned where Gandalf had
been to; for he overheard the words of the wizard to El-

rond. It appeared that Gandalf had been to a great council of the white wizards,[2] masters of lore and good
magic; and that they had at last driven the Necromancer
from his dark hold in the south of Mirkwood.

"Ere long now," Gandalf was saying, "the Forest will
grow somewhat more wholesome. The North will be
freed from that horror for many long years, I hope.[3] Yet
I wish he were banished from the world!"

"It would be well indeed," said Elrond; "but I fear
that will not come about in this age of the world, or for
many after."

When the tale of their journeyings was told, there
were other tales, and yet more tales, tales of long ago,
and tales of new things, and tales of no time at all, till
Bilbo's head fell forward on his chest, and he snored
comfortably in a corner.

He woke to find himself in a white bed, and the moon
shining through an open window. Below it many elves
were singing loud and clear on the banks of the stream.

Sing all ye joyful, now sing all together!
The wind's in the tree-top, the wind's in the heather;
The stars are in blossom, the moon is in flower,
And bright are the windows of Night in her tower.

Dance all ye joyful, now dance all together!
Soft is the grass, and let foot be like feather!
The river is silver, the shadows are fleeting;
Merry is May-time, and merry our meeting.

Sing we now softly, and dreams let us weave him!
Wind him in slumber and there let us leave him!
The wanderer sleepeth. Now soft be his pillow!
Lullaby! Lullaby! Alder and Willow!
Sigh no more Pine, till the wind of the morn!
Fall Moon! Dark be the land!
Hush! Hush! Oak, Ash, and Thorn!
Hushed be all water, till dawn is at hand!

2 The phrasing here concerning Gandalf's attendance at "a great council of the white wizards" is slightly unusual and probably reflects the fact that at the time of writing Tolkien had not fully developed the idea of how many wizards there were, and what their colors might be. In *The Lord of the Rings,* three of the Five Wizards are named: Gandalf the Grey, Saruman the White, and Radagast the Brown. In *Unfinished Tales,* Christopher Tolkien published some writings by his father on the subject of the Istari, or wizards, and there we learn that the other two were "the Blue Wizards." (A few further short writings on the Five Wizards appear in volume twelve of the *History, The Peoples of Middle-earth.*)

In Appendix B ("The Tale of Years") of *The Lord of the Rings,* the "council of the white wizards" is called the White Council and headed by Saruman the White. In 2941 the Council agreed to attack the Necromancer's fortress, Dol Guldur (Sindarin Elvish for "hill of sorcery"), in southwestern Mirkwood. The Necromancer (Sauron) then abandoned Dol Guldur.

3 *1937:* "The North is freed from that horror for many an age" > *1966-Ball:* "The North will be freed from that horror for many long years, I hope"

This revision changes Gandalf's words from an assertion into a statement of hope, which is more appropriate in light of the story of *The Lord of the Rings.*

Bilbo at the end of his adventure. Illustration by Peter Chuklev from the 1979 version of the 1975 Bulgarian edition.

"Well, Merry People!" said Bilbo looking out. "What time by the moon is this? Your lullaby would waken a drunken goblin! Yet I thank you."

"And your snores would waken a stone dragon — yet we thank you," they answered with laughter. "It is drawing towards dawn, and you have slept now since the night's beginning. Tomorrow, perhaps, you will be cured of weariness."

"A little sleep does a great cure in the house of Elrond," said he; "but I will take all the cure I can get. A second good night, fair friends!" And with that he went back to bed and slept till late morning.

Weariness fell from him soon in that house, and he had many a merry jest and dance, early and late, with the elves of the valley. Yet even that place could not long delay him now, and he thought always of his own home. After a week, therefore, he said farewell to Elrond, and giving him such small gifts as he would accept, he rode away with Gandalf.

Even as they left the valley the sky darkened in the West before them, and wind and rain came up to meet them.

"Merry is May-time!" said Bilbo, as the rain beat into his face. "But our back is to legends and we are coming home. I suppose this is the first taste of it."

"There is a long road yet," said Gandalf.

"But it is the last road," said Bilbo.

They came to the river that marked the very edge of the borderland of the Wild, and to the ford beneath the steep bank, which you may remember. The water was swollen both with the melting of the snows at the approach of summer, and with the daylong rain; but they crossed with some difficulty, and pressed forward, as evening fell, on the last stage of their journey.

This was much as it had been before, except that the company was smaller, and more silent; also this time there were no trolls. At each point on the road Bilbo recalled the happenings and the words of a year ago — it seemed to him more like ten – so that, of course, he quickly noted the place where the pony had fallen in the river, and they had turned aside for their nasty adventure with Tom and Bert and Bill.

Not far from the road they found the gold of the trolls, which they had buried, still hidden and untouched. "I have enough to last me my time," said Bilbo, when they had dug it up. "You had better take this, Gandalf. I daresay you can find a use for it."

"Indeed I can!" said the wizard. "But share and share alike! You may find you have more needs than you expect."

So they put the gold in bags and slung them on the ponies, who were not at all pleased about it. After that their going was slower, for most of the time they walked. But the land was green and there was much grass through which the hobbit strolled along contentedly. He mopped his face with a red silk handkerchief – no! not a single one of his own had survived, he had borrowed this one from Elrond – for now June had brought summer, and the weather was bright and hot again.

As all things come to an end, even this story, a day came at last when they were in sight of the country where Bilbo had been born and bred,[4] where the shapes of the land and of the trees were as well known to him as his hands and toes. Coming to a rise he could see his own Hill in the distance, and he stopped suddenly and said:

> *Roads go ever ever on,*
> *Over rock and under tree,*
> *By caves where never sun has shone,*
> *By streams that never find the sea;*
> *Over snow by winter sown,*
> *And through the merry flowers of June,*
> *Over grass and over stone,*
> *And under mountains in the moon.*
> *Roads go ever ever on*
> *Under cloud and under star,*

4 The "country where Bilbo had been born and bred" is not named in *The Hobbit,* though in *The Lord of the Rings* we learn it is called the Shire. In his guide for translators, "Nomenclature of *The Lord of the Rings,*" Tolkien notes that *Shire* is from Old English *scír,* which "seems very early to have replaced the ancient Germanic word for a 'district.'" It is a common element in many county names in England.

Bilbo arrives home during the auction. Illustration by Maret Kernumees for the 1977 Estonian edition.

5 In the first chapter of *The Lord of the Rings,* we are given another verse of the same nature as these two. Whereas the two here tell of the wistfulness of returning home, the other exhibits more of the restlessness of beginning a new journey. It is recited by Bilbo, as he leaves Bag End for the last time:

The Road goes ever on and on
*   Down from the door where it began.*
Now far ahead the Road has gone,
*   And I must follow, if I can,*
Pursuing it with eager feet,
*   Until it joins some larger way*
Where many paths and errands meet.
*   And whither then? I cannot say.*

Frodo repeats this verse, with the change of "eager feet" to "weary feet" in line 5, in Chapter 3, "Three is Company," of *The Fellowship of the Ring.*

In one of the closing chapters of *The Lord of the Rings* ("Many Partings" in *The Return of the King*), Bilbo recites a very different version, showing now a strong desire to leave the questing for others:

The Road goes ever on and on
*   Out from the door where it began.*
Now far ahead the Road has gone,
*   Let others follow it who can!*
Let them a journey new begin,
*   But I at last with weary feet*
Will turn towards the lighted inn,
*   My evening rest and sleep to meet.*

The inspiration for these verses may be a poem entitled "Romance" by E. F. A. Geach, which, as was discovered by Tolkien scholar John D. Rateliff, appears immediately following a reprint of Tolkien's poem "Goblin Feet" in *Fifty New Poems for Children: An Anthology Selected from Books Recently Published by Basil Blackwell* (1922):

Yet feet that wandering have gone
*   Turn at last to home afar.*
Eyes that fire and sword have seen
*   And horror in the halls of stone*
Look at last on meadows green
*   And trees and hills they long have known.* **5**

Gandalf looked at him. "My dear Bilbo!" he said. "Something is the matter with you! You are not the hobbit that you were." **6**

And so they crossed the bridge and passed the mill by the river and came right back to Bilbo's own door.

"Bless me! What's going on?" he cried. There was a great commotion, and people of all sorts, respectable and unrespectable, were thick round the door, and many were going in and out — not even wiping their feet on the mat, as Bilbo noticed with annoyance.

If he was surprised, they were more surprised still. He had arrived back in the middle of an auction! **7** There was a large notice in black and red hung on the gate, stating that on June the Twenty-second Messrs Grubb, Grubb, and Burrowes **8** would sell by auction the effects of the late Bilbo Baggins Esquire, of Bag-End, Underhill, Hobbiton. Sale to commence at ten o'clock sharp. It was now nearly lunchtime, and most of the things had already been sold, for various prices from next to nothing to old songs (as is not unusual at auctions). Bilbo's cousins the Sackville-Bagginses **9** were, in fact, busy measuring his rooms to see if their own furniture would fit. In short Bilbo was "Presumed Dead", and not everybody that said so was sorry to find the presumption wrong.

The return of Mr. Bilbo Baggins created quite a disturbance, both under the Hill and over the Hill, and across the Water; it was a great deal more than a nine days' wonder. **10** The legal bother, indeed, lasted for years. It was quite a long time before Mr. Baggins was in fact admitted to be alive again. The people who had got specially good bargains at the Sale took a deal of convincing; and in the end to save time Bilbo had to buy back quite a lot of his own furniture. Many of his silver spoons mysteriously disappeared and were never accounted for. Personally he suspected the Sackville-Bagginses. On their side they never admitted that the returned Baggins was genuine, and they were not on friendly terms[11] with Bilbo ever after. They really had wanted to live in his nice hobbit-hole so very much.

Indeed Bilbo found he had lost more than spoons — he had lost his reputation. It is true that for ever after he remained an elf-friend, and had the honour of dwarves, wizards, and all such folk as ever passed that way; but he was no longer quite respectable. He was in fact held by all the hobbits of the neighbourhood to be 'queer' — except by his nephews and nieces on the Took side, but even they were not encouraged in their friendship by their elders.

I am sorry to say he did not mind. He was quite content; and the sound of the kettle on his hearth was ever after more musical than it had been even in the quiet days before the Unexpected Party. His sword he hung over the mantelpiece. His coat of mail was arranged on a stand in the hall (until he lent it to a Museum). His gold and silver was largely spent in presents,[12] both useful and extravagant — which to a certain extent accounts for the affection of his nephews and his nieces. His magic ring he kept a great secret, for he chiefly used it when unpleasant callers came.

He took to writing poetry and visiting the elves; and though many shook their heads and touched their foreheads and said "Poor old Baggins!" and though few believed any of his tales, he remained very happy to the end of his days,[13] and those were extraordinarily long.

One autumn evening some years afterwards Bilbo was sitting in his study writing his memoirs[14] — he thought of calling them "There and Back Again, a Hobbit's Hol-

ROMANCE
BY E. F. A. GEACH

Round the Next Corner and in the next street
Adventure lies in wait for you.
Oh, who can tell what you may meet
Round the next corner and in the next street!
Could life be anything but sweet
When all is hazardous and new
Round the next corner and in the next street?
Adventure lies in wait for you.

This poem previously appeared in *Oxford Poetry 1918,* edited by Geach, T. W. Earp, and Dorothy L. Sayers, where Tolkien could also have seen it.

Eleonora Frederika Adolphina (Sgonina) Geach was born in 1896 in Essen, Germany. She had studied at the City of Cardiff High School for Girls, and at Cambridge, before matriculating at Oxford as a Home Student in 1917. Dorothy L. Sayers was one of her tutors. Her short-lived marriage produced one son, the philosopher Peter Geach (b. 1916), who was raised by his father and never knew his mother. E. F. A. Geach published two books of poetry: the first, *-Esques* (1918), in collaboration with Doreen Wallace (1897–1989), who would later become well known as a novelist, and *Twenty Poems* (1931). Both were published by Basil Blackwell. Nothing is known of E. F. A. Geach's life after 1931.

6 Tolkien summed up the central theme of *The Hobbit* in an undated letter to Milton Waldman, probably written late in 1951: "In effect this is the study of simple ordinary man, neither artistic nor noble and heroic (but not without the undeveloped seeds of these things) against a high setting — and in fact (as a critic has perceived) the tone and style change with the Hobbit's development,

passing from fairy-tale to the noble and high and relapsing with the return" (*Letters*, No. 131).

The critic to whom Tolkien refers is probably his friend C. S. Lewis, who wrote in an anonymous review of *The Hobbit* in the *Times Literary Supplement* for October 2, 1937, "No common recipe for children's stories will give you creatures so rooted in their own soil and history as those of Professor Tolkien. . . . Still less will the common recipe prepare us for the curious shift from the matter-of-fact beginnings of the story . . . to the saga-like tone of the later chapters. . . . You must read for yourself to find out how inevitable the change is and how it keeps pace with the hero's journey" (p. 714).

7 In *The Road to Middle-earth,* Tom Shippey suggests that the idea of Bilbo returning home to find an auction taking place, with his house untidy and with people "not even wiping their feet on the mat," is a joking reflection of the phonetically spelled word *okshẹn,* in the dialect of Huddersfield in South Yorkshire. Walter E. Haigh's *A New Glossary of the Dialect of the Huddersfield District,* to which Tolkien contributed a foreword, gives the meaning of *okshẹn* as "any untidy room" — i.e., a mess — and cites the disapproving remark, presumably said by one woman of another, "shu's nout but ẹ slut; er eẹs ẹz ẹ feẹr okshẹn" ["she's nothing but a slut; her house is a fair auction"]. In his foreword, Tolkien specified this particular entry in commenting that, in this glossary, philologists have "the opportunity of observing changes in sense that take place when

iday" — when there was a ring at the door. It was Gandalf and a dwarf; and the dwarf was actually Balin.

"Come in! Come in!" said Bilbo, and soon they were settled in chairs by the fire. If Balin noticed that Mr. Baggins' waistcoat was more extensive (and had real gold buttons), Bilbo also noticed that Balin's beard was several inches longer, and his jewelled belt was of great magnificence.

They fell to talking of their times together, of course, and Bilbo asked how things were going in the lands of the Mountain. It seemed they were going very well. Bard had rebuilt the town in Dale and men had gathered to him from the Lake and from South and West, and all the valley had become tilled again and rich, and the desolation was now filled with birds and blossoms in spring and fruit and feasting in autumn. And Lake-town was refounded and was more prosperous than ever, and much wealth went up and down the Running River; and there was friendship in those parts between elves and dwarves and men.

The old Master had come to a bad end. Bard had given him much gold for the help of the Lake-people, but being of the kind that easily catches such disease he fell under the dragon-sickness, and took most of the gold and fled with it, and died of starvation in the Waste, deserted by his companions.

"The new Master is of wiser kind," said Balin, "and very popular, for, of course, he gets most of the credit for the present prosperity. They are making songs which say that in his day the rivers run with gold."

"Then the prophecies of the old songs have turned out to be true, after a fashion!" said Bilbo.

"Of course!" said Gandalf. "And why should not they prove true? Surely you don't disbelieve the prophecies, because you had a hand in bringing them about yourself? You don't really suppose, do you, that all your adventures and escapes were managed by mere luck, just

The Hall at Bag-End, Residence of B. Baggins Esquire by J.R.R. Tolkien, one of the standard black-and-white illustrations that has appeared in *The Hobbit* since 1937.

In a letter to Allen & Unwin dated February 5, 1937, after the publisher had had the line engraving of this illustration made, Tolkien confessed: "I misguidedly put in a wash shadow [behind the door] reaching right up to the side beam. This has of course come out black (with disappearance of the key) though not right up to the beam. But the print is I think as good as the original allows" (*Letters*, No. 11). In *Artist*, Wayne G. Hammond and Christina Scull note that Tolkien enthusiasts have made many deductions about Hobbit culture and crafts from what can be seen in this picture, and they also observe a discrepancy between the relative proportions of Bilbo and the door: "as drawn the hobbit would have had to stand on a chair to reach the knob" (p. 143).

This illustration appears in *Artist* (No. 139) and *Pictures* (No. 20, left). A version of this illustration colored by H. E. Riddett appeared in *The J.R.R. Tolkien Calendar 1979* (1978) and in *Pictures* (No. 20, right).

for your sole benefit? You are a very fine person, Mr. Baggins, and I am very fond of you; but you are only quite a little fellow in a wide world after all!"

"Thank goodness!" said Bilbo laughing, and handed him the tobacco-jar.

words of more 'learned' origin are adopted and put to everyday use in dialect (see *keęnsil, okshęn, inséns*), an important and interesting part of the life of dialect speech" (p. xiv).

8 In his "Nomenclature of *The Lord of the Rings,*" originally prepared as a guide for translators, Tolkien said that the name *Grubb* was meant to "recall the English verb grub 'dig, root, in the ground.' " It and *Burrowes* would then seem perfect names for the hole-dwelling hobbits; yet one also detects Tolkien's wry smile in using them as names for lawyers.

9 Tolkien commented on the name *Sackville-Baggins* in "Nomenclature of *The Lord of the Rings*": "*Sackville* is an English name (of more aristocratic association than *Baggins*). It is of course joined in the story with *Baggins* because of the similar meaning in English (= Common Speech) *sack* and *bag,* and because of the slightly comic effect of this conjunction." The name Sackville-Baggins inevitably recalls Sackville-West, and especially the writer Vita Sackville-West (1892–1962), who wrote of her aristocratic family and its ancestral home, Knole, in *Knole and the Sackvilles* (1922). Her 1930 novel *The Edwardians,* which details the lives of English aristocrats before the First World War, was a bestseller.

10 A "nine days' wonder" is something that causes a great sensation for a few days and then passes into the limbo of things forgotten. The fourteenth edition of *Brewer's Dictionary of Phrase and Fable* (1989), edited by Ivor H. Evans, cites an old proverb, "A wonder lasts nine days, and then the puppy's eyes are open," which alludes to dogs' being born blind and achieving sight only some days afterward.

11 *1937:* "they were not on speaking terms" > *1966-Ball:* "they were not on friendly terms"

Since the Sackville-Bagginses were invited to Bilbo's Farewell Party in the first chapter of *The Lord of the Rings,* it must be presumed that they were at least on speaking terms with Bilbo.

12 *1937:* "His gold and silver was mostly spent in presents" > *1966-Ball:* "His gold and silver was largely spent in presents"

13 In a letter to Charles Furth at Allen & Unwin dated July 24, 1938, Tolkien referred to the remark here that Bilbo "remained very happy to the end of his days" as "an almost insuperable obstacle to a satisfactory link" between *The Hobbit* and its sequel, *The Lord of the Rings,* which Tolkien had begun in December 1937. Fortunately Tolkien found his way around such an obstacle.

14 Around 1954 Tolkien wrote "The Quest of Erebor," a chapter-length account told from Gandalf's point of view about how he came to arrange the adventure of Bilbo and the Dwarves. (*Erebor* is the Sindarin Elvish name for the Lonely Mountain.) Originally intended to be part of Appendix A to *The Lord of the Rings,* this is a fascinating piece of re-imagining of the story of *The Hobbit.* It was first published in *Unfinished Tales* and also appears as Appendix A of this book.

Appendix A. The Quest of Erebor

Appendix B. On Runes

Bibliography

Map of Wilderland

Appendix A. The Quest of Erebor

"The Quest of Erebor" is essentially Gandalf's explanation of how he arranged Bilbo's adventure as told in *The Hobbit.* It was originally intended to be part of Appendix A in *The Lord of the Rings,* where some portions of it survive in greatly abridged form (cf. pp. 358–60 of *The Return of the King*). It was eventually removed before publication for considerations of space. A version of "The Quest of Erebor" was first published in *Unfinished Tales,* where Christopher Tolkien's account of the textual history is also given. This textual history was subsequently amended in the *History,* as new information was discovered. I give a brief summary here.

The story of "The Quest of Erebor" first emerged in work on Section III, headed "Durin's Folk," of Appendix A, and the earliest manuscript draft leading up to the story is now published in *The Peoples of Middle-earth* (pp. 279–84), which also includes two notes that belong with the earliest manuscript. This early version was unknown to Christopher Tolkien at the time he compiled *Unfinished Tales,* wherein he labeled the next version, a cleaner but also much rewritten and amended manuscript entitled "The History of Gandalf's Dealings with Thráin and Thorin Oakenshield," text A.[1] From A there followed a clean typescript B. It consists of ten pages, with the subtitle ("Gandalf's account of how he came to arrange the expedition to Erebor and send Bilbo with the Dwarves") penciled at the top of the first page, and "The Quest of Erebor" penciled in the top right-hand corner. A subsequent, shortened version of the story is also found as a manuscript, designated C, which lacks a title and the opening section. Version C was possibly composed in an attempt to retain at least a compressed version of the story in the published volume, but in the end it too was rejected for reasons of space.

The main version published in *Unfinished Tales* is text C, while long extracts of B are given after it with Christopher Tolkien's commentary. The version given below is the full version of text B, and I am especially grateful to Christopher Tolkien for allowing it to appear here.

It is difficult to date precisely any of the versions of "The Quest of Erebor." On one of the two early notes mentioned above there is a note by Tolkien referring to actual page numbers of *The Fellowship of the Ring,*[2] which implies that volume one of *The Lord of the Rings* was then already in page proofs if it had not actually appeared in print. The first galleys of *The Fellowship of the Ring* were sent to Tolkien in late July 1953. On September 29, he was sent page proofs, and the book was published on July 29, 1954. A considerable amount of material for the Appendices of *The Lord of the Rings* — known to include at that time family trees and accounts of the languages, alphabets, and calendars — was already in existence by April 11, 1953, when Tolkien wrote to his publisher with the hope that some of this material, however reduced, would appear in volume three. As of May 8, 1954, Tolkien had not finalized the contents of the Appendices and felt that he could not do so until he knew how much space was to be allowed for them. By September 18 he was still worrying over what to select from what he called the too abundant matter. On March 6, 1955, Tolkien expressed hope that he could compress into the remaining space various things, including information about the House of Durin. By April 12, Tolkien had finally delivered the rest of the Appendices, including A, and in May he received galley proofs of Appendix A.

If we accept, on the outside, September 29, 1953 (when Tolkien received the page proofs of *The Fellowship of the Ring*), as terminus a quo for the composition of the earliest notes for "The Quest of Erebor" and April 12, 1955 (when Tolkien had turned in the last of the materials for *The Return of the King*), as terminus ad quem for Tolkien having abandoned the thought of using "The Quest of Erebor" in the Appendices, it follows that all of the versions of "The Quest of Erebor" must date from the time period between October 1953 and mid-April 1955. If, narrowing it down, we accept (as seems likely) that *The Fellowship of the Ring* had been published before Tolkien wrote "The Quest of Erebor," the range of dates becomes late July 1954 through mid-April 1955. Thus it seems probable that "The Quest of Erebor" dates from the later half of 1954, or early 1955.

THE QUEST OF EREBOR

Gandalf's account of how he came to arrange the expedition to Erebor and send Bilbo with the Dwarves

So Thorin Oakenshield became the Heir of Durin, but an heir without hope. At the sack of Erebor he had been too young to bear arms, but at Azanulbizar he had fought in the van of the assault; and when Thráin was lost he was ninety-five, a great Dwarf of proud bearing. He had no Ring, and, for that reason maybe, he seemed content to remain in Eriador. There he laboured long, and trafficked, and gained such wealth as he could; and his people were increased by many of the wandering Folk of Durin that heard of his dwelling and came to him. Now they had fair halls in the mountains, and store of goods, and their days did not seem so hard, though in their songs they spoke ever of the Lonely Mountain far away, and the treasure and the bliss of the Great Hall in the light of the Arkenstone.

The years lengthened. The embers in the heart of Thorin grew hot again, as he brooded on the wrongs of his House and of the vengeance upon the Dragon that was bequeathed to him. He thought of weapons and armies and alliances, as his great hammer rang in his forge; but the armies were dispersed and the alliances broken and the axes of his people were few; and a great anger without hope burned him, as he smote the red iron on the anvil.

Gandalf had not yet played any part in the fortunes of Durin's House. He had not had many dealings with the Dwarves; though he was a friend to those of good will, and liked well the exiles of Durin's Folk who lived in the west. But on a time it chanced that he was passing through Eriador (going to the Shire, which he had not seen for some years) when he fell in with Thorin Oakenshield, and they talked together on the road, and rested for the night at Bree.

In the morning Thorin said to Gandalf: "I have much on my mind, and they say you are wise and know more than most of what goes on in the world. Will you come home with me and hear me, and give me your counsel?"

To this Gandalf agreed, and when they came to Thorin's hall he sat long with him and heard all the tale of his wrongs.

From this meeting there followed many deeds and events of great moment: indeed the finding of the One Ring, and its coming to the Shire, and the choosing of the Ringbearer. Many therefore have supposed that Gandalf foresaw all these things, and chose his time for the meeting with Thorin. Yet we believe that it was not so. For in his tale of the War of the Ring Frodo the Ringbearer left a record of Gandalf's own words on this very point. This is what he wrote.

After the crowning we stayed in a fair house in Minas Tirith with Gandalf, and he was very merry, and though we asked him questions about all that came into our minds, his patience seemed as endless as his knowledge. I cannot now recall most of the things that he told us; often we did not understand them. But I remember this conversation very clearly. Gimli was there with us, and he said to Peregrin:

"There is a thing I must do one of these days: I must visit that Shire of yours. Not to see more Hobbits! I doubt if I could learn anything about them that I do not know already. But no Dwarf of the House of Durin could fail to look with wonder on that land. Did not the recovery of the kingship under the Mountain, and the fall of Smaug, begin there? Not to mention the end of Barad-dûr, though both were strangely woven together. Strangely, very strangely," he said and paused.

Then looking hard at Gandalf he went on: "But who wove the web? I do not think I have ever considered that before. Did you plan all this then, Gandalf? If not, why did you lead Thorin Oakenshield to such an unlikely door? To find the Ring and bring it far away into the West for hiding, and then choose the Ringbearer — and to restore the Mountain Kingdom as a mere deed by the way: was that not your design?"

Gandalf did not answer at once. He stood up, and looked out of the window, west, seawards; and the sun was then setting, and a glow was in his face. He stood so a long while silent.

But at last he turned to Gimli and said: "I do not know the answer. For I have changed since those days, and I am no longer trammelled by the burden of Middle-earth as I was then. In those days I should have answered you with words like those I used to Frodo, only last year in the spring. Only last year! But such measures are meaningless. In that far distant time I said to a small and frightened hobbit: Bilbo was *meant* to find the Ring, and *not* by its maker, and you therefore were *meant* to bear it. And I might have added: and I was *meant* to guide you both to those points.

"To do that, I used in my waking mind only such means as were allowed to me, doing what lay to my hand according to such reasons as I had. But what I knew in my heart, or knew before I stepped on these grey shores: that is another matter. Olórin I was in the West that is forgotten, and only to those who are there shall I speak more openly."

Then I said: "I understand you a little better now, Gandalf, than I did before. Though I suppose that, whether *meant* or not, Bilbo might have refused to leave home, and so might I. You could not compel us. You were not even allowed to try. But I am still curious to know why you did what you did, as you were then, an old grey man as you seemed."

"Why you should want to know that I do not understand," said Gandalf. "But I had, of course, simple reasons for what I did; and, if I may say so, Hobbits were not at first very important among them.

"My chief reason was that of a captain, a member of a Council of War. When I met Thorin I had long known that Sauron had arisen again, and I expected him to declare himself soon. I knew that he was planning a great war, and I surveyed all the lands in my mind. The urgent question was: which would he do first? Try to re-occupy Mordor; or attack the small but powerful strongholds of his chief enemies, Lórien and Rivendell?

"I felt sure that he meant to attack them; it would have been the better move for him. Lórien was near: that would come first. But Rivendell was not out of reach. He only needed to re-occupy the old realm of Angmar, and before long he might find that only too easy. His power was growing fast, and if he sent any great force of his servants that way, between them and the passes of the northern mountains there lay only the Dwarves of the Iron Hills and the remnants of the Men of Dale that lived on the edge of the desolation of Smaug. Smaug he might use with terrible effect.

"The North, then, was a very weak point. There was time yet, but not too much. 'Well,' I said to myself, 'some means must be found of dealing with Smaug. But first of all a direct stroke against Sauron is needed; at least that may force him to make some hasty decisions.'

"That is why, to jump forward, I went off as soon as the expedition against Smaug was well started, and persuaded the Council to attack Dol Guldur first, before he attacked Lórien. We did, and Sauron fled. But he was always ahead of us in his plans. I must confess that I thought he really had retreated again, and that we might have another spell of watchful peace. But it did not last long. Sauron decided to take the next step. He returned at once to Mordor, and in ten years he declared himself.

"Then everything grew dark. And yet that was not his original plan; and it was in the end a terrible mistake. Resistance still had somewhere where it could take counsel free from the Shadow. How could the Ringbearer have escaped, if there had been no Lórien or Rivendell? And those places might have fallen, I think, if Sauron had thrown all his power against them first, and not spent more than half of it in the assault on Gondor.

"Well, there you have it. That was my chief reason. But it is one thing to see what needs doing, and quite another to find the means. I was beginning to be seriously troubled about the situation in the North when I met Thorin Oakenshield one day: in the middle of March 2941, I think. I heard all his tale, and I thought: 'Well, here is an enemy of Smaug at any rate! And one worthy of help. I must do what I can. I should have thought of Dwarves before.'

"And then there was the Shire-folk. I began to have a warm place in my heart for them in the Long Winter, which none of you can remember. They were very hard put to it then: one of the worst pinches they have been in, dying of cold, and starving in the dreadful dearth that followed. But that was the time to see their courage, and their pity one for another. It was by their pity as much as by their tough uncomplaining courage that they survived. I wanted them still to survive. But I saw that the Westlands were in for another very bad time again, sooner or later, though of quite a different sort: pitiless war. To come through that I thought they would need something more than they now had. It is not easy to say what. Well, they would want to know a bit more, understand a bit clearer what it was all about, and where they stood.

"They had begun to forget: forget their own beginnings and legends, forget what little they had known about the greatness of the world. It was not yet gone, but it was getting buried: the memory of the high and the perilous.

"But you cannot teach that sort of thing to a whole people quickly. There was not time. And anyway you must begin at some point, with some one person. I dare say he was 'chosen' and I was only chosen to choose him; but I picked out Bilbo."

"Now that is just what I want to know," said Peregrin. "Why did you do that?"

"How would you select any one Hobbit for such a purpose?" said Gandalf. "I had not time to sort them all out; but I knew the Shire very well by that time, although when I met Thorin I had been away for more than twenty years on less pleasant business. So naturally thinking over the Hobbits that I knew, I said to myself: 'I want a dash of the Took' (but not too much, Master Peregrin), 'I want a good foundation of the stolider sort, a Baggins perhaps.'

"That pointed at once to Bilbo. And I had known him once very well, almost up to his coming of age, better than he knew me. I liked him then. And now I found that he was 'unattached,' — to jump on again; for of course I did not know all this until I went back to the Shire. I learned that he had never married. I thought that odd, though I guessed why it was; and the reason I guessed was *not* the one that most of the Hobbits gave me: that he had early been left very well off and his own master. No, I guessed that he wanted to remain 'unattached' for some reason deep down which he did not understand himself — or would not acknowledge, for it alarmed him. He wanted, all the same, to be free to go when the chance came, or he had made up his courage. I remembered how he used to pester me with questions when he was a

youngster about the Hobbits that had occasionally 'gone off' as they said in the Shire. There were at least two of his uncles on the Took side that had done so.

"But I am getting my tale out of order. Let us go back to my meeting with Thorin. He invited me to go home with him. So I did; and we actually passed through the Shire, though Thorin would not stop long enough for that to be useful. Indeed, I think it was annoyance with his haughty disregard of the Hobbits that first put into my head the idea of entangling him with them. As far as he was concerned they were just food-growers who happened to work the fields on either side of the Dwarves' ancestral road to the mountains.

"Well, I heard his long tale. Some of it I knew before, though the way of Thrór's death, and the disappearance of Thráin, were then only known to the Dwarves. If you do not know about them, you must get Gimli to tell you the story some other time. I was sorry in my heart for Thorin, but I could see little hope of helping him. He was involved, as I saw only too well, in the net of Sauron's designs, a dark strategy beyond his powers, and beyond his grasp. Yet he sat there still talking in a large way, wondering if his cousin Dáin could furnish two thousands, and if the Men of that region would be likely to help, or King Thranduil, and so on, as if he was a king planning a campaign.

"At last I stopped him. 'I will think about all this,' I said. 'I have the hint of a plan in my mind, but there is a piece missing that I want to find if I can. I must go now. I have some business of my own to attend to. But don't be too hopeful. My plan is very different from any of yours, and you may not like it at all.'

"'I will consider it, when you return,' said Thorin. 'Do not be long! my heart burns me.'

"I went straight to the Shire, and gathered all the news I could of events and people. Then I sat alone for a long while and thought. I needed it. I could not get Bilbo out of my mind, though I had not had time to visit him yet. But also Thorin's tale had recalled a strange half-forgotten chance to my mind. It now looked less like chance. You will guess what I mean, since you know Bilbo's story. I remembered the unhappy dying Dwarf in the pits of Dol Guldur, and the old map, and the strange key. Until then I had had no idea who he was. He had a map that had belonged to Durin's Folk in Erebor, and a key that seemed to go with it (though he could not explain it); and he said he had possessed a Ring.

"Nearly all of his ravings were of that: *the last of the seven* he would say over and over again. But all these things he might have come by in many ways. He might have been a messenger caught as he fled; or even a thief trapped by a greater thief. He died, before I escaped myself, and I stowed the things away. By some warning of my heart I kept them always on me, safe but almost forgotten. For I had other business in Dol Guldur more important and perilous than all the treasure of Erebor.

"But I remembered them now, and I saw that I had kept them until time revealed their meaning. I understand now that I had heard the last ravings of Thráin II Thrór's son, though he could not speak his own name nor his son's; and that I had the plan and the key of a secret entrance to Erebor. What should I do about it?

"Well, you know what I decided to do; and it may sound less absurd now than it did then. It seemed so absurd then, even to me, that I laughed at myself, and wondered what made me consider such a plan: to entangle the Shire-folk in the affairs of the Dwarves, and in feuds and disasters on the far frontiers more than two hundred years ago.

"At last I made up my mind, and I went back to Thorin. I found him in conclave with some of his kinsfolk. Balin and Glóin were there, and several others.

"'Well, what have you got to say?' Thorin asked as soon as I came in.

"'This first,' I answered: 'your own ideas are those of a king, Thorin Oakenshield. But your kingdom is gone. If it is to be restored, which I doubt, it must be from small beginnings. Far away here, I wonder if you fully realize the strength of a great dragon. But that is not all: there is a Shadow growing fast in the world far more terrible. They will help one another.' And they certainly would have done so, if I had not attacked Dol Guldur at the same time. 'Open war would be quite useless; and anyway it is impossible for you to arrange it. You will have to try something simpler and yet bolder, indeed something desperate.'

"'You are both vague and disquieting,' said Thorin. 'Speak more plainly!'

"'Well, for one thing,' I said, 'you will have to go on this quest yourself, and you will have to go *secretly*. No messengers, heralds, or challenges, for you, Thorin Oakenshield. At most you can take with you a few kinsmen or faithful followers. But you will need something more, something unexpected.'

"'Name it!' said Thorin.

"'One moment!' I said. 'You hope to deal with a dragon; and he is not only very great, but he is now also old and very cunning. From the beginning of your adventure you must allow for this: his memory, and his sense of smell.'

"'Naturally,' said Thorin. 'Dwarves have had more dealings with dragons than most, and you are not instructing the ignorant.'

"'Very good,' I answered; 'but your own plans did not seem to me to consider this point. My plan is one of stealth. *Stealth.*[3]

"'Smaug does not lie on his costly bed without dreams, Thorin Oakenshield. He dreams of Dwarves! You may be sure that he explores his hall day by day, night by night, until he is sure that no faintest air of a dwarf is near, before he goes to his sleep: his half-sleep, prick-eared for the sound of – dwarf-feet.'

"'You make your *stealth* sound as difficult and hopeless as any open attack,' said Balin. 'Impossibly difficult!'

"'Yes, it is difficult,' I answered. 'But not *impossibly* difficult, or I would not waste my time here. I would say *absurdly* difficult. So I am going to suggest an absurd solution to the problem. Take a hobbit with you! Smaug has probably never heard of hobbits, and he has certainly never smelt them.'

"'What!' cried Glóin. 'One of those simpletons down in the Shire? What use on earth, or under it, could he possibly be? Let him smell as he may, he would never dare to come within smelling distance of the nakedest dragonet new from the shell!'

"'Now, now!' I said, 'that is quite unfair. You do not know much about the Shire-folk, Glóin. I suppose you think them simple, because they are generous and do not haggle; and think them timid because you never sell them any weapons. You are mistaken. Anyway, there is one that I have my eye on as a companion for you, Thorin. He is neat-handed and clever, though shrewd, and far from rash. And I think he has courage. Great courage, I guess, according to the way of his people. They are, you might say, "brave at a pinch." You have to put these hobbits in a tight place before you find out what is in them.'

"'The test cannot be made,' Thorin answered. 'As far as I have observed, they do all that they can to avoid tight places.'

"'Quite true,' I said. 'They are a very sensible people. But this hobbit is rather unusual. I think he could be persuaded to go into a tight place. I believe that in his heart he really desires to – to have, as he would put it, an adventure.'

"'Not at my expense!' said Thorin, rising and striding about angrily. 'This is not advice, it is foolery! I fail to see what any hobbit, good or bad, could do that would repay me for a day's keep, even if he could be persuaded to start.'

"'Fail to see! You would fail to hear it, more likely,' I answered. 'Hobbits move without effort more quietly than any Dwarf in the world could manage, though his life depended on it. They are, I suppose, the most soft-footed of all mortal kinds. You do not seem to have observed that, at any rate, Thorin Oakenshield, as you tramped though the Shire, making a noise (I may say) that the inhabitants could hear a mile away. When I said that you would need stealth, I meant it: professional stealth.'

"'Professional stealth?' cried Balin, taking up my words rather differently than I had meant them. 'Do you mean a trained treasure-seeker? Can they still be found?'

"I hesitated. This was a new turn, and I was not sure how to take it. 'I think so,' I said at last. 'For a reward they will go in where you dare not, or at any rate cannot, and get what you desire.'

"Thorin's eyes glistened as the memories of lost treasures moved in his mind; but 'a paid thief, you mean,' he said scornfully. 'That might be considered, if the reward was not too high. But what has all this to do with one of those villagers? They drink out of clay, and they cannot tell a gem from a bead of glass.'

"'I wish you would not always speak so confidently without knowledge,' I said sharply. 'These villagers have lived in the Shire some fourteen hundred years, and they have learned many things in the time. They had dealings with the Elves, and with the Dwarves, a thousand years before Smaug came to Erebor. None of them are wealthy as your forefathers reckoned it, but you will find some of their dwellings have fairer things in them than you can boast here, Thorin. The hobbit that I have in mind has ornaments of gold, and eats with silver tools, and drinks wine out of shapely crystal.'

"'Ah! I see your drift at last,' said Balin. 'He's a thief, then? That is why you recommend him?'"

"At that I fear I lost my temper and my caution. This dwarvish conceit that no one can have or make anything 'of value' save themselves, and that all fine things in other hands must have been got, if not stolen, from the Dwarves at some time, was more than I could stand at that moment. 'A thief?' I said, laughing. 'Why yes, a professional thief, of course! How else would a Hobbit come by a silver spoon? I will put the thief's mark on his door, and then you will find it.'

"Then being angry I got up, and I said with a warmth that surprised myself: 'You must look for that door, Thorin Oakenshield! I am *serious*.' And suddenly I felt that I was indeed in hot earnest. This queer notion of mine was not a joke, it was *right*. It was desperately important that it should be carried out. The Dwarves must bend their stiff necks.

"'Listen to me, Durin's Folk!' I cried. 'If you persuade this hobbit to join you, you will succeed. If you do not, you will fail. If you refuse even to try, then I have finished with you. You will get no more advice or help from me until the Shadow falls on you!'

"Thorin turned and looked at me in astonishment, as well he might. 'Strong words!' he said. 'Very well, I will come. Some foresight is on you, if you are not merely crazed.'

"'Good!' I said. 'But you must come with good will, not merely in the hope of proving me a fool. You must be patient and not easily put off, if neither the courage nor the desire for adventure that I speak of are plain to see at first sight. He will deny them. He will try to back out; but *you must not* let him.'

"'Haggling will not help him, if that is what you mean,' said Thorin. 'I will offer him a fair reward for anything that he recovers, and no more.'

"It was not what I meant, but it seemed useless to say so. 'There is one other thing,' I went on; 'you must make all your plans and preparations beforehand. Get everything ready! Once persuaded he must have no time for second thoughts. You must go straight from the Shire, east on your quest.'

"'He sounds a very strange creature, this thief of yours,' said a young Dwarf called Fili (Thorin's nephew, as I afterwards learned). 'What is his name, or the one that he uses?'

"'Hobbits use their real names,' I said. 'The only one that he has is Bilbo Baggins.'

"'What a name!' said Fili, and laughed.

"'He thinks it very respectable,' I said. 'And it fits well enough; for he is a middle-aged bachelor, and getting a bit flabby and fat. Food is perhaps at present his main interest. He keeps a very good larder, I am told, and maybe more than one. At least you will be well entertained.'

"'That is enough,' shouted Thorin. 'If I had not given my word, I would not come now. I am in no mood to be made a fool of. For I am serious also. Deadly serious, and my heart is hot within me.'

"I took no notice of this. 'Look now, Thorin,' I said, 'April is passing and Spring is here. Make everything ready as soon as you can. I have some business to do, but I shall be back in a week. When I return, if all is in order, I will ride on ahead and prepare the ground. Then we will all visit him together on the following day.'

"And with that I took my leave, not wishing to give Thorin more chance of second thoughts than Bilbo was to have. The rest of the story is well known to you — from Bilbo's point of view. If I had written the account, it would have sounded rather different. He did not know all that went on: the care, for instance, that I took so that the coming of a large party of Dwarves to Bywater, off the main road and their usual beat, should not come to his ears too soon.

"It was on the morning of Tuesday, April 25 2941, that I called to see Bilbo; and though I knew more or less what to expect, I must say that my confidence was shaken. I saw that things would be far more difficult than I had thought. But I persevered. Next day, Wednesday, April 26 I brought Thorin and his companions to Bag End; with great difficulty so far as Thorin was concerned, he hung back at the last. And of course Bilbo was completely bewildered and behaved ridiculously. Everything in fact went extremely badly for me from the beginning; and that unfortunate business about the 'professional thief', which the Dwarves had got firmly into their heads, only made matters worse.

"I was thankful that I had told Thorin we should all stay the night at Bag End, since we should need time to discuss ways and means. It gave me a last chance. If Thorin had left Bag End before I could see him alone, my plan would have been ruined.

"There were many dangers and difficulties on the road afterwards, but for me I think the most difficult part of all was persuading Thorin that night and next morning to take Bilbo in his company. Thorin was contemptuous and suspicious, and felt that I had deceived him.

"'Thief!' he snorted. 'He is as honest as he is silly. His mother died too soon. And anyway many of the spoons were tin. You are playing some strange game of your own, Master Gandalf. I am sure you have other purposes than helping me.'

"'You are quite right,' I said. 'If I had not other purposes, I should not be helping you at all. Great as your affairs may seem to you, they are only a small strand in the great web. I am concerned with many strands. But that should make my advice more weighty, not less.

"'I know your fame,' said Thorin, 'and I must hope that it is merited. Even so this foolish business of the hobbit might make me wonder whether so many cares had not disordered your wits.'

"'They are certainly enough to do so,' I an-swered; 'and among them I find most exasperating a proud Dwarf who seeks advice from me (without claim on me that I know of), and then speaks to me with insolence. Go your own way, Thorin Oaken-shield, if you will. But you have sought advice, and that cannot be undone. If you flout it, you will do so on your peril. You will walk to disaster. Beware! You and your quest are caught up in a much greater matter. If you succeed, it will be so that other larger causes may be furthered. Curb your pride, and your greed, or you may fall at the end, though your hands be full of gold!'

"He blenched a little at that; but his eyes smouldered. 'Do not threaten me!' he said. 'I will use my own judgement in this matter, as in others.'

"'Do so then,' I said. "I will not argue it further. I have said all that is needed. Except perhaps this. I do not give my love or my trust lightly, Thorin; but I am fond of this hobbit, and I wish him well. Treat him well, and you have my friendship to the end of your days!'

"I said that without hope of persuading him; but it was a good thing to say. Dwarves understand and approve devotion to friends, and gratitude to those that help them. 'Very well,' Thorin said at last. 'Have your way! He shall set out with my company — if he dares (which I doubt). But if you insist on burdening me with him, you must come too and look after your darling.'

"I saw that I had driven him as far as he would go. 'Very good,' I said. 'I will come, and stay with you as long as I can: at least until you have discovered his worth.' It proved well in the end, but at the time I was troubled, for I had the urgent matter of the White Council on my hands, and the attack on Dol Guldur. Well, that is how the Quest of Erebor began; and from that day on the Dwarves and the Hobbits have been wonderfully entangled to-gether on all the chief events of our time."

So Gandalf ended his long account. I remember that Gimli laughed. "It still sounds absurd," he said, "even now that all has turned out more than well. I knew Thorin, of course; and I wish I had been there, but I was away at the time of your first visit to us. And I was not allowed to go on the quest: too young, they said, though at sixty-two I thought myself fit for anything. Well, I am glad to have heard the full tale. If it is full. I do not really suppose that even now you are telling us all you know."

"Of course not," said Gandalf.

"No," said Merry. "What about that map and key, for instance? You never said anything about them to Thorin, when you had heard his tale, though you must have had them then for a hundred years!"

"Nearly ninety-one, to be exact," said Gandalf. "It was ten years after Thráin had left his people that I found him, and he had then been in the pits for five years at least. I do not know how he endured for so long, nor how he had kept these things hidden through all his torments. I think the Dark Power had desired nothing from him except the Ring only, and when he had taken that, he troubled no further, but just flung the broken prisoner into the pits to rave until he died. A small oversight. But it proved fatal. Small oversights often do.

"Well, as I have explained, I did not know for ninety-one years what the value of these things was. When I did, I saw that I had at any rate one good argument for my plan; and if I may say so, I brought it out at the right moment: just when things had become quite hopeless and Bilbo had made a complete fool of himself. From that moment Thorin really made up his mind to follow my plan, as far as a secret expedition went at any rate. Whatever he thought of Bilbo, he would have set out himself.

"The map and the key brought all the past vividly back to him. He was young for a dwarf at the sack of Erebor, a mere twenty-four, but he had often wondered, as he told me, how Thrór and Thráin escaped from their halls. The existence of a secret door, only discoverable by Dwarves, made it seem at least possible to find out something of the dragon's doings, perhaps even to recover some gold, or some heirloom to ease his heart's longings.

"I do not suppose that when he started he had any real hope of destroying Smaug. There was no hope. Yet it came about. But alas! Thorin did not live long enough to enjoy his triumph or his treasure. The pride and the greed overcame him in spite of my warning."

"But surely," I said, "he might have been killed anyway? There would have been an attack of Orcs, however generous Thorin had been with his treasure."

"He might," said Gandalf. "Poor Thorin! He was a great Dwarf of a great House, whatever his faults. And though the Enemy slew him, the Kingdom under the Mountain was restored. Dáin was a worthy successor. My strategy proved right. The main attack was diverted southwards, and yet even so with his far-stretched right hand Sauron could have done terrible harm in the North, while we defended Gondor. Even Rivendell might have been ravaged, if King Brand and King Dáin had not stood in his path. When you think of the great battle of the Pelennor Fields, do not forget the Battle of Dale. Think of what might have been. Dragon-fire and savage swords in Eriador! There might be no Queen in Gondor. We might now only hope to return from our victory here to ashes and regret. But that has been averted – because I met Thorin Oakenshield one morning on the edge of Spring[4] not far from Bree. A chance meeting, as we say in Middle-earth."[5]

NOTES

1. On p. 357 of volume eight of the *History, The War of the Ring,* Christopher Tolkien presents another short passage of "The Quest of Erebor" from an early version (certainly preceding text B, and possibly from A or the earlier version of A) that survives on the lower half of a torn page. Notes on the verso, which Christopher Tolkien makes clear are a secondary use of the page (pp. 357-58), concern distances east of Edoras and may have been recorded in association with the map of Gondor, drawn by Christopher Tolkien in April 1955 and published that October in *The Return of the King.*

2. See volume twelve of the *History, The Peoples of Middle-earth,* p. 283, and p. 287 n. 12. Tolkien also set down some notes, which Christopher Tolkien associates with the original manuscript of "The Quest of Erebor," headed "Dates already fixed in *printed* narrative . . ." These notes also include citations to pages in *The Fellowship of the Ring.* (See Christopher Tolkien's "Note on the date of the Quest of Erebor," *The Peoples of Middle-earth,* pp. 28–89.)

3. In *Unfinished Tales,* Christopher Tolkien notes that "at this point a sentence in the manuscript, A, was perhaps unintentionally omitted in the typescript" (p. 333). The sentence reads: "Also a scent that cannot be placed, at least not by Smaug, the enemy of Dwarves."

4. The text was here originally typed "one winter's morning not far from Bree" but "winter's" is crossed out and "Spring" written in, and underneath that "on the edge of Spring." In the later text C, the line reads: "one evening on the edge of spring."

5. Underneath the typed text there is a penciled note by Tolkien that reads, "Nothing is said to justify the musical instruments that the Dwarves brought to Bag End — nor to explain what became of them."

Appendix B. On Runes

In a letter printed in a London newspaper on February 20, 1938, Tolkien noted that the runes in *The Hobbit* were "similar to, but not identical with, the runes of Anglo-Saxon inscriptions" (*Letters,* No. 25). Tolkien used these runes in three places in *The Hobbit* — twice on Thror's Map (the regular runes and the moon-runes, both of which are repeated in the introductory note added to the book in 1966) and once on the dust jacket of the British edition (see p. 17). These runes from the dust jacket are copied here:

ᚦᛖ ᚺᛖᛒᛒᛁᛏ ᚩᚱ ᚦᛗᚱᛖ ᚨᚾᛞ ᛒᚨᚳᚲ
ᚨᚷᚨᛁᚾ ᛒᛖᛁᚾᚷ ᚦᛖ ᚱᛖᚳᚩᚱᛞ ᚩᚠ ᚨ ᚤᛖᚨᚱᛋ
ᛁᚩᚢᚱᚾᛖᚤ ᛗᚨᛞᛖ ᛒᚤ ᛒᛁᛚᛒᚩ ᛒᚨᚷᚷᛁᚾᛋ
ᚩᚠ ᚺᛖᛒᛒᛁᛏᚩᚾ ᚳᚩᛗᛈᛁᛚᛖᛞ ᚠᚱᚩᛗ
ᚺᛁᛋ ᛗᛖᛗᚩᛁᚱᛋ ᛒᚤ ᛁ ᚱ ᚱ ᛏᚩᛚᚲᛁᛖᚾ
ᚨᚾᛞ ᛈᚢᛒᛚᛁᛋᚺᛖᛞ ᛒᚤ ᚷᛖᚩᚱᚷᛖ
ᚨᛚᛚᛖᚾ ᚨᚾᛞ ᚢᚾᚹᛁᚾ ᛚᛏᛞ:

The runes read (with the underlined pairs of letters below represented by one runic character):

THE HOBBIT OR <u>TH</u>ERE AND BACK
AGAIN BEI<u>NG</u> <u>TH</u>E RECORD OF A YE<u>AR</u>S
JOURNEY MADE BY BILBO BAGGINS
OF HOBBITON COMPILED FROM
HIS MEMOIRS BY J R R TOLKIEN
AND PUBLISHED BY GE<u>OR</u>GE
ALLEN AND UNWIN LTD.

The 1938 American edition of *The Hobbit* had a different dust jacket (see p. 18), but for the 1951 second edition (fifth impression) of the book, the American publisher began importing copies of the British edition with the British dust jacket. Eventually someone noticed that the runes gave the name of the book's British publisher instead of the American one. In 1965, the last five words of the runes were changed on the American edition's jacket to read:

ᚺᛖᚢᚷᚺᛏᚩᚾ ᛗᛁᚠᚠᛚᛁᚾ ᚨᚾᛞ ᚳᚩ:

The publisher is here given as "HOUGHTON MIFFLIN AND CO." This change may have been made in the nineteenth impression (February 1965), of which I have yet to see a copy; the twentieth impression (August 1965) has the updated runes. It is not known whether Tolkien himself changed the runes in this instance.

Tolkien did redraw the runes for the cover of the 1966 Longmans, Green edition of *The Hobbit* (see p. 385), where the shortened inscription is as follows:

These runes read:

THE HOBBIT OR THERE AND BACK AGAIN EDITION FOR SCHOOLS PUBLISHED BY LONGMANS GREEN AND CO.

Tolkien used this system of runes in one other published example, in a 1947 postcard to Katherine Farrer printed in *Letters* (No. 112). In this instance, the usage is somewhat more sophisticated; for example, a dot placed below a rune gives it a doubled value.

The above examples have been used to compile the table given on the right. For further information on these runes as used by the Anglo-Saxons and other Germanic peoples, see Ralph W. V. Elliott's *Runes: An Introduction* (1959; revised edition 1989) and R. I. Page's *An Introduction to English Runes* (1973; revised edition 1999).

In *The Lord of the Rings,* Tolkien presents a much larger table of runes, but there these same runes are assigned different values according to a different mode of usage. For further information, see Section II ("The Cirth") of Appendix E of *The Lord of the Rings,* and Christopher Tolkien's "Appendix on Runes" in volume seven of the *History,*

The Treason of Isengard. See also "The Angerthas and *The Hobbit*" by Paul Nolan Hyde in *Mythlore,* Summer 1987 (13, no. 4; whole no. 50) and Arden R. Smith's "Certhas, Skirditaila, Fuþark: A Feigned History of Runic Origins," in *Tolkien's Legendarium* (2000), edited by Verlyn Flieger and Carl F. Hostetter.

Tolkien was not the first writer to use historical runes in a story for children. Rudyard Kipling, in his *Just So Stories* (1902), gives an illustration of a story carved on an elephant's tusk, with a long inscription in runes.

Bibliography

This bibliography is divided into five main sections. The first is a listing, necessarily selective, of J.R.R. Tolkien's major book publications. The first British and American editions are noted, and subsequent editions with significant differences are also mentioned. Readers interested in a more complete account of Tolkien's published writings (including contributions to books and periodicals, as well as details of the various editions of Tolkien's books) are referred to *J.R.R. Tolkien: A Descriptive Bibliography* (1993), by Wayne G. Hammond with the assistance of Douglas A. Anderson.

The second section concerns Tolkien's revisions to the published text of *The Hobbit* and how they are presented in the annotations to the main portion of this book. The third section contains a listing of translations of *The Hobbit*, while the fourth is a selected listing of criticism of *The Hobbit* in books and periodicals.

In the final section I have given information on the two major societies (one in the United States, the other in England) that focus their especial interests on the works of J.R.R. Tolkien. There are additionally many other international societies devoted to Tolkien, and a listing of these is maintained at the links page at the Tolkien Society Web site, where information about other Tolkien resources can also be found.

I. The Works of J.R.R. Tolkien

Writings About Middle-earth:

The Hobbit, or There and Back Again. London: George Allen & Unwin, 1937. Second edition, 1951; third edition, 1966; fourth edition, 1978; fifth edition: London: HarperCollins, 1995. Boston: Houghton Mifflin Company, 1938. Second American edition, 1951; third American edition, 1966 [paper], 1967 [cloth]; fourth American edition, 1985; fifth American edition, 1999.

The Lord of the Rings:

The Fellowship of the Ring: Being the First Part of The Lord of the Rings. London: George Allen & Unwin, 1954. Second edition, 1966. Boston: Houghton Mifflin Company, 1954. Second American edition, 1965 [paper], 1967 [cloth].

The Two Towers: Being the Second Part of The Lord of the Rings. London: George Allen & Unwin, 1954. Second edition, 1966. Boston: Houghton Mifflin Company, 1955. Second American edition, 1965 [paper], 1967 [cloth].

The Return of the King: Being the Third Part of The Lord of the Rings. London: George Allen & Unwin, 1955. Second edition, 1966. Boston: Houghton Mifflin Company, 1956. Second American edition, 1965 [paper], 1967 [cloth].

[*The Lord of the Rings* is sometimes published in a single volume. For an overview of this work's complex textual and publishing history, see my "Note on the Text" in editions of *The Fellowship of The Ring* and *The Lord of the Rings* currently published by HarperCollins in England and Houghton Mifflin Company in America. The "Note on the Text" has been published in three versions, the earliest dated 1986 and the revised versions dated 1993 and 2002.]

The Adventures of Tom Bombadil and Other Verses from the Red Book. Illustrated by Pauline Baynes. London: George Allen & Unwin, 1962. Boston: Houghton Mifflin Company, 1963.

The Road Goes Ever On: A Song Cycle. Poems by J.R.R. Tolkien set to music by Donald Swann. Boston: Houghton Mifflin Company, 1967. London: George Allen & Unwin, 1968. Second edition, adding a musical setting to the poem "Bilbo's Last Song." London: George Allen & Unwin, 1978. Boston: Houghton Mifflin Company, 1978.

Bilbo's Last Song. Boston: Houghton Mifflin Company, 1974. London: George Allen & Unwin, 1974. A single poem, issued as a poster, with a photograph by Robert Strindberg used as background in the American edition and an illustration by Pauline Baynes in the British edition. The poem was later issued as a book, fully illustrated by Pauline Baynes. London: Unwin Hyman, 1990. Boston: Houghton Mifflin Company, 1990.

The Silmarillion. Edited by Christopher Tolkien. London: George Allen & Unwin, 1977. Boston: Houghton Mifflin Company, 1977. Second edition, adding a long extract from Tolkien's 1951 letter to Milton Waldman (see *Letters,* No. 131), and a "Preface to the Second Edition" by Christopher Tolkien. London: HarperCollins, 1999. Boston: Houghton Mifflin Company, 2001.

Unfinished Tales of Númenor and Middle-earth. Edited by Christopher Tolkien. London: George Allen & Unwin, 1980. Boston: Houghton Mifflin Company, 1980.

The History of Middle-earth. A twelve-volume series, edited by Christopher Tolkien. A single-volume *History of Middle-earth Index* is forthcoming in 2002.

I. *The Book of Lost Tales, Part One.* Edited by Christopher Tolkien. London: George Allen & Unwin, 1983. Boston: Houghton Mifflin Company, 1984.

II. *The Book of Lost Tales, Part Two.* Edited by Christopher Tolkien. London: George Allen & Unwin, 1984. Boston: Houghton Mifflin Company, 1984.

III. *The Lays of Beleriand.* Edited by Christopher Tolkien. London: George Allen & Unwin, 1985. Boston: Houghton Mifflin Company, 1985.

IV. *The Shaping of Middle-earth: The Quenta, the Ambarkanta and the Annals.* Edited by Christopher Tolkien. London: George Allen & Unwin, 1986. Boston: Houghton Mifflin Company, 1986.

V. *The Lost Road and Other Writings: Language and Lore Before* The Lord of the Rings. Edited by Christopher Tolkien. London: Unwin Hyman, 1987. Boston: Houghton Mifflin Company, 1987.

VI. *The Return of the Shadow: The History of* The Lord of the Rings, *Part One.* Edited by Christopher Tolkien. London: Unwin Hyman, 1988. Boston: Houghton Mifflin Company, 1988.

VII. *The Treason of Isengard: The History of* The Lord of the Rings, *Part Two.* Edited by Christopher Tolkien. London: Unwin Hyman, 1989. Boston: Houghton Mifflin Company, 1989.

VIII. *The War of the Ring: The History of* The Lord of the Rings, *Part Three.* Edited by Christopher Tolkien. London: Unwin Hyman, 1990. Boston: Houghton Mifflin Company, 1990.

IX. *Sauron Defeated: The End of the Third Age (The History of* The Lord of the Rings, *Part Four), The Notion Club Papers and The Drowning of Anadûnê.* Edited by Christopher Tolkien. London: HarperCollins, 1992. Boston: Houghton Mifflin Company, 1992. The first section of this book, which relates to *The Lord of the Rings,* has been published separately, beginning in 1998, as a paperback entitled *The End of the Third Age.*

X. *Morgoth's Ring: The Later Silmarillion, Part One: The Legends of Aman.* Edited by Christopher Tolkien. London: HarperCollins, 1993. Boston: Houghton Mifflin Company, 1993.

XI. *The War of the Jewels: The Later Silmarillion, Part Two: The Legends of Beleriand.* Edited by Christopher Tolkien. London: HarperCollins, 1994. Boston: Houghton Mifflin Company, 1994.

XII. *The Peoples of Middle-earth.* Edited by Christopher Tolkien. London: HarperCollins, 1996. Boston: Houghton Mifflin Company, 1996.

Linguistical writings:

I•Lam na•Ngoldathon: The Grammar and Lexicon of the Gnomish Tongue. Edited by Christopher Gilson, Patrick Wynne, Arden R. Smith, and Carl F. Hostetter. Walnut Creek, Calif.: Parma Eldalamberon, 1995. Issue no. XI.

Qenyaqetsa: The Qenya Phonology and Lexicon. Edited by Christopher Gilson, Carl F. Hostetter, Patrick Wynne, and Arden R. Smith. Cupertino, Calif.: Parma Eldalamberon, 1998. Issue no. XII.

The Alphabet of Rúmil & Early Noldorin Fragments. The Alphabet of Rúmil, edited by Arden R. Smith; *Early Noldorin Fragments,* edited by Christopher Gilson, Bill Welden, Carl F. Hostetter, and Patrick Wynne. Cupertino, Calif.: Parma Eldalamberon, 2001. Issue no. XIII.

Non-Middle-earth writings:

Farmer Giles of Ham. Illustrated by Pauline Baynes. London: George Allen & Unwin, 1949. Boston: Houghton Mifflin Company, 1950. Fiftieth anniversary edition, edited by Christina Scull and Wayne G. Hammond, including the previously unpublished first version of the story and Tolkien's notes for a sequel, with an introduction and notes by the editors. London: HarperCollins, 1999. Boston: Houghton Mifflin Company, 1999.

Tree and Leaf. London: George Allen & Unwin, 1964. Boston: Houghton Mifflin Company, 1965. Contains the essay "On Fairy-Stories" and the short story "Leaf by Niggle." Second edition, adding the poem "Mythopoeia" and a "Preface" by Christopher

Tolkien. London: Unwin Hyman, 1988. Boston: Houghton Mifflin Company, 1989. A further edition, adding "The Homecoming of Beorhtnoth," has recently appeared in paperback. London: HarperCollins, 2001.

Smith of Wootton Major. London: George Allen & Unwin, 1967. Boston: Houghton Mifflin Company, 1967.

The Father Christmas Letters. Edited by Baillie Tolkien. London: George Allen & Unwin, 1976. Boston: Houghton Mifflin Company, 1976. An abridged version, published in an oblong format, with envelopes attached to the pages and containing fold-out letters, was published under the title *Letters from Father Christmas.* London: HarperCollins, 1995. Boston: Houghton Mifflin Company, 1995. A minibook version, in three slip-cased volumes, was published as *Father Christmas Letters.* London: HarperCollins, 1994. A single volume minibook version, much abridged, was also published as *Father Christmas Letters.* London: HarperCollins, 1998. Boston: Houghton Mifflin Company, 1998. A much-expanded and redesigned version of the 1976 book, including previously unpublished letters and drawings, appeared under the title *Letters from Father Christmas.* London: HarperCollins, 1999. Boston: Houghton Mifflin Company, 1999.

Mr. Bliss. London: George Allen & Unwin, 1982. Boston: Houghton Mifflin Company, 1983. A children's story, reproduced from Tolkien's illustrated manuscript.

Roverandom. Edited by Christina Scull and Wayne G. Hammond. London: HarperCollins, 1998. Boston: Houghton Mifflin Company, 1998.

Academic work:

A Middle English Vocabulary. Oxford: Clarendon Press, 1922. Designed for use with Kenneth Sisam's *Fourteenth Century Verse and Prose* (Oxford: Clarendon Press, 1921) and published with it subsequently.

Sir Gawain and the Green Knight. Edited by J.R.R. Tolkien and E. V. Gordon. Oxford: Clarendon

Press, 1925. Second edition revised by Norman Davis. Oxford: Clarendon Press, 1967.

Ancrene Wisse: The English Text of the Ancrene Riwle. Edited by J.R.R. Tolkien. London: Oxford University Press, 1962. Early English Text Society, Original Series, no. 249.

Sir Gawain and the Green Knight, Pearl, Sir Orfeo. Translated by J.R.R. Tolkien; edited by Christopher Tolkien. London: George Allen & Unwin, 1975. Boston: Houghton Mifflin Company, 1975.

The Old English Exodus. Text, translation, and commentary by J.R.R. Tolkien; edited by Joan Turville-Petre. Oxford: Clarendon Press, 1981.

Finn and Hengest: The Fragment and the Episode. Edited by Alan Bliss. London: George Allen & Unwin, 1982. Boston: Houghton Mifflin Company, 1983.

The Monsters and the Critics and Other Essays. Edited by Christopher Tolkien. London: George Allen & Unwin, 1983. Boston: Houghton Mifflin Company, 1984. Contains seven essays: "Beowulf: The Monsters and the Critics"; "On Translating Beowulf"; "Sir Gawain and the Green Knight"; "On Fairy-Stories"; "English and Welsh"; "A Secret Vice"; and "Valedictory Address to the University of Oxford."

Beowulf and the Critics. Edited by Michael D. C. Drout. Tempe, Ariz.: Medieval and Renaissance Texts and Studies, 2002.

Miscellaneous:

The Letters of J.R.R. Tolkien. Edited by Humphrey Carpenter, with the assistance of Christopher Tolkien. London: George Allen & Unwin, 1981. Boston: Houghton Mifflin Company, 1981. A much-expanded index, compiled by Christina Scull and Wayne G. Hammond, was added to the British edition in 1995 and to the American edition in 2000.

Artwork:

Pictures by J.R.R. Tolkien. Edited by Christopher Tolkien. London: George Allen & Unwin, 1979. Boston: Houghton Mifflin Company, 1979. A selection of Tolkien's art, based on a series of calendars published in England in the 1970s. Second edition. London: HarperCollins, 1992. Boston: Houghton Mifflin Company, 1992.

J.R.R. Tolkien: Artist and Illustrator. By Wayne G. Hammond and Christina Scull. London: HarperCollins, 1995. Boston: Houghton Mifflin Company, 1995. A comprehensive study of Tolkien as an artist.

Reprint collections:

The Tolkien Reader. New York: Ballantine Books, 1966 [paper]. Contains "The Homecoming of Beohrtnoth," "On Fairy-Stories," "Leaf by Niggle," *Farmer Giles of Ham,* and *The Adventures of Tom Bombadil.*

Smith of Wootton Major and Farmer Giles of Ham. Illustrated by Pauline Baynes. New York: Ballantine Books, 1969 [paper]. Reprint in one volume.

Tree and Leaf, Smith of Wootton Major, The Homecoming of Beorhtnoth. London: Unwin Books, 1975 [paper]. Reprint in one volume.

Farmer Giles of Ham, The Adventures of Tom Bombadil. London: Unwin Books, 1975 [paper]. Reprint in one volume.

Poems and Stories. Illustrated by Pauline Baynes. London: George Allen & Unwin, 1980. Boston: Houghton Mifflin Company, 1994. Contains *The Adventures of Tom Bombadil,* "The Homecoming of Beorhtnoth," "On Fairy-Stories," "Leaf by Niggle," *Farmer Giles of Ham,* and *Smith of Wootton Major.*

Tales from the Perilous Realm. London: HarperCollins, 1997. Contains *Farmer Giles of Ham, The Adventures of Tom Bombadil,* "Leaf by Niggle," and *Smith of Wootton Major.*

A Tolkien Miscellany. Illustrated by Pauline Baynes. Garden City, N.Y.: Science Fiction Book Club, 2002. Contains *Smith of Wootton Major, Farmer Giles of Ham, Tree and Leaf, The Adventures of Tom Bombadil,* and *Sir Gawain and the Green Knight, Pearl, Sir Orfeo.*

 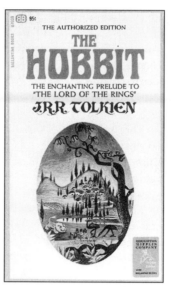 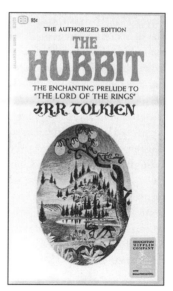

During World War II, publishers in England were severely limited in their output by paper rationing policies. After the bombing of and subsequent fire at Allen & Unwin's warehouse in November 1940, when the remaining stock of unbound copies of *The Hobbit* had been destroyed, the book was temporarily unavailable until the Children's Book Club edition (dated 1942) was released in 1943, following delays at the bindery. The dust jacket (above, left) was redesigned (dropping Tolkien's own illustration), and printed in black, orange, and white. Oddly, the book did not include Thror's Map, though it is referred to in the text. Tolkien commented in a letter to Allen & Unwin of March 18, 1945: "Surely the paper wasted on that hideous dust-cover could have been better used."

II. Revisional Notes on *The Hobbit*

Tolkien's revisions to the published text of *The Hobbit* are given in the annotations throughout this book. These annotations attempt to account for all revisions made from the first edition (1937) through the various resettings of the third edition (1966–67). They do not detail misprints or errors in these editions, save in the instances where an intended change to the text was involved. Each revisional annotation begins with the original 1937 reading and gives the details of change only up to the time when the final reading was first reached. Hence, if a change made in 1951 is given and the text

Above, center: The first American paperback edition of *The Hobbit* (containing the second edition text) was published by Ballantine Books in August 1965. The vignette on the cover, a part of a mural also used on the covers of the three volumes of the 1965 Ballantine edition of *The Lord of the Rings,* strangely includes an absurdly grinning lion with red eyes in the surreal landscape. Tolkien was, with justification, not pleased with this cover. To Rayner Unwin he wrote on September 12, 1965: "I must ask this about the vignette: what has it got to do with the story? Where is this place? Why a lion and emus? And what is the thing in the foreground with pink bulbs?" (*Letters,* No. 277).

The cover artist, Barbara Remington, can't really be blamed for this misrepresentation, for the production of this edition was so rushed that that artist wasn't given time to read the book before making her illustration. After subsequently reading the books, Remington wrote to Tolkien and agreed that her art was inappropriate to the text.

Above, right: For the revised Ballantine edition of *The Hobbit* (containing the third edition text), published in February 1966, the grinning lion was removed, hidden under the yellow-green grass. Strangely, the trees were also widened at this time, though the overall effect of the surreal cover remained unaltered.

remained unaltered from that point, I do not repeat the reading. All through these annotations, the symbol > means "changed to."

In compiling these notes, for the 1937 text I used the first printing (with the bowing hobbit on the title page) of the 1938 American edition published by Houghton Mifflin. This printing was reproduced photographically from the 1937 English first edition and contains the identical text and misprints. (The later printing of the 1938 Houghton Mifflin edition, with a seated figure playing a flute replacing the bowing hobbit on the title page, has a very small number of further differences.)

For the 1951 text I used the Houghton Mifflin "Second Edition (Fifth Impression)," made from English sheets. The Houghton Mifflin second edition, printed at the same time as the Allen & Unwin second edition, was apparently published in the spring of 1951, while the Allen & Unwin second edition came out a few months later in July. Christopher Tolkien photocopied for me the revisions his father made (c. August 1965, for the third edition) in his working copy of *The Hobbit,* a 1954 "Sixth impression" of the Allen & Unwin edition, and a close study of these notes has improved my revisional notes and confirmed some of Tolkien's intended readings.

Tolkien's revisions for the third edition were entered in a somewhat complex manner. They were first sent to the United States for the Ballantine Books paperback edition, which was published in February 1966. Meanwhile, in England, Allen & Unwin used the revisions in a new paperback edition for their Unwin Books imprint, labeled the "Third edition (sixteenth impression) 1966." At the same time Allen & Unwin had licensed a hardcover edition to Longmans, Green for their Heritage of Literature series. Both the Unwin Books and the Longmans editions appeared in June 1966, though the Longmans edition apparently preceded the Unwin Books edition by a few weeks. (The British Library received the Longmans edition on June 6, whereas the publication date for the Unwin Books edition was June 30.) Allen & Unwin also produced a hardcover edition of the revised text, published simultaneously with the Unwin Books edition on June 30. This Allen & Unwin edition ("Sixteenth impression 1966") erroneously labels the "Fifteenth impression 1966" as the "Third edition." (The correct "Fifteenth impression" is dated 1965; it contains the second edi-

The cover of the 1966 Longmans, Green edition of *The Hobbit.* Tolkien himself redrew the runes, but the artist who redrew a portion of Tolkien's dust-jacket design is unknown.

tion text.) These 1966 revisions were finally added to the American hardcover edition, published by Houghton Mifflin, in the "Twenty-fourth printing C" of August 1967.

For what I have called the *1966-Ball* text, I have used the February 1966 "First Printing" by Ballantine Books, and for the *1966-Longmans/Unwin* text, a first printing of the Longmans edition. (The Longmans edition was reprinted four times through 1970). The *1966-A&U* text, labeled the "Sixteenth impression 1966," follows the Longmans/Unwin readings extremely closely, though some differences are noted. For the *1967-HM* text, I have used a "Twenty-fourth" printing of the American hardcover (Houghton Mifflin) edition.

The "Fourth Edition" of 1978 sometimes referred to was published by Allen & Unwin; an American edition uniform with this was published in 1985 (fortieth printing). The text of the "Fourth Edition" is not very reliable, owing to more than a few dozen errors that entered during the resetting of the type.

The 1961 Puffin edition (a British paperback; see

p. 103) is also referred to in a few places. The 1995 HarperCollins edition is technically the fifth edition, though it is not so designated. For this British hardcover edition the text of *The Hobbit* was first entered into a word-processing file; it is referred to once (though other peculiarities of that edition are not discussed). In 1999 this text was photo-offset for Houghton Mifflin editions. However, for the 2001 Houghton Mifflin edition (hardcover and trade paperback, with a Peter Sís cover), the entire text was compared line by line with earlier editions, and errors and oddities of the 1995 edition were cleared up. This most up-to-date corrected text file is the basis for the text used in this book.

For readers interested in studying chronologically the revisions Tolkien made to *The Hobbit,* I append the listings below, which for the most part omit typographical errors. For revisions to the 1951 second edition, see the following annotations:

> Introductory Note: 3.
> Chapter I: 36, 41, 50.
> Chapter III: 14.
> Chapter V: 11–12, 20, 25, 32.
> Chapter VI: 3–5.
> Chapter XVIII: 2.

The annotations concerning changes in the 1961 Puffin edition are as follows:

> Introductory Note: 3.
> Chapter I: 19.
> Chapter V: 17.

For the revisions made to the various resettings of the 1966–67 third edition, see the following annotations:

> Introductory Note: 3.
> Chapter I: 4, 13, 17, 19, 21–23, 26–27, 30–31, 33,
>   39, 42–43, 45–46, 48–51, 53–54.
> Chapter II: 2, 4–11, 13, 18–19, 22, 24–25.
> Chapter III: 1, 4–6, 10–11, 13, 15, 17.
> Chapter IV: 3, 8.
> Chapter V: 2, 4–5, 17.
> Chapter VIII: 1, 20, 23.
> Chapter XII: 6.

> Chapter XIII: 2–3.
> Chapter XIV: 3.
> Chapter XV: 5–7.
> Chapter XVII: 7.
> Chapter XIX: 3, 11–12.

III. Translations and Illustrated Editions of *The Hobbit*

The listing below attempts to include all translations of *The Hobbit* published in book form, as well as all of the various illustrated editions, but it by no means accounts for the many reprints of these editions. It should also be noted that the illustrations in the editions cited are sometimes dropped from subsequent printings, wholly or in part, and such alterations are not always discussed, nor are the many changes in cover art over the years.

The pioneer listing of Tolkien translations was done by Glen H. GoodKnight in "Tolkien in Translation," *Mythlore,* Summer 1982 (9, no. 2; whole no. 32): 22–27. A revised and updated version, retitled "J.R.R. Tolkien in Translation," appeared in *Mythlore,* Summer 1992 (18, no. 3; whole no. 69): 61–69. This version was followed soon after by the section on translations (G) in the *Bibliography.* Since its founding in 1992, *The Tolkien Collector,* edited by Christina Scull, has established itself as the premier journal for those interested in all of the editions of Tolkien's works, British, American, and foreign. In updating my list of *Hobbit* translations (originally published in the 1988 *Annotated Hobbit*), *The Tolkien Collector* has proven invaluable. (For more information on *The Tolkien Collector,* see its Web site at lanfiles.williams.edu/~whammond/collect.html.)

To this listing I have added some comments to call attention to articles (written in English) that discuss aspects of the translations. Many of these are by Arden R. Smith, and they appear in his always interesting column, "Transitions in Translations." This column is a regular feature in *Vinyar Tengwar,* the journal of the Elvish Linguistic Fellowship, a special interest group of the Mythopoeic Society. A more general article by

Smith, "Tolkien on Translation," which is not referenced below and discusses Tolkien's own reactions to the translations, appears in *Vinyar Tengwar,* no. 21 (January 1992): 21–24. (For more information on *Vinyar Tengwar* and other resources on Tolkien's invented languages, see www.elvish.org.)

A few words should be said here about the multiplicity of Russian translations. Many of these were unauthorized, and circulated in underground "samizdat" form before the fall of Communism in the early 1990s made it possible for these translations to appear in book form. The circumstances behind each of these translations reflect the complex political and sociological conditions of the former Soviet Union and of the present Russian Federation. For some understanding of such concerns, see "The Secret War and the End of the Third Age: Tolkien in the (former) USSR," by Maria Kamenkovich, *Mallorn,* no. 29 (August 1992): 33–38; "Problems of Translating into Russian," by Natalia Grigorieva, *Proceedings of the J. R. R. Tolkien Centenary Conference,* edited by Patricia Reynolds and Glen H. GoodKnight (1995): 200–205; and "Russia As a New Context for Tolkien," by Maria Kamenkovich, *Inklings Jahrbuch für Literatur und Ästhetik* 17 (1999): 197–216. The latter essay has also been published as a booklet, *The Trojan Horse: Russia As a New Context for Tolkien* (Flint, Mich.: American Tolkien Society, 1999). As to how these matters relate specifically to the many Russian translations of *The Hobbit,* I especially recommend Mark T. Hooker's "Tolkien Through Russian Eyes" in *Concerning Hobbits and Other Matters: Tolkien Across the Disciplines,* edited by Tim Schindler (St. Paul, Minn.: University of St. Thomas English Department, 2001): 7–31. In the Russian section given below I have, for convenience, grouped the various editions first by translation and then chronologically under each translation.

In making this listing I have consulted the collections of *Hobbit* translations in a few libraries that specialize in collecting Tolkien's works, including the Marion E. Wade Center, Wheaton College, Wheaton, Illinois, and the Department of Special Collections, Marquette University, Milwaukee, Wisconsin. A larger collection of Tolkien translations is also available at the Bodleian Library, Oxford University, Oxford, England, in association with their major holding of Tolkien's own papers.

Armenian

Hobit: Kam Gnaln ou Galû. Yerevan: Sovetakan Grogh, 1984. Translated by Emma Makaryan; illustrated by Mikhail Belomlinskiy.

Breton

An Hobbit, pe eno ha distro. Argenteuil: A.R.D.A., 2001. Translated by Alan Dipode.

Bulgarian

Bilbo Begins, ili, Dotam i obratno. Sofia: Narodna Mladezh, 1975. Translated by Krasimira Todorova (prose) and Asen Todorov (verse); illustrated by Peter Chuklev. This translation appeared in paperback from the same publisher in 1979 with slightly altered illustrations.

Khobit: Bilbo Begins, ili, Dotam i obratno. Sofia: Bard, 1999. Translated by Liubomir Nikolov; illustrated by J.R.R. Tolkien.

[See "Tolkien in Bulgaria" by Christina Scull, *The Tolkien Collector,* no. 4 (August 1993): 18–21.]

Catalan

El Hòbbit, o, Viatge d'anada i tornada. Barcelona: Edicions de la Magrana, 1983. Translated by Francesc Parcerisas.

Chinese

Sheau Aeren Lihshean Jih [tonal spelling] or *Xiao Airen Lixian Ji* [Hanyu Pinyin]. Taipei: Linking, 1996. Translated by Liou Huey Yeou; rewritten by Jang Tsyrjiuan; illustrated by J.R.R. Tolkien.

[*The Hobbit*]. Jinan: Tomorrow Publishing House, 2000. Translated by Xín Píao; illustrated anonymously.

[*The Hobbit*]. Nanjing: Yilin Press, 2001. Translated by Lí Gí.

[*The Hobbit*]. Taipei: Linking, 2001. Translated by Lucifer Chu.

Croatian

Hobit. Zagreb: Algoritam, 1994. Translated by Zlatko Crnković; illustrated by J.R.R. Tolkien.

Czech

Hobit, aneb, Cesta tam a zase zpátky. Prague: Odeon, 1979. Translation credited to Lubomír Dorůžka; illustrated by Jiří Šalamoun. [The Czech translation was initially, for political reasons, credited to Dorůžka, who in fact wrote only the afterword. The translation was actually made by František Vrba, who is credited in later editions.]

The cover of the 1991 reissue of the Czech translation, originally published by Odeon in 1979. Cover art by Jiří Šalamoun.

[See "Works by and about J.R.R. Tolkien in Czech and Slovak," by Karel Makovsky, *The Tolkien Collector,* no. 5 (November 1993): 20–26. Also, in 1996 the Czech Tolkien Society issued a booklet of twenty-three black-and-white illustrations for *The Hobbit* done by the art-ist Jan Václavík (b. 1971) as a master's thesis at the College of Education at Hradec Králové in 1993. The booklet was published under the title *Tam a zase zpátky: There and Back Again.*

Arden R. Smith comments on the expanded use of runes by Šalamoun in illustrating the Czech translation in his column "Transitions in Translations," *Vinyar Tengwar,* no. 32 (November 1993): 26–28.]

Danish

Hobbitten, eller, Ud og hjem igen. Copenhagen: Gyldendal, 1969. Translated by Ida Nyrop Ludvigsen; illustrated by J.R.R. Tolkien.

Dutch

De hobbit, of Daarheen en weer terug. Utrecht: Spectrum, 1960. Translated by Max Schuchart.
De hobbit, of Daarheen en weer terug. Utrecht: Spectrum, 1976. Revised translation by Max Schuchart, illustrated by J.R.R. Tolkien.
[See "Some Comments on the Dutch Translation of *The Hobbit*" by Renée Vink, in *Translations of "The Hobbit" Reviewed,* Quettar Special Publication no. 2 (London: The Tolkien Society, 1988): 8–10. Vink calls the translation "charming."

See also "Dutch Editions of Tolkien's Works," by Johan Vanhecke, *The Tolkien Collector,* no. 12 (February 1996): 20–28; some corrigenda to this article by Vanhecke and Felix Claessens appear in issue no. 14 (October 1996): 5–6. An earlier article by Vanhecke (which predominately concerns *The Lord of the Rings*), "Tolkien in Dutch: A Study of Tolkien's Work in Belgium and The Netherlands," appears in *Mythlore,* Autumn 1992 (18, no. 2; whole no. 70): 53–60.

Arden R. Smith discusses the editions used in Max Schuchart's revised translation of 1976 in his column "Transitions in Translations," in *Vinyar Tengwar,* no. 26 (November 1992): 26–28.]

English

The Hobbit, or There and Back Again. New York: Harry N. Abrams, 1977. Illustrations from the television film by Rankin-Bass Productions, 1977.
The Hobbit, or There and Back Again. London: Folio Society, 1979. Illustrated by Eric Fraser.
The Hobbit, or There and Back Again. London: George

Allen & Unwin, 1984. Boston: Houghton Mifflin, 1984. Illustrated by Michael Hague.

The Annotated Hobbit. London: Unwin Hyman, 1989. Boston: Houghton Mifflin, 1988. Illustrated by many artists.

The Hobbit. Adapted by Charles Dixon and Sean Deming. Forestville, Calif.: Eclipse Books, 1989–1990. Three volumes. Illustrated by David Wenzel. A graphic novel, subsequently published in one volume. New York: Ballantine Books, 1990.

The Hobbit, or There and Back Again. London: HarperCollins, 1997. Boston: Houghton Mifflin, 1997. Illustrated by Alan Lee.

The Hobbit. London: HarperCollins, 1999. New York: HarperFestival 1999. Illustrated by John Howe. A pop-up book, illustrating five scenes from *The Hobbit.*

The cover of the 2000 edition of the Esperanto translation. Cover art by Maŝa Baĵenova [Masha Bazhenova].

Tolkien first studied the international language Esperanto, proposed by L. L. Zamenhof in 1887, when he was in his teens. In 1932, he published a letter supporting Esperanto in *The British Esperantist.* A very interesting study, "Tolkien and Esperanto," by Arden R. Smith and Patrick Wynne, can be found in *Seven: An Anglo-American Literary Review* 17 (2000): 27–46.

Esperanto

Lo hobito, aŭ tien kaj reen. Ekaterinburg: Sezonoj, 2000. Translated by Christopher Gledhill (prose) and William Auld (verse); illustrated by Maŝa Baĵenova [Masha Bazhenova]. [Reviewed by Arden Smith, *Mythprint,* July 2001 (38, no. 7; whole no. 232): 4–6. Smith finds that "the translation of the main text of the book is for the most part a success" but that there are some inexplicable lapses.]

Estonian

Kääbik, ehk, Sinna ja tagasi. Tallinn: Eesti Raamat, 1977. Translated by Lia Rajandi (prose and verse) and Harald Rajamets (co-translator, verse); illustrated by Maret Kernumees.

Faeroese

Hobbin, ella, Út og heim aftur. Hoyvík: Stiðin, 1990. Translated by Axel Tógarð; illustrated by J.R.R. Tolkien. [See Hanus Andreassen's review of the Faeroese translation, "The Dream of Getting Lost," *Mallorn,* no. 30 (September 1993): 46–49, which originally appeared in Faeroese in *Tíðindablaðið Sosialurin,* December 12, 1990. Andreassen comments that "the translation has been carried out in such a way that it never crosses the reader's mind that this is a translation. Which is to say that it is masterly."]

Finnish

Lohikäärmevuori, eli, Erään hoppelin matka sinne ja takaisin. Helsinki: Kustannusosakeyhtiö Tammi, 1973. Translated by Risto Pitkänen; illustrated by Tove Jansson. [The illustrations by Jansson are identical to those published in the 1962 Swedish edition.]

Hobitti, eli, Sinne ja takaisin. Porvoo: Werner Söderström, 1985. Translated by Kersti Juva (prose) and Panu Pekkanen (verse); illustrated by J.R.R. Tolkien. [See Ellen Pakarinen's brief comments on the Finnish translations, headed "Finnish," in *Translations of "The Hobbit" Reviewed,* Quettar Special Publication no. 2 (London: Tolkien Society, 1988): 24. Pakarinen notes that for the 1973 translation the book "was treated very much as a book for children with all the names Finnicized," but for the 1985 edition "the translator Mrs. Kersti Juva received a State Award for it."

Arden R. Smith briefly considers the translation of Bilbo Baggins's name as Kalpa Kassinen in the 1973 Finnish edition in his column "Transitions in Translations," *Vinyar Tengwar,* no. 15 (January 1991): 12; he discusses the Finnicization of Elvish words and names in no. 16 (March 1991): 10–11; and he similarly considers the dwarf-names in no. 19 (September 1991): 26–27.]

French

Bilbo le Hobbit, ou, Histoire d'un aller et retour. Paris: Éditions Stock, 1969. Translated by Francis Ledoux.

Bilbo le Hobbit, ou, Histoire d'un aller et retour. Paris: Hachette, 1976. Translated by Francis Ledoux; illustrated by Chica.

Bilbo le Hobbit, ou, Histoire d'un aller et retour. Paris: Hachette, 1980. Translated by Francis Ledoux; illustrated by J.R.R. Tolkien.

Bilbo le Hobbit, ou, Histoire d'un aller et retour. Paris: Éditions Stock, 1983. Translated by Francis Ledoux; illustrated by Évelyne Drouhin.

Le Hobbit. Paris: Christian Bourgois, 1997. Translated by Francis Ledoux; illustrated by Alan Lee.

[See David Doughan's brief comments, headed "*Bilbo le Hobbit,*" in *Translations of "The Hobbit" Reviewed,* Quettar Special Publication no. 2 (London: Tolkien Society, 1988): 27. Doughan notes that the French translation "has a slight tendency to paunchiness," and that while "sharp cultural differences keep breaking through" he still finds that "in general, it's a good translation." See also "J.R.R. Tolkien in France," by Jean-Marc Bouilly, *The Tolkien Collector,* no. 17 (December 1997): 24–27.]

Galician

O Hobbit. Salamanca: Edicións Xerais de Galicia, 2000. Translated by Moisés R. Barcia; illustrated by J.R.R. Tolkien.

German

Kleiner Hobbit und der grosse Zauberer. Recklinghausen: Paulus Verlag, 1957. Translated by Walter Scherf; illustrated by Horus Engels. Republished in 1967 under the title *Der kleine Hobbit.*

Der kleine Hobbit. Recklinghausen: Georg Bitter, 1971. Revised translation by Walter Scherf; illustrated by Klaus Ensikat. [A reprint of this edition with considerably fewer illustrations has appeared.]

Der kleine Hobbit. Stuttgart: Klett-Cotta, 1991. Second revised translation by Walter Scherf.

Der Hobbit, oder, Hin und zurück. Stuttgart: Klett-Cotta, 1997. Translated by Wolfgang Krege.

[See "The Hobbit in Germany," by Manfred Zimmermann, in *Translations of "The Hobbit" Reviewed,* Quettar Special Publication no. 2 (London: Tolkien Society, 1988): 3–7.

Arden R. Smith discusses the editions used in Walter Scherf's revised translation of 1971 in his column "Transitions in Translations," in *Vinyar Tengwar,* no. 13 (September 1990): 18–19; and no. 15 (January 1991): 11–12. He also discusses differences between the translations of names and phrases that appear in both Scherf's translation of *The Hobbit* and in Margaret Carroux's 1969 German translation of *The Lord of the Rings* in no. 28 (March 1993): 35–38. Follow-up comments by David Bratman and Arden R. Smith appear in no. 30 (July 1993): 28–31; and no. 32 (November 1993): 30.]

Greek

Khompit. Athens: Kedros, 1978. Translated by A. Gabrielide and Kh. Delegianne; illustrated by J.R.R. Tolkien.

[Arden R. Smith discusses the Greek translation in his column "Transitions in Translations," in *Vinyar Tengwar,* no. 11 (May 1990): 16.]

Hebrew

ha-Hobit, o, Le-sham uva-hazarah. Tel Aviv: Zemorah, Bitan, Modan, 1976. Translated by Mosheh ha-Na'ami; illustrated by J.R.R. Tolkien.

Hobit. Tel Aviv: Zemorah, Bitan, Modan, 1977. Translated "by the P.O.W. of the Israeli Air-Force Pilots and their comrades in Abasya Prison, Cairo, 1970–1973."

Hungarian

A babó. Budapest: Móra Könyvkiadó, 1975. Translated by Tibor Szobotka (prose) and István Tótfalusi (verse); illustrated by Tamás Szecskó.

[See Andrea Fazakas's brief comments, headed "Hungarian," in *Translations of "The Hobbit" Reviewed*, Quettar Special Publication no. 2 (London: Tolkien Society, 1988): 24.]

The cover of the 1975 edition of the Hungarian translation. Cover art by Tamás Szecskó.

Icelandic

Hobbit. Reykjavík: Almenna Bókafélagið, 1978. Translated by Úlfur Ragnarsson and Karl Ágúst Úlfsson.

Hobbitinn, eða, Út og Heim Aftur. Reykjavík: Fjölvaútgáfan, 1997. Translated by Þorsteinn Thorarensen; illustrated by Alan Lee.

Indonesian

Hobbit. Jakarta: P. T. Gramedia, 1977. Translated by Anton Adiwiyoto.

Italian

Lo hobbit, o, La riconquista del tesoro. Milan: Adelphi Edizioni, 1973. Translated by Elena Jeronimidis; illustrated by J.R.R. Tolkien. [The translator's name is sometimes given as Elena Jeronimidis Conte.]

Lo hobbit, o, La riconquista del tesoro. Milan: Arnaldo Mandadori Editore, 1986. Translated by Elena Jeronimidis; illustrated by Michael Hague.

Lo Hobbit, o, La riconquista del tesoro. Milan: Rusconi, 1991. *The Annotated Hobbit*, translated by Elena Jeronimidis (Tolkien's text) and Grazia Maria Griffini (annotations); many illustrators, as per the annotated edition.

Japanese

Hobitto no Bôken. Tokyo: Iwanami Shoten, 1965. Translated by Teiji Seta; illustrated by Ryûichi Terashima.

Hobitto no Bôken. Tokyo: Iwanami Shoten, 1983. Revised translation by Teiji Seta; revised illustrations by Ryûichi Terashima. [Tenth impression, with the translation revised and corrected, bringing the reading level slightly higher. Also a small number of illustrations have been redone, particularly those of Gollum, who is drawn to be whiter and thinner but with fatter arms and legs than in the earlier version. And in a couple of illustrations, the door to Bilbo's hobbit-hole is now shown opening inward, rather than outward.]

Hobitto, Yukite kaerishi Monogatari. Tokyo: Hara Shobô, 1997. *The Annotated Hobbit*, translated by Shirô Yamamoto; many illustrators, as per the annotated edition.

[See "The Japanese Hobbit," by Robert Ellwood, *Mythlore*, 1, no. 3 (July 1969): 14–17. Ellwood considers the translation to be "smooth, idiomatic, simple in vocabulary," and praises Terashima's illustrations (a few of which are reprinted with the review). Ellwood also translates some sections from the translator's six-page afterword.

See also "The Japanese *Hobbit*," by Takashi Okunishi, in *Translations of "The Hobbit" Reviewed*, Quettar Special Publication no. 2 (London: Tolkien Society, 1988): 19–20.

In *The Tolkien Collector*, no. 17 (December 1997): 13, it is noted concerning the Japanese edition of *The Annotated Hobbit* that "Makoto Takahashi writes that he finds it a poor translation [of text of the novel, by Yamamoto] which is not in accord with the Japanese *Lord of the Rings*."]

Korean

[*The Hobbit*]. Seoul: Sigongsa, 1997. Translator unknown; illustrated by J.R.R. Tolkien.

Latvian

Hobits, jeb, Turp un atpakaļ. Riga: Sprīdītis, 1991. Translated by Zane Rozenberga; illustrated by Laima Eglīte.

Lithuanian

Hobitas, arba, Ten ir atgal: Apysaka-pasaka. Vilnius: Vyturys, 1985. Translated by Bronė Balčienė; illustrated by Mikhail Belomlinskiy.

Luxembourgish

Den Hobbit. Esch-sur-Sûre: Editions Op der Lay, 2002. Translated by Henry Wickens.

Moldavian

Hobbitul. Kishinev: Literatura Artistike, 1987. Translated by Aleksey Zurhkanu; illustrated by Igor Hmelnickij.

Norwegian

Hobbiten, eller, Fram og tilbake igjen. Oslo: Tiden Norsk Forlag, 1972. Translated by Finn Aasen and Oddrun Grønvik.

Hobbiten, eller, Fram og tilbake igjen. Oslo: Tiden Norsk Forlag, 1997. Translated by Nils Ivar Agøy; illustrated by Alan Lee.

[See "*The Hobbit* in Norwegian" by Nils Ivar Agøy, in *Translations of "The Hobbit" Reviewed*, Quettar Special Publication no. 2 (London: The Tolkien Society, 1988): 11–16. Agøy notes that "two independent translators each prepared part of the book. Finn Aasen started out, but quit on page 197 for reasons the publishers don't wish to talk about, and Oddrun Grønvick took over and translated the rest." He complains that the language of the translation is "mostly ordinary colloquial Norwegian, which is *not* a worthy substitute for Tolkien's elegant, sometimes formal and archaic prose."

Agøy also wrote "Tolkien in Norway" in *Inklings Jahrbuch für Literatur und Ästhetik, 3* (1985): 159–67, and his own translation of *The Hobbit* appeared in 1997.]

Polish

Hobbit, czyli, Tam i z powrotem. Warsaw: Iskry, 1960. Translated by Maria Skibniewska; illustrated by Jan Mlodozeniec.

Hobbit, czyli, Tam i z powrotem. Warsaw: Iskry, 1985. Revised Translation by Maria Skibniewska; illustrated by Maciej Buszewicz.

Hobbit, albo, Tam i z powrotem. Warsaw: Atlantic-Rubicon, 1997. Translated by Paulina Braiter; illustrated by Alan Lee.

[See "A Few Comments on Maria Skibniewska's translation of *The Hobbit*," by Agnieszka Sylwanowicz, in *Translations of "The Hobbit" Reviewed*, Quettar Special Publication no. 2 (London: The Tolkien Society, 1988): 21–23. Sylwanowicz writes that "on the whole, *The Hobbit* is translated very well, its atmosphere is preserved and the impact on the reader is — as far as I can judge — almost identical to the impact the original has on the English-speaking."

See also "Tolkien Boom in Poland," again by Agnieszka Sylwanowicz, *The Tolkien Collector*, no. 18 (June 1998): 21–23.]

Portuguese

O gnomo. Porto: Livraria Civilização, 1962. Translated by Maria Isabel Braga and Mário Braga; illustrated by António Quadros.

O Hobbit. Rio de Janeiro: Artenova, 1976. Translated by Luiz Alberto Monjardim.

O Hobbit. Mem Martins: Publicações Europa-América, 1985. Translated by Fernanda Pinto Rodrigues.

O Hobbit. São Paulo: Martins Fontes, 1995. Translated

by Lenita Maria Rimoli Esteves and Almiro Pisetta.

[Arden R. Smith comments briefly on the 1962 edition in his column "Transitions in Translations," in *Vinyar Tengwar*, no. 8 (November 1989): 10–11; and in no. 10 (March 1990): 16.

Ronald Kyrmse discusses the faults of the 1976 translation by Monjardim in "O Hobbit," *Translations of "The Hobbit" Reviewed*, Quettar Special Publication no. 2 (London: The Tolkien Society, 1988): 17–18.]

Romanian

O poveste cu un hobbit. Bucharest: Editura Ion Creangă, 1975. Translated by Catinca Ralea; illustrated by Livia Rusz.

Povestea Unui Hobbit. Ploieşti: Editura Elit, 1995. Translated by Junona Tutunea; illustrated by Peter Green.

The cover of the 1989 Detskaya Literatura reissue of the Rakhmanova translation into Russian, originally published in 1976. Cover art by Mikhail Belomlinskiy.

Russian

Khobbit, ili, Tuda i obratno. Leningrad: Detskaya Literatura, 1976. Translated by N. Rakhmanova (prose)

and G. Usova and I. Komarova (verse); illustrated by Mikhail Belomlinskiy.

Khobbit, ili, Tuda i obratno. Leningrad: Detskaya Literatura, 1989. Revised translation by N. Rakhmanova (prose) and G. Usova and I. Komarova (verse); illustrated by Mikhail Belomlinskiy.

Khobbit, ili, Tuda i obratno. Novosibirsk: Novosibirskoe Knizhnoe Izdatel'stvo, 1989. Translated by N. Rakhmanova (prose) and G. Usova and I. Komarova (verse); illustrated by A. Shurits.

Khobbit, ili, Tuda i obratno. Published in *Zabytiy den' Rozhdeniya: Skazki Angliyskikh Pisateley* [*The Forgotten Birthday: Fairy Tales by English Writers*], compiled by Olga Aleksandrovna Kolesnikova. Moscow: Pravda, 1990. Translated by N. Rakhmanova (prose) and G. Usova and I. Komarova (verse); illustrated by Il'ya A. Markevich.

Khobbit, ili, Tuda i obratno. St. Petersburg: Severo-Zapad, 1991. Translated by N. Rakhmanova (prose) and G. Usova and I. Komarova (verse); illustrated by Denis Gordeyev.

Khobbit, ili, Tuda i obratno. Minsk: Vyshehjshaya Shkola, 1992. Translated by N. Rakhmanova (prose) and G. Usova and I. Komarova (verse); illustrated by A. G. Zvonarev.

Khobbit, ili, Tuda i obratno. St. Petersburg: Severo-Zapad, 1993. Translated by N. Rakhmanova (prose) and G. Usova and I. Komarova (verse); illustrated by N. Martinova.

Khobbit, ili, Tuda i obratno. Baku: Olimp, 1993. Translated by N. Rakhmanova (prose) and G. Usova and I. Komarova (verse); illustrated by A. V. Koval'.

Khobbit, ili, Tuda i obratno. Moscow: Pedagogika-Press, 1994. Translation by N. Rakhmanova (prose) and G. Usova and I. Komarova (verse); illustrated by Dar'ya Yudina.

Khobbit, ili, Tuda i obratno. Minsk: Kavaler, 1996. Translation by N. Rakhmanova (prose) and G. Usova and I. Komarova (verse); illustrated by Nicolas Bayrachny. [Profusely illustrated. Three of these illustrations are included in *Realms of Tolkien* (London: HarperCollins, 1997).]

Khobbit, ili, Tuda i obratno. Published in *Skazki Veka 2*

[*Fairy Tales of the Century 2*], compiled by Roland A. Bykov. Moscow: Polifakt, 1999. Translated by N. Rakhmanova (prose) and G. Usova and I. Komarova (verse); illustrated by Yu. Tokarev.

Khobbit, ili, Tuda i obratno. Khabarovsk: Amur, 1990. Translated by V. A. M. [Valeriya Aleksandrovna Matorina].

Khobbit, ili, Tuda i obratno. Zaporozhye-Kaliningrad: Izdatel'stvo 'Interbook-Khortitsa', 1994. Revised translation by V. A. M. [Valeriya Aleksandrovna Matorina]; illustrations signed L. A. Dziazdyk (but attributed to her husband, Vladimir Kosyúk; see *The Tolkien Collector*, no. 13 [May 1996]: 14) and L. V. Malinka.

Khobbit, ili, Tuda i obratno. Moscow: Éksmo-Press, 2000. Second revised translation by V. A. M. [Valeriya Aleksandrovna Matorina]; illustrated by I. Pankov. [This edition also includes translations, by a different translator, of *Farmer Giles of Ham*, "Leaf by Niggle," and *Smith of Wootton Major*.]

Khobbit, ili, Tuda i obratno. Moscow: Molodaya Gvardiya, 1991. Translated by Z. Bobyr'; illustrated by M. I. Sivenkova. [This edition also includes a translation of *The Fellowship of the Ring*.]

Khobbit, ili, Tuda i obratno. Perm: Knizhnymir, 1992. Translated by Z. Bobyr'; illustrated by A. Filipova and A. Kytmanova.

Khobbit, ili, Tuda i obratno. St. Petersburg: Terra/Azbuka, 1995. Translated by Mariya Kamenkovich, Valeriy Karrik, and Sergei Stepanov; illustrated by Nikita Badmayev. [This edition is annotated by Kamenkovich and Karrik. *Karrik* is a pseudonym of Valeriy Kamenkovich.]

Khobbit, ili, Tuda i obratno [etc., also with the English title: *The Hobbit and Other Minor Works*]. Moscow: ACT; St. Petersburg: Terra Fantastica, 2000. Translated by K. Korolev (prose) and V. Tikhomirov (verse); illustrations unedited. [This edition also includes translations, by different translators, of *The Adventures of Tom Bombadil*, *Smith of Wootton Major*, *The Father Christmas Letters*, and *Farmer Giles of Ham*.]

Khobbit, ili, Tuda i obratno. Moscow: Armada/Al'fa-Kniga, 2001. Translated by Leonid L. Yakhnin; illustrated by V. S. Krivenko.

Khobbit, ili, Tuda i obratno. Ekaterinburg: Litur Publishers, 2001. Translated by A. A. Gruzberg.

[David Doughan reviewed the 1976 translation by Nataliya Rakhmanova in *Amon Hen*, no. 55 (April 1982): 12–14; and this piece is reprinted in *Translations of "The Hobbit" Reviewed*, Quettar Special Publication no. 2 (London: The Tolkien Society, 1988): 25–26. Doughan finds it "a thoroughly enjoyable translation, which manages to catch the spirit of the original without distorting the letter too much."

Mark T. Hooker has informed me of another Russian translation of *The Hobbit* that has not been published in book form, an anonymous translation that has circulated both in samizdat and as a computerized text on the World Wide Web. The V. A. M., Aleksandr A. Gruzberg, and Zinaida A. Bobyr' translations listed above were also first circulated in samizdat, and the Gruzberg additionally appeared as a CD-Rom in 2000.

Arden R. Smith discusses some of the geographical curiosities of the text and story map in the 1989 revised translation by Rakhmanova in his column, "Transitions in Translations," *Vinyar Tengwar*, no. 29 (May 1993): 25–26.

A graphic novel version of *The Hobbit*, titled *Khobbit* and adapted by N. Utilova, has also been published (Moscow: Avlad, 1992). The illustrations, by R. Ramazanov, A. Shevtsov, and R. Azizov, are fanciful (e.g., Bilbo is portrayed with long rabbitlike ears), and the story is both altered and abridged.

An anonymous comic book adaptation also appeared under the name *Khobbit* (Moscow: Belyj Gorod, 1999).

There have also been three editions of *The Hobbit* published as texts for the use of Russian students in learning English. These editions contain adapted English texts, along with explanatory notes and exercises in Russian. The first came out in 1982 (edited by Yu. P. Tret'yakova, and published by Prosveshchenie in Moscow), the second in 1992 (published by Tekart of

St. Petersburg), and the third in 2000 (edited by S. N. Cherkhanova, illustrated by M. I. Sukharev, and published by Presto in Moscow).]

Serbian

Hobit. Belgrade: Nolit, 1975. Translated by Meri and Milan Milišić.

Slovak

Hobbiti. Bratislava: Mladé Letá, 1973. Translated by Viktor Krupa (prose) and Jana Šimulčíková (verse); illustrated by Nada Rappensbergerová-Jankovičová. [See "Works by and about J.R.R. Tolkien in Czech and Slovak," by Karel Makovsky, *The Tolkien Collector,* no. 5 (November 1993): 20-25.]

Slovenian

Hobit, ali, Tja in spet nazaj. Ljubljana: Mladinska Knjiga, 1986. Translated by Dušan Ogrizek; illustrated by Mirna Pavlovec.

Hobit, ali, Tja in spet nazaj. Ljubljana: Založba Mladinska Knjiga, 2000. Translated by Dušan Ogrizek; illustrated by J.R.R. Tolkien.

Spanish

El hobito. Buenos Aires: Fabril, 1964. Translated by Teresa Sanchez Luevas.

El hobbit. Barcelona: Ediciones Minotauro, 1982. Translated by Manuel Figueroa; illustrated by J.R.R. Tolkien.

El hobbit anotado. (The Annotated Hobbit.) Barcelona: Ediciones Minotauro, 1990. Translated by Manuel Figueroa (Tolkien text) and Rubén Masera (annotations); many illustrators, as per the annotated edition.

El hobbit. Barcelona: Ediciones Minotauro, 1997. Translated by Manuel Figueroa; illustrated by Alan Lee.

[Some of the above editions were also distributed in other Spanish-speaking countries, including Mexico, Cuba, and Argentina.

A 1981 translation by José Valdivieso listed by Glen H. GoodKnight in his original 1982 article on transla-

tions of Tolkien and in the *Bibliography* has been determined to be a ghost entry.]

Swedish

Hompen, eller, En resa dit och tillbaksigen. Stockholm: Kooperativa Förbundets Bokförlag, 1947. Translated by Tore Zetterholm; illustrated by Torbjörn Zetterholm and Charles Sjöblom (cover and maps only).

Bilbo: en hobbits äventyr. Stockholm: Rabén & Sjögren, 1962. Translated by Britt G. Hallqvist; illustrated by Tove Jansson. [Jansson's illustrations also appear in the 1973 Finnish edition.]

Bilbo: en hobbits äventyr. Stockholm: Rabén & Sjögren, 1971. Translated by Britt G. Hallqvist; illustrated by J.R.R. Tolkien.

[See "Tolkien in Sweden," by Anders Stenström, in *Inklings Jahrbuch für Literatur und Ästhetik,* 2 (1984): 43-49. Stenström refers to the Hallqvist translation of *The Hobbit* as "possibly the best Swedish translation of any work by Tolkien."]

The cover of the 1994 Rabén Prisma reissue of the Hallqvist translation into Swedish, originally published in 1962. Cover art by Tove Jansson.

Thai

[*The Hobbit*]. Bangkok: Naiin, 2002. Translator unknown; illustrated by J.R.R. Tolkien.

Turkish

Hobbit, Oradaydık ve şimdi buradayız. Istanbul: Altıkırbeş Yayın / Mitos Yayıncılık, 1996. Translated by Emeli İzmirli.

Hobbit, Oradaydık ve şimdi buradayız. Istanbul: Altıkırbeş Yayın, 1997. Translated by Esra Uzun.

Ukrainian

Hobit, abo, Mandrivka za imlysti hory. Kiev: Veselka, 1985. Translated by Oleksandr Mokrovol's'kiy; illustrated by Mikhail Belomlinskiy.

IV. Selected Criticism of *The Hobbit*

Agøy, Nils Ivar. "*Mr. Bliss:* The Precursor of a Precursor?" *Mallorn,* no. 20 (September 1983): 25–27.

Alderson, Brian. *The Hobbit 50th Anniversary 1937–1987* (London: Unwin Hyman, 1987).

Barnfield, Marie. "The Roots of Rivendell: or, Elrond's House Now Open As a Museum," *þe Lyfe ant þe Auncestrye,* no. 3 (spring 1996): 4–18.

Bibire, Paul. "By Stock or by Stone: Recurrent Imagery and Narrative Pattern in *The Hobbit,*" *Scholarship and Fantasy: Proceedings of "The Tolkien Phenomenon" May 1992, Turku, Finland,* edited by K. J. Battarbee (Turku, Finland: University of Turku, 1993): 203–15.

Bolintineanu, Alexandra. " 'Walkers in Darkness': The Ancestry of Gollum," in *Concerning Hobbits and Other Matters: Tolkien Across the Disciplines,* edited by Tim Schindler (St. Paul, Minn.: University of St. Thomas English Department, 2001): 67–72.

Brunsdale, Mitzi M. "Norse Mythological Elements in *The Hobbit,*" *Mythlore* 9, no. 4 (whole number 34; winter 1983): 49–50, 55.

Burns, Marjorie J. "Echoes of William Morris's Icelandic Journals in J.R.R. Tolkien," *Studies in Medievalism* 3, no. 3 (winter 1991): 367–73.

Chance, Jane. *Tolkien's Art: A Mythology for England, Revised Edition* (Lexington: University of Kentucky Press, 2001). See especially Chapter 2, "The King Under the Mountain: Tolkien's Children's Story."

Christensen, Bonniejean. "Gollum's Character Transformation in *The Hobbit,*" in *A Tolkien Compass,* edited by Jared Lobdell (La Salle, Ill.: Open Court, 1975): 9–28.

———. "Tolkien's Creative Technique: *Beowulf* and *The Hobbit,*" *Mythlore* 15, no. 3 (whole no. 57; spring 1989): 4–10.

Couch, Christopher L. "From Under the Mountains to Beyond the Stars: The Process of Riddling in Leofric's *The Exeter Book* and *The Hobbit,*" *Mythlore* 14, no. 1 (whole no. 51; autumn 1987): 9–13, 55.

Crabbe, Katharyn W. *J.R.R. Tolkien: Revised and Expanded Edition* (New York: Continuum, 1988). See Chapter 2, "The Quest As Fairy Tale: *The Hobbit.*"

Ellison, John A. "The Structure of *The Hobbit,*" *Mallorn,* no. 27 (September 1990): 29–32.

Evans, Jonathan. "The Dragon-Lore of Middle-earth: Tolkien and Old English and Old Norse Tradition," in *J.R.R. Tolkien and His Literary Resonances: Views of Middle-earth,* edited by George Clark and Daniel Timmons (Westport, Conn.: Greenwood Press, 2000): 21–38.

Glenn, Jonathan A. "To Translate a Hero: *The Hobbit* As *Beowulf* Retold," *Publications of the Arkansas Philological Association* 17 (1991): 13–34.

Green, William H. "The Four-Part Structure of Bilbo's Education," *Children's Literature* 8 (1979): 133–140.

———. *The Hobbit: A Journey into Maturity* (New York: Twayne, 1995).

———. "King Thorin's Mines: *The Hobbit* As Victorian Adventure Novel," *Extrapolation* 42, no. 1 (spring 2001): 53–64.

———. " 'Where's Mama?' The Construction of the Feminine in *The Hobbit,*" *The Lion and the Unicorn* 22 (1998): 18–95.

Hammond, Wayne G. "All the Comforts: The Image of Home in *The Hobbit* and *The Lord of the Rings,*" *Mythlore* 14, no. 1 (whole no. 51; autumn 1987): 29–33.

Hieatt, Constance B. "The Text of *The Hobbit:* Putting Tolkien's Notes in Order," *English Studies in Canada* 7, no. 2 (summer 1981): 212–24.

Helms, Randel. *Tolkien's World* (Boston: Houghton Mifflin Company, 1974). See Chapters 2 ("Tolkien's

Leaf: *The Hobbit* and the Discovery of a World") and 3 ("*The Hobbit* As Swain: A World of Myth").

Hodge, James L. "The Heroic Profile of Bilbo Baggins," *Florilegium* 8 (1986): 212–21.

———. "Tolkien's Mythological Calendar in *The Hobbit*," in *Aspects of Fantasy: Selected Essays from the Second International Conference on the Fantastic in Literature and Film,* edited by William Coyle (Westport, Conn.: Greenwood Press, 1986): 141–48.

Hopkins, Lisa. "Bilbo Baggins As a Burglar," *Inklings Jahrbuch für Literatur und Asthetik* 10 (1992): 93–101.

———. "*The Hobbit* and *A Midsummer Night's Dream,*" *Mallorn,* no. 28 (September 1991): 19–21.

Hunnewell, Sumner Gary. "Durin's Day," in *Ravenhill,* Special Mythcon XXX/Bree Moot 4 Issue (August 1, 1999): 1–14.

Kocher, Paul H. *Master of Middle-earth: The Fiction of J.R.R. Tolkien* (Boston: Houghton Mifflin Company, 1972). See Chapter 2, "The Hobbit."

Kuznets, Lois R. "Tolkien and the Rhetoric of Childhood," in *Tolkien: New Critical Perspectives,* edited by Neil D. Isaacs and Rose A. Zimbardo (Lexington: University of Kentucky Press, 1981): 150–62.

McDaniel, Stanley V. *The Philosophical Etymology of Hobbit* (Highland, Mich.: The American Tolkien Society, 1994).

MacIntyre, Jean. " 'Time Shall Run Back': Tolkien's *The Hobbit,*" *Children's Literature Association Quarterly* 13 (1988): 12–17.

Masson, Pat. "Not an Orderly Narrator: Inaccuracies and Ambiguities in the Early Chapters of the Red Book of Westmarch," *Mallorn,* no. 13 (1979): 23–28.

Matthews, Dorothy. "The Psychological Journey of Bilbo Baggins," in *A Tolkien Compass,* edited by Jared Lobdell (La Salle, Ill.: Open Court, 1975): 29–42.

O'Brien, Donald. "On the Origin of the Name 'Hobbit,' " *Mythlore* 16, no. 2 (whole no. 60; winter 1989): 32–38.

Olney, Austin. *The Hobbit Fiftieth Anniversary 1938–1988* (Boston: Houghton Mifflin Company, 1988).

O'Neill, Timothy R. *The Individuated Hobbit: Jung, Tolkien and the Archetypes of Middle-earth* (Boston: Houghton Mifflin Company, 1979). See especially Chapter 4, "The Individuated Hobbit."

Reckford, Kenneth J. " 'There and Back Again' – Odysseus and Bilbo Baggins," *Mythlore* 14, no. 3 (whole no. 53; spring 1988): 5–9.

Rogers, William N., II, and Michael R. Underwood. "Gagool and Gollum: Exemplars of Degeneration in *King Solomon's Mines* and *The Hobbit,*" in *J.R.R. Tolkien and His Literary Resonances: Views of Middle-earth,* edited by George Clark and Daniel Timmons (Westport, Conn.: Greenwood Press, 2000): 121–31.

Rosebury, Brian. *Tolkien: A Critical Assessment* (London: Macmillan; New York: St. Martin's, 1992). See the section on *The Hobbit* in "Minor Works, 1914–1973."

Rossenberg, René van. "Tolkien's Golem: A Study in Gollumology," *Lembas Extra 1995* (1995): 57–71.

Russom, Geoffrey. "Tolkien's Versecraft in *The Hobbit* and *The Lord of the Rings,*" in *J.R.R. Tolkien and His Literary Resonances: Views of Middle-earth,* edited by George Clark and Daniel Timmons (Westport, Conn.: Greenwood Press, 2000): 53–69.

Sarjeant, William A. S. "The Shire: Its Bounds, Food and Farming," *Mallorn,* no. 39 (September 2001): 33–37.

——— "Where Did the Dwarves Come from?" *Mythlore* 19, no. 1 (whole no. 71; winter 1993): 43, 64.

Scull, Christina. "Dragons from Andrew Lang's Retelling of Sigurd to Tolkien's Chrysophylax," in *Leaves from the Tree: J.R.R. Tolkien's Shorter Fiction,* edited anonymously (London: The Tolkien Society, 1991), 49–62.

———. "The Fairy-Tale Tradition," *Mallorn,* no. 23 (Summer 1986): 30–36.

———. "*The Hobbit* and Tolkien's Other Pre-War Writings," *Mallorn,* no. 30 (September 1993): 14–20.

———. "*The Hobbit* Considered in Relation to Children's Literature Contemporary with Its Writings and Publication," *Mythlore* 14, no. 2 (whole no. 52; winter 1987): 49–56.

Shippey, T. A. (Tom). *J.R.R. Tolkien: Author of the Century* (London: HarperCollins, 2000). See

Chapter 1, "*The Hobbit:* Re-Inventing Middle-earth."

———. *The Road to Middle-earth,* second edition (London: Grafton, 1992). See Chapter 3, "The Bourgeois Burglar."

Sibley, Brian. *There and Back Again: The Map of* The Hobbit. Illustrated by John Howe. London: HarperCollins, 1995.

Stenström, Anders ("Beregond"). "The Figure of Beorn," *Arda 1987,* 7 (1992): 44–83.

———. "Some Notes on Giants," *Scholarship and Fantasy: Proceedings of "The Tolkien Phenomenon" May 1992, Turku, Finland,* edited by K. J. Battarbee (Turku, Finland: University of Turku, 1993): 53–71.

———. "Striking Matches," *Arda 1985,* 5 (1988): 56–69.

Stevens, David. "Trolls and Dragons Versus Pocket Handkerchiefs and 'Polite Nothings': Elements of the Fantastic and the Prosaic in *The Hobbit,*" in *The Scope of the Fantastic – Culture, Biography, Themes, Children's Literature: Selected Essays from the First International Conference on the Fantastic in Literature and Film,* edited by Robert A. Collins and Howard D. Pearce (Westport, Conn.: Greenwood Press, 1985): 249–55.

Thomas, Paul Edmund. "Some of Tolkien's Narrators," in *Tolkien's Legendarium: Essays on The History of Middle-earth,* edited by Verlyn Flieger and Carl F. Hostetter (Westport, Conn.: Greenwood Press, 2000): 161–81.

Thompson, Kristin. "*The Hobbit* As a Part of *The Red Book of Westmarch,*" *Mythlore* 15, no. 2 (whole no. 56; winter 1988): 11–16.

Tolkien, Christopher. "Note on the Differences in Editions of *The Hobbit* Cited by Mr. David Cofield," *Beyond Bree* (newsletter of the Mensa Tolkien Special Interest Group), July 1986: 1–3. Comments on an article "Changes in Hobbits: Textual Differences in Editions of *The Hobbit*" by David Cofield, in the April 1986 issue of *Beyond Bree.*

———. "Foreword," in *The Hobbit,* by J.R.R. Tolkien. Special fiftieth anniversary edition (London: Unwin Hyman, 1987).

Wytenbroek, J. R. "Rites of Passage in *The Hobbit,*" *Mythlore* 13, no. 4 (whole no. 50; summer 1987): 5–8, 40.

V. Societies

The Mythopoeic Society is an international literary organization devoted to the study of the works of J.R.R. Tolkien, C. S. Lewis, and Charles Williams (members of the Oxford literary circle known as the Inklings), and also to the study of the literary traditions previous to and descending from the works of these three men. Founded in 1967 by Glen H. GoodKnight, the society sponsors an annual Mythopoeic Conference (at which are presented the society's annual Fantasy and Scholarship Awards) and publishes the quarterly journal *Mythlore* and the monthly bulletin *Mythprint.* For further information, see the society's Web site: www.mythsoc.org.

The Tolkien Society was founded by Vera Chapman in London in 1969. It is dedicated to the furtherance of interest in the life and works of J.R.R. Tolkien, who in 1972 agreed to become the honorary president and who remains so "in perpetuo." The society holds two international meetings in the United Kingdom, the Annual General Meeting in the spring and the Oxonmoot in Oxford in the early autumn. The society publishes an annual journal, *Mallorn,* and a bimonthly bulletin, *Amon Hen.* For further information, see the society's Web site: www.tolkiensociety.org.

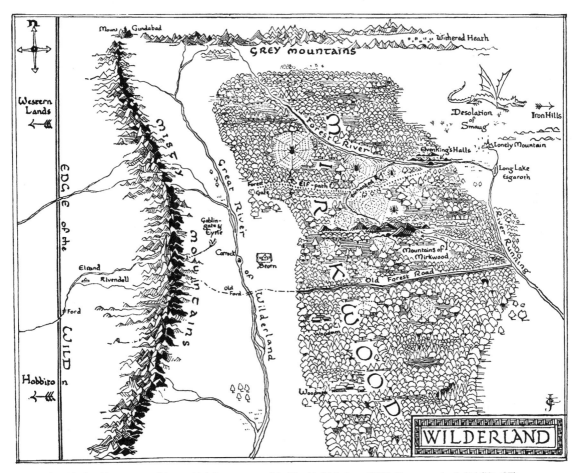

Map of *Wilderland* by J.R.R. Tolkien, which has appeared in *The Hobbit* since 1937. It appears in *Artist* (No. 87), where an earlier version can also be found (No. 84). A version colored by H. E. Riddett was published as a poster (which also included "Thror's Map") by Allen & Unwin in 1979.

The drawing of Smaug in the upper right corner is a close copy of the dragon in Tolkien's drawing *The White Dragon pursues Roverandom & the Moondog,* which appears in *Roverandom* and in *Artist* (No. 75).